CASTLE WARLOCK

CORAGE GOD MEND AL
EX LIBRIS
GEORGE MACDONALD

CASTLE WARLOCK

A Homely Romance

George MacDonald

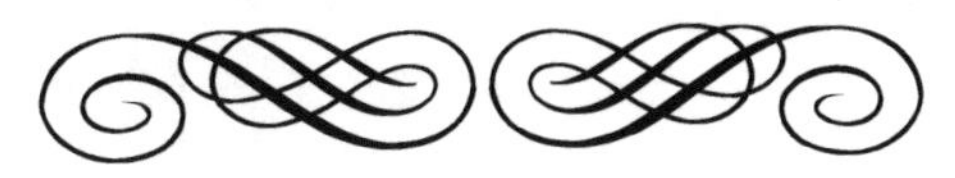

With Side-By-Side English/Scots Dialogue
Translated and Illustrated by David Jack

Warlock of Glenwarlock is a production of The Works of George MacDonald (worksofmacdonald.com)

The redesigned replica of George MacDonald's bookplate inside the front cover was provided by Michael Phillips, who notes that "it shows an old man entering his tomb through the door of death, and emerging from it with a new body of strength into the light of eternity."

Scots dialogue translated by David Jack
Translator's Preface by David Jack
Cover art and design by Melissa Alvey
Illustrations by David Jack
Interior design by Tracy Wilson

ISBN:1718873980
ISBN 13:9781718873988
Library of Congress Control Number:
CreateSpace Independent Publishing Platform North Charleston, South Carolina

MacDonald's Scottish Novels

David Elginbrod

Alec Forbes of Howglen

Robert Falconer

Malcolm

The Marquis of Lossie

Sir Gibbie

Castle Warlock

Donal Grant

What's Mine's Mine

The Elect Lady

Heather and Snow

Salted With Fire

GEORGE MACDONALD'S SCOTTISH NOVELS:
THE SCOTS-ENGLISH EDITIONS

> The man who loves the antique speech...of his childhood, and knows how to use it, possesses therein a certain kind of power over the hearts of men, which the most refined and perfect of languages cannot give, inasmuch as it has travelled farther from the original sources of laughter and tears.
>
> *-Sir Gibbie*

"George MacDonald writes of homely things and simple people who saw, in the stuff of a shepherd's cottage or a fisherman's arduous work on the cold sea, the love of God."

-Elisabeth Elliot

"All his life he continued to love the rock from which he had been hewn. All that is best in his novels carries us back to that 'kaleyard' world of granite and heather, of bleaching greens beside burns that look as if they flowed not with water but with stout, to the thudding of wooden machinery, the oatcakes, the fresh milk, the pride, the poverty, and the passionate love of hard-won learning."

-C S Lewis

"Among the many men of genius Scotland produced in the nineteenth century, there was only one...who really represented what Scottish religion should have been, if it had continued the colour of the Scottish medieval poetry. In his particular type of literary work, he did indeed realize the apparent paradox of a St. Francis of Aberdeen."

-G K Chesterton

"While MacDonald's current reputation rests largely on his mythopoeic genius, the reader who would truly know him cannot afford to neglect the twelve novels set in his native Scotland. Full of the spiritual wisdom characterising all his work, there is a further element of oracular power drawn from the very soil itself, so strong was his bond to the land that reared him. As soon might we separate Dickens from London, Hardy from Wessex, or Tolstoy from the heart of Russia, as think of George MacDonald without picturing the Aberdeenshire he brought to life in these stories."

-David Jack

∞

TO THE MEMORY OF MARVIN D. HEATON

1927-2017

THIS BOOK IS DEDICATED BY THE TRANSLATOR

AND HIS WIFE, MARVIN'S GRANDDAUGHTER,

JESSICA LAUREN JACK (NÉE HEATON)

"What wad ye say to bein' made yoong again, auld freen'?"
Chapter VI, p.27

TABLE OF CONTENTS

ACKNOWLEDGEMENTS

George MacDonald's extensive use of Scots in many of his novels has been a stumbling block for many potential readers. That is what we set out to remedy through a new series of books featuring the original, unaltered text, but featuring English translations side-by-side with the original Scots.

This new edition of *Castle Warlock* is the second of the series, following our publication of *Robert Falconer* in late 2016. It is the result of more than a year of effort by an extraordinary team on both sides of the Atlantic. My heartfelt thanks go to our translator, Scotsman David Jack, who also provided a number of illustrations to accompany the text; to his wife Jessica, who created the one-column/two-column formatting in Word; to Melissa Alvey, for her beautiful artwork and design of the front and back covers; to Michael Phillips, who over the past four decades has transformed countless people's lives by introducing them to George MacDonald, for his superb introduction; and to graphic artist Tracy Wilson, who took Word documents and and incorporated countless edits to create a splendid final product.

A special word of thanks also to Barbara Amell, editor of Wingfold, the quarterly journal which provides invaluable research on George MacDonald, who identified Tilquhillie castle as the model MacDonald used for Castle Warlock; and to Abby Palmisano, who tracked down the footnote for 'arture' from MacDonald's annotated edition of Shakespeare's Hamlet.

We are well along with the third book in the series, *Sir Gibbie*, which we hope to release by Christmas, 2018.

Blessings to all,
Jess Lederman
jess@worksofmacdonald.com

TRANSLATOR'S PREFACE
BY DAVID JACK

In my introductory remarks to *Robert Falconer*, my first MacDonald translation, I claimed that the hero's search for a father was the novel's central theme. The reason I have chosen *Castle Warlock* as its successor is that there is, if not a similitude, at least a kind of parallel between the two stories. Fatherhood remains at the very heart of the tale; but Robert's youth was defined by its absence, and Cosmo's by its life-giving presence. MacDonald said of his own father that he was his "refuge from all the ills of life, even sharp pain itself" and he advised those who took no pleasure in the name *father* to "interpret the word by all that you have missed in life. Every time a man might have been to you a refuge from the wind, a covert from the tempest, the shadow of a great rock in a weary land, that was a time when a father might have been a father indeed." In at least one sense, *Warlock* can be seen as a reimagining of *Falconer*, as if MacDonald had set himself to write a tale wherein the great lack in Robert's life was pre-eminently supplied for another of his fictional heroes. At any rate, the contrast is there: through all his adventures, challenges, and wanderings, Cosmo's abiding strength and solace is indeed that "great rock", as firm as the castle they both call home, the love of his father.

Great good also came of Robert's hardships in the end, but, to quote C S Lewis, it was "not the good that [God] had prepared" and "what was lost [we] have not seen."[1] Well, here, in *Castle Warlock*, we spend a whole novel seeing it: the good that God intends for a child who grows up in the sunshine of a strong and loving paternal presence. The old laird's devotion is no cold philanthropy or detached benignity (one thinks of the efforts of Grannie Falconer to help Robert, or of the minister in *Alec Forbes* to assuage the sufferings of Annie.) Here is loving fatherhood indeed: potent, venerable, and real—and only growing as the story unfolds. It is noteworthy too, that while the desolate Robert was raised in *relative* material comfort (as a rule, all of MacDonald's heroes are what we would call poor) and was well clothed and fed by the unstinting hand of his grandmother, Cosmo and his father sometimes look literal starvation in the face together. But the "together" is all. Reading the two stories, I wonder if there is anyone who would consider the ample meals and cosy parlour of grannie Falconer worth exchanging for the shared privations of the grim old castle.

I have given my attention first to what I think most important, but before turning to translation matters, it is only fitting to briefly touch on the story itself and the other characters belonging to it. Many people know MacDonald chiefly (if they know him at all) as a writer of fantasies; and within the story of *Castle Warlock* are elements of the supernatural worthily handled by the master. The ghostly tale of the old captain, with his riddling-rhyme "catch your horse and pull his tail..." is admirable in itself, and is deftly woven into the other themes of romance and what Cosmo aptly calls "castle-building" (his dreams of restoring the fallen fortunes of his house.) This eerie tale, however, while the most significant, is not the only fantastic or mythic allusion; there are several "stories within the story" which leave their mark on us, not unlike *The Gray Wolf* in *Robert Falconer*, or the many fairy tales in *Adela Cathcart*. As for characters, even the minor ones are memorable, such as the exasperatingly loquacious watchmaker Jeames Merson, or the displaced Scottish gardener at Cairncarque, whose saturnine disposition is something of a throwback to Scott's Andrew Fairservice. When it comes to Grizzie and Aggie, however, MacDonald is simply lyrical (in the former case, literally so.) One in their tireless loving devotion to the lairds, they are otherwise almost opposites—the irascible old servant who speaks in involuntary rhyming couplets, and the peasant-protectress

1 *Perelandra*, chapter 9. The original context of the quote is not the same (as MacDonald himself once wrote, "I should be sorry to be supposed so far out in my classics") but it struck me as being very applicable here.

who proudly stands in the stead of both mother and sister to Cosmo. These two are a delight in themselves, and they serve as ample testament to the inexhaustible invention of the author.

Turning our attention now to the translation, the reader will notice that one of the defining features of *Warlock* is the frequent appearance of verse, from the old captain's scrap of equestrian poetry to the aforementioned rhyming couplets affected by Grizzie. This of course presented a potential challenge from a language perspective: a rhyme in Scots having no guarantee of surviving after translation into English. By a happy chance, the captain's riddle "Catch yer naig an' pu' his tail" did, in fact, transpose with rhyme intact, and the short poem beginning "Whan the coo lowps ower the mune" I considered to be sufficiently free of jar, even without its rhyme, that I was happy to leave it in blank verse. With Grizzie's "rimes" I have had to be creative, but have endeavoured on all occasions to retain the *sense* of what's being said even when having to diverge from the original wording. The following may serve as an example:

Whaur's naither sun nor mune Laich things come abune	Where's neither sun nor moon Low things turn up soon

"Soon" is superfluous in that it doesn't appear in the Scots, but "Low things come above" (a word-for-word translation) would of course have dispensed with the rhyme. Here again though, a happy chance came to my aid: having chosen the phrase "turn up", I realised that it has connotations of ploughed fields, and the *turning up* of the soil, thus I have been able to convey not only the "coming to light" of the "low things", but equally their elevation.

A brief mention might also be made here about character names. I cannot now remember if I had any set approach in mind during *Robert Falconer,* but here, where a name has been written in Scots in preference to its English equivalent (such as Jeames rather than James) I have seen no occasion to meddle. The nickname (Lord) Lick-my-loof I have opted to translate only the first time it appears, and have again let the Scots stand thereafter, since Lick-my-palm simply lacks the pith which the original conveys. I have, however, placed that single translation in brackets in the main body of the text, rather than in a footnote, in hopes that it will the more easily lodge itself in the reader's memory.

On a more general note, certain questions arising from the translation project as a whole, some of which have been put to me in the interval between *Falconer* and *Warlock,* also deserve attention. They are of purely technical interest, and the answers to them can be found in the two books themselves, as I shall explain. Firstly, for those new to Scots, it must be understood that it is a quite separate language from Gaelic. The latter is spoken predominantly in the highlands and islands of Scotland, and even in MacDonald's native Huntly it would be a rare thing to find a fluent speaker. Grannie Falconer, who speaks exclusively in Scots, illustrates the point when she admits that she "never could understand Erse (Gaelic.)" The second general point to be made is that Scots is a language like Gaelic or English, not a dialect of the latter tongue. There are numerous dialects *within* Scots—the Aberdeenshire Doric used by MacDonald being one—just as English has its own multiplicity of regional tongues—but the equivalency therefore is between Scots and English, not between Scots and Cockney, for example. My intentional omission of a second column when Cosmo is in Yorkshire is an acknowledgement of this fact: his conversations with the locals there no more merit translation than do the comparable passages in *Jane Eyre, Wuthering Heights* or *The Secret Garden.*

David Jack
hoopydave@hotmail.com

Introduction by Michael Phillips

How fascinating it is that four of George MacDonald's most thoroughly "Scottish" novels were written after he and his family built a new home in Italy and were spending most of their time there. Even from the sunny Mediterranean, Scotland was never far from MacDonald's heart.

The second of these intensely Scottish novels, variously titled *Warlock O'Glenwarlock* and *Castle Warlock* for different editions, was published in 1882. Its opening scene, indeed the entire opening chapter, gives one of MacDonald's most pithy and colorful descriptions of those lonely spaces that probably only a Highlander can love as they ought to be loved.

It is one of my favorite passages in all MacDonald's writings.

A rough, wild glen it was, to which, far back in times unknown to its annals, the family had given its name, taking in return no small portion of its history, and a good deal of the character of its individuals. It lay in the debatable land between highlands and lowlands; most of its inhabitants spoke both Scotch and Gaelic; and there was often to be found in them a notable mingling of the chief characteristics of the widely differing Celt and Teuton. The country produced more barley than wheat, more oats than barley, more heather than oats, more boulders than trees, and more snow than anything. It was a solitary, thinly peopled region, mostly of bare hills, and partially cultivated glens, each with its small stream, on the banks of which grew here and there a silver birch, a mountain ash, or an alder tree, but with nothing capable of giving giving much shade or shelter, save cliffy banks and big stones. From many a spot you might look in all directions and not see a sign of human or any other habitation. Even then however, you might, to be sure, most likely smell the perfume—to some nostrils it is nothing less than perfume—of a peat fire, although you might be long in finding out whence it came; for the houses, if indeed the dwellings could be called houses, were often so hard to be distinguished from the ground on which they were built, that except the smoke of fresh peats were coming pretty freely from the wide-mouthed chimney, it required an experienced eye to discover the human nest. The valleys that opened northward produced little; there the snow might some years be seen lying on patches of oats yet green, destined now only for fodder; but where the valley ran east and west, and any tolerable ground looked to the south, there things put on a different aspect. There the graceful oats would wave and rustle in the ripening wind, and in the small gardens would lurk a few cherished strawberries, while potatoes and peas would be tolerably plentiful in their season.

What a masterful piece of prose! The descriptive power of this passage takes my breath away.

The Highlands naturally figure into many of MacDonald's stories, and nowhere more poignantly or descriptively than in the two intensely "Highland" tales, *Castle Warlock* and *What's Mine's Mine.*

MacDonald himself was not exactly a Highlander. All that can be said was that his hometown of Huntly lay near the outlying edges of the Grampian Highlands. Though most of his life was lived in or near London, MacDonald treasured his north-Scotland roots, loved his homeland's Highland history, considered himself a "son of Glencoe," and at least in part always thought like a Highlander.

In his reminiscence *From A Northern Window,* MacDonald's son Ronald writes:

"In George MacDonald's blood the Gael at least preponderated very largely; and I cannot doubt that the tradition which existed in his family of escape from the Glencoe massacre affected his imagination strongly, giving him a heart equally open to the Highland and the Lowland appeal…his occasional picture of a Highlander will stand out from the camera with great distinction, and it may be doubted whether he ever equaled in clarity of characterization or profundity of loving humour his Duncan MacPhail, the blind piper of Portlossie...at once the type of the Celt for his author, and the reconstruction...of the influence upon his author of Highland tradition. Much that Duncan relates of Glencoe and Culloden, as well as certain passages in *Robert Falconer*...is family history...

"Although George MacDonald's working life was almost entirely spent outside Scotland... he was, I think, in habit of mind, and in swift brilliance of fancy, radically a Gael."

C.S. Lewis's description of MacDonald's homeland is almost as descriptive as MacDonald's of Glen Warlock. In the Preface to his *George MacDonald, An Anthology,* Lewis writes:

"All his life he continued to love the rock from which he had been hewn. All the best in his novels carries us back to that 'kaleyard' world of granite and heather, of bleaching greens beside burns that look as if they flowed not with water but with stout, to the thudding of wooden machinery, the oatcakes, the fresh milk, the pride, the poverty, the passionate love of hard-won learning."

Like most of MacDonald's novels, *Castle Warlock* possesses elements of autobiography that increase our interest. We instantly recognize in young Cosmo Warlock the same thoughtfulness of Robert Falconer, and indeed the boy George MacDonald himself. Cosmo has grown up without his mother, reminding us of the death of George MacDonald's mother when he was eight. As Cosmo matures, he goes to college, turns to writing poems, and takes a job as a tutor—all of which parallel MacDonald's own experience. The description of the tutorship is almost purely autobiographical, revealing insight into what we know of MacDonald's first thankless job in London after graduating from university in 1845. And like MacDonald's, Cosmo's father managed a small estate of land whose fortunes were on the decline.

Most striking of all, however, is the love which exists between Cosmo and his aging father, in the heart of which pulsed the earliest attraction of the boy toward the heartbeat of God himself. Through this relationship the inheritance of God is passed from father to son. MacDonald unquestionably draws upon the memory of his own long relationship with his father when he writes in *Castle Warlock:* "Nobody knows what the relation of father and son may yet come to. Those who accept the relationship in Christian terms are bound to recognize that there must be in it depths more infinite than our eyes can behold, ages away from being fathomed yet. For is it not a small and finite reproduction of the loftiest mystery in human ken—that of the infinite Father and infinite Son? If man be made in the image of God, then must not human fatherhood and sonship be the earthly image of the eternal relation between God and Jesus?"

The desire of his father's heart is particularly moving: "But gien I've ever had onything to ca' an ambition, Cosmo, it has been that my son should be ane o' the wise, wi' faith to believe what his father had learned afore him, an' sae start farther on upo' the narrow way than his father had startit."

And out of that dear old man's mouth comes one of the most succinct statements of bull's-eye life-focus since Jesus spoke the Golden Rule, and one of my favorite nuggets of spiritual wisdom left us in the entire MacDonald legacy:

"I don't doubt there have been some in it who would count me a foolish man...but those of them who are up there don't. They see that the business of life is not to get as much as you can, but to do justly, and love mercy, and walk humbly with your God."

As reflected in Warlock's words, the Doric dialect is an intrinsic part of this book's unique Highland flavor. This "flavor," however, has for years been one of the primary stumbling-blocks to contemporary readers of George MacDonald's dialect-heavy Scottish novels. This new edition, with the Doric placed side-by-side with a more readable translation, offers readers both new to MacDonald as well as seasoned MacDonald veterans the opportunity to penetrate MacDonald's meaning more deeply.

I have long been a proponent of the production of new and creatively helpful editions of MacDonald's works that allow his books to reach wider audiences. This is just such a "creatively helpful" edition, and I heartily recommend and endorse it! I guarantee you will enjoy it.

I'm sure you will find your reading of this timeless story enhanced by enjoying it in this new format.

Michael Phillips

CASTLE WARLOCK CAST OF CHARACTERS

THE WARLOCK HOUSEHOLD

Cosmo Warlock, or 'The Young Laird'
The Laird of Glenwarlock: Cosmo's father
Grandmother Warlock
Griselda (Grizzie): The faithful family servant

THE GRACIE FAMILY

Agnes (Aggie) Gracie: Cosmo's childhood friend
Jeames Gracie: Aggie's grandfather
Mistress Gracie: Aggie's grandmother
'Grannie': Aggie's aged great-grandmother

THE MERGWAINS

Lord Mergwain: A drunken English lord
Lady Joan: His beautiful daughter
Borland/Constantine: Joan's brother and Lord Mergwain's heir

The Old Captain:
An ancestor of Cosmo's, whose ghost is believed to haunt Castle Warlock

Lord Lick-My-Loof:
A local landed proprietor, and antagonist to the Warlocks

The Schoolmaster:
Cosmo's teacher at the time of the novel's commencement

Peter Simon:
Takes over Cosmo's education from the schoolmaster

Jeames Merson:
The local watchmaker

Mr. Burns:
An Aberdeen jeweller whom Cosmo befriends

Charles Jermyn:
An English doctor and suitor of Lady Joan's

Elspeth (Elsie):
A farmer's daughter who falls in love with Cosmo

Chapter I
Castle Warlock

A rough, wild glen it was, to which, far back in times unknown to its annals, the family had given its name, sharing in return no small portion of its history, and a good deal of the character of its individuals. It lay in the debatable land between highlands and lowlands; most of its inhabitants spoke both Scotch and Gaelic, and there was often to be found in them a notable mingling of the chief characteristics of the widely differing Celt and Teuton. The country produced more barley than wheat, more oats than barley, more heather than oats, more boulders than trees, and more snow than anything. It was a solitary, thinly peopled region, mostly of bare hills and partially cultivated glens, each with its small stream, on the banks of which grew here and there a silver birch, a mountain ash, or an alder tree, but with nothing capable of giving much shade or shelter, save cliffy banks and big stones. From many a spot you might look in all directions and not see a sign of human or any other habitation. Even then however, you might, to be sure, most likely smell the perfume—to some nostrils it is nothing less than perfume—of a peat fire, although you might be long in finding out whence it came; for the houses, if indeed the dwellings could be called houses, were often so hard to be distinguished from the ground on which they were built, that except the smoke of fresh peats were coming pretty freely from the wide-mouthed chimney, it required an experienced eye to discover the human nest. The valleys that opened northward produced little; there the snow might some years be seen lying on patches of oats yet green, destined now only for fodder; but where the valley ran east and west, and any tolerable ground looked to the south, there things put on a different aspect. There the graceful oats would wave and rustle in the ripening wind, and in the small gardens would lurk a few cherished strawberries, while potatoes and peas would be tolerably plentiful in their season.

Upon a natural terrace in such a slope to the south stood Castle Warlock. But it turned no smiling face to the region whence came the warmth and the growth. A more grim, repellent, unlovely building would be hard to find; and yet, from its extreme simplicity, its utter indifference to its own looks, its repose, its weight, and its gray historical consciousness, no one who loved houses would have thought of calling it ugly. It was like the hard-featured face of a Scotch matron, suggesting no end of story, of life, of character: she holds a defensive if not defiant face to the world, but within she is warm, tending carefully the fires of life. Summer and winter the chimneys of that desolate looking house smoked; for though the country was inclement, and the people that lived in it were poor, the great, sullen, almost unhappy-looking hills held clasped to their bare cold bosoms, exposed to all the bitterness of freezing winds and summer hail, the warmth of household centuries: their peat-bogs were the store closets and wine-cellars of the sun, for the hoarded elixir of physical life. And although the walls of the castle, as it was called, were so thick that in winter they kept the warmth generated within them from wandering out and being lost on the awful wastes of homeless hillside and moor, they also prevented the brief summer heat of the wayfaring sun from entering with freedom, and hence the fires were needful in the summer days as well—at least at the time my story commences, for then, as generally, there were elderly and aged people in the house, who had to help their souls to keep their bodies warm.

The house was very old. It had been built for more kinds of shelter than need to be thought of in our days. For the enemies of our ancestors were not only the cold, and the fierce wind, and the rain, and the snow; they were men also—enemies harder to keep out than the raging storm or the creeping frost. Hence the more hospitable a house could be, the less must it look what it was: it must wear its face haughty, and turn its smiles inward. The house of Glenwarlock, as it was also sometimes called, consisted of three massive, narrow, tall blocks of building, which showed little connection with each other beyond juxtaposition, two of them standing end to end, with but a few feet of space between, and the third at right angles to the two. In the two which stood end to end, and were originally the principal parts, hardly any windows were to be seen on the side that looked out into the valley; while in the third, which, though looking much of the same age, was of later build, were more windows, but none in the lowest story. Narrow as were these buildings, and four stories high, they had a solid, ponderous look, suggesting a thickness of the walls such as to leave little of a hollow within for the indwellers—like great marine shells for a small mollusk. On the other side was a kind of a court, completed by the stables and cow-houses, and towards this court were most of the windows—many of them for size more like those in the cottages around, than suggestive of a house built by the lords of the soil. The court was now merely that of a farmyard.

There must have been at one time outer defences to the castle, but they were no longer to be distinguished by the inexperienced eye; and indeed the windowless walls of the house itself seemed strong enough to repel any attack without artillery—except indeed the assailants had got into the court. There were however some signs of the windows there having been enlarged if not increased at a later period.

In the block that stood angle-wise to the rest was the kitchen, the door of which opened immediately on the court; and behind the kitchen, in that part which had no windows to the valley, was the milk-cellar, as they called the dairy, and places for household storage. A rough causeway ran along the foot of the walls, connecting the doors in the different blocks. Of these, the kitchen door for the most part stood open: sometimes the snow would be coming fast down the wide chimney, with little soft hisses in the fire, and the business of the house going on without a thought of closing it, though from it you could not have seen across the yard for the falling flakes.

But when my story opens, the summer held the old house and the older hills in its embrace. The sun was pouring torrents of light and heat into the valley, and the slopes of it were covered with green. The bees were about, contenting themselves with the flowers, while the heather was getting ready its bloom for them, and a boy of fourteen was sitting in a little garden that lay like a dropped belt of beauty about the feet of the grim old walls. This was on the other side—that to the south, parting the house from the slope where the corn began—now with the ear half-formed. The boy sat on a big stone, which once must have had some part in the house itself, or its defences, but which he had never known except as a seat for himself. His back leaned against the hoary wall, and he was in truth meditating, although he did not look as if he were. He was already more than an incipient philosopher, though he could not yet have put into recognizable shape the thought that was now passing through his mind. The bees were the primary but not the main subject of it. It came thus: he thought how glad the bees would be when their crop of heather was ripe; then he thought how they preferred the heather to the flowers; then, that the one must taste nicer to them than the other; and last awoke the question whether their taste of sweet was the same as his. "For," said he, "if their honey is sweet to them with the same sweetness with which it is sweet to me, then there is something in the make of the bee that's the same with the make of me; and perhaps then a man might some day, if he wanted, try the taste of being a bee all out for a little while." But to see him, nobody would have thought he was doing anything but basking in the sun. The scents of the flowers all about his feet came and went on the eddies of the air, paying my lord many a visit in his antechamber, his brain; the windy noises of the insects, the watery noises of the pigeons, the noises from the poultry-yard, the song of the mountain river, visited him also through the portals of his ears; but at the moment the boy seemed lost in the mere fundamental satisfaction of existence.

Neither, although broad summer was on the earth, and all the hill-tops and as much of the valleys as their shadows did not hide were bathed in sunlight, although the country was his native land, and he loved it with the love of his country's poets, was the consciousness of the boy free from a certain strange kind of trouble connected with, if not resulting from the landscape before him. A Celt through many of his ancestors, and his mother in particular, his soul, full of undefined emotion, was aware of an ever-recurring impulse to song, ever checked and broken, ever thrown back upon itself. There were a few books in the house, amongst them certain volumes of verse—a copy of Cowly, whose notable invocation of Light he had instinctively blundered upon, one of Milton, the translated Ossian; Thomson's Seasons—with a few more; and from the reading of these, among other results had arisen this—that, in the midst of his enjoyment of the world around him, he found himself every now and then sighing after a lovelier nature than that before his eyes. There he read of mountains, if not wilder, yet loftier and more savage than his own, of skies more glorious, of forests of such trees as he knew only from one or two old engravings in the house, on which he looked with a strange, inexplicable reverence: he would sometimes wake weeping from a dream of mountains, or of tossing waters. Once with his waking eyes he saw a mist, afar off between the hills that ramparted the horizon, grow rosy after the sun was down, and his heart filled as with the joy of a new discovery. Around him, it is true, the waters rushed well from their hills, but their banks had little beauty. Not merely did the want of trees distress him, but the nature of their channel; most of them, instead of rushing through rocks, cut their way only through beds of rough gravel and their bare surroundings were desolate without grandeur—almost mean to eyes that had not yet pierced to the soul of them. Nor had he yet learned to admire the lucent brown of the bog-waters. There seemed to be in the boy a strain of some race used to a richer home, and yet all the time the frozen regions of the north drew his fancy tenfold more than Italy or Egypt.

His name was Cosmo, a name brought from Italy by one of the line who had sold his sword and fought for strangers. Not a few of the younger branches of the family had followed the same evil profession and taken foreign pay chiefly from poverty and prejudice combined, but not a little in some cases from the inborn love of fighting that seems to characterize the Celt. The last soldier of them had served the East India Company both by sea and land: tradition more than hinted that he had chiefly served himself. Since then the heads of the house had been peaceful farmers of their own land, contriving to draw what to many farmers nowadays would seem but a scanty subsistence from an estate which had dwindled to the twentieth part of what it had been a few centuries before, though even then it could never have made its proprietor rich in anything but the devotion of his retainers.

Growing too hot between sun and wall, Cosmo rose, and passing to the other side of the house beyond the court-yard, and crossing a certain heave of grass, came upon one unfailing delight in his lot—a preacher whose voice, inarticulate it is true, had, ever since he was born, been at most times louder in his ear than any other. It was a mountain stream, which, through a channel of rock, such as nearly satisfied his most fastidious fancy, went roaring, rushing, and sometimes thundering, with an arrow-like, foamy swiftness, down to the river in the glen below. The rocks were very dark, and the foam shone brilliant against them. From the hill-top above it came, sloping steep from far. When you looked up, it seemed to come flowing from the horizon itself, and when you looked down, it seemed to have suddenly found it could no more return to the upper regions it had left too high behind it, and in disgust to shoot headlong to the abyss. There was not much water in it now, but plenty to make a joyous white rush through the deep-worn brown of the rock: in the autumn and spring it came down gloriously, dark and fierce, as if it sought the very centre, wild with greed after an absolute rest.

The boy stood and gazed, as was his custom. Always he would seek this endless water when he grew weary, when the things about him put on their too ordinary look. Let the aspect of this be what it might, it seemed still inspired and sent forth by some essence of mystery and endless possibility. There was in him an unusual combination of the power to read the hieroglyphic internal aspect of things, and the scientific nature that bows before fact. He knew that the stream was in its second stage when it rose from the earth and rushed past the house, that it was gathered first from the great ocean, through millions of smallest ducts, up to the reservoirs of the sky, thence to descend in snows and rains and wander down and up through the veins of the earth; but the sense of its mystery had not hitherto begun to withdraw. Happily for him, the poetic nature was not merely predominant in him, but dominant, sending itself, a pervading spirit, through the science that else would have stifled him. Accepting fact, he found nothing in its outward relations by which a man can live, any more than by bread; but this poetic nature, illuminating it as with the polarized ray, revealed therein more life and richer hope. All this was as yet however as indefinite as it was operative in him, and I am telling of him what he could not have told of himself.

He stood gazing now in a mood different from any that had come to him before: he had begun to find out something fresh about this same stream, and the life in his own heart to which it served as a revealing phantasm. He recognised that what in the stream had drawn him from earliest childhood, with an infinite pleasure, was the vague sense, for a long time an ever growing one, of its *mystery*—the form the infinite first takes to the simplest and liveliest hearts. It was because it was *always* flowing, that he loved it, because it could not stop: whence it came was utterly unknown to him, and he did not care to know. And when at length he learned that it came flowing out of the dark hard earth, the mystery only grew. He imagined a wondrous cavity below in black rock, where it gathered and gathered, nobody could think how—not coming from anywhere else, but beginning just there, and nowhere beyond. When, later on, he had to shift its source, and carry it back to the great sky, it was no less marvellous, and more lovely; it was a closer binding together of the gentle earth and the awful withdrawing heavens. These were a region of endless hopes and ever recurrent despairs: that his beloved, an earthly finite thing, should rise there, was added joy, and gave a mighty hope with respect to the unknown and appalling. But from the sky, he was sent back to the earth in further pursuit; for, whence came the rain, his books told him, but from the sea? That sea he had read of, though never yet beheld, and he knew it was magnificent in its might; gladly would he have hailed it an intermediate betwixt the sky and the earth—so to have the sky come first! but, alas! the ocean came first in order. And then, worse and worse! how was the ocean fed but from his loved torrent? How was the sky fed but from the sea? How was the dark fountain fed but from the sky? How was the torrent fed but from the fountain? As he sat in the hot garden, with his back against the old gray wall, the nest of his family for countless generations, with the scent of the flowers in his nostrils, and the sound of the bees in his ears, it had begun to dawn upon him that he had lost the stream of his childhood, the mysterious, infinite idea of endless, inexplicable, original birth, of outflowing because of essential existence within! There was no production any more, nothing but a mere rushing around, like the ring-sea of Saturn, in a never ending circle of formal change! Like a great dish, the mighty ocean was skimmed in particles invisible, which were gathered aloft into sponges all water and no sponge; and from this, through many an airy, many an earthly channel, deflowered of its mystery, his ancient, self-producing fountain to a holy, merry river, was *fed*—only *fed!* He grew very sad, and well he might. Moved by the spring eternal in himself, of which the love in his heart was but a river-shape, he turned away from the deathened stream, and without knowing why, sought the human elements about the place.

CHAPTER II
THE KITCHEN

He entered the wide kitchen, paved with large slabs of slate. One brilliant gray-blue spot of sunlight lay on the floor. It came through a small window to the east, and made the peat-fire glow red by the contrast. Over the fire, from a great chain, hung a three-legged pot, in which something was slowly cooking. Between the fire and the sun-spot lay a cat, content with fate and the world. At the corner of the fire sat an old lady, in a chair high-backed, thick-padded, and covered with striped stuff. She had her back to the window that looked into the court, and was knitting without regarding her needles. This was Cosmo's grandmother. The daughter of a small laird in the next parish, she had started in life with an overweening sense of her own importance through that of her family, nor had she lived long enough to get rid of it. I fancy she had clung to it the more that from the time of her marriage nothing had seemed to go well with the family into which she had married. She and her husband had struggled and striven, but to no seeming purpose; poverty had drawn its meshes closer and closer around them. They had but one son, the present laird, and he had succeeded to an estate yet smaller and more heavily encumbered. To all appearance he must leave it to Cosmo, if indeed he left it, in no better condition. From the growing fear of its final loss, he loved the place more than any of his ancestors had loved it, and his attachment to it had descended yet stronger to his son.

But although Cosmo the elder fought and wrestled against encroaching poverty, and with little success, he had never forgot small rights in anxiety to be rid of large claims. What man could, he did to keep his poverty from bearing hard on his dependents, and never master or landlord was more beloved. Such being his character and the condition of his affairs, it is not very surprising that he should have passed middle age before thinking seriously of marriage. Nor did he then fall in love, in the ordinary sense of the phrase; he reflected with himself that it would be cowardice so far to fear poverty as to run the boat of the Warlocks aground, and leave the scrag end of a property and a history without a man to take them up, and possibly bear them on to redemption; for who could tell what life might be in the stock yet! Anyhow, it would be better to leave an heir to take the remnant in charge, and at least carry the name a generation farther, even should it be into yet deeper poverty than hitherto. A Warlock could face his fate. Thereupon, with a sense of the fitness of things not always manifested on such occasions, he had paid his addresses to a woman of five and thirty, the daughter of the last clergyman of the parish, and had by her been accepted with little hesitation. She was a capable and brave woman, and, fully informed of the state of his affairs, married him in the hope of doing something to help him out of his difficulties. A few pounds she had saved up, and a trifle her mother had left her, she placed unreservedly at his disposal, and he in his abounding honesty, spent it on his creditors, bettering things for a time, and, which was of much more consequence, greatly relieving his mind, and giving the life in him a fresh start. His marriage was of infinitely more salvation to the laird than if it had set him free from all his worldly embarrassments, for it set him growing again—and that is the only final path out of oppression.

Whatever were the feelings with which he took his wife home, they were at least those of a gentleman; and it were a good thing indeed, if, at the end of five years, the love of most pairs who marry for love were equal to that of Cosmo Warlock to his middle-aged wife; and now that she was gone, his reverence for her memory was something surpassing. From the day almost of his marriage the miseries of life lost half their bitterness, nor had it returned at her death. Instinctively he felt that outsiders, those even who respected him as an honest man, believed that, somehow or other, they could only conjecture how, he must be to blame for the circumstances he was in—either this, or Providence did not take care of the just man. Such was virtually the unuttered conclusion of many, who nevertheless imagined they understood the Book of Job, and who would have counted Glenwarlock's rare honesty, pride or fastidiousness or unjustifiable free-handedness. Hence they came to think and speak of him as a poor creature, and soon the man, through the keen sensitiveness of his nature, became aware of the fact. But to his sense of the misprision of neighbours and friends, came the faith and indignant confidence of his wife like the closing and binding up and mollifying of a wound with ointment. The man was of a far finer nature than any of those who thus judged him, of whom some would doubtless have got out of their difficulties sooner than he—only he was more honourable in debt than they were out of it. A woman of strong sense, with an undeveloped stratum of poetry in the heart of it, his wife was able to appreciate the finer elements of his nature; and she let him see very plainly that she did. This was strength and a lifting up of the head to the husband, who in his youth had been oppressed by the positiveness, and in his manhood by the opposition, of his mother, whom the neighbours regarded as a woman of strength and faculty. And now, although all his life since, he had had to fight the wolf as constantly as ever, things, even after his wife's death, continued very different from what they had been before he married her; his existence looked a far more acceptable thing seen through the regard of his wife than through that of his neighbours. They had been five years married before she brought him an heir to his poverty, and she lived five years more to train him—then, after a short illness, departed, and left the now aging man virtually alone with his little child, coruscating spark of fresh vitality amidst the ancient surroundings. This was the Cosmo who now, somewhat sore at heart from the result of his cogitations, entered the kitchen in search of his kind.

Another woman was sitting on a three-legged stool, just inside the door, paring potatoes—throwing each, as she cut off what the old lady, watching, judged a paring far too thick, into a bowl of water. She looked nearly as old as her mistress, though she was really ten years younger. She had come with the late mistress from her father's house, and had always taken, and still took her part against the opposing faction—namely the grandmother.

A second seat—not over easy, but comfortable enough, being simply a wide arm-chair of elm, with a cushion covered in horse-hair, stood at the opposite corner of the fire. This was the laird's seat, at the moment, as generally all the morning till dinner time, empty: Cosmo, not once looking up, walked straight to it, diagonally across the floor, and seated himself like one verily lost in thought. Now and then, as she peeled, Grizzie would cast a keen glance at him out of her bright blue eyes, round whose fire the wrinkles had gathered like ashes: those eyes were sweet and pleasant, and the expression of her face was one of lovely devotion; but otherwise she was far from beautiful. She gave a grim smile to herself every time she glanced up at him from her potatoes, as much as to say she knew well enough what he was thinking, though no one else did. "He'll be a man yet!" she said to herself.

The old lady also now and then looked over her stocking at the boy, where he sat with his back to the white deal dresser, ornate with homeliest dishes.

"It'll be lang or ye fill that chair, Cossie, my man!" she said at length,—but not with the smile of play, rather with the look of admonition, as if it was the boy's first duty to grow in breadth in order to fill the chair, and restore the symmetry of the world.

Cosmo glanced up, but did not speak, and presently was lost again in the thoughts from which his grandmother had roused him as one is roused by a jolt on the road.

"It'll be long ere you fill that chair, Cossie, my man!" she said at length,—but not with the smile of play, rather with the look of admonition, as if it was the boy's first duty to grow in breadth in order to fill the chair, and restore the symmetry of the world.

Cosmo glanced up, but did not speak, and presently was lost again in the thoughts from which his grandmother had roused him as one is roused by a jolt on the road.

"What are ye dreaming about, Cossie?" she said again, in a tone wavering but imperative.

"What are you dreaming about, Cossie?" she said again, in a tone wavering but imperative.

Her speech was that of a gentlewoman of the old time, when the highest born in Scotland spoke Scotch.

Not yet did Cosmo reply. Reverie does not agree well with manners, but it would besides have been hard for him to answer the old lady's question—not that he did not know something at least of what was going on in his mind, but that, he knew instinctively, it would have sounded in her ears no hair better than the jabber of Jule Sandy.[1]

"Mph!" she said, offended at his silence, "Ye'll hae to learn manners afore ye're laird o' Glenwarlock, young Cosmo!"

"Mph!" she said, offended at his silence, "You'll have to learn manners before you're laird of Glenwarlock, young Cosmo!"

A shadow of indignation passed over Grizzie's rippled, rather than wrinkled face, but she said nothing. There was a time to speak and a time to be silent; nor was Grizzie indebted to Solomon, but to her own experience and practice, for the wisdom of the saw. Only the pared potatoes splashed louder in the water as they fell. And the old lady knew as well what that meant, as if the splashes had been articulate sounds from the lips of the old partisan.

The boy rose, and coming forward, rather like one walking in his sleep, stood up before his grandmother, and said,

"What was ye sayin', gran'mamma?"

"I was sayin' what ye wadna hearken till, an' that's enouch," she answered, willing to show offence.

"Say 't again, gran'mamma, if you please. I wasna noticin'."

"Na! I s' warran' ye frae noticin'! There ye winna gang, whaur yer ain fule fancy doesna lead the w'y. Cosmo, ye gie ower muckle tether to wull thoucht; an' someday ye'll be laid i' the dub, followin' what has naither sense intil't nor this warl's guid—What was ye thinkin' aboot the noo? Tell me that, an' I s' lat ye gang."

"I was thinkin' aboot the burnie, gran'mamma."

"It wad be tellin' ye to lat the burnie rin, an' stick to yer buik, laddie!"

"The burnie wull rin, gran'mamma, and the buik 'ill bide," returned Cosmo, perhaps not very clearly understanding himself.

"Ye're gettin' on to be a man, noo," said his grandmother, heedless of the word of his defence, "an' ye maun learn to put awa' bairnly things. There's a heap depen'in' upo' ye, Cosmo. Ye'll be the fift o' the name i' the family, an' I'm feart ye may be the last. It's but

"What were you saying, grandmamma?"

"I was saying what you wouldn't listen to, and that's enough," she answered, willing to show offence.

"Say it again, grandmamma, if you please. I wasn't noticing."

"Na! I'll bet you weren't! You won't go where your own foolish fancy doesn't lead the way. Cosmo, you give too much tether to stray thought; and someday you'll be laid in the mire, following what has neither sense in it, nor this world's good—What were you thinking about just now? Tell me that, and I'll let you go."

"I was thinking about the burn (stream) grandmamma."

"It would be better for you to let the burn run, and stick to your book, laddie!"

"The burn will run, grandmamma, and the book will wait," returned Cosmo, perhaps not very clearly understanding himself.

"You're getting on to be a man, now," said his grandmother, heedless of the word of his defence, "and you must learn to put away childish things. There's a lot depending upon you, Cosmo. You'll be the fifth of the name in the family, and I'm afraid you may be the last.

1 JULE SANDY: a character MacDonald seems to have invented solely for the purpose of this reference by Cosmo's grandmother. See also Meg Scroggie (chapt IX)

sma' honour, laddie, to ony man to be the last; an' gien ye dinna gaither the wit ye hae, an' du the best ye can, ye winna lang be the laird o' Glenwarlock. Gien it wasna for Grizzie there, wha has no richt to owerhear the affairs o' the family, I micht think the time had come for enlichtenin' ye upo' things it's no shuitable ye sud gang ignorant o'. But we'll put it aff till a mair convanient sizzon, atween oor ain twa lanes."

It's but small honour, laddie, to any man to be the last; and if you don't gather the wit you have, and do the best you can, you won't long be the laird of Glenwarlock. If it wasn't for Grizzie there, who has no right to overhear the affairs of the family, I might think the time had come for enlightening you upon things it's not suitable you should be ignorant of. But we'll put it off till a more convenient season, between our own two selves."

"An' a mair convanient spokesman, I houp, my leddy," said Grizzie, deeply offended.

"And a more convenient spokesman, I hope, my lady," said Grizzie, deeply offended.

"An' wha sud that be?" rejoined her mistress.

"And who should that be?" rejoined her mistress.

"Ow, wha but the laird himsel'?" answered Grizzie. "Wha's to come atween father an' son wi' licht upo' family-affairs? No even the mistress hersel' wad hae prezhunt upo' that ?"

"Oh, who but the laird himself?" answered Grizzie. "Who's to come between father and son with light upon family-affairs? Not even the mistress herself would have presumed upon that?"

"Keep your own place, Grizzie," said the old lady with dignity.

And Grizzie, who had gone farther in the cause of propriety than propriety itself could justify, held her peace. Only the potatoes splashed yet louder in the bowl. Her mistress sat grimly silent, for though she had had the last word and had been obeyed, she was rebuked in herself. Cosmo, judging the specialty of the interview over, turned and went back to his father's chair; but just as he was seating himself in it, his father appeared in the doorway.

The form was that of a tall, thin man, a little bent at the knees and bowed in the back, who yet carried himself with no small dignity, cloaked in an air of general apology—as if he would have said, "I am sorry my way is not yours, for I see very well how wrong you must think it." He wore large strong shoes—I think a description should begin with the feet rather than the head—fit for boggy land; blue, ribbed, woollen stockings; knee breeches of some home-made stuff; all the coarser cloth they wore, and they wore little else, was shorn from their own sheep, and spun, woven, and made at home; an old blue dress-coat with bright buttons; a drab waistcoat which had once been yellow; and to crown all, a red woollen nightcap, hanging down on one side with a tassel.

"Weel, Grizzie!" he said, in a gentle, rather sad voice, as if the days of his mourning were not yet ended, "I'm ower sune the day."

"Well, Grizzie!" he said, in a gentle, rather sad voice, as if the days of his mourning were not yet ended, "I'm too early today."

He never passed Grizzie without greeting her, and Grizzie's devotion to him was like that of slave and sister mingled.

"Na, laird," she answered, "ye can never be ower sune for yer ain fowk, though ye may be for yer ain stamack. The taties winna be lang bilin' the day. They're some sma'."

"Na, laird," she answered, "you can never be too early for your own folk, though you may be for your own stomach. The potatoes won't take long to boil today. They're pretty small."

"That's because you pare them so much, Grizzie," said the grandmother.

"That's because you pare them so much, Grizzie," said the grandmother.

Grizzie vouchsafed no reply.

Grizzie vouchsafed no reply.

The moment young Cosmo saw whose shadow darkened the doorway, he rose in haste, and standing with his hand upon the arm of the chair, waited for his father to seat himself in it. The laird acknowledged his attention with a smile, sat down, and looked like the last sitter grown suddenly old. He put out his hand to the boy across the low arm of the chair, and the boy laid his hand in his father's, and so they remained, neither saying a word. The laird leaned back, and sat resting. All were silent.

Notwithstanding the oddity of his dress, no one who had any knowledge of humanity could have failed to see in Cosmo Warlock, the elder, a high bred gentleman. His face was small, and the skin of it was puckered into wrinkles innumerable; his mouth was sweet, but he had lost his teeth, and the lips had fallen in; his chin, however, was large and strong; while his blue eyes looked out from under his narrow high forehead with a softly piercing glance of great gentleness and benignity. A little gray hair clustered about his temples and the back of his head—the red nightcap hid the rest. There was three days' growth of gray beard on his chin, for *now that he had nobody,* he would say, he had not the heart to shave every morning.

For some time he sat looking straight before him, smiling to his mother's hands as they knitted, she casting on him now and then a look that seemed to express the consciousness of blame for not having made a better job of him, or for having given him too much to do in the care of himself. For neither did his mother believe in him farther than that he had the best possible intentions in what he did, or did not do. At the same time she never doubted he was more of a man than ever his son would be, seeing they had such different mothers.

"Grizzie," said the laird, "hae ye a drappy o' soor milk? I'm some dry."

"Ay, that hae I, sir!" answered Grizzie with alacrity, and rising went into the darker region behind the kitchen, whence presently she emerged with a white basin full of rich milk—half cream, it was indeed. Without explanation or apology she handed it to her master, who received and drank it off.

"Hoots, woman!" he said, "ye wad hae me a shargar! That's no soor milk!"

"I'm vexed it's no to yer taste, laird!" returned Grizzie coolly, "but I hae nane better."

"Ye tellt me ye had soor milk!" insisted the laird—without a particle of offence, rather in the tone of apology for having by mistake made away with something too good for him.

"Weel, laird," replied Grizzie, "it's naething but the guidman's milk; an' gien ye dinna ken what's guid for ye at your time o' life, it's weel there sud be anither 'at does. What has a man o' your 'ears to du drinkin' soor milk—eneuch to turn a' soor thegither i' the inside o' ye! It's true I min' ye weel a sma' bairn i' my leddy's airms—"

"Ye may weel du that!" interrupted her mistress.

"I wasna weel intil my teens, though, my leddy!" returned Grizzie. "An' I'm sure," she

"Grizzie," said the laird, "have you a drop of sour milk? I'm fairly parched."

"Ay, that I have, sir!" answered Grizzie with alacrity, and rising went into the darker region behind the kitchen, whence presently she emerged with a white basin full of rich milk—half cream, it was indeed. Without explanation or apology she handed it to her master, who received and drank it off.

"Heavens, woman!" he said, "you would take me for a starveling! That's not sour milk!"

"I'm vexed it's not to your taste, laird!" returned Grizzie coolly, "but I have none better."

"You told me you had sour milk!" insisted the laird—without a particle of offence, rather in the tone of apology for having by mistake made away with something too good for him.

"Well, laird," replied Grizzie, "it's nothing but the goodman's milk; and if you don't know what's good for you at your time of life, it's well there should be another that does. Why should a man of your age be drinking sour milk—enough to turn all sour together inside of you! It's true I well remember you a small child in my lady's arms—"

"You may well do that!" interrupted her mistress.

"I wasn't well into my teens, though, my lady!" returned Grizzie. "And I'm sure," she added in revenge for the insinuation as to her age, "it wad ill become ony wuman to grudge a man o' the laird's stan'in a drap o' the best milk in 's ain cellar!"

"Who spoke of refusing it to him?" said his mother.

"Ye spak yersel' sic an' siclike," answered Grizzie.

"Hoots, Grizzie! haud yer tongue, my wuman," said the laird, in the gentlest tone, yet with reproof in it. "Ye ken weel it's no my mother wad grudge me the milk ye wad gie me. It was but mysel' 'at didna think mysel' worthy o' that same, seein' it's no a week yet sin' bonny Hawkie de'ed!"

"An' wad ye hae the Lord's anintit depen' upo' Hawkie?" cried Grizzie with indignation.

added in revenge for the insinuation as to her age, "it would ill become any woman to grudge a man of the laird's standing a drop of the best milk in his own cellar!"

"Who spoke of refusing it to him?" said his mother.

"You spoke in suchlike way yourself," answered Grizzie.

"Heavens, Grizzie! hold your tongue, my woman," said the laird, in the gentlest tone, yet with reproof in it. "You know well my mother wouldn't grudge me the milk you would give me. It was I who didn't think myself worthy of it, seeing it's not a week yet since bonny Hawkie[2] died!"

"And would you have the Lord's anointed depend upon Hawkie?" cried Grizzie with indignation.

The contest went no farther, and Grizzie had had the best of it, as none knew better than she. In a minute or two the laird rose and went out, and Cosmo went with him.

Before Cosmo's mother died, old Mrs. Warlock would have been indignant at the idea of sitting in the kitchen, but things had combined to bring her to it. She found herself very lonely seated in state in the drawing-room, where, as there was no longer a daughter-in-law to go and come, she learned little or nothing of what was doing about the place, and where few that called cared to seek her out, for she had never been a favourite with the humbler neighbours. Also, as time went on, and the sight of money grew rarer and rarer, it became more desirable to economize light in the winter. They had not come to that with firing, for, as long as there were horses and intervals of less labour on the farm, peats were always to be had, though at the same time, the drawing room could not be made so warm as the kitchen. But for light, even for train-oil to be burned in the simplest of lamps, money had to be paid—and money was of all ordinary things the seldomest seen at Castle Warlock. From these operative causes it came by degrees, that one winter, for the sake of company, of warmth, of economy, Mistress Warlock had her chair carried to the kitchen; and the thing once done, it easily and naturally grew to a custom, and extended itself to the summer as well; for she who had ceased to stand on ceremony in the winter, could hardly without additional loss of dignity reascend her pedestal only because it was summer again. To the laird it was a matter of no consequence where he sat, ate, or slept. When his wife was alive, wherever she was, that was the place for him; when she was gone, all places were the same to him. There was, besides, that in the disposition of the man which tended to the homely:—anyone who imagines that in the least synonymous with the coarse, or discourteous, or unrefined, has yet to understand the essentials of good breeding. Hence it came that the other rooms of the house were by degrees almost neglected. Both the dining-room and drawing-room grew very cold, cold as with the coldness of what is dead; and though he slept in the same part of the house by choice, not often did the young laird enter either. But he had concerning them, the latter in particular, a notion of vastness and grandeur; and along with that a vague sense of sanctity, which it is not quite easy to define or account for. It seems however to have the same root with all veneration for place—for if there were not a natural inclination to venerate place, would any external reason make men capable of it? I

2 HAWKIE: a pet name for a cow.

think we shall come at length to feel all places, as all times and all spaces, venerable, because they are the outcome of the eternal nature and the eternal thought. When we have God, all is holy, and we are at home.

CHAPTER III
THE DRAWING-ROOM

As soon as they were out of the kitchen-door, the boy pushed his hand into his father's; the father's grasped it, and without a word spoken, they walked on together. They would often be half a day together without a word passing between them. To be near, each to the other, seemed enough for each.

Cosmo had thought his father was going somewhere about the farm, to see how things were getting on; but, instead of crossing to the other side of the court, where lay the sheds and stables, etc., or leaving it by the gate, the laird turned to the left, and led the way to the next block of building, where he stopped at a door at the farther end of the front of it. It was a heavy oak door, studded with great broad iron knobs arranged in angular patterns. It was set deep in the thick wall, but there were signs of there having been a second, doubtless still stronger, flush with the external surface, for the great hooks of the hinges remained, with the deep hole in the stone on the opposite side for the bolt. The key was in the lock, for, except to open the windows, and do other necessary pieces of occasional tendance, it was seldom anybody entered the place, and Grizzie generally turned the key, and left it in the lock. She would have been indignant at the assertion, but I am positive it was not *always* taken out at night. In this part of the castle were the dining and drawing rooms, and immediately over the latter, a state bedroom in which nobody had slept for many years.

It was into a narrow passage, no wider than itself, the door led. From this passage, a good-sized hall opened to the left—very barely furnished, but with a huge fireplace, and a great old table, that often had feasted jubilant companies. The walls were only plastered, and were stained with damp. Against them were fixed a few mouldering heads of wild animals—the stag and the fox and the otter—one ancient wolfs-head also, wherever that had been killed. But it was not into this room the laird led his son. The passage ended in a stone stair that went up between containing walls. It was much worn, and had so little head-room that the laird could not ascend without stooping. Cosmo was short enough as yet to go erect, but it gave him always a feeling of imprisonment and choking, a brief agony of the imagination, to pass through the narrow curve, though he did so at least twice every day. It was the oldest looking thing about the place—that staircase.

At the top of it, the laird turned to the right, and lifted the latch—all the doors were latched—of a dark-looking door. It screaked dismally as it opened. He entered and undid a shutter, letting an abiding flash of the ever young light of the summer day into the ancient room. It was long since Cosmo had been in it before. The aspect of it affected him like a withered wall-flower.

It was a well-furnished room. A lady with taste must at one time at least have presided in it—but then withering does so much for beauty—and that not of stuffs and *things* only! The furniture of it was very modern compared with the house, but not much of it was younger than the last James, or Queen Anne, and it had all a stately old-maidish look. Such venerable rooms have been described, and painted, and put on the stage, and dreamed about, tens of thousands of times, yet they always draw me afresh as if they were as young as the new children who keep the world from growing old. On the floor was an old, old carpet, wondrously darned and skilfully patched, with all its colours faded into a sweet, faint ghost-like harmony. Several spider-legged inlaid tables stood about the room, but most of the chairs were of a sturdier make, one or two of the rich carved work of India, no doubt a great rarity when first brought to Glenwarlock. The walls had once had colour, but it was so retiring and indistinct in the little light that came through the one small deep-set window whose shutter had been opened, that you could not have said what it was. There were three or four cabinets—one of them old Japanese; and on a table a case of gorgeous humming-birds. The scarlet cloth that covered the table was faded to a dirty orange, but the birds were as bright as when they darted like live jewels through tropical sunlight. Exquisite as they were however, they had not for the boy half the interest of a faded old fire-screen, lovelily worked in silks by hands to him unknown, long ago returned to the earth of which they were fashioned. A variety of nick-nacks and ornaments, not a few of which would have been of value in the eyes of a connoisseur, crowded the chimney-piece—which stood over an iron grate with bulging bars, and a tall brass fender. How still and solemn-quiet it all was in the middle of the great triumphant sunny day—like some far-down hollow in a rock, the matrix of a gem! It looked as if it had done with life—as much done with life as if it were a room in Egyptian rock, yet was it full of the memories of keenest life, and Cosmo knew there was treasure upon treasure of wonder and curiosity hid in those cabinets, some of which he had seen, and more he would like to see. But it was not to show him any of these that his father had now brought him to the room.

Not once yielding the right hand of the boy which was clasped to and in his own, the laird closed the door of the room, and advancing the whole length of it, stopped at a sofa covered with a rich brocade, and seating himself thereon, slowly, and with a kind of care, drew him between his thin knees, and began to talk to him. Now there was this difference between the relation of these two and that of most fathers and sons, that, thus taken into solemn solitude by his old father, the boy felt no dismay, no sense of fault to be found, no troubled expectation of admonition. Reverence and love held about equal sway in his feeling towards his father. And while the grandmother looked down on Cosmo as the son of his mother, for that very reason his father in a strange lovely way reverenced his boy: the reaction was utter devotion.

Cosmo stood and looked in his father's eyes—their eyes were of the same colour—that bright, sweet, soft Norwegian blue—his right hand still clasped in his father's left, and his left hand leaning gently on his father's knee. Then, as I say, the old man began to talk to the young one. A silent man ordinarily, it was from no lack of the power of speech, for he had a Celtic gift of simple eloquence.

"This is your birthday, my son," he said.

"Yes, papa."

"You are now fourteen."

"Yes, papa."

"You are growing quite a man."

"I don't know, papa."

"So much of a man, at least, my Cosmo, that I am going to treat you like a man this day, and tell you some things that I have never talked about to anyone since your mother's death.—You remember your mother, Cosmo?"

This question he was scarcely ever alone with the boy without asking—not from forgetfulness, but from the desire to keep the boy's remembrance of her fresh, and for the pure pleasure of talking of her to the only one with whom it did not seem profane to converse concerning his worshipped wife.

"Yes, papa, I do."

The laird always spoke Scotch to his mother, and to Grizzie also, who would have thought him seriously offended had he addressed her in book-English; but to his Marion's son he always spoke in the best English he had, and Cosmo did his best in the same way in return.

"Tell me what you remember about her," said the old man.

He had heard the same thing again and again from the boy, yet every time it was as if he hoped and watched for some fresh revelation from the lips of the lad—as if, truth being one, memory might go on recalling, as imagination goes on foreseeing.

"I remember," said the boy, "a tall beautiful woman, with long hair, which she brushed before a big, big looking-glass."

The love of the son, kept alive by the love of the husband, glorifying through the mists of his memory the earthly appearance of the mother, gave to her the form in which he would see her again, rather than that in which he had actually beheld her. And indeed the father saw her after the same fashion in the memory of his love. Tall to the boy of five, she was little above the middle height, yet the husband saw her stately in his dreams: there was nothing remarkable in her face except the expression, which after her marriage had continually gathered tenderness and grace, but the husband as well as the child called her absolutely beautiful.

"What colour were her eyes, Cosmo?"

"I don't know; I never saw the colour of them; but I remember they looked at me as if I should run into them."

"She would have died for you, my boy. We must be very good, that we may see her again some day."

"I will try. I do try, papa."

"You see, Cosmo, when a woman like that condescends to be wife to one of us and mother to the other, the least we can do when she is taken from us, is to give her the same love and the same obedience after she is gone as when she was with us. She is with her own kind up in heaven now, but she may be looking down and watching us. It may be God lets her do that, that she may see of the travail of her soul and be satisfied—who can tell? She can't be very anxious about me now, for I am getting old, and my warfare is nearly over; she may be getting things ready to rest me a bit. She knows I have for a long time now been trying to keep the straight path, so far as I could see it, though sometimes the grass and heather has got the better of it, so that it was hard to find. But *you* must remember, Cosmo, that it is not enough to be a good boy, as I shall tell her you have always been: you've got to be a good man, and that is a rather different, and sometimes a harder thing. For, as soon as a man has to do with other men, he finds they expect him to do things they ought to be ashamed of doing themselves; and then he has got to stand on his own honest legs, and not move an inch for all their pushing and pulling; and especially where a man loves his fellow-man, and likes to be on good terms with him, that is not easy. The thing is just this, Cosmo—when you are a full-grown man, you must be a good boy still—that's the difficulty. For a man to be a boy, and a good boy still, he must be a thorough man. The man that's not manly can never be a good boy to his mother. And you can't keep true to your mother except you remember no man can be right manly, no man can keep true to his mother, except he remember Him who is father and mother both to all of us. I wish my Marion were here to teach you as she taught me. She taught me to pray, Cosmo, as I have tried to teach you—when I was in any trouble, just to go into my closet, and shut to the door, and pray to my Father who is in secret—the same Father who loved you so much as to give you my Marion for a mother. But I am getting old and tired, and shall soon go where I hope to learn faster. Oh, my boy! hear your father who loves you, and never do the thing you would be ashamed for your mother or me to know. Remember, nothing drops out; everything hid shall be revealed. But, of all things, if ever you should fail or fall, don't lie still because you are down: get up again—for God's sake, for your mother's sake, for my sake—get up and try again.

"And now it is time you should know a little about the family of which you come. I don't doubt there have been some in it who would count me a foolish man for bringing you up as I have done, but those of them who are up there with your mother don't. They see that the business of life is not to get as much as you can, but to do justly, and love mercy, and walk humbly with your God—with your mother's God, my son. They may say I've made a poor thing of it, but I shall not hang my head before the public of that country because I've let the land slip from me that I couldn't keep any more than this weary old carcase that's now crumbling away from about me. Some would tell me I ought to shudder at the thought of leaving you to such poverty, but I am too anxious about yourself, my boy, to think much about the hardships that may be waiting you. I should be far more afraid about you if I were leaving you rich. I have seen rich people do things I never knew a poor gentleman do. I don't mean to say anything against the rich—there's good and bad of all sorts; but I just can't be so very sorry that I am leaving you to poverty, though, if I might have had my way, it wouldn't have been so bad. But he knows best who loves best. I have struggled hard to keep the old place for you; but there's hardly an acre outside the garden and close (courtyard) but was mortgaged before I came into the property. I've been all my life trying to pay off, but have made little progress. The house is free, however, and the garden; and don't you part with the old place, my boy, except you see you *ought*. But rather than anything not out and out honest, anything the least doubtful, sell every stone. Let all go, if you should have to beg your way home to us. Come clean, my son, as my Marion bore you."

Here Cosmo interrupted his father, to ask what *mortgaged* meant. This led to an attempt on the part of the laird to instruct him in the whole state of the affairs of the property. He showed him where all the papers were kept, and directed him to whom to go for any requisite legal advice. Weary then of business, of which he had all his life had more than enough, he turned to pleasanter matters, and began to tell him anecdotes of the family.

"What in mercy can hae come o' the laird, think ye, my leddy?" said Grizzie to her mistress. "It's the yoong laird's birthday, ye see, an' they aye haud a colloguin' thegither upo' that same, an' I kenna whaur to gang to cry them til their denner."

"Run an' ring the great bell," said the grandmother, mindful of old custom.

"'Deed I s' du naething o' the kin'!" said Grizzie to herself; "it's eneuch to raise a regiment—gien it camna doon upo' my heid!"

"What in mercy can have come of the laird, do you think, my lady?" said Grizzie to her mistress. "It's the young laird's birthday, you see, and they always have a talk together on that day, and I don't know where to go to call them to their dinner."

"Run and ring the great bell," said the grandmother, mindful of old custom.

"Indeed, I'll do nothing of the kind!" said Grizzie to herself; "it's enough to raise a regiment—if it didn't come down upon my head!"

But she had her suspicion, and finding the great door open, ascended the stair. The two were sitting at a table, with the genealogical tree of the family spread out before them, the father telling tale after tale, the son listening in delight. I must confess, however—let it tell against the laird's honesty as it may—that, his design being neither to glorify his family, nor teach its records, but to impress all he could find of ancestral nobility upon his boy, he made a choice, and both communicated and withheld. So absorbed were they, that Grizzie's knock startled them both a good deal.

"Yer denners is ready, laird," she said, standing erect in the doorway.

"Verra weel, Grizzie, I thank ye," returned the laird.—

"Cosmo, we'll take a walk together this evening, and then I'll tell you more about that brother of my grandfather's. Come along to dinner now—I houp ye hae something in honour o' the occasion, Grizzie," he added in a whisper when he reached the door, where the old woman waited to follow them.

"Your dinners are ready, laird," she said, standing erect in the doorway.

"Very well, Grizzie, I thank you," returned the laird.—

"Cosmo, we'll take a walk together this evening, and then I'll tell you more about that brother of my grandfather's. Come along to dinner now—I hope you have something in honour of the occasion, Grizzie," he added in a whisper when he reached the door, where the old woman waited to follow them.

"I teuk it upo' me, laird," answered Grizzie in the same tone, while Cosmo was going down the stair, "to put a cock an' a leek thegither, an' they'll be nane the waur that ye hae keepit them i' the pot a while langer—Cosmo," she went on when they had descended, and overtaken the boy, who was waiting for them at the foot, "the Lord bless ye upo' this bonnie day! An' may ye be aye a comfort to them 'at awes ye, as ye hae been up to this present."

"I took it upon me, laird," answered Grizzie in the same tone, while Cosmo was going down the stair, "to put a cock and a leek together, and they'll be none the worse that you've kept them in the pot a while longer—Cosmo," she went on when they had descended, and overtaken the boy, who was waiting for them at the foot, "the Lord bless you upon this bonnie day! And may you always be a comfort to those you belong to, as you have been up to now."

"I houp sae, Grizzie," responded Cosmo humbly; and all went together to the kitchen.

"I hope so, Grizzie," responded Cosmo humbly; and all went together to the kitchen.

There the table was covered with a clean cloth of the finest of homespun, and everything set out with the same nicety as if the meal had been spread in the dining-room. The old lady, who had sought to please her son by putting on her best cap for the occasion, but who had in truth forgot what day it was until reminded by Grizzie, sat already at the head of the table, waiting their arrival. She made a kind speech to the boy, hoping he would be master of the place for many years after his father and she had left him. Then the meal commenced. It did not last long. They had the soup first, and then the fowl that had been boiled in it, with a small second dish of potatoes—the year's baby Kidneys, besides those Grizzie had pared. Delicate pancakes followed—and dinner was over—except for the laird, who had a little toddy after. But as yet Cosmo had never even tasted strong drink—and of course he never desired it. Leaving the table, he wandered out, pondering some of the things his father had been telling him.

CHAPTER IV
AN AFTERNOON SLEEP

Presently, without having thought whither he meant to go, he found himself out of sight of the house—in a favourite haunt, but one in which he always had a peculiar feeling of strangeness and even expatriation. He had descended the stream that rushed past the end of the house, till it joined the valley river, and followed the latter up, to where it took a sudden sharp turn, and a little farther. Then he crossed it, and was in a lonely nook of the glen, with steep hills about him on all sides, some of them covered with grass, others rugged and unproductive. He threw himself down in the clover, a short distance from the stream, and straightway felt as if he were miles from home. No shadow of life was to be seen. Cottage-chimney, nor any smoke was visible—no human being, no work of human hands, no sign of cultivation except the grass and clover.

Now whether it was that in childhood he had learned that here he was beyond his father's land, or that some early sense of loneliness in the place had been developed by a brooding fancy into a fixed feeling, I cannot well say; but certainly, as often as he came—and he liked to visit the spot, and would sometimes spend hours in it—he felt like a hermit of the wilderness cut off from human society, and was haunted with a vague sense of neighbouring hostility. Probably it came of an historical fancy that the nook ought to be theirs, combined with the sense that it was not. But there had been no injury done *ab extra:* the family had suffered from the inherent moral lack of certain of its individuals.

This sense of *away-from-homeness,* however, was not strong enough to keep Cosmo from falling into such a dreamful reverie as by degrees naturally terminated in slumber. Seldom is sleep far from one who lies on his back in the grass, with the sound of waters in his ears. And indeed a sleep in the open air was almost an essential ingredient of a holiday such as Cosmo had been accustomed to make of his birthday: constantly active as his mind was, perhaps in part because of that activity, he was ready to fall asleep any moment when warm and supine.

When he woke from what seemed a dreamless sleep, his half roused senses were the same moment called upon to render him account of something very extraordinary which they could not themselves immediately lay hold of. Though the sun was yet some distance above the horizon, it was to him behind one of the hills, as he lay with his head low in the grass; and what could the strange thing be which he saw on the crest of the height before him, on the other side of the water? Was it a fire in a grate, thinned away by the sunlight? How could there be a grate where there was neither house nor wall? Even in heraldry the combination he beheld would have been a strange one. There stood in fact a frightful-looking creature half consumed in light—yet a pale light, seemingly not strong enough to burn. It could not be a phoenix, for he saw no wings, and thought he saw four legs. Suddenly he burst out laughing, and laughed that the hills echoed. His sleep-blinded eyes had at length found their focus and clarity.

"I see!" he said, "I see what it is! It's Jeames Gracie's coo 'at's been loupin' ower the mune, an 's stucken upo' 't !"	"I see!" he said, "I see what it is! It's Jeames Gracie's cow that's been leaping over the moon, and has stuck upon it!"

In very truth there was the moon between the legs of the cow! She did not remain there long however, but was soon on the cow's back, as she crept up and up in the face of the sun. He bethought him of a couplet that Grizzie had taught him when he was a child:

"Whan the coo loups ower the mune, The reid gowd rains intil men's shune."	"When the cow leaps over the moon, The red gold rains into men's shoes."

And in after-life he thought not unfrequently of this odd vision he had had. Often, when, having imagined he had solved some difficulty of faith or action, presently the same would return in a new shape, as if it had but taken the time necessary to change its garment, he would say to himself with a sigh, "The coo's no ower the mune yet!" ("The cow's not over the moon yet!") and set himself afresh to the task of shaping a handle on the infinite small enough for a finite to lay hold of.

Grizzie, who was out looking for him, heard the roar of his laughter, and, guided by the sound, spied him where he lay. He heard her footsteps, but never stirred till he saw her looking down upon him like a benevolent gnome that had found a friendless mortal asleep on ground of danger.

"Eh, Cosmo, laddie, ye'll get yer deid o' caul'!" she cried. "An' preserve's a'! what set ye lauchin' in sic a fearsome fashion as yon? Ye're surely no fey!"

"Eh, Cosmo, laddie, you'll get your death of cold!" she cried. "And preserve us all! What set you laughing in such a fearsome fashion as that? You're surely not fey!"[3]

"Na, I'm no fey, Grizzie. Ye wad hae lauchen yersel' to see Jeames Gracie's coo wi' the mune atween the hin' an' the fore legs o' her. It was terrible funny."

"Na, I'm not fey, Grizzie. You would have laughed yourself to see Jeames Gracie's cow with the moon between her hind and fore legs. It was terribly funny."

"Hoots ! I see naething to lauch at i' that. The puir coo cudna help whaur the mune wad gang. The haivenly boadies is no to be restricket."

"Heavens! I see nothing to laugh at in that. The poor cow couldn't help where the moon would go. The heavenly bodies are not to be restricted."

Again Cosmo burst into a great laugh, and this time Grizzie, seriously alarmed lest he should be in reality *fey*, grew angry, and seizing hold of him by the arm, pulled lustily.

"Get up, I tell ye!" she cried. "Here's the laird speirin' what's come o' ye 'at ye come na hame to yer tay!"

"Get up, I tell you!" she cried. "The laird's been asking what's come of you that you don't come home to your tea!"

But Cosmo instead of rising only laughed the more, and went on until at length Grizzie made use of a terrible threat.

"As sure's sowens!"[4] she said, "gien ye dinna haud yer tongue wi' that menseless-like lauchin', I'll no tell ye anither auld-warld tale afore Marti'mas."

"As sure as sowens!"[4] she said, "if you don't hold your tongue with that foolish laughing, I won't tell you another old-world tale before Martinmas."

"Will ye tell me ane the nicht gien I haud my tongue an' gang hame wi' ye?"

"Will you tell me one tonight if I hold my tongue and go home with you?"

"Aye, that will I—that's gien I can min' upo' ane."

"Aye, that I will—that's if I can remember one."

He rose at once, and laughed no more. They walked home together in the utmost peace.

After tea, his father went out with him for a stroll, and to call on Jeames Gracie, the owner of the cow whose *inconstellation* had so much amused him. He was an old man, with an elderly wife, and a granddaughter—a weaver to trade, whose father and grandfather before him had for many a decade done the weaving-work, both in linen and wool, required by "them at the castle." He had been on the land, in the person of his ancestors, from time almost immemorial, though he had only a small cottage, and a little bit of land, barely enough to feed the translunar cow. But poor little place as Jeames's was, if the laird would have sold it, the price would have gone a good way towards clearing the rest of his property of its encumbrances. For the situation of the little spot was such as to make it specially desirable in the eyes of the next proprietor, on

3 FEY: considered doomed to die, as signified by odd or erratic behaviour.
4 SOWENS: a dish made from oats and fine meal. An alternative spelling is 'sowans'.

the border of whose land it lay. He was a lord of session, and had taken his title from the place, which he inherited from his father; who, although a laird, had been so little of a gentleman, that the lordship had not been enough to make one of his son. He was yet another of those trim, orderly men, who will sacrifice anything—not to beauty—of that they have in general no sense—but to tidiness: tidiness in law, in divinity, in morals, in estate, in garden, in house, in person,—tidiness is in their eyes the first thing—seemingly because it is the highest creative energy of which they are capable. Naturally the dwelling of Jeames Gracie was an eyesore to this man, being visible from not a few of his windows, and from almost anywhere on the private road to his house; for decidedly it was not tidy. Neither in truth was it dirty, while to any life-loving nature it was as pleasant to know as it was picturesque to look at. But the very appearance of poverty seems to act as a reproach on some of the rich—at least why else are they so anxious to get it out of their sight?—and Lord Lickmyloof *(Lickmypalm)*—that was not his real title, but he was better known by it than by the name of his land: it came of a nasty habit he had, which I need not at present indicate farther—Lord Lickmyloof could not bear the sight of the cottage which no painter would have consented to omit from the landscape. It haunted him like an evil thing.

CHAPTER V
THE SCHOOL

The next morning, by the steep farm road, and the parish road, which ran along the border of the river and followed it downward, Cosmo, on his way to school, with his books in a green baize bag, hung by the strings over his shoulder, came out from among the hills upon a comparative plain. But there were hills on all sides round him yet—not very high—few of them more than a couple of thousand feet—but bleak and bare, even under the glow of the summer sun, for the time of heather was not yet, when they would show warm and rich to the eye of poet and painter. Most of the farmers there, however, would have felt a little insulted by being asked to admire them at any time: whatever their colour or shape or product, they were incapable of yielding crops and money! In truth many a man who now admires, would be unable to do so, if, like those farmers, he had to struggle with nature for little more than a bare living. The struggle there, what with early, long-lasting, and bitter winters, and the barrenness of the soil in many parts, was a severe one.

Leaving the river, the road ascended a little, and joined the highway, which kept along a level, consisting mostly of land lately redeemed from the peat-moss. It went straight for two miles, fenced from the fields in many parts by low stone walls without mortar, abhorrent to the eye of Cosmo; in other parts by walls of earth, called dykes, which delighted his very soul. These were covered with grass for the vagrant cow, sprinkled with loveliest little wild flowers for the poet-peasant, burrowed in by wild bees for the adventurous delight of the honey-drawn schoolboy. Glad I am they had not quite vanished from Scotland before I was sent thither, but remained to help me get ready for the kingdom of heaven: those dykes must still be dear to my brothers who have gone up before me. Some of the fields had only a small ditch between them and the road, and some of them had no kind of fence at all. It was a dreary road even in summer, though not therefore without its loveable features—amongst which the dykes; and wherever there is anything to love, there is beauty in some form.

A short way past the second milestone, he came to the first straggling houses of the village. It was called Muir of Warlock, after the moor on which it stood, as the moor was called after the river that ran through it, and that named after the glen, which took its name from the family—so that the Warlocks had scattered their cognomen all around them. A somewhat dismal-looking village it was—except to those that knew its people: to some of them it was beautiful—as the plainest face is beautiful to him who knows a sweet soul inside it. The highway ran through it—a broad fine road, fit for the richest country under the sun; but the causeway along its edges, making of it for the space a street, was of the poorest and narrowest. Some of the cottages stood immediately upon the path, some of them receded a little. They were almost all of one story, built of stone, and rough-cast—*harled*, they called it there, with roofs of thick thatch, in which a half-smothered pane of glass might hint at some sort of room beneath. As Cosmo walked along, he saw all the trades at work; from blacksmith to tailor, everybody was busy. Now and then he was met by a strong scent, as of burning leather, from the oak-bark which some of the housewives used for fuel, after its essence had been exhausted in the tan-pit, but mostly the air was filled with the odour of burning peat. Cosmo knew almost everybody, and was kindly greeted as he went along—none the less that some of them, hearing from their children that he had not been at school the day before, had remarked that his birthday hardly brought him enough to keep it with. The vulgarity belonging to the worship of Mammon, is by no means confined to the rich; many of these, having next to nothing, yet thought possession the one thing—money, houses, lands, the only inheritances. It is a marvel that even world-loving people should never see with what a load they oppress the lives of the children to whom, instead of bringing them up to earn their own living, and thus enjoy at least *the game* of life, they leave a fortune enough to sink a devil yet deeper in hell. Was it nothing to Cosmo to inherit a long line of ancestors whose story he knew—their virtues, their faults, their wickedness, their humiliation?—to inherit the nobility of a father such as his? the graciousness of a mother such as that father caused him to remember her? Was there no occasion for the laird to rejoice in the birth of a boy whom he believed to have inherited all the virtues of his race, and left all their vices behind? But none of the villagers forgot, however they might regard the holiday, that Cosmo was the "young laird" notwithstanding the poverty of his house; and they all knew that in old time the birthday of the heir had been a holiday to the school as well as to himself, and remembered the introduction of the change by the present master. Indeed, throughout the village, although there were not a few landed proprietors in the neighbourhood whose lands came nearer, all of whom of course were lairds, and although the village itself had ceased to belong to the family, Glenwarlock was always called *the* laird; and the better part in the hearts of even the money-loving and money-trusting among its inhabitants honoured him as the best man in the country, "thof he hed sae little skeel at haudin' his ain nest thegither;" ("though he had so little skill at holding his own nest together;") and though, besides, there is scarce a money-making man who does not believe poverty the cousin, if not the child of fault; and the more unscrupulous, *within the law,* a man has been in making his money, the more he regards the man who seems to have lost the race he has won, as somehow or other to blame: "People with nought are naughty." Nor is this judgment confined to the morally unscrupulous. Few who are themselves permitted to be successful, care to conjecture that it may be the will of the power, that in part through their affairs, rules men, that some should be, in that way, unsuccessful: better can be made of them by preventing the so-called success. Some men rise with the treatment under which others would sink. But of the inhabitants of Muir of Warlock, only a rather larger proportion than of the inhabitants of Mayfair would have taken interest in such a theory of results.

They all liked, and those who knew him best, loved the young laird; for if he had no lands, neither had he any pride, they said, and was as happy sitting with any old woman, and sharing her tea, as at a lord's table. Nor was he was less of a favourite at school, though, being incapable of self-assertion, his inborn consciousness of essential humanity rendering it next to impossible for him to him to *claim* anything, some of the bigger boys were less than friendly with him. One point in his conduct was in particular distasteful to them: he seemed to scorn even an honest advantage. For in truth he never could bring himself, in the small matters of dealing that pass between boys at school, to make the least profit. He had a passion for fair play, which, combined with love to his neighbour, made an advantage, though perfectly understood and recognized, almost a physical pain: he shrank from it with something like disgust. I may not, however, conceal my belief, that there was in it a rudimentary tinge of the pride of those of his ancestors who looked down upon commerce, though not upon oppression or even on robbery. But the true man will change to nobility even the instincts derived from strains of inferior moral development in his race—as the oyster makes, they say, of the sand grain a pearl.

Greeting the tailor through his open window, where he sat cross-legged on his table, the shoemaker on his stool, which, this lovely summer morning, he had brought to the door of his cottage, and the smith in his nimbus of sparks, through the half-door of his smithy, and receiving from each a kindly response, the boy walked steadily on till he came to the school. There, on the heels of the master, the boys and girls were already crowding in, and he entered along with them. The religious preliminaries over, consisting in a dry and apparently grudging recognition of a sovereignty that required the homage, and the reading of a chapter of the Bible in class, the *secular* business was proceeded with; and Cosmo was sitting with his books before him, occupied with a hard passage in *Caesar,* when the master left his desk and came to him.

"You'll have to make up for lost time to-day, Cosmo," he said.

Now if anything was certain to make Cosmo angry, it was the appearance, however slight, or however merely implied, of disapproval of anything his father thought, or did, or sanctioned. His face flushed, and he answered quickly,

"The time wasn't lost, sir."

This reply made the master in his tum angry, but he restrained himself.

"I'm glad of that! I may then expect to find you prepared with your lessons for to-day."

"I learned my lessons for yesterday," Cosmo answered; "but my father says it's no play to learn lessons."

"Your father's not master of this school."

"He's maister o' me," ("He's master of me,") returned the boy, relapsing into the mother-tongue, which, except it be spoken in good humour, always sounds rude.

The master took the youth's devotion to his father for insolence to himself.

"I shall say no more," he rejoined, still using the self-command which of all men an autocrat requires, "till I find how you do in your class. That you are the best scholar in it, is no reason why you should be allowed to idle away hours in which you might have been laying up store for the time to come."—It was a phrase much favoured by the master—in present application foolish.—"But perhaps your father does not mean to send you to college?"

"My father hasna said, an' I haena speirt," answered Cosmo, with his eyes on his book.

"My father hasn't said, and I haven't asked," answered Cosmo, with his eyes on his book.

Still misinterpreting the boy, the conceit and ill-temper of the master now overcame him, and caused him to forget the proprieties altogether.

"Haud on that gait, laddie, an' ye'll be as great a fule as yer father himsel'," he said.

"Keep on that way, laddie, and you'll be as great a fool as your father himself," he said.

Cosmo rose from his seat, white as the wall behind him, looked in the master's eyes, caught up his *Caesar,* and dashed the book in his face. Most boys would then have made for the door, but that was not Cosmo's idea of bearing witness. The moment the book left his hand, he drew himself up, stood still as a statue, looked full at the master, and waited. Not by a motion would he avoid any consequence of his act.

He had not long to wait. A corner of the book had gone into the master's eye; he clapped his hand to it, and for a moment seemed lost in suffering. The next, he clenched for the boy a man's fist, and knocked him down. Cosmo fell backward over the form, struck his head hard on the foot of the next desk, and lay where he fell.

A shriek arose, and a girl about sixteen came rushing up. She was the granddaughter uf James Gracie, befriended of the laird.

"Go to your seat, Agnes!" shouted the master, and turning from her, stood, with his handkerchief to one eye, looking down on the boy. So little did he know him, he suspected him of pretending to be more hurt than he was.

"Touch me gien yc daur," cried Agnes, as she stooped to remove his legs from the form.

"Touch me if you dare," cried Agnes, as she stooped to remove his legs from the form.

"Leave him alone," shouted the master, and seizing her, pulled her away, and flung her from him that she almost fell.

But by this time the pain in his eye had subsided a little, and he began to doubt whether indeed the boy was pretending as he had imagined. He began also to feel not a little uneasy as to the possible consequences of his hasty act—not half so uneasy, however, as he would have felt had the laird been as well-to-do as his neighbour, Lord Lickmyloof—who would be rather pleased than otherwise, the master thought, at any grief that might befall either Cosmo or the lass Gracie. Therefore, although he would have been ready to sink had the door then opened and the laird entered, he did not much fear any consequences to be counted serious from the unexpected failure of his self-command. He dragged the boy up by the arm, and set him on his seat, before Agnes could return; but his face was as that of one dead, and he fell forward on the desk. With a second great cry, Agnes again sprang forward. She was a strong girl, accustomed to all kinds of work, out-door and in-door. She caught Cosmo round the waist from behind, pulled him from the seat, and drew him to the door, which because of the heat stood open. The master had had enough of it, and did not attempt to hinder her. There she took him in her arms, and literally ran with him along the street.

CHAPTER VI
GRANNIE'S COTTAGE

But she had not to pass many houses before she came to that of her grandfather's mother, an aged woman, I need not say, but in very tolerable health and strength nevertheless. She sat at her spinning wheel with her door wide open. Suddenly, and, to her dulled sense, noiselessly, Aggie came staggering in with her burden. She dropped him on the old woman's bed, and herself on the floor, her heart and lungs going wildly.

"I' the name o' a'!" ("In the name of all!") cried her great-grandmother, stopping her wheel, breaking her thread, and letting the end twist madly up amongst the revolving iron teeth, emerging from the mist of their own speed, in which a moment before they had looked ethereal as the vibration-film of an insect's wings.

She rose with a haste marvellous for her years, and approaching, looked down on the prostrate form of the girl.

"It can never be my ain Aggie," she faltered, "to rush intil my quaiet hoose that gait, fling a man upo' my bed, an' fa' her len'th upo' my flure!"

"It can never be my own Aggie," she faltered, "to rush into my quiet house that way, fling a man upon my bed, and fall her length upon my floor!"

But Agnes was not yet able to reply. She could only sign with her hand to the bed, which she did with such energy that her great-grandmother—*Grannie*, she called her, as did the whole of the village—turned at once thitherward. She could not see well, and the box-bed was dark, so she did not at first recognize Cosmo, but the moment she suspected who it was, she too uttered a cry—the cry of old age, feeble and wailful.

"The Michty be ower 's! what's come to my bairn?" she said.

"The maister knockit him doon," gasped Agnes.

"Eh, lassie! rin for the doctor."

"No," came feebly from the bed. "I dinna want ony notice ta'en o' the business."

"Are ye sair hurtit, my bairn?" asked the old woman.

"My heid's some sair, an' throughither-like; but I'll jist lie still a wee, an' syne I'll be able to gang hame. I'm some sick. I winna gang back to the school the day."

"Na, my bonny man, that ye sanna!" cried Grannie, in a tone of mingled pity and indignation.

"The Almighty be over us! what's come to my child?" she said.

"The master knocked him down," gasped Agnes.

"Eh, lassie! run for the doctor."

"No," came feebly from the bed. "I don't want any notice taken of the business.

"Are you badly hurt, my child?" asked the old woman.

"My head's pretty sore, and confused; but I'll just lie still for a bit, and then I'll be able to go home. I'm quite sick. I won't go back to the school today."

"Na, my bonny man, that you shan't!" cried Grannie, in a tone of mingled pity and indignation.

A moment more, and Agnes rose from the earth, for earth it was, quite fresh; and the two did all they could to make him comfortable. Aggie would have gone at once to let his father know; she was perfectly able, she said, and in truth seemed nothing the worse for her fierce exertion. But Cosmo said, "Bide a wee, Aggie, an' we'll gang hame thegither. I'll be better in twa or three minutes." ("Stay a bit, Aggie, and we'll go home together. I'll be better in two or three minutes.") But he did not get better so fast as he expected, and the only condition on which Grannie would consent not to send for the doctor, was, that Agnes should go and tell his father.

"But eh, Aggie!" said Cosmo, "dinna lat him think there's onything to be fleyt aboot. It's naething but a gey knap o' the heid; an'

"But eh, Aggie!" said Cosmo, "don't let him think there's anything to be frightened about. It's nothing but a good rap on the head;

I'm sure the maister didna inten' duin' me ony sarious hurt. But my father's sure to gie 'im fair play! He gies a'body fair play."

and I'm sure the master didn't intend doing me any serious hurt. But my father's sure to give him fair play! He gives everyone fair play."

Agnes set out, and Cosmo fell asleep.

He slept a long time, and woke better. She hurried to Glenwarlock, and in the yard found the laird.

"Weel, lassie!" he said, "what brings ye here this time o' day? What for are ye no at the school? Ye'll hae little eneuch o' 't by an' by whan the hairst 's come."

"Well, lassie!" he said, "what brings you here this time of day? Why aren't you at the school? You'll have little enough of it by and by when the harvest is come."

"It's the yoong laird!" said Aggie and stopped.

"It's the young laird!" said Aggie, and stopped.

"What's come till 'im?" asked the laird, in the sharpened tone of anxiety.

"What's happened to him?" asked the laird, in the sharpened tone of anxiety.

"It's no muckle, he says himsel'. But his heid's some sair yet."

"It's not much, he says himself. But his head's quite sore yet."

"What maks his heid sair? He was weel eneuch whan he gaed this mornin'."

"What makes his head sore? He was well enough when he went this morning."

"The maister knockit 'im doon."

"The master knocked him down."

The laird started as if one had struck him in the face. The blood reddened his forehead, and his old eyes flashed like two stars. All the battle-fury of the old fighting race seemed to swell up from ancient fountains amongst the unnumbered roots of his being, and rush to his throbbing brain. He clenched his withered fist, drew himself up straight, and made his knees strong. For a moment he felt as in the prime of life and its pride. The next his fist relaxed, his hand fell by his side, and he bowed his head.

"The Lord hae mercy upo' me!" he murmured. "I was near takin' the affairs o' ane o' his intil *my* han's!"

"The Lord have mercy upon me!" he murmured. "I was near taking the affairs of one of his into *my* hands!"

He covered his face with his wrinkled hands, and the girl stood beside him in awe-filled silence. But she did not quite comprehend, and was troubled at seeing him stand thus motionless. In the trembling voice of one who would comfort her superior, she said,

"Dinna greit, laird. He'll be better, I'm thinkin', afore ye win till 'im. It was Grannie gart me come—no him."

"Don't cry, laird. He'll be better, I'm thinking, before you get to him. It was Grannie made me come—not him."

Speechless the laird turned, and without even entering the house, walked away to go to the village.

He had reached the valley-road before he discovered that Agnes was behind him.

"Dinna ye come, Aggie," he said; "ye may be wantit at hame."

"Don't you come, Aggie," he said, "you may be wanted at home."

"Ye dinna think I wad ley ye, laird!—'cep' ye was to think fit to sen' me frae ye. I'm 'maist as guid's a man to gang wi' ye—wi' the advantage o' bein' a wuman, as my mither tells me:"—She called her grandmother, *mother.*—"Ye see we can daur mair nor ony man—but, Guid forgie me!—no mair nor the yoong laird whan he flang his *Caesar* straucht i' the maister's face this verra mornin'."

"You don't think I would leave you, laird!—except you were to think fit to send me from you. I'm almost as good as a man to go with you—with the advantage of being a woman, as my mother tells me:"—She called her grandmother, *mother.*—"You see we can dare more than any man—but, God forgive me!—not more than the young laird when he flung his *Caesar* straight in the master's face this very morning."

The laird stopped, turned sharply round, and looked at her.

"What did he that for?" he asked.

"'Cause he ca'd yersel' a fule," answered the girl, with the utmost simplicity, and no less reverence.

"What did he do that for?" he asked.

"Because he called you a fool," answered the girl, with the utmost simplicity, and no less reverence.

The laird drew himself up once more, and looked twenty years younger. But it was not pride that inspired him, nor indignation, but the father's joy at finding in his son his champion.

"Mony ane's ca'd me that, I weel believe, lassie, though no to my ain face or that o' my bairn. But whether I deserv't or no, nane but ane kens. It's no by the word o' man I stan' or fa'; but it's hoo my maister luiks upo' my puir endeevour to gang by the thing he says. Min' this, lassie—lat fowk say as they like, but du ye as *he* likes, an', or a' be dune, they'll be upo' their knees to ye. An' sae they'll be yet to my bairn—though I'm some tribbled he sud hae saired the maister—e'en as he deserved."

"Many a one has called me that, I well believe, lassie, though not to my own face or that of my child. But whether I deserve it or not, none but one knows. It's not by the word of man I stand or fall; but it's how my master looks upon my poor endeavour to go by the thing he says. Remember this, lassie—let folk say as they like, but you do as *he* likes, and, before all's done, they'll be upon their knees to you. And so they'll be yet to my child—though it troubles me he should have served the master—even as he deserved."

"What cud he du, sir? It wasna for himsel' he strack! An' syne he never muved an inch, but stud there like a rock, an' liftit no a han' to defen' himsel', but jist loot the maister tak his wull o' 'im."

"What could he do, sir? It wasn't for himself he struck! And then he never moved an inch, but stood there like a rock, and didn't lift a hand to defend himself, but just let the master take his will of him."

The pair tramped swiftly along the road, heeding nothing on either hand as they went, Aggie lithe and active, the laird stooping greatly in his forward anxiety to see his injured boy, but walking much faster "than his age afforded." Before they reached the village, the mid-day recess had come, and everybody knew what had happened. Loud were most in praise of the boy's behaviour, and many were the eyes that from window and door watched the laird, as he hurried down the street to "Grannie's", where all had learned the young laird was lying. But no one spoke, or showed that he was looking, and the laird walked straight on with his eyes to the ground, glancing neither to the right hand nor the left; and as did the laird, so did Aggie.

The door of the cottage stood open. There was a step down, but the laird knew it well. Turning to the left through a short passage, in the window of which stood a large hydrangea, over two wooden pails of water, he lifted the latch of the inner door, bowed his tall head, and entered the room where lay his darling. With a bow to Grannie, he went straight up to the bed, speedily discovered that Cosmo slept, and stood regarding him with a full heart. Who can tell but him who knows it, how much more it is to be understood by one's own, than by all the world beside! By one's own one learns to love all God's creatures, and from one's own one gets strength to meet the misprision of the world.

The room was dark though it was summer, and although it had two windows, one to the street, and one to the garden behind: both ceiling and floor were of a dark brown, for the beams and boards of the one were old and interpenetrated with smoke, and the other was of hard-beaten clay, into which also was wrought much smoke and an undefinable blackness, while the windows were occupied with different plants favoured of Grannie, so that little light could get in, and that little was half-swallowed by the general brownness. A tall eight-day clock stood in one corner, up to which whoever would learn from it the time, had to advance confidentially, and consult its face on tiptoe with peering eyes. Beside it was a beautifully polished chest of drawers; a nice tea-table stood in the centre, and some dark-shiny wooden chairs against the walls. A closet opened at the head of the bed, and at the foot of it was the door of the room and the passage, so that it stood in a recess, to which were wooden doors, seldom closed. A fire, partly of peat, partly of tan, burned on the little hearth.

Cosmo opened his eyes, and saw those of his father looking down upon him. He stretched out his arms, and drew the aged head upon his bosom. His heart was too full to speak.

"How do you find yourself, my boy?" said the father, gently releasing himself. "I know all about it; you need not trouble yourself to tell me more than just how you are."

"Better, father, much better," answered Cosmo. "But there is one thing I must tell you. Just before it happened, we were reading in the Bible-class about Samson—how the spirit of the Lord came upon him, and with the jaw-bone of an ass he slew ever so many of the Philistines; and when the master said that bad word about you, it seemed as if the spirit of the Lord came upon me; for I was not in a rage, but filled with what seemed a holy indignation; and as I had no ass's jaw-bone handy, I took my *Caesar*, and flung it as hard and as straight as I could in the master's face. But I am not so sure about it now."

"Tak ye nae thoucht anent it, Cosmo, my bairn," said the old woman, taking up the word; "it's no a hair ayont what he deserved 'at daured put sic a word to the best man in a' the country. By the han' o' a babe, as he did Goliah o' Gath, heth the Lord rebuked the enemy. The Lord himsel' 's upo' your side, laird, to gie ye siccan a brave son."

"Don't think about it, Cosmo, my child," said the old woman, taking up the word; "it's not a hair beyond what he deserved who dared put such a word to the best man in all the country. By the hand of a babe, as he did Goliath of Gath, hath the Lord rebuked the enemy. The Lord himself is on your side, laird, to give you such a brave son."

"I never kent him lift his han' afore," said the laird, as if he would fain mitigate judgment on youthful indiscretion,—"excep' it was to the Kirkmalloch bull whan he ran at him an' me as gien he wad hae pitcht 's ower the wa' o' the warl'."

"I never knew him lift his hand before," said the laird, as if he would fain mitigate judgment on youthful indiscretion,—"except it was to the Kirkmalloch bull when he ran at him and me as if he would have pitched us over the wall of the world."

"The mair like it *was* the speerit o' the Lord, as the bairn himsel' was jaloosin," remarked Grannie, in a tone of confidence to which the laird was ready enough to yield; "an' whaur the speerit o' the Lord is, there's leeberty," she added, thinking less of the suitableness of the quotation, than of the aptness of words in it. Glenwarlock stooped and kissed the face of his son, and went to fetch the doctor.

"The more likely it *was* the spirit of the Lord, as the child himself suspected," remarked Grannie, in a tone of confidence to which the laird was ready enough to yield; "and where the spirit of the Lord is, there's liberty," she added, thinking less of the suitableness of the quotation, than of the aptness of words in it. Glenwarlock stooped and kissed the face of his son, and went to fetch the doctor.

Before he returned, Cosmo was asleep again. The doctor would not have him waked. From his pulse and the character of his sleep he judged he was doing well. He had heard all about the affair before, but heard all now as for the first time, assured the laird there was no danger, said he would call again, and recommended him to go home. The boy must remain where he was for the night, he said, and if the least ground for uneasiness should show itself, he would ride over, and make his report.

"I don't know what to think," returned the laird; "it would be trouble and inconvenience to Grannie."

"I don't know what to think," returned the laird; "it would be trouble and inconvenience to Grannie."

"'Deed, laird, ye sud be ashamt to say sic a thing: it'll be naething o' the kin'!" cried the old woman. "Here he s' bide—wi' your leave,

"Indeed, laird, you should be ashamed to say such a thing: it'll be nothing of the kind!" cried the old woman. "Here he'll stay—with

sir, an' no muv frae whaur he lies! There's anither bed i' the cloaset there. But, troth, what wi' the rheumatics, an'—an'—the din o' the rottans, we s' ca 't, mony's the nicht I gang to nae bed ava'; an' to hae the yoong laird sleepin' i' my bed, an' me keepin' watch ower 'im, 'ill be jist like haein' an angel i' the hoose to luik efter. I'll be somebody again for ae nicht, I can tell ye! An' oh! it's a lang time, sir, sin' I was onybody i' this warl'! I houp sair they'll hae something for auld fowk to du i' the neist."

"Hoots, Mistress Forsyth," returned the laird, "there'll be naebody auld there!"

"Hoo am I to win in than, sir? *I'm* auld, gien onybody ever was auld! An' hoo's yersel' to win in, sir—for ye maun be some auld yersel' by this time, thof I min' weel yer father a bit loonie in a tartan kilt?"

"What wad ye say to bein' made yoong again, auld freen'?" suggested the laird, with a smile of wonderful sweetness.

"Eh, sir! There's naething to that effec' i' the word."

"Hoot!" rejoined the laird, "wad ye hae me plaguit to tell the laddie there a'thing I wad du for him, as gien he hadna a hert o' his ain to tell 'im a score o' things—ay, hun'ers o' things? Dinna ye ken 'at the speerit o' a man 's the can'le o' the Lord?"

"But sae mony for a' that follows but their ain fancies!—That ye maun alloo, laird! An' what comes o' yer can'le than?"

"That's sic as never luik whaur the licht fa's, but aye some ither gait, for they carena to walk by the same. But them 'at orders their w'ys by what licht they hae, there's no fear o' them. Even sud they stummle, they sanna fa'."

"'Deed, laird, I'm thinkin' ye may be richt. I hae stummlet mony's the time, but I'm no doon yet; I hae a guid houp 'at maybe, puir dissiple as I am, the Maister may lat on 'at he kens me, whan that great and terrible day o' the Lord comes."

your leave, sir, and not move from where he lies! There's another bed in the closet there. But, honestly, what with the rheumatics, and—and—the noise of the rats, we'll call it, many's the night I go to no bed at all; and to have the young laird sleeping in my bed, and me keeping watch over him, will be just like having an angel in the house to look after. I'll be somebody again for one night, I can tell you! And oh! it's a long time, sir, since I was anybody in this world! I only hope they'll have something for old folk to do in the next.

"Heavens, Mistress Forsyth," returned the laird, "there'll be nobody old there!"

"How will I get in then, sir? *I'm* old, if anybody ever was old! And how are you to get in yourself, sir—for you must be pretty old yourself by this time, though I well remember your father a little boy in a tartan kilt?"

"What would you say to being made young again, old friend?" suggested the laird, with a smile of wonderful sweetness.

"Eh, sir! There's nothing to that effect in the word."

"Heavens!" rejoined the laird, "would you have me plagued to tell the laddie there everything I would do for him, as if he hadn't a heart of his own to tell him a score of things—ay, hundreds of things? Don't you know that the spirit of a man is the candle of the Lord?"

"But so many for all that follow but their own fancies!—That you must admit, laird! And what comes of your candle then?"

"They're such as never look where the light falls, but always somewhere else, for they don't care to walk by the same. But those who order their ways by what light they have, there's no fear of them. Even should they stumble, they won't fall."

"Indeed, laird, I'm thinking you may be right. I have stumbled many a time, but I'm not down yet; I have good hope that maybe,poor disciple as I am, the Master may admit that he knows me, when that great and terrible day of the Lord comes."

Cosmo began to stir. His father went to the bed-side, and saw at a glance that the boy was better. He told him what the doctor had decreed. Cosmo said he was quite able to get up and go home that minute. But his father would not hear of it.

"I can't bear to think of you walking back all that way alone, papa," objected Cosmo.

"Ye dinna think, Cosmo," interposed Aggie, "'at I'm gauin' to lat the laird gang hame himlane, an' me here to be his body-gaird! I ken my duty better nor that."

"I can't bear to think of you walking back all that way alone, papa," objected Cosmo.

"You don't think, Cosmo," interposed Aggie, "that I'm going to let the laird go home himself, and me here to be his body-guard! I know my duty better than that."

But the laird did not go till they had all had tea together, and the doctor had again come and gone, and given his decided opinion that all Cosmo needed was a little rest, and that he would be quite well in a day or two. Then at length his father left him, and, comforted, set out with Aggie for Glenwarlock.

CHAPTER VII
DREAMS

The gloamin' came down much sooner in Grannie's cottage than on the sides of the eastward hills, but the old woman made up her little fire, and it glowed a bright heart to the shadowy place. Though the room was always dusky, it was never at this season quite dark any time of the night. It was not absolutely needful, except for the little cooking required by the invalid—for as such, in her pride of being his nurse, Grannie regarded him—but she welcomed the excuse for a little extra warmth to her old limbs during the night watches. Then she sat down in her great chair, and all was still.

"What for arena ye spinnin', Grannie?" said Cosmo. "I like fine to hear the wheel singin' like a muckle flee upo' the winnock. It spins i' my heid lang lingles o' thouchts, an' dreams, an' *wad-be's*. Neist to hearin' yersel' tell a tale, I like to hear yer wheel gauin'. It has a w'y o' 'ts ain wi' me."

"Why aren't you spinning, Grannie?" said Cosmo. "I like well to hear the wheel singing like a great fly upon the window. It spins in my head long threads of thoughts, and dreams, and *would-be's*. Next to hearing yourself tell a tale, I like to hear your wheel going. It has a way of its own with me."

"I was feart it micht vex ye wi' the soomin' o' 't," answered Grannie, and as she spoke, she rose, and lighted her little lamp, though she scarcely needed light for her spinning, and sat down to her wheel.

"I was afraid it might vex you with its humming," answered Grannie, and as she spoke, she rose, and lighted her little lamp, though she scarcely needed light for her spinning, and sat down to her wheel.

For a long unweary time, Cosmo lay and listened, an aerial Amphion, building castles in the air to its music, which was so monotonous that, like the drone of the bag-pipes, he could use it for accompaniment to any dream-time of his own.

When a man comes to trust in God thoroughly, he shrinks from castle-building, lest his faintest fancy should run counter to that loveliest Will; but a boy's dreams are nevertheless a part of his education. And the true heart will not leave the blessed conscience out, even in its dreams.

Those of Cosmo were mostly of a lovely woman, much older than himself, who was kind to him, and whom he obeyed and was ready to serve like a slave. These came, of course, first of all, from the heart that needed and delighted in the thought of a mother, but they were bodied out from the memory, faint, far-off and dim, of his own mother, and the imaginations of her roused by his father's many talks with him concerning her. He dreamed now of one, now of another beneficent power, of the fire, the air, the earth, or the water—each of them a gracious woman, who favoured, helped, and protected him, through dangers and trials innumerable. Such imaginings may be—nay, must be unhealthy for those who will not attempt the right in the face of loss and pain and shame; but to those who labour in the direction of their own ideal, dreams will do no hurt, but foster rather the ideal.

When at length the spinning-wheel ceased with its hum, the silence was to Cosmo like the silence after a song, and his thoughts refused to do their humming alone. The same moment he fell—from a wondrous region where he dwelt with sylphs in a great palace, built on the tree—tops of a forest ages old ; where the buxom air bathed every limb, and was to his ethereal body as water—sensible as a liquid; whose every room rocked like the baby's cradle of the nursery rime, but equilibrium was the merest motion of the will; where the birds nested in its cellars, and the squirrels ran up and down its stairs, and the woodpeckers pulled themselves along its columns and rails by their beaks; where the winds swung the whole city with a rhythmic roll, and the sway as of tempest waves, music-ruled to ordered cadences; where, far below, lower than the cellars, the deer, and the mice, and the dormice, and the foxes, and all the wild things of the forest, ran in its caves—from this high city of the sylphs, watched and loved and taught by the most gracious and graceful and tenderly ethereal and powerful of beings, he fell supine into Grannie's box-bed, with the departed hum of her wheel spinning out its last thread of sound in his disappointed brain.

In after years when he remembered the enchanting dreams of his boyhood, instead of sighing after them as something gone forever, he would say to himself, "what matter they are gone? In the heavenly kingdom my own mother is waiting me, fairer and stronger and real. I imagined the elves; God imagined my mother."

The unconscious magician of the whole mystery, who had seemed to the boy to be spinning his very brain into dreams, rose, and, drawing near the bed, as if to finish the ruthless destruction, and with her long witch-broom sweep down the very cobwebs of his airy phantasy, said,

"Is ye waukin', Cosmo, my bairn?"

"Ay am I," answered Cosmo, with a faint pang, and a strange sense of loss: when should he dream its like again?

"Soon, soon, Cosmo," he might have heard, could he have interpreted the telephonic signals from the depths of his own being; "wherever the creative pneuma can enter, there it enters, and no door stands so wide to it as that of the obedient heart."

"Weel, ye maun hae yer supper, an' syne ye maun say yer prayers, an' hae dune wi' Tyseday, an' gang on til' Wudensday."

"I'm nae wantin' ony supper, thank ye," said the boy.

"Ye maun hae something, my bonny man; for them 'at aits ower little, as weel's them 'at aits ower muckle, the night-mear rides—an' she's a fearsome horse. Ye can never win upo' the back o' her, for as guid a rider as ye're weel kent to be, my bairn. Sae wull ye hae a drappy parritch an' ream? or wad ye prefar a sup of fine gruel, sic as yer mother used to like weel frae my han', whan it sae happent I was i' the hoose?" The offer seemed to the boy to bring him a little nearer the mother whose memory he worshipped, and on the point of saying, for the sake of saving her trouble, that he would have the porridge, he chose the gruel.

"Are you awake, Cosmo, my child?"

"Ay, I am," answered Cosmo, with a faint pang, and a strange sense of loss: when should he dream its like again?

"Soon, soon, Cosmo," he might have heard, could he have interpreted the telephonic signals from the depths of his own being; "wherever the creative pneuma can enter, there it enters, and no door stands so wide to it as that of the obedient heart."

"Well, you must have your supper, and then you must say your prayers, and have done with Tuesday, and go on till Wednesday."

"I'm not wanting any supper, thank you," said the boy.

"You must have something, my bonny man; for those that eat too little, as well as those that eat too much, the nightmare rides—and she's a fearsome horse. You can never get upon the back of her, for as good a rider as you're well known to be, my child. So will you have a drop of porridge and cream? Or would you prefer a sup of fine gruel, such as your mother used to like well from my hand, when I happened to be in the house?" The offer seemed to the boy to bring him a little nearer the mother whose memory he worshipped, and on the point of saying, for the sake of saving her trouble, that he would have the porridge, he chose the gruel.

He watched from his nest the whole process of its making. It took a time of its own, for one of the secrets of good gruel is a long acquaintance with the fire.—Many a time the picture of that room returned to him in far different circumstances, like a dream of quiet and self-sustained delight—though his one companion was an aged woman.

When he had taken it, he fell asleep once more, and when he woke again it was in the middle of the night. The lamp was nearly burned out: it had a long, red, disreputable nose, that spoke of midnight hours and exhausted oil. The old lady was dozing in her chair. The clock had struck something, for the sound of its bell was yet faintly pulsing in the air. He sat up, and looked out into the room. Something seemed upon him—he could not tell what. He felt as if something had been going on besides the striking of the clock, and were not yet over—as if something was even now being done in the room. But there the old woman slept, motionless, and apparently in perfect calm! It could not, however, have been perfect as it seemed, for presently she began to talk. At first came only broken sentences, occasionally with a long pause; and just as he had concluded she would say nothing more, she would begin again. There was something awful to the fancy of the youth in the issuing of words from the lips of one apparently unconscious of surrounding things; her voice was like the voice of one speaking from another world. Cosmo was a brave boy where duty was concerned, but conscience and imagination were each able to make him tremble. To tremble, and to turn back, are, however, very different things: of the latter, the thing deserving to be called cowardice, Cosmo knew nothing; his hair began to rise upon his head, but that head he never hid beneath the bed-clothes. He sat and stared into the gloom, where the old woman lay in her huge chair, muttering at irregular intervals.

Presently she began to talk a little more continuously. And now also Cosmo's heart had got a little quieter, and no longer making such a noise in his ears, allowed him to hear better. After a few words seemingly unconnected, though probably with a perfect dependence of their own, she began to murmur something that sounded like verses. Cosmo soon perceived that she was saying the same thing over and over, and at length he had not only made out every word of the few lines, but was able to remember them. This was what he afterwards recalled—by that time uncertain whether the whole thing had not been a dream.

Catch yer naig an' pu' his tail:
In his hin' heel ca' a nail;
Rug his lugs frae ane anither—
Stan' up, an' ca' the king yer brither.

Catch your horse and pull his tail:
In his hind heel drive a nail;
Pull his ears from one another—
Stand up, and call the king your brother.

When first he repeated them entire to himself, the old woman still muttering them, he could not help laughing, and the noise, though repressed, yet roused her. She woke, not, like most young people, with slow gradation of consciousness, but all at once was wide awake. She sat up in her chair.

"Was I snorin', laddie, 'at ye leuch?" she asked, in a tone of slight offence.

"Was I snoring, laddie, that you laughed?" she asked, in a tone of slight offence.

"Eh, na!" replied Cosmo. "It was only 'at ye was sayin' something rael funny—i' yer sleep, ye ken-a queer jingle o' poetry it was."

"Eh, na!" replied Cosmo. "It was only that you were saying something really funny—in your sleep, you know-a strange jingle of poetry it was."

Therewith he repeated the rime, and Grannie burst into a merry laugh—which, however, sobered rather suddenly.

"I dinna won'er I was sayin' ower thae fule words," she said, "for 'deed I was dreamin' o' the only ane I ever h'ard say them an' that was whan I was a lass—maybe aboot thirty. Onybody micht hae h'ard him sayin' them—ower an' ower til himsel, as gien he cudna weary o' them, but naebody but mysel' seemed to hae ta'en ony notice o' the same. I used whiles to won'er whether he fully un'erstude what he was sayin'—but troth! hoo cud there be ony sense in sic havers?"

"I don't wonder I was saying over those foolish words," she said, "for in fact I was dreaming of the only one I ever heard say them and that was when I was a lass—maybe about thirty. Anybody might have heard him saying them—over and over to himself, as if he couldn't weary of them, but nobody but myself seemed to have taken any notice of the same. I used sometimes to wonder whether he fully understood what he was saying—but honestly! how could there be any meaning in such nonsense?"

"Was there ony mair o' the ballant?" asked Cosmo.

"Gien there was mair, I h'ard na 't," replied Grannie. "An' weel I wat! he wasna ane to sing, the auld captain! Did ye never hear tell o' 'im, laddie?"

"Gien ye mean the auld brither o' the laird o' that time, him 'at cam hame frae his seafarin' to the East Indies—"

"Ay, ay; that's him! Ye hae h'ard tell o' 'im ! He had a ship o' 's ain, an' made mony a voyage afore any o' 's was born, an' was an auld man whan at len'th hame cam he, as the sang says—ower auld to haud by the sea ony mair. I'll never forget the luik o' the man whan first I saw 'im, nor the hurry an' the scurry, the rinnin' here an' the routin' there, 'at there was whan the face o' 'm came in at the gett ! Ye see, they a' thoucht he was hame wi' a walth ayont figures—stowed awa' somewhaur—naebody kent whaur. Eh, but he was no a bonny man, an' fowk said he dee'd na a fairstrae deith: hoo that may be, I dinna weel ken: there war unco things aboot the affair—things 'at winna weel bide speykin o'. Ae thing's certain, an' that is, 'at the place has never thriven sin syne. But, for that maitter, it hedna thriven for mony a lang afore. An' there was a fowth o' awfu' stories reengin' the country, like ghaists 'at naebody cud get a grup o'—as to hoo he had gotten the said siller, an' sic like—the siller 'at naebody ever saw; for upo' that siller, as I tell ye, naebody ever cuist an e'e. Some said he had been a pirate upo' the hie seas, an' had ta'en the siller in lumps o' gowd frae puir ships 'at hadna men eneuch to haud the grip o't; some said he had been a privateer; an' ither some said there was sma' differ atween the twa. An' some wad hae't he was ane o' them 'at tuik an' sauld the puir black fowk, 'at cudna help bein' black, for as ootlandish as 't maun luik,—I never saw nane o' the nation mysel'—ony mair nor a corbie can help his feathers no bein' like a doo's ; an' gien they turnt black for ony deevilry o' them 'at was their forbeirs, I kenna, an' it maks naething to me or mine—I wad fain an' far raither du them a guid turn nor tak an' sell them; for gien their parents had sinned, the mair war they to be pitied.

"Was there any more of the poem?" asked Cosmo.

"If there was more, I didn't hear it," replied Grannie. "And I can tell you! he wasn't one to sing, the old captain! Did you never hear tell of him, laddie?"

"If you mean the old brother of the laird of that time, him that came home from his seafaring to the East Indies—"

"Ay, ay; that's him! You have heard tell of him! He had a ship of his own, and made many a voyage before any of us were born, and was an old man when at length he came home, as the song says—too old to follow the sea any more. I'll never forget the look of the man when first I saw him, nor the hurry and the scurry, the running here, and the routing there, that there was when his face came in at the gate! You see they all thought he was home with a wealth beyond figures—stowed away somewhere—nobody knew where. Eh, but he wasn't a bonny man, and folk said he died a dubious death: how that may be, I don't well know: there were strange things about the affair—things that won't much bear speaking of. One thing's certain, and that is, that the place has never thriven since. But, for that matter, it hadn't thriven for a long time before. And a number of awful stories were ranging the country, like ghosts that nobody could get a grip of—as to how he had gotten the said money, and such like—the money that nobody ever saw; for upon that money, as I tell you, nobody ever cast an eye. Some said he had been a pirate upon the high seas, and had taken the money in lumps of gold from poor ships that hadn't men enough to keep hold of it; some said he had been a privateer; and others still that there was small difference between the two. And some would have it he was one of those that took and sold the poor black folk, that couldn't help being black, for as outlandish as it must look—I never saw any of the nation myself—any more than a raven can help his feathers not being like a dove's; and if they turned black for any devilry of them that were their forebears, I don't know, and it's nothing to me or mine—I would fain and far rather do them a good turn than take

But as I was sayin', naebody kent hoo he had gethert his siller, the mair by token 'at maybe there was nane, for naebody, as I was tellin' ye, ever had the sma'est glimp o' siller aboot 'im. For a close-loofed near kin' o' man he was, gien ever ony! Aye ready was he to borrow a shillin' frae ony fule 'at wad len' 'im ane, an' lang had him 'at len't it forgotten to luik for 't, er' he thoucht o' peyin' the same. It was mair nor ae year or twa 'at he leeved aboot the place, an' naebody cared muckle for his company, though a'body was ower feart to lat 'im ken he wasna welcome here or there; for wha cud tell he micht oot wi' the swoord he aye cairriet, an' mak an en' o' 'im! For 'deed he feardna God nor man, ony mair nor the jeedge i' the Scriptur'. He drank a heap—for a'body at he ca'd upo' aye hed oot the whisky-bottle—well willun' to please the man they war feart at."

and sell them; for if their parents had sinned, the more were they to be pitied. But as I was saying, nobody knew how he had gathered his money, especially since maybe there was none, for nobody, as I was telling you, ever had the smallest glimpse of money about him. For a close-fisted near kind of man he was, if ever any! Ever ready was he to borrow a shilling from any fool that would lend him one, and long had the lender forgotten to look for it, ere he thought of paying the same. It was more than a year or two that he lived about the place, and nobody cared much for his company, though all were too scared to let him know he wasn't welcome here or there; for who could tell—he might pull out the sword he always carried, and make an end of him! For indeed he had no fear of God or man, any more than the judge in the Scripture. He drank a heap—for everyone he called upon always offered him whisky—well willing to please the man they were afraid of."

The voice of the old woman went sounding in the ears of the boy, on and on in the gloom, and through it, possibly from the still confused condition of his head, he kept constantly hearing the rimes she had repeated to him. They seemed to have laid hold of him as of her, perhaps from their very foolishness, in an odd inexplicable way:—

Catch yer naig an' pu" his tail;
In his hin' heel ca' a nail;
Rug his lugs frae ane anither—
Stan' up, an' ca' the king yer brither.

Catch your horse and pull his tail;
In his hind heel drive a nail;
Tug his ears from one another—
Stand up, and call the king your brother.

On and on went the rime, and on and on went the old woman's voice.

"Weel, there cam a time whan an English lord begud to be seen aboot the place, an' that was nae common sicht i' oor puir country. He was a frien', fowk said, o' the yoong Markis o' Lossie, an' that was hoo he cam to sicht. He gaed fleein' aboot, luikin' at this, an' luikin' at that ; an' whaur or hoo he fell in wi' him, I dinna ken, but or lang the twa o' them was a heap thegither. They playt cairts thegither, they drank thegither, they drave oot thegither—for the auld captain never crossed beast's back—an' what made sic frien's o' them naebody could imaigine. For the tane was a rouch sailor chield, an' the tither was a yoong lad—little mair, an' a fine gentleman as weel's a bonny man. But the upshot o' 't a' was an ill ane ; for, efter maybe aboot a month or sae

"Well, there came a time when an English lord began to be seen about the place, and that was no common sight in our poor country. He was a friend, folk said, of the young Marquis of Lossie, and that was how he came on the scene. He went flying about, looking at this, and looking at that; and where or how he fell in with him, I don't know, but before long the two of them were much together. They played cards together, they drank together, they drove out together—for the old captain never rode a horse—and what made such friends of them nobody could imagine. For the one was a rough sailor fellow, and the other was a young lad—little more, and a fine gentleman as well as a bonny man. But the upshot of it all was a bad one; for, after maybe about a month or so of o' sic friendship as was atween them, there cam a nicht 'at brouchtna the captain hame; for ye maun un'erstan', wi' a' his rouch w'ys, an' his drinkin', an' his cairt-playin', he was aye hame at nicht, an' safe intil 's bed, whaur he sleepit i' the best chaumer i' the castle. Ay, he wad come hame—aften as drunk as man cud be, but hame he cam! Sleep intil the efternune o' the neist day he wad, but never oot o' 's nain bed—or if no aye in his ain nakit *bed*, for I fan' him ance mysel' lyin' snorin' upo' the flure, it was aye intil 's ain room, as I say, an' no in ony strange place, drunk or sober. Sae there was some surprise at his no appearin', an' fowk spak o' 't, but no that muckle, for naebody cared i' their hert what cam o' the man. Still, whan the men gaed oot to their wark, they bude to gie a luik gien there was ony sign o' 'im. It was easy to think 'at he micht hae been at last ower sair owertaen to be able to win hame. But that wasna it, though whan they cam upo' 'im lyin' on 's back i' the howe yon'er 'at luiks up to my dauchter's bit gerse for her coo, they thoucht he bude to hae sleepit there a' nicht. Sae he had, but it was the sleep 'at kens no waukin—at least no the kin' o' waukin' 'at comes wi' the mornin'!"

such friendship as was between them, there came a night that brought no captain home; for you must understand, with all his rough ways, and his drinking, and his card-playing, he was always home at night, and safe in his bed, where he slept in the best chamber in the castle. Ay, he would come home—often as drunk as man could be, but home he came! He'd sleep into the afternoon of the next day, but never out of his own bed—or if not always in his own naked *bed,* for I found him once myself lying snoring upon the floor, it was always in his own room, as I say, and not in any strange place drunk or sober. So there was some surprise at his not appearing, and people spoke of it, but not that much, for nobody cared in their heart what came of the man. Still, when the men went out to their work, they had to look and see if there was any sign of him. It was easy to think that he might have finally drunk himself into such a stupor that he couldn't get home. But that wasn't it, though when they came upon him lying on his back in the hollow yonder that looks up to my daughter's patch of grass for her cow, they thought he must have slept there all night. So he had, but it was the sleep that knows no waking—at least not the kind of waking that comes with the morning!"

Cosmo recognized with a shudder his favourite spot, where on his birthday, as on many a day before, he had fallen asleep. But the old woman went on with her story.

"Deid was the auld captain—as deid as ever was man 'at had nane left to greit for him. But thof there was nae greitin', no but sic a hullabaloo as rase upo' the discovery! They rade an' they ran; the doctor cam, an' the minister, and the lawyer an' the grave-digger. But whan a man's deid, what can a the warl' du for 'im but berry 'im? puir hin'er en' thof it be to him 'at draws himsel' up, an' blaws himsel' oot! There was mony a conjectur as to hoo he cam by his deith, an' mony a doobt it wasna by fair play. Some said he dee'd by his ain han', driven on till 't by the enemy; an' it was true the blade he cairriet was lyin' upo' the gerse aside 'im; but ither some, 'at exem't him, said the hole i' the side o' 'im wasna made wi' that. But o' a' 'at cam to speir efter 'im, the English lord was nane. He hed vainished the country.

"Dead was the old captain—as dead as ever was man that had none left to cry for him. But though there was no crying, yet such a hullabaloo as rose upon the discovery! They rode and they ran; the doctor came, and the minister, and the lawyer, and the grave-digger. But when a man's dead, what can all the world do but bury him? poor latter end though it be to him that draws himself up, and blows himself out! There was many a conjecture as to how he came by his death, and many a doubt it wasn't by fair play. Some said he died by his own hand, driven on to it by the enemy; and it was true the blade he carried was lying upon the grass beside him; but others that examined him, said the hole in his side wasn't made with that. But of all that came to ask about him, the English lord was none. He had vanished the

The general opingon sattled doon to this, 'at they twa bude till hae fa'en oot at cairts, an' fouchten it oot, an' the auld captain, for a' his skeel an' exparience, had had the warst o' 't, an' sae there they faun' 'im—But I reckon, Cosmo, yer father 'ill hae tellt ye a' aboot the thing, mony's the time, or noo, an' I'm jist deivin' ye wi' my clavers, an' haudin' ye ohn sleepit!"

"Na, Grannie," answered Cosmo, "he never tellt me what ye hae tellt me noo. He did tell me 'at there was sic a man, an' the ill en' he cam til; an' I think he was jist gaein' on to tell me mair, whan Grizzie cam to say the denner was ready. That was only yesterday—or the day afore, I'm thinkin', by this time.—But what think ye could hae been in 's heid wi' yon jingle aboot the horsie?"

"Ow, what wad be intil 't but jist fulish nonsense? Ye ken some fowk has a queer trick o' sayin' the same thing ower an' ower again to themsel's wi'oot ony sense intil 't. There was the auld laird himsel'; he was ane o' sic. Aye an' ower again, he wad be sayin' til himsel', 'A hun'er poun'! Ay, a hun'er poun'!' It maittered na what he wad be speikin' aboot, or wha til, in it wad come!—i' the middle o' onything, ye cudna tell whan or whaur,—'A hun'er poun'!' says he; 'Ay, a hun'er poun'!' Fowk leuch at the first, but sune gat used til't, an' cam hardly to ken 'at he said it, for what has nae sense has little hearin'. An' I doobtna thae rimes wasna even a verse o' an auld ballant, but jist a cletter o' clinkin' styte 'at he had learnt frae some blackamore bairn, maybe, an' cudna get oot o' 's heid ony ither gait, but bude to say 't, to hae dune wi' 't—jist like a cat whan it gangs scrattin' at the door, ye hae to get up whether ye wull or no an' lat the cratur oot."

country. The general opinion settled down to this, that the two of them must have fallen out at cards, and fought each other, and the old captain, for all his skill and experience, had had the worst of it, and so there they found him.—But I reckon, Cosmo, your father will have told you all about the thing, many's the time, ere now, and I'm just deafening you with my prattle, and keeping you from sleep!"

"Na, Grannie," answered Cosmo, "he never told me what you've told me now. He did tell me that there was such a man, and the bad end he came to; and I think he was just going on to tell me more, when Grizzie came to say the dinner was ready. That was only yesterday—or the day before, I think, by this time.—But what do you think could have been in his head with that jingle about the horse?"

"Oh, what would be in it but just foolish nonsense? You know some folk have an odd trick of saying the same thing over and over again to themselves without any sense in it. There was the old laird himself; he was one of such. Always and ever, he would be saying to himself, 'A hundred pounds! Ay, a hundred pounds!' It didn't matter what he would be speaking about, or who to, in it would come!—in the middle of anything, you couldn't tell when or where,—'A hundred pounds!' says he; 'Ay, a hundred pounds!' Folk laughed at first, but soon got used to it, and came hardly to know that he said it, for what has no sense has little hearing. And I've no doubt those rhymes weren't even a verse of an old poem, but just a clatter of clanking nonsense, that he had learned from some foreign child, maybe, and couldn't get out of his head any other way, but had to say it to have done with it—just like a cat when it goes scratching at the door, you have to get up, whether you will or not, and let the creature out."

Cosmo did not feel quite satisfied with the explanation, but he made no objection to it.

"I maun alloo, hooever," the old woman went on, "'at ance ye get a haud o' *them,* they tak' a grip o' *you,* an' hae a queer w'y o' hauntin' ye like, as they did the man himsel', sae 'at ye canna get rid o' them. It comes only at noos an' thans, but whan the fit's upo' me, I canna

"I must allow, however," the old woman went on, "that once you get a hold of *them,* they take a grip of *you,* and have a strange way of haunting you, like they did the man himself, so that you can't get rid of them. It comes only now and then, but when the fit's upon me, I

get them oot o' my heid. The verse gangs on tum'lin' ower an' ower intil 't, till I'm jist scunnert wi' 't. Awa' it winna gang, maybe for a haill day, an syne it mayna come again for months."	can't get them out of my head. The verse goes on tumbling over and over inside it, till I'm just sick of it. It won't go away, maybe for a whole day, and then it mightn't come again for months."

True enough, the rime was already running about in Cosmo's head like a mouse, and he fell asleep with it ringing in the ears of his mind. Before he woke again, which was in the broad daylight, he had a curious dream. He dreamed that he was out in the moonlight. It was a summer night—late. But there was something very strange about the night: right up in the top of it was the moon, looking down as if she knew all about it, and something was going to happen. He did not like the look of her—he had never seen her look like that before! And he went home just to get away from her. As he was going up the stairs to his chamber, something moved him—he could not tell what—to stop at the door of the drawing-room, and go in. It was flooded with moonlight, but he did not mind that, so long as he could keep out of her sight. Still it had a strange, eerie look, with its various pieces of furniture casting different shadows from those that by rights belonged to them. He gazed at this thing and that, as if he had never seen it before. The place seemed to cast a spell on him, so that he could not leave it. He seated himself on the ancient brocaded couch, and sat staring, with a sense, which by degrees grew dreadful, that he was where he would not be, and that if he did not get up and go, something would happen. But he could not rise—not that he felt any physical impediment, but that he could not make a resolve strong enough—like one in irksome company, who wants to leave, but waits in vain a fit opportunity. Delay grew to agony, but still he sat. He became aware that he was not alone. His whole skin seemed to contract with a shuddering sense of presence. Gradually, as he gazed straight in front of him, slowly, in the chair on the opposite side of the fire-place, grew visible the form of a man, until he saw it quite plainly—that of a seafaring man, in a blue coat, with a red sash round his waist, in which were pistols and a dagger. He too sat motionless, fixing on him the stare of fierce eyes, black, yet glowing, as if set on fire of hell. They filled him with fear, but something seemed to sustain him under it. He almost fancied, when first on waking he thought over it, that a third must have been in the room—for his protection. The face that stared at him was a brown and red and weather-beaten face, cut across with a great scar, and wearing an expression of horror trying not to look horrible. His fear threatened to turn him into clay, but he met it with scorn, strove against it, would not and did not yield. Still the figure stared, as if it would fascinate him into limpest submission. Slowly at length it rose, and with a look that seemed meant to rivet the foregone stare—a look of mingled pain and fierceness, turned, and led the way from the room, whereupon the spell was so far broken or changed that he was able to rise and follow him: even in his dreams he was a boy of courage, and feared nothing so much as yielding to fear. The figure went on, nor ever turned its head, up the stair to the room over that they had left—the best bedroom, the guest-chamber of the house—not often visited, and there it entered. Cosmo entered also. The figure walked across the room, as if making for the bed, but in the middle of the floor suddenly turned, and went round by the foot of the bed to the other side of it, where the curtains hid it. Cosmo followed, but when he reached the other side, the shade was nowhere to be seen, and he woke, his heart beating terribly.

By this time Grannie was snoring in her chair, or very likely, in his desire to emerge from its atmosphere, he would have told her his dream. For a while he lay looking at the dying fire, and the streak from the setting moon, that stole in at the window, and lay weary at the foot of the wall. Slowly he fell fast asleep, and slept far into the morning: long after lessons were begun in the school, and village affairs were in the full swing of their daily routine, he slept; nor had he finished his breakfast, when his father entered.

"I'm quite well, papa," answered the boy to his gentle yet eager inquiry;—"perfectly able to go to school in the afternoon."

"I don't mean you to go again, Cosmo," replied his father gravely. "It could not be pleasant either for yourself or for the master. The proper relation between you is destroyed."

"If you think I was wrong, papa, I will make an apology."

"If you had done it for yourself, I should unhesitatingly say you must. But as it was, I am not prepared to say so."

"What am I to do then? How am I to get ready for college?"

The laird gave a sigh, and made no answer. Alas! there were more difficulties than that in the path to college.

He turned away, and went to call on the minister, while Cosmo got up and dressed: except a little singing in his head when he stooped, he was aware of no consequences of the double blow.

Grannie was again at her wheel, and Cosmo sat down in her chair to await his father's return.

"Whaur said ye the captain sleepit whan he was at the castle?" he inquired across the burr and whiz and hum of the wheel. Through the low window, betwixt the leaves of the many plants that shaded it, he could see the sun shining hot upon the bare street; but inside was soft gloom filled with murmurous sound.

"Whaur but i' the best bedroom?" answered Grannie. "Naething less wad hae pleased *him,* I can assure ye. For ance 'at there cam the markis to the hoose—whan things warna freely sae scant aboot the place as they hae been sin' yer father cam to the throne—there cam at his back a fearsome storm sic as comes but seldom in a life lang as mine, an' sic 'at his lordship cudna win awa'. Thereupon yer father, that is yer gran'father—or wad it be yer grit-gran'father?—I'm turnin' some confused amo' ye: ye aye keep comin'!—onyhoo, he gae the auld captain a hent like, 'at he wad du weel to offer his room til 's lordship. But wad he, think ye? Na, no him! He grew reid, an' syne as white's the aisse, an' luikit to be in the awfu'est inside rage 'at mortal wessel cud weel haud. Sae yer gran'father, no 'at he was feart at 'im, for I s' be bun' he never was feart afore the face o' man, but jist no wullin' to anger his ain kin, an' maybe no wullin' onybody sud say he was a respecter o' persons, heeld his tongue an' said nae mair, an' the markis hed the second best bed, for he sleepit in Glenwarlock's ain."

"Where did you say the captain slept when he was at the castle?" he inquired across the burr and whiz and hum of the wheel. Through the low window, betwixt the leaves of the many plants that shaded it, he could see the sun shining hot upon the bare street; but inside was soft gloom filled with murmurous sound.

"Where but in the best bedroom?" answered Grannie. "Nothing less would have pleased *him,* I can assure you. For once when the marquis came to the house—when things weren't quite so scanty about the place as they have been since your father came to the throne—there came at his back a fearsome storm such as comes but seldom in a life long as mine, and such that his lordship couldn't get away. Thereupon your father, that is your grandfather—or would it be your great-grandfather?—I'm growing quite confused among you: you just keep coming!—anyway, he gave the old captain a hint that he would do well to offer his room to his lordship. But would he, do you think? Na, not him! He grew red, and then as white as ash, and appeared to be in the most awful inside rage that mortal vessel could hold. So your grandfather, not that he feared him, for I'll swear he never was afraid before the face of man, but just unwilling to anger his own kin, and maybe not wishing to be thought a respecter of persons, held his tongue and said no more, and the marquis had the second best bed, for he slept in Glenwarlock's own."

Cosmo then told her the dream he had had in the night, describing the person he had seen in it as closely as he could. Now all the time Grannie had been speaking, it was to the accompaniment of her wheel, but Cosmo had not got far with his narrative when she ceased spinning, and sat absorbed—listening as to a real occurrence, not the feverish dream of a boy. When he ended—

"It maun hae been the auld captain himsel'!" ("It must have been the old captain himself!") she said under her breath, and with a sigh; then shut up her mouth, and remained silent, leaving Cosmo in doubt whether it was that she would take no interest in such a foolish thing, or found in it something to set her thinking; but he could not help noting that there seemed a strangeness about her silence; nor she did break it until his father returned.

CHAPTER VIII
HOME

Cosmo was not particularly fond of school, and he was particularly fond of holidays; hence his father's resolve that he should go to school no more, seemed to him the promise of an endless joy. The very sun seemed swelling in his heart as he walked home with his father. A whole day of home and its pleasures was before him—only the more welcome that he had had a holiday so lately, and that so many more lay behind it. Every shadow about the old place was a delight to him. Never human being loved more the things into which he had been born than did Cosmo. The whole surrounding had to him a sacred look, such as Jerusalem, the temple, and its vessels bore to the Jews, even those of them who were capable of loving little else. There was hardly anything that could be called beauty about the building—strength and gloom were its main characteristics—but its very stones were dear to the boy. There never were such bees, there never were such thick walls, there never were such storms, never such a rushing river, as those about his beloved home! And this although, all the time, as I have said, he longed for more beauty of mountain and wood than the country around could afford him. Then there were the books belonging to the house!—was there any such a collection in the world besides! They were in truth very few—all contained in a closet opening out of his father's bedroom; but Cosmo had a feeling of inexhaustible wealth in them—partly because his father had not yet allowed him to read everything there, but restricted him to certain of the shelves—as much to cultivate self-restraint in him as to keep one or two of the books from him—partly because he read books so that they remained books to him, and he believed in them after he had read them, nor imagined himself capable of exhausting them. But the range of his taste was certainly not a limited one. While he revelled in *The Arabian Nights*, he read also, and with no small enjoyment, the *Night Thoughts*—books, it will be confessed, considerably apart both in scope and in style. But while thus, for purest pleasure, fond of reading, to enjoy life it was to him enough to lie in the grass; in certain moods, the smell of the commonest flower would drive him half crazy with delight. On a holiday his head would be haunted with old ballads like a sunflower with bees: on other days they would only come and go. He rejoiced even in nursery rimes, only in his head somehow or other they got glorified. The swing and hum and *bizz* of a line, one that might have to him no discoverable meaning, would play its tune in him as well as any mountain-stream its infinite water-jumbled melody. One of those that this day kept—not coming and going, but coming and coming, just as Grannie said his foolish rime haunted the old captain, was that which two days before came into his head when first he caught sight of the moon playing bo-peep with him betwixt the cow's legs:

Whan the coo loups ower the mune, The reid gowd rains intil men's shune.	When the cow leaps over the moon, The red gold rains into men's shoes.

I think there must at one time have been a poet in the Glenwarlock nursery, for there were rimes, and modifications of rimes, floating about the family, for which nobody could account. Cosmo's mother too had been, in a fragmentary way, fond of verse; and although he could not remember many of her favourite rimes, his father did, and delighted in saying them over and over to her child—and that long before he was capable of understanding them. Here is one :—

Make not of thy heart a casket,
Opening seldom, quick to close;
But of bread a wide-mouthed basket,
And a cup that overflows.

Here is another:

The gadfly makes the horse run swift:
"Speed," quoth the gadfly, "is my gift."

One more, and it shall be the last for the present: They serve as dim lights on the all but vanished mother, of whom the boy himself knew so little.

In God alone, the perfect end,
Wilt thou find thyself or friend.

Cosmo's dream of life was, to live all his days in the house of his forefathers—or at least and worst, to return to it at last, however long soever he might have been compelled to be away from it. In his castle building, next to that of the fairy-mother-lady, his fondest fancy was—not the making of a fortune, but the returning home with one to make the house of his fathers beautiful, and the heart of his father glad. About the land he did not think so much yet: the country was open to him as if it had been all his own. Still, he had quite a different feeling for that portion which yet lay within the sorely contracted marches; to have seen any smallest nook of that sold would have been like to break his heart. In him the love of place was in danger of becoming a disease. There was in it something, I fear, of the nature, if not of the avarice that grasps, yet of the avarice that clings. He was generous as few in the matter of money, but then he had had so little—not half enough to learn to love it! Nor had he the slightest idea of any mode in which to make it. Most of the methods he had come in contact with, except that of manual labour, in which work was done and money paid immediately for it, repelled him, as having elements of the unhandsome where not the dishonest: he was not yet able to distinguish between substance and mode in such matters. The only way in which he ever dreamed of coming into possession of money—it was another of his favourite castles—was finding in the old house a room he had never seen or heard of before, and therein a hoard of riches incredible. Such things had been—why might it not be?

As they walked, his father told him he had been thinking all night what it would be best to do with him, now that the school was closed against him; and that he had come to the conclusion to ask his friend Peter Simon—the wits of the neighbourhood called him Simon Peter— to take charge of his education.

"He is a man of peculiar opinions," he said, "as I dare say you may have heard; but everything in him is, practice and theory, on a scale so grand, that to fear harm from him would be to sin against the truth. A man must learn to judge for himself, and he will teach you that. I have seen in him so much that I recognize as good and great, that I am compelled to believe in him where the things he believes appear to me out of the way, or even extravagant."

"I have heard that he believes in ghosts, papa!" said Cosmo.

His father smiled, and made him no answer. He had been born into an age whose incredulity, taking active form, was now fast approaching its extreme, and becoming superstition; and the denial of many things that had long been believed in the country had penetrated at last even to the remote region where his property lay: like that property, his mind, because of the age, lay also in a sort of border-land. An active believer in the care and providence of God, with no conscious difficulty in accepting any miracle recorded in the Bible, he was, where the oracles were dumb, in a measure inclined to scepticism, which yet was limited to the region of his intellect;— his imagination turned from its conclusions, and cherished not a little so-called weakness for the so-called supernatural—so far as any glimmer of sense or meaning or reason would show itself therein. And in the history of the world, the imagination has, I fancy, been quite as often right as the intellect, and the things in which it has been right have been of much the greater importance. Only, unhappily, wherever Pegasus has shown the way through a bog, the pack-horse which followed gets the praise of crossing it; while the blunders with which the pack-horse is burdened, are, the moment each is discovered, by the plodding leaders of the pair transferred to the space betwixt the wings of Pegasus, without regard to the beauty of his feathers. The laird was unable to speak with authority respecting such things, and was not particularly anxious to influence the mind of his son concerning them. Happily, in those days the platitudes and weary vulgarities of what they call spiritualism had not been heard of in those quarters, and the soft light of imagination yet lingered about the borders of that wide region of mingled false and true, commonly called Superstition. It seems to me the most killing poison to the imagination must be a strong course of "spiritualism." For myself, I am not so set upon entering the Unknown, as, instead of encouraging what holy visitations faith, not in the spiritual or the immortal, but in the living God, may bring, to creep through the sewers of it to get in. I care not to encounter its mud-larkes, and lovers of garbage, its thieves, impostors, liars, and canaille, in general. That they are on the other side, that they are what men call dead, does not seem to me sufficient reason for taking them into my confidence, courting their company, asking their advice. A well-attested old fashion ghost story, where such is to be had, is worth a thousand séances.

"Do you believe in ghosts, papa?" resumed Cosmo, noting his father's silence, and remembering that he had never heard him utter an opinion on the subject. "The master says none but fools believe in them now; and he makes such a face at anything he calls superstition, that you would think it must be somewhere in the commandments."

"Mr. Simon remarked the other day in my hearing," answered his father, "that the dread of superstition might amount to superstition, and become the most dangerous superstition of all."

"Do you think so, papa?"

"I could well believe it. Besides, I have always found Mr. Simon so reasonable, even where I could not follow him, that I am prejudiced in favour of anything he thinks."

The boy rejoiced to hear his father talk thus, for he had a strong leaning to the marvellous, and hitherto, from the school master's assertion and his father's silence, had supposed nothing was to be accepted for belief but what was scientifically probable or was told in the bible. That we live in a universe of marvels of which we know only the outsides, and which we turn into the incredible by taking the mere outsides for all, even while we know the roots of the seen remain unseen—these spiritual facts now began to dawn upon him, and fell in most naturally with those his mind had already conceived and entertained. He was therefore delighted at the thought of making the closer acquaintance of a man like Mr. Simon—a man of whose peculiarities even, his father could speak in such terms. All day long he brooded on the prospect, and in the twilight went out wandering over the hills.

There was no night there at this season, any more than all the year through in heaven. Indeed, we have seldom real positive night in this world—so many provisions have been made against it. Every time we say, "What a lovely night!" we speak of a breach, a rift in the old night. There is light more or less, positive light, else were there no beauty. Many a night is but a low starry day, a day with a softened background, against which the far-off suns of millions of other days show themselves: when the near vision vanishes, the farther hope awakes. It is nowhere said of heaven, there shall be no twilight there.

CHAPTER IX
THE STUDENT

The twilight had not yet reached the depth of its mysteriousness, when Cosmo, returning home from casting a large loop of wandering over several hills, walked up to James Gracie's cottage, thinking whether they would not all be in bed.

But as he passed the window, he saw a little light, and went on to the door and knocked: had it been the daytime, he would have gone straight in. Agnes came, and opened cautiously, for there were occasionally such beings as tramps about.

"Eh! it's you?" she cried with a glad voice, when she saw the shape of Cosmo in the dimness. "There's naething wrong, I houp," she added, changing her tone.

"Na, naething," answered Cosmo. "I only wantit to lat ye ken 'at I wasna gaein' back to the schuil ony mair."

"Weel, I dinna won'er at that!" returned Agnes with a little sigh. "Efter the w'y the maister behaved til ye, the laird cud ill lat ye gang there again. But what's he gaein' to du wi' ye, Maister Cosmo, gien a body micht speir 'at has nae richt to be keerious?"

"He's sen'in' me to Maister Simon," answered Cosmo.

"I wuss I was gaein' tu," sighed Aggie. "I'm feart 'at I come to hate the maister efter ye're no to be seen there, Cosmo. An' we maunna hate, for that, ye ken, 's the hin'er en' o' a'thing. But it wad be a heap easier no to hate him gien I had naething to du wi' him."

"That maun be confest," answered Cosmo.—"But," he added, "the hairst-play 'ill be here sune, an' syne the hairst itsel'; an' whan ye gang back ye'll hae won ower 't."

"Na, I doobt no, Cosmo; for, ye see, as I hae h'ard my father say, the Gracies are a' terrible for min'in'. Na, there's nae forgetting' o' naething. What for sud onything be forgotten? It''s a cooardly kin' o' a w'y to forget."

"Some things, I doobt, hae to be forgotten," returned Cosmo, thoughtfully. "Gien ye forgie a body, for enstance, ye maun forget tu—no sae muckle, I'm thinkin', for the sake o' them 'at did ye the wrang, for wha wad tak up again a fool thing ance it was drappit?—but for yer ain sake; for what ye hae dune richt, my father says, maun be forgotten oot o' sight for fear o'

"Eh! it's you?" she cried with a glad voice, when she saw the shape of Cosmo in the dimness. "There's nothing wrong, I hope," she added, changing her tone.

"Na, nothing," answered Cosmo. "I only wanted to let you know that I wasn't going back to the school any more."

"Well, I don't wonder at that!" returned Agnes with a little sigh. "After the way the master behaved to you, the laird could hardly let you go there again. But what's he going to do with you, Master Cosmo, if a person might ask that has no right to be curious?"

"He's sending me to Master Simon," answered Cosmo.

"I wish I was going too," sighed Aggie. "I'm afraid I'll come to hate the master after you've left, Cosmo. And we mustn't hate, for that, you know, is when everything falls apart. But it would be much easier not to hate him if I had nothing to do with him."

"That must be confessed," answered Cosmo.—"But," he added, "the harvest-holiday will be here soon, and then the harvest itself; and when you go back you'll have conquered it."

"Na, I doubt it, Cosmo; for you see, as I have heard my father say, the Gracies are all terrible for remembering. No, there's no forgetting anything. Why should anything be forgotten? It's cowardly to forget."

"Some things, I suspect, have to be forgotten," returned Cosmo, thoughtfully. "If you forgive someone, for instance, you must forget too—not so much, I think, for the sake of them that did you the wrong, for who would take a foul thing up again once it was dropped?—but for your own sake; for what you've done right, my father says, must be corruption, for naething comes to stink waur nor a guid deed hung up i' the munelicht o' the memory."

"Eh!" exclaimed Aggie, "but ye're unco wice for a lad o' yer 'ears!"

"I wad be an unco gowk," remarked Cosmo, "gien I kent naething, wi' sic a father as yon o' mine. What wad ye think o' yersel', gien the dochter o' Jeames Gracie war nae mair wice-like nor Meg Scroggie?"

Agnes laughed, but made no reply, for the voice of her mother came out of the dark.

"Wha's that, Aggie, ye're haudin' sic a confab wi' i' the middle o' the nicht? Ye tellt me ye had to sit up to yer lessons!"

"I was busy at them, mither, whan Maister Cosmo chappit at the door."

"Weel, what for lat ye him stan' there? Ye may hae yer crack wi' *him* as lang's ye like—in rizzon, that is. Gar him come in."

"Na, na, Mistress Gracie," answered Cosmo; "I maun awa' hame; I hae had a gey lang walk. It's no 'at I'm tired, but I'm gey an sleepy. Only I was sae pleased 'at I was gaein' to learn my lessons wi' Maister Simon, 'at I bude to tell Aggie. She micht hae been won'erin', an' thinkin' I wasna better, gien she hadna see me at the schuil the morn."

"I s' warran' her ohn gane to the schuil ohn speirt in at the Castle the first thing i' the mornin', an' seein' gien the laird had ony eeran' to the toon. Little cares she for the maister, gien onybody at the Hoose be in want o' her!"

"Is there naething I cud help ye wi', Aggie, afore I gang?" asked Cosmo. "Somebody tellt me ye was tryin' yer han' at algebra."

"Naebody had ony business to tell ye ony sic a thing," returned Aggie, rather angrily. "It's no at the schuil I wad think o' sic a ploy. They wad a' lauch fine! But I *wad* fain ken what's intil the thing. I can*not* un'erstan' hoo fowk can coont wi' letters an' crosses an' strokes in place o' figgers. I hae been at it a haill ook noo—by mysel', ye ken—an' I'm nane nearer til 't yet. I can add an' subtrac, accordin' to

forgotten out of sight for fear of corruption, for nothing comes to stink worse than a good deed hung up in the moonlight of the memory."

"Eh!" exclaimed Aggie, "but you're very wise for a lad of your years!"

"I'd be very stupid," remarked Cosmo, "if I knew nothing, with such a father as mine. What would you think of yourself, if the daughter of James Gracie was no wiser than Meg Scroggie?"

Agnes laughed, but made no reply, for the voice of her mother came out of the dark.

"Who's that, Aggie, you're holding such a confab with in the middle of the night? You told me you had to stay up for your homework!"

"I was busy at it, mother, when Master Cosmo knocked at the door."

"Well, why do you let him stand there? You may have your news with *him* as long as you like—in reason, that is. Make him come in."

"Na, na, Mistress Gracie," answered Cosmo; "I must get home; I've had a good long walk. It's not that I'm tired, but I'm very sleepy. Only I was so pleased that I was going to learn my lessons with Master Simon, that I had to tell Aggie. She might have been wondering, and thinking I wasn't better, if she hadn't seen me at the school tomorrow."

"I know she wouldn't go to the school without asking at the Castle, the first thing in the morning, if the laird had any errand to the town. Little she cares for the master, if anybody at the House be in want of her!"

"Is there nothing I could help you with, Aggie, before I go?" asked Cosmo. "Somebody told me you were trying your hand at algebra."

"Nobody had any business to tell you any such thing," returned Aggie, rather angrily. "It's not at the school I would think of such a ploy. They would all fairly laugh! But I *would* gladly know the meaning of it. I can*not* understand how folk can count with letters and crosses and strokes in place of figures. I've been at it a whole week now—by myself, you know—and I'm no nearer to it yet. I can add

the rules gien, but that's no un'erstan'in', an' un'erstan' I canna."

and subtract, according to the rules given, but that's not understanding, and understanding's beyond me."

"I'm thinkin' it's something as gien x was a horse, an' y was a coo, an' z was a cairt, or onything ither ye micht hae to ca' 't; an' ye bargain awa' aboot the x an' the y an' the z, an' ley the horse i' the stable, the coo i' the byre, an' the cairt i' the shed, till ye hae sattlet a'."

"I'm thinking it's something as if x was a horse, and y was a cow, and z was a cart, or anything other you might have to call it, and you bargain away about the x and the y and the z, and leave the horse in the stable, the cow in the barn, and the cart in the shed, till you've settled it all."

"But *ye* ken aboot algébra"—she pronounced the word with the accent on the second syllable, "divna ye, Maister Cosmo?"

"But *you* know about algébra"—she pronounced the word with the accent on the second syllable, "don't you, Master Cosmo?"

"Na, no the half, nor the hun'ert pairt. I only ken eneuch to haud me gaein' on to mair. A body maun hae lairnt a heap o' onything afore the licht breaks oot o' 't. Ye maun win throuw the wa' first. I doubt gien onybody un'erstan's a thing oot an' oot, sae lang's he's no ready at a moment's notice to gar anither see intil the hert o' 't; an' I canna gar ye see what's intil 't the minute ye speir 't at me!"

"Na, not the half, nor the hundredth part. I only know enough to keep me at it till I get to more. You need to learn a great deal of anything before the light breaks out of it. You have to get through the wall first. I doubt if anybody understands a thing thoroughly, so long as he's not ready at a moment's notice to make another see into the heart of it; and I can't make you see what's in it the moment you ask me!"

"I'm thinkin', hooever, Cosmo, a body maun be nearhan' seein' o' himsel' afore anither can lat him see onything."

"I'm thinking, however, Cosmo, that a person would have to be close to seeing himself before another could let him see anything."

"Ye may be richt there," yielded Cosmo. "—But jist lat me see whaur ye are," he went on. "I may be able to help ye, though I canna lat ye see a' at ance. It wad be an ill job for them 'at needs help, gien naebody could help them but them 'at kent a' aboot a thing."

"You may be right there," yielded Cosmo. "—But just let me see where you are," he went on. "I may be able to help you, though I can't let you see all at once. It would be a bad state of things for those that need help, if nobody could help them but those that knew all about a thing."

Without a word, Aggie turned and led the way to the "but-end" (kitchen). An iron lamp, burning the coarsest of train-oil, hung against the wall, and under that she had placed the one moveable table in the kitchen, which was white as scouring could make it. Upon it lay a slate and a book of algebra.

"My cousin Willie lent me the buik," said Aggie.

"My cousin Willie lent me the book," said Aggie.

"What for didna ye come to me to len' ye ane? I could hae gien ye a better nor that," expostulated Cosmo.

"Why didn't you come to me to lend you one? I could have given you a better than that," expostulated Cosmo.

Aggie hesitated, but, open as the day, she did not hesitate long. She turned her face from him, and answered,

"I wantit to gie ye a surprise, Maister Cosmo. Divna ye min' tellin' me ance 'at ye saw no rizzon hoo a lassie sudna un'erstan' jist as weel's a laddie? I wantit to see whether ye was richt or wrang; an' as algébra luikit the

"I wanted to give you a surprise, Master Cosmo. Don't you remember telling me once that you saw no reason why a lassie shouldn't understand just as well as a laddie? I wanted to see whether you were right or wrong; and

maist oonlikely thing, I thoucht I wad taikle that, an' sae sattle the queston at ance. But, eh me! I'm sair feart ye was i' the wrang, Cosmo!"

as algébra looked the most unlikely thing, I thought I would tackle that, and so settle the question at once. But, oh! I'm much afraid you were wrong, Cosmo!"

"I maun du my best to pruv mysel' i' the richt!" returned Cosmo. "I never said onybody cud learn a' o' themsel's, wantin' help, ye ken. There's nae mony laddies cud do that, an' feower still wad try."

"I must do my best to prove myself in the right!" returned Cosmo. "I never said anybody could learn all by themselves, without help, you know. There's not many laddies could do that, and fewer still would try."

They sat down together at the table, and in half an hour or so Aggie had begun to see the faint light of at least the false dawn, as they call it, through the thickets of algebra. It was nearly midnight when Cosmo rose, and then Aggie would not let him go alone, but insisted on accompanying him to the gate of the court.

It was a curious relation between the two. While Agnes looked up to Cosmo, about two years her junior, as immeasurably her superior in all that pertained to the intellect and its range, she assumed over him a sort of general human superiority, something like that a mother will assert over the most gifted of sons. One has seen, with a kind of sacred amusement, the high priest of many literary and artistic circles, set down with rebuke by his mother, as if he had been still a boy! And I have heard the children of this world speak with like superiority of the child of light whom they loved—allowing him wondrous good, but regarding him as a kind of God's chicken: nothing is so mysterious to the children of this world as the ways of the children of light, though to themselves they seem simple enough. That Agnes never treated Cosmo with this degree of protective condescension, arose from the fact that she was very nearly as much a child of light as he; only, being a woman, she was keener of perception, and being older, felt the more of the mother that every woman feels, and made the most of it. It was to her therefore a merely natural thing to act his protector. Indeed with respect to the Warlock family in general, she counted herself possessed of the right to serve any one of them to the last drop of her blood. From infancy she had heard the laird spoken of—without definite distinction between the present and the last—as the noblest, best, and kindest of men, as the power which had been for generations over the Gracies, for their help and healing; and hence it was impressed upon her deepest consciousness, that one of the main reasons of her existence was her relation to the family of Glenwarlock.

Notwithstanding the familiarity I have shown between them—Agnes had but lately begun to put the *Master* before Cosmo's name, and as often forgot it,—the girl, as they went towards the castle, although they were walking in deep dusk, and entirely alone, kept a little behind the boy—not behind his back, but on his left hand in the next rank. No spy most curious could have detected the least love-making between them, and their talk, in the still, dark air, sounded loud all the way as they went. Strange talk it would have been counted by many, and indeed unintelligible, for it ranged over a vast surface, and was the talk of two wise children, wise not above their own years only, but immeasurably above those of the prudent. Riches indubitably favour stupidity; poverty, where the heart is right, favours mental and moral development. They parted at the gate, and Cosmo went to bed.

But although his father allowed him such plentiful liberty, and would fain have the boy feel the night holy as the day—so that no one ever asked where he had been, or at what hour he had come home—a question which, having no watch, he would have found it hard to answer—not an eye was closed in the house until his entering footsteps were heard. The grandmother lay angry at the unheard of liberty her son gave his son; it was neither decent nor in order; it was against all ancient rule of family life; she must speak about it! But she never did speak about it, for she was now in her turn afraid of the son who, without a particle of obstinacy in his composition, yet took what she called his own way. Grizzie kept grumbling to herself that the lad was sure to come to "mischief;" but the main forms of "mischief" that ruled in her imagination were tramps, precipices, and spates. The laird, for his part, spent most of the time his son's absence kept him awake, in praying for him—not that he might be the restorer of the family, but that he might be able to accept the will of God as the best thing for family as for individual. If his boy might but reach the spirit-land unsoiled and noble, his prayers were ended.

In such experiences, the laird learned to understand how the catholics come to pray to their saints, and the Chinese to their parents and ancestors; for he frequently found himself, more especially as drowsiness began to steal upon his praying soul, seeming to hold council with his wife concerning their boy, and asking her help toward such strength for him as human beings may minister to each other.

But Cosmo went up to bed without a suspicion that the air around him was full of such holy messengers heavenward for his sake. He imagined none anxious about him—either with the anxiety of grandmother or of servant-friend or of great-hearted father.

As he passed the door of the spare room, immediately above which was his own, his dream, preceded by a cold shiver, came to his memory. But he scorned to quicken his pace, or to glance over his shoulder, as he ascended the second stair. Without any need of a candle, in the still, faint twilight, which is the ghosts' day, he threw off his clothes, and was presently buried in the grave of his bed, under the sod of the blankets, lapt in the death of sleep.

The moment he woke, he jumped out of bed: a new era in his life was at hand, the thought of which had been subjacently present in his dreams, and was operative the instant he became conscious of waking life. He hurried on his clothes without care, for this dressing was but temporary. Going down the stairs like a cataract, for not a soul slept in that part but himself, and there was no fear of waking any one, then in like manner down the hill, he reached the place where, with a final dart, the torrent shot into the quiet stream of the valley, in whose channel of rock and gravel, it had hollowed a deep basin. This was Cosmo's bath—and a splendid one. His clothes were off again more quickly than he put them on, and headforemost he shot like the torrent into the boiling mass, where for a few moments he yielded himself the sport of the frothy water, and was tossed and tumbled about like a dead thing. Soon however, down in the heart of the boil, he struck out, and shooting from under the fall, rose to the surface beyond it, panting and blowing. To get out on the bank was then the work of one moment, and to plunge in again that of the next. Half a dozen times, with scarce a pause between, he thus plunged, was tossed and overwhelmed, struggled, escaped, and plunged again. Then he ran for a few moments up and down the bank to dry himself—he counted the use of a towel effeminacy—and dressing again, ran home to finish his simple toilet. If after that, he read a chapter of his Bible, it was no more than was required by many a parent of many a boy who got little good of the task; but Cosmo's father had never enjoined it on him; and when next he knelt down at his bedside, he did not merely "say his prayers." Then he took his slate, to try after something Aggie had made him know he did not understand:—for the finding of our own intellectual defects, nothing is like trying to teach another. But before long, certain sensations began to warn him there was an invention in the world called breakfast, and laying his slate aside, he went to the kitchen, where he found Grizzie making the porridge.

"Min' ye pit saut eneuch in 't the day, Grizzie," he said. "It was unco wersh yesterday."

"An' what was't like thestreen, Cosmo?" asked the old woman, irritated at being found fault with in a matter wherein she counted her

"Mind you put enough salt in it today, Grizzie," he said. "It was very bland yesterday."

"And what was it like last night, Cosmo?" asked the old woman, irritated at being found fault with in a matter wherein she counted her self as near perfection as ever mortal could come.

self as near perfection as ever mortal could come.

"I had nane last nicht, ye min'," answered Cosmo. "I was oot a' the evenin'."

"I had none last night, remember," answered Cosmo. "I was out all the evening."

"An' whaur got ye yer supper?"

"And where did you get your supper?"

"Ow, I didna want nane. Hoot! I'm forgettin'! Aggie gied me a quarter o' breid as I cam by, or rather as I cam awa', efter giein' her a han' wi' her algebra."

"Oh, I didn't want any. Heavens! I'm forgetting! Aggie gave me a quarter loaf as I came by, or rather as I came away, after giving her a hand with her algebra."

"What ca' ye that for a lass-bairn to be takin' up her time wi'? I never h'ard o' sic a thing! What's the natur o' 't Cosmo?"

"What kind of thing do you call that for a young lass to be taking up her time with? I never heard of such a thing! What's the nature of it Cosmo?"

He tried to give her some far-off idea of the sort of thing algebra was, but apparently without success, for she cried at length,

"Na, sirs! I hae h'ard o' cairts, an' bogles, an' witchcraft, an' astronomy, but sic a thing as this ye bring me noo, I never did hear tell o'! What can the warl' be comin' til!—An' dis the father o' ye, laddie, ken what ye spen' yer midnicht hoors gangin' teachin' to the lass-bairns o' the country roon'?"

"Na, sirs! I've heard of cards, and spectres, and witchcraft, and astronomy, but such a thing as this you bring me now, I never did hear tell of! What can the world be coming to!—And does your father, laddie, know what you spend your midnight hours going teaching to the young lassies of the country round?"

She was interrupted by the entrance of the laird, and they sat down to breakfast. The grandmother within the last year had begun to take hers in her own room.

Grizzie was full of anxiety to know what the laird would say to the discovery she had just made, but she dared not hazard allusion to the *conduct* of his son, and must therefore be content to lead the conversation in the direction of it, hoping it might naturally appear. So, about the middle of Cosmo's breakfast, that is about two minutes after he had attacked his porridge, she approached her design, if not exactly the object she desired, with the remark,

"Did ye never hear the auld saw, sir—

Whaur's neither sun nor mune,
Laich things come abune?"

"Did you never hear the old saw, sir—

Where's neither sun nor moon,
Low things turn up soon?"

"I 'maist think I hae, Grizzie," answered the laird. "But what gars ye come ower 't the noo?"

"I almost think I have, Grizzie," answered the laird. "But what makes you repeat it now?"

"I canna but think, sir," answered Grizzie, "as I lie i' the mirk, o' the heap o' things 'at gang to nae kirk, oot 'an aboot as sharp as a gled, whan the yoong laird is no in his bed—oot wi' 's algibbry, an' astronomy, an' a' that kin' o' thing! 'Deed, sir, it wadna be canny gien they cam to ken o' 't!"

"I can't but think, sir," answered Grizzie, "as I lie half asleep, of the unhallowed things that aren't of God's sheep, out and about as sharp as a kite, when your son the laird is wakeful at night—out with his algebra, and astronomy, and all that kind of thing! Indeed, sir, it wouldn't be canny if they came to know of it!"

"Wha come to ken o' what, Grizzie?" asked the laird, with a twinkle in his eye, and a glance at Cosmo, who sat gazing curiously at the old woman.

"Who come to know of what, Grizzie?" asked the laird, with a twinkle in his eye, and a glance at Cosmo, who sat gazing curiously at the old woman.

"Them 'at the saw speyks o', sir," said Grizzie, answering the first part of the double question, as she placed two boiled eggs before her master.

The laird smiled: he was too kind to laugh. Not a few laughed at old Grizzie, but never the laird.

"Did *ye* never hear the auld saw, Grizzie," he said:

> "Throu the heather an' how gaed the creepin' thing,
> But abune was the waught o' an angel's wing?"

"Ay, I hae h'ard it,—naegait 'cep' here i' this hoose," answered Grizzie: she would disparage the authority of the saying by a doubt as to its genuineness. "But, sir, ye sud never temp' Providence. Wha kens what may be oot i' the nicht?"

"To *him*, Grizzie, the nicht shineth as the day."

"Weel, sir," cried Grizzie, "ye jist pit me 'at I dinna ken mysel'! Is't poassible ye hae forgotten what's sae weel kent to a' the cuintry roon'?—the auld captain, 'at canna lie still in's grave because o'—because o' whatever the rizzon may be? Onygait, he's no laid yet; an' some thinks he's doomed to haunt the hoose till the day o' jeedgement."

"I suspec' there winna be muckle o' the hoose left for him to haunt 'gen that time, Grizzie," said the laird. "But what for sud ye pit sic fule things intil the bairn's heid? And gien the ghaist haunt the hoose, isna he better oot o' 't? Wad ye hae him come hame to sic company?"

"Those that the saw speaks of, sir," said Grizzie, answering the first part of the double question, as she placed two boiled eggs before her master.

The laird smiled: he was too kind to laugh. Not a few laughed at old Grizzie, but never the laird.

"Did *you* never hear the old saw, Grizzie," he said:

> "Through the heather and dale went the creeping thing,
> But above was the waft of an angel's wing?"

"Ay, I've heard it—nowhere except here in this house," answered Grizzie: she would disparage the authority of the saying by a doubt as to its genuineness. "But, sir, you should never tempt Providence. Who knows what may be out in the night?"

"To *him*, Grizzie, the night shineth as the day."

"Well, sir," cried Grizzie, "you just make me not to know myself! Is it possible you've forgotten what's so well known to all the country round?—the old captain, that can't lie still in his grave because of—because of whatever the reason may be? Anyway, he's not laid yet; and some think he's doomed to haunt the house till the day of judgement."

"I suspect there won't be much of the house left for him to haunt by that time, Grizzie," said the laird. "But why should you put such foolish things in the boy's head? And if the ghost haunts the house, isn't he better out of it? Would you have him come home to such company?"

This posed Grizzie, and she held her peace for the time.

"Come, Cosmo," said the laird, rising; and they set out together for Mr. Simon's cottage.

CHAPTER X
PETER SIMON

This man was not a native of the district, but had for some two years now been a dweller in it. Report said he was the son of a small tradesman in a city at no great distance, but, to those who knew him, he made no secret of the fact, that he had been found by such a man, a child of a few months, lying on the pavement of that city one stormy desolate Christmas-eve, when it was now dark, with the wind blowing bitterly from the north, and the said tradesman seemingly the one inhabitant of the coldest city in Scotland who dared face it. He had just closed his shop, had carried home to one of one of his customers a forgotten order, and was returning to his wife and a childless hearth, when he all but stumbled over the infant. Before stooping to lift him, he looked all about to see if there was nobody to do it instead. There was not a human being, or even what comes next to one, a dog in sight, and the wind was blowing like a blast from a frozen hell. There was no help for it: he must take up the child! He did, and carried it home, grumbling all the way. What right had the morsel to be lying there, a trap and a gin for his character, in the dark and the cold, where there was positively nobody but himself! What would his wife say? And what would the neighbours think? All the way home he grumbled.

What happened there, how his wife received him with his burden, how she scolded and he grumbled, how it needed but the one day—the Christmas Day, in which nothing could well be done—to reconcile them to the gift, and how they brought him up, blessing the day when they found him, would be a story fit to make the truehearted of my readers both laugh and cry; but I have not room or time for it.

Of course, as they were in poor circumstances, hardly able indeed, not merely to make both ends meet, but to bring them far enough round the parcel of their necessities to let them see each other, their friends called their behaviour in refusing to hand over the brat to the parish authorities—which they felt as a reflection upon all who in similar circumstances would have done so—utter folly. But when the moon-struck pair was foolish enough to say they did not know that he might not have been sent them instead of the still-born child that had hitherto been all their offspring, this was entirely too much for the nerves of the neighbours in general—that peculiar people often better acquainted with one's affairs, down to his faults and up to his duties, than he is himself. It was rank superstition! It was a flying in the face of Providence! How could they expect to prosper, when they acted with so little foresight, rendering the struggle for existence severer still! They did not reckon what strength the additional motive, what heart the new love, what uplifting the hope of help from on high, kindled by their righteous deed, might give them—for God likes far better to help people from the inside than from the outside. They did not think that this might be just the fresh sting of life that the fainting pair required. To mark their disapproval, some of them immediately withdrew what little custom they had given them: one who had given them none, promised them the whole of hers, the moment they sent the child away; while others, with equal inconsistency, doubled theirs, and did what they could to send them fresh customers: they were a pair of good-natured fools, but they ought not to be let starve! From that time they began to get on a little better. And still as the boy grew, and wanted more, they had the little more. For it so happened that the boy turned out to be one of God's creatures, and it looked as if the Maker of him, who happened also to be the ruler of the world, was not altogether displeased with those who had taken him to their hearts, instead of leaving him to the parish. The child was the light of the house and of the shop, a beauty to the eyes and a joy in the heart of both. But perhaps the best proof that they had done right, lay in the fact that they began to love each other better from the very next day after they took him in for, to tell the truth, one cause of their not getting on well had been that they did not pull well together. Thus we can explain the improvement in their circumstances by reference to merest "natural causes," without having recourse to the distasteful idea that a power in the land of superstition, with a weakness called a special providence, was interested in the matter.

But foolishness such as theirs is apt to increase with years; and so they sent the foundling to the grammar-school, and thence to college—not a very difficult affair in that city. At college he did not greatly distinguish himself, for his special gifts, though peculiar enough, were not of a kind to *distinguish* a man much, either in that city or in this world. But he grew and prospered nevertheless, and became a master in one of the schools. His father and mother, as he called them, would gladly have made a minister of him, but of that he would never hear. He lived with them till they died, always bringing home to them his salary, minus only the little that he spent on books. His life, his devotion and loving gratitude, so wrought upon them, that the kingdom of heaven opened its doors to them, and they were the happiest old couple in that city. Of course this was all an accident, for the kingdom of heaven being but a dream, the dignity of natural cause can scarcely consent to work to the end of delusion; but the good-natured pair were foolish enough to look upon their miserable foundling as a divine messenger, an angel entertained not for long unawares, and the cause of all the good luck that followed his entrance. They never spent a penny of his salary, but added to it, and saved it up, and when they went, very strangely left all they had to this same angel of a beggar, instead of to their own relations, who would have been very glad of it, for they had a good deal more of their own.

The foundling did not care to live longer in any city, but sought a place as a librarian, and was successful. In the family of an English lord he lived many years, and when time's changes rendered it necessary he should depart, he retired to the cottage on the Warlock. There he was now living the quietest of quiet lives, cultivating the acquaintance of but a few—chiefly that of the laird, James Gracie, and the minister of the parish. Among the people of the neighbourhood he was regarded as "no a'thegither there." (*"not altogether there."*) This judgment possibly arose in part from the fact that he not unfrequently wandered about the fields from morning to night, and sometimes from night to morning. Then he never drank anything worthy of the name of drink—seldom anything but water or milk! That he never ate animal food was not so notable where many never did so from one year's end to another's. As he was no propagandist, few had any notion of his opinions, beyond a general impression that they were unsound.

Cosmo had heard some of the peculiarities attributed to him, and was filled with curious expectation as to the manner of man he was about to meet, for, oddly enough, he had never seen him except at a distance; but anxiety, not untinged with awe, was mingled with his curiosity.

Mr. Simon's cottage was some distance up the valley, at an angle where it turned westward. It stood on the left bank of the Warlock, at the foot of a small cliff that sheltered it from the north, while in front the stream came galloping down to it from the sunset. The immediate bank between the cottage and the water was rocky and dry, but the ground on which the cottage stood was soil washed from the hills. There Mr. Simon had a little garden for flowers and vegetables, with a summer-seat in which he smoked his pipe of an evening—for, however inconsistent the habit may seem with the rest of the man, smoke he did: slowly and gently and broodingly did the man smoke, thinking a great deal more more than he smoked, and making his one pipe last a long time. His garden was full of flowers, but of the most ordinary kinds; rarity was no recommendation to him. Some may think that herein he was unlike himself, seeing his opinions were of the rarest; but in truth never once did Peter Simon, all his life, adopt an opinion because of its strangeness. He never *adopted* an opinion at all; he believed—he loved what seemed to him true: how it looked to others he concerned himself little.

The cottage was of stone and lime, nowise the less thoroughly built that the stones were unhewn. It was *harled*, that is rough-cast, and shone very white both in sun and moon. It contained but two rooms and a closet between, with one under the thatch for the old woman who kept house for him. Altogether it was a very ordinary, and not very promising abode.

When they were shown through to the parlour, Cosmo was struck with nothing less than astonishment: the walls from floor to ceiling were covered with books. Not a square foot all over was vacant. Even the chimney-piece was absorbed, assimilated, turned into a book-shelf, and so obliterated. Mr. Simon's pipe lay on the hob; and there was not another spot where it could have lain. There was not a shelf, a cupboard to be seen. Books, books everywhere, and nothing but books! Even the door that led to the closet where he slept was covered over, and, like the mantelshelf, obliterated with books. They were but about twelve hundred in all; to the eyes of Cosmo it seemed a mighty library—a treasure-house for a royal sage.

There was no one in the room when they entered, and Cosmo was yet staring in mute astonishment, when suddenly Mr. Simon was addressing his father. But the door had not opened, and how he came in seemed inexplicable. To the eyes of the boy, the small man before him assumed gigantic proportions.

But he was in truth below the middle height, somewhat round-shouldered, with long arms, and small, well-shaped hands. His hair was plentiful, grizzled, and cut short. His head was large and his forehead wide, with overhanging brows; his eyes were small, dark, and brilliant; his nose had a certain look of decision—but a nose is a creature beyond description; his mouth was large, and his chin strong; his complexion dark, and his skin rugged. The only *fine* features about him were his two ears, which were delicate enough for a lady. His face was not at first sight particularly attractive; indeed it was rather gloomy—till he smiled, not a moment after; for that smile was the true interpreter of the mouth, and, through the mouth, of the face, which was never the same as before to one that had seen it.

After a word or two about a book he had borrowed, the laird took his departure, saying the sooner he left master and pupil to themselves the better. Mr. Simon acquiesced with a smile, and presently Cosmo was facing his near future, not without some anxiety.

CHAPTER XI
THE NEW SCHOOLING

Without a word, Mr. Simon opened a drawer, and taking from it about a score of leaves of paper, handed one of them to Cosmo. Upon it, in print, was a stanza—one, and no more.

"Read that," he said, with a glance that showed through his eyes the light burning inside him, "and tell me if you understand it. I don't want you to ponder over it, but to say at a reading whether you know what it means."

Cosmo obeyed, and read.

"I dinna mak heid nor tail o' 't, sir," ("I don't make head nor tail of it, sir,") he answered, looking over the top of the paper like a prisoned sheep.

Mr. Simon took it from him, and handed him another.

"Try that," he said.

Cosmo read, put his hand to his head, and looked troubled.

"Don't distress yourself," said Mr. Simon. "The thing is of no consequence for judgment; it is only for discovery."

The remark conveyed but little consolation to the pupil, who would gladly have stood well in his own eyes before his new master.

One after another Mr. Simon handed him the papers he held. About the fifth or sixth, Cosmo exclaimed,

"I do understand that, sir,"

"Very well," returned Mr. Simon, without showing any special satisfaction, and immediately handed him another.

This was again a non-luminous body, and indeed cast a shadow over the face of the embryo student. One by one Mr. Simon handed him all he held. Out of the score there were three Cosmo said he understood, and four he thought he should understand if he were allowed to read them over two or three times. But Mr. Simon laid them all together again, and back into the drawer.

"Now I shall know what I am about," he said. "Tell me what you have been doing at school."

Were my book a treatise on education, it might be worth while to give some account of Peter Simon's ways of furthering human growth. But intellectual development is not my main business or interest, and I mean to say little more concerning Cosmo's than that, after about six weeks' work, the boy one day begged Mr. Simon to let him look at those papers, and found to his delight that he understood all but three or four of them.

That first day, Mr. Simon gave him an ode of Horace, and a poem by Wordsworth to copy—telling him to put in every point as it was in the book exactly, but to note any improvement he thought might be made in the pointing. He told him also to look whether he could see any resemblance between the two poems.

As he sat surrounded by the many books, Cosmo felt as if he were in the heart of a cloud of witnesses.

The first day was sufficient to make the heart of the boy cleave to his new master. For one thing, Mr. Simon always, in anything done, took note first of the things that pleased him, and only after that proceeded to make remark on the faults—most of which he treated as imperfections, letting Cosmo see plainly that he understood how he had come to go wrong.

Such an education as Mr. Simon was thus attempting with Cosmo, is hardly to be given to more than one at a time; and indeed there are not a great many boys on whom it would be much better than lost labour. Cosmo, however, was now almost as eager to go to his lessons, as before to spend a holiday. Mr. Simon never gave him anything to do at home, heartily believing it the imperative duty of a teacher to leave room for the scholar to grow after the fashion in which he is made, and that what a boy does by himself is of greater import than what he does with any master. Such leisure may indeed be of comparatively small consequence with regard to the multitude of boys, but it is absolutely necessary wherever one is born with his individuality so far determined, as to be on the point of beginning to develop itself. When Cosmo therefore went home, he read or wrote what he pleased, wandered about at his will, and dreamed to his heart's content. Nor was it long before he discovered that his dreams themselves were becoming of greater import to him—that they also were being influenced by Mr. Simon. And there were other witnesses there, quite as silent as those around him in the library, and more unseen, who would not remain speechless or invisible always.

One day Cosmo came late, and to say there were traces of tears on his cheeks would hardly be correct, for his eyes were swollen with weeping. His master looked at him almost wistfully, but said nothing until he had settled for a while to his work, and was a little composed. He asked him then what was amiss, and the boy told him. To most boys it would have seemed small ground for such heart-breaking sorrow.

Amongst the horses on the farm, was a certain small mare, which, although she worked as hard as any, was yet an excellent one to ride, and Cosmo, as often as there was not much work doing, rode her where he would, and boy and mare were much attached to each other. Sometimes he would have her every day for several weeks, and that would be in the prime of the summer weather, when the harvest was drawing nigh, and the school had its long yearly holiday. Summer, the harvest—"play" and Linty!—oh, large bliss! My heart swells at the thought. They would be out for hours together, perhaps not far from home all the time—on the top of a hill it might be, whence Cosmo could see when he would the castle below. There, the whole sleepy afternoon, he would lie in the heather, with Linty, the mare, feeding amongst it, ready to come at his call, receive him on her back, and carry him where he would!

But alas! though supple and active, Linty was old, and the day could not be distant when they must part company: she was then nine and twenty. And now—the night before she had been taken ill: there was a disease amongst the horses. The men had been up with her all night, and Grizzie too: she had fetched her own pillow and put it under her head, then sat by it for hours. When Cosmo left, she was a little better, but great fears were entertained as to the possibility of her recovery.

"She's sae terrible aul', ye see, sir!" said Cosmo, as he ended his tale of woe, and burst out crying afresh.

"Cosmo," said Mr. Simon,—and to a southern ear the issuing of such sweet solemn thoughts in such rough northern speech, might have seemed strange, though, to be sure, the vowels were finely sonorous if the consonants were harsh,—"Cosmo, your heart is faithful to your mare, but is it equally faithful to him that made your mare?"

"I ken it's his wull," answered Cosmo:—his master never took notice whether he spoke in broad Scotch or bastard English—"I ken mears maun dee, but eh! *she* was sic a guid ane!—Sir! I canna bide it."

"She's so terribly old, you see, sir!" said Cosmo, as he ended his tale of woe, and burst out crying afresh.

"Cosmo," said Mr. Simon,—and to a southern ear the issuing of such sweet solemn thoughts in such rough northern speech, might have seemed strange, though, to be sure, the vowels were finely sonorous if the consonants were harsh,—"Cosmo, your heart is faithful to your mare, but is it equally faithful to him that made your mare?"

"I know it's his will," answered Cosmo:—his master never took notice whether he spoke in broad Scotch or bastard English— "I know mares must die, but eh! *she* was such a good one!—Sir! I can't stand it!"

"Ye ken wha sits by the deein' sparrow?" said Mr. Simon, himself taking to the dialect. "Cosmo! there was a better nor Grizzie, an' nearer to Linty a' the lang nicht. Things warna gangin' sae ill wi' her as ye thoucht. Life's an awfu' mystery, Cosmo, but it's jist the ae thing the maker o' 't can haud nearest til, for it's nearest til himsel' i' the mak o' 't—Fowk may tell me," he went on, more now as if he were talking to himself than to the boy, "'at I sud content mysel' wi' what I see an' hear, an' lat alane sic eeseless speculations! wi' deein' men an' mears a' aboot me, hoo can I! They're onything but eeseless to me, for gien I had naething but what I see an' hear, gran' an' bonny as a heap o' 't is, I wad jist smore for want o' room."

"But what's the guid o' 't a', whan I'll never see her again?" sobbed Cosmo.

"Wha says sic a thing, laddie?"

"A'body," answered Cosmo, a good deal astonished at the question.

"Maister A'body has a heap o' the gowk in him yet, Cosmo," rejoined his master. "In fac', he's scarce mair nor an infant yet, though he wull speyk as gien the haill universe o' wisdom an' knowledge war open til 'im! There's no a word o' the kin' i' the haill Bible, nor i' the hert o' man—nor i' the hert o' the Maker, do I, i' the hert o' me, believe. Cosmo, can *ye* believe 'at that wee bit foal o' an ass 'at cairriet the maister o' 's a' alang yon hill ro'd frae Bethany to Jerus'lem, cam to sic an ill hin'er en' as to be forgotten by him he cairriet? No more can I believe that jist 'cause it cairriet him it was ae hair better luikit efter nor ony ither bit assie foalt i' the lan' o' Isr'el."

"The disciples micht hae min't it to the cratur, an' luikit efter him for 't," suggested Cosmo.

His master looked pleased.

"They could but work the wull o' him that made the ass," he said, "an' does the best for a'thing an' a'body. Na, na, my son! gien I hae ony pooer to read the trowth o' things, the life 'at's gien is no taen; an' whatever come o' the crater, the love it waukent in a human breist 'ill no more be lost than the objec' o' the same. That

"You know who sits by the dying sparrow?" said Mr. Simon, himself taking to the dialect. "Cosmo! There was a better than Grizzie, and nearer to Linty all the long night. Things weren't going so ill with her as you thought. Life's an awful mystery, Cosmo, but it's just the one thing the maker of it can hold nearest to, for it's nearest to himself in the make of it—Folk may tell me," he went on, more now as if he were talking to himself than to the boy, "that I should content myself with what I see and hear, and let alone such useless speculations! with dying men and mares all about me, how can I! They're anything but useless to me, for if I had nothing but what I see and hear, grand and bonny as much of it is, I would just be smothered for want of room."

"But what's the good of it all, when I'll never see her again?" sobbed Cosmo

"Who says such a thing, laddie?"

"Everyone," answered Cosmo, a good deal astonished at the question.

"Master Everyone has a deal of the fool in him yet, Cosmo," rejoined his master. "In fact, he's scarce more than an infant yet, though he will speak as if the whole universe of wisdom and knowledge were open to him! There's not a word of the kind in the whole Bible, nor in the heart of man—nor in the heart of the Maker, do I, in the heart of me, believe. Cosmo, can *you* believe that that wee foal of an ass that carried our master along that hill road from Bethany to Jerusalem, came to such a bad end as to be forgotten by him he carried? No more can I believe that just because it carried him it was one hair better looked after than any other wee ass-foal in the land of Israel."

"The disciples might have remembered what it did, and looked after him for it," suggested Cosmo.

His master looked pleased.

"They could but work the will of him that made the ass," he said, "and does the best for everything and everyone. Na, na, my son! if I have any power to read the truth of things, the life that's given is not taken; and whatever come of the creature, the love it wakened in a human breast will no more be lost than the

a thing can love an' be loved—an' that's yer bonnie mearie, Cosmo—is jist a' ane to sayin' 'at it's immortal, for God is love, an' whatever partakes o' the essence o' God canna dee, but maun gang on livin' till it please him to say haud, an' that he'll never say."

object of the same. That a thing can love and be loved—and that's your bonnie mare, Cosmo—is just all one to saying that it's immortal, for God is love, and whatever partakes of the essence of God can't die, but must go on living till it please him to say hold, and that he'll never say."

By this time the face of the man was glowing like an altar on which had descended the fire of the highest heaven. His confidence entered the heart of Cosmo, and when the master ceased he turned, with a sigh of gladness and relief, to his work, and wept no more. The possible entrance of Linty to an enlarged existence, widened the whole heaven of his conscious being; the well-spring of personal life within him seemed to rush forth in mighty volume; and through that grief and its consolation, the boy made a great stride towards manhood.

One day in the first week of his new schooling, Cosmo took occasion to mention Aggie's difficulty with her algebra, and her anxiety to find whether it was true that a girl could do as well as a boy. Mr. Simon was much interested, and with the instinct of the true hunter, whose business it is to hunt death for the sake of life, began to think whether here might not be another prepared to receive. He knew her father well, but had made no acquaintance with Agnes yet, who indeed was not a little afraid of him, for he looked as if he were always thinking about things nobody else knew of, although, in common with every woman who saw it, she did find his smile reassuring. No doubt the peculiar feeling of the neighbours concerning him had caused her involuntarily to associate with him the idea of something "not canny." Not the less, when she heard from Cosmo what sort of man his new master was, would she have given all she possessed to learn of him. And before long, she had her chance. Old Dorothy, Mr. Simon's servant and housekeeper, was one day taken ill, and Cosmo mentioning the fact in Aggie's hearing, she ran, with a mere word to her mother, and not a moment's cogitation, to offer her assistance till she was better.

It turned out that "old Dorty," as the neighbours called her, not without some hint askance at the quality of her temper, was not very seriously ailing, yet sufficiently so to accept a little help for the rougher work of the house; and while Aggie was on her knees washing the slabs of the passage that led through the back door, the master, as she always called him now that Cosmo was his pupil, happened to come from his room, and saw and addressed her. She rose in haste, mechanically drying her hands in her apron.

"How's the algebra getting on, Agnes?" he said.

"Naething's getting' on verra weel sin' maister Cosmo gaed frae the schuil, sir. I dinna seem to hae the hert for the learnin' 'at I had sae lang as he was there, sae far aheid o' me, but no a'thegither oot o' my sicht, like. It soon's a conceitit kin' o' a thing to say, but I'm no meanin' onything o' that natur', sir."

"I understand you very well, Agnes," returned the master. "Would you like to have some lessons with me? I don't say along with Cosmo; you would hardly be able for that at present, I fancy—but at such times as you could manage to come—odd times, when you were not wanted."

"How's the algebra getting on, Agnes?" he said.

"Nothing's getting on very well since master Cosmo left the school, sir. I don't seem to have the heart for the learning that I had as long as he was there, so far ahead of me, but not altogether out of my sight. It sounds a conceited kind of a thing to say, but I'm not meaning anything of that nature, sir."

"I understand you very well, Agnes," returned the master. "Would you like to have some lessons with me? I don't say along with Cosmo; you would hardly be able for that at present, I fancy—but at such times as you could manage to come—odd times, when you were not wanted."

"There's naething upo' the airth, sir," said Aggie, "'at I wad like half sae weel. There's jist a kin' o' a hoonger upo' me for un'erstan'in' things. It's frae bein' sae muckle wi' Maister Cosmo, I'm thinkin'—ever sin' he was a bairn, ye ken, sir; for bein' twa year aul'er nor him, I was a kin' o' a wee nursie til him; an' ever sin' syne we hae had nae secrets frae ane anither; an' ye ken what he's like—aye wantin' to win at the boddom o' things—an' that's infeckit me, sae 'at I canna rist whan I see any body un'erstan'in' a thing till I set aboot getting' a grip o' 't mysel'."

"There's nothing upon the earth, sir," said Aggie, "that I would like half so well. There's just a kind of hunger upon me for understanding things. It's from being so much with Master Cosmo, I'm thinking—ever since he was a child, you know, sir; for being two years older than him, I was a kind of nurse to him; and ever since then we've had no secrets from each other; and you know what he's like—always wanting to get to the bottom of things—and that's infected me, so that I can't rest when I see anybody understanding a thing till I set about getting a grip of it myself."

"A very good infection to take, Agnes," replied the master, with a smile of thorough pleasure, "and one that will do more for you than the cow-pox! Come to me as often as you can—and as you like. I think I shall be able to tell you some things that will make you happier."

"A very good infection to take, Agnes," replied the master, with a smile of thorough pleasure, "and one that will do more for you than the cow-pox! Come to me as often as you can—and as you like. I think I shall be able to tell you some things that will make you happier."

"'Deed, sir, I'm no in want o' happiness!—O' that I hae full mair nor I deserve; but I want a heap for a' that. I canna say what it is, for the hoonger is for what I haena."

"Indeed, sir, I'm not in want of happiness! I've much more of that than I deserve; but there's much I want for all that. I can't say what it is, for the hunger's for what I don't have."

"Another of God's children," said the master to himself, "and full of the groanings of the spirit! The wilderness and the solitary place shall be glad for them."

"Another of God's children," said the master to himself, "and full of the groanings of the spirit! The wilderness and the solitary place shall be glad for them."

He often quoted scripture as the people of the New Testament did—not much minding the original application of the words. Those that are filled with the spirit have always taken liberties with the letter.

That very evening before she went home, they had a talk about algebra, and several other things. Agnes went no more to school, but almost every day to see the master, avoiding the hours when Cosmo would be there.

CHAPTER XII
GRANNIE'S GHOST STORY

Things went on very quietly. The glorious days of harvest came and went, and left the fields bare for the wintry revelling of great blasts. The potatoes were all dug up, and again buried—deeper than before, in pits, with sheets of straw and blankets of earth to protect them from the biting of the frost. Their stalks and many weeds with them were burned, and their ashes scattered. Some of the land was ploughed, and some left till the spring. Before the autumn rains the stock of peats was brought from the hill, where they had been drying through the hot weather, and a splendid stack they made. Coal was carted from the nearest sea-port, though not in such quantity as the laird would have liked, for money was as scarce as ever, and that is to put its lack pretty strongly. Everything available for firewood was collected, and, if of any size, put under saw and axe, then stored in the house. Good preparation was thus made for the siege of the winter.

In their poverty, partly no doubt from consideration, they seemed to be much forgotten. The family was like an old thistle-head, withering on its wintry stalk, alone in a wind-swept field. All the summer through, not a single visitor, friend or stranger, had slept in the house. A fresh face was more of a wonder to Cosmo than to desert-haunting Abraham. The human heart, like the human body, can live without much variety to feed on, but its house is built on a lordly scale for hospitality, and is capable of welcoming every new face as a new revelation. Steadily Cosmo went to his day's work with the master, steadily returned to his home; saw nothing new, yet learned day by day as he went and came, to love yet more not the faces of the men and women only, but the aspects of the country in which he was born, to read the lines and shades of its varying beauty: if it was not luxuriant enough to satisfy his ideal, it had yet endless loveliness to disclose to him who already loved enough to care to understand it. When the autumn came, it made him sad, for it was not in harmony with the forward look of his young life, which, though not ambitious, was vaguely expectant. But when the hoar-frosts appeared, when the clouds gathered, when the winds began to wail, and the snows to fall, then his spirits rose to meet the invading death. The old castle grew grayer and grayer outside, but ruddier and merrier within. Oh, that awful gray and white Scottish winter—dear to my heart as I sit and write with window wide open to the blue skies of Italy's December!

Cosmo kept up his morning bath in "the pot" as long as he could, but when sleet and rain came, and he could no longer dry himself by running about, he did not care for it longer, but waited for the snow to come in plenty, which was a sure thing, for then he had a substitute. It came of the ambition of hardy endurance, and will scarcely seem credible to some of my readers. In the depth of the winter, when the cold was at its strongest, provided only the snow lay pretty deep, he would jump from his warm bed with the first glimmer of the morning, and running out, in a light gray with the grayness of what is frozen, to a hollow on the hill-side a few yards from the house, there pull off his night-garment and roll in the snow, kneading handfuls of it, and rubbing himself with it all over. Thus he believed he strengthened himself to stand the cold of the day; and happily he was strong enough to stand the strengthening, and so increased his hardihood: what would have been death to many was to him invigoration. He knew nothing of boxing, or rowing, or billiards, but he could run and jump well, and ride very fairly, and, above all, he could endure. In the last harvest he had for the first time wielded a scythe, and had held his own with the rest, though, it must be allowed, with a fierce struggle. The next spring—I may mention it here—he not only held the plough, but by patient persistence and fearless compulsion trained two young bulls to go in it, saving many weeks' labour of a pair of horses. It filled his father with pride, and hope for his boy's coming fight with the world. Even the eyes of his grandmother would after that brighten at the mention of him; she began to feel proud that she had a share in the existence of the lad: if he did so well when a hobbledehoy, he might be something by the time he was a man! But one thing troubled her: he was no sportsman; he never went out to hunt the otter, or to shoot hares or rabbits or grouse or partridges! and that was unnatural! The fact was, ever since that talk with the master about Linty, he could not bear to kill anything, and was now and then haunted by the dying eyes of the pigeon he shot the first time he handled a gun. The grandmother thought it a defect in his manhood that he did not like shooting; but, woman, and old woman as she was, his heart was larger and tenderer than hers, and got in the way of the killing.

His father had never troubled his young life with details concerning the family affairs; he had only let him know that, for many years, through extravagance and carelessness in those who preceded his father, things had been going from bad to worse. But this was enough to wake in the boy the desire, and it grew in him as he grew, to rescue what was left of the estate from its burdens, and restore it to independence and so to honour. He said nothing of it, however, to his father, feeling the presumption of proposing to himself what his father had been unable to effect.

He went oftener to the village this winter than before, and rarely without going to see Mistress Forsyth, whom he, like the rest, always called Grannie. She suffered much from rheumatism, which she described as a sorrow in her bones. But she never lost her patience, and so got the good of a trouble which would seem specially sent as the concluding discipline of old people for this world, that they may start well in the next. Before the winter set in, the laird had seen that she was provided with peats—that much he could do because it cost him nothing but labour: and indeed each of the several cart-loads Cosmo himself had taken, with mare Linty between the shafts. But no amount of fire could keep the frost out of the old woman's body, or the sorrow out of her bones. Hence she had to be a good deal in bed, and needed her great-grandchild, Agnes, to help her to bear her burden. When the bitter weather came, soon after Christmas, Agnes had to be with her almost constantly. She had grown a little graver, but was always cheerful, and, except for anxiety lest her mother should be overworked, or her father take cold, seemed as happy with her grandmother as at home.

One afternoon, when the clouds were rising, and the wind blew keen from the north, Cosmo left Glenwarlock to go to the village—mainly to see Grannie. He tramped the two miles and a half in all the joy of youthful conflict with wind and weather, and reached the old woman's cottage radiant. The snow lay deep and powdery with frost, and the struggle with space from a bad footing on the world had brought the blood to his cheeks and the sparkle to his eyes. He found Grannie sitting up in bed, and Aggie getting her tea—to which Cosmo contributed a bottle of milk he had carried her—an article rare enough in the winter when there was so little grass for the cows. Aggie drew the old woman's chair to the fire for him, and he sat down and ate barley-meal scones, and drank tea with them. Grannie was a little better than usual, for every disease has its inconsistencies, and pain will abate before an access; and so, with storm at hand, threaded with fiery flying serpents for her bones, she was talking more than for days previous. Her voice came feebly from the bed to Cosmo's ears, where he leaned back in her great chair, and Aggie was removing the tea-things.

"Did ye ever dream ony mair aboot the auld captain, Cosmo?" she asked: from her tone he could not tell whether she spoke seriously, or was amusing herself with the idea.	"Did you ever dream any more about the old captain, Cosmo?" she asked: from her tone he could not tell whether she spoke seriously, or was amusing herself with the idea.
"No ance," he answered. "What gars ye speir, Grannie?"	"Not once," he answered. "What makes you ask, Grannie?"

She said nothing for a few minutes, and Cosmo thought she had dismissed the subject. Aggie had returned to her seat, and he was talking with her about Euclid, when she began again; and this time her voice revealed that she was quite in earnest.

"Ye're weel nigh a man noo, Cosmo," she said, "A body may daur speyk to ye aboot things a body wadna be wullin' to say till a bairn for fear o' frichtin' o' 'im mair nor the bit hert o' 'm cud stan'. Whan a lad can warstle wi' a pair o' bills, an' get the upper han' o' them, an' gar them du his biddin', he wadna need to tak fricht at—"

"You're well nigh a man now, Cosmo," she said, "A person may dare speak to you about things they wouldn't be willing to say to a child for fear of frightening him more than his young heart could stand. When a lad can wrestle with a pair of bulls, and get the upper hand of them, and make them do his bidding, he wouldn't need to take fright at—"

This preamble was enough in itself-not exactly to bring Cosmo's heart into his mouth, but to send a little more of his blood from his brain to his heart than was altogether welcome there. His imagination, however, was more eager than apprehensive, and his desire to hear far greater than his dread of the possible disclosure. He looked at Aggie as much as to say, "What can be coming?" and she stared at him again in turn with dilated pupils, as if something dreadful were about to be evoked by the threatened narrative. Neither spoke a word, but their souls got into their ears, and there sat listening. The hearing was likely to be frightful when so prefaced by Grannie.

"There's no guid ever cam o' ca'in' things oot o' their ain names," she began, "an' it's my min' 'at gien ever ae man was a willain, an' gien ever ae man had rizzon no to lie quaiet whan he was doon, that man was yer father's uncle—his gran'-uncle, that is—the auld captain, as we ca'd him. Fowk said he saul' his sowl to the ill ane: hoo that may be, I wadna care to be able to tell; but sure I am 'at his was a sowl ill at ease—baith here an' herefter. Them 'at sleepit aneth me, for there was twa men servan's aboot the hoose at that time—an' troth there was need o' them an' mair, sic war the gangin's on!—an' they sleepit whaur I'm tauld ye sleep noo, Cosmo—them 'at sleepit there tellt me 'at never a nicht passed 'at they h'ardna soons aneth them 'at there was no mainner o' accoontin' for, nor explainin', as fowk's sae set upo' duin' nooadays wi' a'thing. That explainin' I canna bide: it's jist a love o' leasin', an' taks the bluid oot' o' a'thing, lea'in' life as wersh and fusionless as kail wantin' saut. Them 'at h'ard it tellt me 'at there was *no* accoontin' for the reemish they baith h'ard—whiles douf-like dunts, an' whiles speech o' mou' beggin' an' groanin', as gien the enemy war bodily present to the puir sinner."

"There's no good ever came of calling things by false names," she began, "and to my mind if ever one man was a villain, and if ever one man had reason not to lie quiet when he was down, that man was your father's uncle—his grand-uncle, that is—the old captain, as we called him. Folk said he sold his soul to the devil: how that may be, I wouldn't care to think; but sure I am that his was a soul ill at ease—both here and hereafter. Those that slept beneath me, for there were two men-servants about the house at that time—and truly there was need of them and more, such were the goings on!—and they slept where I'm told you sleep now, Cosmo—those that slept there told me that never a night passed that they didn't hear sounds beneath them that there was no manner of accounting for, nor explaining, as folks are so set upon doing nowadays with everything. That explaining I can't stand: it's just a love of system, and takes the blood out of everything, leaving life as drab and tasteless as cabbages wanting salt. Those that heard it told me that there was *no* accounting for the romage they both heard—sometimes dull-sounding blows, and sometimes spoken words begging and groaning, as if the enemy were bodily present to the poor sinner."

"He micht hae been but jabberin' in 's sleep," Cosmo, with his love of truth, ventured

"He might have simply been jabbering in his sleep," Cosmo, with his love of truth,

to suggest: Aggie gave him a nudge of warning.

"Ay micht he," returned the old woman with calm scorn; "an' it micht, nae doobt, hae been snorin', or a cat speykin' wi' man's tongue, or ony ane o' mony things 'cep' the trowth 'at ye're no wullin' to hear."

"I *am* wullin'—to hear the warst trowth ye daur tell me, Grannie," cried Cosmo, terrified lest he had choked the fountain. He was more afraid of losing the story than of hearing the worst tale that could be told even about the room he slept in last night, and must go back to sleep in again tonight.

Grannie was mollified, and went on.

"As I was sayin', he micht weel be ill at ease, the auld captain, gien ae half was true 'at was said o' 'im; but I 'maist think yer father coontit it priven 'at he had led a deevilich life amo' the pirates. Only, gien he did, whaur was the wauges o' his ineequity? Nae doobt he got the wauges 'at the apostle speyks o', whilk is, as ye weel ken, deith—'the wauges o' sin is deith.'—But, maistly, sic-like sinners get first wauges o' anither speckle frae the maister o' them. For troth! He has no need to be near in's dealin's wi' them, seein' there's nae buyin' nor sellin' whaur he is, an' a' the gowd he has doon yon'er i' the booels o' the yird wad jist lie there duin' naething, gien he sentna 't up abune whaur maist pairt it works his wull. Na, he seldom scrimps 't to them 'at follows his biddin'. But i' this case, whaur, I say, was the wauges? Natheless, he aye cairriet himsel' like ane 'at cud lay doon the law o' this warl', an' cleemt no sma' consideration; yet was there never sign or mark o' the proper fundation for sic assumption o' the richt to respec'.

"It turnt oot, or cam to be said, 'at the Englishman 'at fowk believed to hae killt him, was far-awa' sib to the faimily, an' the twa had come thegither afore, somewhaur i' foreign pairts. But that's neither here nor there, nor what for he killed him, or wha's faut was that same: aboot a' that, naething was ever kent for certain.

"Weel, it was an awfu' like thing, you may be sure, to quaiet fowk, sic as we was a'—'cep'

ventured to suggest: Aggie gave him a nudge of warning.

"Ay he might," returned the old woman with calm scorn; "and it might, no doubt, have been snoring, or a cat speaking with man's tongue, or any one of many things except the truth that you're not willing to hear."

"I *am* willing—to hear the worst truth you dare tell me, Grannie," cried Cosmo, terrified lest he had choked the fountain. He was more afraid of losing the story than of hearing the worst tale that could be told even about the room he slept in last night, and must go back to sleep in again tonight.

Grannie was mollified, and went on.

"As I was saying, he might well be ill at ease, the old captain, if one half was true that was said of him; but I almost think your father counted it proven that he had led a devilish life among the pirates. Only, if he did, where were the wages of his iniquity? No doubt he got the wages that the apostle speaks of, which is, as you well know, death—'the wages of sin is death.'—But such sinners tend first to get another kind of wages from their master. For, faith! He has no need to be near in his dealings with them, seeing there's no buying or selling where he is, and all the gold he has down yonder in the bowels of the earth would just lie there doing nothing, unless he sent it up above where mostly it works his will. Na, he seldom scrimps it to those that follow his bidding. But in this case, where, I say, were the wages? Nonetheless, he always carried himself like one that could lay down the law of this world, and claimed no small consideration; yet was there never sign or mark of the proper foundation for such assumption of the right to respect.

"It turned out, or came to be said, that the Englishman that folk believed to have killed him, was a distant relation of the family, and the two had come together before, somewhere in foreign parts. But that's neither here nor there, nor why he killed him, or whose fault it was: about all that, nothing was ever known for certain.

"Well, it was an awful thing, you may be sure, to quiet folk, such as we all were—except for the drinkin' an' sic like, sin ever the auld captain cam, wi' his reprobate w'ys—it was a sair thing, I'm sayin', to hae a deid man, a' at ance upo' oor han's; for, lat the men du 'at they like, the warst o 't aye comes upo' the women. Lat a bairn come to mischance, or the guidman turn ower the kettle, an' it's aye, 'Rin for Jean this, or Bauby that,' to set richt what they hae set wrang. Even whan a man kills a body, it's the women hae to mak the best o' 't, an' the corp luik dacent. An' there's some o' them no that easy to mak luik dacent! Troth, there's mony ane luiks bonnier died nor alive, but that wasna the case wi' the auld captain, for he lookit as gien he had dee'd cursin', as he bude to du, gien he dee'd as he lived. His moo was drawn fearfu', as gien his last aith had chokit him. Nae doubt they said 'at wad hae't they kent, 'at hoo that's the w'y wi' deith frae slayin' wi' the swoord; but I wadna hear o't; I kenned better. An' whether he had fair play or no, the deith he dee'd was a just ane; for them 'at draws the swoord maun periss by the swoord. Whan they faun' 'im, the richt han' o' the corp was streekit oot, as gien he was cryin' to somebody rinnin' awa' to bide an' tak 'im wi' 'im. But there was anither at han' to tak 'im wi' 'im. Only, gien he took 'im that same nicht, he cudna hae carried him far. 'Deed, maybe, the auld sinner was ower muckle aven for *him.*

for the drinking and suchlike, since ever the old captain came, with his reprobate ways—it was a sore thing, I say, to have a dead man all at once upon our hands; for, let the men do what they like, the worst of it always comes upon the women. Let a child come to mischance, or the goodman knock the kettle over, and it's always, 'Run for Jean this, or Bauby that,' to set right what they have set wrong. Even when a man kills someone, it's the women have to make the best of it, and the corpse look decent. And there's some of them that aren't so easy to make look decent! Indeed, there's many a one looks bonnier dead than alive, but that wasn't the case with the old captain, for he looked as if he had died cursing, as he must have done, if he died as he lived. His mouth was drawn something fearful, as if his last oath had choked him. No doubt they said who would have it they knew, that that's the way with death by the sword, but I wouldn't hear of it; I knew better. And whether he had fair play or not, the death he died was a just one; for whoever draws the sword must perish by the sword. When they found him, the right hand of the corpse was stretched out, as if he was calling to somebody running away to stay and take him with him. But there was another at hand to take him with him. Only, if he took him that same night, he couldn't have carried him far. Indeed, maybe, the old sinner was too much even for *him.*

"They broucht him hame, an' laid the corp o' him upo' his ain bed, whaur, I reckon, up til this nicht, he had tried mair nor he had sleepit. An' that verra nicht, wha sud I see—but I'm jist gaein' to tell ye a' aboot it, an' hoo it was, an' syne ye can say yersel's. Sin' my ain auld mither dee'd, I haena opent my moo' to mortal upo' the subjec'."

"They brought him home, and laid his corpse upon his own bed, where, I reckon, up till this night, he had tried more than he had slept. And that very night, who should I see—but I'm just going to tell you all about it, and how it was, and then you can say yourselves. Since my own old mother died, I haven't opened my mouth to mortal man upon the subject."

The minds of the two listeners were fixed upon the narrator in the acme of expectation. A real ghost-story, from the lips of one they knew, and must believe in, was a thing of dread delight. Like ghosts themselves, they were all-unconscious of body, rapt in listening.

"Ye may weel believe," resumed the old woman after a short pause, "'at nane o' 's was ower wullin' to sit up wi' the corp oor lane, for, as I say, he wasna a comely corp to be a body's lane wi'. Sae auld auntie Jean an' mysel, we

"You may well believe," resumed the old woman after a short pause, "that none of us were over-willing to sit up by the corpse ourselves, for, as I say, he wasn't a comely corpse to be alone with. So old auntie Jean and myself, agreed 'at we wud tak the thing upo' oorsel's, for, huz twa, we cud lippen til ane anither no to be ower feart to min' 'at there was twa o''s. There hadna been time yet for the corp to be laid intil the coffin, though, i' the quaiet o' the mirk, we thoucht, as we sat, we cud hear the tap-tappin' as they cawed the braiss nails intil't, awa' ower in Geordie Lumsden's chop, at the Muir o' Warlock, a twa mile, it wad be! We war sittin', auntie Jean an' mysel, i' the mids o' the room, no wi' oor backs til the bed, nor yet wi' oor faces, for we dauredna turn aither o' them til't. I' the ae case, wha cud tell what we micht see, an' i' the ither, wha cud tell what micht be luikin' at hiz? We war sittin', I say, wi' oor faces to the door o' the room, an' auntie was noddin' a wee, for she was turnin' gey an' auld, but *I* was as wide waukin' as ony baudrins by a moose-hole, whan suddent there cam a kin' o' a dirlin' at the sneck 'at sent the verra sowl o' me up intil the garret o' my heid; an afore I had time to ken hoo sair frichtit I was, the door begud to open; an, glower as I wad, no believin' my ain e'en, open that door did, langsome, langsome, quaiet, quaiet, jist as my auld grannie used to tell o' the deid man comin' doon the lum, bit an' bit, an' jinin' thegither upo' the flure. I was turnt to stane, like, 'at I didna believe I cud hae fa'en frae the cheir gien I had swarfed clean awa'. An' eh, but it tuik a time to open that door! But at last, as sure as ye sit there, you twa, an' no anither,—" At the word, Cosmo's heart came swelling up into his throat, but he dared not look round to assure himself that they were indeed two sitting there and not another,—"in cam the auld captain, ae fit efter anither! Speir gien I was sure o' 'im! Didna I ken him as weel as my ain father—as weel's my ain minister—as weel as my ain man? He cam in, I say, the auld captain himsel'—an' eh, sic an evil luik!—the verra luik deith had frozen upo' the face o' the corp! The live bluid turned to dubs i' my inside. He cam on an' on, but no straucht for whaur we sat, or I dinna think the sma' rizzon I had left wad hae bidden wi' me, but as gien he war haudin' for 's bed. To tell God's trowth, for I daurna lee, for fear o' haein' to luik upo' his like again,

we agreed that we would take the thing upon ourselves, for, we two, we could trust to one another not to be too frightened to remember that there were two of us. There hadn't been time yet for the corpse to be laid in the coffin, though, in the quiet of the night, we thought, as we sat, we could hear the tap-tapping as they drove the brass nails into it, away over in Geordie Lumsden's shop, at the Moor of Warlock, two miles away! We were sitting, auntie Jean and myself, in the middle of the room, not with our backs to the bed, nor yet with our faces, for we dared turn neither of them to it. In the one case, who could tell what we might see, and in the other, who could tell what might be looking at us? We were sitting, I say, with our faces to the door of the room, and auntie was nodding a bit, for she was turning very old, but *I* was as wide waking as any cat by a mouse-hole, when suddenly there came a kind of a rattling at the latch that sent my very soul up into the garret of my head; and before I had time to know how badly I was frightened, the door began to open; and, stare as I would, not believing my own eyes, open that door did, slowly, slowly, quiet, quiet, just as my old grannie used to tell of the dead man coming down the chimney, bit by bit, and joining together upon the floor. I was so petrified that I didn't believe I could have fallen from the chair, if I had fainted clean away. And eh, but it took some time to open that door! But at last, as sure as you sit there, you two and not another—" At the word, Cosmo's heart came swelling up into his throat, but he dared not look round to assure himself that they were indeed two sitting there and not another,-"in came the old captain, one foot after another! Ask if I was sure of him! Didn't I know him as well as my own father—as well as my own minister—as well as my own husband? He came in, I say, the old captain himself—and eh, such an evil look!—the very look death had frozen upon the face of the corpse! The live blood turned to mud in my veins. He came on and on, but not straight for where we sat, or I don't think the small reason I had left would have stayed with me, but as if he were making for his bed. To tell God's truth, for I

my auld auntie declaret efterhin 'at she saw naething. She bude til hae been asleep, an' a mercifu' thing it was for her, puir body! but she didna live lang efter. He made strauch for the bed, as I thoucht. 'The Lord preserve 's!' thoucht I, 'is he gaein' to lie doon wi' 's ain corp?' but he turnt awa, an roon' the fit o' the bed to the ither side o' 't, an' I saw nae mair; an' for a while, auntie Jean sat her lane wi' the deid, for I lay upo' the flure, an' naither h'ard nor saw. But whan I cam to mysel', wasna I thankfu' 'at I wasna deid, for he micht hae gotten me than, an' there was nae sayin' what he micht hae dune til me! But, think ye, wad auntie Jean believe 'at I had seen him, or that it was onything but a dream 'at had come ower me, atween waukin' an' sleepin'! Na, no she! For she had sleepit throu' 't hersel'!"

daren't lie, for fear of having to look upon his like again, my old auntie declared afterwards that she saw nothing. She must have been asleep, and a merciful thing it was for her, poor woman! but she didn't live long after. He made straight for the bed, as I thought. 'The Lord preserve us!' thought I, 'is he going to lie down with his own corpse?' but he turned away, and round the foot of the bed to the other side of it, and I saw no more; and for a while, auntie Jean sat by herself with the dead, for I lay upon the floor, and neither heard not saw. But when I came to myself, wasn't I thankful that I wasn't dead, for he might have gotten me then, and there was no saying what he might have done to me! But do you think auntie Jean would believe that I had seen him, or that it was anything but a dream that had come over me, between waking and sleeping! Na, not she! For she had slept through it herself!"

For some time silence reigned, as befitted the close of such a story. Nothing but the solemn tick of the tall clock was to be heard. On and on it went, as steady as before. Ghosts were nothing special to the clock: it had to measure out the time both for ghosts and unghosts.

"But what cud the ghaist hae been wantin'? No the corp, for he turnt awa', ye tell me, frae hit," Cosmo ventured at length to remark.

"But what could the ghost have been wanting? Not the corpse, for he turned away, you tell me, from it," Cosmo ventured at length to remark.

"Wha can say what ghaists may be efter, laddie? But, troth to tell, whan ye see live fowk sae gien ower to the boady 'at they're never happy but whan they're aitin' or drinkin' or sic like—an' the auld captain was seldom throu' wi' his glaiss, 'at he wasna cryin' for the whisky or the het watter for the neist—whan the boady's the best half o' them, like, an' they maun aye be duin' something wi' 't, ye needna won'er 'at the ghaist o' ane sic like sud fin' himsel' geyan eerie an' lanesome like wantin' his seck to fill, an' sae try to win back to hae a luik hoo it was weirin'!"

"Who can say what ghosts may be after, laddie? But, truth to tell, when you see live folk so given over to the body that they're never happy but when they're eating or drinking or suchlike—and the old captain was seldom through with his glass, that he wasn't calling for the whisky or the hot water for the next—when the body's the best half of them, like, and they must always be doing something with it, you needn't wonder that the ghost of such a one should find himself rather eerie and lonesome without his sack to fill, and so try to get back to have a look at the state of it!"

"But he gaedna to the corp," Cosmo insisted.

"But he didn't go to the corpse," Cosmo insisted.

"'Cause he wasna alloot," said Grannie: "He wad hae been intil 't again in a moment, ye may be certain, gien it had been in his pooer. But the deevils cudna gang intil the swine wantin' leave."

"Because he wasn't allowed," said Grannie: "He would have been into it again in a moment, you may be certain, if it had been in his power. But the devils couldn't go into the swine without leave."

"Ay, I see," said Cosmo.

"Aye, I see," said Cosmo.

"But jist ye speir at yer new maister," Grannie went on, "what he thinks aboot it, for I ance h'ard him speyk richt wice words to my gudeson, Jeames Gracie, anent sic things. I min' weel 'at he said the only thing 'at made agen the viouw I tuik—though I spakna o' the partic'lar occasion—was, 'at naebody ever h'ard tell o' the ghaist o' an alderman wha they say's some grit Lon'on man, sair gien to the fillin' o' the seck."

"But just you ask your new master," Grannie went on, "what he thinks about it, for I once heard him speak very wise words to my son-in-law, Jeames Gracie, about such things. I clearly remember him saying that the only thing counting against the view I took—though I didn't speak of the particular occasion—was, that nobody ever heard tell of the ghost of an alderman who they say is some great London man, obsessed with filling his sack."

CHAPTER XIII
THE STORM-GUEST

Again a deep silence descended on the room. The twilight had long fallen, and settled down into the dark. The only thing that acknowledged and answered the clock was the red glow of the peats on the hearth. To Cosmo, as he sat sunk in thought, the clock and the fire seemed to be holding a silent talk. Presently came a great and sudden blast of wind, which roused Cosmo, and made him bethink himself that it was time to be going home. And for this there was another reason besides the threatening storm: he had the night before begun to read aloud one of Sir Walter's novels to the assembled family, and Grizzie would be getting anxious for another portion of it before she went to bed.

"I'm glaid to see ye sae muckle better, Grannie," he said. "I'll say guid nicht noo, and luik in again the morn."

"Weel, I'm obleeged to ye," replied the old woman. "There's been but feow o' yer kin, be their fau'ts what they micht, wad forget ony 'at luikit for a kin' word or a kin' deed!—Aggie, lass, ye'll convoy him a bittock, willna ye?"

All the few in whom yet lingered any shadow of retainership towards the fast-fading chieftainship of Glenwarlock, seemed to cherish the notion that the heir of the house had to be tended and cared for like a child—that that was what they were in the world for. Doubtless a pitying sense of the misfortunes of the family had much to do with the feeling. "There's nae occasion," and "I'll du that," said the two young people in a breath.

"I'm glad to see you so much better, Grannie," he said. "I'll say good night now, and look in again tomorrow."

"Well, I'm obliged to you," replied the old woman. "There's been but few of your kin, be their faults what they might, who'd forget any that looked for a kind word or a kind deed!—Aggie, lass, you'll go some of the way with him, won't you?"

All the few in whom yet lingered any shadow of retainership towards the fast-fading chieftainship of Glenwarlock, seemed to cherish the notion that the heir of the house had to be tended and cared for like a child—that that was what they were in the world for. Doubtless a pitying sense of the misfortunes of the family had much to do with the feeling. "There's no occasion," and "I'll do that," said the two young people in a breath.

Cosmo rose, and began to put on his plaid, crossing it over back and chest to leave his arms free: that way the wind would get least hold on him. Agnes went to the closet for her plaid also—of the same tartan, and drawing it over her head and pinning it under her chin, was presently ready for the stormy way. Then she turned to Cosmo, and was pinning his plaid together at the throat, when the wind came with a sudden howl, rushed down the chimney, and drove the level smoke into the middle of the room. It could not shake the cottage—it was too lowly: neither could it rattle its windows—they were not made to open; but it bellowed over it like a wave over a rock, and as in contempt blew its smoke back into its throat.

"It'll be a wull nicht, I'm doobtin', Cosmo!" said Agnes; "an' I wuss ye safe at the ingle-neuk wi' yer fowk."

Cosmo laughed. "The win' kens me," he said.

"Guid forbid!" cried the old woman from the bed. "Kenna ye wha's the prence o' 't, laddie? Makna a jeist o' the pooers 'at be."

"Gien they binna ordeent o' God, what are they but a jeist?" returned Cosmo. "Eh, but ye

"It'll be a wild night, I'm thinking, Cosmo!" said Agnes; "and I wish you safe at the fireside with your family."

Cosmo laughed. "The wind knows me," he said.

"God forbid!" cried the old woman from the bed. "Don't you know who's the prince of it, laddie? Make no jest of the powers that be."

"If they're not ordained by God, what are they but a jest?" returned Cosmo. "Eh, but you wad mak a bonny munsie o' me, Grannie, to hae me feart at the deil an' a'! I canna a'thegither help it wi' the ghaists, an' I'm ashamet o' mysel' for 't, but I *am not* gaein' to heed the deil. I defy him an' a' his works. He's but a cooard, ye ken, Grannie, for whan ye resist him, he rins."

would make a fine fool of me, Grannie, to have me afraid of the devil and all! I can't altogether help it with the ghosts, and I'm ashamed of myself for it, but I *am not* going to heed the devil. I defy him and all his works. He's but a coward, you know, Grannie, for when you resist him, he runs."

She made no answer. Cosmo shook hands with her, and went, followed by Agnes, who locked the door behind her, and put the key in her pocket.

It was indeed a wild night. The wind was rushing from the north, full of sharp stinging pellicles, something between snow-flakes and hail-stones. Down the wide village street it came right in their faces. Through it, as through a thin shifting sheet, they saw on both sides the flickering lights of the many homes, but before them lay darkness, and the moor, a chaos, a carnival of wind and snow. Worst of all, the snow on the road was not binding, and their feet felt as if walking on sand. As long as the footing is good, one can get on even in the face of a northerly storm; but to heave with a shifting fulcrum is hard. Nevertheless Cosmo, beholding with his mind's eye the wide waste around him, rejoiced; invisible through the snow, it was not the less a presence, and his young heart rushed to the contest. There was no fear of ghosts in such a storm! The ghosts might be there, but there was no time to heed them, and that was as good as their absence—perhaps better, if we knew all.

"Bide a wee, Cosmo," ("Wait a bit, Cosmo,") cried Agnes, and leaving him in the middle of the street where they were walking, she ran across to one of the houses, and entered—lifting the latch without ceremony. No neighbour troubled another to come and open the door; if there was no one at home, the key in the lock outside showed it.

Cosmo turned his back to the wind, and stood waiting. From the door which Aggie opened, came through the wind and snow the sound of the shoemaker's hammer on his lapstone.

"Cud ye spare the mistress for an hoor, or maybe twa an' a half, to haud Grannie company, John Nauchty?" said Agnes.

"Weel that," answered the *sutor*, hammering away. He intended no reflection on the bond that bound the mistress and himself.

"I dinna see her," said Aggie.

"She'll be in in a meenute. She's run ower the ro'd to get a doup o' can'le," returned the man.

"Gien she binna the speedier, she'll hae to licht it to fin' her ain door," said Agnes merrily, to whom the approaching fight with the elements was as welcome as to Cosmo. She had made up her mind to go with him all the way, let him protest as he might.

"Ow, na! she'll hearken an' hear the hemmer," replied the shoemaker.

"Weel, tak the key, an' ye winna forget, John?" said Aggie, laying the key amongst his tools. "Grannie's lyin' there her lee-lane,

"Could you spare the mistress for an hour, or maybe two and a half, to keep Grannie company, John Nauchty?" said Agnes.

"Easily," answered the cobbler, hammering away. He intended no reflection on the bond that bound the mistress and himself.

"I don't see her," said Aggie.

"She'll be in in a minute. She's run over the road to get a candle-end," returned the man.

"If she doesn't hurry, she'll have to light it to find her own door," said Agnes merrily, to whom the approaching fight with the elements was as welcome as to Cosmo. She had made up her mind to go with him all the way, let him protest as he might.

"Na, na! she'll listen and hear the hammer," replied the shoemaker.

"Well, take the key, and you won't forget, John?" said Aggie, laying the key amongst his tools. "Grannie's lying there all alone, and if an' gien the hoose was to tak fire, what wad come o' her?"

"Guid forbid onybody sud forget Grannie!" rejoined the man heartily; "but fire wad hae a sma' chance the nicht."

the house was to catch fire, what would become of her?"

"God forbid anyone should forget Grannie!" rejoined the man heartily; "but fire would have little chance tonight."

Agnes thanked and left him. All the time he had not missed a single stroke of his hammer on the ben-leather between it and his lapstone.

When she rejoined Cosmo, where he stood leaning his back against the wind in the middle of the road—

"Come nae farther, Aggie," he said. "It's an ill nicht, an' grows waur. There's nae guid in't naither, for we winna hear ane anither speyk ohn stoppit an' turnt oor back til't. Gang to yer grannie; she'll be feart aboot ye."

"Nae a bit. I maun see ye oot o' the toon."

"Come no farther, Aggie," he said. "It's a bad night, and it grows worse. There's no good in it either, for we won't hear one another speak without stopping and turning our backs to it. Go to your Grannie; she'll be afraid for you."

"Not a bit. I must see you out of the town."

They fought their way along the street, and out on the open moor, the greater part of which was still heather and swamp. Peat-bog and ploughed land was all one waste of snow. Creation seemed but the snow that had fallen, the snow that was falling, and the snow that had yet to fall; or, to put it otherwise, a fall of snow between two outspread worlds of snow.

"Gang back noo, Aggie," said Cosmo again. "What's the guid o' twa whaur ane only need be, an' baith hae to fecht for themsel's?"

"I'm no gaein' back yet," persisted Aggie. "Twa's better at onything nor ane himlane. The sutor's wife's gaein' in to see Grannie, an' Grannie 'll like her cracks a heap better nor mine. She thinks I hae nae mair brains nor a hen, 'cause I canna min' upo' things 'at war nearhan' forgotten or I was born."

"Go back now, Aggie," said Cosmo again. "What's the good of two where one only need be, and both have to fight for themselves?"

"I'm not going back yet," persisted Aggie. "Two are better at anything than one by himself. The cobbler's wife's going in to see Grannie, and Grannie'll like speaking with her much better than me. She thinks I have no more brains than a hen, because I can't remember things that were nearly forgotten before I was born."

Cosmo desisted from useless persuasion, and they struggled on together, through the snow above and the snow beneath. At this Aggie was more than a match for Cosmo. Lighter and smaller, and perhaps with stronger lungs in proportion, she bored her way through the blast better than he, and the moment he began to expostulate, would increase the distance between them, and go on in front where he knew she could not hear a word he said. At last, being then a little ahead, she turned her back to the wind, and waited for him to come up.

"Noo, ye've had eneuch o' 't!" he said, "an' I maun turn an' gang back wi' ye, or ye'll never win hame."

Aggie broke into a loud laugh that rang like music through the storm.

"A likly thing!" she cried, "an' me wi' my back a' the ro'd to the win'! Gang back yersel', Cosmo, an' sit by Grannie's fire, an' I'll gang on to the castle, an' lat them ken whaur ye are. Gien ye dinna that, I tell ye ance for a', I'm no gaein' to lea' ye till I see ye safe inside yer ain wa's."

"Now, you've had enough of it!" he said, "and I must turn and go back with you, or you'll never get home."

Aggie broke into a loud laugh that rang like music through the storm.

"A likely thing!" she cried, "and me with my back all the road to the wind! Go back yourself, Cosmo, and sit by Grannie's fire, and I'll go on to the castle, and let them know where you are. If you don't, I tell you once and for all, I'm not going to leave you till I see you safe inside your own walls."

"But Aggie," reasoned Cosmo, with yet greater earnestness, "what'll ye gar fowk think o' me, 'at wad hae a lassie to gang hame wi' me, for fear the win' micht blaw me intil the sea? Ye'll bring me to shame, Aggie."

"But Aggie," reasoned Cosmo, with yet greater earnestness, "what'll you make folk think of me, that would have a lassie to go home with me, for fear the wind might blow me into the sea? You'll bring me to shame, Aggie."

"A lassie! say ye?" cried Aggie,—"I think I hear ye!—an' me auld eneuch to be yer mither! I s' tak guid care there s' be nae affront intil 't. Haud yer hert quaiet, Cosmo; ye'll hae need o' a' yer breath afore ye win to yer ain fireside."

"A lassie! you say?" cried Aggie,—"I think I hear you!—and me old enough to be your mother! I'll take good care there's no affront in it. Calm yourself down, Cosmo; you'll need all your breath before you reach your own fireside."

As she spoke, the wind pounced upon them with a fiercer gust than any that had preceded. Instinctively they grasped each other, as if from the wish, if they should be blown away, to be blown away together.

As she spoke, the wind pounced upon them with a fiercer gust than any that had preceded. Instinctively they grasped each other, as if from the wish, if they should be blown away, to be blown away together.

"Eh, that's a rouch ane!" said Cosmo, and again Aggie laughed merrily.

"Eh, that's a rough one!" said Cosmo, and again Aggie laughed merrily.

While they stood thus, with their backs to the wind, the moon rose. Far indeed from being visible, she yet shed a little glimmer of light over the plain, revealing a world as wild as ever the frozen north outspread—as wild as ever poet's despairing vision of desolation. I see it! I see it! but how shall I make my reader see it with me? It was ghastly. The only similitude of life was the perplexed and multitudinous motion of the drifting, falling flakes. No shape was to be seen, no sound but that of the wind was to be heard. It was like the dream of a delirious child after reading the ancient theory of the existence of the world by the rushing together of fortuitous atoms. Wan and thick, tumultuous, innumerable to millions of angels, an interminable tempest of intermingling and indistinguishable vortices, it stretched on and on, a boundless hell of cold and shapelessness—white thinned with gray, and fading into gray blackness, into tangible darkness.

The moment the fury of the blast abated, Agnes turned, and without a word began again her boring march, forcing her way through the palpable obstructions of wind and snow. Unable to prevent her, Cosmo followed. But he comforted himself with the thought that, if the storm continued, he would get his father to use his authority against her attempting a return before the morning. The cobbler's wife was one of Grannie's best cronies, and there was no fear of her being deserted through the night.

Aggie kept the lead she had taken till there could be no more question of going back, and they were now drawing near the road that struck off to the left, along the bank of the Warlock river, leading up among the valleys and low hills, most of which had once been the property of the house of Warlock, when she stopped suddenly, this time without turning her back to the wind, and Cosmo was immediately beside her.

"What's yon, Cosmo?" ("What's that, Cosmo?") she said—and Cosmo fancied consternation in the tone. He looked sharply forward, and saw what seemed a glimmer, but might be only something whiter in the whiteness. No! it was certainly a light—but whether on the road, he could not tell. There was no house in that direction! It moved!—yet not as if carried in human hand! Now it was gone! There it was again! There were two of them—two huge pale eyes, rolling from side to side. Grannie's warning about the Prince of the power of the air, darted into Cosmo's mind. It was awful! But anyhow the devil was not to be run from! That was the easiest measure, no doubt, yet not the less the one impossible to take. And now it was plain that the something was not away on the moor, but on the road in front of them, and coming towards them. It came nearer and nearer, and grew vaguely visible—a huge blundering mass—animal or what, they could not tell, but on the wind came sounds that might be human—or animal human—the sounds of encouragement and incitation to horses. And now it approached no more. With common impulse they hastened towards it.

It was a travelling carriage—a rare sight in those parts at any time, and rarer still in winter. Both of them had certainly seen one before, but as certainly, never a pair of lighted carriage-lamps, with reflectors to make of them fiendish eyes. It had but two horses, and, do what the driver could, which was not much, they persisted in standing stock-still, refusing to take a single step farther. Indeed they could not. They had tried and tried, and done their best, but finding themselves unable to move the carriage an inch, preferred standing still to spending themselves in vain struggles, for all their eight legs went slipping about under them.

Cosmo looked up to the box. The driver was little more than a boy, and nearly dead with cold. Already Aggie had a forefoot of the near horse in her hand. Cosmo ran to the other.

"Their feet's fu' o' snaw," said Aggie.

"Their feet are full of snow," said Aggie.

"Ay; it's ba'd hard!" said Cosmo. "They maun hae come ower a saft place: it wadna ba' the nicht upo' the muir."

"Ay; it's balled hard!" said Cosmo. "They must have come over a soft place: it wouldn't ball tonight upon the moor."

"Hae ye yer knife, Cosmo?" asked Aggie.

"Have you your knife, Cosmo?" asked Aggie.

Here a head was put out of the carriage-window. It was that of a lady, in a swansdown travelling-hood. She had heard an unintelligible conversation—and one intelligible word. They must be robbers! How else should they want a knife in a snowstorm? Why else should they have stopped the carriage? She gave a little cry of alarm. Aggie dropped the hoof she held, and went to the window.

"What's yer wull, mem?" she asked.

"What's your will, ma'am?" she asked.

"What's the matter?" the lady returned in a trembling voice, but not a little reassured at the sight, as she crossed the range of one of the lamps, of the face of a young girl. "Why doesn't the coach man go on?"

"What's the matter?" the lady returned in a trembling voice, but not a little reassured at the sight, as she crossed the range of one of the lamps, of the face of a young girl. "Why doesn't the coachman go on?"

"He canna, mem," answered Agnes. "The horses canna win throu the snaw. They hae ba's o' 't i' their feet, an' they canna get a grip wi' them, nae mair nor ye cud yersel', mem, gien the soles o' yer shune war roon' an' made o' glaiss. But we'll sune set that richt.—Hoo far hae ye come, mem, gien I may speir? Aigh, mem, it's an unco nicht!"

"He can't, ma'am," answered Agnes. "The horses can't get through the snow. They have balls of it in their feet, and they can't get a grip with them, no more than you could yourself, ma'am, if the soles of your shoes were round and made of glass. But we'll soon set that right.—How far have you come, ma'am, if I might ask? Ah, ma'am, it's a terrible night!"

The lady did not understand much of what Aggie said, for she was English, returning from her first visit to Scotland, but, half guessing at her question, replied, that they had come from Cairntod, and were going on to Howglen. She told her also, now entirely reassured by Aggie's voice, that they had been much longer on the way than they had expected, and were now getting anxious.

"I doubt sair gien ye'll win to Howglen the nicht," said Aggie. "But ye're not yer lone?" she added, trying to summon her English, of which she had plenty of a sort, though not always at hand.

"I hardly expect you'll get to Howglen tonight," said Aggie. "But you're not alone?" she added, trying to summon her English, of which she had plenty of a sort, though not always at hand.

"My father is with me," replied the lady, looking back into the dark carriage, "but I think he is asleep, and I don't want to wake him while we are standing still."

"My father is with me," replied the lady, looking back into the dark carriage, "but I think he is asleep, and I don't want to wake him while we are standing still."

Peeping in, Aggie caught sight of somebody muffled, leaning back in the other corner of the carriage, and breathing heavily.

To Aggie's not altogether unaccustomed eye, it seemed he might have had more than was good for him in the way of refreshment.

Cosmo was busy clearing the snow from the horses' hoofs. The driver, stupid or dazed, sat on the box, helpless as a parrot on a swinging perch.

"You'll never win to Howglen to-night, mem," said Aggie.

"You'll never get to Howglen to-night, ma'am," said Aggie.

"We must put up where we can, then," answered the lady.

"We must put up where we can then," answered the lady.

"I dinna know of a place nearer, fit for gentlefowk, mem."

"I don't know of a place nearer, fit for gentlefolk, ma'am."

"What are we to do, then?" asked the lady, with subdued, but evident anxiety.

"What are we to do then?" asked the lady, with subdued, but evident anxiety.

"What's the guid o' haein' a father like that—sleepin' and snorin' whan maist ye're in want o' 'im!" thought Aggie to herself; but what she replied was, "Bide, mem, till we hear what Cosmo has to say til't."

"What's the good of having a father like that—sleeping and snoring when most you're in want of him!" thought Aggie to herself; but what she replied was, "Wait, ma'am, till we hear what Cosmo has to say about it."

"That is a peculiar name!" remarked the lady, brightening at the sound of it, for it could, she thought, hardly belong to a peasant.

"That is a peculiar name!" remarked the lady, brightening at the sound of it, for it could, she thought, hardly belong to a peasant.

"It's the name the lairds o' Glenwarlock hae borne for generations," answered Aggie; "though doobtless it's no a name, as the maister wad say, indigenous to the country. Ane o' them broucht it frae Italy, the place whaur the Pop' o' Rom' bides."

"It's the name the lairds of Glenwarlock have borne for generations," answered Aggie; "though doubtless it's not a name, as the master would say, indigenous to the country. One of them brought it from Italy, the place where the Pope of Rome lives."

"And who is this Cosmo whose advice you would have me ask?"

"And who is this Cosmo whose advice you would have me ask?"

"He's the yoong laird himsel', mem:—eh! but ye maun be a stranger no to ken the name o' Warlock!"

"He's the young laird himself, ma'am:—eh! but you must be a stranger not to know the name of Warlock!"

"Indeed I am a stranger—and I can't help wishing, if there is much more of this weather between us and England, that I had been more of a stranger still."

"Indeed I am a stranger—and I can't help wishing, if there is much more of this weather between us and England, that I had been more of a stranger still."

"'Deed, mem, we hae a heap o' weather up here as like this as ae snaw-flake is til anither! But we tak what's sent, an' makna mony remarks. Though to be sure the thing's different whan it's o' a body's ain seekin'!"

"Indeed, ma'am, we have a heap of weather up here as like this as one snow-flake is to another! But we take what's sent, and make few remarks. Though to be sure the thing's different when it's of a person's own seeking!"

This speech—my reader may naturally think it not over-polite—was happily not over-intelligible to the lady. Aggie, a little wounded by the reflection on the weather of her country, had in her emotion aggravated her Scottish tone.

"And where is this Cosmo? How are we to find him?"

"He'll come onsoucht, mem. It's only 'at he's busy cleanin' oot yer puir horse's hivs 'at he disna p'y his respec's to ye. But he'll be blythe eneuch!"

"I thought you said he was a lord!" remarked the lady.

"Na, I saidna that, mem. He's nae lord. But he's a laird, an' some lairds is better nor 'maist ony lords; an' *he's* Warlock o' Glenwarlock—at least he wull be—an' may it be lang or come the day!"

"And where is this Cosmo? How are we to find him?"

"He'll come unsought, ma'am. It's only that he's busy cleaning out your poor horse's hooves that he doesn't pay his respects to you. But he'll be happy to do so!"

"I thought you said he was a lord!" remarked the lady.

"Na, I didn't say that ma'am. He's no lord. But he's a laird, and some lairds are better than almost any lords; and *he's* Warlock of Glenwarlock—at least he will be—and may the day be long in coming!"

Hard as the snow was packed in them, all the eight hoofs were now cleared out with Cosmo's busy knife, which he had had to use carefully lest he should hurt the frog. The next moment his head appeared a little behind that of Aggie, and in the light of the lamp the lady saw the handsome face of a lad seemingly about sixteen.

"Here he is, mem! This is the yoong laird. Ye speir at *him* what ye're to du, and du jist as he tells ye." said Aggie, and drew back, that Cosmo might take her place.

"Is that girl your sister?" asked the lady, with not a little abruptness, for the *best bred* are not always the most polite.

"No, my lady," answered Cosmo, who had learned from the lad on the box her name and rank; "she is the daughter of one of my father's tenants."

"Here he is, ma'am! This is the young laird. You ask *him* what you're to do, and do just as he tells you." said Aggie, and drew back, that Cosmo might take her place.

"Is that girl your sister?" asked the lady, with not a little abruptness, for the *best bred* are not always the most polite.

"No, my lady," answered Cosmo, who had learned from the lad on the box her name and rank; "she is the daughter of one of my father's tenants."

Lady Joan Scudamore thought it very odd that the youth should be on such familiar terms with the daughter of one of his father's tenants—out alone with her in the heart of a hideous storm! No doubt the girl looked up to him, but apparently from the same level, as one sharing in the pride of the family! Should she take her advice, and seek his? or should she press on for Howglen? There was, alas! no counsel to be had from her father just at present: if she woke him, he would but mutter something not so much unlike an oath as it ought to be, and go to sleep again!

"We want very much to reach Howglen—I think that is what you call the place," she said.

"You can't get there to-night, I'm afraid," returned Cosmo. "The road is, as you see, no road at all. The horses would do better if you took their shoes off, I think—only then, if they came on a bit of frozen mud, it might knock their hoofs to pieces in such a frost."

The lady glanced round at her sleeping companion with a look expressive of no small perplexity.

"My father will make you welcome, my lady," continued Cosmo, "if you will come with us. We can give you only what English people must think poor fare, for we're not—"

She interrupted him.

"I should be glad to sit anywhere all night, where there was a fire. I am nearly frozen."

"We can do a little better for you than that, though not so well as we should like. Perhaps, as we can't make any show, we are the more likely to do our best for your comfort."

Their pinched circumstances had at one time and another given rise to conversation in which the laird and his son sought together to sound the abysses of hospitality: the old-fashioned sententiousness of the boy had in it nothing of the prig.

"You are very kind. I will promise to be comfortable," said the lady. She began to be a trifle interested in this odd specimen of the Scotch calf.

"Welcome then to Glenwarlock!" said Cosmo. "Come, Aggie; tak ane o' them by the heid: they're gaein' wi' 's.—We must turn the horses' heads, my lady. I fear they won't like to face the wind they've only had their backs to yet. I can't make out whether your driver is half dead or half drunk or more than half frozen; but Aggie and I will take care of them, and if he tumble off, nobody will be the worse."

"Welcome then to Glenwarlock!" said Cosmo. "Come, Aggie; take one of them by the head: they're going with us.—We must turn the horses' heads, my lady. I fear they won't like to face the wind they've only had their backs to yet. I can't make out whether your driver is half dead or half drunk or more than half frozen; but Aggie and I will take care of them, and if he tumble off, nobody will be the worse."

"What a terrible country!" said the lady to herself. "The coachmen get drunk! the boys are prigs! there is no distinction between the owners of the soil and the tenants who farm it! and it snows from morning to night, and from one week's end to another!"

Aggie had taken the head of the near horse, and Cosmo took that of the off one. Their driver said nothing, letting them do as they pleased. With some difficulty, for they had to be more than ordinarily cautious, the road being indistinguishable from the ditches they knew here bounded it on both sides, they got the carriage round. But when the weary animals received the tempest in their faces, instead of pulling they backed, would have turned again, and for some time were not to be induced to front it. Agnes and Cosmo had to employ all their powers of persuasion, first to get them to stand still, and then to advance a little. Gradually, by leading, and patting, and continuous encouraging in language they understood, they were coaxed as far as the parish road, and there turning their sides to the wind, and no longer their eyes and noses, they began to move with a little will of their own; for horses have so much hope, that the mere fact of having made a turn is enough to revive them with the expectation of cover and food and repose. They reached presently a more sheltered part of the road, and if now and then they had to drag the carriage through deeper snow, they were no longer buffeted by the cruel wind or stung by its frost-arrows.

All this time the gentleman inside slept—nor was it surprising; for, lunching at the last town, and not finding the wine fit to drink, he had fallen back upon an accomplishment of his youth, and betaken himself to toddy. That he had found that at least fit to drink was proved by the state in which he was now carried along.

They reached at last the steep ascent from the parish road to Castle Warlock. The two conductors, though they had no leisure to confer on the subject, were equally anxious as to whether the horses would face it; but the moment their heads came round, whether only that it was another turn with its fresh hope, or that the wind brought some stray odour of hay or oats to their wide nostrils, I cannot tell, but finding the ground tolerably clear, they took to it with a will, and tore up with the last efforts of all but exhausted strength, Cosmo and Aggie running along beside them, and talking to them all the way. The only difficulty was to get the lad on the box to give them their heads.

CHAPTER XIV
THE CASTLE INN

The noise of their approach, heard from the bottom of the ascent, within the lonely winter castle, awoke profound conjecture, and Grizzie proceeded to light the lantern that she might learn the sooner what catastrophe could cause such a phenomenon: something awful must have taken place! Perhaps they had cut off the king's head as they did in France! But such was the rapidity of the horses' ascent in the hope of rest, and warmth, and supper, that the carriage was in the close and rattling up to the door, ere she had got the long wick of the tallow candle to acknowledge the dominion of fire. The laird rose in haste from his arm-chair, and went to the door. There stood the chaise, in the cloud of steam that rose from the quick-heaving sides of the horses. And there were Cosmo and Agnes at the door of it, assisting somebody to descend. The laird was never in a hurry. He was too thorough a gentleman to trouble approach by uneasy advance, and he had no fear of anything Cosmo had done. He stood therefore in the kitchen door, calmly expectant.

A long-cloaked lady got down, and, turning from the assistant hand of his son, came towards him—a handsome lady, tall and somewhat stately, but weary, and probably in want of food as well as rest. He bowed with old-fashioned worship, and held out his hand to welcome her. She gave him hers graciously, and thanked him for the hospitality his son had offered them.

"Come in, come in, madam," said the old man. "the fireside is the best place for explanations. Welcome to a poor house, but a warm hearth! So much we can yet offer stranger-friends."
He led the way, and she followed him into the kitchen. On a small piece of carpet before the fire, stood the two chairs of state, each protected by a large antique screen. From hers the grandmother rose with dignified difficulty, when she perceived the quality of the entering stranger.

"Mother," said the laird, "it is not often we have the pleasure of visitors at this time of the year!"

"The more is the rare foot welcome!" answered she, and made lady Joan as low a courtesy as she dared: she could not quite reckon on her power of recovery.

Lady Joan returned her salute, little impressed with the honour done her, but recognizing that she was in the presence of a gentlewoman. She took the laird's seat at his invitation, and leaning forward, gazed wearily at the fire.

The next minute a not very pleasant-looking old man entered, supported on one side by Cosmo and on the other by Agnes. They had had no little difficulty in waking him up, and he entered vaguely supposing they had arrived at an inn where they were to spend the night. If his grumbling and swearing as he advanced was *sotto voce*, the assuagement was owing merely to his not being sufficiently awake to use more vigour. The laird left the lady and advanced to meet him, but he took no notice of him, regarding his welcome as the obsequiousness of a landlord, and turned shivering towards the fire, where Grizzie was hastening to set him a chair.

"The fire's the best flooer i' the gairden, an' the pig's the best coo i' the herdin', my lord," she said—an old saw to which his lordship might have been readier to respond, had he remembered that the *pig* sometimes meant the stone jar that held the whisky.

"The fire's the best flower in the garden, and the pig's the best cow in the herding, my lord," she said—an old saw to which his lordship might have been readier to respond, had he remembered that the *pig* sometimes meant the stone jar that held the whisky.

As soon as Lord Mergwain was seated, Cosmo drew his father aside, told him the names of their guests, and in what difficulty he had found them, and added that the lady and the horses were sober enough, but for the other two he would not answer.

"We have been spending some weeks at Canmore Castle in Ross-shire, and are now on our way home," said lady Joan to Mistress Warlock.

"You have come a long way round," remarked the old lady, not so pleased with the manners of her male visitor, on whom she kept casting, every now and then, a full glance.

"We have," replied Lady Joan. "We turned out of our way to visit an old friend of papa's, and have been storm-bound till he—I mean papa—could bear it no longer. We sent our servants on this morning. They are, I hope, by this time, waiting us at Howglen."

The fire had been thawing the sleep out of Lord Mergwain, and now at length he was sufficiently awake to be annoyed that his daughter should hold so much converse with the folk of the inn.

"Can't you show us to a room?" he said gruffly, "and get us something to eat?"

"We are doing the best we can for your lordship," replied the laird. "But we were not expecting visitors, and one of the rooms you will have to occupy, has not been in use for some time. In such weather as this, it will take two or three hours of a good fire to render it fit to sleep in. But I will go myself, and see that the servant is making what haste she can."

He put on his hat over his night-cap, and made for the door.

"That's right, landlord!" cried his lordship; "always see to the comfort of your guests yourself—But bless me! you don't mean we have to go out of doors to reach our bedrooms?"

"I am afraid we cannot help it," returned the laird, arresting his step. "There used to be a passage connecting the two houses, but for some reason or other—I never heard what—it was closed in my father's time."

"He must have been an old fool!" remarked the visitor.

"My lord!"

"I said your father must have been an old fool," repeated his lordship testily.

"You speak of my husband!" said Mistress Warlock, drawing herself up with dignity.

"I can't help that. *I* didn't give you away. Let's have some supper, will you? I want a tumbler of toddy, and without something to eat it might make me drunk."

Lady Joan sat silent, with a look half of contempt, half of mischievous enjoyment on her handsome face. She had too often to suffer from her father's rudeness not to enjoy its bringing him into a scrape. But the laird was sharper than she thought him, and seeing both the old man's condition and his mistake, humoured the joke. His mother rose, trembling with indignation. He gave her his arm, and conducted her to a stair which ascended immediately from the kitchen, whispering to her on the way, that the man was the worse for drink, and he must not quarrel with him. She retired without leave-taking. He then called Cosmo and Agnes, who were talking together in a low voice at the other end of the kitchen, and taking them to Grizzie in the spare room, told them to help her, that she might the sooner come and get the supper ready.

"I am afraid, my lord," he said, returning, "we are but poorly provided for such guests as your lordship, but we will do what we can."

"A horrible country!" growled his lordship; "but, look you, I don't want jaw—I want drink."

"What drink would your lordship have? If it be in my power—"

"I'll doubt, for all your talk, if you've got anything but your miserable whisky!" interrupted Lord Mergwain.

Now the laird had some remnants of old wine in the once well stored cellar, and, thankless as his visitor seemed likely to turn out, his hospitality would not allow him to withhold what he had.

"I have a few bottles of claret," he said, "—if it should not be over-old!—I do not understand much about wine myself."

"Let's have it up!" cried his lordship. "We'll see. If you don't know good wine, I do. I'm old enough for any wine."

The laird would have had more confidence in recommending his port, which he had been told was as fine as any in Scotland, but he thought claret safer for one in his lordship's condition—one who having drunk would drink again. He went therefore to the wine-cellar, which had once been the dungeon of the castle, and brought thence a most respectable-looking magnum, dirty as a burrowing terrier, and to the eye of the imagination hoary with age. The eyes of the toper glistened at the sight. Eagerly he stretched out both hands towards it. They actually trembled with desire. Hardly could he endure the delay of its uncorking. No sooner did the fine promissory note of the discharge of its tompion reach his ear, than he cried out, with the authority of a field-officer at least—

"Decant it. Leave the last glass in the bottom."

The laird filled a decanter, and set it before him.

"Haven't you a magnum-jug?"

"No, my lord."

"Then fill another decanter, and mind the last glass."

"I have not another decanter, my lord."

"Not got two decanters, you fool?" sneered his lordship, enraged at not having the whole bottle set down to him at once. "But after all," he resumed, "it mayn't be worth a rush, not to say a decanter. Bring the bottle. Set it down. Here!—Carefully! Bring a glass. You should have brought the glasses first. Bring three; I like to change my glass. Make haste, will you!"

The laird did make haste, smiling at the exigence of his visitor. Lord Mergwain listened to the glug-glug in the long neck of the decanter as if it had been a song of love, and the moment it was over, was holding the glass to his nose.

"Humph! Not much aroma here!" he growled, "I ought to have made the old fool—the laird must have been some fifteen years younger than he—"set it down before the fire, only what would have become of me while it was thawing? It's no wonder though! By the time I've been buried as long, I shall want thawing too!"

The wine, however, turned out more satisfactory to the palate of the toper than to his nostrils—which in truth, so much had he drunk that day, were at present incapable of doing it justice—and he set himself to enjoy it. How that should be possible to a man for whom the accompanying dried olives of memory could do so little, I find it difficult to understand. One would think, to enjoy his wine alone, a man must have either good memories or good hopes: Lord Mergwain had forgotten the taste of hope; and most men would shrink from touching the spring that would set a single scene of such a panorama unrolling itself, as made up the past of Lord Mergwain. However there he sat, and there he drank, and, truth to tell, now and then smiled grimly.

The laird set a pair of brass candlesticks on the table—there were no silver utensils anymore in the house of Glenwarlock; years ago the last of them had vanished—and retired to a wooden chair at the end of the hearth, under the lamp that hung on the wall. But on his way he had taken from a shelf an old, much-thumbed folio which Mr. Simon had lent him—the Journal of George Fox, and the panorama which then for a while kept passing before his mind's eye was not a little different from that passing before Lord Mergwain's. What a study to a spirit able to watch the unrolling of the two side by side!

In a few minutes Grizzie entered, carrying a fowl newly killed, its head all but touching the ground at the end of its long, limp neck. She seated herself on a stool, somewhere about the middle of the large space, and proceeded to pluck, and otherwise prepare it for the fire. Having, last of all, split it open from end to end, turning it into something like an illegible heraldic crest, she approached the fire, the fowl in one hand, the gridiron in the other.

"I doubt I maun get his lordship to sit a wee back frae the fire," she said. "I maun jist bran'er this chuckie for his supper."

"I think his lordship will have to sit back from the fire a bit," she said. "I just have to brander this chicken for his supper."

Lady Joan had taken Mrs. Warlock's chair, and her father had taken the laird's, and pulled it right in front of the fire, where a small deal table supported his bottle, his decanter, and his three glasses.

"What does the woman mean?" said his lordship. "—Oh! I see; a spread-eagle! But is my room not ready yet? Or haven't you one to sit in? I don't relish feasting my nose so much in advance of my other senses."

"What does the woman mean?" said his lordship. "—Oh! I see; a spread-eagle! But is my room not ready yet? Or haven't you one to sit in? I don't relish feasting my nose so much in advance of my other senses."

"Ow! nae fear o' yer lordship's nose, 'cep' it be frae yer lordship's hose, my lord!" said Grizzie, "for I doobt ye're birstlin' yer lordship's shins! I'll tak the cratur oot to the cairt-shed, an' sing' 't there first. But 'deed I wadna advise ye to gang to yer room a minute afore ye need, for it winna be that warm the nicht. I hae made a fire 'at's baith big an' bricht—an' fit to ro'st Belzebub—an' I beg yer pardon, laird—but it's some days—I micht say ooks—sin' there was a fire intil 't, an' the place needs time to tak the heat intil its auld neuks."

"Oh! no fear of your lordship's nose, except it be from your lordship's hose, my lord!" said Grizzie, "for I expect you're scorching your lordship's shins! I'll take the bird out to the cart-shed, and singe it there first. But I wouldn't advise going to your room a minute before you need, for it won't be that warm tonight. I've made a fire that's both big and bright—and fit to roast Beelzebub—and I beg your pardon, laird—but it's some days—I might say weeks—since there was a fire in it, and the place needs time to take the heat into its old nooks."

She might have said years not a few, instead of some weeks, but her truthfulness did not drive her so far. She turned, and left the house, carrying with her the fowl to singe.

"Here," said his lordship to his host, "move back this table and chair a bit, will you? I don't relish having the old witch fussing about my knees. What a mistake it is not to have rooms ready for whoever may come!"

The laird rose, laid his book down, and moved the table, then helped his guest to rise, moved his chair, and placed the screen again betwixt him and the door. Lord Mergwain re-settled himself to his bottle.

In the meantime, in the guest-chamber, which had for so long entertained neither friend nor stranger, Cosmo and Aggie were busy—too busy to talk much—airing the linen, dusting the furniture, setting things tidy, and keeping up a roaring fire. For this purpose the remnants of an old broken-down cart, of which the axle was anciently greasy, had been fetched from the winter-store, and the wood and peats together, with a shovelful of coal to give the composition a little body, had made a glorious glow. But the heat had hardly yet begun to affect sensibly the general atmosphere of the place. It was a large room, the same size as the drawing-room immediately under it, and still less familiar to Cosmo. For, if the latter filled him with a kind of loving awe, the former caused him a kind of faint terror, so that, in truth, even in broad daylight, at no time was he willing to enter it. Now and then he would open the door in passing, and for a moment stand peering in, with a stricken, breath-bating enjoyment of the vague atmosphere of dread, which, issuing, seemed to envelop him in its folds; but to go in was too much, and he neither desired nor endured even the looking in for more than a few seconds. For so long it was to him like a page in a book of horrors: to go to the other end of it, and in particular to approach the heavily curtained bed, was more than he cared to do without cogent reason. At the same time he rejoiced to think there was such a room in the house, and attached to it an idea of measureless value—almost as if it had a mysterious window that looked out upon the infinite. The cause of this feeling was not to himself traceable. Until old Grannie's story, he had heard no tale concerning it that he remembered: he may have heard hints—a word dropped may have made its impression, and roused fancies outlasting the memory of their origin; for feelings, like memories of scents and sounds, remain, when the related facts have vanished. What it was about the room that scared him, he could not tell, but the scare was there. With a companion like Aggie, however, even after hearing Grannie's terrible reminiscence, he was able to be in the room without experiencing worse than that same milder, almost pleasant degree of dread, caused by the mere looking through the door into the strange brooding silence of the place. But, I must confess, this applies only to the space on the side of the bed next the fire. The bed itself—not to mention the shadowy region beyond it—on which the body of the pirate had lain, he could not regard without a sense of the awfully gruesome: itself looked scared at its own consciousness of the fact, and of the feeling it caused in the beholder.

In the strength of Aggie's presence, he was now able to take a survey of the room such as never before. Over walls, floor, and ceiling, his eyes were wandering, when suddenly a question arose on which he desired certainty: "Is there," he said to himself, "a door upo' the ither side o' the bed?" "Did Grannie mak mention o' sic a door?" he asked himself next, and could not be certain of the answer. He gazed around him, and saw no door other than that by which they had entered, but at the head of the bed, on the other side, was a space hidden by the curtain: it might be there! When they went to put the sheets on the bed, he would learn! He dared not go till then! "Dare not!" he repeated to himself—and went at once.

In the strength of Aggie's presence, he was now able to take a survey of the room such as never before. Over walls, floor, and ceiling, his eyes were wandering, when suddenly a question arose on which he desired certainty: "Is there," he said to himself, "a door upon the other side of the bed?" "Did Grannie make mention of such a door?" he asked himself next, and could not be certain of the answer. He gazed around him, and saw no door other than that by which they had entered, but at the head of the bed, on the other side, was a space hidden by the curtain: it might be there! When they went to put the sheets on the bed, he would learn! He dared not go till then! "Dare not!" he repeated to himself—and went at once.

He saw and trembled. It was the strangest feeling. If it was not fear, it was something very like it, but with a mixture of wondrous pleasure: there was the door! The curtains hid Aggie, and for a moment he felt as if he were miles alone, and must rush back to the refuge of her presence. But he would not yield to the folly—compelled himself to walk to the door.

Whether he was more disappointed or relieved, he could not, the first instant, have told: instead of a door, scarcely leaning against the wall, was an old dark screen, in stamped leather, from which the gilding was long faded. Disappointment and not relief was then his only sense.

"Aggie," he called, still on the farther side of the bed—he called gently, but trembled at the sound of his own voice—"did ye ever hear—did Grannie mak mention o' a door 'at the auld captain gaed oot at?"

"Whisht, whisht!" cried Aggie, in a loud hissing whisper, which seemed to pierce the marrow of Cosmo's bones. "I rede ye say naething aboot that i' this chaumer. Bide till we're oot o' 't: I hae near dune. Syne we'll steek the door, an' lat the fire work. It'll hae eneuch

"Aggie," he called, still on the farther side of the bed—he called gently, but trembled at the sound of his own voice—"did you ever hear—did Grannie make mention of a door that the old captain went out at?"

"Shush, shush!" cried Aggie, in a loud hissing whisper, which seemed to pierce the marrow of Cosmo's bones. "Take my advice, and don't speak of that here. Wait till we're out of it: I'm nearly done. Then we'll shut the door, and let the fire work. It'll

adu afore it mak the place warm: the cauld until this room's no a coamon ane. There's something by ord'nar' intil 't."

have trouble enough to make the place warm: the cold in it's not a common one. There's something strange in it."

Cosmo could no longer endure having the great, old, hearse-like bed between him and Aggie. With a shiver in the very middle of his body, he hastened to the other side: there lay the country of air, and fire, and safe earthly homeliness: the side he left was the dank region of the unknown, whose march-ditch was the grave.

They hurried with the rest of their work. Aggie insisted on being at the farther side of the bed when they made it. Not another word was spoken between them, till they were safe from the room, and had closed its door behind them.

They went up to Cosmo's room, to make it something fitter for a lady's bower. Opening a certain chest, they took from it—stored there by his mother, Cosmo loved to think—another set of curtains, clean blankets, fine sheets, and a counterpane of silk patchwork, and put them all on the bed. With these, a white toilet-cover, and a chair or two from the drawing-room, they so changed the room that Cosmo declared he would not have known it. They then filled the grate with as much fuel as it would hold, and running fast down the two stairs, went again to the kitchen. At the door of it, however, Aggie gave her companion the slip, and set out to go back to her grannie at Muir o' Warlock.

Cosmo found the table spread for supper, the English lord sitting with his wine before him, and the lady in his grandmother's chair, leaning back, and yawning wearily. Lord Mergwain looked muddled, and his daughter cast on him now and then a look that had in it more of annoyance than affection. He was not now a very pleasant lord to look on, whatever he might once have been. He was red-faced and blear-eyed, and his nose, partly from the snuff he took in large quantity, was much injured in shape and colour: closer description the historical muse declines. His eyes had once been blue, but tobacco, potations, revellings day and night—everything but tears, had washed from them almost all the colour. It added much to the strange unpleasantness of his appearance, that he wore a jet-black wig, so that to the unnatural came the untimely, and enhanced the withered. His mouth, which was full of false teeth, very white, and ill-fitting, had a cruel expression, and Death seemed to look out every time he grinned.

As soon as he and Lady Joan were seated at the supper-table, with Grizzie to wait upon them, the laird and Cosmo left the kitchen and went to the spare-room, for the laird judged that, in the temper and mistake her father was in, the lady would be more comfortable in their absence.

"Cosmo," he said, standing with his back to the fire when he had again made it up, "I cannot help feeling as if I had known that man before. But I can recall no circumstances, and it may be a mere fancy. *You* have never seen him before, my boy, have you?"

"I don't think I have, papa; and I don't care if I never see him again," answered Cosmo. "The lady is pretty, but not very pleasant, I think, though she is a lord's daughter."

"Ah, but such a lord, Cosmo!" returned his father. "When a man goes on drinking like that, he is no better than a cheese under the spigot of a wine-cask; he lives to keep his body well soaked—that it may be the nicer, or the nastier for the worms. Cosmo, my son, don't you learn to drown your soul in your body, like the poor Duke of Clarence in the wine-butt.

The material part of us ought to keep growing gradually thinner, to let the soul out when its time comes, and the soul to keep growing bigger and stronger every day, until it bursts the body at length, as a growing nut does its shell; when, instead, the body grows thicker and thicker, lessening the room within, it squeezes the life out of the soul, and when such a man's body dies, his soul is found a shrivelled thing, too poor to be a comfort to itself or to anybody else. Cosmo, to see that man drink, makes me ashamed of my tumbler of toddy. And now I think of it, I don't believe it does me any good; and, just to make sure that I am in earnest, from this hour I will take no more.—Then," he added, after a short pause, "I shall be pretty sure you will not take it."

"Oh, papa!" cried Cosmo, "take your toddy all the same: I promise you—and a Warlock will not break his word—never to taste strong drink while I live."

"I should prefer the word of a man to that of a Warlock," said his father. "A Warlock is nothing except he be a man. Some Warlocks have been men."

From that day, I may here mention, the laird drank nothing but water, much to the pleasure of Peter Simon, who was from choice a water-drinker.

"What a howling night it is, Cosmo!" he resumed. "If that poor old drinker had tried to get on to Howglen, he would have been frozen to death; when the drink is out of the drunkard, he has nothing to resist with."

By this time Lord Mergwain had had his supper, and had begun to drink again. Grizzie wanted to get rid of him that she might "redd up"[5] her kitchen. But he would not move. He was quite comfortable where he was, he said, and though it was the kitchen! he wouldn't stir a peg till he had finished the magnum. My lady might go when she pleased; the magnum was better company than the whole houseful!

Grizzie was on the point of losing her temper with him altogether, when the laird returned to the kitchen. He found her standing before him with her two hands on her two hips, and lingered a moment at the door to hear what she was saying.

"Na, na, my lord!" expostulated Grizzie, "I canna lea' ye here. Yer lordship 'll sune be past takin' care o' yersel'—no 'at ye wad be a witch at it this present! Ye wad be thinkin' ye was i' yer bed whan ye was i' the mids' o' the middin', or pu'in' the blankets o' the deuk-dub ower yer heid! Lord! my lord, ye micht set the hoose o' fire, an' burn a', baith stable an' byre, an' horses an' cairts an' cairt-sheds, an' hiz a' to white aisse in oor nakit beds!"

"Na, na, my lord!" expostulated Grizzie, "I can't leave you here. Your lordship'll soon be past taking care of yourself—not that you would be a witch at it now! You would be thinking you were in your bed when you were in the midst of the dunghill, or pulling the blankets of the duck pond over your head! Lord! my lord, you might set the house on fire, and burn all, both stable and cow-shed, and horses and carts and cart-sheds, and all of us to white ash in our naked beds!"

"Hold your outlandish gibberish," returned his lordship, "Go and fetch me some whisky. This stuff is too cold to go to sleep on in such weather."

"Hold your outlandish gibberish," returned his lordship, "Go and fetch me some whisky. This stuff is too cold to go to sleep on in such weather."

"Deil a drap o' whusky, or oucht else, yer lordship s' hae frae my han' this nicht—nae mair nor gien ye war a bairn 'at wantit poother to blaw himsel' up wi'! Ye hae had ower muckle a'ready, gien ye war but cawpable o' un'erstan'in' 't, or failin' that, o' believin' an honest wuman 'at kens what state ye are in better nor ye du yersel'!—A bonny lordship!" she muttered to herself as she turned from him.

"Devil a drop of whisky, or anything else, shall your lordship have from me this night—no more than if you were a child that wanted gunpowder to blow himself up with! You have had too much already, if you were but capable of understanding it, or failing that, of believing an honest woman that knows what state you're in better than you do yourself!—A fine lordship!" she muttered to herself as she turned from him.

The laird thought it time to show himself, and went forward. Lord Mergwain had understood not the half of what Grizzie said; but had found sufficient provocation in the tone, and was much too angry for any articulate attempt at speech beyond swearing.

5 REDD UP: tidy, put in order

"My lord," said the laird, "I think you will find your room tolerably comfortable now: shall I have the pleasure of showing you the way?"

"No, indeed! I'm not going to stir. Fetch me a bottle of your whisky—that's pretty safe to be good."

"Indeed, my lord, you shall have no more drink to-night," said the laird, and taking the bottle, which was nearly empty, carried it from the table.

Though nearly past everything else, his guest was not yet too far gone to swear with vigour, and the volley that now came pouring from his outraged heart was such, that, for the sake of Grizzie and Cosmo, the laird took the bottle again in his hand, and said, that, if his lordship would drink it in his own room, he should have what was left of it.

Not too drunk to see where his advantage lay, Lord Mergwain yielded; the thunder of imprecation from bellowing sank to growling, then to muttering, and the storm gradually subsided. The laird gave him one arm, Cosmo another, and Grizzie came behind, ready to support or push, and so in procession they moved from the kitchen along the causeway, his lordship grumbling and slipping, hauled, carried, and shoved—through the great door as they called it, up the stairs, past the drawing-room, and into "the muckle chaumer" (the great chamber). There he was deposited in an easy chair, before the huge fire, and was fast asleep in a moment. Lady Joan had followed them, and while they were in her father's room, had passed up to her own, so that when they re-entered the kitchen, there was nobody there.

With a sigh of relief, the laird sank into his mother's chair. After a little while, he sent Cosmo to bed, and, rejoicing in the quiet, got again the journal of George Fox, and began to read. When Grizzie had pottered about for a while, she too went to bed, and the laird was alone. When he had read about an hour, he thought it time to see after his guest, and went to his room. He found him still asleep in his chair before the fire; but he could not be left there through such a night, for the fire would go out, and then a pack of wolves would hardly be worse than the invading cold. It was by no means an easy task to rouse him, however, and indeed remained in large measure unaccomplished—so far so, that, after with much labour and contrivance relieving him of his coat and boots, the laird had to satisfy his hospitality with getting him into bed in the remainder of his clothes. He then heaped fresh fuel on the fire, put out the candles, and left him to what repose there might be for him. Returning to his chair and his book, the laird read for another hour, and then went to bed. His room was in the same block, above that of his mother.

CHAPTER XV
THAT NIGHT

Cosmo's temporary quarters were in one of two or three chambers above his own, formerly occupied by domestics, when there were many more of them about the place. He went to bed, but, after about three hours, woke very cold—so cold that he could not go to sleep again. He got up, heaped on his bed everything protective he could find, and tried again. But it was of no avail. Cosmo could keep himself warm enough in the open air, or if he could not, he did not mind; but to be cold in bed was more than he would willingly endure. He got up again—with an idea. Why should he not amuse himself, rather than lie shivering on couch inhospitable? When anything disturbed him on a summer night, as a matter of course he got up and went out; and although naturally he was less inclined on such a night as this, when the rooks would be tumbling dead from the boughs of the fir-trees, he yet would, rather than lie sleepless with cold.

On the opposite side of the court, in a gap between the stable and the byre, the men had heaped up the snow from the rest of the yard, and in the heap Cosmo had been excavating. For snow-balling he had little inclination, but the snow as a plastic substance, a thing that could be compelled into shapes, was an endless delight to him, and in connection with this mound he had conceived a new fancy, which, this very night, but for the interruption of their visitors, he would already have put to the test.

Into the middle of the mound he had bored a tunnel, and then hollowed out what I may call a negative human shape—the mould, as it were, of a man, of life-size, with his arms thrown out, and his feet stretched straight, like one that had fallen and lay in weariness. His object was to illuminate it, in the hope of "a man all light, a seraph man," shining through the snow. That very night he had intended, on his return from Muir of Warlock, to light him up; and now that he was driven out by the cold, he would brave, in his own den, in the heart of the snow, the enemy that had roused him, and make his experiment.

He dressed himself, crept softly out, and, for a preparation, would have a good run. He trotted down the hill, beating his feet hard, until he reached the more level road, where he set out at full speed, and soon was warm as any boy need care to be.

About three o'clock in the morning, the laird woke suddenly, without knowing why. But he was not long without knowing why he must not go to sleep again. From a distance, as it seemed, through the stillness of the night, in rapid succession, came three distinct shrieks, one close on the other, as from the throat of a human being in mortal terror. Never had such shrieks invaded his ears. Whether or not they came from some part of his own house, he could not tell. He sprung upon the floor, thinking first of his boy, and next of the old man whom he had left drunk in his bed, and dressed as fast as he could, expecting every moment a fresh assault of horrible sound. But all he heard was the hasty running of far-off feet. He hurried down, passing carefully his mother's door, but listening as he passed, in the hope of finding she had not been disturbed. He heard nothing, and went on. But in truth the old lady lay trembling, too terrified to move or utter a sound. In the next room he heard Grizzie moving, as if, like himself, getting up with all speed. Down to the kitchen he ran, in haste to get out and reach the great door. But when he opened the kitchen door, a strange sight met his eyes, and for a moment arrested him.

The night was dark as pitch, for, though the snow had ceased to fall, great clouds of it yet filled the vault of the sky, and behind them was no moon from which any smallest glimmer might come soaking through. But, on the opposite side of the court, the heap of snow familiar to his eyes was shining with an unknown, a faint, phosphorescent radiance. The whole heap was illuminated, and was plainly visible: but the strangest thing was, that the core of light had a vague *shadowy* resemblance—if one may use the word of a shape of *light*—to the form of a man. There were the body and outstretched limbs of one who had cast himself supine in sorest weariness, ready for the grave which had found him. The vision flickered, and faded and revived, and faded again, while, in his wonder forgetting for one brief moment the cries that had roused him, the laird stood and gazed. It was the strangest, ghostliest thing he had ever seen! Surely he was on the point of discovering some phenomenon hitherto unknown! What Grizzie would have taken it for, unhappily we do not know, for, just as the laird heard her footsteps on the stair, and he was himself starting to cross the frozen space between, the light, which had been gradually paling, suddenly went out. With its disappearance he bethought himself, and hurried towards the great door, with Grizzie now at his heels.

He opened it. All was still. Feeling his way in the thick darkness, he went softly up the stair. Cosmo had but just left the last remnants of his candle-ends burning, and climbed glowing to his room, delighted with the success of his experiment, when those quick-following, hideous sounds rent the night, like flashes from some cloud of hellish torture. His heart seemed to stand still. Without knowing why, involuntarily he associated them with what he had been last about, and for a moment felt like a murderer. The next he caught up his light and rushed from the room, to seek, like his father, that of their guest.

As he reached the bottom of the first stair, the door of his own room opened, and out came Lady Joan, with a cloak thrown over her nightgown, and looking like marble, with wide eyes. But Cosmo felt it was not she who had shrieked, and passing her without a second look, led the way down, and she followed.

When the laird reached the door of the guest-chamber, there was his boy in his clothes, with a candle in his hand, and the lady in her nightgown, standing in the middle of the floor, and looking down with dismayed countenances. There lay Lord Mergwain!—or was it but a thing of nought—the deserted house of a living soul? The face was drawn a little to one side, and had a mingled expression, of horror—which came from within, and of ludicrousness, which had an outside formal cause. Upon closer investigation the laird almost concluded he was dead; but on the merest chance something must be done. Cosmo seemed dazed, and Lady Joan stood staring with lost look, more of fright than of sorrow, but there was Grizzie, peeping through between them, with bright searching eyes! On her countenance was neither dismay, anxiety, nor distraction. She nodded her head now and then as she gazed, looking as if she had expected it all, and here it was.

"Rin an' fess het watter as fest's ye can, Grizzie," (Run and bring hot water as fast as you can, Grizzie,") said the laird. "My dear Lady Joan, go and dress, or you will be frozen to death. We will do all we can. Cosmo, get the fire up as quickly as possible—it is not quite out. But first you and I must get him into bed, and cover him up warm, and I will rub his hands and feet till the hot water comes."

As the laird said every one did. A pail of hot water was soon brought, the fire was soon lighted, and the lady soon returned more warmly clad. He made Grizzie put the pail on a chair by the bed-side, and they got his feet in without raising him, or taking him out of the blankets. Before long he gave a deep sigh, and presently showed other signs of revival. When at length he opened his eyes, he stared around him wildly, and for a moment it seemed to all of them he had lost his reason. But the laird said he might not yet have got over the drink he had taken, and if he could be got to sleep, he would probably wake better. They removed some more of his clothes, laid him down again, and made him as comfortable as they could, with hot bottles about him. The laird said he would sit with him, and call Lady Joan if needful. To judge by her behaviour, he conjectured such a catastrophe was not altogether strange to her. She went away readily, more like one relieved than anxious.

But there had arisen in the mind of the laird a fear: might not Cosmo unwittingly have had some share in the frightful event? When first he entered the room, there was Cosmo, dressed, and with a light in his hand: the seeming phosphorescence in the snow must have been one of his *ploys,* and might that not have been the source of the shock to the dazed brain of the drinker?

His lordship was breathing more softly and regularly, though every now and then half waking with a cry—a dreadful thing to hear from a sleeping *old man.* They drew their chairs close to the fire and to each other, and Cosmo, as was usual with him, laid his hand on his father's knee.

"Did you observe that peculiar appearance in the snow-heap, on the other side of the court, Cosmo?" asked the laird.

"Yes, papa," replied the boy: "I made it myself." And therewith he told him all about it. "You're not vexed with me, are you, papa?" he added, seeing the laird look grave.

"No, my son," answered his father; "I am only uneasy lest that should have had anything to do with this sad affair."

"How could that be, papa?" asked Cosmo.

"He may have looked out of the window and seen it, and, in the half-foolish state he was in, taken it for something supernatural."

"But why should that have done him any harm?"

"It may have terrified him."

"Why should it terrify him?" said Cosmo.

"There may be things we know nothing of," replied his father, "to answer that question. I cannot help feeling rather uneasy about it."

"Did *you* see anything frightful about my man of light, papa?" inquired Cosmo.

"No," answered his father thoughtfully; "but the thing, you see, was in the shape of a man—a man lying at full length as if he were dead, and indeed in his grave: he might take it for his wraith—an omen of his coming end."

"But he is an Englishman, papa, and the English don't believe in the second sight."

"That does make it less likely.—Few lowlanders do."

"Do you believe in it, papa?"

"Well, you see," returned the laird, with a small smile, "I, like yourself, am neither pure highlander nor pure lowlander, and the natural consequence is, I am not very sure whether I believe in it or not. I have heard stories difficult to explain."

"Still," said Cosmo, "my lord would be more to blame than me, for no man with a good conscience would have been so frightened as that, even if it had been his wraith."

"That may be true;—still, a man cannot help being especially sorry anything should happen to a stranger in his house. You and I, Cosmo, would have our house a place of refuge.—But you had better go to bed now. There is no reason in tiring two people, when one is enough."

"But, papa, I got up because I was so cold I could not sleep. If you will let me, I would much rather sit with you. I shall be much more comfortable here."

That his son should have been cold in the night distressed the laird. He felt as if, for the sake of strangers, he had neglected his own—the specially sent. He would have persuaded Cosmo to go to his father's bed, which was in a warmer room, but the boy begged so to be allowed to remain, that he yielded.

They had talked in a low voice for fear of disturbing the sleeper, and now were silent. Cosmo rolled himself in his plaid, lay down at his father's feet, and was soon fast asleep: with his father there, the chamber had lost its terrors, and was just like any other home-feeling room of the house. Many a time in after years did that night, that room, that fire, and the feeling of his father over his head, while the bad lord lay snoring within the dark curtains, rise before him; and from the memory he would try to teach himself, that, if he were towards his great Father in his house as he was then towards his earthly father in his, he would never fear anything.

To know one's self as safe amid storm and darkness, amid fire and water, amid disease and pain, even during the felt approach of death, is to be a Christian, for that is how the Master felt in the hour of darkness, because he knew it a fact.

All night long, at intervals, the old man moaned, and every now and then would mutter sentences unintelligible to the laird, but sown with ugly, sometimes fearful words. In the gray of the morning he woke.

"Bring me brandy," he cried in a voice of discontent.

The laird rose and went to him. When he saw the face above him, a horror came upon his—a look like that they found frozen on it.

"Who are you?" he gasped. "Where am I?"

"You came here in the storm last night, my lord," said the laird.

"Cursed place! I never had such horrible dreams in my life. Where am I—do you hear? Why don't you answer me?"

"You are at Castle Warlock, my lord," replied the laird.

At this he shrieked, and, throwing off the clothes, sprung from the bed.

"I entreat you, my lord, to lie down again. You were very ill in the night," expostulated the laird.

"I don't stop another hour in the blasted hole!" roared his guest, in a fierce quaver. "Out of my way, you fool! Where's Joan? Tell her to get up and come directly. I'm off, tell her. I'd as soon go to bed in the drifts as stop another hour in this abominable old lime-kiln."

The laird let him rave on: it was useless to oppose him. He flew at his clothes to dress himself, but his poor old hands trembled with rage, fear, drink, and eagerness. The laird did his best to help him, but he seemed nowise recognizant.

"I will get you some hot water, my lord," he said at length, and was moving towards the door.

"No, damn you! Damn everybody!" shrieked the old man. "If you go out of that door, I will throw myself out of this window."

The laird turned at once, and in silence waited on him again like a servant. "He must be in a fit of delirium tremens!" he said to himself. He poured him out some cold water, but he would not use it. He would neither eat nor drink nor wash till he was out of the horrible dungeon, he said. The next moment he cried for water, drank three mouthfuls eagerly, threw the tumbler from him, and broke it on the hearth.

The instant he was dressed, he dropped into the great chair and closed his eyes.

"Your lordship must allow me to fetch some fuel," said the laird; "the room is growing cold."

"No, I tell you!" cried lord Mergwain, opening his eyes and sitting up. "When I'm cold I'll go to hell and get warm again. If you attempt to leave the room, I'll send a bullet after you.—God have mercy! What's that at my feet?'"

"It is only my son," replied the laird gently. "We have been with you all night—since you were taken ill, that is."

"When was that? What do you mean by that?" he said, looking up sharply, with a face of more intelligence than he had yet shown.

"Your lordship had some sort of fit in the night, and if you do not compose yourself, I dread a return of it."

"You well may, if I stop here," he returned—then, after a pause, "Did I talk?" he asked.

"Yes, my lord—a good deal."

"What did I say?"

"Nothing I could understand, my lord."

"And you did your best, I don't doubt!" rejoined his lordship, with a sneer. "But you know nothing is to be made of what a man says in a fit."

"I have told your lordship I heard nothing."

"No matter; I don't sleep another night under your roof."

"That will be as it may, my lord."

"What do you mean?"

"Look at the weather, my lord.—Cosmo!"

The boy was asleep, but at the sound of his name from his father's lips, he started at once to his feet.

"Go and wake Grizzie," said the laird. "and tell her to get breakfast ready as fast as she can. Then bring some peat for the fire, and some hot water for his lordship."

Cosmo ran to obey. Grizzie had been up for more than an hour, and was going about with the look of one absorbed in a tale of magic and devilry. Her mouth was pursed up close, as if worlds should not make her speak, but her eyes were wide and flashing, and now and then she would nod her head, as for the Q.E.D. to some unheard argument. Whatever Cosmo required, she attended to at once, but not one solitary word did she utter.

He went back with the fuel, and they made up the fire. Lord Mergwain was lying back exhausted in his chair, with his eyes closed.

"Why don't you bring me my brandy—do you hear?" all at once he cried. "—Oh, I thought it was my own rascal! Get me some brandy, will you?"

"There is none in the house, my lord," said his host.

"What a miserable sort of public to keep! No brandy!"

"My lord, you are at Castle Warlock—not so good a place for your lordship's needs."

"Oh, that's it, yes! I remember! I knew your father, or your grandfather, or your grandson, or somebody—the more's my curse! Out of this I must be gone, and that at once! Tell them to put the horses to. Little I thought when I left Cairntod where I was going to find myself! I would rather be in hell and have done with it! Lord! Lord! to think of a trifle like that not being forgotten yet! Are there no doors out? Give me brandy, I say. There's some in my pocket somewhere. Look you! I don't know what coat I had on yesterday! Or where it is!"

He threw himself back in his chair. The laird set about looking if he had brought the brandy of which he spoke: it might be well to let him have some. Not finding it, he would have gone to search the outer garments his lordship had put off in the kitchen; but he burst out afresh:

"I tell you—and confound you, I say, that you have to be told twice—I will not be left alone with that child! He's as good as nobody! What could he do if—?" Here he left the sentence unfinished.

"Very well, my lord," responded the laird, "I will not leave you. Cosmo shall go and look for the brandy-flask in your lordship's greatcoat."

"Yes, yes, good boy! you go and look for it. You're all Cosmos, are you? Will the line never come to an end! A cursed line for me—if it shouldn't be a rope-line! But I had the best of the game after all!—though I did lose my two rings. Confounded old cheating son of a porpus! It was doing the world a good turn and Glenwarlock a better to—Look you! what are you listening there for!—Ha! ha! ha! I say, now—would you hang a man, laird—I mean, when you could get no good out of it—not a ha'p'orth for yourself or your family?"

"I've never had occasion to consider the question," answered the laird.

"Ho! ho! haven't you? Let me tell you it's quite time you considered it. It's no joke when a man has to decide without time to think. He's pretty sure to decide wrong."

"That depends, I should think, my lord, on the way in which he has been in the habit of deciding."

"Come now! none of your Scotch sermons to me! You Scotch always were a set of down-brown hypocrites! Confound the whole nation!"

"To judge by your last speech, my lord,—"

"Oh, by my last speech, eh?—my dying declaration? Then I tell you 'tis fairer to judge a man by anything sooner than his speech. That only serves to hide what he's thinking. I wish I might be judged by mine, though, and not by my deeds! I've done a good many things in my time I would rather forget, now age has clawed me in his clutch. So have you; so has everybody. I don't see why I should fare worse than the rest."

Here Cosmo returned with the brandy-flask, which he had found in his greatcoat. His lordship stretched out both hands to it, more eagerly even than when he had welcomed the cob-webbed magnum of claret—hands trembling with feebleness and hunger for strength. Heedless of his host's offer of water and a glass, he put it to his mouth, and swallowed three great gulps hurriedly. Then he breathed a deep sigh, seemed to say with Macbeth, "Ourselves again!" drew himself up in a chair, and glanced around him with a look of gathering arrogance. A kind of truculent question was in his eyes—as much as to say, "Now then, what do you make of it all? What's your candid notion about me and my extraordinary behaviour?" After a moment's silence,—

"What puzzles me is this," he said, "how the deuce I came, of all places, to come just here! I don't believe, in all my wicked life, I ever made such a fool of myself before—and I've made many a fool of myself too!"

Receiving no answer, he took another pull at his flask. The laird stood a little behind and watched him, harking back upon old stories, putting this and that together, and resolving to have a talk with old Grannie.

A minute or two more, and his lordship got up, and proceeded to wash his face and hands, ordering Cosmo about after the things he wanted, as if he had been his valet.

"Richard's himself again!" he said in a would-be jaunty voice, the moment he had finished his toilet, and looked in a crow-cocky kind of way at the laird. But the latter thought he saw trouble still underneath the look.

"Now, then, Mr. Warlock, where's this breakfast of yours?" he said.

"For that, my lord," replied the laird, "I must beg you to come to the kitchen. The dining-room in this weather would freeze the very marrow of your bones."

"And, look you! it don't want freezing," said his lordship, with a shudder. "The kitchen, to be sure!—I don't desire a better place. I'll be hanged if I enter this room again!" he muttered to himself—not too low to be heard. "My tastes are quite as simple as yours, Mr. Warlock, though I have not had the same opportunity of indulging them."

He seemed rapidly returning to the semblance of what he would have called a gentleman. He rose, and the laird led the way. Lord Mergwain followed; and Cosmo, coming immediately behind, heard him muttering to himself all down the stairs: "Mere confounded nonsense! Nothing whatever but the drink!—I must say I prefer the daylight after all.—Yes! That's the drawing-room.—What's done's done—and more than done, for it can't be done again!"

It was a nipping and an eager air into which they stepped from the great door. The storm had ceased, but the snow lay much deeper, and all the world seemed folded in a lucent death, of which the white mounds were the graves. All the morning it had been snowing busily, for no footprints were between the two doors but those of Cosmo.

When they reached the kitchen, there was a grand fire on the hearth, and a great pot on the fire, in which the porridge Grizzie had just made was swelling in huge bubbles that burst in sighs. Old Grizzie was bright as the new day, bustling and deedy. Her sense of the awful was nowise to be measured by the degree of her dread: she believed and did not fear—much. She had an instinctive consciousness that a woman ought to be, and was a match for the devil.

"I am sorry we have no coffee for your lordship," said the laird, "To tell the truth, we seldom take anything more than our country's porridge. I hope you can take tea? Our Grizzie's scons are good, with plenty of butter."

His lordship had in the meantime taken yet another pull at the brandy-flask, and was growing more and more polite.

"The man would be hard to please," he said, "who would not be enticed to eat by such a display of good victuals. Tea for me, before everything!—How am I to pretend to swallow the stuff?" he murmured, rather than muttered, to himself.—"But," he went on aloud, "didn't that cheating rascal leave you—"

He stopped abruptly, and the laird saw his eyes fixed upon something on the table, and following their look, saw it was a certain pepper-pot, of odd device—a piece of old china in the shape of a clumsily made horse, with holes between the ears for the issue of the pepper.

"I see, my lord," he said, "you are amused with the pepper-pot. It is a curious utensil, is it not? It has been in the house a long time—longer than anybody knows. Which of my great-grandmothers let it take her fancy, it is impossible to say; but I suppose the reason for its purchase, if not its manufacture, was, that a horse passant has been the crest of our family from time immemorial."

"Curse the crest, and the horse too!" said his lordship.

The laird started. His guest had for the last few minutes been behaving so much like a civilized being, that he was not prepared for such a sudden relapse into barbarity. But the entrance of Lady Joan, looking radiant, diverted the current of things.

The fact was, that, Lord Mergwain had fallen into such a habit of speaking in his worse moods without the least restraint, that in his better moods, which were indeed only good by comparison, he spoke in the same way, without being aware of it, and of himself seldom discovering that he had spoken.

The rest of the breakfast passed in peace. The visitors had tea, oatcake, and scons, with fresh butter and jam; and Lady Joan, for all the frost and snow, had yet a new-laid egg—the only one; while the laird and Cosmo ate their porridge and milk—the latter very scanty at this season of the year, and tasting not a little of turnip—and Grizzie, seated on a stool some distance from the table, took her porridge with treacle. Mrs. Warlock had not yet left her room.

When the meal was over, Lord Mergwain turned to his host, and said,

"Will you oblige me, Mr. Warlock, by sending orders to my coachman to have the horses put to as quickly as possible: we must not trespass more on your hospitality.—Confound me if I stop an hour longer in this hole of a place, though it be daylight!"

"Papa!" cried Lady Joan.

His lordship understood, looked a little confused, and with much readiness sought to put the best face on his blunder.

"Pardon me, Mr. Warlock," he said; "I have always had a bad habit of speech, and now that I am an old man, I don't improve on it."

"Don't mention it, my lord," returned the laird. "I will go and see about the carriage; but I am more than doubtful.

He left the kitchen, and Cosmo followed him. Lord Mergwain turned to his daughter and said,

"What does the man mean? I tell you, Joan, I am going at once. So don't you side with him if he wants us to stop. He may have his reasons. I knew this confounded place before you were born, and I hate it."

"Very good, papa!" replied Lady Joan, with a slight curl of her lip, "I don't see why you should fancy I should like to stop."

They had spoken aloud, regardless of the presence of Grizzie.

"May it be lang afore ye're in a waur an' a warmer place, my lord an' my leddy," ("May it be long before you're in a worse and a warmer place, my lord and my lady,") said the old woman, with the greatest politeness of manner she knew how to assume. When people were rude, she thought she had a right to be rude in return. But they took no more notice than if they had not heard.

CHAPTER XVI
THROUGH THE DAY

It was a glorious morning. The wind had fallen quite, and the sun was shining as if he would say, "Keep up your hearts; I am up here still. I have not forgotten you. By and by you shall see more of me." But Nature lay dead, with a great white sheet cast over face and form. Not dead?—Just as much dead as ever was man, save for the inner death with which he kills himself, and which she cannot die. It is only to the eyes of his neighbours that the just man dies: to himself, and to those on the other side, he does not die, but is born instead: "He that liveth and believeth in me shall never die." But the poor old lord felt the approaching dank and cold of the sepulchre as the end of all things to him—if indeed he would be permitted to lie there, and not have to get up and go to worse quarters still.

"I am sorry to have to tell you, my lord," said the laird, re-entering, "that both our roads and your horses are in such a state that it is impossible you should proceed to-day."

His guest turned white through all the discoloration of his countenance. His very soul grew too white to swear. He stood silent, his pendulous under lip trembling.

"Though the wind fell last night," resumed the laird, "the snow came on again before the morning, and it seems impossible you should get through. To attempt it would be to run no small risk of your lives."

"Joan," said lord Mergwain, "go and order the rascal to put the horses to."

Lady Joan rose at once, took her shawl, put it over her head, and went. Cosmo ran to open the door for her. The laird looked on, and said not a word: the headstrong old man would find the thing could not be done!

"Will you come and find the coachman for me, Cosmo?" said Lady Joan when they reached the door—with a flash of her white teeth and her dark eyes that bewitched the boy. Then first, in the morning light and the brilliance of the snow-glare, he saw that she was beautiful. When the shadows were dark about her, the darkness of her complexion obscured itself; against the white sheen she stood out darkly radiant. Specially he noted the long eyelashes that made a softening twilight round the low, horizon-like luminousness of her eyes.

Through the deep snow between the kitchen and the stable, were none but his father's footsteps. He cast a glance at her small feet, daintily shod in little more than sandals: she could not put down one of them anywhere without sinking beyond her ankle!

"My lady," he said, "you'll get your feet soaking wet! They're so small they'll just dibble the snow! Please ask your papa if I mayn't go and give his message. It will do just as well."

"I must go myself," she answered. "Sometimes he will trust nobody but me."

"Stop then a moment," said Cosmo. "Just come to the drawing-room. I won't keep you more than two minutes. The path there, you see, is pretty well trodden."

He led the way, and she followed.

The fire was alight, and burning well; for Grizzie, foreseeing how it must be, and determined she would not have strangers in the kitchen all day, had lighted it early. Lady Joan walked straight to it, and dropped, with a little shiver, into a chair beside it. To Cosmo the sight of the blaze brought a strange delight, like the discovery of a new loveliness in an old friend. To Lady Joan the room looked old-fashioned dreariness itself, to Cosmo an ancient marvel, ever fresh. He left her, and ran to his own room, whence presently he returned with a pair of thick woollen stockings, knitted in green and red by the hands of his grandmother. These he carried to Lady Joan, where she sat on the low chair, and kneeling before her, began, without apology or explanation, to draw one of them over the dainty foot placed on the top of the other in front of the fire. She gave a little start, and half withdrew her foot; then looking down at the kneeling figure of service before her, recognized at once the utterly honest and self-forgetful earnestness of the boy, and submitted. Carefully he drew the stockings on, and she neither opposed nor assisted him. When he had done, he looked up in her face with an expression that seemed to say—"There now! Can't I do it properly?" She thanked him, rose, and went out, and Cosmo conducted her to the stable, where he heard the coachman, as she called him, not much better than than a stable-boy, whistling. She gave him her father's order.

The lad stared with open mouth, and pointed to one of the stalls. There stood an utterly wretched horse, swathed in a cloth, with his head hanging down, heedless of the food before him. It was clear no hope lay there. She turned and looked at Cosmo.

"The better for us, my lady!" replied Cosmo to her look; "we shall have your beautiful eyes the longer! They were lost in the dark last night, because they are made out of it, but now we see them, we don't want to part with them."

She looked at him and smiled, saying to herself the boy would be dangerous by and by, and together they went back to the kitchen, where since they left not a word had been spoken. Grizzie was removing the breakfast things; Lord Mergwain was seated by the fire, staring into it; and the laird had got his Journal of George Fox, and was reading diligently: when nothing was to be done, the deeper mind of the laird grew immediately active.

When Lady Joan entered, her father sat up straight in his chair: he expected opposition!

"One of the horses, my lord, is quite unfit," she said.

"Then, by my soul! We'll start with the other," he replied, in a tone that sounded defiance to heaven or earth or whatever said him nay.

"As your lordship pleases," returned Joan.

My lord," said the laird, lowering his book to his knee, "if I thought four cart-horses would pull you through to Howglen to-night, you should have them; but you would simply stick fast, horses and all, in the snow-wreaths."

The old man uttered an exclamation with an awful solemnity, and said no more, but collapsed, and sat huddled up, staring into the fire.

"You must just make the best of your quarters here; they are entirely at your service, my lord," said the laird. "We shall not starve. There are sheep on the place, pigs and poultry, and plenty of oatmeal, though very little flour. There is milk too—and a little wine, and I think we shall do well enough."

Lord Mergwain made no answer, but in his silence seemed to be making up his mind to the ineludible.

"Have you any more of that claret?" he asked. "Not much, I am sorry to say," answered the laird, "but it is your lordship's while it lasts."

"If this lasts, I shall drink your cellar dry," returned his lordship with a feeble grin. "I may as well make a clean breast of it. From my childhood I have never known what it was not to be thirsty. I believe thirst to be the one unfailing birth-mark of the family. I was what the Methodists call a drunkard before I was born. My father died of drink. So did my grandfather. You must have some pity on me, if I should want more than seems reasonable. The only faculty ever cultivated in our strain was drinking, and I am sorry to say it has not been brought to perfection yet. Perfection is to get drunk and never know it; but I have bad dreams, sir! I have bad dreams! And the worst of it is, if once I have a bad dream, I am sure to have it again; and if it come first in a strange place, it will come every night until I leave that place. I had a very bad one last night, as you know. I grant it came because I drank too much yesterday, but that won't keep it from coming again to-night."

He started to his feet, the muscles of his face working frightfully.

"Send for your horses, Glenwarlock," he cried. "Have them put to at once. Four of them, you said. At once—at once! Out of this I must go. If it be to hell itself, go I must and will."

"My lord," said the laird, "I cannot send you from my house in this weather. As my guest, I am bound to do my best for you; especially as I understand the country, and you do not. I said you should have my horses if I thought they could take you through, but I do not think it. Besides, the change, in my judgment, is a deceitful one, and this night may be worse than the last. Poor as your accommodation is, it is better than the open road between this and Howglen; though, doubtless, before to-morrow morning you would be snug in the heart of a snow-wreath."

"Look here, sir," said Lord Mergwain, and rising, he went up to the laird, and laid his hand on his shoulder; "if I stop, will you give me another room, and promise to share it with me to-night? I am aware it is an odd request to make, but, as I tell you, we have been drinking for generations, and my nerves are the worse for it. It's rather hard that the sins of the fathers should be visited on the children! Before God, I have enough to do with my own, let alone my father's! Every one should bear his own burden. I can't bear mine. If I could, it's not much my father's would trouble me!"

"My lord, I will do anything I can for you—anything but consent to your leaving Castle Warlock to-day."

"You will spend the night with me, then?"

"I will."

"But not in that room, you know!"

"Anywhere you please in the house, my lord, except my mother's room."

"Then I'll stop.—Joan, you may amuse yourself; we are not going till to-morrow."

The laird smiled; he could not flatter himself with the hope of so speedy a departure. Joan turned to Cosmo.

"Will you take me about the place?" she said.

"If you mean indoors," interposed the laird. "It is a curious old house, and might interest you a little."

"I should like nothing better. May I go with Cosmo?"

"Certainly: he will be delighted to attend your ladyship.—Here are the keys of the cabinets in the drawing-room, Cosmo. Her ladyship may like to look at some of their contents."

"I hardly know enough about them," returned Cosmo. "Won't you come yourself, father, and show them to us?"

It was the first time the boy used the appellation.

"If they are not worth looking at in themselves, the facts about them cannot be of much consequence to a stranger, my boy," answered the laird.

He was unwilling to leave Lord Mergwain. Lady Joan and Cosmo went without him.

"Perhaps we may follow you by and by," said the laird.

"Is the place very old, Cosmo?" asked Lady Joan on their way.

"Nobody knows how old the oldest part of it is," answered Cosmo, "though dates are assigned to the most of what you will see to-day. But you must ask my father; I do not know much of the history of it. I know the place itself, though, as well as he does. I fancy I know nearly every visible stone of it."

"You are very fond of it, then?"

"There never could be any place like it to me, my lady. I know it is not very beautiful, but I love it none the less for that. I sometimes think I love it the more for its ruggedness—ugliness, if you please to call it so. If my mother had not been beautiful, I should love her all the same."—"and think there wasn't anybody like her," he was going to add, but checked himself, remembering that of course there was not.

Arrived in the drawing-room, whither Cosmo led her first, Lady Joan took her former place by the fire, and sat staring into it. She did not know what to make of what she saw and heard. How could people be happy, she thought, in such a dreary, cold, wretched country, with such poverty-stricken home-surroundings, and nothing to amuse them from one week's end to another? Yet they seemed to be happy to a degree she knew nothing of! For alas, her home was far from a blessed one; and as she had no fountain open in herself, but looked entirely to foreign supply for her life-necessities, and as such never can be so supplied, her life was not a flourishing one.

There are souls innumerable in the world, as dry as the Sahara desert—souls which, when they look most gay and summer-like, are only flaunting the flowers gathered from other people's gardens, stuck without roots into their own unproducing soil. Oh, the dreariness, the sandy sadness of such poor arid souls! They are hungry and eat husks; they are thirsty, and drink hot wine; their sleep is a stupor, and their life, if not an unrest, then a yielded decay. Only when praised and admired do they feel as if they lived! But Joan was not yet of such. She had had too much discomfort to have entered yet into their number. There was water not yet far from the surface of her consciousness.

With no little pleasure and some pride, Cosmo proceeded to take the family treasures from their shelves; but alas! Most of them were common to the eyes of one who also had a family and a history, lived in a much larger, if not half so old a house, and had had amongst her ancestors more than one with a liking for antiquities, oddities, and *bibelots*. Lady Joan regarded them listlessly, willing to seem to attend to the boy, but with her thoughts far away, while now and then she turned a weary gaze towards the next window: all she saw thence was a great, mounded country, dreary as sunshine and white cold could make it. Storm, driving endless whirls of spectral snow, would have been less dreary to her than the smiling of this cold antagonism. It was a picture of her own life. Evil greater than she knew had spread a winter around her. If her father suffered for the sins of his fathers, she suffered for his, and had for them to dwell in desolation and loneliness.

One thing after another Cosmo brought her, but none of them seemed much to interest her. She knew the sort of most of them.

"This is said to be solid silver," he remarked, as he laid on a chair beside her a curious little statuette of a horse, trapped and decorated in Indian graving, and having its whole surface covered with an involved and rich ornamental design. Its eyes were, or seemed to be rubies, and saddle and bridle and housing were studded with small gems. There was little merit in the art of it beyond the engraving, but Cosmo saw the eyes of the lady fixed upon it, with a strange look in them.

"That is the only thing they say the old captain ever gave his brother, my great-grandfather," said Cosmo. "But I beg your pardon," he added, "I have never told you the story of the old captain!"

The boy already felt as if he had known their guest of a night for years; the hearts of the young are divinely hospitable, which is one of the things that make children the *such* of the kingdom of heaven.

Lady Joan took the horse in her hand, and looked at it more closely.

"It is very heavy!" she remarked.

"It is said to be solid silver," repeated Cosmo.

She laid it down, and put her hand to her forehead, but said nothing.

They heard the steps and voices of the two gentlemen ascending the stair. Lady Joan caught up the horse, rose hastily, and holding it out to Cosmo, said,

"Quick! quick! put it away. Don't let my father see it."

Cosmo cast on her one look of surprise, and obeyed at once, restored it to its place, and had just closed the doors of the cabinet, when Lord Mergwain and his father entered the room.

They were a peculiar-looking pair—Lord Mergwain in antiquated dress, not a little worn, and neither very clean nor in very good condition—a snuffy, dilapidated, miserable, feeble old man, with a carriage where doubt seemed rooted in apprehension, every other moment casting about him a glance of enquiry, as if an evil spirit came running to the mouth of his eye-caves, looked out, and retreated; and the laird behind him, a head higher, crowned with his red nightcap, and dressed as I have already described, looking older than his years, but bearing on his face the repose of discomfort accepted, his eye keen and clear, and, when turned on his guest, filled with compassion rather than hospitality. He was walking more erect than usual, either in recognition of the lady's presence, or from a feeling of protection towards her father. "Now, my lord," he said, as they advanced from the door, "we will set you in a warm corner by the fire, and you must make the best of it. We can't have things all as we should like them. That is not what the world was made for."

His lordship returned him no answer, but threw a queer look from under his black wig—a look of superior knowledge—of the wisdom of this world.

"You are an old fool," it said; "but you are master here! Ah! how little you know!"

He walked tottering to the fire where Cosmo had already set for him a chair. Something in the look of it displeased him. He glanced round the room.

"Fetch me *that* chair, my boy," he said, not unkindly, and Cosmo hastened to substitute the one he indicated. The laird placed a tall screen behind it. His lordship dropped into the chair, and began to rub his knees with his hands, and gaze into the fire. Lady Joan rearranged her skirts, and for a moment the little circle looked as if each was about to settle down to some mild mutual enjoyment of the others. Cosmo drew a chair as near Lady Joan as he judged politeness would permit. The laird made up the fire, and turned away, saying he must go and see the sick horse.

"Mr. Warlock!" said Lord Mergwain, and spoke with a snarl, "you will not deprive us of the only pleasure we have—that of your company?"

"I shall be back in a few minutes, my lord," replied his host; and added, "I must see about lunch too."

"That was wonderful claret!" said his lordship, thoughtfully.

"I shall see to the claret, my lord."

"If I *might* suggest, let it be brought here. A gentle airing under my own eye, just an introduction to the fire, would improve what is otherwise perfect.—And look here," he added, as, with a kindly bow of assent, the laird was going, "—you haven't got a pack of cards, have you?"

"I believe there is a pack somewhere in the house," replied the laird, "but it is very old, and I fear too much soiled for your lordship's hands."

"Oh, confound the dirt!" said his lordship. "Let us have them. They're the only thing to make the time pass."

"Have you a library?" asked Lady Joan—mainly to say something, for she was not particularly fond of books; like most people she had not yet learned to read.

"What do you want with a library?" growled her father. "Books are nothing but a pack of lies, not half so good for killing time as a pack of cards. You're going to play a rubber, not to read books!"

"With pleasure, papa," responded Lady Joan.

"*I* don't want to kill the time. I should like to keep it alive for ever," said Cosmo, with a worshipping look at the beautiful lady—a summer-bird of heaven that had strayed into their lonely winter.

"Hold your tongue; you are an idiot!" said his lordship angrily. "—Old and young," he went on, unaware of utterance, "the breed is idiotic. 'Tis time it were played out."

Cosmo's eyes flashed. But the rudesby was too old to be served as he had served the schoolmaster! He was their guest too, and the father of the lady by his side!

The hand of the lady stole to his, and patting it gently, said, as plainly as if it had been her mouth, "Don't mind him; he is an old man, and does not know what he is saying." He looked up in her face, and his anger was gone.

"Come with me," he said, rising; "I will show you what books we have. There may be one you would like another time. We shall be back before the cards come."

"Joan!" cried her father, "sit still."

She glanced an appeal for consideration to Cosmo, and did not move. Cosmo sat down again. A few minutes passed in silence. Father and daughter stared into the fire. So did Cosmo. But into what different three worlds did the fire stare! The old man rose and went to the window.

"I *must* get away from this abominable place," he said, "if it cost me my life."

He looked out and shuddered. The world seemed impassable as a dead world on which the foot of the living could take no hold, could measure no distance, make no progress. Not a print of man or of beast was visible. It was like a world not yet discovered.

"I am tied to the stake; I hear the fire roaring!" he muttered. "My fate has found me—caught me like a rat, and is going to make an end of me! In my time nobody believed such things! Now they seem to be coming into fashion again!"

Whoever would represent what is passing in a mind, must say more than the man himself knows how to say.

The laird re-entered.

"Well, have you brought the cards?" said Lord Mergwain, turning from the window.

"I have, my lord. I am sorry it is such a poor pack, but we never play.—I think, Cosmo, you had better come with me."

"Hold you, laird, we're going to have a rubber!"

"Cosmo does not understand the game"

"I will teach him,'" said Lady Joan. "He shall be live dummy for a few rounds; that will be enough."

"My lord will not care to play for counters," persisted the laird, "and we cannot play for money."

"I don't care what the points are," said Lord Mergwain, "—sixpence, if you like—so long as it is money. None but a fool cares for victory where nothing is to be got by it."

"I am sorry to disappoint your lordship," returned the laird, but play for money neither my son nor myself will. But perhaps you would like a game of draughts, or backgammon?"

"Will you bet on the game or the gammon?"

"On nothing, my lord."

"Oh, confound you!"

He turned again and went to the window.

"This is frightful!" he said to himself. "Nothing whatever to help one forget! If the day goes on like this, I shall out with everything.—Maybe I had better!—How the clodpoles would stare!—I believe I should laugh in the middle of it.—And that fellow lurking somewhere all the time about the place, watching his chance when the night comes!—It's horrible. I shall go mad!" This last he spoke aloud.

"Papa!" said his daughter sharply.

Lord Mergwain started, and looked troubled. What he might have uttered, he could not tell.

"A rubber, then," he said, approaching the fire again, "—on any terms, or no terms at all!"

He took up the cards.

"Ha, there's blood on them," he cried, and dashing them on the table, turned once more to the window.

He was like a bird in a cage that knows he cannot get out, and yet keeps trying, as if he dared not admit the impossibility. Twenty times that morning he went to the window, saying, "I must get out of this!" and returned again to his seat by the fire. The laird had removed the pack, and he said nothing more about a rubber. Lady Joan tried to talk, and Cosmo did his best to amuse her. The laird did his endeavour with his lordship, but with small success. And so the morning crept away. It might have been a pleasant one to the rest, but for the caged lord's misery. At last came Grizzie.

"Sir, an' my lord," she said, "come ye doon the stair. The kail's het, an' the cheirs is set, an' yer denner's waitin' ye there."

"Sir, and my lord," she said, "come downstairs. The kail's hot, and the chairs on their spots, and your dinner's waiting you there."

It may have been already remarked that to Grizzie came not unfrequently an odd way of riming what she said. She was unaware of this peculiarity. The suggestion of sound by sound was as hidden from her as it was deep-seated in her and strong. And this was not all: the riming might have passed unperceived by others too, but for the accompanying tendency to rhythm as well. Nor was this by any means all yet: there was in her a great leaning to poetic utterance generally, and that arising from a poetic habit of thought. She had in her everything essential to the making of a poetess; yet of the whole she was profoundly ignorant; and had any one sought to develop the general gift, I believe all would have shrunk back into her being.

The laird rose, and offered his arm to Lady Joan. Lord Mergwain gave a grunt, and looked only a little pleased at the news: no discomfort or suffering, mental or spiritual, made him indifferent to luncheon or dinner—for after each came the bottle; but the claret had not been brought to the drawing-room as he had requested!

When they reached the kitchen, he looked first eagerly, then uneasily round him: no bottle, quart or magnum was to be seen! A cloud gathered, lowering and heavy, on the face of the toper. The laird saw it, remembered that in his anxiety to amuse him, he had forgotten his dearest delight, and vanished in the region behind.

Mrs. Warlock, according to her custom, was already seated at the head of the table. She bowed just her head to his lordship, and motioned him to a chair on her right hand. He took it with a courteous acknowledgment, of which he would hardly have been capable, had he not guessed on what errand his host was gone: he had no recollection of having given her offence.

"I hope your ladyship is well this morning?" he said.

"Ye revive an auld custom, my lord," returned his hostess, not without sign of gratification, "—clean oot o' fashion nooadays, excep' amang the semple. A laird's wife has no richt to be ca'd *my leddy* 'cep' by auncient custom."

"Oh, if you come to that," returned his lordship, "three fourths of the titles in use are merely of courtesy. Joan there has no more right than yourself to be called *my lady.* Neither has my son Borland the smallest right to the title; it is mine, and mine only, as much as Mergwain."

"I hope your ladyship is well this morning?" he said.

"You revive an old custom, my lord," returned his hostess, not without sign of gratification, "—clean out of fashion nowadays, except among the commoners. A laird's wife has no right to be called *my lady* except by ancient custom."

"Oh, if you come to that," returned his lordship, "three fourths of the titles in use are merely of courtesy. Joan there has no more right than yourself to be called *my lady.* Neither has my son Borland the smallest right to the title; it is mine, and mine only, as much as Mergwain."

The old lady turned her head, and fixed a stolen but searching gaze on her guest, and to the end of the meal took every opportunity of regarding him unobserved. Her son from the other end of the table saw her looks, and guessed her suspicions; saw also that she did not abate her courtesy, but little thought to what her calmness was owing.

Mrs. Warlock, ready to welcome anything marvellous, had held with Grizzie much conference concerning what had passed in the night—one accidental result of which was the disappearance for the time of all little rivalries and offences between them in the common interest of an awful impending *denoument.* She had never heard, or had forgotten the title to which Lord Borland of the old time was heir; and now that all doubt as to the identity of the man was over, although, let her strain her vision as she might, she could not, through the deformation of years, descry the youthful visage, she felt that all action on the part of the generation in possession was none the less forestalled and precluded by the presence of one in the house who had evidently long waited his arrival, and had certainly but begun his reprisals. More would be heard ere the next dawn, she said to herself; and with things in such a train she would not interfere by the smallest show of feud or offence. Who could tell how much that certain inmate of the house—she hesitated to call him a member of the family—and, in all righteous probability, of a worse place as well, had to do with the storm that drove Borland thither, and the storms that might detain him there! Already there were signs of a fresh onset of the elements! The wind was rising; it had begun to moan in the wide chimney; and from the quarter whence it now blew, it was certain to bring more storm, that is snow!

The dinner went on. The great magnum before the fire was gathering genial might from the soft insinuation of limpid warmth, renewing as much of its youth as was to be desired in wine; and redeveloping relations, somewhat suppressed, with the slackening nerves and untwisting fibres of an old man's earthly being!

But there was not a drop to drink on the table, except water; and the toper found it hard to lay solid foundation enough for the wine that was to follow, and grumbled inwardly. The sight of the bottle before the fire, however, did much to enable him, not to be patient, but to suppress the shows of impatience. He eyed it, and loved it, and held his peace. He saw the water at his elbow, and hated it the worse that it was within his reach—hated its cold staring rebuke as he hated virtue—hated it as if its well were in the churchyard where the old captain was buried sixty years ago.—Confound him! Why wouldn't he lie still? He made some effort to be polite to the old hag, as he called her, in that not very secret chamber of his soul, whose door was but too ready to fall ajar, and allow its evil things to issue. He searched his lumber-room for old stories to tell, but found it difficult to lay hold on any fit for the ears present, though one of the ladies was an old woman—old enough, he judged, not to be startled at anything, and the other his own daughter, who ought to see no harm when her father made the company laugh! It was a miserable time for him, but, like a much enduring magician awaiting the moment of his power, he kept eying the bottle, and gathering comfort.

Grizzie eyed him from behind, almost as he eyed the bottle. She eyed him as she might the devil caught in the toils of the arch-angel; and if she did not bring against him a railing accusation, it was more from cunning than politeness. "Ah, my fine fellow," her eyes said, "he is after you! he will be here presently!"

Grizzie afforded a wonderfully perfect instance of a relation which is one of the loveliest in humanity—absolute service without a shade of servility. She would have died for her master, but even to him she must speak her mind. Her own affairs were nothing to her, and those of her master as those of the universe, but she was vitally one of his family, as the toes belong to the head! In truth, she was of the family like a poor relation, with few priviliges, and no end of duties; and she thought ten times more of her duties than her priviliges. She would have fed, and sometimes did feed with perfect satisfaction on the poorest scraps remaining from meals, but a doubt of the laird's preference of her porridge to that of any maker in broad Scotland, would have given her a sore heart. She would have wept bitter tears had the privilege of washing the laird's feet been taken from her. If reverence for the human is an essential element of greatness, then at least greatness was possible to Grizzie. She dealt with no abstractions; she worshipped one living man, and that is the first step toward the love of all men; while some will talk glowingly about humanity, and be scornful as a lap-dog to the next needy embodiment of it that comes in their way. Such as Grizzie will perhaps prove to be of those last foredoomed to be first. With the tenderness of a ministering angel and mother combined, her eyes waited upon her master. She took her return beforehand in the assurance that the laird would follow her to the grave, would miss her, and at times think nobody could do something or other so much to his mind as old Grizzie. And if, like the old captain, she might be permitted to creep about the place after night-fall, she desired nothing better than the chance of serving him still, if but by rolling a stone out of his way. The angels might bear him in their hands—she could not aspire to that, but it would be much the same whether she got the stone out of the way of his foot, or they lifted his foot above the stone!

Dinner over, the laird asked his guest whether he would take his wine where he was, or have it carried to the drawing-room. The offering of this alternative, the old lady, to use an Elizabethan phrase, took in snuff; for although she never now sat in the drawing-room, and indeed rarely crossed its threshold, it was *her* room; and, ladies having been banished from the dining-room while men drank, what would be left them if next, bottle in hand, the men invaded the drawing-room? But happily their guest declined the proposal, and that on the very ground of respect for her ladyship's apartment; the consequence of which was that she very nearly forgave him the murder of which she never doubted him guilty, saying to herself that, whatever he might be when disguised, poor man—and we all had our failings—he knew how to behave when sober, and that was more than could be said for everybody! So the old lord sat in the kitchen and drank his wine; and the old lady sat by the fire and knitted her stocking, went to sleep, and woke up, and went to sleep again a score of times, and enjoyed her afternoon. Not a word passed between the two: now, in his old age, Lord Mergwain never talked over his bottle; he gave his mind to it. The laird went and came, unconsciously anxious to be out of the way of his guest, and consciously anxious not to neglect him, but nothing was said on either side. The old lady knitted and dozed, and his lordship sat and drank, now and then mingling the aesthetic with the sensual, and holding his glass to the light to enjoy its colour and brilliancy,—doing his poor best to encourage the presence of what ideas he counted agreeable, and prevent the intrusion of their opposites. And still as he drank, the braver he grew, and the more confident that the events of the past night were but the foolish consequences of having mingled so many liquors, which, from the state of the thermometer, had grown cold in his very stomach, and bred rank fancies! "With two bottles like this under my belt," he said to himself, "I would defy them all, but this wretched night-capped curmudgeon of a host will never fetch me a second! If he had not been so niggardly last night, I should have got through well enough!" Lady Joan and Cosmo had been all over the house, and were now sitting in the drawing-room, silent in the firelight. Lady Joan did not yet find Cosmo much of a companion, though she liked to have him beside her, and would have felt the dreariness more penetrating without him. But to Cosmo her presence was an experience as marvellous and lovely as it was new and strange. He had never save in his dreams before been with one who influenced him with beauty; and never one of his dreams came up to the dream-like reality that now folded him about with bliss. For he sat, an isolating winter stretched miles and miles around him, in the old paradise of his mother's drawing-room, in the glorious twilight of a peat and wood fire, the shadows flickering about at their own wild will over all the magic room, at the feet of a lady, whose eyes were black as the night, but alive with a radiance such as no sun could kindle, whose hand was like warm snow, whose garments lovely as the clouds that clothe a sunset, and who inhabited an atmosphere of evanescent odours, that were themselves dreams from a region beyond the stars, while the darkness that danced with the firelight played all sorts of variations on the theme of her beauty.

How long he had sat lost in the dream-haunted gorgeous silence he did not know, when suddenly he bethought himself that he ought to be doing something to serve or amuse, or at least interest the heavenly visitant. Strangers and angels must be entertained, nor must the shadow of loneliness fall upon them. Now to that end he knew one thing always good, always at hand, and specially fitting the time.

"Shall I tell you a story, my lady?" he said, looking up to her from the low stool on which he had taken his place at her feet.

"Yes, if you please," she answered, finding herself in a shoal of sad thoughts, and willing to let them drift.

"Then I will try. But I am sorry I cannot tell it so well as Grizzie told it me. Her old-fashioned way suits the story. And then I must make English of it for your ladyship, and that goes still worse with it."

Alas! Alas! The speech of every succeeding generation is a falling away from the pith and pathos of the preceding. Speech gains in scope, but loses in intensity.

"There was once a girl in the Highlands," began Cosmo, "—not very far from here it was, who was very beautiful, so that every young man in the neighbourhood fell in love with her. She was as good as she was beautiful, and of course would not let more than one be her lover, and said no to everyone else; and if after that they would go on loving her, she could not help it. She was the daughter of a sheep-farmer, who had a great many sheep that fed about over the hills, and she helped her father to look after them, and was as good and obedient as any lamb of his flock. And her name was Mary. Her other name I do not know.

"Now her father had a young shepherd, only a year or two older than Mary, and he of course was in love with her as well as the rest, and more in love with her than any of them, because he was the most to be trusted of all in that country-side. He was very strong and very handsome, and a good shepherd. He was out on the hills all day, from morning to night, seeing that the sheep did their duty, and ate the best grass, so as to give plenty of good wool, and good mutton when it was wanted.—That's the way Grizzie tells the story, my lady, though not so that you would understand her.—When any of the lambs were weakly or ill, they were brought home for Mary to nurse, and that was how the young shepherd came to know Mary, and Mary to know him. And so it came to pass that they grew fond of each other, and saw each other as often as they could; and Mary promised, if her father would let her, she would marry Alister. But her father was too well-off to show favour to a poor shepherd lad, for his heart had got so full of his money that there was not room enough for the blood in it. If Alister had had land and sheep like himself, he would have had no objection to giving him Mary; but a poor son-in-law, however good he might be, would make him feel poor, whereas a rich son-in-law, if he were nothing but an old miser, would make him feel rich! He told Alister, therefore, that he had nothing to say to him, and he and Mary must have nothing to say to each other. Mary felt obliged to do what her father told her, but in her heart she did not give up Alister, and felt sure Alister did not give up her, for he was a brave and honest youth.

"Of course Alister was always wanting to see Mary, and often he saw her when nobody, not even Mary herself, knew it. One day she was out rather late on the hill, and when the gloaming came down, sat wishing in her heart that out of it Alister would come, that she might see him, though she would not speak to him. She was sitting on a stone, Grizzie says, with the gloamin' coming down like a gray frost about her; and by the time it grew to a black frost, out of it came some one running towards her.

"But it was not Alister; it was a farmer who wanted to marry her. He was a big, strong man, rich and good-looking, though twice Mary's age. Her father was very friendly to him. But people said he was a coward.

"Now just at that time, only it had not yet reached the glen, a terrible story was going about the country, of a beast in the hills, that went biting every living thing he could get at, and whatever he bit went raving-mad. He never ate any creature he attacked, never staid to kill it, but just came up with a rush, bit it, and was out of sight in a moment. It was generally in the twilight he came. He appeared—nobody ever saw from where—made his gnash, and was gone. There was great terror and dismay wherever the story was heard, so that people would hardly venture across their thresholds after sun-down, for terror lest the beast should dash out of the borders of the dark upon them, and leave his madness in them. Some said it was a sheep-dog, but some who thought they had seen it, said it was too large for any collie, and was, they believed, a mad wolf; for though there are no wolves in Scotland now, my lady, there were at one time, and this is a very old story."

Lady Joan gaped audibly.

"I am wearying you, my lady!" said Cosmo, penitently.

"No, no! dear boy," answered Lady Joan, sorry, and a little ashamed. "It is only that I am very weary. I think the cold tires one."

"I will tell you the rest another time," said Cosmo cheerily. "You must lie down on the sofa, and I will cover you up warm."

"No, no; please go on. Indeed I want to hear the rest of it."

"Well," resumed Cosmo, "the news of this wolf, or whatever it was, had come to the ears of the farmer for the first time that day at a fair, and he was hurrying home with his head and his heart and his heels full of it, when he saw Mary sitting on the white stone by the track, feeling as safe as if she were in paradise, and as sad as if she were in purgatory.—That's how Grizzie tells it—I suppose because some of her people are papists.—But, for as much as he wanted to marry her, you could hardly say he was in love with her—could you, Lady Joan?—when I tell you that, instead of stopping and taking her and her sheep home, he hurried past her, crying out, 'Gang hame, Mary. There's a mad beast on the hill. Rin, rin—a' 'at ye can. Never min' yer sheep.' ('Go home, Mary. There's a mad beast on the hill. Run, run—all that you can. Never mind your sheep.') His last words came from the distance, for he never stayed a step while he spoke.

"Mary got up at once. But you may be sure, my lady, a girl like that was not going to leave her sheep where she dared not stop herself. She began to gather them together to take them out of harm's way, and was just setting out with them for home, when a creature like a huge dog came bounding upon her out of the edge of the night. The same instant, up from behind a rock, a few yards away, jumped Alister, and made at the beast with his crook; and just as the wolf was upon Mary, for Alister was not near enough to get between the beast and her, he heaved a great blow at him, which would have knocked him down anyhow. But that instant Mary threw herself towards Alister, and his terrible blow came down upon her, and not upon the wolf, and she fell dead in his arms—that's what Grizzie says—and away went the wolf, leaping and bounding, and never uttering a cry.

"What Alister did next, Grizzie never says—only that he came staggering up to her father's door with dead Mary in his arms, carried her in, laid her on the bed, and went out again. They found the blow on her head, and when they undressed her, they found also the bite of the wolf; and they soon guessed how it had been, and said it was well she had died so, for it was much better than going mad first; it was kind of Death, they said, to come and snatch her away out of the arms of Madness. But the farmer, because he hated Alister, and knew that Alister must have seen him running away, gave it out, that he himself was rushing to defend Mary, and that the blow that killed her was meant for him. Nobody however believed him.

"What people might think, was, however, a matter of little consequence to Alister, for from that day he never spoke to human being, never slept under a roof. He left his shepherding, and gave himself to the hunting of the mad wolf: such a creature should not be allowed to live, and he must do some good thing for Mary's sake. Mary was so good, that any good thing done would be a thing done for her. So he followed and followed, hunting the horrible creature to destroy him. Some said he lived on his hate of the wolf, and never ate anything at all. But some of the people on the hills, when they heard he had been seen, set out of their doors at night milk and cakes; and in the morning, sometimes, they would be gone, and taken as if by a human being, and not an animal.

"By and by came a strange story abroad. For a certain old woman, whom some called a witch, and whom all allowed to have the second sight, told that, one night late, as she was coming home from her daughter's house, she saw Alister lying in the heather, and another sitting with him; Alister she saw plainly with her first or bodily eyes; but with her second eyes, in which lay the second sight, she saw his head lying on a woman's lap—and that woman was Mary, whom he had killed. He was fast asleep, and whether he knew what pillow he had, she could not tell; but she saw the woman as plainly as if with her bodily eyes,—only with the difference which there always was, she said, and which she did not know how to describe, between the things seen by the one pair of eyes, and the things seen by the other. She stood and regarded them for some time, but neither moved. It was in the twilight, and as it grew darker she could see Alister less and less clearly, but always Mary better and better—till at last the moon rose, and then she saw Alister again, and Mary no more. But, through the moonlight, three times she heard a little moan, half very glad, and half a little sad

"Now the people had mostly a horror of Alister, and had shunned him—even those who did not believe him to blame for what he had done—because of his having killed a human being, one made like himself, and in the image of God; but when they heard the wise woman's story, they began to feel differently towards Alister, and to look askance upon Mary's father, whose unkindness had kept them asunder. They said now it had all come through him, and that God had sent the wolf to fetch Mary, that he might give her and Alister to each other in spite of him—for God had many a way of doing a thing, every one better than another.

"But that did not help Alister to find the wolf. The winter came, however, and that did help him, for the snow let him see the trail, and follow faster. The wonder was that the animal, being mad, lived so long; but some said that, although the wolf was mad, he was not mad in any ordinary way—if he had been, he would indeed have been dead long ago; he was a wolf into which an evil spirit had entered; and had he been a domestic animal, or one for the use of man, he would immediately have destroyed himself; but, being a wild and blood-thirsty animal, he went on very much like his natural self, without knowing what sort of a fellow-tenant he had with him in the house.

"At last, one morning in the month of December, when the snow lay heavy on the ground, some men came upon a track which they all agreed must be that of the wolf. They went and got their weapons, and set out in chase. They followed, and followed, and better than followed, and the trail led them high into the hills, wondering much at the huge bounds with which the beast had galloped up the steepest places. They concluded that Alister had been after him, and that the beast knew it, and had made for the most inaccessible spot he was acquainted with. They came at length to a point where a bare-foot human track joined that of the wolf for a little way, and after that they came upon it again and again. Up and up the mountain they went—sometimes losing the track from the great springs the wolf took—now across a great chasm which they had to go round the head of, now up the face of a rock too steep for the snow to lie upon, so that there was no print of his horrid feet.

"But at last, almost at the top of the mountain, they saw before them two dark spots in a little hollow, and when they reached it, there was the wolf, dead in a mass of frozen blood and trampled snow. It was a huge, gaunt, gray, meagre carcass, with the foam frozen about its jaws, and stabbed in many places, which showed the fight had been a close one. All the snow was beaten about, as if with many feet, which showed still more plainly what a tussle it had been. A little farther on lay Alister, as if asleep, stretched at full length, with his face to the sky. He had been dead for many hours, they thought, but the smile had not faded which his spirit left behind as it went. All about his body were the marks of the brute's teeth—everywhere almost except on his face. That had been bespattered with blood, but it had been wiped away. His dirk[6] was lying not far off, and his skene dhu[7] close by his hand.

"There is but one thing more—and I think that is just the thing that made me want to tell you the story. The men who found Alister declared when they came home, and ever after when they told the story—Grizzie says her grandmother used always to say so—that, when they lifted him to bring him away, they saw in the snow the mark of the body, deep-pressed, but only as far as the shoulders; there was no mark of his head whatever. And when they told this to the wise woman, she answered only,

'Of coorse! Of coorse!—Gien I had been wi' ye, lads, I wad hae seen mair.' When they pressed her to speak more plainly, she only shook her head, and muttered, 'Dull-hertit gowks!'—That's all, my lady."

'Of course! Of course!—If I had been with you, lads, I would have seen more.' When they pressed her to speak more plainly, she only shook her head, and muttered, 'Dull-hearted fools!'—That's all, my lady."

In the kitchen, things were going on even more quietly than in the drawing-room. In front of the fire sat the English lord over his wine; Mistress Warlock sat in her arm-chair, knitting and dozing—between her evanescent naps wide awake, and ever and anon sliding her eyes from the stocking which did not need her attention to the guest who little desired it; the laird had taken his place at the other corner, and was reading the journal of George Fox; and Grizzie was bustling about with less noise than she liked, and wishing heartily she were free of his lordship, that she might get on with her work. Scarcely a word was spoken.

It began to grow dark; the lid of the night was closing upon them ere half a summer-day would have been over. But it mattered little: the snow had stayed the work of the world. Grizzie put on the kettle for her mistress's tea. The old lady turned her forty winks into four hundred, and slept outright, curtained in the shadows. All at once his lorsdship became alive to the fact that the day was gone, shifted uneasily in his chair, poured out a bumper of claret, drank it off hurriedly, and hitched his chair a little nearer to the fire. His hostess saw these movements with satisfaction: he had appeased her personal indignation, but her soul was not hospitable towards him, and the devil in her was gratified with the sight of his discomposure: she hankered after talion, not waited on penitence. Her eyes sought those of Grizzie.

"Gang to the door, Grizzie," she said, "an' see what the nicht's like. I'm thinkin' by the cry o' the win', it'll be a wull mirk again. What think ye, laird?"

"Go to the door, Grizzie," she said, "and see what the night's like. I'm thinking by the cry of the wind, it'll be a wild night again. What think you, laird?"

Her son looked up from his book, where he had been beholding a large breadth of light

6 DIRK: a dagger worn by Scottish Highlanders as a personal sidearm and utility tool from around the early 1800s.

7 SKENE DHU: a small knife worn inside the stocking as part of full Highland dress

on the spiritual sky, and answered, somewhat abstractedly, but with the gentle politeness he always showed her.

"I should not wonder if it came on to snow again!" Lord Mergwain shifted uneasily.

"I should not wonder if it came on to snow again!" Lord Mergwain shifted uneasily.

Grizzie returned from her inspection of the weather.

Grizzie returned from her inspection of the weather

"It's black theroot, an' dingin' oot, wi' great thuds o' win'," she said.

"It's black out there, and pelting down fair, with great thuds of wind," she said.

"God bless me!" murmured his lordship, "what an abominable country!"

"God bless me!" murmured his lordship, "what an abominable country!"

"Had we not better go to the drawing-room, my lord?" said the laird. "I think, Grizzie," he went on, "you must get supper early.-And Grizzie," he added, rising, "mind you bring Lady Joan a cup of tea—if your mistress will excuse her," he concluded, with a glance to his mother.

Mistress Warlock was longing for a talk with Grizzie, and had no wish for Lady Joan's presence at tea.

"An old woman is bare company for a young one, Cosmo," she said.

His lordship sat as if he did not mean to move.

"Will you not come, Lord Mergwain?" said the laird. "We had better go before the night gets worse."

"I will stay where I am."

"Excuse me, my lord, that can hardly be. Come, I will carry your wine. You will finish your bottle more at your ease there, knowing you have not to move again."

"The bottle is empty," replied his lordship, gruffly, as if reproaching his host for not being aware of the fact, and having another at hand to follow.

"Then—" said the laird, and hesitated.

"Then you'll fetch me another!" adjoined his lordship, as if answering an unpropounded question that ought not to be put. Seeing, however, that the laird stood in some hesitation still, he added definitively, "I don't stir a peg without it. Get me another bottle—another *magnum,* I mean, and I will go at once."

Yet a moment the laird reflected. He said to himself that the wretched man had not had nearly so much to drink that day as he had the day before; that he was used to soaking, and a great diminution of his customary quantity might in its way be dangerous; and that anyhow it was not for him to order the regimen of a passing guest, to whom first of all he owed hospitality.

"I will fetch it, my lord," he said, and disappeared in the milk-cellar, from which a steep stone-stair led down to the ancient dungeon.

"The maister's gane wantin' a licht," muttered Grizzie; "I houp he winna see onything."

"The master's gone without a light," muttered Grizzie; "I hope he won't see anything."

It was an enigmatical utterance, and angered Lord Mergwain.

"What the deuce should he see, when he has got to feel his way with his hands?" he snarled.

"What the deuce should he see, when he has got to feel his way with his hands?" he snarled.

"There's some things, my lord, 'at can better affoord to come oot i' the dark nor the licht," replied Grizzie.

"There's some things, my lord, that can better afford to come out in the dark than the light," replied Grizzie.

His lordship said nothing in rejoinder, but kept looking every now and then towards the door of the milk-cellar—whether solely in anxiety for the appearance of the magnum, may be doubtful. The moment the laird emerged from his dive into darkness, bearing with him the pearl-oyster of its deep, his lordship rose, proud that for an old man he could stand so steady, and straightened himself up to his full height, which was not great. The laird set down the bottle on the table, and proceeded to wrap him in a plaid, that he might not get a chill, nor heeded that his lordship, instead of showing recognition of his care, conducted himself like an ill-conditioned child, to whom his mother's ministrations are unwelcome. But he did not resist, he only grumbled. As soon as the process was finished, he caught up the first bottle, in which, notwithstanding his assertion, he knew there was yet a glass or two, while the laird resumed the greater burden of the second, and gave his guest an arm, and Grizzie, leaving the door open to cast a little light on their way, followed close behind, to see them safe in.

When they reached the drawing-room, his lordship out of breath with the long stair, they found Lady Joan teaching and Cosmo learning backgammon, which they immediately abandoned until they had him in his former chair, with a small table by him, on it the first bottle, and the fresh one at his feet before the fire: with the contents of one such inside him, and another coming on, he looked more cheerful than since first he entered the house. But a fluctuating trouble was very visible in his countenance notwithstanding.

A few poverty-stricken attempts at conversation followed, to which Lord Mergwain contributed nothing. Lost in himself, he kept his eyes fixed on the ripening bottle, waiting with heroic self-denial, nor uttering a single audible oath, until the sound of its opening should herald the outbursting blossom of the nightly flower of existence. The thing hard to bear was, that there were no fresh wine-glasses on the table—only the one he had taken care to bring with the old bottle.

Presently Grizzie came with the tea-things, and as she set them down, remarked, with cunningly devised look of unconsciousness:

"It's a gurly nicht; no a pinch o' licht, an' the win' blawin' like deevils; the Pooer o' the air, he's oot wi' a rair, an' the snaw rins roon' upo' sweevils."

"It's a stormy night; not a pinch of light, and the wind blowing like devils; the Power of the air, roars out from his lair, and the snow runs round in swirls."

"What do you mean, woman? Would you drive me mad with your gibberish?" cried his lordship, getting up, and going to the window.

"What do you mean, woman? Would you drive me mad with your gibberish?" cried his lordship, getting up, and going to the window.

"Ow na, my lord!" returned Grizzie quietly; "mad's mad, but there's waur nor mad."

"Oh no, my lord!" returned Grizzie quietly; "mad's mad, but there's worse than mad."

"Grizzie!" said the laird, and she did not speak again.

"Grizzie!" said the laird, and she did not speak again.

Lurking in Grizzie was the suspicion, less than latent in the minds of the few who had any memory of the old captain, that he had been robbed as well as murdered—though nothing had ever been missed that was known to belong to him, except indeed an odd walking-stick he used to carry; and if so, then the property, whatever it was, had been taken to the loss of his rightful heir, Warlock o' Glenwarlock. Hence mainly arose Grizzie's desire to play upon the fears of the English lord; for might he not be driven by terror to make restitution? Therefore, although, obedient to the will of her master, she left the room in silence, she cast on the old man, as she turned away, a look, which, in spite of the wine he had drunk, and the wine he hoped to drink, he felt freeze his very vitals—a look it was of inexplicable triumph, and inarticulate doom.

The final effect of it on her victim, however, was different from what she intended. For it roused suspicion. What if, he thought with himself, he was the victim of a conspiracy? What if the something frightful that befell him the night before, of which he had but a vague recollection, had been contrived and executed by the people of the house? This horrible old hag might remember else-forgotten things? What if they had drugged his wine? The first half of the bottle he had yesterday was decanted!—But the one he had just drunk had not been touched!

And this fresh one before the fire should not be carried from his sight! He would not take his eyes off it for a moment! He was safe so far as these were concerned! Only if after all—if there should be no difference—if something were to happen again all the same—ah, then indeed!—then it would only be so much the worse!—Better let them decant the bottle, and then he would have the drug to fall back upon!

Just as he heard the loud bang of Grizzie's closure of the great door, the wind rushed all at once against the house, with a tremendous bellow, that threatened to drive the windows into the room. An immediate lull followed, through which as instantly came strange sounds, as of a distant staccato thunder. The moment the laird heard the dull thuds, he started to his feet, and made for the door, and Cosmo rose to follow.

"Stop! stop!" shouted Lord Mergwain, in a quavering, yet, through terror, imperative voice, and looked as if his hair would have stood on end, only that it was a wig.

Lady Joan gave Cosmo a glance of entreaty: the shout was ineffectual, the glance was not. The laird scarcely heard his visitor's cry, and hastened from the room, taking huge strides with his long thin legs; but Cosmo resumed his seat as if nothing were the matter.

Lord Mergwain was trembling visibly; his jaw shook, and seemed ready to drop.

"Don't be alarmed, my lord," said Cosmo; "it is only one of the horses kicking against his stall."

"But why should the brute kick?" said his lordship, putting his hand to his chin, and doing his best to hide his agitation.

"My father will tell us. He will soon set things right. He knows all about horses. Jolly may have thrown his leg over his halter, and got furious. He's rather an ill-tempered horse."

Lord Mergwain swallowed a great glass of wine, the last of the first bottle, and gave a little shiver

"It's cold! Cold!" he said.

The wine did not seem to be itself somehow this evening!

The game interrupted, Lady Joan forgot it, and stared into the fire. Cosmo gave his eyes a glorious holiday on her beautiful face.

It was some time before the laird returned. He brought the news that one of the strange horses was very ill.

"I thought he looked bad this morning," said Cosmo.

"Only it's not the same horse, my boy," answered his father. "I believe he has been ill all day; the state of the other has prevented its being noticed. He was taken suddenly with violent pain; and now he lies groaning. They are doing what they can for him, but I fear, in this weather, he will not recover. Evidently he has severe inflammation; the symptoms are those of the worst form of the disease now about."

"Hustled here in the dark to die like a rat!" muttered his lordship.

"Don't make a trap of the old place, my lord," said the laird cheerily. "The moment the roads will permit, I will see that you have horses."

"I don't doubt you'll be glad enough to get rid of me."

"We shall not regret your departure so much, my lord, as if we had been able to make your lordship comfortable," said the laird.

With that there came another great howling onset of wind. Lord Mergwain started almost to his feet, but sat down instantly, and said with some calmness,

"I should be obliged, Mr. Warlock, if you would order a wine-glass or two for me. I am troublesome, I know, but I like to change my glass; and the wine will be the worse every moment more it stands there.—I wish you would drink! We should make a night of it."

"I beg your pardon, my lord," said the laird. "What was I thinking of!—Cosmo, run and fetch wine-glasses—and the cork-screw."

But while Cosmo was returning, he heard the battery of iron shoes recommence, and ran to the stable. Just as he reached the door of it, the horse half reared, and cast himself against the side of his stall. With a great crash it gave way, and he fell upon it, and lay motionless.

"He's deid!" cried one of the men, and Cosmo ran to tell his father.

"He's dead!" cried one of the men, and Cosmo ran to tell his father.

While he was gone, the time seemed to the toper endless. But the longer he could be kept from his second magnum, the laird thought it the better, and was not troubled at Cosmo's delay.

A third terrible blast, fiercer and more imperious than those that preceded it, shook the windows as a dog shakes a rat: the house itself it could shake no more than a primeval rock. The next minute Cosmo entered, saying the horse was dead.

"What a beastly country!" growled his lordship.

But the wine that was presently gurgling from the short neck of the apoplectic magnum, soon began to console him. He liked this bottle better than the last, and some composure returned to him.

The laird fetched a book of old ballads, and offered to read one or two to make the time pass. Lord Mergwain gave a scornful grunt; but Lady Joan welcomed the proposal: the silent worship of the boy, again at her feet, was not enough to make her less than very weary. For more than an hour, the laird read ballad after ballad; but nobody, not even himself, attended much-the old lord not at all. But the time passed. His lordship grew sleepy, began to nod, and seemed to forget his wine. At length he fell asleep. But when the laird would have made him more comfortable, with a yell of defiance he started to his feet wide awake. Coming to himself at once, he tried to laugh, and said from a child he had been furious when waked suddenly. Then he settled himself in the chair, and fell fast asleep.

Still the night wore on, and supper-time came. His lordship woke, but would have no supper, and took to his bottle again. Lady Joan and Cosmo went to the kitchen, and the laird had his porridge brought to the drawing-room.

At length it was time to go to bed. Lady Joan retired. The laird would not allow Cosmo to sit up another night, and he went also. The lord and the laird were left together, the one again asleep, and dreaming who knows what! the other wide awake, but absorbed in the story of a man whose thoughts, fresh from above, were life to himself, and a mockery to his generation.

CHAPTER XVII
THAT SAME NIGHT

The wind had now risen to a hurricane—a rage of swiftness. The house was like a rock assaulted by the waves of an ocean-tempest. The laird had closed all the shutters, and drawn the old curtains across them: through windows and shutters, the curtains waved in the penetrating blasts. The sturdy old house did not shake, for nothing under an earthquake could have made it tremble. The snow was fast gathering in sloped heaps on the window-sills, on the frames, on every smallest ledge where it could lie. In the midst of the blackness and the roaring wind, the house was being covered with spots of silent whiteness, resting on every projection, every roughness even, of the building. In his own house as he was, a sense of fierce desolation, of foreign invasion and siege, took possession of the soul of the laird. He had made a huge fire, and had heaped up beside it great store of fuel, but, though his body was warm and likely to be warm, his soul inside it felt the ravaging cold outside—remorseless, and full of mock, the ghastly power of negation and unmaking. He had got together all the screens he could find, and with them inclosed the fireplace, so that they sat in a citadel within a fortress. By the fire he had placed for his lordship the antique brocade-covered sofa, that he might lie down when he pleased, and himself occupied the great chair on the other side. From the centre of this fire-defended heart, the room itself outside looked cold and waste: it demanded almost courage to leave the stockade of the screens, and venture into the campaign of the floor beyond. And then the hell of wind and snow that raved outside that! and the desert of air surrounding it, in which the clouds that garnered the snow were shaken by mad winds, whirled and tossed and buffeted, to make them yield their treasures! Lord Mergwain heard it, and drank. The laird listened, and lifted up his heart. Not much passed between them. The memories of the English lord were not such as he felt it fit to share with the dull old Scotchman beside him, who knew nothing of the world—knew neither how pitilessly selfish, nor how meanly clever a man of this world might be and bate not a jot of his self admiration! Men who salute a neighbour as a man of the world, paying him the greatest compliment they know in acknowledging him of their kind, recoil with a sort of fear from the man alien to their thoughts, and impracticable for their purposes. They say "He is beyond me," and despise him. So is there a great world beyond them with which they yet hold a frightful relationship—that of unrecognized, unattempted duty! Lord Mergwain regarded the odd-looking laird as a fool; the laird looked on him with something of the pity an angel must feel for the wretch to whom he is sent to give his last chance, ere sorer measures be taken in which angels are not the ministers.

But the wine was at last beginning to work its too oft repeated and now nearly exhausted influence on the sagging and much frayed nerves of the old man. A yellowish remnant of withered rose began to smear his far-off west: he dared not look to the east; that lay terribly cold and gray; and he smiled with a little curl of his lip now and then, as he thought of this and that advantage he had had in the game of life, for alas! it had never with him risen to the dignity of a battle. He was as proud of a successful ruse, as a hero of a well fought and well won field. "I had him there!" stood with him for the joy of work done and salvation wrought. It was a repulsive smile—one that might move even to hatred the onlooker who was not yet divine enough to let the outrushing waves of pity swamp his human judgment. It only curled the cruel-looking upper lip, while the lower continued to hang thick, and sensual, and drawn into a protuberance in the middle.

Gradually he seemed to himself, as he drank, to be recovering the common sense of his self-vaunted, vigorous nature. He assured himself that now he saw plainly the truth and fact of things—that his present outlook and vision were the true, and the horrors of the foregone night the weak soul-gnawing fancies bred of a disordered stomach. He was a man once more, and beyond the sport of a foolish imagination.

Alas for the man who draws his courage from wine! the same alas for the man whose health is its buttress! the touch of a pin on this or that spot of his mortal house, will change him from a leader of armies, or a hunter of tigers in the jungle, to one who shudders at a centipede! That courage also which is mere insensibility crumbles at once before any object of terror able to stir the sluggish imagination. There is a fear, this for one, that for another, which can appal the stoutest who is not one with the essential.

Lord Mergwain emerged from the influence of his imagination and his fears, and went under that of his senses and himself. He took his place beside the Christian in his low, common moods, when the world, with its laws and its material insistence, presses upon him, and he does not believe that God cares for the sparrow, or can possibly count the hairs of his head; when the divine power, and rule, and means to help, seem nowhere but in a passed-away fancy of the hour of prayer. Only the Christian in them is miserable, and Lord Mergwain was relieved; for did he not then come to himself? and did he know anything better to arrive at than just that wretched self of his?

A glass or two more, and he laughed at the terror by night. He had been a thorough fool not to go to bed like other people, instead of sitting by the fire with a porridge-eating Scotchman, who regarded him as one of the wicked, afraid of the darkness. The thought may have passed from his mind to that of his host, for the self-same moment the laird spoke:

"Don't you think you had better go to bed when you have finished your bottle, my lord?"

With the words, a cold swell, as from the returning tide of some dead sea, so long ebbed that men had ploughed and sown and built within its bed, stole in, swift and black, filling every cranny of the old man's conscious being.

"My God!" he cried; "I thought better of you than that, laird! I took you for a man of your word! You promised to sit up with me!"

"I did, my lord, and am ready to keep my promise. I only thought you looked as if you might have changed your mind; and in such a night as this, beyond a doubt, bed is the best place for everybody that has one to go to."

"That depends," answered his lordship, and drank. The laird held his peace for a time, then spoke again:

"Would your lordship think me rude if I were to take a book?"

I don't want a noise. It don't go well with old wine like this: such wine wants attention! It would spoil it. No, thank you."

"I did not propose to read aloud, my lord—only to myself."

Oh! That alters the matter! That I would by no means object to. I am but poor company!"

The laird got his "Journal," and was soon lost in the communion of a kindred soul.

By and by, the boat of his lordship's brain was again drifting towards the side of such imagination as was in him. The half-tide restoring the physical mean was past, and intoxication was setting in. He began to cast uneasy glances towards the book the laird was reading. The old folio had a look of venerable significance about it, and whether it called up some association of childhood, concerned in some fearful fancy, or dreamfully he dreaded the necromancer's art, suggested by late experience, made him uneasy.

"What's that you are reading?" he said at length. "It looks like a book of magic."

"On the contrary," replied the laird, "it is a religious book of the very best sort."

"Oh, indeed! Ah! I have no objection to a little religion—in its own place. There it is all right. I never was one of those mockers—those Jacobins, those sans-culottes! Arrogant fools they always seemed to me!"

"Would your lordship like to hear a little of the book then?"

"No, no; by no means! Things sacred ought not to be mixed up with things common—with such an uncommon bottle of wine, for instance. I dictate to no one, but for my own part I keep my religion for church. That is the proper place for it, and there you are in the mood for it. Do not mistake me; it is out of respect I decline."

He drank, and the laird dropt back into the depths of his volume. The night wore on. His lordship did not drink fast. There was no hope of another bottle, and the wine must cover the period of his necessity: he dared not encounter the night without the sustaining knowledge of its presence. At last he began to nod, and by slow degrees sank on the sofa. Very softly the laird covered him, and went back to his book.

The storm went raging on, as if it would never cease. The sense of desolation it produced in the heart of the laird when he listened to it was such, that with an inward shudder he closed his mind against it, and gave all his attention to George Fox, and the thoughts he roused. The minutes crawled slowly along. He lost all measure of time, because he read with delight, and at last he found himself invaded by that soft physical peace which heralds the approach of sleep. He roused himself; he wanted to read: he was in one of the most interesting passages he had yet come to. But presently the sweet enemy was again within his outworks. Once more he roused himself, heard the storm raving on—over buried graves and curtained beds, heedless of human heeding—fell a-listening to its shriek-broken roar, and so into a soundless and dreamless sleep.

He woke so suddenly that for a moment he knew himself only for somebody he knew. There lay upon him the weight of an indefinable oppression—the horror of a darkness too vague to be combated. The fire had burned low, and his very bones seemed to shiver. The candle-flames were down in the sockets of the candlesticks, and the voice of the storm was like a scream of victory. Had the cold then won its way into the house? Was it having its deathly will of them all? He cast his eyes on his guest. Sleeping still, he half lay, half leaned in the corner of the sofa, breathing heavily. His face was not to be well seen, because of the flapping and flickering of the candle-flames, and the shadows they sent waving huge over all, like the flaunting of a black flag. Through the flicker and the shadow the laird was still peering at him, when suddenly, without opening his eyes, the old man raised himself to a sitting posture—all of a piece, like a figure of wood lifted from behind. The laird then saw his face, and upon it the expression as of one suffering from some horrible nightmare—so terrified was it, so wrathful, so disgusted, all in one—and rose in haste to rouse him from a drunken dream. But ere he reached him he opened his eyes, and his expression changed—not to one of relief, but to utter collapse, as if the sleep-dulled horrors of the dream had but grown real to him as he woke. His under lip trembled like a dry yellow leaf in a small wind; his right arm rose slowly from the shoulder and stuck straight out in the direction of his host, while his hand hung from the wrist; and he stared as upon one loosed from hell to speak of horrors. But it did not seem to the laird that, although turned straight towards him, his eyes rested on him; they did not appear to be focused for him, but for something beyond him. It was like the stare of one demented, and it invaded—possessed the laird. A physical terror seized him. He felt his gaze returning that of the man before him, like to like, as from a mirror. He felt the skin of his head contracting; his hair was about to stand on end! The spell must be broken! He forced himself forward a step to lay his hand on Lord Mergwain, and bring him to himself. But his lordship uttered a terrible cry, betwixt a scream and a yell, and sank back on the sofa. The same instant the laird was himself again, and sprang to him.

Lord Mergwain lay with his mouth wide open, and the same look with which they found him the night before prostrate in the guest-chamber. His arm stuck straight out from his body. The laird pressed it down, but it rose again as soon as he left it. He could not for a moment doubt the man was dead; there was that about him that assured him of it, but what it was he could not have told.

The first thought that came to him was, that his daughter must not see him so. He tied up his jaw, laid him straight on the sofa, lighted fresh candles, left them burning by the dead, and went to call Grizzie: a doctor was out of the question.

He felt his way down the dark stair, and fought it through the wind to the kitchen, whence he climbed to Grizzie's room. He found she was already out of bed, and putting on her clothes. She had not been asleep, she said, and added something obscure, which the laird took to mean that she had been expecting a summons.

"Whan Ane's oot, there's nane in!" she said. "Hoo's the auld reprobate, laird—an' I beg yer pardon?"

"When One's out, there's none in!" she said. "How's the old reprobate, laird—and I beg your pardon?"

"He's gane til's accoont, Grizzie," answered the laird, in a trembling voice.

"He's gone to his account, Grizzie," answered the laird, in a trembling voice.

"Say ye sae, laird?" returned Grizzie with perfect calmness. "Oh, sirs!"

"Say you so, laird?" returned Grizzie with perfect calmness. "Oh, sirs!"

Not a single remark did she then offer. If she was cool, she was not irreverent before the thought of the awful thing that lay waiting her.

"Ye winna wauk the hoose, will ye, sir?" she added presently. "I dinna think it wad be ony service to deid or livin'."

"You won't wake the house, will you, sir?" she added presently. "I don't think it would be any service to dead or living."

"I'll no du that, Grizzie; but come ye an' luik at him," said the laird, "an' tell me what ye think. I makna a doubt he's deid, but gien ye hae ony, we'll du what we can; an' we'll sit up wi' the corp thegither, an' lat yoong an' auld tak the rist they hae mair need o' nor the likes o' you an' me."

"I won't do that, Grizzie; but come and look at him," said the laird, "and tell me what you think. I make no doubt that he's dead, but if you have any, we'll do what we can; and we'll sit up with the corpse together, and let young and old take the rest they have more need of than the likes of you and me."

It was a proud moment in Grizzie's life, one never forgotten, when the laird addressed her thus. She was ready in a moment, and they went together.

It was a proud moment in Grizzie's life, one never forgotten, when the laird addressed her thus. She was ready in a moment, and they went together.

"The prince is haein' his ain w'y the nicht!" she murmured to herself, as they bored their way through the wind to the great door.

"The prince is having his own way tonight!" she murmured to herself, as they bored their way through the wind to the great door.

When she came where the corpse lay, she stood for some moments looking down upon it without uttering a sound, nor was there any emotion in the fixed gaze of her eye. She had been brought up in a stern and nowise pitiful school. She made neither solemn reflection, nor uttered hope which her theology forbade her to cherish.

"Ye think wi' me 'at he's deid—dinna ye, Grizzie?" said the laird, in a voice that seemed to himself to intrude on the solemn silence.

"You think with me that he's dead—don't you, Grizzie?" said the laird, in a voice that seemed to himself to intrude on the solemn silence.

She removed the handkerchief, and the jaw fell.

She removed the handkerchief, and the jaw fell.

"He's gane til's accoont," she said. "It's a great amoont; an' mair on ae side nor he'll weel bide. It's sair eneuch, laird, whan we hae to gang at the Lord's call, but whan the messenger comes frae the laich yet, we maun

"He's gone to his account," she said. "It's a great amount; and more one one side than he'll take in stride. It's hard enough, laird, when we have to go at the Lord's call, but when the messenger comes from the low gate, jist lat gang an' forget. But sae lang's he's a man, we maun do what we can—an' that's what we did last nicht; sae I'll rin an' get het watter."

we must let go and bow to fate. But so long as he's a man, we must do what we can—and that's what we did last night; so I'll run and get hot water."

She did so, and they used every means they could think of for his recovery, but at length gave it up, heaped him over with blankets, for the last chance of spontaneous revival, and sitting down, awaited the slow-travelling, feeble dawn.

After they had sat in silence for nearly an hour, the laird spoke:

"We'll read a psalm thegither, Grizzie," he said

"We'll read a psalm together, Grizzie," he said.

"Ay, du ye that, laird. It'll haud them awa' for the time bein', though it can profit but little i' the hin'er en'."

"Ay, do that, laird. It'll keep them away for the time being, though it can profit but little at the last."

The laird drew from his pocket a small, much worn bible which had been his Marion's, and by the body of the dead sinner, in the heart of the howling storm and the waste of the night, his voice, trembling with a strange emotion, rose upborne upon the glorious words of the ninety-first psalm.

When he ended, they were aware that the storm had begun to yield, and by slow degrees it sank as the morning came on. Till the first faintest glimmer of dawn began to appear nothing more was said between them. But then Grizzie rose in haste, like one that had overslept herself, and said:

"I maun to my wark, laird—what think ye?" ("I must see to my work, laird—what think you?")

The laird rose also, and by a common impulse they went and looked at the corpse—for corpse it now was, beyond all question, cold as the snow without. After a brief, low-voiced conference, they proceeded to carry it to the guest-chamber, where they laid it upon the bed, and when Grizzie had done all that custom required, left it covered with a sheet, dead in the room where it dared not sleep, a mound cold and white as any snow-wreath outside. It looked as if Winter had forced his way into the house, and left this one drift, in signal of his capture. Grizzie went about her duties, and the laird back to his book.

A great awe fell upon Cosmo when he heard what visit and what departure had taken place in the midst of the storm and darkness. Lady Joan turned white as the dead, and spoke not a word. A few tears rolled from the luminous dark of her eyes, like the dew slow-gathering in a night of stars, but she was very still. The bond between her and her father had not been a pleasant one; she had not towards him that reverence which so grandly heightens love. She had loved him pitifully—perhaps, dreadful thought! a little contemptuously. The laird persuaded her not to see the body; taking every charge concerning it.

All that day things went on in the house much as usual, with a little more silence where had been much. The wind lay moveless on the frozen earth; the sun shone cold as a diamond; and the fresh snow glittered and gleamed and sparkled like a dead sea of lightning.

The laird was just thinking which of his men to send to the village, when the door opened and in came Agnes. Grannie had sent her, she said, to enquire after them. Grannie had had a troubled night, and the moment she woke began to talk about the laird, and his visitors, and what the storm must have been round lonely Castle Warlock. The drifts were tremendous, she said, but she had made her way without much difficulty. So the laird, partly to send Cosmo from the house of death into the world of life, told him to go with Aggie, and give directions to the carpenter, for the making of a coffin.

How long the body might have to lie with them, no one could tell, for the storm had ceased in a hard frost, and there could be no postal communication for many days. The laird judged it better, therefore, as soon as the shell arrived, to place the body in a death-chapel prepared for it by nature herself. With their spades he and Cosmo fashioned the mound, already hollowed in sport, into the shape of a huge sarcophagus, then opened wide the side of it, to receive the coffin as into a sepulchre in a rock. The men brought it, laid it in, and closed the entrance again with snow. Where Cosmo's hollow man of light had shone, lay the body of the wicked old nobleman.

CHAPTER XVIII
A WINTER IDYLL

Lady Joan the same day wrote to her brother Borland, now Mergwain, telling him what had taken place. But it must be some time before she received his answer, for the post from England reached the neighbouring city but intermittently, and was there altogether arrested, so far as Howglen and Muir o' Warlock were concerened. The laird told her she must have patience, and assured her that to them her presence was welcome.

And now began for Cosmo an episode of enchantment, as wondrous as any dream of tree-top, or summer wave city—for if it was not so full of lighter marvel around, it had at the heart of it a deeper marvel, namely a live and beautiful lady.

She was a girl of nearly eighteen, but looked older—shapely, strong, and graceful. But both her life-consciousness and her spirits—in some only do the words mean the same thing—had been kept down by the family relations in which she found herself. Her father loved her with what love was in him, and therefore was jealous; trusted, and therefore enslaved her; could make her useful, and therefore oppressed her. Since his health began to decline he would go nowhere without her, though he spoke seldom a pleasant, and often a very unpleasant word to her. He never praised her to her face, but swore deeply to her excellence in ears that cared little to hear of it. When at home she must always be within his reach, if not within his call; but he was far from slow to anger with her, and she dreaded his anger, not so much from love or fear as from nicety, because of the ugly things he would say when he was offended with her. One hears of ruling by love and ruling by fear, but this man ruled by disgust. At home he lived much as we have seen him in the house of another, cared for nobody's comfort but his own, and was hard to keep in good humour—such good humour as was possible to him. He paid no attention to business or management: his estates had long been under trustees; lolled about in his room, diverting himself with a horrible monkey which he taught ugly tricks; drank almost constantly; and would throw dice by himself for an hour together—doing what he could, which was little, towards the poor object of killing Time. He kept a poor larder but a rich cellar; almost always without money, he yet contrived to hold his bins replenished, and that from the farther end: he might have been expecting to live to a hundred and twenty, for of visitors he had none, except an occasional time-belated companion of his youth, whom the faint, muddled memories of old sins would bring to his door, when they would spend a day or two together, soaking, and telling bad stories, at times hardly restrained until Joan left the room—that is, if her brother was not present, before whom her father was on his good behaviour.

The old man was in bad repute with the neighbours, and they never called upon him—which they would have found it hard to justify, seeing some who were not better were quite respectable. No doubt he was the dilapidated old reprobate they counted him, but if he had not made himself poor, they would have found his morals no business of theirs. They pitied the daughter, or at least spoke pityingly of her, but could not for her sake countenance the father! Neglecting their duty towards her, they began to regard her with a blame which was the shadow of their neglect, thinking of her as defiled in her father's defilement. The creeping things—those which God hath not yet cleansed—call the pure things unclean. But it was better to be so judged than to run the risk of growing after the pattern of her judges. I suspect the man who leads a dissolute, and the man who leads a commonly selfish life, will land from the great jump pretty nearly in the same spot. What if those who have despised each the other's sins, are set down to stare at them together, until each finds his own iniquity to be hateful.

Of the latter, the respectably selfish class, was Borland her brother. He knew his presence a protection to his sister, yet gave himself no trouble to look after her. As the apple of his eye would he cherish the fluid in which he hoped to discover some secret process of nature; but he was not his sister's keeper, and a drop of mud more or less cast into her spirit was to him of no consequence. Yet he would as soon have left a woman he wanted to marry within reach of the miasms that now and then surrounded Joan, as unwarned in the dark by the cage of a tiger.

At home, therefore, because of the poverty of the family, the ill-repute of her father, and the pride and self-withdrawal of her brother, she led a lonely life where everything around her was left to run wild. The lawn was more of a meadow than a lawn, and the park a mere pasture for cattle. The shrubbery was an impassable tangle, and the flower garden a wilderness. She could do nothing to set things right, and lived about the place like a poor relation. At school, which she left at fifteen, she had learned nothing so as to be of any vital use to her—possibly left it a little less capable than she went. For some of her natural perceptions could hardly fail to be blunted by the artificial, false, and selfish judgements and regards which had there surrounded her. Without a mother, without a companion, she had to find what solace, what pastime she could. In the huge house there was not a piano fit to play upon; and her only source of in-door amusement was a library containing a large disproportion of books in old French bindings, with much tarnished gilding on the backs. But a native purity of soul kept her lovely, and capable of becoming lovelier.

The mystery of all mysteries is the upward tendency of so many souls through so much that clogs and would defile their wings, while so many others seem never even to look up. Then, having so begun with the dust, how do these ever come to raise their eyes to the hills? The keenest of us moral philosophers are but poor, mole-eyed creatures! One day, I trust, we shall laugh at many a difficulty that now seems insurmountable, but others will keep rising behind them.

Lady Joan did not like ugly things, and so shrank from evil things. She was the less in danger from liberty, because of the disgust which certain tones and words of her father had repeatedly occasioned her. She learned self-defence early—and alone, without even a dog to keep her company, and help her to the laws of the world outside herself.

With none of the conventionalities of society, Lady Joan saw no reason for making a difficulty when, the day after that on which her father died, Cosmo proposed a walk in the snow. He saw her properly provided for what seemed to her an adventure—with short skirts, and stockings over her shoes—and they set out together, in the brilliant light of a sun rapidly declining toward the western horizon, though it had but just passed the low noon. The moment she stepped from the threshold, Joan was invaded by an almost giddy sense of freedom. The keen air and the impending snow sent the warm blood to her cheeks, and her heart beat as if new-born into a better world. She was annoyed with herself, but in vain she called herself heartless; in vain she accused herself of indifference to the loss of her father, said to herself she was a worthless girl: there was the sun in the sky—not warm, but dazzling-bright and shining straight into her very being! while the air, instinct with life, was filling her lungs like water drunk by a thirsty soul, and making her heart beat like the heart of Eve when first she woke alive, and felt what her maker had willed! Life indeed was good! it was a blessed thing for the eyes to behold the sun!—Let death do what it can, there is just one thing it cannot destroy, and that is life. Never in itself, only in the unfaith of man, does life recognize any sway of death.—A fresh burst of healthy vigour seemed born to answer each fresh effort. Over the torrent they walked on a bridge of snow, and listening could hear, far down, below the thick white blanket, the noise of its hidden rushing. Away and up the hill they went; the hidden torrent of Joan's blood flowed clearer; her heart sang to her soul; and everything began to look like a thing in a story—herself a princess, and her attendant a younger brother, travelling with her to meet the tide of in-flowing lovely adventure. Such a brother was a luxury she had never had—very different from an older one. He talked so strangely too—now like a child, now like an old man!

She felt a charm in both, but understood neither. Capable, through confidence in his father, of receiving wisdom far beyond what he could have thought out for himself, he sometimes said things because he understood them, which seemed to most who heard them beyond his years. Some people only understand enough of a truth to reject it, but Cosmo's reception by faith turned to sight, as all true faith does at last, and formed a soil for thought more immediately his own.

They had been climbing a steep ascent, very difficult in the snow, and had at length reached the top, where they stood for a moment panting, with another ascent beyond them.

"Aren't you always wanting to climb and climb, Lady Joan?" said the boy.

"Call me Joan, and I will answer you."

"Then, Joan,—how kind you are! Don't you always want to be getting up?—up higher than you are?"

"No; I don't think I do."

"I believe you do, only you don't know it. When I get on the top of yon hill there, it always seems to me such a little way up!—and Mr. Simon tells me I should feel much the same, if it were the top of the highest peak in the Himalayas."

Lady Joan did not reply, and Cosmo too was silent for a time.

"Don't you think," he began again, "though life is so very good—to me especially with you here—you would get very tired if you thought you had to live in this world always—for ever and ever and ever, and never, never get out of it?"

"No, I don't," said Joan. "I can't say I find life so nice as you think it, but one keeps hoping it may turn to something better."

She was amused with what she counted childish talk for a boy of his years—so manly too beyond his years!

"That is very curious!" he returned. "Now I am quite happy; but this moment I should feel just in a prison, if I thought I should never get to another world; for what you can never get out of, is your prison—isn't it?"

"Yes—but if you don't want to get out?"

"Ah, that is true! But as soon as that comes to a prisoner, it is a sign that he is worn out, and has not life enough in him to look the world in the face. I was talking about it the other day with Mr. Simon, else I shouldn't have got it so plain. The blue roof so high above us there, is indeed very different from the stone vault of a prison, for there is no stop or end to it. But if you can never get away from under it, never get off the floor at the bottom of it, I feel as if it might almost as well be something solid that held me in. There would be no promise in the stars then: they look now like promises, don't they? I do not believe God would ever show us a thing he did not mean to give us."

"You are a very odd boy, Cosmo. I am almost afraid to listen to you. You say such presumptuous things!"

Cosmo laughed a little gentle laugh.

"How can you love God, Joan, and be afraid to speak before him? I should no more dream of his being angry with me for thinking he made me for great and glad things, and was altogether generous towards me, than I could imagine my father angry with me for wishing to be as wise and good as he is, when I know it is wise and good he most wants me to be."

"Ah, but he is your father, you know, and that is very different!"

"I know it is very different—God is so much, much more my father than is the laird of Glenwarlock! He is so much more to me, and so much nearer to me, though my father is the best father that ever lived! God, you know, Joan, God is more than anybody knows what to say about. Sometimes, when I am lying in my bed at night, my heart swells in me, that I hardly know how to bear it, with the thought that here I am, come out of God, and yet not *out* of him—close to the very life that said to everything *be*, and it was!—you think it strange that I talk so?"

"Rather, I must confess! I don't believe it can be a good thing at your age to think so much about religion. There is a time for everything. You talk like one of those good little children in books that always die—at least I have heard of such books—I never saw any of them."

Cosmo laughed again.

"Which of us is the merrier—you or me? Which of us is the stronger, Joan? The moment I saw you, I thought you looked like one that hadn't enough of something—as if you weren't happy; but if you knew that the great beautiful person we call God was always near you, it would be impossible for you to go on being sad."

Joan gave a great sigh: her heart knew its own bitterness, and there was little joy in it for a stranger to intermeddle with. But she said to herself the boy would be a gray-haired man before he was twenty, and began to imagine a mission to help him out of these morbid fancies.

"You must understand, Cosmo," she said, "that, while we are in this world, we must live as people of this world, not of another."

"But you can't mean that the people of this world are banished from Him who put them in it! He is all the same, in this world and in every other. If anything makes us happy, it must make us much happier to know it for a bit of frozen love—for the love that gives is to the gift as water is to snow. Ah, you should hear our torrent sing in summer, and shout in the spring! The thought of God fills me so full of life that I want to go and do something for everybody. I am never miserable. I don't think I shall be when my father dies."

"Oh, Cosmo!—with such a good father as yours! I am shocked."

Her words struck a pang into her own heart, for she felt as if she had compared his father and hers, over whom she was not miserable. Cosmo turned, and looked at her. The sun was close upon the horizon, and his level rays shone full on the face of the boy.

"Lady Joan," he said slowly, and with a tremble in his voice, "I should just laugh with delight to have to die for my father. But if he were taken from me now, I should be so proud of him, I should have no room to be miserable. As God makes me glad though I cannot see him, so my father would make me glad though I could not see him. I cannot see him now, and yet I am glad because my father *is*—away down there in the old castle; and when he is gone from me, I shall be glad still, for he will be *somewhere* all the same—with God as he is now. We shall meet again one day, and run at each other."

It was an odd phrase with which he ended, but Lady Joan did not laugh.

The sun was down, and the cold, gray twilight came creeping up from the east. They turned and walked home, through a luminous dusk. It would not be dark all night, though the moon did not rise till late, for the snow gave out a ghostly radiance. Surely it must be one of those substances that have the power of drinking and hoarding the light of the sun, that with their memories of it they may thin the darkness! I suspect everything does it more or less. Far below were the lights of the castle, and across an unbroken waste of whiteness the gleams of the village. The air was keen as an essence of points and edges, and the thought of the kitchen fire grew pleasant. Cosmo took Joan's hand, and down the hill they ran swiftly descending what they had toilsomely climbed.

As she ran, the thought that one of those lights was burning by the body of her father, rebuked Joan afresh. She was not glad, and she could not be sorry! If Cosmo's father were to die, Cosmo would be both sorry and glad! But the boy turned his face, ever and again as they ran, up to hers—she was a little taller than he—and his every look comforted her. An attendant boy-angel he seemed, whose business it was to rebuke and console her. If he were her brother, she would be well content never more to leave the savage place! For the strange old man in the red night-cap was such a gentleman! and this odd boy, absolutely unnatural in his goodness, was nevertheless charming! She did not yet know that goodness is the only nature. She regarded it as a noble sort of disease—as something at least which it was possible to have too much of. She had not a suspicion that goodness and nothing else is life and health—that what the universe demands of us is to be good boys and girls.

To judge religion we must have it—not stare at it from the bottom of a seeming interminable ladder. When she reached the door, she felt as if waking out of a dream, in which she had been led along strange paths by a curious angel. But not to himself was Cosmo like an angel! For indeed he was a strong, vigorous, hopeful, trusting boy of God's in this world, and would be just such a boy in the next—one namely who did his work, and was ready for whatever was meant to come.

When, from all that world of snow outside, Joan entered the kitchen with its red heart of fire, she knew for a moment how a little bird feels when creeping under the wing of his mother. Those old Hebrews—what poets they were! Holy and homely and daring, they delighted in the wings of the Almighty; but the Son of the Father made the lovely image more homely still, likening himself to the hen under whose wings the chickens would not creep for all her crying and calling. Then first was Joan aware of simple confidence, of safety and satisfaction and loss of care; for the old man in the red night-cap would see to everything! Nought would go amiss where he was at the head of affairs! And hardly was she seated when she felt a new fold of his protection about her: he told her he had had her room changed, that she might be near his mother and Grizzie, and not have to go out to reach it.

Cosmo heard with delight that his father had given up his room to Lady Joan, and would share his. To sleep with his father was one of the greatest joys the world held for him. Such a sense of safety and comfort—of hen's wings—was nowhere else to be had on the face of the great world! It was the full type of conscious well-being, of softness and warmth and peace in the heart of strength. His father was to him a downy nest inside a stone-castle.

They all sat together round the kitchen fire. The laird fell into a gentle monologue, in which, to Joan's thinking, he talked even more strangely than Cosmo. Things born in the fire and the smoke, like the song of the three holy children, issued from the furnace clothed in softest moonlight. Joan said to herself it was plain where the boy got his oddity; but what she called oddity was but sense from a deeper source than she knew the existence of. He read them also passages of the book then occupying him so much: Joan wondered what attraction such a jumble of good words and no sense could have for a man so capable in ordinary affairs. Then came supper; and after that, for the first time in her life, Joan was present when a man had the presumption to speak to his Maker direct from his own heart, without the mediation of a book. This she found odder than all the rest; she had never even heard of such a thing! So peculiar, so unfathomable were his utterances, that it never occurred to her the man might be meaning something; farther from her still was the thought, that perhaps God liked to hear him, was listening to him and understanding him, and would give him the things he asked. She heard only an extraordinary gibberish, supposed suitable to a religious observance—family prayers, she thought it must be! She felt confused, troubled, ashamed—so grievously out of her element that she never knew until they rose, that the rest were kneeling while she sat staring into the fire. Then she felt guilty and shy, but as nobody took any notice, persuaded herself they had not observed. The unpleasantness of all this, however, did not prevent her from saying to herself as she went to bed, "Oh, how delightful it would be to live in a house where everybody understood, and loved, and thought about everybody else!" She did not know that she was wishing for nothing more, and something a little less, than the kingdom of heaven—the very thing she thought the laird and Cosmo so strange for troubling their heads about. If men's wishes are not always for what the kingdom of heaven would bring them, their miseries at least are all for the lack of that kingdom.

That night Joan dreamed herself in a desert island, where she had to go through great hardships, but where everybody was good to everybody, and never thought of taking care except of each other; and that, when a beautiful ship came to carry her away, she cried, and would not go.

Three weeks of all kinds of weather, except warm, followed, ending with torrents of rain, and a rapid thaw; but before that time Joan had got as careless of the weather as Cosmo, and nothing delighted her more than to encounter any sort of it with him. Nothing kept her indoors, and as she always attended to Grizzie's injunctions the moment she returned, she took no harm, and grew much stronger. It is not encountering the weather that is dangerous, but encountering it when the strength is not equal to the encounter. These two would come in wet from head to foot, change their clothes, have a good meal, sleep well, and wake in the morning without the least cold. They would spend the hours between breakfast and dinner ascending the bank of a hill stream, dammed by the snow, swollen by the thaw, and now rushing with a roar to the valley; or fighting their way through wind and sleet to the top of some wild expanse of hill-moorland, houseless for miles and miles—waste bog, and dry stony soil, as far as eye could reach, with here and there a solitary stalk or bush, bending low to the ground in the steady bitter wind—a hopeless region, save that it made the hope in their hearts glow the redder; or climbing a gully, deep-worn by the few wheels of a month but the many of centuries, and more by the torrents that rushed always down its trench when it rained heavily, or thawed after snow—hearing the wind sweep across it above their heads, but feeling no breath of its presence, till emerging suddenly upon its plane they had to struggle with it for very foot-hold upon the round earth. In such contests Lady Joan delighted. It was so nice, she said, to have a downright good fight, and nobody out of temper! She would come home from the windy war with her face glowing, her eyes flashing, her hair challenging storm from every point of the compass, and her heart merry with very peacefulness. Her only thoughts of trouble were, that her father's body lay unburied, and that Borland would come and take her away.

When the thaw came at last, the laird had the coffin brought again into the guest-chamber, and there placed on trestles, to wait the coming of the new Lord Mergwain.

Outstripping the letter that announced his departure, he arrived at length, and with him his man of business. Lady Joan's heart gave a small beat of pleasure at sight of him, then lay quiet, sad, and apprehensive: the cold proper salute he gave her seemed, after the life she had of late been living, to belong rather to some sunless world than the realms of humanity. He uttered one commonplace concerning his father's death, and never alluded to it again; behaved in a dignified, recognizant manner to the laird, as to an inferior to whom he was under more obligation than he saw how to wipe out; and, after the snub with which he met the boy's friendly approach, took no farther notice of Cosmo. Seated three minutes, he began to require the laird's assistance towards the removal of the body; could not be prevailed upon to accept refreshment; had a messenger despatched instantly to procure the nearest hearse and four horses; and that same afternoon started for England, following the body, and taking his sister with him.

CHAPTER XIX
AN INTERLUNAR CAVE

And so the moon died out of Cosmo's heaven. But it was only the moon. The sun remained to him—his father—visible type of the great sun, whose light is too keen for souls, and heart and spirit only can bear. But when he had received Joan's last smile, when she turned away her face, and the Ungenial, who had spoiled everything at Glenwarlock, carried her away, then indeed for a moment a great cloud came over the light of his life, and he sought where to hide his tears. It was a sickening time, for suddenly she had come, suddenly entered his heart, and suddenly departed. But such things are but clouds, and cannot but pass. Ah, reader! It may be your cloud has not yet passed, and you scorn to hear it called one, priding yourself that your trouble is eternal. But just because you are eternal, your trouble cannot be. You may cling to it, and brood over it, but you cannot keep it from either blossoming into a bliss, or crumbling to dust. Be such while it lasts, that, when it passes, it shall leave you loving more, not less.

There was this difference between Cosmo and most young men of clay finer than ordinary, that, after the first few moments of the seemingly unendurable, he did not wander about moody, nursing his sorrow, and making everybody uncomfortable because he was uncomfortable; but sought the more the company of his father, and of Mr. Simon, from whom he had been much separated while Lady Joan was with them. For such a visit was an opportunity most precious in the eyes of the laird. With the sacred instinct of a father he divined what the society of a lady would do for his boy—for the ripening of his bloom, and the strengthening of his volition. Two days had not passed before he began to be aware of a softening and clearing of his speech; of greater readiness and directness in his replies; of an indescribable sweetening of the address, that had been sweet, with a rose-shadow of gentle apology cast over every approach; of a deepening of the atmosphere of his reverence, which yet as it deepened grew more diaphanous. And when now the episode of angelic visitation was over, with his usual wisdom he understood the wrench her abrupt departure must have given his whole being, and allowed him plenty of time to recover himself from it. Once he came upon him weeping: not with faintest overshadowing did he rebuke him, not with farthest hint suggest weakness in his tears. He went up to him, laid his hand gently on his head, stood thus a moment, then turned without a word, and left him. Nowise because of his sorrow did he regret the freedom he had granted their intercourse. He knew what the sharp things of life are to the human plant; that its frosts are as needful as its sunshine, its great passion-winds as its gentle rains; that a divine result is required, and that his son was being made divinely human; that in aid of this end the hand of man must humbly follow the great lines of Nature, ready to withhold itself, anxious not to interfere. Most people resist the marvellous process; call in the aid of worldly wisdom for low ends; and bring the experience of their own failures to bear for the production of worse. But there is no escaping the mill that grinds slowly and grinds small; and those who refuse to be living stones in the living temple, must be ground into mortar for it.

The next day, of his own choice, Cosmo went to Mr. Simon. He also knew how to treat the growing plant. He set him such work as should in a measure harmonize with his late experience, and so drew him gently from his past: mere labour would have but driven him deeper into it. Yesterday is as much our past as the bygone century, and sheltering in it from an uncongenial present, we are lost to our morrow. Thus things slid gently back with him into their old grooves. An era of blessedness had vanished, but was not lost; it was added to his life, gathered up into his being; it was dissolved into his consciousness, and interpenetrated his activity. Where there is no ground of regret, or shame, or self-reproach, new joy casts not out the old; and now that the new joy was old, the older joys came softly trooping back to their attendance. Nor was this all. The departing woman left behind her a gift that had never been hers—the power of verse: he began to be a poet. The older I grow the more am I filled with marvel at the divine idea of the mutual development of the man and the woman. Many a woman has made of a man, for the time at least, and sometimes for ever, a poet, caring for his verses never a cambric handkerchief or pair of gloves! A wretched man to whom a poem is not worth a sneer, may set a woman singing to the centuries!

Any gift of the nature of poetry, however poor or small, is of value inestimable to the development of the individual, ludicrous even though it may show itself, should conceit clothe it in print. The desire of fame, so vaunted, is the ruin of the small, sometimes of the great poet. The next evil to doing anything for love of money, is doing it for the love of fame. A man may have a wife who is all the world to him, but must he therefore set her on a throne? Cosmo, essentially and peculiarly practical, never thought of the world and his verses together, but gathered life for himself in the making of them.

These children of his, like all real children, strengthened his heart, and upheld his hands. In them Truth took to him shape; in them she submitted herself to his contemplation. He grew faster, and from the days of his mourning emerged more of a man, and abler to look the world in the face.

From that time also he learned and understood more rapidly, though he never came to show any great superiority in the faculties most prized of this world, whose judgement differs from that of God's kingdom in regard to the comparative value of intellectual gifts almost as much as it does in regard to the relative value of the moral and the intellectual. Not the less desirable however did it seem in the eyes of both his father and his tutor, that, if it could anyhow be managed, he should go the next winter to college. As to how it could be managed, the laird took much serious thought, but saw no glimmer of light in the darkness of apparent impossibility. An unsuspected oracle was however at hand.

Old servants of the true sort have, I fancy, a kind of family instinct. From the air about them almost, from the personal carriage, from words dropped that were never meant for them, from the thoughtful, troubled, or eager look, and the sought or avoided conference, they get possessed by a notion both of how the wind is blowing, and of how the ship wants to sail. But Grizzie was capable of reasoning from what she saw. She marked the increase of care on the brow of her master; noted that it was always greater after he and Mr. Simon had had a talk at which Cosmo, the beloved of both, was not present; and concluded that their talk and the laird's trouble, must be about Cosmo. She noted also that both were as much pleased with him as ever, and concluded therefore it was his prospects and not his behaviour that caused the uneasiness. Then again she noted how fervently at prayers her master entreated guidance to do neither more nor less than the right thing; and from all put together, and considered in the light of a tolerably accurate idea of the laird's circumstances, Grizzie was able not only to arrive at a final conclusion, but to come to the resolution of offering—not advice—that she would never have presumed upon—but a suggestion.

CHAPTER XX
CATCH YER NAIG

One night the laird sat in the kitchen revolving in his mind the whole affair for the many hundredth time. Was it right to spend on his son's education what might go to the creditors? Was it not better for the world, for the creditors, and for all, that one of Cosmo's vigour should be educated? Was it not the best possible investment of any money he could lay hold of? As to the creditors, there was the land! the worst for him would be the best for them; and for the boy it was infinitely better he should go without land than without education! But, all this granted and settled, *where was the money to come from?* That the amount required was small, made no difference, when it was neither in hand, nor, so far as he could see, anywhere near his hand.

He sat in his great chair, with his book open upon his knees. His mother and Cosmo were gone to bed, and Grizzie was preparing to follow them: the laird was generally the last to go. But Grizzie, who had been eying him at intervals for the last half hour, having now finished her preparations for the morning, drew near, and stood before him, with her hands and bare arms under her apron. Her master taking no notice of her, she stood thus in silence for a moment, then began. It may have been noted that her riming tendency appeared mostly in the start of a speech, and mostly vanished afterwards.

"Laird," she said, "ye're in trouble, for ye're sittin' double, an' castna a leuk upo' yer buik. Gien ye wad lat a body speyk 'at kens naething, 'cep' 'at oot o' the moo' o' babes an' sucklin's—an' troth I'm naither babe nor sucklin' this mony a lang, but I'm a muckle eneuch gowk to be ane o' the Lord's innocents, an' hae him perfec' praise oot o' the moo' o' me!—"

She paused a moment, feeling it was time the laird should say something—which immediately he did.

"Say awa', Grizzie," he answered; "I'm hearin' ye. There's nane has a better richt to say her say i' this hoose; what ither hae ye to say't intil!"

"I hae *no* richt," retorted Grizzie, almost angrily, "but what ye alloo me, laird; and I wadna wuss the Lord to gie me ony mair. But whan I see ye in tribble—eh, mony's the time I haud my tongue till my hert's that grit it's jist swallin' in blobs an' blawin' like the parritch whan it's dune makin', afore I tak it frae the fire! for I hae naething to say, an' naither coonsel nor help intil me. But last nicht, whan I leukitna for't, there cam a thoucht intil my heid, an' seein' it was a stranger, I bad it walcome. It micht hae come til a far wysser heid nor mine, but seein' it did come to mine, it wad luik as gien the Lord micht hae pitten

"Laird," she said, "you're in trouble, for you're sitting double, and cast not a look upon your book. If you would let one speak that knows nothing, except that out of the mouth of babes and sucklings—and I've been neither babe nor suckling this many a year, but I'm a big enough fool to be one of the Lord's innocents, and have him perfect praise out of my mouth!—"

She paused a moment, feeling it was time the laird should say something—which immediately he did.

"Say on, Grizzie," he answered; "I'm hearing you. There's none has a better right to say her say in this house; what other have you to say it in!"

"I have *no* right," retorted Grizzie, almost angrily, "but what you allow me, laird; and I wouldn't wish the Lord to give me any more. But when I see you in trouble—eh, many's the time I hold my tongue till my heart's that great it's just swelling in blobs and blowing like the porridge when it's just been made, before I take it from the fire! for I have nothing to say, and neither counsel nor help in me. But last night, unasked-for, there came a thought into my head, and seeing it was a stranger, I bade it welcome. It might have come to a far wiser head than mine, but seeing it did come to mine, it would look as if the Lord might have

’t there—to the comfort an’ consolation o’ ane, ’at, gien she be a gowk, is muckle the same as the Lord made her wi’ ’s ain bliss-it han’. Sae, quo’ I, I s’ jist submit the thing to the laird. He’ll sune discern whether it be frae the Lord or mysel’!”

“Say on, Grizzie,” returned the laird, when again she paused. “It sud surprise nane to get a message frae the Lord by the mou’ o’ ane o’ his handmaidens.”

“Weel, it’s this, laird.—I hae aften been i’ the gran’ drawin’ room, whan ye wad be lattin’ the yoong laird, or somebody or anither ye wantit to be special til, see the bonny things ye hae sic a fouth o’ i’ the caibinets again the wa’s; an’ I hae aye h’ard ye say o’ ane o’ them—yon bonnie little horsie, ye ken, ’at they say the auld captain, ’at’s no laid yet, gied to yer gran’father—I hae aye h’ard ye say o’ that ’at hoo it was solid silver—*‘said to be’* ye wad aye tack to the tail o’ ’t.”

“True! true!” said the laird, a hopeful gleam beginning to break upon his darkness.

“Weel, ye see, laird,” Grizzie went on, “I’m no sic a born idiot as think ye wad set the possession o’ sic a playock again the yoong laird’s edication; sae ye maun hae some rizzon for no meltin’ ’t doon—seein’ siller maun aye be worth siller—an’ gowd, gien there be eneuch o’ ’t.—Sae, like the minister, I come to the conclusion—But I hae yer leave, laird, to speyk?”

“Gang on, gang on, Grizzie,” said the laird, almost eagerly. “Weel, laird—I winna say *feart,* for I never saw yer lairdship”—she had got into the way of saying *lordship,* and now not unfrequently said *lairdship!*—“feart afore bull or bully, but I cud weel believe ye wadna willin’ly anger ane ’at the Lord lats gang up and doon upo’ the earth, whan he wad be far better intil’t, ristin’ in ’s grave till the resurrection—only he was never ane o’ the sancts! But anent that, michtna ye jist ca’ to min’, laird, ’at a gi’en gift’s yer ain, to du wi’ what ye like; an’ I wadna heed man, no to say a cratur ’at belongs richtly to nae warl’ ava’, ’at wad play the bairn, an’ want back what he had

put it there—to the comfort and consolation of one, that, if she be a goose, is much the same as the Lord made her with his own blessed hand. So, said I, I’ll just submit the thing to the laird. He’ll soon discern whether it be from the Lord or myself!”

“Say on, Grizzie,” returned the laird, when again she paused. “It should surprise none to get a message from the Lord by the mouth of one of his handmaidens.”

“Well, it’s this, laird. I have often been in the grand drawing room, when you would be letting the young laird, or somebody or another you wanted to treat specially, see the bonny things you have so many of in the cabinets against the walls; and I have always heard you say of one of them—that bonnie little horse, you know, that they say the old captain, that’s not at rest yet, gave to your grandfather—I’ve always heard you say of that, that it was solid silver—*‘said to be’* you would always end by saying.”

“True! true!” said the laird, a hopeful gleam beginning to break upon his darkness.

“Well, you see, laird,” Grizzie went on, “I’m not such a born idiot as think you would set the possession of such a plaything against the young laird’s education; so you must have some reason for not melting it down—seeing silver’s worth silver coin—and gold, if there be enough of it.—So, like the minister, I come to the conclusion—But I have your leave, laird, to speak?”

“Go on, go on, Grizzie,” said the laird, almost eagerly. “Well, laird—I won’t say *frightened,* for I never saw your lairdship”—she had got into the way of saying *lordship,* and now not unfrequently said *lairdship!*—“afraid before bull or bully, but I could well believe you wouldn’t willingly anger one that the Lord lets roam up and down upon the earth, when he would be far better in it, resting in his grave till the resurrection—only he was never one of the saints! But about that, mightn’t you just call to mind, laird, that a given gift’s your own, to do with what you like; and I wouldn’t heed man, not to say a creature that belongs rightly to no world at all, that would play the child,

gi'en. For him, he's a mere deid man 'at winna lie still. Mony a bairn canna sleep, 'cause he's behavet himsel' ill the day afore! But gien, by coortesy, like, he hed a word i' the case, he cudna objec'—that is, gien he hae onything o' the gentleman left intil him, which nae doubt may weel be doobtfu'—for wasna he a byous expense wi' his drink an' the gran' ootlandish dishes he bude to hae! Aften hae I h'ard auld Grannie say as muckle, an' she kens mair aboot that portion o' oor history nor ony ither, for, ye see, I cam rather late intil the family mysel'. Sae, as I say, it wad be but fair the auld captain sud contreebit something to the needcessities o' the hoose, war it his to withhaud, which I mainteen it is not."

and want back what he had given. For him, he's a mere dead man that won't lie still. Many a child can't sleep, because he's behaved himself badly the day before! But if, by courtesy, he had a word in the case, he couldn't object—that is, if he has anything of the gentleman left in him, which no doubt may well be doubtful—for wasn't he a great expense with his drink and the grand outlandish dishes he had to have! Often have I heard old Grannie say as much, and she knows more about that portion of our history than any other, for, you see, I came rather late into the family myself. So, as I say, it would be but fair the old captain should contribute something to the necessities of the house, were it his to withhold, which I maintain it is not."

"Weel rizzont, Grizzie!" cried the laird. "An' I thank ye mair for yer thoucht nor yer rizzons; the tane I was in want o', yer rizzons I was na. The thing sall be luikit intil, an' that the first thing the morn's mornin'! The bit playock cam never i' my heid! I maun be growin' auld, Grizzie, no to hae thoucht o' a thing sae plain! But it's the w'y wi a' the best things! They're sae guid whan ye get a grip o' them, 'at ye canna un'erstan' hoo ye never thoucht o' them afore."

"Well reasoned, Grizzie!" cried the laird. "And I thank you more for your thought than your reasons; the one I was in want of, your reasons I was not. The thing shall be looked into, and that the first thing tomorrow morning! The little toy never entered my head! I must be growing old, Grizzie, not to have thought of a thing so plain! But it's the way with all the best things! They're so good when you get a grip of them, that you can't understand how you never thought of them before."

"I'm aul'er nor you, sir; sae it maun hae been the Lord himsel' 'at pat it intil me."

"I'm older than you, sir; so it must have been the Lord himself that put it into me."

"We'll see the morn, Grizzie. I'm no that sure there's onything mair intil 't nor a mere fule word. For onything I ken, the thing may be nae better nor a bit o' braiss. I hae thoucht mony a time it luikit, in places, unco like braiss. But I s' tak it the morn's mornin' to Jeemie Merson. We'll see what he says til 't. Gien ony body i' these pairts hae ony authority in sic maitters, it's Jeemie. An' I thank ye hertily, Grizzie."

"We'll see tomorrow, Grizzie. I'm not that sure there's anything more in it than a mere foolish word. For anything I know, the thing may be no better than a bit of brass. I have thought many a time it looked, in places, very like brass. But I'll take it tomorrow morning to Jamie Merson. We'll see what he says to it. If any body in these parts has any authority in such matters, it's Jamie. And I thank you heartily, Grizzie."

But Grizzie was not well pleased that her master should so lightly pass the reasoned portion of her utterance; like many another prophet, she prized more the part of her prophecy that came from herself, than the part that came from the Lord.

"Sae plain as he cam an' gaed, laird, I thoucht ye micht hae been considerin' him."

"So plain as he came and went, laird, I thought you might have been considering him."

The laird replied to her tone rather than her words.

"Hoots, Grizzie, wuman!" he said, "wasna ye jist tellin' me no to heed him a hair? An' no ae hair wad I heed him, 'cep' it wad gie ony rist til 's puir wan'erin' sowl."

"Heavens, Grizzie, woman!" he said, "weren't you just telling me not to heed him a hair? And not one hair would I heed him, except it would give any rest to his poor wandering soul."

"I but thoucht the thing worth a thoucht, laird," said Grizzie, humbly and apologetically; and with a kind "Guid nicht to ye, laird," turned away, and went up the stairs to her room.

"I but thought the thing worth a thought, laird," said Grizzie, humbly and apologetically; and with a kind "Good night to you, laird," turned away, and went up the stairs to her room.

The moment she was gone, the laird fell on his knees, and gave God thanks for the word he had received by his messenger—if indeed it pleased him that such Grizzie should prove to be.

"O Lord," he said, "with thee the future is as the present, and the past as the future. In the long past it may be thou didst provide this supply for my present need—didst even then prepare the answer to the prayers with which thou knewest I should assail thine ear. Never in all my need have I so much desired money as now for the good of my boy. But if this be but one of my hopes, not one of thy intents, give me the patience of a son, O Father."

With these words he rose from his knees, and taking his book, read and enjoyed into the dead of the night.

That same night, Cosmo, who, again in his own chamber, was the more troubled with the trouble of his father that he was no longer with him in his room, dreamed a very odd, confused dream, of which he could give himself but little account in the morning—something about horses shod with shoes of gold, which they cast from their heels in a shoe-storm as they ran, and which anybody might have for the picking up. And throughout the dream was diffused an unaccountable flavour of the old villain, the sea-captain, although nowhere did he come into the story.

When he came down to breakfast, his father told him, to his delight, that he was going to Muir o' Warlock, and would like him to go with him. He ran like a hare up the waterside to let Mr. Simon know, and was back by the time his father was ready.

CHAPTER XXI
THE WATCHMAKER

It was a lovely day. There would be plenty of cold and rough weather yet, but the winter was over and gone, and even to that late region of the north, the time of the singing of birds was come. The air was soft, with streaks of cold in it. The fields lay about all wet, but there was the sun above them, whose business it was to dry them. There were no leaves yet on the few trees and hedges, but preparations had long been made, and the sap was now rising in their many stems, like the mercury in all the thermometers. Up also rose the larks, joy fluttering their wings and quivering their throats. They always know when the time to praise God is come, for it is when they begin to feel happy: more cannot be expected of them. And are they not therein already on the level of most of us Christians, who in this mood and that praise God? And indeed are not the birds and the rest of the creatures Christians in the same way as the vast mass of those that call themselves such? Do they not belong to the creation groaning after a redemption they do not know? Men and women groan in misery from not being yet the sons and daughters of God, who regard nothing else as redemption, but the getting of their own way, which the devil only would care to give them.

As they went, the laird told Cosmo what was taking him to the village, and the boy walked by his father's side as in a fairy tale; for had they not with them a strange thing that might prove the talismanic opener of many doors to treasure-caves?

They went straight to the shop, if shop it could be called, of Jeames Merson, the watchmaker of the village. There all its little ornamental business was done—a silver spoon might be engraved, a new pin put to a brooch, a wedding ring of sterling gold purchased, or a pair of earrings of lovely glass, representing amethyst or topaz. There a second-hand watch might be had, with choice amongst a score, taken in exchange from ploughmen or craftsmen. Jeames was poor, for there was not much trade in his line, and so was never able to have much of a stock; but he was an excellent watchmaker—none better in the great city—so at least his townfolk believed, and in the village it soon appears whether a watchmaker has got it in him.

He was a thin, pale man, with a mixed look of rabbit and ferret, a high narrow forehead, and keen gray eyes. His work-shop and show-room was the kitchen, partly for the sake of his wife's company, partly because there was the largest window the cottage could boast. In this window was hung almost his whole stock, and a table before it was covered with his work and tools. He was stooping over it, his lens in his eye, busy with a watch, of which several portions lay beside him protected from the dust by footless wine-glasses, when the laird and Cosmo entered. He put down his pinion and file, pushed back his chair, and rose to receive them.

"A fine mornin', Jeames!" said the laird. "I houp ye're weel, and duin' weel."	"A fine morning, Jeames!" said the laird. "I hope you're well, and doing well."
"Muckle the same as usual, laird, an' I thank ye," answered Jeames, with a large smile. "I'm no jist upo' the ro'd to be what they ca' a millionaire, an' I'm no jist upon the perris—something atween the twa, I'm thinkin'."	"Much the same as usual, laird, and I thank you," answered Jeames, with a large smile. "I'm not quite upon the road to be what they call a millionaire, and I'm not quite upon the parish—something between the two, I'm thinking."
"I doobt there's mair o' 's in like condition, Jeames," responded the laird, "or we wad na be comin' to tax yer skeel at this present."	"I suspect there are more of us in like condition, Jeames," responded the laird, "or we wouldn't be coming to tax your skill just now."

"Use yer freedom, laird; I'm yer heumble servan'. It wadna be a watch for the yoong laird? I kenna—"

He stopped, and cast an anxious eye towards the window.

"Na, na," interrupted the laird, sorry to have raised even so much of a vain hope in the mind of the man, "I'm as far frae a watch as ye are frae the bank. But I hae here i' my pooch a bit silly playock, 'at 's been i' the hoose this mony a lang; an' jist this last nicht it was pitten intil my heid there micht be some guid intil the chattel, seein' i' the tradition o' the family it's aye been hauden for siller. For my ain pairt I hae my doobts; but gien onybody here aboot can tell the trowth o' 't, yersel' maun be the man; an sae I hae brought it, to ken what ye wad say til 't."

"I'll du my best to lowse yer doobt, laird," returned Jeames. "Lat's hae a luik at the article."

The laird took the horse from his pocket, and handed it to him. Jeames regarded it for some time with interest, and examined it with care.

"It's a bonny bit o' carved work," he said; "—a bairnly kin' o' a thing for shape—mair like a timmer horsie; but whan ye come to the ornamentation o' the same, it's o' anither character frae the roon' spots o' reid paint—an' sae's the sma' rubies an' stanes intil 't. This has taen a heap o' time, an' painfu' labour—a deal mair nor some o' 's wad think it worth, I doobt! It's the w'y o' the haithens wi' their graven eemages, but what for a horsie like this, I dinna ken. Hooever, that's naither here nor there: ye didna come to me to speir hoo or what for it was made; it's what is 't made o' 's the question. It's some yallow-like for siller; an' it's unco black, which is mair like it—but that may be wi' dirt.—An' dirt I'm thinkin' it maun be, barkit intil the gravin'" he went on, taking a tool and running the point of it along one of the fine lines. "Troth ohn testit, I wadna like to say what it was. But it's an unco weicht!—I doobt—na, I mair nor doobt it canna be siller."

"Use your freedom, laird; I'm your humble servant. It wouldn't be a watch for the young laird? I don't know—"

He stopped, and cast an anxious eye towards the window.

"Na, na" interrupted the laird, sorry to have raised even so much of a vain hope in the mind of the man, "I'm as far from a watch as you are from the bank. But I have here in my pocket a silly wee toy, that's been in the house this long time; and just this last night it was put in my head that there might be some good in the chattel, since the family tradition has always taken it for silver. For my own part I have my doubts; but if anyone here about can tell the truth of it, you must be the man; and so I have brought it, to know what you would say to it."

"I'll do my best to relieve your doubt, laird," returned Jeames. "Let's have a look at the article."

The laird took the horse from his pocket, and handed it to him. Jeames regarded it for some time with interest, and examined it with care.

"It's a bonny bit of carved work," he said; "—a childish kind of a thing for shape—more like a wooden horse; but when you come to its ornamentation, it's of another character from the round spots of red paint—and so are the small rubies and stones in it. This has taken a deal of time, and painful labour—a deal more than some of us would think it worth, I expect! It's the way of the heathens with their graven images, but why a horse like this, I don't know. However, that's neither here nor there: you didn't come to me to ask how or why it was made; it's what is it made of that's the question. It's quite yellowish for silver; and it's very black, which is more like it—but that may be with dirt.—And dirt I'm thinking it must be, barked into the graving," he went on, taking a tool and running the point of it along one of the fine lines. "Honestly without testing, I wouldn't like to say what it was. But it's a great weight!—I suspect—na, I more than suspect it can't be silver."

So saying he carried it to his table, put it down, and went to a corner-cupboard. Thence he brought a small stoppered phial. He gave it a little shake, and took out the stopper. It was followed by a dense white fume. With the stopper he touched the horse underneath, and looked closely at the spot. He then replaced the stopper and the bottle, and stood by the cupboard, gazing at nothing for a moment. Then turning to the laird, he said, with a peculiar look and a hesitating expression:

"Na, laird, it's no siller. Aquafortis winna bite upo' 't. I wad mix 't wi' muriatic, an' try that, but I hae nane handy, an' forby it wad tak time to tell. Ken ye whaur it cam frae?—Ae thing I'm sure o'—it's no siller!"

"I'm sorry to hear it," rejoined the laird, with a faint smile and a little sigh.—"Well, we're no worse off than we were, Cosmo!—But poor Grizzie! She'll be dreadfully disappointed.—Gie me the bit horsie, Jeames; we'll e'en tak' him hame again. It's no his fau't, puir thing, 'at he's no better nor he was made!"

"Wad ye no tell me whaur the bit thing cam frae, or is supposit to hae come frae, sir? H'ard ye it ever said, for enstance, 'at the auld captain they tell o' had broucht it?"

"That's what I hae h'ard said," answered the laird.

"Weel, sir," returned Jeames, "gien ye had nae objection, I wad fain mak' oot what the thing *is* made o'."

"It matters little," said the laird, "seein' we ken what it's *no* made o'; but tak' yer wull o' 't, Jeames."

"Sit ye doon than, laird, gien ye hae naething mair pressin', an' see what I mak' o' 't," said the watchmaker, setting him a chair.

"Wullin'ly," replied the laird, "—but I dinna like takin' up yer time."

"Ow, my time's no sae dooms precious! I can aye win throu' wi' my work ohn swatten," said Jeames, with a smile in which mingled a half comical sadness. "An' it wad set me to waur 't better to my ain min' nor servin' yersel', i' the sma'est, sir."

The laird thanked him, and sat down. Cosmo placed himself on a stool beside him.

"Na, laird, it's not silver. Aquafortis won't bite upon it. I would mix it with muriatic, and try that, but I have none handy, and besides it would take time to tell. Do you know where it came from?—One thing I'm sure of—it's not silver!"

"I'm sorry to hear it," rejoined the laird, with a faint smile and a little sigh.—"Well, we're no worse off than we were, Cosmo!—But poor Grizzie! She'll be dreadfully disappointed.—Give me the wee horse, Jeames; we'll just take him home again. It's not his fault, poor thing, that he's no better than he was made!"

"Would you not tell me where the wee thing came from, or is supposed to have come from, sir? Did you ever hear it said, for instance, that the old captain they tell of had brought it?"

"That's what I have heard said," answered the laird.

"Well, sir," returned Jeames, "if you had no objection, I would fain make out what the thing *is* made of."

"It matters little," said the laird, "seeing we know what it's *not* made of; but do what you like with it, Jeames."

"Sit down then, laird, if you have nothing more pressing, and see what I make of it," said the watchmaker, setting him a chair.

"Willingly," replied the laird, "—but I don't like taking up your time."

"Oh, my time's not so very precious! I can always get through with my work without sweating," said Jeames, with a smile in which mingled a half comical sadness. "And it would puzzle me to spend it better to my own mind than serving yourself, in the smallest matter, sir."

The laird thanked him, and sat down. Cosmo placed himself on a stool beside him.

"I hae naething upo' han' the day," Jeames Merson went on, "but a watch o' Jeames Gracie's, up at the Know—ane o' yer ain fowk, laird. He tells me it was your gran'father, sir, gied it til his gran'father. It 's a queer kin' o' a thing—some complicat; an' whiles it's 'maist ower muckle for me. Ye see auld age is aboot the warst disease horses an' watches can be taen wi': there's sae little left to come an' gang upo'!"

While the homely assayer thus spoke, he was making his preparations.

"What for no men as weel 's horses an' watches?" suggested the laird.

"I wadna meddle wi' men. I lea' them to the doctors an' the ministers," replied Jeames, with another wide, silent laugh.

"I have nothing on hand today," Jeames Merson went on, "but a watch of Jeames Gracie's, up at the Know (Hilltop)—one of your own folk, laird. He tells me it was your grandfather, sir, gave it to his grandfather. It's a queer kind of thing—quite complicated; and sometimes it's almost too much for me. You see old age is about the worst disease horses and watches can be taken with: there's so little left to come and go upon!"

While the homely assayer thus spoke, he was making his preparations.

"Why not men as well as horses and watches?" suggested the laird.

"I wouldn't meddle with men. I leave them to the doctors and the ministers," replied Jeames, with another wide, silent laugh.

By this time he had got a pair of scales carefully adjusted, a small tin vessel in one of them, and balancing weights in the other. Then he went to the rack over the dresser, and mildly lamenting his wife's absence and his own inability to lay his hand on the precise vessels he wanted, brought thence a dish and a basin. The dish he placed on the table with the basin in it and filled the latter with water to the very brim. He then took the horse, placed it gently in the basin, which was large enough to receive it entirely, and set basin and horse aside. Taking then the dish into which the water had overflowed, he poured its contents into the tin vessel in the one scale, and added weights to the opposite until they balanced each other, upon which he made a note with a piece of chalk on the table. Next, he removed everything from the scales, took the horse, wiped it in his apron, and weighed it carefully. That done, he sat down, and leaning back in his chair, seemed to his visitors to be making a calculation, only the conjecture did not quite fit the strange, inscrutable expression of his countenance. The laird began to think he must be one of those who delight to plaster knowledge with mystery.

"Weel, laird," said Jeames at length, "the weicht o' what ye hae laid upo' me, maks me doobtfu' whaur nae doobt sud be. But I'm b'un' to say, ootside the risk o' some mistak, o' the gr'un's o' which I can ken naething, for else I wadna hae made it, 'at this bit horsie o' yours, by a' 'at my knowledge or skeel, which is neither o' them muckle, can tell me—this bit horsie—an' gien it binna as I say, I cannot see what for it sudna be sae—only, ye see, laird, whan we think we ken a'thing, there's a heap ahint oor *a'thing;* an' feow ken better, at least feow hae a richt to ken better, nor I du mysel', what a puir cratur is man, an hoo liable to mak mistaks, e'en whan he's duin' his best to be i' the richt; an for oucht 'at I ken, there may hae been grit discoveries made, ohn ever come to my hearin', 'at upsets a'thing I ever was gien to

"Well, laird," said Jeames at length, "the weight of what you have laid upon me, makes me doubtful where no doubt should be. But I'm bound to say, outside the risk of some mistake, of the grounds of which I can know nothing, for else I wouldn't have made it, that this wee horse of yours, by all that my knowledge or skill, which is neither of them much, can tell me—this wee horse—and if it be not as I say, I cannot see why it shouldn't be so—only, you see, laird, when we think we know all, there's a heap behind our *all;* and few know better, at least few have a right to know better, than I do myself, what a poor creature is man, and how liable to make mistakes, even when he's doing his best to be in the right; and for anything I know, there may have been great discoveries made, without me ever hearing them, that tak, an' haud by for true; an' yet I daurna withhaud the conclusion I'm driven til, for maybe whiles the hert o' man may gang the wrang gait by bein' ower wise in its ain conceit o' expeckin' ower little, jist as weel's in expeckin' ower muckle, an' sae I'm b'un' to tell ye, laird, 'at yer expectations frae this knot o' metal,—for metal we maun alloo it to be, whatever else it be or bena—yer expectations, I say, are a'thegither wrang, for it's no more siller nor my wife's kitchie-poker."

"Weel, man!" said the laird, with a laugh that had in it just a touch of scorn, "gien the thing be sae plain, what gars ye gang that gait aboot the buss to say't? Du ye tak me and Cosmo here for bairns 'at wad fa' a greetin' gien ye tellt them their ba-lamb wasna a leevin' ane—naething but a fussock o' cotton—oo', rowed roon' a bit stick? We're neither o' 's complimentit.—Come, Cosmo.—I'm nane the less obleeged to ye, Jeames," he added as he rose, "though I cud weel wuss yer opignon had been sic as wad hae pitten 't i' my pooer to offer ye a fee for 't."

"The less said aboot that the better, laird!" replied Jeames with imperturbability, and his large, silent smile; "the trowth's the trowth, whether it's paid for or no. But afore ye gang it's but fair to tell ye—only I wadna like to be hauden ower strickly accountable for the opignon, seein' it's no my profession, as they ca' 't, but I hae dune my best, an gien I be i' the wrang, I neither hae nor had ony ill design intil 't.—"

"Bless my soul!" cried the laird, with more impatience than Cosmo had ever seen him show, "is the man mad, or does he take me for a fool?"

"There's some things, laird," resumed Jeames, "that hae to be approcht oontil, wi' circumspection an' a proaper regaird to the impression they may mak. Noo, disclaimin' ony desire to luik like an ill-bred scoon'rel, whilk I wad rather luik to onybody nor to yersel', laird, I venture to jaloose 'at maybe the matter o' a feow poun's micht be o' some consequence to ye—"

upset all I was ever given to take, and hold by for true; and yet I daren't withhold the conclusion I'm driven to, for maybe sometimes the heart of man may go wrong by being over wise in its own conceit of expecting too little, just as well as in expecting too much, and so I'm bound to tell you, laird, that your expectations from this knot of metal,—for metal we must allow it to be, what ever else it is or is not—your expectations, I say, are altogether wrong, for it's no more silver than my wife's kitchen poker."

"Well, man!" said the laird, with a laugh that had in it just a touch of scorn, "if the thing be so plain, what makes you go that way about the bush to say it? Do you take me and Cosmo here for children that would fall a crying if you told them their ba-lamb wasn't a living one—nothing but a bundle of cotton wool, rolled round a stick? We're neither of us complimented.—Come, Cosmo.—I'm none the less obliged to you, Jeames," he added as he rose, "though I could well wish your opinion had been such as would have put it in my power to offer you a fee for it."

"The less said about that the better, laird!" replied Jeames with imperturbability, and his large, silent smile; "the truth's the truth, whether it's paid for or not. But before you go, it's but fair to tell you—only I wouldn't like to be held too strictly accountable for the opinion, seeing it's not my profession, as they call it, but I have done my best, and if I be in the wrong, I neither have nor had any ill design in it.—"

"Bless my soul!" cried the laird, with more impatience than Cosmo had ever seen him show, "is the man mad, or does he take me for a fool?"

"There's some things, laird," resumed Jeames, "that have to be approached, with circumspection and a proper regard to the impression they may make. Now, disclaiming any desire to look like an ill-bred scoundrel, which I would rather look to anybody than to yourself, laird, I venture to suspect that maybe the matter of a few pounds might be of some consequence to you—"

"Ilka fule i' the country kens that 'at kens Glenwarlock," interrupted the laird, and turned hastily. "Come, Cosmo."

Cosmo went to open the door, troubled to see his father annoyed with the unintelligibility of the man.

"Weel, gien ye *wull* gang," said Jeames, "I maun jist tak my life i' my han', an'—"

"Hoot, man! tak yer tongue i' yer teeth; it'll be mair to the purpose," cried the laird laughing, for he had got over his ill humour already. "My life i' my han', quo' he!—Man, I haena carriet a dirk this mony a day! I laid it aff wi' the kilt."

"Weel, it micht be the better 'at ye hadna, gien ye binna gaein hame afore nicht, for I saw some cairds o' the ro'd the day.—Ance mair, gien ye wad but hearken til ane 'at confesses he oucht to ken, even sud he be i' the wrang, I tell ye that horsie is *not* siller—na, nor naething like it."

"Plague take the man!—what is it, then?" cried the laird.

"What for didna ye speir that at me afore?" rejoined Jeames. "It wad hae gien me leeberty to tell ye—to the best o' my abeelity that is. Whan I'm no cocksure—an' it's ower muckle a thing to be cocksure aboot—I wadna volunteer onything. I wadna say naething till I was adjured like an evil speerit."

"Weel," quoth the laird, entering now into the humour of the thing, "herewith I adjure thee, thou contrairy and inarticulate speerit, that thou tell me whereof and of what substance this same toy-horse is composed, manufactured, or made up."

"Toy here, toy there!" returned Jeames; "sae far as ony cawpabeelity o' mine, or ony puir skeel I hae, will alloo o' testimony—though min' ye, laird, I winna tak the consequences o' bein' i' the wrang—though I wad rather tak them, an' ower again, nor be i' the wrang,—"

"Every fool in the country knows that that knows Glenwarlock," interrupted the laird, and turned hastily. "Come, Cosmo."

Cosmo went to open the door, troubled to see his father annoyed with the unintelligibility of the man.

"Well, if you *will* go," said Jeames, "I must just take my life in my hand, and—"

"Heavens, man! take your tongue in your teeth; it'll be more to the purpose," cried the laird laughing, for he had got over his ill humour already. "My life in my hand, said he!—Man, I haven't carried a dirk[6] this many a day! I laid it off with the kilt."

"Well, it might be the better if you hadn't, if you're not going home before night, for I saw some tinkers on the road today.—Once more, if you would but listen to one that confesses he ought to know, even should he be in the wrong, I tell you that horse is *not* silver—na, nor anything like it."

"Plague take the man!—what is it, then?" cried the laird.

"Why didn't you ask me that before?" rejoined Jeames. "It would have given me liberty to tell you—to the best of my ability that is. When I'm not cocksure—and it's too great a thing to be cocksure about—I wouldn't volunteer anything. I wouldn't say anything till I was adjured like an evil spirit."

"Well," quoth the laird, entering now into the humour of the thing, "herewith I adjure thee, thou contrary and inarticulate spirit, that thou tell me whereof and of what substance this same toy-horse is composed, manufactured, or made up."

"Toy here, toy there!" returned Jeames; "so far as any capability of mine, or any poor skill I have, will allow of testimony—though remember, laird, I won't take the consequences of being in the wrong—though I would rather take them, and over again, than be in the wrong,—"

The laird turned and went out, followed by Cosmo. He began to think the man must have lost his reason. But when the watchmaker saw them walking steadily along the street in the direction of home, he darted out of the door and ran after them.

"Gien ye *wad* gang, laird," he said, in an injured tone, "ye micht hae jist latten me en' the sentence I had begun!"

"If you *would* go, laird," he said, in an injured tone, "you might have just let me end the sentence I had begun!"

"There's nae en' to ony o' yer sentences, man!" said the laird; "that's the only thing i' them 'at was forgotten, 'cep' it was the sense."

"There's no end to any of your sentences, man!" said the laird; "that's the only thing in them that was forgotten, except it was the sense."

"Weel, guid day to ye, laird!" returned Jeames. "Only," he added, drawing a step nearer, and speaking in a subdued confidential voice, "dinna lat yer horsie rin awa' upo' the r'od hame, for I sweir til ye, gien there be ony trowth i' the laws o' natur, he's no siller, nor onything like it—"

"Well, good day to you, laird!" returned Jeames. "Only," he added, drawing a step nearer, and speaking in a subdued confidential voice, "don't let your horse run away upon the road home, for I swear to you, if there be any truth in the laws of nature, he's not silver, nor anything like it—"

"Hoots!" said the laird, and turning away, walked off with great strides.

"Heavens!" said the laird, and turning away, walked off with great strides.

"But," the watchmaker continued, almost running to keep up with him, and speaking in a low, harsh, hurried voice, as if thrusting the words into his ears, "naither mair nor less nor solid gowd—pure gowd, no a grain o' alloy!"

"But," the watchmaker continued, almost running to keep up with him, and speaking in a low, harsh, hurried voice, as if thrusting the words into his ears, "neither more nor less than solid gold—pure gold, not a grain of alloy!"

That said, he turned, went back at the same speed, shot himself into his cottage, and closed the door.

The father and son stopped, and looked at each other for a moment. Then the laird walked slowly on. After a minute or two, Cosmo glanced up in his face, but his father did not return the glance and the boy saw that he was talking to another. By and by he heard him murmur to himself, "The gifts of God are without repentance."

Not a word passed between them as they went home, though all the time it seemed to both father and son that they were holding closest converse. The moment they reached the castle, the laird went to his room—to the closet where his few books lay, and got out a volume of an old cyclopaedia, where he read all he could find about gold. Thence descending to the kitchen, he rummaged out a rusty old pair of scales, and with their help arrived at the conclusion that the horse weighed about three pounds avoirdupois: it might be worth about a hundred and fifty pounds. Ready money, this was a treasure in the eyes of one whose hand had seldom indeed closed upon more than ten pounds at once. Here was large provision for the four years of his boy's college life! Nor was the margin it would leave for his creditors by any means too small for consideration! It is true the golden horse, hoofs, and skin, and hair of jewels, could do but little towards the carting away of the barrow of debt that crushed Glenwarlock; but not the less was it a heavenly messenger of good will to the laird. There are who are so pitiful over the poor man, that, finding they cannot lift him beyond the reach of the providence which intends there shall always be the poor on the earth, will do for him nothing at all.

"Where is the use?" they say. They treat their money like their children, and would not send it into a sad house. If they had themselves no joys but their permanent ones, where would the hearts of them be? Can such have a notion of the relief, the glad rebound of the heart of the poor man, the inburst of light, the re-creation of the world, when help, however temporary, reaches him? A man like the laird of Glenwarlock, capable of a large outlook, one that reaches beyond the wide-spread skirts of his poverty, sees in it an arc of the mighty rainbow that circles the world, a well in the desert he is crossing to the pastures of red kine and wooly sheep. It is to him a foretaste of the final deliverance. While the rich giver is saying "Poor fellow, he will be just as bad next month again!" the poor fellow is breathing the airs of paradise, reaping more joy of life in half a day than his benefactor in half a year, for help is a quick seed and of rapid growth, and burgeons in a moment into the infinite aeons. Everything in this world is but temporary: why should temporary help be undervalued? Would you not pull out a drowning bather because he will bathe again tomorrow? The only question is—*does it help?* Jonah might grumble at the withering of his gourd, but if it had not grown at all, would he ever have preached to Nineveh? It set the laird on a Pisgah-rock, whence he gazed into the promised land.

The rich, so far as money-needs are concerned, live under a cloudless sky of summer—dreary rather and shallow, it seems to me, however lovely its blue light; when for the poor man a breach is made through a vaporous firmament, he sees deeper into the blue because of the framing clouds—sees up to worlds invisible in the broad glare. I know not how the born-rich, still less those who have given themselves with success to the making of money, can learn that God is the all in all of men, for this world's needs as well as for the eternal needs. I know they may learn it, for the Lord has said that God can even teach the rich, and I have known of them who seemed to know it as well as any poor man; but speaking generally, the rich have not the same opportunity of knowing God—nor the same conscious need of him—that the poor man has. And when, after a few years, all, so far as things to have and to hold are concerned, are alike poor, and all, as far as any need of them is concerned, are alike rich, the advantage will all be on the side of such as, neither having nor needing, do not desire them. In the meantime, the rich man who, without pitying his friend that he is not rich also, cheerfully helps him over a stone where he cannot carry him up the hill of his difficulty, rejoicing to do for him what God allows, is like God himself, the great lover of his children, who gives a man infinitely, though he will not take from him his suffering until strength is perfected in his weakness.

The laird called Cosmo, and they went out together for a walk in the fields, where they might commune in quiet. There they talked over the calculation the laird had made of the probable worth of the horse; and the father, unlike most prudent men, did not think it necessary to warn his son against too sure an expectation, and so prepare him for the consequence of a possible mistake; he did not imagine that disappointment, like the small-pox, required the vaccination of apprehension—that a man, lest he should be more miserable afterwards, must make himself miserable now. In matters of hope as well as fear, he judged the morrow must look after itself; believed the God who to-day is alive in to-morrow, looks after our affairs there where we cannot be. I am far from sure that the best preparation for a disappointment is not the hope that precedes it.

Friends, let us hold by our hopes. All colours are shreds of the rainbow. There is a rainbow of the cataract, of the paddle-wheel, of the falling wave: none of them is the rainbow, yet they are all of it; and if they vanish, so does the first, the arch-rainbow, the bow set in the cloud, while that which set it there, and will set it again, vanishes never. All things here pass; yet say not they are but hopes. It is because they are not the thing hoped for that they are precious—the very opals of the soul. By our hopes are we saved. There is many a thing we could do better without than the hope of it, for our hopes ever point beyond the thing hoped for. The bow is the damask flower on the woven tear-drops of the world; hope is the shimmer on the dingy warp of the trouble shot with the golden woof of God's intent. Nothing almost sees miracles but misery. Cosmo never forgot that walk in the fields with his father. When the money was long gone after the melted horse, that hour spent chiefly amongst the great *horse-gowans* that adorned the thin soil of one of the few fields yet in some poor sense their own, remained with him—to be his forever—a portion of the inheritance of the meek. The joy had brought their hearts yet closer to each other, for one of the lovelinesses of true love is that it may and must always be more. In a gravelly hollow, around which rose hillocks, heaped by far off tides in times afar, they knelt together on the thin grass, among the ox-eyes, and gave God thanks for the golden horse on which Cosmo was to ride to the temple of knowledge.

After, they sat a long time talking over the strange thing. All these years had the lump of gold been lying in the house, ready for their great need! For what was lands, or family, or ancient name, to the learning that opens doors, the hand-maiden of the understanding, which is the servant of wisdom, who reads in the heart of him who made the heaven and the earth and the sea and the fountains of water and the conscience of man! Then they began to imagine together how the thing had come to pass. It could hardly be that the old captain did not know what a thing he gave! Doubtless he had intended sometime, perhaps in the knowledge of approaching death, to say something concerning it, and in the meantime, probably, with cunning for its better safety, had treated it as a thing of value, but of value comparatively slight! How had it come into existence, they next asked each other. Either it had belonged to some wealthy prince, they concluded, or the old captain had got it made for himself, as a convenient shape in which to carry with him, if not ready money, yet available wealth. Cosmo suggested that possibly, for better concealment, it had been silvered; and the laird afterwards learned from the jeweller to whom he sold it, that such was indeed the case. I may mention also that its worth exceeded the laird's calculation, chiefly because of the tiny jewels with which it was studded.

Cosmo repeated to his father the rime he had learned from dreaming Grannie, and told him how he heard it that time he lay a night in her house, and what Grannie herself said about it, and now the laird smiled, and now he looked grave; but neither of them saw how to connect the rime with the horse of gold. For one thing, great as was the wealth it brought them, the old captain could hardly have expected it to embolden any one to the degree of arrogance specified. What man would call the king his brother on the strength of a hundred and fifty pounds?

When Grizzie learned the result of her advice, she said "Praise be thankit!" ("Thank Heavens!") and turned away. The next moment Cosmo heard her murmuring to herself,

"Whan the coo loups ower the mune,	"When the cow jumps over the moon,
The reid gowd rains intil men's shune."	The red gold rains into men's shoes."

CHAPTER XXII
THE LUMINOUS NIGHT

That night Cosmo could not sleep. It was a warm summer night, though not yet summer—a soft dewy night, full of genial magic and growth—as if some fire-bergs of summer had drifted away out into the spring, and got melted up in it. He dressed himself, and went out. It was cool, deliciously cool, and damp, but with no shiver. The stars were bright-eyed as if they had been weeping, and were so joyously consoled that they forgot to wipe away their tears. They were bright but not clear—large and shimmering, as if reflected from some invisible sea, not immediately present to his eyes. The gulfs in which they floated were black-blue with profundity. There was no moon, but the night was yet so far from dark, that it seemed conscious throughout of some distant light that illumined it without shine. And his heart felt like the night, as if it held a deeper life than he could ever know. He wandered on till he came to the field where he had so lately been with his father. He was not thinking; any effort would break the world-mirror in which he moved! For the moment he would be but a human plant, gathering comfort from the soft coolness and the dew, when the sun had ceased his demands. The coolness and the dew sank into him, and made his soul long for the thing that waits the asking. He came to the spot where his father and he had prayed together, and there kneeling lifted up his face to the stars. Oh, mighty, only church! whose roof is a vaulted infinitude! whose lights come burning from the heart of the Maker! church of all churches—where the Son of Man prayed! In the narrow temple of Herod he taught the people, and from it drove the dishonest traders; but here, under the starry roof, was his house of prayer! church where not a mark is to be seen of human hand! church that is all church, and nothing but church, built without hands, despised and desecrated through unbelief! church of God's building! thou alone in thy grandeur art fitting type of a yet greater, a yet holier church, whose stars are the burning eyes of unutterable, self-forgetting love, whose worship is a ceaseless ministration of self-forgetting deeds—the one real ideal church, the body of the living Christ, built of the hearts and souls of men and women of every nation and every creed, through all time and over all the world, redeemed alike from Judaism, paganism, and all the false Christianities that darken and dishonour the true.

Cosmo, I say, knelt, and looked up. Then will awoke, and he lifted up his heart, sending aloft his soul on every holy sail it could spread, on all the wings it could put forth, as if, through the visible, he would force his way to the invisible.

Softly through the blue night came a gentle call:

He started, not with fear, looked round, but saw no one.

"Cosmo!" came the call again.

The sky was shining with the stars, and that other light that might be its own; other than the stars and the sky he saw nothing. He looked all round his narrow horizon, the edge of the hollow between him and the sky, where the heaven and the earth met among the stars and the grass, and the stars shimmered like glow-worms among the thin stalks: nothing was there; its edge was unbroken by other shape than grass, daisies, ox-eyes and stars. A soft dreamy wind came over the edge, and breathed once on his cheek. The voice came again—

"Cosmo!"

It seemed to come from far away, so soft and gentle was it, and yet it seemed near.

"It has called me three times!" said Cosmo, and rose to his feet.

There was the head of Simon Peter, as some called him, rising like a dark sun over the top of the hollow! In the faint light Cosmo knew him at once, gave a cry of pleasure, and ran to meet him.

"You called so softly," said Cosmo, "I did not know your voice."

"And you are disappointed! You thought it was a voice from some region beyond this world! I am sorry. I called softly, because I wanted to let you know I was coming, and was afraid of startling you."

"I confess," replied Cosmo, "a little hope was beginning to flutter, that perhaps I was called from somewhere in the unseen—like Samuel, you know; but I was too glad to see you to be much disappointed. I do sometimes wonder though, that, if there is such a world beyond as we sometimes talk about, there should be so little communication between it and us. When I am out in the still time of this world, and there is nothing to interfere,—when I am not even thinking, so as to close my doors, why should never anything come? Never in my life have I had one whisper from that world."

"You are saying a great deal more than you can possibly know, Cosmo," answered Mr. Simon. "You have had no communication recognized by you as such, I grant. And I, who am so much older than you, must say the same. If there be any special fitness in the night, in its absorbing dimness, and isolating silence, for such communication—and who can well doubt it?—I have put myself in the heart of it a thousand times, when, longing after an open vision, I should have counted but the glimpse of a ghostly garment the mightiest boon, but never therefrom has the shadow of a feather fallen upon me. Yet here I am, hoping no less, and believing no less! The air around me may be full of ghosts—I do not know; I delight to think they may somehow be with us, for all they are so unseen; but so long as I am able to believe and hope in the one great ghost, the Holy Ghost that fills all, it would trouble me little to learn that betwixt me and the visible centre was nothing but what the senses of men may take account of. If there be a God, he is all in all, and filleth all things, and all is well. What matter where the region of the dead may be? Nowhere but here are they called the dead. When, of all paths, that to God is alone always open, and alone can lead the wayfarer to the end of his journey, why should I stop to peer through the fence either side of that path? If he does not care to reveal, is it well I should make haste to know? I shall know one day, why should I be eager to know now?"

"But why might not something show itself once—just for once, if only to give one a start in the right direction?" said Cosmo.

"I will tell you one reason," returned Mr. Simon, "—the same why everything is as it is, and neither this nor that other way—namely, that it is best for us it should be as it is. But I think I can see a little way into it. Suppose you saw something strange—a sign or a wonder—one of two things, it seems to me likely, would follow:—you would either doubt it the moment it had vanished, or it would grow to you as one of the common things of your daily life—which are indeed in themselves equally wonderful. Evidently, if visions would make us sure, God does not care about the kind of sureness they can give, or for our being made sure in that way. A thing that, gained in one way, might be of less than no value to us, gained in another, might, as a vital part of the process, be invaluable. God will have us sure of a thing by knowing the heart whence it comes; that is the only worthy assurance. To know, he will have us go in at the great door of obedient faith; and if anybody thinks he has found a back-stair, he will find it land him at a doorless wall. It is the assurance that comes of inmost beholding of himself, of seeing what he is, that God cares to produce in us. Nor would he have us think we know him before we do, for thereby thousands walk in a vain show. At the same time I am free to imagine if I imagine holily—that is, as his child. And I imagine space full of life invisible; imagine that the young man needed but the opening of his eyes to see the horses and chariots of fire around his master, an inner circle to the horses and chariots that encompassed the city to take him. As I came now through the fields, I lost myself for a time in the feeling that I was walking in the midst of lovely people I have known, some in person, some by their books. Perhaps they were with me—are with me—are speaking to me now. For if all our thoughts, from whatever source, whether immediately from God, or through ourselves, seem to enter the chamber of our consciousness by the same door, why may it not be so with some that come to us from other beings? Why may not the dead speak to me, and I be unable to distinguish their words from my thoughts? The moment a thought is given me, my own thought rushes to mingle with it, and I can no more part them. Some stray hints from the world beyond may mingle even with the folly and stupidity of my dreams."

"But if you cannot distinguish, where is the good?" Cosmo ventured to ask.

"Nowhere for deductive certainty. Nor, if the things themselves are not worth remembering, or worthy of influencing us, is there any good in enquiring concerning them. Shall I mind a thing that is not worth minding, because it came to me in a dream or was told me by a ghost? It is the quality of a thing, not how it arrived, that is the point. But true things are often mingled with things grotesque. For aught I know, at one and the same time, a spirit may be taking advantage of the door set ajar by sleep, to whisper a message of love or repentance, and the troubled brain or heart or stomach may be sending forth fumes that cloud the vision, and cause evil echoes to mingle with the hearing. When you look at any bright thing for a time, and then close your eyes, you still see the shape of it, but in different colours. This figure has come to you from the outside world, but the brain has altered it. Even the shape itself is reproduced with but partial accuracy: some imperfection in the recipient sense, or in the receptacle, sends imperfection into the presentation. In a way something similar may our contact with the dwellers beyond fare in our dreams. My unknown mother may be talking to me in my sleep, and up rises some responsive but stupid dream-cloud of my own, and mingles with and ruins the descended grace. But it is well to remind you again that the things around us are just as full of marvel as those into which you are so anxious to look. Our people in the other world, although they have proved these earthly things before, probably now feel them strange, and full of a marvel the things about them have lost. All is well. The only thing worth a man's care is the will of God, and that will is the same whether in this world or in the next. That will has made this world ours, not the next; for nothing can be ours until God has given it to us. Curiosity is but the contemptible human shadow of the holy thing wonder. No, my son, let us make the best we can of this life, that we may become able to make the best of the next also."

"And how make the best of this?" asked Cosmo.

"Simply by falling in with God's design in the making of you. That design must be worked out—cannot be worked out without you. You must walk in the front of things with the will of God—not be dragged in the sweep of his garment that makes the storm behind him! To walk with God is to go hand in hand with him, like a boy with his father. Then, as to the other world, or any world, as to the past sorrow, the vanished joy, the coming fear, all is well; for the design of the making, the loving, the pitiful, the beautiful God, is marching on towards divine completion, that is, a never ending one. Yea, if it please my sire that his infinite be awful to me, yet will I face it, for it is his. Let your prayer, my son, be like this: 'O maker of me, go on making me, and let me help thee. Come, Father! here I am; let us go on. I know that my words are those of a child, but it is thy child who prays to thee. It is thy dark I walk in; it is thy hand I hold.'"

The words of his teacher sank into the heart of Cosmo, for his spirit was already in the lofty condition of capacity for receiving wisdom direct from another. It is a lofty condition, and they who scorn it but show they have not reached it—nor are likely to reach it soon. Such as will not be taught through eye or ear, must be taught through the skin, and that is generally a long as well as a painful process. All Cosmo's superiority came of his having faith in those who were higher than he. True, he had not yet been tried; but the trials of a pure, honest, teachable youth, must, however severe, be very different from those of one unteachable. The former are for growth, the latter for change.

CHAPTER XXIII
AT COLLEGE

The summer and autumn had yet to pass before he left home for the university of the north. He spent them in steady work with Mr. Simon. But the steadier his work, and the greater his enjoyment of it, the dearer was his liberty, and the keener his delight in the world around him. He worked so well that he could afford to dream too; and his excursions and his imaginings alike took wide and wider sweeps; while for both, ever in the near or far distance, lay the harbour, the nest of his home. It drew him even when it lay behind him, and he returned to it as the goal he had set out to seek. It was as if, in every excursion or flight, he had but sought to find his home afresh, to approach it by a new path. But—the wind-fall?—nay, the God-send of the golden horse, gave him such a feeling of wealth and freedom, that he now began to dream in a fresh direction, namely, of things he would do if he were rich; and as he was of a constructive disposition, his fancies in this direction turned chiefly on the enlarging and beautifying of the castle—but always with the impossibility understood of destroying a feature of its ancient dignity and historic worth.

A portion of the early summer he spent in enlarging the garden on the south side, or back of the house. One portion of the ground there seemed to him to have been neglected—the part which lay between the block in which was the kitchen, and that in which was the drawing-room. These stood at right-angles to each other, their gables making two sides of a square. But he found the rock so near the surface, that he could not utilize much of it. This set him planning how the space might be used for building. In the angle, the rock came above ground entirely, and had been made the foundation of a wall connecting the two corners, to defend the court—a thick strong wall of huge stones, that seemed as solid as the rock. He grew fond of the spot, almost forsaking for it his formerly favoured stone, and in the pauses of his gardening would sit with his back against this wall, dreaming of the days to come. Here also he would bring his book, and read or write for hours, sometimes drawing plans of the changes and additions he would make, of the passages and galleries that might be contrived to connect the various portions of the house, and of the restoration of old defences. The whole thing was about as visionary as his dream of Tree-top city, but it exercised his constructive faculty, and exercise is growth, and growth in any direction, if the heart be true, is growth in all directions.

The days glided by. The fervid Summer slid away round the shoulder of the world, and made room for her dignified matron sister; my lady Autumn swept her frayed and discoloured train out of the great hall-door of the world, and old brother Winter, who so assiduously waits upon the house, and cleans its innermost recesses, was creeping around it, biding his time, but eager to get to his work. The day drew near when Cosmo must leave the house of his fathers, the walls that framed almost all his fancies, the home where it was his unchanging dream to spend his life, until he went to his mother in heaven.

I will not follow his intellectual development. The *real* education of the youth is enough for my narrative.

His mind was too much filled with high hopes and lofty judgements, to be tempted like a common nature in the new circumstances in which he found himself. There are not a few who, believing of others as they are themselves, and teaching as they practice, represent the youth of the nation as necessarily vile; but let not the pure thence imagine there is no one pure but himself. There is life in our nation yet, and a future for her yet, none the less that the weak and cowardly and self-indulgent neither enter into the kingdom of God, nor work any salvation in the earth. Cosmo left the university at least as clean as he went to it.

He had few companions. Those whom he liked best could not give him much. They looked up to him far more than he knew, for they had a vague suspicion that he was a genius; but they ministered almost only to his heart. The unworthy amongst his fellow-students scorned him with looks askance, and called him Baby Warlock—for on more than one of them he had literally turned his back when his conversation displeased him. None of them however cared to pick a quarrel with him. The devil finds it easier to persuade fools that there is dignity in the knowledge of evil, and that ignorance of it is contemptible, than to give them courage. Truly, if ignorance is the foundation of any man's goodness, it is not worth the wind that upsets it, but in its mere self, ignorance of evil is a negative good. It is those who do not love good that require to be handed over to evil. The grinders did not care about Cosmo, for neither was he of their sort. Now and then, however, one of them would be mildly startled by a request from him for assistance in some passage, which, because he did not *go in* for what they counted scholarship, they could hardly believe him interested. Cosmo regarded everything from amidst associations of which they had none. In his instinctive reach after life, he assimilated all food that came in his way. His growing life was his sole impulsive after knowledge. And already he saw a glimmer here and there in regions of mathematics from which had never fallen a ray into the corner of an eye of those grinding men. That was because he read books of poetry and philosophy of which they had never heard. For the rest, he passed his examinations creditably, and indeed, in more than one case, with unexpected as unsought distinction. I must mention, however, that he did all his set work first, and thoroughly, before giving himself what he hungered after.

Of society in the city he had no knowledge. Amongst the tradespeople he made one or two acquaintances.

His father had been so much pleased with the jeweller to whom he parted with the golden horse, that he requested Cosmo to call upon him as soon as he was settled. Cosmo found him a dignified old gentleman—none the less of a gentleman, and all the more of a man, that he had in his youth worked with his own hands. He took a liking to Cosmo, and, much pleased with his ready interest in whatever he told him, for Cosmo was never tired of listening to anyone who talked of what he knew, made him acquainted with many things belonging to his trade, and communicated many of his experiences. Indifferent to the opinion of any to whom he had not first learned to look up, nobody ever listened better than Cosmo to any story of human life, however humble. Everybody seemed to him of his own family. The greater was the revulsion of his feeling when he came upon anything false in character or low in behaviour. He was then severe, even to utter breach. Incapable of excusing himself, he was incapable also of excusing others. But though gentleness towards the faults of others is an indispensable fruit of life, it is perhaps well it should be a comparatively late one: there is danger of foreign excuse reacting on home conduct. Excuse ought to be rooted in profoundest obedience, and outgoing love. To say *anything* is too small to matter, is of the devil; to say anything is too great to forgive, is not of God. He who would soonest die to divide evil and his fellows, will be the readiest to make for them all *honest* excuse.

Cosmo liked best to hear Mr. Burns talk about precious stones. There he was great, for he had a passion for them, and Cosmo was more than ready to be infected with it. By the hour together would he discourse of them; now on the different and comparative merits of individual stones which had at one time and another passed through his hands, and on the way they were cut, or ought to have been cut; now on the conditions of size, shape, and water, as indicating the special best way of cutting them; now on the various settings, as bringing out the qualities of different kinds and differing stones.

One day he came upon the subject of the weather in relation to stones: on such a sort of day you ought to buy this or that kind of stone; on such another you must avoid buying this or that kind, and seek rather to sell.

To study hard – constantly

Up to this moment, and the mention of this last point, Cosmo had believed Mr. Burns an immaculate tradesman, but here the human gem was turned at that angle to the light which revealed the flaw in it. There are tradesmen not a few, irreproachable in regard to money, who are not so in regard to the quality of their wares in relation to the price: they take and do not give the advantage of their superior knowledge; and well can I imagine how such a one will laugh at the idea that he ought not: to him every customer is more or less of a pigeon.

"If I could but buy plenty of such sapphires," said Mr. Burns, "on a foggy afternoon like this, when the air is yellow as a cairngorm, and sell them the first summer-like day of spring, I should make a fortune in a very few years."

"But you wouldn't do it, Mr. Burns?" Cosmo ventured to suggest, in some foreboding anxiety, caused by the tone in which the man had spoken: he would fain have an express repudiation of the advantage thus to be obtained.

"Why not?" rejoined Mr. Burns, lifting his keen gray eyes, with some wonder in them, and looking Cosmo straight in the face. His mind also was crossed by a painful doubt: was the young man a mere innocent? Was he *"no a' there?"* ("not all there")

"Because it is not honest," replied Cosmo.

"Not honest!" exclaimed the jeweller, in a tone loud with anger, and deep with a sense of injury—whether at the idea that he should be capable of a dishonest thing, or at the possibility of having, for honesty's sake, to yield a money-making principle, I do not know; "I present the thing as it is, and leave my customer to judge according to his knowledge. Is mine to be worth nothing to me? There is no deception in the affair. A jeweller's business is not like a horse-dealer's. The stone is as God made it, and the day is as God made it, only my knowledge enables me to use both to better purpose than my neighbour can."

"Then a man's knowledge is for himself alone—for his own behoof exclusively—not for the common advantage of himself and his neighbour?" said Cosmo.

"Mine is so far for my neighbour, that I never offer him a stone that is not all I say it is. He gets the advantage of his knowledge, let us say, in selling me wine, which he understands to fit my taste with; and I get the advantage of my knowledge in selling him the ring that pleases him. Both are satisfied. Neither asks the other what he paid for this or that. But why make any bones about it; the first acknowledged principle in business is, to buy in the cheapest market and sell in the dearest."

"Where does the love of your neighbour come in then?"

"That has nothing to do with business; it belongs to the relations of social life. No command must be interpreted so as to make it impossible to obey it. Business would come to a stand-still—no man could make a fortune that way."

"You think then that what we are sent here for is to make a fortune?"

"Most people do. I don't know about *sent for.* That's what, I fancy, I find myself behind this counter for. Anyhow the world would hardly go on upon any other supposition."

"Then the world had better stop. It wasn't worth making," said Cosmo.

"Young man," rejoined Mr. Burns, "if you are going to speak blasphemy, it shall not be on my premises."

Bewildered and unhappy, Cosmo turned away, left the shop, and for years never entered it again.

Mr. Burns had been scrupulous to half a grain in giving Mr. Warlock the full value of his gold and of his stones. Nor was this because of the liking he had taken to the old gentleman. There are not a few who will be carefully honest, to a greater or less compass, with persons they like, but leave those they do not like to protect themselves. But Mr. Burns was not of their sort. His interest in the laird, and his wounded liking for Cosmo, did, however, cause him to take some real concern in the moral condition of the latter; while, at the same time, he was willing enough to think evil of him who had denounced as dishonest one of his main principles in the conduct of affairs. It but added venom to the sting of Cosmo's words that although the jeweller was scarcely yet conscious of the fact, he was more unwilling to regard as wrong the mode he had defended, than capable of justifying it to himself. That same evening he wrote to the laird that he feared his son must have taken to keeping bad company, for he had that day spoken in his shop in a manner most irreverent and indeed wicked—so as he would never, he was certain, have dared to speak in his father's hearing. But college was a terrible place for ruining the good principles learned at home. He hoped Mr. Warlock would excuse the interest he took in his son's welfare. Nothing was more sad than to see the seed of the righteous turning from the path of righteousness—and so on.

The laird made reply that he was obliged to Mr. Burns for his communication and the interest he took in his boy, but could only believe there had been some mistake, for it was impossible his boy should have been guilty of anything to which his father would apply the epithets used by Mr. Burns. And so little did the thing trouble the laird, that he never troubled Cosmo with a word on the matter—only, when he came home, asked him what it meant.

But in after days Cosmo repented of having so completely dropped the old gentleman's acquaintance; he was under obligation to him; and if a man will have to do only with the perfect, he must needs cut himself first, and go out of the world. He had learned a good deal from him, but nothing of art: his settings were good, but of the commonest ideas. In the kingdom of heaven tradesmen will be teachers, but on earth it is their business to make fortunes! But a stone, its colour, light, quality, he enjoyed like a poet. Many with a child's delight in pure colours, have no feeling for the melodies of their arrangement, or the harmonies of their mingling. So are there some capable of delight in a single musical tone, who have but little reception for melody or complicate harmony. Whether a condition analogical might not be found in the moral world, and contribute to the explanation of such as Mr. Burns, I may not now inquire.

The very rainbow was lovelier to Cosmo after learning some of the secrets of precious stones. Their study served also his metaphysico-poetic nature, by rousing questions of the relations between beauty fixed and beauty evanescent; between the beauty of stones and the beauty of flowers; between the beauties of art, and the beauties of sunsets and faces. He saw that where life entered, it brought greater beauty, with evanescence and reproduction,—an endless fountain flow and fall. Many were the strange, gladsome, hopeful, corrective thoughts born in him of the gems in Mr. Burns's shop, and he owed the reform much to the man whose friendship he had cast from him. For every question is a door-handle.

Cosmo lived as simply as at home—in some respects more hardly, costing a sum for his maintenance incredibly small. Some may hint that the education was on a par with the expense; and, if education consists in the amount and accuracy of facts learned, and the worth of money in that poor country be taken into the account, the hint might be allowed to pass. But if education is the supply of material to a growing manhood, the education there provided was all a man needed who was man enough to aid his own growth; and for those who have not already reached that point, it is matter of infinite inconsequence what they or their parents find or miss. But I am writing of a period long gone by.

In his second year, willing to ease his father however little, he sought engagements in teaching; and was soon so far successful that he had two hours every day occupied—one with a private pupil, and the other in a public school. The master of that school used afterwards to say that the laird of Glenwarlock had in him the elements of a real teacher. But indeed Cosmo had more teaching power than the master knew, for not in vain had he been the pupil of Peter

Simon—whose perfection stood in this, that he not only taught, but taught to teach. Life is propagation. The perfect thing, from the spirit of God downwards sends itself onward, not its work only, but its life. And in the reaction Cosmo soon found that, for making a man accurate, there is nothing like having to impart what he possesses. He learned more by trying to teach what he thought he knew, than by trying to learn what he was sure he did not know.

In his third year it was yet more necessary he should gain what money he could. For the laird found that his neighbour, Lord Lick-my-loof, had been straining every means in his power to get his liabilities all into his own hands, and had in great part succeeded. The discovery sent a pang to the heart of the laird, for he could hardly doubt his lordship's desire was to foreclose every mortgage, and compel him to yield the last remnant of the possessions of his ancestors. He had refused him James Gracie's cottage, and he would have his castle! But the day was not yet come; and as no one knew what was best for his boy, no one could foretell what would come to pass, or say what deliverance might not be in store for them! The clouds must break somehow, and then there was the sun! So, as a hundred times before, he gathered heart, and went on, doing his best, and trusting his hardest.

The summers at home between the sessions, were times of paradise to Cosmo. Now first he seemed to himself to begin to understand the simple greatness of his father, and appreciate the teaching of Mr. Simon. He seemed to descry the outlines of the bases on which they stood so far above him.

And now the question came up, what was Cosmo to do after he had taken his degree. It was impossible he should remain at home. There was nothing for him to do there, except the work of a farm labourer. That he would have undertaken gladly, had the property been secure, for the sake of being with his father; but the only chance of relieving the land was to take up some profession. The only one he had a leaning to was that of chemistry. This science was at the time beginning to receive so much attention in view of agricultural and manufacturing purposes, that it promised a sure source of income to the man who was borne well in front upon its rising tide. But alas, to this hope, money was yet required! A large sum must yet be spent on education in that direction, before his knowledge would be of money-value, fit for offer in the scientific market! He must go to Germany to Leibig, or to Edinburgh to Gregory! There was no money, and the plan was not, at least for the present, to be entertained. There was nothing left but to go on teaching.

CHAPTER XXIV
A TUTORSHIP

It cannot but be an unpleasant change for a youth, to pass from a house and lands where he is son—ah, how much better than master! and take a subordinate position in another; but the discipline is invaluable. To meet what but for dignity would be humiliation, to do one's work in spite of misunderstanding, and accept one's position thoroughly, intrenching it with recognized duty, is no easy matter. As to how Cosmo stood this ordeal of honesty, I will only say that he never gave up trying to do better.

His great delight and consolation were his father's letters, which he treasured as if they had been a lover's, as indeed they were in a much deeper and truer sense than most love-letters. The two wrote regularly, and shared their best and deepest with each other. The letters also of Mr. Simon did much to uplift him, and enable him to endure and strive.

Nobody knows what the relation of father and son may yet come to. Those who accept the Christian revelation are bound to recognise that there must be in it depths infinite, ages off being fathomed yet. For is it not a reproduction in small of the loftiest mystery in human ken—that of the infinite Father and infinite Son? If man be made in the image of God, then is the human fatherhood and sonship the image of the eternal relation between God and Jesus.

One happy thing was that he had a good deal of time to himself. He set his face against being with the children beyond school hours, telling their parents it would be impossible for him otherwise to do his work with that freshness which was as desirable for them as for him.

The situation his friends of the university had succeeded in finding for him, was in the south of Scotland, almost on the borders. His employers were neither pleasant nor interesting—but more from stupidity than anything worse. Had they had some knowledge of Cosmo's history, they would have taken pains to be agreeable to him, for, having themselves nothing else, they made much of birth and family. But Cosmo had no desire to come nearer where it was impossible to be near, and was content with what they accorded him as a poor student and careful teacher. They lived in the quietest way; for the heir of the house, by a former marriage, was a bad subject, and kept them drained of more than the superfluous money about the place. Cosmo remained with them two years, and during that time did not go home, for so there was the more money to send; but as he entered his third year, he began to feel life growing heavy upon him, and longed unspeakably after his father.

One day, the last of the first quarter, Mr. Baird sent a message, desiring his presence, and with some hesitation and difficulty informed him that, because of certain circumstances over which unhappily he had no control, he was compelled to dispense with his services. He regretted the necessity much, he said, for the children were doing well with him. He would always be glad to hear from him, and know that he was getting on. A little indignant, for his father's sake more than his own, Cosmo remarked that it was customary, he believed, to give a tutor a quarter's notice, which brought the reply, that nothing would please Mr. Baird better than that he should remain another quarter—if it was any convenience to him; but he had had great misfortunes within the last month, and had no choice but beg him to excuse some delay in the payment of his quarter's salary now due. In these circumstances he had thought it the kindest thing to let him look out for another situation.

Hearing this, Cosmo was sorry, and said what he could to make the trouble, so far as he was concerned, weigh lightly. He did not know that what he had fairly earned went to save a rascal from the punishment he deserved—the best thing man could give him. Mr. Baird judged it more for the honour of his family to come between the wicked and his deserts, than to pay the workman his wages. Of that money Cosmo never received a farthing. The worst of it to him was, that he had almost come to the bottom of his purse—had not nearly enough to take him home.

He went to his room in no small perplexity. He could not, would not trouble his father. There are not a few sons, I think, who would be more considerate, were they trusted like Cosmo from the first, and allowed to know thoroughly the circumstances of their parents. The sooner mutual confidence is initiated the better. A servant knocked at the door, and, true to the day, came the expected letter from his father—this time enclosing one from Lady Joan.

The Warlocks and she had never had sight of each other since the dreary day she left them, but they had never lost hearing of each other. Lady Joan retained a lively remembrance of her visit, and to both father and son the occasional letter from her was a rare pleasure. Some impression of the dignity and end of life had been left with Joan from their influences, old man as was the one, and child as was the other; and to the imagination of Cosmo she was still the type of all beauty—such as his boyish eyes had seen her, and his boyish heart received her. But from her letters seemed to issue to the inner ear of the laird a tone of oppression for which they gave him no means of accounting; while she said so little concerning her outward circumstances, hardly ever even alluding to her brother, that he could not but fear things did not go well with her at home. The one he had now sent was even sad, and had so touched his heart, that in his own he suggested the idea of Cosmo's paying her a visit in his coming holidays. It might comfort her a little, he said, to see one who cared so much, though he could do so little for her.

Cosmo jumped up, and paced about the room. What better could he do than go at once! He had not known what to do next, and here was direction! He was much more likely to find a situation in England than in Scotland! And for his travelling expenses, he knew well how to make a little go a great way! He wrote therefore to his father telling him what had occurred, and saying he would go at once. The moment he had dispatched his letter, he set about his preparations. Like a bird the door of whose cage had been opened, he could hardly endure his captivity one instant longer. To write and wait a reply from Joan was simply impossible. He must start the very next morning. Alas, he had no wings either real or symbolic, and must foot it! It would take him days to reach Yorkshire, on the northern border of which she lived, but the idea of such a journey, with such a goal before him, not to mention absolute release from books and boys, was entrancing. To set out free, to walk on and on for days, not knowing what next would appear at any turn of the road—it was like reading a story that came to life as you read it! And then in the last chapter of it to arrive at the loveliest lady in the world, the same whose form and face mingled with his every day-dream—it was a chain of gold with a sapphire at the end of it—a flowery path to the gate of heaven!

That night he took his leave of the family, to start early in the morning. The father and mother were plainly sorry; the children looked grave, and one of them cried. He wrote to Mr. Baird once after, but had no answer—nor ever heard anything of them but that they had to part with everything, and retire into poverty,

It was a lovely spring morning when with his stick and his knapsack he set out, his heart as light as that of the sky-lark that seemed for a long way to accompany him. It was one after another of them that took up the song of his heart and made it audible to his ears. Better convoy in such mood no man could desire. He walked twenty miles that day for a beginning, and slept in a little village, whose cocks that woke him in the morning seemed all to have throats of silver, and hearts of golden light. He increased his distance walked every day, and felt as if he could go on so for years.

But before he reached his destination, what people call a misfortune befell him. I do not myself believe there is any misfortune; what men call such is merely the shadow-side of a good.

He had one day passed through a lovely country, and in the evening found himself upon a dreary moorland. As night overtook him, it came on to rain, and grew very cold. He resolved therefore to seek shelter at the first house he came to; and just ere it was quite dark, arrived at some not very inviting abodes on the brow of the descent from the moor, the first of which was an inn. The landlady received him, and made him as comfortable as she could, but as he did not find his quarters to his taste, he rose even earlier than he had intended, and started in a pouring rain. He had paid his bill the night before, intending to break his fast at the first shop where he could buy a loaf.

The clouds were sweeping along in great gray masses, with yellow lights between, and every now and then they would let the sun look out for a moment, and the valley would send up the loveliest smile from sweetest grass or growing corn, all wet with the rain that made it strong for the sun. He saw a river, and bridges, and houses, and in the distance the ugly chimneys of a manufacturing town. Still it rained and still the sun would shine out. He had grown very hungry before at length he reached a tiny hamlet, and in it a cottage with a window that displayed loaves. He went in, took the largest he saw, and was on the point of tearing a great piece out of it, when he thought it would be but polite to pay for it first, and put his hand in his pocket. It was well he did so, for in his pocket was no purse! Either it had been stolen at the inn, or he had lost it on the way. He put down the loaf.

"I am very sorry," he said, "but I find that I have lost my purse."

The woman looked him in the face with keen enquiring eyes; then apparently satisfied with her scrutiny, smiled, and said,

"Ne'er trouble yoursel', sir. Yo can pey mo as yo coom back. Aw hope you 'n lost noan so mich?"

"Not much, but all I had," answered Cosmo. "I am much obliged to you, but I'm not likely ever to be this way again, so I can't accept your kindness. I am sorry to have troubled you, but after all, I have the worst of it," he added, smiling, "for I am very hungry."

As he spoke, he turned away, and had laid his hand on the latch of the door, when the woman spoke again.

"Tak th' loaf," she said; "it'll be aw the same in less than a hunder year."

She spoke crossly, almost angrily. Cosmo seemed to himself to understand her entirely. Had she looked well-to-do, he would have taken the loaf, promising to send the money; but he could not bring himself to trouble the thoughts of a poor woman, possibly with a large family, to whom the price of such a loaf must be of no small consequence. He thanked her again, but shook his head. The woman looked more angry than before: having constrained herself to give, it was hard to be refused.

"Yo micht tak what's offered yo!" she said.

Cosmo stood thinking: was there any way out of the difficulty? Almost mechanically he began searching his pockets: he had very few *things* either in his pockets or anywhere else. All his fingers encountered was a penknife too old and worn to represent any value, a stump of cedar-pencil, and an ancient family-seal his father had given him when he left home. This last he took out, glanced at it, felt that only the duty of saving his life could make him part with it, put it back, turned once more, said "Good morning," and left the shop.

He had not gone many steps when he heard the shop-bell ring; the woman came running after him. Her eyes were full of tears. What fountain had been opened, I cannot tell; perhaps only that of sympathy with the hungry youth.

"Tak th' loaf," she said again, but in a very different voice this time, and held it out to him. "Dunnot be vexed with a poor woman. Sometimes hoo dunnot knaw wheer to get the bread for her own."

"That's why I wouldn't take it," rejoined Cosmo. "If I had thought you were well off, I would not have hesitated."

"Oh! Aw'm noan so pinched at present," she answered with a smile. "Tak th' loaf, an' welcome, an' pey mo when yo' can."

Cosmo put down her name and address in his pocket-book, and as he took the loaf, kissed the toil-worn hand that gave it him. She uttered a little cry of remonstrance, threw her apron over her head, and went back to the house, sobbing.

The tide rose in Cosmo's heart too, but he left the hamlet eating almost ravenously. Another might have asked himself where dinner was to come from, and spared a portion; but that was not Cosmo's way. He would have given half his loaf to any hungry man he met, but he would not save the half of it in view of a possible need that might never come. Every minute is a to-morrow to the minute that goes before it, and is bound to it by the same duty-roots that make every moment one with eternity; but there is no more occasion to bind minute to minute with the knot-grass of anxiety, than to ruin both to-day and the grand future with the cares of a poor imaginary to-morrow. To-day's duty is the only true provision for to-morrow; and those who are careful about the morrow are but the more likely to bring its troubles upon them by the neglect of duty which care brings. Some say that care for the morrow is what distinguishes the man from the beast; certainly it is one of the many things that distinguish the slave of Nature from the child of God.

Cosmo ate his loaf with as hearty a relish as ever Grizzie's porridge, and that is saying as much for his appetite, if not necessarily for the bread, as words can. He had swallowed it almost before he knew, and felt at first as if he could eat another, but after a drink of water from a well by the road-side, found that he had had enough, and strode on his way, as strong and able as if he had had coffee and eggs and a cutlet, and a dozen things besides.

He was passing the outskirts of the large manufacturing town he had seen in the distance, leaving it on one hand, when he became again aware of the approach of hunger. One of the distinguishing features of Cosmo's character, was a sort of childlike boldness towards his fellow-men; and coming presently to a villa with a smooth-shaven lawn, and seeing a man leaning over the gate that opened from the road, he went up to him and said,

"Do you happen to have anything you want done about the place, sir? I want my dinner and have no money."

The man, one with whom the world seemed to have gone to his wish, looked him all over.

"A fellow like you ought to be ashamed to beg," he said.

"That is precisely what I was not doing," returned Cosmo—"—except as everybody more or less must be a beggar. It is one thing to beg for work, and another to beg for food. I didn't ask you to make a job for me; I asked if there was any work about the place you wanted done. Good morning, sir."

He turned, and the second time that day was stopped as he went.

"I say!—if you can be as sharp with your work as you are with your tongue, I don't care if I give you a job. Look here: my coachman left me in a huff this morning, and it was time too, as I find now he is gone. The stable is in a shocking mess: if you clean it out, and set things to rights—but I don't believe you can—I will give you your dinner."

"Very well, sir," returned Cosmo. "I give you warning I'm very hungry; only on the other hand, I don't care what I have to eat."

"Look here," said the man: "your hands look a precious sight more like loafing than work! I don't believe your work will be worth your dinner."

"Then don't give me any," rejoined Cosmo, laughing. "If the proof of the pudding be in the eating, the proof of the stable must be in the cleaning. Let me see the place."

Much pondering what a fellow scouring the country with a decent coat and no money could be, the dweller in the villa led the way to his stable.

In a mess that stable certainly was.

"The new man is coming this evening," said the man, "and I would rather he didn't see things in such a state. He might think anything good enough after this! The rascal took to drink—and that, young man," he added in a monitory tone, "is the end of all things."

"I'll soon set the place to rights," said Cosmo. "Let's see—where shall I find a graip?"

"A grape? What the deuce do you want with grapes in a stable?"

"I forgot where I was, sir," answered Cosmo, laughing. "I am a Scotchman, and so I call things by old-fashioned names. That is what we call a three or four-pronged fork in my country. The word comes from the same root as the German *greifen,* and our own *grip,* and *gripe,* and *grope,* and *grab*—and *grub* too!" he added, "which in the present case is significant."

"Oh, you are a scholar—are you? Then you are either a Scotch gardener on the tramp after a situation, or a young gentleman who has made a bad use of his priviliges!"

"Do you found that conclusion on my having no money, or on my readiness to do the first honest piece of work that comes to my hand?" asked Cosmo, who having lighted on a tool to serve his purpose, was already at work. "—But never mind! Here goes for a clean stable and a good dinner."

"How do you know your dinner will be good?"

"Because I am so ready for it."

"If you're so sharp-set, I don't mind letting you have a snack before you go further," said his employer.

"No, thank you, sir," replied Cosmo; "I am too self-indulgent to enjoy my food before I have finished my work."

"Not a bad way of being self-indulgent, that!" said the man. "—But what puzzles me is, that a young fellow with such good principles should be going about the country like—"

"Like a tinker—would you say, sir—or like Abraham of old when he had no abiding city?"

"You seem to know your Bible too!—Come now, there must be some reason for your being adrift like this!"

"Of course there is, sir; and if I were sure you would believe me, I would tell you enough to make you understand it."

"A cautious Scotchman!"

"Yes. Whatever I told you, you would doubt; therefore I tell you nothing."

"You have been doing something wrong!" said the man.

"You are rude," returned Cosmo quietly, without stopping his work.—"But," he resumed, "were *you* never in any difficulty? Have you always had your pockets full when you were doing right? It is not just to suspect a man because he is poor. The best men have rarely been rich." Receiving no reply, Cosmo raised his head. The man was gone.

"Somebody has been telling him about me!" he said to himself, and went. For the stable Cosmo was then cleaning out, the horses that lived in it, and the house to which it belonged, were the proceeds of a late judicious failure.

He finished the job, set everything right as far as he could, and going to the kitchen door, requested the master might be invited to inspect his work. But the master only sent orders to the cook to give the young man his dinner, and let him go about his business.

Cosmo ate none the less heartily, for it was his own; and cook and maid were more polite than their master. He thanked them and went his way, and in the strength of that food walked many miles into the night—for now he set no goal before him but the last.

It was a clear, moonless, starry night, cold after the rain, but the easier to walk in. The wind now and then breathed a single breath and ceased; but that breath was piercing. He buttoned his coat, and trudged on. The hours went and went. He could not be far from Cairncarque, and hoped by break of day to be, if not within sight of it, at least within accurate hearing of it.

Midnight was not long past when a pale old moon came up, and looked drearily at him. For some time he had been as if walking in a dream; and now the moon mingled with the dream right strangely. Scarce was she above the hill when an odd-shaped cloud came upon her; and Cosmo's sleep-bewildered eyes saw in the cloud the body and legs of James Gracie's cow, straddling across the poor, withered heel-rind of the moon. Then another cloud, high among the stars, began to drop large drops of rain upon his head. "That's the reid gowd rainin'" ("That's the red gold raining,") he said to himself. He was gradually sinking under the power of invading sleep. Every now and then he would come to himself for the briefest instant, and say he must seek some shelter. The next moment he was asleep again. He had often wondered that horses could get over the road and sleep: here he was doing it himself and not wondering at all! The wind rose, and blew sharp stings of rain in his face, which woke him up a little. He looked about him. Had he been going through a town, who would have taken him in at that time of the midnight-morning? And here he was in a long lane without sign of turning! To him it had neither beginning nor end, like a lane in a dream. It might be a lane in a dream! He could remember feeling overwhelmed with sleep in a dream! Still he did not think he was dreaming: for one thing, he had never been so uncomfortable in a dream!

The lane at last opened on a triangular piece of sward, looking like a village green. In the middle of it stood a great old tree, with a bench round it. He dropped on the bench and was asleep in a moment.

The wind blew, and the rain fell. Cold and discomfort ruled his dim consciousness, but he slept like one of the dead. When the sun rose, it found him at full length on the bare-worn earth at the foot of the tree. But, shining full upon him, it did not for a long time break his sleep. When at last it yielded and he came to himself, it was to the consciousness of a body that was a burden, of a tabernacle that ached as if all its cords were strained, yet all its stakes loosened. With nightmare difficulty he compelled his limbs to raise him, and then was so ill able to govern them, that he staggered like a drunken man, and again and again all but dropped. Such a night's-rest after such a day's-weariness had all but mastered him.

Seeing a pond in the green, he made for it, and having washed his face, felt a little revived. On the other side of the green, he saw a little shop, in the unshuttered window of which was bread. Mechanically he put his hand in his pocket. To his surprise, he found there sixpence: the maid that waited on him at dinner had dropped it in. Rejoiced by the gift, he tried to run, to get some warmth into his limbs, but had no great success. The moment the shop was opened, he spent his sixpence, and learned that he was but about three miles off the end of his journey. He set out again therefore with good courage; but alas! The moment he tried to eat, mouth and throat and all refused their office. He had no recollection of any illness, but this was so unlike his usual self, that he could not help some apprehension. As he walked he got a little better, however, and trudged manfully on. By and by he was able to eat a bit of bread, and felt better still. But as he recovered, he became aware that with fatigue and dirt his appearance must be disreputable in the extreme. How was he to approach Lady Joan in such a plight? If she recognised him at once, he would but be the more ashamed! What could she take him for but a ne'er-do-weel, whose character had given way the moment he left the guardianship of home, and who now came to sponge upon her! And if he should be ill! He would rather lie down and die on the roadside than present himself dirty and ill at Cairncarque!—rather go to the workhouse, than encounter even the momentary danger of such a misunderstanding! These reflections were hardly worthy of the faith he had hitherto shown, but he was not yet perfect, and unproved illness had clouded his judgement.

Coming to a watering-place for horses on the roadside, he sat down by it, and opening his bag, was about to make what little of a toilet was possible to him—was thinking whether he might venture, as it seemed such a lonely road, to change his shirt, when round a near corner came a lady, walking slowly, and reading as she came. It was she! And there he stood without coat or waistcoat! To speak to her thus would be to alarm her! He turned his back, and began to wash in the pool, nor once dared look round. He heard her slowly pass, fancied he heard her stop one step, felt her presence from head to foot, and washed the harder. When he thought she was far enough off, he put on the garments he had removed, and hastened away, drying himself as he went.

At the turn of the road, all at once rose the towers of Cairncarque. There was a castle indeed!—something to call a castle!—with its huge square tower at every corner, and its still huger two towers in the middle of its front, its moat, and the causeway where once had been its drawbridge!—Yes! There were the spikes of the portcullis, sticking down from the top of the gateway, like the long upper teeth of a giant or ogre! That was a real castle—such as he had read of in books, such as he had seen in pictures! Castle Warlock would go bodily into half a quarter of it—would be swallowed up like a mouthful, and never seen again! Castle Warlock was twice as old—that was something! But why had not Lady Joan told him hundreds of stories about Cairncarque, instead of letting him gabble on about their little place? But she could not love her castle as he did his, for she had no such father in it! That must be what made the difference! That was why she did not care to talk about it! Was he actually going to see her again? And would she be to him the same as before? For him, the years between had vanished; the entrancing shadows of years far away folded him round, and he was no more a man, but the boy who had climbed the wintry hills with her, and run down them again over the snow hand in hand with her. But as he drew nigh the great pile, which grew as he approached it, his heart sank within him. His head began to ache: a strange diffidence seized him; he could not go up to the door. He would not mind, he said to himself, if Joan would be there the moment the door opened. But would any servant in England admit a fellow like him to the presence of a grand lady? How could he walk up to the great door in the guise of one who had all night had his lodging on the cold ground! He would reconnoitre a little, find some quiet way of approaching the house, perhaps discover some shelter where he might rectify what was worst in his personal appearance! He turned away therefore from the front of the castle, and following the road that skirted the dilapidated remnants of fortification, passed several farm-like sheds, and arrived at a door in a brick wall, apparently that of a garden—ancient, and green and gray with lichens. Looking through it with the eyes of his imagination, he saw on the other side the loveliest picture of warmth, order, care, and ancient peace,—regions stately with yews and cedars, fruit-trees and fountains, clean-swept walks and shady alleys. The red wall, mottled and clouded with its lichens, and ruffed with many a thread weed, looked like the reverse of some bit of gorgeous brocade, on the sunny side of which must hang blossoming peaches and pears, nectarines and apricots and apples, on net-like trees, that spread out great obedient arms and multitudinous twigs against it, holding on by it, and drinking in the hot sunshine it gathered behind them. Ah, what it would be to have such a garden at Glenwarlock!

He turned to the door, with difficulty opened it, and the vision vanished. Not a few visions vanish when one takes them for fact, and not for the vision of fact that has to be wrought out with the energy of a God-born life.

CHAPTER XXV
THE GARDENER

There was a garden indeed, but a garden whose ragged, ugly, degraded desolation looked as if the devil had taken to gardening in it. Rather than a grief, it was a pain and disgust to see. Fruit-trees there were on the wall, but run wild with endless shoots, which stuck like a hog's mane over the top of it, and out in every direction from the face of it with a look of impertinent daring. All the fastenings were broken away, and only the old branches, from habit, kept their places against it. Everything all about seemed striving back to a dear disorder and salvage liberty. The walks were covered with weeds, and almost impassable with unpruned branches, while here lay a heap of rubbish, there a smashed flower-pot, here a crushed water-pot, there a broken dinner-plate. Following a path that led away from the wall, he came upon a fountain without any water, in a cracked basin dry as a lizard-haunted wall, a sundial without a gnomon, leaning wearily away from the sun, a marble statue without a nose, and streaked about with green: like an army of desolation in single file, they revealed to Cosmo the age-long neglect of the place. Next appeared a wing built out from the back of the inner court of the castle—in a dilapidated, almost dangerous condition. Then he came to a great hedge of yew, very lofty, but very thin, like a fence of old wire that had caught cart-loads of withered rubbish in its meshes. Here he heard the sound of a spade, and by the accompanying sounds judged the implement was handled by an old man. He peeped through the hedge, and caught sight of him. Old he was—bent with years, but tough, wiry, and sound, and it seemed to Cosmo that the sighs and groans, or rather grunts, which he uttered, were more of impatience and discontent than oppression or weakness. As he stood regarding him for a moment, anxious to discover with what sort of man he had to deal, he began to mutter. Presently he ceased digging, drew himself up as straight as he could, and, leaning on his spade, went on, as if addressing his congregation of cabbages over the book-board of a pulpit. And now his muttering took, to the ears of Cosmo, an indistinct shape like this:

"Wha cares for an auld man like me? I kenna what for there sud be auld men made! The banes o' me micht melt i' the inside o' me, an' never a sowl alive du mair for me nor berry me to get rid o' the stink! No 'at I'm that dooms auld i' mysel' them 'at wad hae my place wad hae me!"

"Who cares for an old man like me? I don't know why old men should be made! My bones might melt inside me, and never a soul alive do more for me than bury me to get rid of the stink! Not that I'm so very old in myself as those that would have my place would imagine!"

Here was a chance for him, Cosmo thought; for at least here was a fellow-countryman. He went along the hedge therefore until he found a place where he could get through, and approached the man, who had by this time resumed his work, though after a listless fashion, turning over spadeful after spadeful, as if neither he nor the cabbages cared much, and all would be in good time if done by the end of the world. As he came nearer, Cosmo read peevishness and ill-temper in every line of his countryman's countenance, yet he approached him with confidence, for Scotchmen out of their own country are of good report for hospitality to each other.

"Hoo's a' wi' ye?" he cried, sending his mother-tongue as a pursuivant in advance.

"Wha's speirin'? an' what richt hae ye to speir?" returned the old man in an angry voice, and lifting himself quickly, though with

"How's all with you?" he cried, sending his mother-tongue as a pursuivant in advance.

"Who's asking? and what right have you to ask?" returned the old man in an angry voice, and lifting himself quickly, though with an aching sigh, looked at him with hard blue eyes.

an aching sigh, looked at him with hard blue eyes.

"A countryman o' yer ain," answered Cosmo.

"A countryman of your own," answered Cosmo.

"Mony ane's that 'at 's naething the better nor the walcomer. Gie an accoont o' yersel', or the doags 'll be lowsed upo' ye here in a jiffy. Haith, this is no the place for lan'loupers!

"Many are that, and are none the better nor the welcomer. Give an account of yourself, or the dogs will be loosed on you here in a jiffy. Faith, this is not the place for vagrants!"

"Hae ye been lang aboot the place?" asked Cosmo.

"Have you been long about the place?" asked Cosmo.

"Langer nor ye're like to be, I'm thinkin', gien ye keep na the ceeviler tongue i' yer heid, my man—Whaur come ye frae?"

"Longer than you're like to be, I think, if you don't keep a more civil tongue in your head, my man—Where do you come from?"

The old man had dropt his spade; Cosmo took it up, and began to dig.

"Lay doon that spaud," cried its owner, and would have taken it from him, but Cosmo delayed rendition.

"Lay down that spade," cried its owner, and would have taken it from him, but Cosmo delayed rendition.

"Hoot, man!" he said, "I wad but lat ye see I'm nae lan'louper, an' can weel han'le a spaud. Stan' ye by a bit, an' rist yer banes, till I caw throuw a trifle o' yer wark."

"Heavens, man!" he said, "I would but let you see I'm no vagrant, and can handle a spade well. Stand by a bit, and rest your bones, till I get through a trifle of your work."

"An' what du ye expec' to come o' that? Ye're efter something, as sure's the devil at the back yett though ye're nae freely sae sure to win at it."

"And what do you expect to come of that? You're after something, as sure as the devil at the back gate, though you're not quite so sure of getting at it."

"What I expec', it wad be ill to say; but what I dinna expec' is to be traitit like a vaggabon. Come, I'll gie ye a guid hoor's wark for a place to wash mysel', an' put on a clean sark."

"What I expect, it would be hard to say; but what I don't expect is to be treated like a vagabond. Come, I'll give you a good hour's work for a place to wash myself, and put on a clean shirt."

"Hae ye the sark?"

"Have you the shirt?"

"I hae 't here i' my bag."

"I have it here in my bag."

"An' what du ye want to put on a clean sark for? What'll ye du whan ye hae 't on?"

"And what do you want to put on a clean shirt for? What'll you do when you have it on?"

"Gie ye anither hoor's wark for the heel o' a loaf an' a drink o' watter."

"Give you another hour's work for the heel of a loaf and a drink of water."

"Ye'll be wantin' to be taen on, I s' wad ye a worm!"

"You'll be wanting to be hired, I'll bet you a worm!"

"Gien ye cud gie me a day's wark, or maybe twa—" began Cosmo, thinking how much rather he would fall in with Lady Joan about the garden than go up to the house.

"If you could give me a day's work, or maybe two—" began Cosmo, thinking how much rather he would fall in with Lady Joan about the garden than go up to the house.

"I weel thoucht there sud be mair intil't nor appear! Ye wad fain hae the auld man's shune, an' mak sur o' them afore he kickit them frae him! Ay! It's jist like the likes o' ye! Mine's a place the like o' you's keen set efter!

"I thought there was more in it than there seemed! You'd gladly have the old man's shoes, and make sure of them before he kicked them from him! Ay! It's just like the likes of you! Mine's a place the like of you's keen to seize!

Ye think it's a' ait an' play! Gang awa' wi' ye, an' latna me see the face o' ye again, or I s' ca' to them 'at 'll tak accoont o' ye."

"Hoot, man!" returned Cosmo, and went on turning the ground over, "ye're unco hard upon a neebor!"

"Neebor! Ye're no neebor o' mine! Gang awa' wi' ye, I tell ye!"

"Did naebody never gie *you* a helpin' han', 'at ye're sae dooms hard upo' ane 'at needs ane?"

"Gien onybody ever did, it wasna you."

"But dinna ye think ye're a kin' o' b'un' to du the like again?"

"Ay, to him 'at did it—but I tell ye ye're no the man; sae gang aboot yer business."

"Someday ye may want somebody ance mair to du ye a guid turn!"

"I hae dune a heap to gie me a claim on consideration. I hae grown auld upo' the place. What hae *ye* dune, my man?"

"I wadna hae muckle chance o' duin' onything, gien a'body was like you. But did ye never hear tell o' ane 'at said: 'Ye wad du naething for nane o' mine, sae ye refeesed mysel'?"

"'Deed, an' I wull refeese yersel'," returned the old man. "Sic a chield for jaw an' cheek—saw I never nane—as the auld sang says! Whaur on this earth cam ye frae?"

You think it's all eating and playing! Go along with you, and don't show your face again, or I'll call to them that'll deal with you."

"Heavens, man!" returned Cosmo, and went on turning the ground over, "You're very hard upon a neighbour!"

"Neighbour! You're no neighbour of mine! Go along with you, I say!"

"Did no one ever give *you* a helping hand, that you're so awfully hard on one that needs one?"

"If anyone ever did, it wasn't you."

"But don't you think in a way you're obliged to do the like again?"

"Ay, to him that did it—but I tell you you're not the man; so go about your business."

"Someday you may want somebody to do you another good turn!"

"I've done a lot to give me a claim on consideration. I've grown old upon the place. What have *you* done, my man?"

"I wouldn't have much chance of doing anything, if everyone was like you. But did you never hear tell of one who said: 'You would do nothing for any of mine, so you refused myself?"

"Indeed, and I will refuse yourself," returned the old man. "Such a man for jaw and cheek, as I never saw—as the old song says! Where on this earth did you come from?"

As he spoke, he gave Cosmo a round punch on the shoulder next him that made him look from his work, and then began eying him up and down in the most supercilious manner. He was a small, withered, bowed man, with a thin wizened face, crowned by a much worn fur cap. His mouth had been so long drawn down at each corner as by weights of discontent, that it formed nearly a half-circle. His eyebrows were lifted as far as they would go above his red-lidded blue eyes, and there was a succession of ripply wrinkles over each of them, which met in the middle of his forehead, so that he was all over arches. Under his cap stuck out enormous ears, much too large for his face. Huge veiny hands hung trembling by his sides, but they trembled more from anger than from age.

"I tellt ye a'ready," answered Cosmo; "I come frae the auld country."

"Deil tak the auld country! What care I for the auld country! It's a braid place, an' langer nor it's braid, an' there's mony ane intil't an' oot on't 'at's no warth the parritch his mither pat intil 'im. Eh, the fowth o' fushionless beggars I hae seen come to me like yersel'!—

"I told you already," answered Cosmo; "I come from the old country."

"Devil take the old country! What do I care for it! It's a broad place, and longer than it's broad, and there's many in it and out upon it that aren't worth the porridge their mother put into them. Eh, the number of worthless beggars I've seen come to me like yourself!—

Ow ay! It was aye wark they wad hae!—an' cudna du mair nor a flea amo' traicle!—What coonty are ye frae, wi' the lang legs an' the lang back-bane o' ye?"

Cosmo told him. The hands of the old man rose from his sides, and made right angles of his elbows.

"Weel," he said slowly, "that's no an ill coonty to come frae. I may say *that,* for I belang til't mysel'. But what pairt o' 't ran ye frae whan ye cam awa'?"

"I ran frae nae pairt, but I cam frae hame i' the north pairt o' that same," answered Cosmo, and bent again to his work.

The man came a step nearer, and Cosmo, without looking up, was aware he was regarding him intently.

"Ay! Ay!" he said at last, in a tone of reflection mingled with dawning interest, "I ance kent a terrible rascal cam frae owerby that gait: what ca' they the perris ye're frae?"

Cosmo told him.

"Lord bless me!" cried the old man, and came close up to him—"But na!" he resumed, and stepped a pace back, "Somebody's been tellin ye!"

Cosmo gave him no answer. He stood a moment expecting one, then broke out in a rage.

"What for mak ye nae answer whan a body speirs ye a question? That wasna mainners whan I was a bairn. Lord! Ye micht as weel be ceevil! Isna it easy eneuch to lee?"

"I would answer no man who was not prepared to believe me," said Cosmo quietly.

The dignity of his English had far more effect on the man than the friendliness of their mother-tongue.

"Maybe ye wadna objec' to mak mention by name o' the toon nearest to ye whan ye was at hame?" said the old man, and from his altered manner and tone Cosmo felt he might reply.

"It was ca'd Muir o' Warlock," he answered.

"Lord, man! come into the hoose. Ye maun be sair in need o' something to put intil

Oh ay! It was always work they would have!—and couldn't do more than a flea in treacle!—What county are you from, with your long legs and back-bone?"

Cosmo told him. The hands of the old man rose from his sides, and made right angles of his elbows.

"Well," he said slowly, "that's not a bad county to come from. I may say *that,* for I belong to it myself. But what part of it did you run from when you came away?"

"I ran from no part, but I came from home in the north part of that same," answered Cosmo, and bent again to his work.

The man came a step nearer, and Cosmo, without looking up, was aware he was regarding him intently.

"Ay! Ay!" he said at last, in a tone of reflection mingled with dawning interest, "I once knew a terrible rascal who came from down that way: what do they call the parish you're from?"

Cosmo told him.

"Lord bless me!" cried the old man, and came close up to him.—"But na!" he resumed, and stepped a pace back, "Somebody's been telling you!"

Cosmo gave him no answer. He stood a moment expecting one, then broke out in a rage.

"Why don't you answer when someone asks you a question? That wasn't manners when I was a child. Lord! You might as well be civil! Isn't it easy enough to lie?"

"I would answer no man who was not prepared to believe me," said Cosmo quietly.

The dignity of his English had far more effect on the man than the friendliness of their mother-tongue.

"Maybe you wouldn't object to mention the name of the town nearest to you when you were at home?" said the old man, and from his altered manner and tone Cosmo felt he might reply.

"It was called Muir o' Warlock," he answered.

"Lord, man! Come into the house. You must be as hungry as a wolf! All the way from

ye! A' the gait frae Muir o' Warlock! A toonsman o' my ain! Scotlan's a muckle place—but Muir o' Warlock! Guid guide 's! Come in, man; come in!"

Muir o' Warlock! A townsman of my own! Scotland's a great size—but Muir o' Warlock! Goodness! Come in, man; come in!"

So saying he took the spade from Cosmo's hands, threw it down with a contemptuous cast, and led the way towards the house.

The old man had a heart after all! Strange the power of that comparatively poor thing, local association, to bring to light the eternal love at the root of the being! Wonderful sign also of the presence of God wherever a child may open eyes! This man's heart was not yet big enough to love a Scotsman, but it was big enough to love a Muir-o'-Warlock-man; and was not that a precious beginning?—a beginning as good as any? It matters nothing where or how one begins, if only one does begin! There are many, doubtless, who have not yet got farther in love than their own family; but there are others who have learned that for the true heart there is neither Frenchman nor Englishman, neither Jew nor Greek, neither white nor black—only the sons and daughters of God, only the brothers and sisters of the one elder brother. There may be some who have learned to love all the people of their own planet, but have not yet learned to look with patience upon those of Saturn and Mercury; while others there must be, who, wherever there is a creature of God's making, love each in its capacity for love—from the arch-angel before God's throne, to the creeping thing he may be compelled to destroy—from the man of this earth to the man of some system of worlds which no human telescope has yet brought within the ken of heaven-poring sage. And to that it must come with every one of us, for not until then are we true men, true women—the children, that is, of him in whose image we are made.

Cosmo followed very willingly, longing for water and a clothes-brush rather than for food. The cold and damp, fatigue and exposure of the night were telling upon him more than he knew, and all the time he was at work, he had been cramped by hitherto unknown pains in his limbs.

The gardener brought him to the half-ruinous wing already mentioned, to a small kitchen, opening under a great sloping buttress, and presented him to his wife, an English woman, some ten years younger than himself. She received him with a dignified retraction of the feelers, but the moment she understood his needs, ministered to them, and had some breakfast ready for him by the time he had made his toilet. He sat down by her little fire, and drank some tea, but felt shivery, and could not eat. In dread lest, if he yielded a moment to the invading sickness, it should at once overpower him, he made haste to get out again into the sun, and rejoined the old man, who had gone back to his cabbage-ground. There he pulled off his coat, and once more seized the spade, for work seemed the only way of meeting his enemy hand to hand. But the moment he began, he was too hot, and the moment he took breath he was ready to shiver. As long as he could stand, however, he would not give in.

"How many years have you been gardener here?" he asked, forcing himself to talk.

"How many years have you been gardener here?" he asked, forcing himself to talk.

"Five an' forty year, an' I'm nearhan' tired o' 't."

"Five and forty years, and I'm almost tired of it."

"The present lord is a young man, is he not?"

"The present lord is a young man, is he not?"

"Ay; he canna be muckle ayont five an' thirty."

"Ay; he can't be much over five and thirty."

"What sort of a man is he?"

"What sort of a man is he?"

"Weel, it's hard to say. He's ane o' them 'at

"Well, it's hard to say. He's one of those

naebody says weel o', an' naebody's begud to say ill o'—yet."

that nobody speaks well of, and nobody's begun to speak ill of—yet."

"There can't be much amiss with him then, surely!"

"There can't be much amiss with him then, surely!"

"Weel, I wadna gang freely sae far as say that. You 'at's a man o' sense, maun weel un'erstan', gien it was only frae yer carritchis, 'at there's baith sins o' o-mission, an' sins o' co-mission. Noo, what sins o' co-mission may lie at my lord's door, I dinna ken, an feow can ken, an' we're no to jeedge; but for the o-mission, ye hae but to see hoo he neglects that bonny sister o' his, to be far eneuch frae thinkin' a sant o 'im."

"Well, I wouldn't go quite so far as that. You that's a man of sense, must easily understand, if it was only from your catechism, that there's both sins of o-mission, and sins of co-mission. Now, what sins of co-mission may lie at my lord's door, I don't know, and few can know, and we're not to judge; but for the o-mission, you have but to see how he neglects that bonny sister of his, to be far enough from thinking him a saint."

Silence followed. Cosmo would go no farther in that direction: it would be fair neither to Lady Joan nor the gardener, who spoke as to one who knew nothing of the family.

"Noo the father," resumed his new friend, "—puir man, he's deid an' damned this mony a day!—an' eh, but he was an ill ane!—but as to Leddy Joan, he wad hardly bide her oot o' his sicht. He cudna be jist that agreeable company to the likes o' her, puir leddy! For he was a rouch-spoken, sweirin' auld sinner as ever lived, but sic as he had he gae her, an' was said to hae been a fine gentleman in 's yoong days. Some wad hae 't he cheenged a' thegither o' a suddent. An' they wad hae 't it cam o' bluid-guitiness—for they said he had liftit the reid han' agen his neebor. An' they warnt me, lang as it was sin' I left it, no to lat 'im ken I cam frae yon pairt o' the country, or he wad be rid o' me in a jiffy, ae w'y or anither.—Ay, it was a gran' name that o' Warlock i' thae pairts! Though they tell me it gangs na for sae muckle noo. I hae h'ard said, 'at ever sin' the auld lord here made awa' wi' the laird o' Glenwarlock, the family there never had ony luck. I wad like to ken what you, as a man o' sense, think o' that same. It appears to me a some queer kin' o justice! No 'at I'm daurin' or wad daur to say a word agen the w'y 'at the warl' 's goverrnt, but there's some things 'at naebody can un'erstan'—I defy them!—an' yon's ane o' them—what for, cause oor graceless auld lord—he was young than—tuik the life o' the laird o' Glenwarlock, the family o' Warlock sud never thrive frae that day to this!—Read me that riddle, yoong man, gien ye can."

"Now the father," resumed his new friend, "—poor man, he's dead and damned this many a day!—and eh, but he was a bad one!—but as to Lady Joan, he would hardly stand her out of his sight. He couldn't be agreeable company to the likes of her, poor lady! For he was a rough-spoken, swearing old sinner as ever lived, but such as he had he gave her, and was said to have been a fine gentleman in his young days. Some would have it he changed altogether of a sudden. And they would have it it came of blood-guiltiness—for they said he had lifted the red hand against his neighbour. And they warned me, long as it was since I left it, not to let him know I came from that part of the country, or he would be rid of me in a jiffey, one way or another.—Ay, it was a grand name that of Warlock in those parts! Though they tell me it goes for little now. I have heard said, that ever since the old lord here made away with the laird of Glenwarlock, the family there never had any luck. I would like to know what you, as a man of sense, think of that same. It appears to me a strange kind of justice! Not that I'm daring or would dare to say a word against the way that the world's governed, but there's some things that nobody can understand—I defy them!—and that's one of them—why, because our graceless old lord—he was young then—took the life of the laird of Glenwarlock, the family of Warlock should never thrive from that day to this!—Read me that riddle, young man, if you can."

"Maybe it was to haud them 'at cam efter frae ony mair keepin' o' sic ill company," Cosmo ventured to suggest; for, knowing what his father was, and something also of what most of those who preceded him were, he could see no such inscrutable dispensation in the fact mentioned.

"Maybe it was to prevent those who came after from keeping such bad company," Cosmo ventured to suggest; for, knowing what his father was, and something also of what most of those who preceded him were, he could see no such inscrutable dispensation in the fact mentioned.

"That wad be hard lines, though," insisted the gardener, unwilling to yield the unintelligibility of the ways of providence.

"That would be rough luck, though," insisted the gardener, unwilling to yield the unintelligibility of the ways of providence.

"But," said Cosmo, "they say doon there, it was a brither o' the laird, no the laird himsel' 'at the English lord killt."

"But," said Cosmo, "they say down there, it was a brother of the laird, not the laird himself that the English lord killed."

"Na, na; they're a' wrang there, whaever says that. For auld Jean, wham I min' a weel faured wuman, though doobtless no sae bonny as whan he broucht her wi' 'im a yoong lass—maybe to gar her haud her tongue—auld Jean said as I say. But that was lang efter the thing was ower auld to be ta'en ony notice o' mair. Forby, you 'at's a man o' sense, gien it wasna the laird himsel' 'at he killt, hoo wad there, i' that case, be onything worthy o' remark i' their no thrivin' efter't? I' that case, the no thrivin' cud hae had naething ava to du wi' the killin'. Na, na, it was the laird himsel' 'at the maister killt—the father o' the present laird, I'm thinkin'. What aged-man micht he be—did ye ever hear tell?"

"Na, na; they're all wrong there, whoever says that. For old Jean, whom I remember a good looking woman, though doubtless not so bonny as when he brought her with him a young lass—maybe to make her hold her tongue—old Jean said as I say. But that was long after the thing was too old to be taken any more notice of. Besides, you that's a man of sense, if it wasn't the laird himself that he killed, how would there, in that case, be anything worthy of remark in their not thriving after it? In that case, the not thriving could have had nothing at all to do with the killing. Na, na, it was the laird himself that the master killed—the father of the present laird, I'm thinking. What age might the man be—did you ever hear tell?"

"He's a man well on to seventy," answered Cosmo, with a pang at the thought.

"He's a man well on to seventy," answered Cosmo, with a pang at the thought.

"Ay; that'll be aboot it! There can be no doobt it was his father oor lord killt—an' as little 'at efter he did it he gaed doon the braid ro'd to the deevil as fest 's ever he cud rin. It was jist like as wi' Judas—he maun gang till's ain. Some said he had sellt himsel' to the deevil, but I'm thinkin' that wasna necessar'. He was to get him ony gait! An' wad ye believe't, it's baith said an' believt—'at he cam by 's deith i' some exterordnar w'y, no accoontable for, but plainly no canny. Ae thing's sure as deith itsel', he was ta'en suddent, an' i' the verra hoose whaur, mony a lang year afore, he commitit the deed o' darkness!"

"Ay; that'll be about it! There can be no doubt it was his father our lord killed—and as little that after he did it he went down the broad road to the devil as fast as ever he could run. It was just like as with Judas—he must go to his own. Some said he had sold himself to the devil, but I'm thinking that wasn't necessary. He was to get him anyway! And would you believe it, it's both said and believed—that he came by his death in some extraordinary way, not accountable for, but plainly not canny. One thing's sure as death itself, he was taken suddenly, and in the very house where, many a long year before, he committed the deed of darkness!"

A pause followed, and then the narrator, or rather commentator, resumed.

"I'm thinkin' whan he begud to ken himsel' growin' auld, his deed cam back upon 'im fresh-like, an' that wad be hoo he cudna bide to hae my lady oot o' the sicht o' his een, or at least ayont the cry o' his tongue. Troth! He wad whiles come aboot the place after her, whaur I wad be at my wark, as it micht be the day, cursin' an' sweirin' as gien he had sellt his sowl to a' the devils thegither, an' sae micht tak his wull o' onything he cud get his tongue roon'! But I never heedit him that muckle, for ye see it wasna him 'at peyt me—the mair by token 'at gien it had been him 'at had the peyin o' me, it's never a baubee wad I hae seen o' my ain siller; but the trustees peyt me, ilka plack, an' sae I was indepen'ent like, an' luit him say his say. But it was aye an oonsaitisfactory kin' o' a thing, for the trustees they caredna a bodle aboot keepin' the place dacent, an' tuik sae sma' delicht in ony pleesurin' o' the auld lord, 'at they jist allooed him me, an' no a man mair nor less—to the gairden, that is. That's hoo the place comes to be in sic a disgracefu' condeetion. Gien it hadna been for rizzons o' my ain, I wad hae gane, mony's the time, for the sicht o' the ruin o' things was beyon' beirin'. But I bude to beir't; sae I bore't an' bore't till I cam by beirin' o' 't to tak it verra quaiet, an' luik upo' the thing as the wull o' a Providence 'at sudna be meddlet wi'. I broucht mysel' in fac' to that degree o' submission, 'at I gae mysel' no trouble more, but jist confint my ainergies to the raisin' o' the kail an' cabbage, the ingons an' pitawtas wantit aboot the place."

"And are things no better," asked Cosmo, "since the present lord succeeded?"

"No a hair—'cep' it be 'at there's no sae mony ill words fleein' aboot the place. My lord never sets his nose intil the gairden, or speirs—no ance in a twalmonth, hoo's things gangin' on. He does naething but rowt aboot in 's boaratory as he ca's 't—bore-a-whig, or bore-a-tory, it's little to me—makin' stinks there fit to scomfish a whaul, an' gar 'im stick his nose aneth the watter for a glamp o' fresh air. He's that hard-hertit 'at he never sae muckle as aits his denner alongside o' his ain sister, 'cep' it be whan he has company, an' wad luik like ither

"I'm thinking when he began to know himself growing old, his deed came back upon him fresh-like, and that would be why he couldn't stand to have my lady out of his eyesight, or at least beyond his call. Faith! He would sometimes come about the place after her, where I would be at my work, as it might be today, cursing and swearing as if he had sold his soul to all the devils together, and so might have his way with anything he could get his tongue around! But I never gave him much heed, for you see it wasn't him that paid me—and if it had been, I would never have seen a penny of my own money; but the trustees payed me, every coin, and so I was independent, and let him say his say. But it was always an unsatisfactory kind of a thing, for the trustees cared nothing about keeping the place decent, and took such small delight in any pleasuring of the old lord, that they just allowed him myself, and not a man more nor less—to the garden, that is. That's how the place comes to be in such a disgraceful condition. If it hadn't been for reasons of my own, I would have gone, many's the time, for the sight of the ruin of things was beyond bearing. But I had to bear it; so I bore it and bore it, till I came by bearing it to take it very quietly, and look upon the thing as the will of a Providence that shouldn't be meddled with. I brought myself in fact to that degree of submission, that I gave myself no more trouble, but just confined my energies to the raising of the kale and cabbage, the onions and potatoes wanted about the place."

"And are things no better," asked Cosmo, "since the present lord succeeded?"

"Not a hair—except that there's not so many bad words flying about the place. My lord never sets his nose into the garden, or asks—not once in a twelvemonth, how things are going on. He does nothing but rummage about in his boaratory as he calls it—bore-a-whig, or bore-a-tory, it's little to me—making stinks there fit to sicken a whale, and make him stick his nose under water for a gasp of fresh air. He's that hard-hearted that he never so much as eats his dinner alongside his own sister, except when he has company, and

fowk. Gien it gaedna ower weel wi' her i' the auld man's time, it gangs waur wi' her noo; for sae lang as he was abune the yird there was aye somebody to ken whether she was livin' or deid. To see a bonnie lass like her strayin' aboot the place nae better companied nor wi' an auld buik—it's jist eneuch to brak a man's hert, but that age kills rage."

"Do the neighbours take no notice of her?"

"Nane o' her ain dignity, like. Ye see she's naething but bonny. She has naething. An' though she's as guid a crater as ever lived, the cauld grun' o' her poverty gaithers the fog o' an ill report. Troth, for her faimily, the ill's there, report or no report; but, a' the same, gien she had been rich, an' her father—I'll no say the hangman, but him 'at he last hangt, there wad be fowth o' coonty-fowk wad hae her til her denner wi' them. An' I'm thinkin' maybe she's the prooder for her poverty, an' winna gang til her inferriors sae lang as her aiquals dinna invete her. She gangs whiles to the doctor's—but he's a kin' o' a freen' o' the yerl's, 'cause he likes stinks—but that's the yoong doctor."

"Does her brother never go out to dinner anywhere, and take her with him?"

"Naebody cares a bodle aboot his lordship i' the haill country-side, sae far as I can learn. There's ane or twa-great men, I daursay—whiles comes doon frae Lon'on, to smell hoo he's getting' on wi's stinks, but deil a neebor comes nigh the hoose. Ow, he's a great man, I mak nae doobt, awa' frae hame! He's aye writin' letters to the newspapers, an' they prent them—aboot this an' aboot that—aboot beasties i' the watter, an' lectreesity, an' I kenna what a'; an' some says 'at hoo he'll be a rich man some day, the moment he's dune fin'in' oot something or ither he's been warslin' at for the feck o' a ten year or sae; but the gentry never thinks naething o' a man sae lang as he's only duin' his best—or his warst, as the case may be—to lay his han' upo' the siller 'at's fleein' aboot him like a snaw-drift. Bide ye a bit, though! *Whan* he's gotten't, it's doon they're a' upo' their k-nees til 'im thegither.

would look like other folk. If it didn't go very well with her in the old man's time, it goes worse with her now; for so long as he was above ground there was always somebody to know whether she was living or dead. To see a bonnie lass like her straying about the place no better companied than with an old book—it's just enough to break a man's heart, but that age kills rage."

"Do the neighbours take no notice of her?"

"None of her own dignity. You see she's nothing but bonny. She has nothing. And though she's as good a creature as ever lived, the cold ground of her poverty gathers the fog of an ill report. Indeed, for her family, the ill's there, report or no report; but, all the same, if she had been rich, and her father—I won't say the hangman, but him that he last hanged, there would be plenty of county-folk who'd have her to dinner with them. And I'm thinking maybe she's the prouder for her poverty, and won't go to her inferiors so long as her equals don't invite her. Sometimes she goes to the doctor's—but he's a kind of friend of the earl's, because he likes stinks—but that's the young doctor."

"Does her brother never go out to dinner anywhere, and take her with him?"

"Nobody cares a thing about his lordship in the whole country-side, so far as I can learn. There's one or two—great men, I daresay—who sometimes come down from London, to smell how he's getting on with his stinks, but devil a neighbour comes nigh the house. Oh, he's a great man, I make no doubt, away from home! He's always writing letters to the newspapers, and they print them—about this and about that—about creatures in the water, and electricity, and I don't know what all; and some say he'll be a rich man some day, the moment he's done finding out something or other he's been wrestling over for about ten years or so; but the gentry never think anything of a man so long as he's only doing his best—or his worst, as the case may be—to lay his hand upon the money that's flying about him like a snow-drift. Stay a bit, though! *When* he's got it, they're all

But gien they be prood, he's prooder, an' lat him ance get his heid up, an' rid o' the trustees, an' fowk upo' their marrow-banes til 'im, haith, he'll lat them sit there, or I'm mistaen in 'im."

"Then has my lady no companions at all?"

"She gangs whiles to see the doctor's lass, an' whiles she comes here an' has her denner wi' her, themsel's twa: never anither comes near the place."

down upon their knees to him together. But if they're proud, he's prouder, and let him once get his head up, and rid of the trustees, and folk upon their marrow-bones to him, my, he'll let them sit there, or I mistake him."

"Then has my lady no companions at all?"

"She sometimes goes to see the doctor's lass, and sometimes she comes here and has her dinner with her, just those two: never another comes near the place."

All this time, Cosmo had been turning over the cabbage-ground, working the harder that he still hoped to work off the sickness that yet kept growing upon him. The sun was hot, and his head, which had been aching more or less all day, now began to throb violently.

The spade dropt from his hands, and he fell on his face in the soft mould.

"What's this o' 't?" cried the old man, going up to him in a fright.

"What's this?" cried the old man, going up to him in a fright.

He caught hold of him by an arm, and turned him on his back. His face was colourless, and the life seemed to have gone out of him.

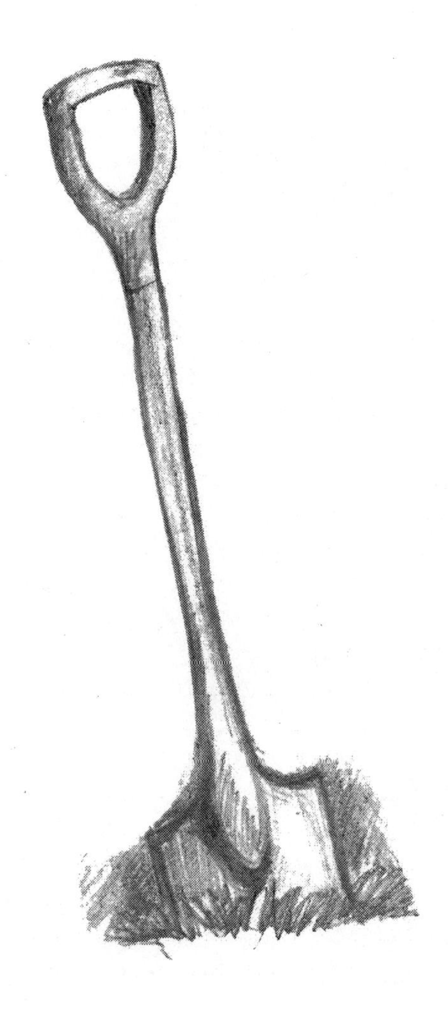

CHAPTER XXVI
LOST AND FOUND

When Cosmo came to himself, he had not a notion where he was, hardly indeed knew what he was. His chief consciousness was of an emptiness and a weight combined, that seemed to paralyze him. He would have turned on his side, but felt as if a ponderous heap of bed-clothes prevented him from even raising an arm—and yet he was cold. He tried to think back, to find what he knew of himself last, but could for a long time recall only a confused dream of multitudinous discomfort and painful effort. At last, however, came the garden, the spade-work, and the old man's talk; and then it seemed as if the cracked complaining voice had never left his ears.

"I've been ill" he said to himself. "Perhaps I dropped down. I hope they haven't buried me!" With a straining agony of will he got in motion an arm, which was lying like that of another man outside the coverlid, and felt feebly about him. His hand struck against something solid, and what seemed a handful of earth fell with a hollow rumble. Alas, this seemed ominous! Where could he be but in his coffin? The thought was not a pleasant one, certainly, but he was too weak, and had been wandering too long in the miserable limbo of vain fancies, to be much dismayed. He said to himself he would not have to suffer long—he must soon go to sleep, and so die.

Fatigued with that one movement, he lay for some time motionless. His eyes were open, though he did not know it, and by and by he became aware of light. Thin, dim, darkly gray, a particle at a time, it grew about him. For some minutes his eyes seemed of themselves, without any commission from him, to make inquiry of his surroundings. They discovered that, if he was in a coffin, or even in a sepulchre without a coffin, it was a large one: there was a wall—miles away! The light grew, and with it the conviction that he was in no sepulchre. But there the consolation ceased, for the still growing light revealed no sign of ministration or comfort. Above him was a bare, dirty, stained ceiling, with a hole in it, through which stuck skeleton ribs of lath; around him were bare, dirty-white walls, that seemed to grow out of the gray light of a wet morning as the natural deposit from such a solution. Two slender poles, meant to support curtains, but without a rag of drapery upon them, rose at his feet, like the masts of a Charon's boat. Was he indeed in the workhouse he had preferred to Cairncarque? It could hardly be, for there was the plaster fallen in great patches from the walls as well as the ceiling, and surely no workhouse would be allowed to get into such a disrepair! He tried again, and this time succeeded in turning on his side, discovering in the process how hard the bed was, and how sharp his bones. A wooden chair stood a little beyond his reach, and upon it a bottle and teacup. Not another article could he discover. Right under the hole in the ceiling a board was partly rotted away in the floor, and a cold, damp air, smelling of earth, and decaying wood, seemed to come steaming up through it. A few minutes more, he said to himself, and he would get up, and out of the hideous place, but he must lie a little longer first, just to come to himself!—Now he would try!—What had become of his strength? Was it gone utterly? Could one night's illness have reduced him thus?

He seemed to himself unable to think, yet the profoundest thought went on as if thinking itself in him. Where had his strength lain before he lost it? Could that ever have been *his* which he could not keep? If a thing were ours, nothing could ever take it from us! Was his strength ever his then? Yes, for God had given it him. Then he could not have lost it! He had it still! The branches of it were gone, but the root remained, hid in God. All was well. If God chose that his child should lie there, for this day, and to-morrow, or till the next year, or if it pleased him that he should never rise again with the same body, was that a thing to trouble him? He turned his back on the ugly room, and was presently fast asleep again.

Not a few read the poems of a certain king brought up a shepherd lad. From Sunday to Sunday they read them. Amongst them, in their turn, they read these: "I will both lay me down in peace and sleep, for thou, Lord, only makest me to dwell in safety." Yet not only do these readers never have such a feeling in their own hearts in consequence, but they never even imagine that David really had it in his. Deeper and grander things still, uttered by this same shepherd-warrior, do they read, and yet in their wisdom will declare it preposterous that any Scotch lad should have such a feeling towards God as I have represented! "Doth God care for oxen?" says St. Paul. Doth God care for kings? I ask, or for Jew-shepherds? Or does he not care all over for all of us—oxen and kings and sparrows and Scotch lairds? According to such blind seers, less is to be expected of humanity since the son of David came, than it was capable of in his father David. Such men build stone houses, but never a spiritual nest. They cannot believe the thing possible which yet another man *does.* Nor ever may they believe it before they begin to do it. I wonder little at so many rejecting Christianity, while so many would-be champions of it hold theirs at arm's length—in their bibles, in their theories, in their church, in their clergyman, in their prayer-books, in the last devotional page they have read—a separable thing—not in their hearts on their beds in the stillness; not their comfort in the night-watches; not the strength of their days, the hope and joy of their conscious being! God is nearer to me than the air I breathe, nearer to me than the heart of wife or child, nearer to me than my own consciousness of myself, nearer to me than the words in which I speak to him, nearer than the thought roused in me by the story of his perfect son—or he is no God at all. The unbelievers might well rejoice in the loss of such a God as many Christians would make of him. But if he be indeed the Father of our Lord Christ, of that Jew who lived and died doing the will of his Father, and nothing but that will, then, to all eternity, "Amen, thy will be done, O God! and nothing but thy will, in or through me!"

Cosmo had been ill a whole week—in fever and pain, and was now helpless almost as an infant. The old man had gone for his wife, and between them they had persuaded him, though all but unconscious, to exert himself sufficiently to reach the house. This effort he could recall, in the shape of an interminable season during which he supported the world for Atlas, that he might get a little sleep; but it was only the aching weight of his own microcosm that he urged Atlantean force to carry. They took him direct to the room where he now lay, for they had themselves but one chamber, and if they took him there, what would become of the old bones to which the gardener was so fond of referring in his colloquies with himself? Also, it might be some fever he had taken, and their own lives were so much the more precious that so much of them was gone! Like most of us, they were ready to do *their next best* for him. They spared some of their own poor comforts to furnish the skeleton bed for him; and there he lay, like one adrift in a rotten boat on the ebbing ocean of life, while the old woman trudged away to the village to tell the doctor that there was a young Scotch gardener taken suddenly ill at their quarters in the castle.

The doctor sent his son, a man about thirty, who after travelling some years as a medical attendant to a nobleman, had settled in his native village as his father's partner. He prescribed for Cosmo, and gave hope that there was nothing infectious about the case. Every day during the week he had come to see him, and the night before had been with him from dark to dawn. The gardener's wife had informed Lady Joan that a young Scotchman who had come to her husband seeking employment, had been taken suddenly ill, and was lying in a room in the old wing; and Lady Joan had said she would speak to the housekeeper to let her have whatever she wanted for him. The doctor saw Lady Joan almost every time he came to see Cosmo, and she would enquire how his patient was going on; she would also hear the housekeeper's complaints of the difficulty she had in getting wine from the butler—of which there was no lack, only he grudged it, for he was doing his best to drink up the stock the old lord had left behind him, intending to take his departure with the last bottle—but she took no farther interest in the affair. The castle was like a small deserted village, and there was no necessity for a person in one part of it knowing what was taking place in another.

But that same morning she had a letter from the laird, saying he was uneasy about his boy. He had been so inconsiderate, he informed her, as to set out to visit her without asking her leave, or even warning her of his intent; and since the letter announcing his immediate departure, received a fortnight before, he had not heard of or from him. This set Joan thinking. And the immediate result was, that she went to the gardener's wife, and questioned her concerning the appearance of her patient. In the old woman's answers she certainly could recognize no likeness to Cosmo; but he must have altered much in seven years, and she could not be satisfied without seeing the young man.

Cosmo lay fast asleep, and dreaming—but pleasant dreams now, for the fever gone, life was free to build its own castles. He thought he was dead, and floating through the air at his will, volition all that was necessary to propel him like a dragon-fly, in any direction he desired to take. He was about to go to his father, to receive his congratulations on his death, and to say to him that now the sooner he too died the better, that the creditors might have the property, everybody be paid, and they two and his mother be together for always. But first, before he set out, he must have one sight of Lady Joan, and in that hope was now hovering about the towers of the castle. He was slowly circling the two great ones of the gateway, crossing a figure of eight over the gallery where stood the machinery of the portcullis, when down he dropped, and lay bruised and heavy, unable by fiercest effort of the will to move an inch from the spot. He was making the reflection how foolish it was to begin to fly before assuring himself that he was dead, and was resolving to be quite prudent another time, when he felt as if a warm sunny cloud came over him, which made him open his eyes. They gradually cleared, and above him he saw the face of his many dreams—a little sadder than it was in them, but more beautiful.

Cosmo had so much of the childlike in him that illness made him almost a very child again, and when he saw Joan's face bending over him like a living sky, just as any child might have done, he put his arms round her neck, and drew her face down to his. Hearts get uppermost in illness, and people then behave as they would not in health. More is in it than is easily found. There is such a dumb prayer in the spirit to be *taken!*

Till he opened his eyes Lady Joan had been unable to satisfy herself whether the pale, worn, yet grand-looking youth could indeed be the lad Cosmo, and was not at all prepared for such precipitate familiarity: the moment she was released, she drew back with some feeling, if not of offence, yet of annoyance. But a smile flooded Cosmo's face, mingled with such a pleading look of apology and excuse, which seemed to say, "How could I help it?" that she was ashamed of herself. It was the same true face as the boy's, with its old look of devotion and gentle worship! To make all right she stooped of her own accord, and kissed his forehead.

"Thank you," murmured Cosmo, his own voice sounding to him like that of another. "Don't be vexed with me. I am but a baby, and have no mother. When I saw you, it was as if heaven had come down into hell, and I did not think to help it. How beautiful you are! How good of you to come to me!"

"Oh, Cosmo!" cried Lady Joan—and now large silent tears were running down her cheeks—"to think of the way you and your father took me and mine in, and here you have been lying ill—I don't know how long—in a place not fit for a beggar!"

"That's just what I am!" returned Cosmo with a smile, feeling already almost well. "I have such a long story to tell you, Joan! I remember all about it now."

"Why didn't you write,—?" said Joan, and checked herself, for alas! If he had written, what would she not have found herself compelled to do!—"Why didn't you send for me at once? They told me there was a young gardener lying ill, and of course I never dreamed it could be you. But I know if you had heard at Castle Warlock that a stranger was lying ill somewhere about the place, you would have gone to him at once! It was very wrong of me, and I am sorely punished!"

"Never mind," said Cosmo; "it's all right now. I have you, and it makes me well again all at once. When I see you standing there, looking just as you used, all the time between is shrivelled up to nothing, and the present joins right on to the past. But you look sad, Joan!—I *may* call you Joan still, mayn't I?"

"Surely, Cosmo. What else? I haven't too many to call me Joan!"

"But what makes you look sad?"

"Isn't it enough to think how I have treated you?"

"You didn't know it was me," said Cosmo.

"That is true. But if, as your father taught you, I had done it to *Him*—"

"Well, there's one thing, Joan—you'll do differently another time."

"I can't be sure of that, for my very heart grows stupid, living here all alone."

"Anyhow, you will have trouble enough with me for awhile, fast as your eyes can heal me," said Cosmo, who began to be aware of a reaction.

Lady Joan's face flushed with pleasure, but the next moment grew pale again at the thought of how little she could do for him.

"The first thing," she said, "is to write to your father. When he knows I have got you, he won't be uneasy. I will go and do it at once."

Almost the moment she left him, Cosmo fell fast asleep again.

But now was Lady Joan, if not in perplexity, yet in no small discomfort. It made her miserable to think of Cosmo in such a place, yet she could not help saying to herself it was well he had not written, for she must then have asked him not to come: now that he was in the house, she dared not tell her brother; and were she to move him to any comfortable room in the castle, he would be sure to hear of it from the butler, for the less faith carried, the more favour curried! One thing only was in her power: she could make the room he was in comparatively comfortable. As soon, therefore, as she had written a hurried letter to the laird, she went hastily through some of the rooms nearest the part in which Cosmo lay, making choice of this and of that for her purpose: in the great, all but uninhabited place there were naturally many available pieces of stuff and of furniture. These she then proceeded, with her own hands, and the assistance of the gardener and his wife, to carry to his room; and when she found he was asleep, she put forth every energy to get the aspect of the place altered before he should wake. With noiseless steps she entered and left the room fifty times; and by making use of a door which had not been opened for perhaps a hundred years, she avoided attracting the least attention.

CHAPTER XXVII
A TRANSFORMATION

When Cosmo the second time opened his eyes, he was afresh bewildered. Which was the dream—that vision of wretchedness, or this of luxury? If it was not a dream, how had they moved him without once disturbing his sleep? It was as marvellous as anything in the Arabian Nights! Could it be the same chamber? Not a thing seemed the same, yet in him was a doubtful denial of transportance. Yes, the ceiling was the same! The power of the good fairy had not reached to the transformation of that! But the walls! Instead of the great hole in the plaster close by the bed, his eyes fell on a piece of rich old tapestry! Curtains of silk damask, all bespotted with quaintest flowers, each like a page of Chaucer's poetry, hung round his bed, quite other than fit sails for the Stygian boat. They had made the bed as different as the vine in summer from the vine in winter. A quilt of red satin lay in the place of the patchwork coverlid. Everything had been changed. He thought the mattress felt soft under him—but that was only a fancy, for he saw before the fire the feather-bed intended to lie between him and it. He felt like a tended child, in absolute peace and bliss—or like one just dead, while yet weary with the struggle to break free. He seemed to recall the content, of which some few vaguest filaments, a glance and no more, still float in the summer-air of many a memory, wherein the child lies, but just awakened to consciousness and the mere bliss of being, before wrong has begun to cloud its pure atmosphere. For Cosmo had nothing on his conscience to trouble it; his mind was stored with lovely images and was fruitful in fancies, because in temperament, faith, and use, he was a poet; the evil vapours of fever had just lifted from his brain, and were floating away in the light of the sun of life; he felt the pressure of no duty—was like a bird of the air lying under its mother's wing, and dreaming of flight; his childhood's most cherished dream had grown fact: there was the sylph, the oriad, the naiad of all his dreams, a living lady before his eyes—nor the less a creature of his imagination's heart; from her, as the centre of power, had all the marvellous transformation proceeded; and the lovely strength had kissed him on the forehead! The soul of Cosmo floated in rapturous quiet, like the evening star in a rosy cloud.

But I return to the earthly shore that bordered this heavenly sea. The old-fashioned, out-swelling grate, loose and awry in its setting, had a keen little fire burning in it, of which, summer as it was, the mustiness of the atmosphere, and the damp of the walls, more than merely admitted. The hole in the floor had vanished under a richly faded Turkey carpet; and a luxurious sofa, in blue damask, faded almost to yellow, stood before the fire, to receive him the moment he should cease to be a chrysalis. And there in an easy chair by the corner of the hearth, wonder of all loveliest wonders, sat the fairy-godmother herself, as if she had but just waved her wand, and everything had come to her will!—the fact being, however, that the poor fairy was not a little tired in legs and arms and feet and hands and head, and preferred contemplating what she had already done, to doing anything more for the immediate present.

Cosmo lay watching her. He dared not move a hand, lest she should move; for, though it might be to rise and come to him, would it not be to change what he saw?—and what he saw was so much enough, that he would see it forever, and desired nothing else. She turned her eyes, and seeing the large orbs of the youth fixed upon her, smiled as she had not smiled before, for a great weight was off her heart now that the room gave him a little welcome. True, it was after all but a hypocrite of a room,—a hypocrite, however, whose meaning was better than its looks! He put out his hand, and she rose and came and laid it in hers. Suddenly he let it go.

"I beg your pardon," he said. "I don't know when my hands were washed! The last I remember is digging in the garden. I wish I might wash my face and hands!"

"You mustn't think of it! you can't sit up yet," said Lady Joan. "But never mind: some people are always clean. You should see my brother's hands sometimes! I will, if you like, bring you a towel with a wet corner. I dare say that will do you good."

She poured water into a basin from a kettle on the hob, and dipping the corner of a towel in it, brought it to him. He tried to use it, but his hands obeyed him so ill that she took it from him, and herself wiped with it his face and hands, and then dried them—so gently, so softly, he thought that must be how his mother did with him when he was a baby. All the time, he lay looking up at her with a grateful smile. She then set about preparing him some tea and toast, during which he watched her every motion. When he had had the tea, he fell asleep, and when he woke next he was alone.

An hour or so later, the gardener's wife brought him a basin of soup, and when he had taken it, told him she would then leave him for the night: if he wanted anything, as there was no bell, he must pull the string she tied to the bed-post. He was very weary, but so comfortable, and so happy, his brain so full of bright yet soft-coloured things, that he felt as if he would not mind being left ages alone. He was but two and twenty, with a pure conscience, and an endless hope—so might he not well lie quiet in his bed?

By the middle of the night, however, the tide of returning health showed a check; there came a strong reaction, with delirium; his pulse was high, and terrible fancies tormented him, through which passed continually with persistent recurrence the figure of the old captain, always swinging a stick about his head, and crooning to himself the foolish rime,

"Catch yer naig an' pu' his tail	"Catch your horse and pull his tail;
In his hin' heel caw a nail;	In his hind heel drive a nail;
Rug his lugs frae ane anither;	Tug his ears from one another;
Stan' up, an' ca' the king yer brither."	Stand up, and call the king your brother."

At last, at the moment when once more his persecutor was commencing his childish ditty, he felt as if, from the top of a mountain a hundred miles away, a cold cloud came journeying through the sky, and descended upon him. He opened his eyes: there was Joan, and the cold cloud was her soft cool hand on his forehead. The next thing he knew was that she was feeding him like a child. But he did not know that she never left him again till the morning, when, seeing him gently asleep, she stole away like a ghost in the gray dawn.

The next day he was better, but for several nights the fever returned, and always in his dreams he was haunted by variations on the theme of the old captain; and for several days he felt as if he did not want to get better, but would lie forever a dreamer in the enchanted palace of the glamoured ruin. But that was only his weakness, and gradually he gained strength.

Every morning and every afternoon Lady Joan visited him, waited on him, and staid a longer or shorter time, now talking, now reading to him; and seldom would she be a whole evening absent—then only on the rare occasions when Lord Mergwain, having some one to dine with him of the more ordinary social stamp, desired her presence as lady of the house. Even then she would almost always have a peep at him one time or another. She did not know much about books, but would take up this or that, almost as it chanced to her hand in the library; and Cosmo cared little what she read, so long as he could hear her voice, which often beguiled him into the sweetest sleep with visions of home and his father. If the story she read was foolish, it mattered nothing; he would mingle with it his own fancies, and weave the whole into the loveliest of foolish dreams, all made up of unaccountably reasonable incongruities: the sensible look in dreams of what to the waking mind is utterly incoherent, is the most puzzling of things to him who would understand his own unreason. And the wild *marchenhaft* lovelinesses that fashioned themselves thus in his brain, outwardly lawless, but inwardly so harmonious as to be altogether credible to the dreamer, were not lost in the fluttering limbo of foolish invention, but, in altered shape and less outlandish garments, appeared again, when, in after years, he sought vent for the all but unspeakable. During this time he would often talk verse in his sleep, such as to Lady Joan, at least, sometimes seemed lovely, though she never could get a hold of it, she said; for always, just as she seemed on the point of understanding it, he would cease, and her ears would ache with the silence.

One warm evening, when now a good deal better, and able to sit up a part of the day, Cosmo was lying on the sofa, watching her face as she read. Through the age-dusted window came the glowing beams of the setting sun, lined and dulled and blotted. They fell on her hands, and her hands reflected them, in a pale rosy gleam, upon her face.

"How beautiful you are in the red light, Joan!" said Cosmo.

"That's the light, not me," she returned.

"Yes, it is you. The red light shows you more as you are. In the dark even you do not look beautiful. Then you may say if you like, 'That is the dark, not me.' Don't you remember what Portia says in The Merchant of Venice,

> 'The crow doth sing as sweetly as the lark
> When neither is attended; and I think
> The nightingale, if she should sing by day
> When every goose is cackling, would be thought
> No better a musician than the wren.
> How many things by reason reasoned are
> To their right praise and true perfection!'

You see he says, not that beautiful things owe their beauty, but the right seeing of their beauty, to circumstance. So the red light makes me see you more beautiful—not than you are—that could not be—but than I could see you in another light—a gray one for instance."

"You mustn't flatter me, Cosmo. You don't know what harm you may do me."

"I love you too much to flatter you," he said.

She raised the book, and began to read again.

Cosmo had gone on as he began—had never narrowed the channels that lay wide and free betwixt his soul and his father and Mr. Simon; Lady Joan had no such aqueducts to her ground, and many a bitter wind blew across its wastes; it ought not therefore to be matter of surprise that, although a little younger, Cosmo should be a good way ahead of Joan both in knowledge and understanding. Hence the conversations they now had were to Joan like water to a thirsty soul—the hope of the secret of life, where death had seemed waiting at the door. She would listen to the youth, rendered the more enthusiastic by his weakness, as to a messenger from the land of truth. In the old time she had thought Cosmo a wonderful boy, saying the strangest things like common things everybody knew: now he said more wonderful things still, she thought, but as if he knew they were strange, and did his best to make it easier to receive them. She wondered whether, if he had been a woman with a history like hers, he would have been able to keep that bright soul shining through all the dreariness, to see through the dusty windows the unchanged beauty of things, and save alive his glorious hope. She began to see that she had not begun at the beginning with anything, had let things draw her this way and that, nor put forth any effort to master circumstance by accepting its duty.

On Cosmo's side, the passion of the believer in the unseen had laid hold upon him; and as the gardener awaits the blossoming of some strange plant, of whose loveliness marvellous tales have reached his ears, so did he wait for something entrancing to issue from the sweet twilight sadness of her being, the gleams that died into dusk, the deep voiceless ponderings into which she would fall.

They talked now about any book they were reading, but it mattered little more what it was, for even a stupid book served as well as another to set their own fountains flowing. That afternoon Joan was reading from one partly written, partly compiled, in the beginning of the century, somewhat before its time in England. It might have been the work of an imitator at once of la Motte Fuoque, and the old British romancers. And this was what she read.

CHAPTER XXVIII
THE STORY OF THE KNIGHT WHO SPOKE THE TRUTH

There was once a country in which dwelt a knight whom no lady of the land would love, and that because he spake the truth. For the other knights, all in that land, would say to the ladies they loved, that of all ladies in the world they were the most beautiful, and the most gracious, yea in all things the very first; and thereby the ladies of that land were taught to love their own praise best, and after that the knight who was the best praiser of each, and most enabled her to think well of herself in spite of doubt. And the knight who would not speak save truly, they mockingly named Sir Verity, which name some of them did again miscall *Severity*—for the more he loved, the more it was to him impossible to tell a lie. And thus it came about that one after another he was hated of them all. For so it was, that, greedy of his commendation, this lady and that would draw him on to speak of that wherein she made it her pleasure to take to herself excellences; but nowise so could any one of them all gain from him other than a true judgement. As thus: one day said unto him a lady "Which of us, think you, Sir Verity, hath the darkest eyes of all the ladies here at the court of our lord the king?" And he thereto made answer, "Verily, me thinketh the queen." Then said she unto him, "Who then hath the bluest eyes of all the ladies at the court of our lord the king?"—for that her own were the colour of the heavens when the year is young. And he answered, "I think truly the Lady Coryphane hath the bluest of all their blue eyes." Then said she, "And I think truly by thine answer, Severity, that thou lovest me not, for else wouldst thou have known that mine eyes are as blue as Coryphane's." "Nay truly," he answered; "for my heart knoweth well that thine eyes are blue, and that they are lovely, and to me the dearest of all eyes, but to say they are the bluest of all eyes, that I may not, for therein should I be no true man." Therewith was the lady somewhat shamed, and seeking to cover her vanity, did answer and say, "It may well be, sir knight, for how can I tell who see not mine own eyes, and would therefore know of thee, of whom men say, some that thou speakest truly, other some that thou speakest naughtily. But be the truth as it may, every knight yet saith to his own mistress that in all things she is the paragon of the world." "Then," quoth the knight, "she that knoweth that every man saith so, must know also that only one of them all saith the thing that is true. Not willingly would I add to the multitude of the lies that do go about the world!" "Now verily am I sure that thou dost not love me," cried the lady; "for all men do say of mine eyes—" Thereat she stayed words, and said no more, that he might speak again. "Lady," said Sir Verity, and spake right solemnly, "as I said before I do say again, and in truth, that thine eyes are to me the dearest of all eyes. But they might be the bluest or the blackest, the greenest or the grayest, yet would I love them all the same. For none of those colours would they be dear to me, but for the cause that they were thine eyes. For I love thine eyes because they are thine, not thee because thine eyes are this or that." Then that lady brake forth into bitter weeping, and would not be comforted, neither thereafter would hold converse with the knight. For in that country it was the pride of a lady's life to lie lapt in praises, and breathe the air of the flatteries blown into her ears by them who would be counted her lovers. Then said the knight to himself, "Verily, and yet again, her eyes are not the bluest in the world! It seemeth to me as that the ladies in this land should never love man aright, seeing, alas! They love the truth from no man's lips; for save they may each think herself better than all the rest, then is not life dear unto them. I will forsake this land, and go where the truth may be spoken nor the speaker thereof hated." He put on his armour, with never lady nor squire nor page to draw thong or buckle spur, and mounted his horse and rode forth to leave the land. And it came to pass, that on his way he entered a great wood. And as he went through the wood, he heard a sobbing and a crying in the wood. And he said to himself, "Verily, here is some one wronged and lamenteth greatly! I will go and help."

So about he rode searchingly, until he came to the place whither he was led. And there, at the foot of a great oak, he found an old woman in a gray cloak, with her face in her hands, and weeping right on, neither ceased she for the space of a sigh. "What aileth thee, good mother?" he said. "I am not good, and I am not thy mother," she answered, and began again to weep. "Ah!" thought the knight, "here is one woman that loveth the truth, for she speaks the truth, and would not that aught but the truth be spoken!—How can I help thee, woman," he said then, "although in truth thou art not my mother, and I may not call thee good?" "By taking thyself from me," she answered. "Then will I ride on my way," said the knight, and turning, rode on his way. Then rose the woman to her feet, and followed him. "Wherefore followest thou me," said the knight, "if I may do nothing to serve thee?" "I follow thee," she answered him, "because thou speakest the truth, and because thou art not true." "If thou speakest the truth, in a mystery speakest thou it," said he. "Wherefore then ridest thou about the world?" she asked. And he replied, "Verily, to succour them that are oppressed, for I have no mistress to whom I may do honour." "nay, sir knight," said she, "but to get thee a name and great glory, thou ridest about the world. Verily thou art a man who loveth not the truth." At these words of the woman the knight clapped spurs to horse, and would have ridden from her, for he loved not to be reviled, and so he told her. But she followed him, and kept by his stirrup, and said to him as she ran, "Yea, thine own heart whispereth unto thee that I speak but the truth. It is from thyself thou wouldst flee." Then did the knight listen, and lo! his own heart was telling him that what the woman said was indeed so. Then drew he the reins of his bridle, and looked down upon the woman and said to her, "Verily thou hast well spoken, but if I be not true, yet would I be true. Come with me. I will take thee upon my horse behind me, and together we will ride through the world; thou shalt speak to me the truth, and I will hear thee, and with my sword will plead what cause thou hast against any; so shall it go well with thee and me, for fain would I not only love what is truly spoken, but be in myself the true thing." Then reached he down his hand, and she put her hand in his hand, and her foot upon his foot, and so sprang lightly up behind him, and they rode on together. And as they rode, he said unto her, "Verily thou art the first woman I have found who hath to me spoken the truth, as I to others. Only thy truth is better than mine. Truly thou must love the truth better than I!" But she returned him no answer. Then said he to her again, "Dost thou not love the truth?" And again she gave him no answer, whereat he marvelled greatly. Then said he unto her yet again, "Surely it may not be thou art one of those who speak the truth out of envy and ill-will, and on their own part love not to hear it spoken, but are as the rest of the children of vanity! Woman, lovest thou the truth, nor only to speak it when it is sharp?" "If I love not the truth," she answered, "yet I love them that love it. But tell me now, sir knight, what thinkest thou of me?" "Nay," answered the knight, "that is what even now I would fain have known from thyself, namely what to think of thee." "Then will I now try thee," said she, "whether indeed thou speakest the truth or no.—Tell me to my face, for I am a woman, what thou thinkest of that face." Then said the knight to himself, "Never surely would I, for the love of pity, of my own will say to a woman she was evil-favoured. But if she will have it, then must she hear the truth."

"Nay, nay!" said the woman, "but thou wilt not speak the truth." "Yea, but I will," answered he. "Then I ask thee again," she said, "what thinkest thou of me?" And the knight replied, "Truly I think not of thee as of one of the well-favoured among women." "Dost thou then think," said she, and her voice was full of anger, which yet it seemed as she would hide, "that I am not pleasant to look upon? Verily no man hath yet said so unto me, though many have turned away from me, because I spoke unto them the truth!" "Now surely thou sayest the thing that is not so!" said the knight, for he was grieved to think she should speak the truth but of contention, and not of love to the same, inasmuch as she also did seek that men should praise her. "Truly I say that which is so," she answered. Then was the knight angered, and spake to her roughly, and said unto her, "Therefore, woman, will I tell thee that which thou demandest of me: Verily I think of thee as one, to my thinking, the worst favoured, and least to be desired among women whom I have yet looked upon; nor do I desire ever to look upon thee again." Then laughed she aloud, and said to him, "Nay, but did I not tell thee thou didst not dare speak the thing to my face? for now thou sayest it not to my face, but behind thine own back!" And in wrath the knight turned him in his saddle, crying, "I tell thee, to thy ill-shaped and worse-hued countenance, that—" and there ceased, and spake not, but with open mouth sat silent. For behind him he saw a woman the glory of her kind, more beautiful than man ever hoped to see out of heaven. "I told thee," she said, "thou couldst not say the thing to my face!" "For that it would be the greatest lie ever in this world uttered," answered the knight, "seeing that verily I do believe thee the loveliest among women, God be praised! Nevertheless will I not go with thee one step farther, so to peril my soul's health, except, as thou thyself hast taught me to inquire, thou tell me thou lovest the truth in all ways, in great ways as well as small." "This much will I tell thee," she answered, "that I love thee because thou lovest the truth. If I say not more, it is that it seemeth to me a mortal must be humble speaking of great things. Verily the truth is mighty, and will subdue my heart unto itself." "And wilt thou help me to do the truth?" asked the knight. "So the great truth help me!" she answered. And they rode on together, and parted not thereafter. Here endeth the story of the knight that spoke the truth.

Lady Joan ceased, and there was silence in the chamber, she looking back over the pages, as if she had not quite understood, and Cosmo, who had understood entirely, watching the lovely, dark, anxious face. He saw she had not mastered the story, but, which was next best, knew she had not. He began therefore to search her difficulty, or rather to help it to take shape, and thereon followed a conversation neither of them ever forgot concerning the degrees of truth: as Cosmo designated them—the truth of fact, the truth of vital relation, and the truth of action.

CHAPTER XXIX
NEW EXPERIENCE

Soon Cosmo began to recover more rapidly—as well he might, he told Joan, with such a heavenly servant to wait on him! The very next day he was up almost the whole of it. But that very day was Joan less with him than hitherto, and therefrom came not so often and stayed a shorter time. She would bring him books and leave them, saying he did not require a nurse any more now that he was able to feed himself. And Cosmo, to his trouble, could not help thinking sometimes that her manner towards him was also a little changed. What could have come between them he asked himself twenty times a day. Had he hurt her anyhow? Had he unconsciously put on the schoolmaster with her? Had he presumed on her kindness? With such questions he plagued himself, but found to them no answer. At times he could even have imagined her a little cross with him, but that never lasted. Yet still when they met, Joan seemed farther off than when they parted the day before. It is true they almost always seemed to get back to nearly the same place before they parted again, and Cosmo tried to persuade himself that any change there might be was only the result of growing familiarity; but not the less did he find himself ever again mourning over something that was gone—a delicate colour on the verge of the meeting sky and sea of their two natures.

But how differently the hours went when she was with him, and when he lay thinking whether she was coming! His heart swelled like a rose-bud ready to burst into a flaming flower when she drew near, and folded itself together when she went, as if to save up all its perfume and strength for her return! Everything he read that pleased him, must be shared with Joan—must serve as an atmosphere of thought in which to draw nigh to each other. Everything beautiful he saw twice—with his own eyes namely, and as he imagined it in the eyes of Joan: he was always trying to see things as he thought she would see them. Not once while recovering did he care to read a thing he thought she would not enjoy—though everything he liked, he said to himself, she must enjoy some day.

Soon he made a discovery concerning himself that troubled him greatly: not once since he was ill had he buried himself in the story of Jesus! not once had he lost himself in prayer! not once since finding Joan had he been flooded with a glory as from the presence of the living One, or had any such vision of truth as used every now and then to fill him like the wine of the new world which is the old! Lady Joan saw that he was sad, and questioned him. But even to her he could not open his mind on such a matter: near as they were, they had not yet got near enough to each other for that.

In the history, which is the growth, of the individual man, epochs of truth and moods of being follow in succession, the one for the moment displacing the other, until the mind shall at length have gained power to blend the new at once with the preceding whole. But this can never be until our idea of the Absolute Life is large enough and intense enough to fill and fit into every necessity of our nature. A new mood is as a dry well for the water of life to fill. The man who does not yet understand God as the very power of his conscious as well as unconscious being, as more in him than intensest consciousness of bliss or of pain, must have many a treeless expanse, many a mirage-haunted desert, many an empty cistern and dried up river, in the world of his being! There was not much of this kind of waste in Cosmo's world, but God was not yet inside his growing love to Joan—that is, consciously to him—and his spirit was therefore of necessity troubled. Was it not a dreadful thing, he thought with himself, and was right in so thinking, that love to any lovely thing—how much more to the loveliest being God had made!—whose will is the soul of all loveliness, should cause him, in any degree, or for any time, to forget him and grow strange to the thought of him? The lack was this, that, having found his treasure, he had not yet taken it home to his Father! Jesus, himself, after he was up again, could not be altogether at home with his own, until he had first been home to his Father and their Father, to his God and their God. For as God is the source, so is he the bond of all love. There are Christians who in portions of their being, of their life, their judgements, and aims, are absolute heathens, for with these, so far as their thought or will is concerned, God has nothing to do. There God is not with them, for there they are not with God. Do they heed St. Paul when he says, "Whatsoever is not of faith is sin"?

So, between these two, an unrest had come in, and they were no more sure of ease in each other's presence, although sometimes, for many minutes together, thought and word would go well between them, and all would be as simple and shining as ever.

CHAPTER XXX
CHARLES JERMYN

The only house in the neighbouring village where Lady Joan sometimes visited, was, as the gardener had told Cosmo, that of the doctor, with whose daughter she had for some years, if not cultivated, yet admitted a sort of friendship. Their relation however would certainly have been nothing such, so different were the two, had it not been that Joan had no other acquaintance of her own age, and that Miss Jermyn had reasons for laying herself out to please her—the principal of which was that her brother, a man about thirty, had a great admiration for Lady Joan, and to please him his sister would do almost anything. Their father also favoured his son's ambition, for he hated the earl, and would be glad of his annoyance, while he liked Lady Joan, and was far from blind to the consequence his family would gain by such an alliance. But he had no great hope, for experience, of which few have more than a country doctor, had taught him that, in every probability, his son's first advance would be for Lady Joan the signal to retire within the palisades of her rank; for there are who will show any amount of familiarity and friendliness with agreeable inferiors up to the moment when the least desire of a nearer approach manifests itself: that moment the old Adam, or perhaps rather the old Satan, is up in full pride like a spiritual turkey-cock, with swollen neck, roused feathers, and hideous gabble. His experience however did not bring to his mind in the company of this reflection the fact that such a reception was precisely that which he had himself given to a prayer for the hand of his daughter from one whom he counted her social inferior. But the younger man, who also had had his experiences, reflected that the utter isolation of Lady Joan, through the ill odour of her family, the disgraceful character of her father, the unamiability of her brother, and the poverty into which they had sunk, gave him incalculable advantages.

The father had been for many years the medical adviser of the house; and although Lord Mergwain accorded the medical practice of his day about the same relation to a science of therapeutics that old alchemy had to modern chemistry, yet the moment he felt ill, he was sure to send for young Jermyn. Charles had also attended Lady Joan in several illnesses, for she had not continued in such health as when she used to climb hills in snow with Cosmo. It is true she had on these occasions sent for the father, but for one reason and another, more likely to be false than true, he had always, with many apologies, sent his son in his stead. She was at first annoyed, and all but refused to receive him; but from dislike of seeming to care, she got used to his attendance, and to him as well. He gained thus the opportunity of tolerably free admission to her, of which he made use with what additional confidence came of believing that at least he had no rival.

Nor indeed was there anything absurd in his aspiring in those her circumstances to win her. He was a man of good breeding, and more than agreeable manners—with a large topographical experience, and a social experience far from restricted, for, as I have already mentioned, he had travelled much, and in the company of persons of high position; and had Joan been less ignorant of things belonging to her proper station, she would have found yet more to interest her in him. But being a man of some insight, and possessed also of considerable versatility, so that, readily discovering any peculiarity, he was equally ready to meet it, he laid himself out to talk to her of the things, and in the ways, which he thought she would like. To discover, however, is not to understand. No longer young enough, as he said to himself, to be greatly interested in anything but *getting on*, he could yet, among the contents of the old property-room in his brain, easily lay his hands on many things to help him in the part he chose as the fittest to represent himself. The greater part of conventionally honest men try to look the thing they would like to be—that being at the same time the way they would like others to see them;

others, along with what they would like to be, act that which they would only like to appear; the downright rascal cares only to look what will serve his purpose; and the honest man thinks only of being, and of being to his fellows.

But even had Jermyn only taken upon him to imagine himself in love with a woman like Lady Joan, he must soon have become, more or less, actually in love with her. This did not however destroy his caution; and so far as his attentions had gone, they were pleasant to her;—they were at least a break in the ennui of her daily life, helping her to reach the night in safety. She was not one of those who, unable to make alive the time, must kill it lest it kill them; but neither was she of those who make their time so living, that the day is too short for them. Hence it came when he called, that by and by she would offer him tea, and when he went, would walk with him into the garden, and at length even accompany him as far as the lodge on his way home.

Charles Jermyn was a tall, well-made man, with a clever and refined face, which, if not much feeling, expressed great intelligence. By the ladies of the neighbourhood he was much admired, by some of them pronounced very manly and good-looking, by others declared to be *beautiful*. Certain of them said he was much too handsome for a doctor. He had a jolly air with him, which was yet far from unrefined, and a hearty way of shaking hands which gave an impression of honesty; and indeed I think honesty would have been comparatively easy to him, had he set himself to cultivate it; but he had never given himself trouble about anything except "getting on." You might rely on his word if he gave it solemnly, but not otherwise. Absolute truth he would have felt a hindrance in the exercise of his profession, neither out of it did he make his yea yea, and his nay nay. His oath was better than his word, and that is a human shame.

Women, even more than men, I presume, see in any one who interests them, not so much what is there, as a reflection of what they construct from the hints that please them. Some of them it takes a miserable married lifetime to undeceive; for some, not even that will serve; they continue to see, if not an angel, yet a very pardonable mortal, therefore altogether loveable man, in the husband in whom everybody else sees only a vile rascal. Whether sometimes the wife or the world be nearer the truth, will one day come out: the wife *may* be a woman of insight, and see where no one else can.

In his youth the doctor had read a good deal of poetry, and enjoyed it in a surface-sort of fashion: discovering that Lady Joan had a fine taste in verse, he made use of his acquaintance there; and effected the greater impression, that one without experience is always ready to take familiarity as indicative of real knowledge, and think that he, for instance, who can quote largely, must have vital relation with the things he quotes. But it had never entered the doctor's head that poetry could have anything to do with life—even in the case of the poet himself—how much less in that of his admirer! Never once had it occurred to him to ask how he could be such a fool as enjoy anything false—beingless save in the brain of a poet—a mere lie! For that which has nothing to do with life, what can it be but a lie? Not the less Jermyn got down book after book, for many a day undusted on his shelves, and read and re-read many a passage which had once borne him into the seventh heaven of feeling, suggesting somewhere a better world, in which lovely things might be had *without too much trouble:* now as he read, he was struck with a mild surprise at finding how much had lost even the appearance of the admirable; how much of what had seemed bitter, he could thoroughly accept. He did not ask whether the change came of a truer vision or a sourer judgement, put all down to the experience that makes a man wise, none to a loss within. He was not able to imagine himself in anything less than he had been, in anything less than he would be. Yet poetry was to him now the mere munition of war! mere feathers for the darts of Cupid!—that was how the once poetic man to himself expressed himself! He was laying in store of weapons, he said! For when a man will use things in which he does not believe, he cannot fail to be vulgar. But Lady Joan saw no vulgarity in the result—it was hid in the man himself. To her he seemed a profound lover of poetry, who knew much of which she had never even heard. Once he contrived to spend a whole afternoon with her in the library, for of the outsides of books, their title-pages, that is, he had a good deal of knowledge, and must make opportunity to show it. One of his patients, with whom he first travelled, then for a time resided, was a book-collector, and with him he learned much, chiefly from old-book-catalogues. With Lady Joan this learning, judiciously poured out, passed for a marvellous knowledge of books, and the country doctor began to assume in her eyes the proportions of a man of universal culture. He knew at least how to bring all he had into use, and succeeded in becoming something in the sweet lonely life, so ignorant and unsupported. He could play the violin too, and that with no mean expression—believing only in the expression, nowise in the feeling expressed: this accomplishment also he contrived she should, as if by accident, become acquainted with.

In the judgement of most who knew him, he was an excellent and indeed admirable man. "No nonsense about him, don't you know?—able to make himself agreeable, but not losing sight of the main chance either!" men would say; and "A thorough family-doctor, knowing how to humour patients out of their fancies!" would certain mammas add, who, instead of being straight-forward with their children, were always scheming, and dodging, and holding private confabulations about them with doctor and clergyman.

In that part of his professional duty which bordered on that of the nurse, the best that was in Jermyn came out. Few men could handle a patient at the same time so firmly and tenderly as he; few were less sparing of self in the endeavour to make him comfortable. And from the moment when the simple-minded Cosmo became aware of his attendance and ministration, his heart went out to him—from the moment, that is, when, in the afternoon of the same day on which Joan transformed his chamber, he lifted him in his arms that the gardener and his wife might place a feather-bed and mattress under him, obliterating in softness the something which had seemed to find out every bone in his body: as soon as he was laid down again, his spirit seemed to rise on clouds of ease to thank his minister. And Cosmo was one in whom the gratitude was as enduring as ready. Next to the appearance of Lady Joan, all the time he was recovering, he looked for the daily visit of the doctor. Nor did the doctor ever come without receiving his reward in an interview with the lady. And herein Jermyn gained another advantage. For Joan found herself compelled to take him into her confidence concerning her brother's ignorance of the presence of Cosmo in the house; and so he shared a secret with her. He did not, of course, altogether relish the idea of this Scotch cousin, but plainly he was too young for Joan, and he would soon find out whether there was any need to beware of him, by which time he would know also what to do with him, should action be necessary.

For the first week or so Joan did not mind how often the doctor found her with Cosmo, but after that she began to dislike it, she could scarcely have told why, and managed to be elsewhere when he came. After the third time the doctor began to cherish suspicion, and called cunning to his aid. Having mentioned an hour at which he would call the next day, he made his appearance an hour earlier, and with an excuse on his lips for the change he had been "compelled to make," walked into the room without warning, as of course he might without offence, where his patient was a young man. There, as he had feared, was Lady Joan. But she had heard or felt his coming, and as he entered she was handing Cosmo the newspaper, with the words,

"There! You are quite able to read to yourself today. I will go and have another search for the book you wanted;" and with that she turned, and gave a little start, for there stood the doctor!

"Oh, Doctor Jermyn!" she exclaimed, "I did not know you were there!" and held out her hand. "Our patient is going on wonderfully now. You will let me see you before you leave the castle?"

Therewith she left the room, and hastening to her own, saw in the mirror the red of a lie, said to herself, "What will Cosmo think?" and burst into tears—the first she had shed since the day she found him.

The doctor was not taken in, but Cosmo was troubled and puzzled. In Jermyn's talk, however, and his own simplicity, he soon forgot the strangeness of this her behaviour.

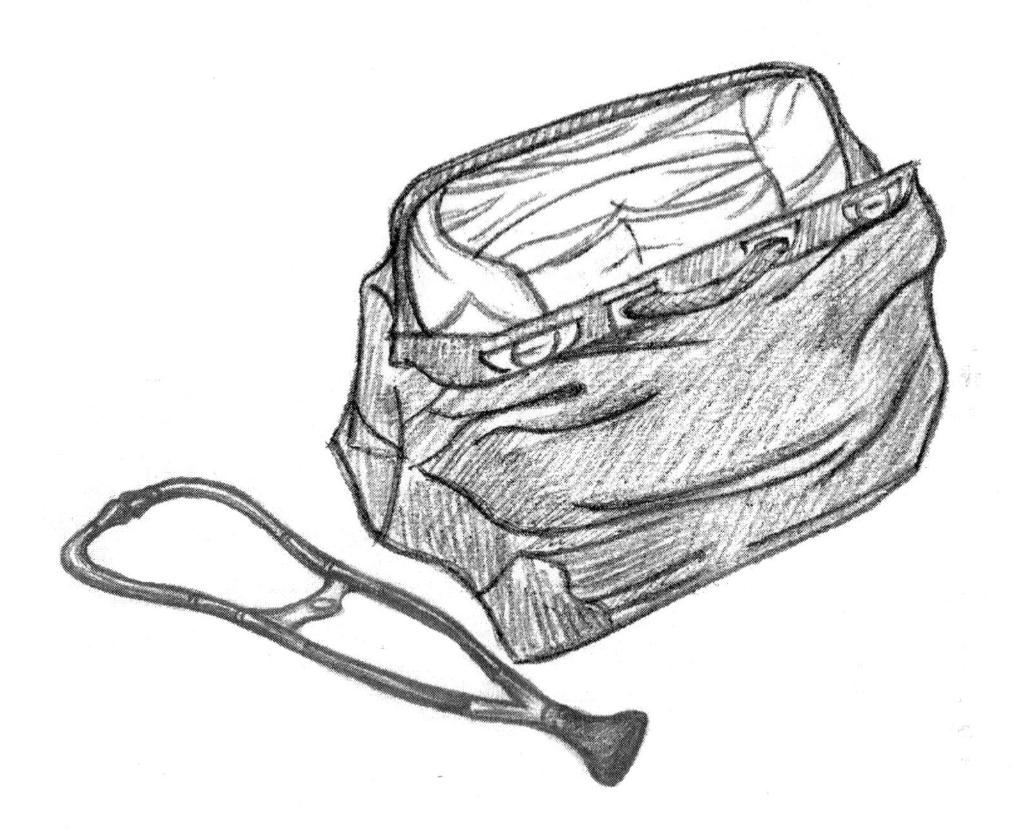

CHAPTER XXXI
COSMO AND THE DOCTOR

To the eyes of Jermyn, Cosmo appeared, mainly from his simplicity, younger than he was, while the doctor's manners, and his knowledge of the world, made Cosmo regard him as a much greater man than, in any sense or direction, he really was. His kindness having gained the youth's heart, he was ready to see in him everything that love would see in the loved.

"You are very good to me, Doctor Jermyn," he said, one day, "—so good, that I am the more sorry, though the less unwilling—"—The doctor could not keep hold of the thread of Cosmo's speech, yet did not interrupt him.—"to tell you what is now weighing on my mind: I do not know how or when I shall be able to hand you your fees. I hope you will not come to see me once more than is necessary; and the first money I earn, you shall be paid part at least of what I owe you."

The doctor laughed. It was such a school-boy speech, he thought! It was a genuine relief to Cosmo to find him take the thing so lightly.

"You were robbed on the way, Lady Joan tells me," Jermyn said.

"I am not sure that I was robbed," returned Cosmo; "but in any case, even had I brought every penny I started with, I could not have paid you. My father and I are very poor, Mr. Jermyn."

"And my father and I are pretty well to do," said the doctor, laughing again.

"But," resumed Cosmo, "neither condition is a reason why you should not be paid. Mine is only the cause why you are not paid at once."

"My dear fellow," said the doctor, laying his hand on the boy's, "I am not such a very old man—it is not so very long since I was a student myself—in your country too—at Edinburgh—that I should forget what it is to be a student, or how often money is scarce in the midst of every other kind of plenty and refinement."

"But I am not exactly a student now. I have been making a little money as tutor; only—"

"Don't trouble your head about it, I beg of you," interrupted the doctor. "It is the merest trifle. Besides, I should never have thought of taking a fee from you! I am well paid in the pleasure of making your acquaintance.—But there is one way," he added, "in which you could make me a return."

"What is that?" asked Cosmo eagerly.

"To borrow a little money of me for a few months? I am not at all hard up at present. I had to borrow many a time when I was in Edinburgh."

The boy-heart of Cosmo swelled in his bosom, and for a time he could not answer. He thought with himself, "Here is a man of the true sort!—a man after my father's own heart! who in the ground of his rights plants fresh favours, and knows the inside of a fellow's soul as well as his body! This is a rare man!"

But he felt it would be to do Joan a wrong to borrow money from the doctor and not from her. So with every possible acknowledgement he declined the generous offer. Now the doctor was quite simple in behaving thus to Cosmo. He was a friendly man and a gentleman, and liked Cosmo as no respectable soul could help liking him. It had not yet entered into him to make him useful. That same night, however, he began to ask himself whether he might not make Cosmo serve instead of hindering his hope, and very soon had thought the matter out. He was by no means too delicate to talk at once about his love, but would say nothing of it until he had made more sure of Cosmo, and good his ground by sowing another crop first: he must make himself something in the eyes of the youth, plant himself firmly in his estimation, cause his idea of him to blossom; and for the sake of this he must first of all understand the boy!

Nor was it long before the doctor imagined he did understand the boy; and indeed, sceptical as both his knowledge of himself and of the world had made him, he did so far understand him as to believe him as innocent of evil as the day he was born. His eyes could not shine so, his mouth could not have that childlike—the doctor called it childish—smile otherwise. He put out various feelers to satisfy himself there was no pretence, and found his allusions either passed over him like a breath of the merest air, or actually puzzled him. It was not always that Cosmo did not know what the suggestion might mean, but that he could not believe Jermyn meant that; and perceiving this, the doctor would make haste to alter the shadow into something definitely unobjectionable. Jermyn had no design of corrupting the youth; he was above that, even could he have fancied anything to be gained by it, whereas his interest lay in the opposite direction, his object being to use the lad unconsciously to himself. He discovered also concerning him that he had lofty ideas of duty in everything; that he was very trusting, and unready to doubt; and that with him poetry was not, as with Lady Joan, a delight, but an absolute passion. After such discoveries, he judged it would not be hard to make for himself, as for an idol, a high place in the imagination of the boy. For this end he brought to bear upon him his choicest fragments of knowledge, and all his power to interest; displayed in pleasing harmonies his acquaintance with not a few of the more delicate phases of humanity, and his familiarity with the world of imagination as embodied in books; professed much admiration he did not feel, in the line of Cosmo's admiration, going into raptures, for instance, over Milton's profoundest gems, whose beauty he felt only in a kind of reflected cold-moony way, through the external perfection of their colour and carving; brought to his notice Wordsworth's *Happy Warrior,* of which he professed, and truly, that he had pasted it on his wall when a student, that at any moment he might read it; and introduced him to the best poems of Shelley, a favour for which alone Cosmo felt as if he must serve him for life.

Cosmo was so entire, so utterly honest, so like a woman, that he could not but regard the channel through which anything reached him, as of the nature of that which came to him through it; how could that serve to transmit which was not one in spirit with the thing transmitted? To his eyes, therefore, Jermyn sat in the reflex glory of Shelley, and of every other radiant spirit of which he had widened his knowledge. How could Cosmo for instance regard him as a common man through whom came to him first that thrilling trumpet-cry, full of the glorious despair of a frustrate divinity, beginning,

O wild west wind, thou breath of autumn's being,

—the grandest of all pagan pantheistic utterances he was ever likely to hear! The whole night, and many a night after, was Cosmo haunted with the Aeolian music of its passionate, self-pitiful self-abandonment. And in his dreams, the "be thou me, impetuous one!" of the poem, seemed fulfilled in himself—for he and the wind were one, careering wildly along the sky, combing out to their length the maned locks of the approaching storm, and answering the cry of weary poets everywhere over the world.

As he sat by his patient's bed, Jermyn would also tell him about his travels, and relate passages of adventure in various parts of the world; and he came oftener, and staid longer, and talked more and more freely, until at length in Cosmo's vision, the more impressible perhaps from his weakness, the doctor seemed a hero, an admirable Chrichton; a paragon of doctors.

In all this, Jermyn, used to his own dignified imagery, was preparing an engine of assault against the heart of the lady. He had no very delicate feeling of the relation of man and woman, neither any revulsion from the loverly custom in low plays of making a friend of the lady's maid, and bribing her to chaunt the praises of the briber in the ears of her mistress. In his intercourse with Lady Joan, something seemed always to interfere and prevent him from showing himself to the best advantage—which he never doubted to be the truest presentation; but if he could send her a reflection of him in the mind of such an admirer as he was making of Cosmo, she would then see him more as he desired to be seen, and as he did not doubt he was.

CHAPTER XXXII
THE NAIAD

At length Cosmo was able to go out, and Joan did not let him go by himself. For several days he walked only a very little, but sat a good deal in the sun, and rapidly recovered strength. At last, one glorious morning of summer, they went out together, intending to have a real little walk. Lady Joan had first made sure that her brother was occupied in his laboratory, but still she dared not lead her patient to any part of the garden or grounds ever visited by him. She took him, therefore, through walks, some of them wide, and bordered with stately trees, but all grown with weeds and moss, to the deserted portion with which he had already made a passing acquaintance. There all lay careless of the present, hopeless of the future, and hardly dreaming of the past. It was long since foot of lady had pressed these ancient paths, long since laugh or merry speech had been heard in them. Nothing is lovelier than the result of the half-neglect which often falls upon portions of great grounds, when the owner's fancy has changed, and his care has turned to some newer and more favoured spot; when there is moss on the walks, but the weeds are few and fine; when the trees stand in their old honour, yet no branch is permitted to obstruct a path; when flowers have ceased to be sown or planted, but those that bloom are not disregarded; while yet it is only through some stately door that admission is gained, and no chance foot is free to stray in. But here it was altogether different. That state of neglect was long past. The place was ragged, dirty, overgrown. There was between the picture I have drawn and this reality, all the painful difference between stately and beautiful matronhood, and the old age that, no longer capable of ministering to its own decencies, has grown careless of them.

"At this time of the day there is plenty of sun here." said his nurse, in a tone that seemed to savour of apology.

"I think," said Cosmo, "the gardener told me some parts of the grounds were better kept than this."

"Yes," answered Joan, "but none of them are anything like what they should be. My brother is so poor."

"I don't believe you know what it is to be poor," said Cosmo.

"Oh, don't I!" returned Joan with a sigh. "You see Constantine requires for his experiments all the little money the trustees allow."

"I know this part," said Cosmo. "I made acquaintance with it the last thing as I was growing ill. It looks to me so melancholy! If I were here, I should never rest till I had with my own hands got it into some sort of order."

"Are you as strong as you used to be, Cosmo—I mean when you are well?" asked Joan, willing to change the direction of the conversation.

"A good deal stronger, I hope," answered Cosmo. "But I am glad it is not just this moment, for then I should have no right to be leaning on you, Joan."

"Do you like to lean on me, Cosmo?"

"Indeed I do; I am proud of it!—But tell me why you don't take me to a more cheerful part." She made him no answer. He looked in her face. It was very pale, and tears were in her eyes.

"Must I tell you, Cosmo?" she said.

"No, certainly, if you would rather not."

"But you might think it something wrong."

"I should never imagine you doing anything wrong, Joan."

"Then I must tell you, lest it should be wrong.—My brother does not know that you are here."

Now Cosmo had never imagined that Lord Mergwain did not know he was at the castle. It was true he had not come to see him, but nothing was simpler if Lord Mergwain desired to see Cosmo as little as Cosmo desired, from his recollection of him at Caslte Warlock, to see Lord Mergwain. It almost took from him what little breath he had to learn that he had been all this time in a man's house without his knowledge. No doubt, in good sense and justice, the house was Joan's too, however little the male aristocracy may be inclined to admit such a statement of rights, but there must be some one at the head of things, and, however ill he might occupy it, that place was was naturally his lordship's, and he had at least a right to know who was in the house. Huge discomfort thereupon invaded Cosmo, and a restless desire to be out of the place. His silence frightened Joan.

"Are you very angry with me, Cosmo?" she said.

"Angy! No, Joan! How could I be angry with you? Only it makes me feel myself where I have no business to be—rather like a thief in fact."

"Oh, I am so sorry! But what could I do? You don't know my brother, or you would not wonder. He seems to have a kind of hatred to your family!—I do not in the least know why. Could my father have said anything about you that he misunderstood?—But no, that could not be!—And yet my father did say he knew your house many years before!"

"I don't care how Lord Mergwain regards me," said Cosmo; "what angers me is that he should behave so to you that you dare not tell him a thing. Now I am sorry I came without writing to you first!—I don't know though!—and I can't say I am sorry I was taken ill, for all the trouble I have been to you; I should never have known otherwise how beautiful and good you are."

"I'm not good! and I'm not beautiful!" cried Joan, and burst into tears of humiliation and sore-heartedness. What a contrast their house and its hospitality, she thought, to those in which Cosmo lived one heart and one soul with his father!

"But," she resumed the next moment, wiping away her tears, "you must not think I have no right to do anything for you. My father left all his personal property to me, and I know there was money in his bureau, saved up for me—I *know* it; and I know too that my brother took it! I said never a word about it to him or any one—never mentioned the subject before; but I can't have you feeling as if you had been taking what I had no right to give!"

They had come to the dry fountain, with its great cracked basin, in the centre of which stood the parched naiad, pouring an endless nothing from her inverted vase. Forsaken and sad she looked. All the world had changed save her, and left her a memorial of former thoughts, vanished ways, and forgotten things: she, alas! could not alter, must be still the same, the changeless centre of change. All the winters would beat upon her, all the summers would burn her; but never more would the glad water pour plashing from her dusty urn! never more would the birds make showers with their beating wings in her cool basin! The dead leaves would keep falling year after year to their rest, but she could not fall, must, through the slow ages, stand, until storm and sunshine had wasted her atom by atom away.

On the broad rim of the basin they sat down. Cosmo turned towards the naiad, such thoughts as I have written throbbing in his brain like the electric light in an exhausted receiver, Joan with her back to the figure, and her eyes on the ground, thinking Cosmo brooded vexed on his newly discovered position. It was a sad picture. The two were as the type of Nature and Art, the married pair, here at strife—still together, but only the more apart—Oberon and Titania, with ruin all about them. Through the straggling branches appeared the tottering dial of Time where not a sun-ray could reach it; for Time himself may well go to sleep where progress is but disintegration. Time himself is nothing, does nothing; he is but the medium in which the forces work. Time no more cures our ills, than space unites our souls, because they cross it to mingle.

Had Cosmo suspected Joan's thought, he would have spoken; but the urn of the naiad had brought back to him his young thoughts and imaginations concerning the hidden source of the torrent that rushed for ever along the base of Castle Warlock: the dry urn was to him the end of all life that knows not its source—therefore, when the water of its consciousness fails, cannot go back to the changeless, ever renewing life, and unite itself afresh with the self-existent, parent spring. A moment more and he began to tell Joan what he was thinking—gave her the whole metaphysical history of the development in him of the idea of life in connection with the torrent and its origin ever receding, like a decoy-hope that entices us to the truth, until at length he saw in God the one only origin, the fountain of fountains, the Father of all lights—that is, of all things, and all true thoughts.

"If there were such an urn as that," he said, pointing to the naiad's, "ever renewing the water inside it without pipe or spring, there would be what we call a miracle, because, unable to follow the appearance farther back, we should cease thought, and wonder only in the presence of the making God. And such an urn would be a true picture of the heart of God, ever sending forth life of itself, and of its own will, into the consciousness of us receiving the same."

He grew eloquent, and talked as even Joan had never heard him before. And she understood him, for the lonely desire after life had wrought, making her capable. She felt more than ever that he was a messenger to her from a higher region, that he had come to make it possible for her to live, to enlarge her being, that it might no more be but the half life of mere desire after something unkown and never to be attained.

Suddenly, with that inexplicable breach in the chain of association over which the electric thought seems to leap, as over a mighty void of spiritual space, Cosmo remembered that he had not yet sent the woman whose generous trust had saved him from long pangs of hunger, the price of her loaf. He turned quickly to Joan: was not this a fresh chance of putting trust in her? What so precious thing between two lives as faith? It is even a new creation in the midst of the old. Would he not be wrong to ask it from another? And ask it he must; for there was the poor woman, on whom he had no claim of individual, developed friendship, in want of her money! Would he not feel that Joan wronged him, if she asked some one else for any help he could give her? He told her therefore the whole story of his adventures on his way to her, and ending said, "Lend me a half-sovereign—please—to put in a letter for the first woman. I will find something for the girl afterwards."

Joan burst into tears. It was some time before she could speak, but at last she told him plainly that she had no money, and dared not ask her brother, because he would want to know first what she meant to do with it.

"Is it possible?" cried Cosmo. "Why, my father would never ask me what I wanted a little money for!"

"And you would be sure to tell him without his asking!" returned Joan. "But I dare not tell Constantine. Last week I could have asked him, because then, for your sake, I would have told a lie; but I dare not do that now."

She did not tell him she gave her last penny to a beggar on the road the day he came, or that she often went for months without a coin in her pocket.

Cosmo was so indignant he could not speak; neither must he give shape in her hearing to what he thought of her brother. She looked anxiously in his face.

"Dear Cosmo," she said, "do not be angry with me. I will borrow the money from the housekeeper. I have never done such a thing, but for your sake I will. You shall send it tomorrow."

"No, no, dearest Joan!" cried Cosmo. "I will not hear of such a thing. I should be worse than Lord Mergwain to lay a feather on the burden he makes you carry."

"I shouldn't mind it *much*. It would be sweet to hurt my pride for your sake."

"Joan, if you do," said Cosmo, "I will not touch it. Don't trouble your dear heart about it. God is taking care of the woman as well as of us. I will send it afterwards."

They sat silent—Cosmo thinking how he was to escape from this poverty-stricken grandeur to his own humble heaven—as poor, no doubt, but full of the dignity lacking here. He knew the state of things at home too well to imagine his father could send him the sum necessary without borrowing it, and he knew also how painful that would be to him who had been so long a borrower ever struggling to pay.

Joan's eyes were red with weeping when at length she looked pitifully in his face. Like a child he put both his arms about her, seeking to comfort her. Sudden as a flash came a voice, calling her name in loud, and as it seemed to Cosmo, angry tones. She turned white as the marble on which they sat, and cast a look of agonized terror on Cosmo.

"It is Constantine!" said her lips, but hardly her voice.

The blood rushed in full tide from Cosmo's heart, as it had not for many a day, and coloured all his thin face. He drew himself up, and rose with the look of one ready for love's sake to meet danger joyously. But Joan threw her arms round him now, and held him.

"No, no!" she said; "—this way! this way!" and letting him go, darted into the pathless shrubbery, sure he would follow her.

Cosmo hated turning his back on any person or thing, but the danger here was to Joan, and he must do as pleased her. He followed instantly.

CHAPTER XXXIII
THE GARDEN-HOUSE

She threaded and forced her way swiftly through the thick-grown shrubs, regardless of thorns and stripping-twigs. It was a wilderness for many yards, but suddenly the bushes parted, and Cosmo saw before him a neglected building, overgrown with ivy, of which it would have been impossible to tell the purpose, for it was the product of a time when everything was made to look like something else. The door of it, thick with accumulated green paint, stood half open, as if the last who left it had failed in a feeble endeavour to shut it. Like a hunted creature Joan darted in, and up the creaking stair before her. Cosmo followed, every step threatening to give way under him.

The place was two degrees nearer ruin than his room. Great green stains were on the walls; plaster was lying here and there in a heap; the floors, rotted everywhere with damp, were sinking in all directions. Yet there had been no wanton destruction, for the glass in the windows was little broken. Merest neglect is all that is required to make of both man and his works a heap; for will is at the root of well-being, and nature speedily resumes what the will of man does not hold against her.

At the top of the stair, Joan turned into a room, and keeping along the wall, went cautiously to the window, and listened.

"I don't think he will venture here," she panted. "The gardener tells me his lordship seems as much afraid of the place as he and the rest of them. I don't mind it much—in the daytime.—You are never frightened, Cosmo!"

As she spoke, she turned on him a face which, for all the speed she had made, was yet pale as that of a ghost.

"I don't pretend never to be frightened," said Cosmo; "all I can say is, I hope God will help me not to turn my back on anything, however frightened I may be."

But the room he was in seemed to him the most fearful place he had ever beheld. His memory of the spare room at home, with all its age and worn stateliness and evil report, showed mere innocence beside this small common-looking, square room. If a room dead and buried for years, then dug up again, be imaginable, that is what this was like. It was furnished like a little drawing-room, and many of the nicities of work and ornament that are only to be seen in a lady's room, were yet recognizable here and there, for everything in it was plainly as it had been left by the person who last occupied it. But the aspect of the whole was indescribably awful. The rottenness and dust and displacement by mere decay, looked enough to scare even the ghosts, if they had any scare left in them. No doubt the rats had at one time their share in the destruction, but it was long since they had forsaken the house. There was no disorder. The only thing that looked as if the room had been abandoned in haste, was the door of a closet standing wide open. The house had a worse repute than ghost could give it—worse than Joan knew, for no one had ever told her what must add to her father's discredit.

Something in a corner of the closet just mentioned, caught Cosmo's eyes, and he had taken one step towards it, when a sharp moan from the lips of his companion arrested him. He turned, saw her face agonized with fresh fear, and was rushing to the window, when she ran *at* him, pushed him back, and stood shaking. He thought she would have fallen, and supported her. They stood listening speechless, with faces like two moons in the daytime. Presently Cosmo heard the rustling of twigs, and the sounds of back-swinging branches. These noises came nearer and nearer. Joan gazed with expanding eyes of terror in Cosmo's face, as if anywhere else she must see what would kill her.

"Joan!" cried the same voice Cosmo had heard in the garden. She shook, and held so to Cosmo's arm that she left as sure marks of her fingers there as ever did ghost. The sympathy of her fear invaded him. He would have darted to meet the enemy, but she would not let him go. The shudder of a new resolve passed through her, and she began to pull him towards the closet. Involuntarily for a moment he resisted, for he feared the worse risk to her; but her action and look were imperative, and he yielded.

They entered the closet and he pulled the door to close it upon them. It resisted; he pulled harder; a rusted hinge gave way, and the door dropped upon its front corner, so that he had partly to lift it to get it to. Just as he succeeded, Joan's name on the voice of her fear echoed awfully through the mouldy silences of the house. In the darkness of the closet, where there was just room for two to stand, she clung like a child to Cosmo, trembling in his arms like one in a fit of the ague. It is mournful to think what a fear many men are to the women of their house. The woman-fear in the world is one of its most pitiful outcries after a saviour.

Hesitating steps were heard below. They went from one to another of the rooms, then began to ascend the stair.

"Now, Joan," said Cosmo, holding her to him, "whatever you do, keep quiet. Don't utter a sound. Please God, I will take care of you."

She pressed his shoulder, but did not speak.

The steps entered the room. Both Cosmo and Joan seemed to feel the eyes that looked all about it. Then the steps came towards the closet. Now was the decisive moment! Cosmo was on the point of bursting out, with the cry of a wild animal, when something checked him, and suddenly he made up his mind to keep still to the very last. He put a hand on the lock, and pressed the door down against the floor. In the faint light that came through the crack at the top of it, he could see the dark terror of Joan's eyes fixed on his face. A hand laid hold of the lock, and pulled, and pulled, but in vain. Probably then Mergwain saw that the door was fallen from its hinge. He turned the key, and the door had not altered its position too far for his locking them in. Then they heard him go down the stair, and leave the house.

"He's not gone far!" said Cosmo. "He will have this closet open presently. You heard him lock it! We must get out of it at once! Please, let me go, Joan, dear! I must get the door open."

She drew back from him as far as the space would allow. He put his shoulder to the door, and sent it into the middle of the room with a great crash, then ran and lifted it.

"Come, Joan! Quick!" he cried. "Help me to set it up again."

The moment something was to be done, Joan's heart returned to her. In an instant they had the door jammed into its place, with the bolt in the catch as Mergwain had left it.

"Now," said Cosmo, "we must get down the stair, and hide somewhere below, till he passes, and comes up here again."

They ran to the kitchen, and made for a small cellar opening off it. Hardly were they in it when they heard him re-enter and go up the stair. The moment he was safely beyond them, they crept out, and keeping close to the wall of the house, went round to the back of it, and through the thicket to a footpath near, which led to the highway. It was a severe trial to Cosmo's strength, now that the excitement of adventure had relaxed, and left him the weaker. Again and again Joan had to urge him on, but as soon as she judged it safe, she made him sit, and supported him.

"I believe," she said, "that wretched man of his has put him up to it. Constantine has found out something. I would not for the world he should learn all! You don't know—you are far too good to know what he would think—yes, and tell me to my face! It was not an easy life with my father, Cosmo, but I would rather be with him now, wherever he is, than go on living in that house with my brother."

"What had we better do?" said Cosmo, trying to hide his exhaustion.

"I am going to take you to the Jermyns'. They are the only friends I have. Julia will be kind to you for my sake. I will tell them all about it. Young Dr. Jermyn knows already."

Alas, it was like being let down out of paradise into purgatory! But when we cannot stay longer in paradise, we must, like our first parents, make the best of our purgatory.

"You will be able to come and see me, will you not, Joan," he said sadly.

"Yes, indeed!" she answered. "It will be easier in some ways than before. At home I never could get rid of the dread of being found out. As soon as I get you safe in, I must hurry home. Oh, dear! how shall I keep clear of stories! Only, when you are safe, I shall not care so much."

In truth, although she had seemed to fear all for herself, her great dread had been to hear Cosmo abused.

"What you must have gone through for me!" said Cosmo. "It makes me ache to think of it!"

"It will be only pleasant to look back upon, Cosmo," returned Joan with a sad smile. "But oh for such days again as we used to have on the frozen hills! There are the hills again every winter, but will the old days ever come again, Cosmo?"

"The old days never come again," answered Cosmo. "But do you know why, Joan?"

"No," murmured Joan, very sadly.

"Because they would be getting in the way of the new better days, whose turn it is," replied Cosmo. "You tell God, Joan, all about it; he will give us better days than those. To some, no doubt, it seems absurd that there should be a great hearing Life in the world; but it is what you and I need so much that we don't see how, by any possibility, to get on without it! It cannot well look absurd to us! And if you should ever find you cannot pray any more, tell me, and I will try to help you. I don't think that time will ever come to me. I can't tell—but always hitherto, when I have seemed to be at the last gasp, things have taken a turn, and it has grown possible to go on again."

"Ah, you are younger than me, Cosmo!" said Joan, more sadly than ever.

Comso laughed.

"Don't you show me any airs on that ground," he said. "Leave that to Agnes. She is two years older than I, and used always to say when we were children, that she was old enough to be my mother."

"But I am more than two years older than you, Cosmo," said Joan.

"How much, then—exactly?" asked Cosmo.

"Three years and a whole month," she answered.

"Then you must be old enough to be my grandmother! But I don't mean to be sat upon for that. Agnes gave me enough of that kind of thing!"

Whether Joan began to feel a little jealous of Agnes, or only more interested in her, it would be hard to say, but Cosmo had now to answer a good many questions concerning her; and when Joan learned what a capable girl Agnes was, understanding Euclid and algebra, as Mr. Simon said, better than any boy, Cosmo himself included, he had ever had to teach, the earl's daughter did feel a little pain at the heart because of the cottar's.[8]

They reached at last the village and the doctor's house, where, to Joan's relief, the first person they met was Charles, to whom at once she told the main part of their adventures that day. He proposed just what Joan wished, and was by no means sorry at the turn things had taken—putting so much more of the game, as he called it, into his hands.

Things were speedily arranged, all that was necessary told his father and sister, and Joan invited to stay to lunch, which was just ready. This she thought it better to do, especially as Jermyn and his sister would then walk home with her. What the doctor would say if he saw

8 COTTAR: a farm labourer provided with a cottage in return for their work on the land.

Mergwain, she did not venture to ask: she knew he would tell any number of stories to get her out of a scrape, while Cosmo would only do or endure anything, from thrashing her brother to being thrashed himself.

A comfortable room was speedily prepared for Cosmo, and Jermyn made him go to bed at once. Nor did he allow him to see Joan again, for he told her he was asleep, and she had better not disturb him—which was not true—but might have been, for all the doctor knew as he had not been to see.

Joan did not fall in with her brother for a week, and when she saw him he did not allude to the affair. What was in his mind she did not know for months. Always, however, he was ready to believe that the mantle of wickedness of his fathers, which he had so righteously refused to put on, had fallen upon his sister instead. Only he had no proof.

CHAPTER XXXIV
CATCH YOUR HORSE

When Cosmo was left alone in his room, with orders from the doctor to put himself to bed, he sank wearily on a chair that stood with its back to the light; then first his eye fell upon the stick he carried. Joan had brought him his stick when he was ready to go into the garden, but this was not that stick. He must have caught it up somewhere instead of his own! Where could it have been? He had no recollection either of laying down his own, or of thinking he took it again. After a time he recalled this much, that, in the horrible room they had last left, at the moment when Joan cried out because of the sound of her brother's approach, he was walking to the closet to look at something in it that had attracted his attention—seeming in the dusk, from its dull shine, the hilt of a sword. The handle of the walking stick he now held must be that very thing! But he could not tell whether he had caught it up with any idea of defence, or simply in the dark his hand had come into contact with it and instinctively closed upon it, he could not even conjecture. But why should he have troubled his head so about a stick? Because this was a notably peculiar one: the handle of that stick was in form a repetition of the golden horse that had carried him to the university! Their common shape was so peculiar, that not only was there no mistaking it, but no one who saw the two could have avoided the conviction that they had a common origin, and if any significance, then a common one. There was an important difference however: even if in substance this were the same as the other, it could yet be of small value: the stick thus capped was a bamboo, rather thick, but handle and all, very light.

Proceeding to examine it, Cosmo found that every joint was double-mounted and could be unscrewed. Of joints there were three, each forming a small box. In the top one were a few grains of snuff, in the middle one a little of something that looked like gold dust, and the third smelt of opium. The top of the cane had a cap of silver, with a screw that went into the lower part of the horse, which thus made a sort of crutch-handle to the stick. He had screwed off, and was proceeding to replace this handle, when his eye was arrested, his heart seemed to stand still, and the old captain's foolish rime came rushing into his head. He started from his chair, took the thing to the window, and there stood regarding it fixedly. Beyond a doubt this was his great grand-uncle's, the old captain's stick, the only thing missed when his body was found! but whence such an assured convition? and why did the old captain's rime, whose application to the golden horse his father and he had rejected, return at sight of this one, so much its inferior? In a word, whence the eagerness of curiosity that now possessed Cosmo?

In turning the handle upside down, he saw that from one of the horse's delicately finished shoes, a nail was missing, and its hole left empty. It was a hind shoe too!

"Catch yer naig, an' pu' his tail; In his hin' heel caw a nail!	"Catch your horse and pull his tail; In his hind heel drive a nail!

I do believe," he said to himself, "this is the horse that was in the old villain's head every time he uttered the absurd rime!"

There must then be in the cane a secret, through which possibly the old man had overreached himself! Had that secret, whatever it was, been discovered, or did it remain for him now to discover?

A passion of curiosity seized him, but something held him back. What was it? The stick was not his property; any discovery concerning or by means of it, ought to be made with the consent and in the presence of the owner of it—her to whom the old lord had left his personal property!

And now Cosmo had to go through an experience as strange as it was new, for, in general of a quietly expectant disposition, he had now such a burning desire to conquer the secret of the stick, as appeared to him to savour of *possession.* It was so unlike himself, that he was both angry and ashamed. He set it aside and went to bed. But the haunting eagerness would not let him rest; it kept him tossing from side to side, and was mingled with the strangest fears lest the stick should vanish as mysteriously as it had come—lest when he woke he should find it had been carried away. He got out of bed, unscrewed the horse, and placed it under his pillow. But there it tormented him like an aching spot. It went on drawing him, tempting him, mocking him. He could not keep his hands from it. A hundred times he resolved he would not touch it again, and of course kept his resolution so long as he thought of it; but the moment he forgot it, which he did repeatedly in wondering why Joan did not come, the horse would be in his hand. Every time he woke from a moment's sleep, he found it in his hand.

On his return from accompanying Lady Joan, Jermyn came to him, found him feverish, and prescribed for him. Disappointed that Joan was gone without seeing him, his curiosity so entirely left him that he could not recall what it was like, and never imagined its possible return. Nor did it appear so long as he was awake, but all through his dreams the old captain kept reminding him that the stick was his own. "Do it; do it; don't put off," he kept saying; but as often as Cosmo asked him what, he could never hear his reply, and would wake yet again with the horse in his hand. In the morning he screwed it on the stick again, and set it by his bed-side.

CHAPTER XXXV
PULL HIS TAIL

About noon, when both the doctors happened to be out, Joan came to see him, and was more like her former self than she had been for many days. Hardly was she seated when he took the stick, and said,

"Did you ever see that before, Joan?"

"Do you remember showing me a horse just like that one, only larger?" she returned. "It was in the drawing-room."

"Quite well," he answered.

"It made me think of this," she continued, "which I had often seen in that same closet where I suppose you found it yesterday."

Cosmo unscrewed the joints and showed her the different boxes.

"There's nothing in them," he said; "but I suspect there is something about this stick more than we can tell. Do you remember the silly Scotch rime I repeated the other day, when you told me I had been talking poetry in my sleep?"

"Yes, very well," she answered.

"Those are words an uncle of my father, whom you may have heard of as the old captain, used to repeat very often."—At this Joan's face turned pale, but her back was to the light, and he did not see it.—"I will say them presently in English, that you may know what sense there may be in the foolishness of them. Now I must tell you that I am all but certain this stick once belonged to that same great uncle of mine—how it came into your father's possession I cannot say—and last night, as I was looking at it, I saw something that made me nearly sure this is the horse, insignificant as it looks, that was in my uncle's head when he repeated the rime. But I would do nothing without you."

"How kind of you, Cosmo!"

"Not kind; I had no right; the stick is yours."

"How can that be, if it belonged to your great uncle?" said Joan, casting down her eyes.

"Because it was more than fifty years in your father's possession, and he left it to you. Besides, I cannot be absolutely certain it is the same."

"Then I give it to you, Cosmo."

"I will not accept it, Joan—at least before you know what it is you want to give me.—And now for this foolish rime—in English!"

"Catch your horse and pull his tail;
In his hind heel drive a nail;
Pull his ears from one another:
Stand up and call the king your brother!

What's to come of it, I know no more than you do, Joan," continued Cosmo; "but if you will allow me, I will do with this horse what the rime says, and if they belong to each other, we shall soon see."

"Do whatever you please, Cosmo," returned Joan, with a tremble in her voice.

Cosmo began to screw off the top of the stick. Joan left her chair, drew nearer to the bed, and presently sat down on the edge of it, gazing with great wide eyes. She was more moved than Cosmo; there was a shadow of horror in her look; she dreaded some frightful revelation. Her father's habit of muttering his thoughts aloud, had given her many things to hear, although not many to understand. When the horse was free in Cosmo's hand, he set the stick aside, looked up, and said,

"The first direction the rime gives, is to pull his tail."

With that he pulled the horse's tail—of silver, apparently, like the rest of him—pulled it hard; but it seemed of a piece with his body, and there was no visible result. The first shadow of approaching disappointment came creeping over him, but he looked up at Joan, and smiled as he said,

"He doesn't seem to mind that! We'll try the next thing—which is, to drive a nail in his hind heel.—Now look here, Joan! Here, in one of his hind shoes, is a hole that looks as if one of the nails had come out! That is what struck me, and brought the rime into my head! But how drive a nail into such a hole as that?"

"Perhaps a tack would go in," said Joan, rising. "I shall pull one out of the carpet."

"A tack would be much too large, I think," said Cosmo. "Perhaps a brad out of the gimp of that chair would do.—Or, stay, I know! Have you got a hair-pin you could give me?"

Joan sat down again on the bed, took off her bonnet, and searching in her thick hair soon found one. Cosmo took it eagerly, and applied it to the hole in the shoe. Nothing the least larger would have gone in. He pushed it gently, then a little harder—felt as if something yielded a little, returning his pressure, and pushed a little harder still. Something gave way, and a low noise followed, as of a watch running down. The two faces looked at each other, one red, and one pale. The sound ceased. They waited a little, in almost breathless silence. Nothing followed.

"Now," said Cosmo, "for the last thing!"

"Not quite the last," returned Joan, with what was nearly an hysterical laugh, trying to shake off the fear that grew upon her; "the last thing is to stand up and call the king your brother."

"That much, as non-essential, I daresay we shall omit," replied Cosmo.—"The next then is, to pull his ears from each other."

He took hold of one of the tiny ears betwixt the finger and thumb of each hand, and pulled. The body of the horse came asunder, divided down the back, and showed inside of it a piece of paper. Cosmo took it out. It was crushed, rather than folded, round something soft. He handed it to Joan.

"It is your turn now, Joan," he said; "you open it. I have done my part."

Cosmo's eyes were now fixed on the movements of Joan's fingers undoing the little parcel, as hers had been on his while he was finding it. Within the paper was a piece of cotton wool. Joan dropped the paper, and unfolded the wool. Bedded in the middle of that were two rings. The eyes of Cosmo fixed themselves on one of them—the eyes of Joan upon the other. In the one Cosmo recognized a large diamond; in the other Joan saw a dark stone engraved with the Mergwain arms.

"This is a very valuable diamond," said Cosmo, looking closely at it.

"Then that shall be your share, Cosmo," returned Joan. "I will keep this if you don't mind."

"What have you got?" asked Cosmo.

"My father's signet-ring, I believe," she answered. "I have often heard him—bemoan the loss of it."

Lord Mergwain's ring in the old captain's stick! Things began to put themselves together in Cosmo's mind. He lay thinking.

The old captain had won these rings from the young lord and put them for safety in the horse; Borland suspected, probably charged him with false play; they fought, and his lordship carried away the stick to recover his own; but had failed to find the rings, taking the boxes in the bamboo for all there was of stowage in it.

It was by degrees, however, that this theory formed itself in his mind; now he saw only a glimmer of it here and there.

In the meantime he was not a little disappointed. Was this all the great mystery of the berimed horse? It was as if a supposed opal had burst, and proved but a soap-bubble!

Joan sat silent, looking at the signet-ring, and the tears came slowly in her eyes.

"I *may* keep this ring, may I not, Cosmo?" she said.

"My dear Joan!" exclaimed Cosmo, "the ring is not mine to give anybody, but if you will give me the stick, I shall be greatly obliged to you."

"I will give it to you on one condition, Cosmo," answered Joan, "—that you take the ring as well. I do not care about rings."

"I do," answered Cosmo; "but sooner than take this from you, Joan, I would part with the hope of ever seeing you again. Why, dear Joan, you don't know what this diamond is worth!—and you have no money!"

"Neither have you," retorted Joan. "—What is the thing worth?"

"I do not like to say lest I should be wrong. If I could weigh it, I should be better able to tell you. But its worth must anyhow be, I think—somewhere towards two hundred pounds."

"Then take it, Cosmo. Or if you won't have it, give it to your father, with my dear love."

"My father would say to me—'How could you bring it, Cosmo!' But I will not forget to give him the message. That he will be delighted to have."

"But, Cosmo! it is of no use to me. How could I get the money you speak of for it? If I were to make an attempt of the kind, my brother would be sure to hear of it. It would be better to give it him at once."

"That difficulty is easily got over," answered Cosmo. "When I go, I will take it with me; I know where to get a fair price for it—not always easy for anything; I will send you the money, and you will be quite rich for a little while."

"My brother opens all my letters," replied Joan. "I don't think he cares to read them, but he sees who they are from."

"Do you have many letters, Joan?"

"Not many. Perhaps about one a month, or so."

"I could send it to Dr. Jermyn."

Joan hesitated a moment, but did not object. The next instant they heard the doctor's step at the door, and his hand on the lock. Joan rose hastily, caught up her bonnet, and sat down a little way off. Cosmo drew the ring and the pieces of the horse under the bed-clothes.

Jermyn cast a keen glance on the two as he entered, took for confusion the remains of excitement, and said to himself he must make haste. He felt Cosmo's pulse, and pronounced him feverish, then, turning to Joan, said he must not talk, for he had not got over yesterday; it might be awkward if he had a relapse. Joan rose at once, and took her leave, saying she would come and see him the next morning. Jermyn went down with her, and sent Cosmo a draught. When he had taken it, he felt inclined to sleep, and turned himself from the light. But the stick, which was leaning against the head of the bed, slipped, and fell on a part of the floor where there was no carpet; the noise startled and roused him, and the thought came that he had better first of all secure the ring—for which purpose undoubtedly there could be no better place than the horse! There, however, the piece of cotton wool would again be necessary, for without it the ring would rattle. He put the ring in the heart of it, replaced both in the horse, and set about discovering how to close it again.

This puzzled him not a little. Spring nor notch, nor any other means of attachment between the two halves of the animal, could he find. But at length he noted that the tail had slipped a little way out, and was loose; and experimenting with it, by and by discovered that by holding the parts together, and winding the tail round and round, the horse—how, he could not tell—was restored to its former apparent solidity.

And now where would the horse be safest? Clearly in its own place on the stick. He got out of bed therefore to pick the stick up, and in so doing saw on the carpet the piece of paper which had been round the cotton. This he picked up also, and getting again into bed, had begun to replace the handle of the bamboo, when his eyes fell again on the piece of paper, and he caught sight of crossing lines on it, which looked like part of a diagram of some sort. He smoothed it out, and saw indeed a drawing, but one quite unintelligible to him. It must be a sketch or lineation of something—but of what? or of what kind of thing? It might be of the fields constituting a property; it might be of the stones in a wall; it might be of an irregular mosaic; or perhaps it might be only a school-boy's exercise in trigonometry for land-measuring. It must mean something; but it could hardly mean anything of consequence to anybody! Still it had been the old captain's probably—or perhaps the old lord's: he would replace it also where he had found it. Once more he unscrewed the horse from the stick, opened it with Joan's hair-pin, placed the paper in it, closed all up again, and lay down, glad that Joan had got such a ring, but thinking the old captain had made a good deal of fuss about a small matter. He fell fast asleep, slept soundly, and woke much better.

In the evening came the doctor, and spent the whole of it with him, interesting and pleasing him more than ever, and displaying one after another traits of character which Cosmo, more than prejudiced in his favour already, took for additional proofs of an altogether exceptional greatness of character and aim. Nor am I capable of determining how much or how little Jermyn may have deceived himself in regard of the same.

Now that Joan had this ring, and his personal attachment to the doctor had so greatly increased, Cosmo found himself able to revert to the offer Jermyn once made of lending him a little money, which he had then declined. He would take the ring to Mr. Burns on his way home, and then ask Joan to repay Dr. Jermyn out of what he sent her for it. He told Jermyn therefore, as he sat by his bedside, that he found himself obliged after all to accept the said generous proposal, but would return the money before he got quite home.

The doctor smiled, with reasons for satisfaction more than Cosmo knew, and taking out his pocket-book, said, as he opened it,

"I have just cashed a cheque, fortunately, so you had better have the money at once.—Don't bother yourself about it," he added, as he handed him the notes; "there is no hurry. I know it is safe."

"This is too much," said Cosmo.

"Never mind; it is better to have too much than too little; it will be just as easy to repay." Cosmo thanked him, and put the money under his pillow. The doctor bade him good night, and left him.

The moment he was alone, a longing greater than he had ever yet felt, arose in his heart to see his father. The first hour he was able to travel, he would set out for home! His *camera obscura* haunted with flashing water and speedwells and daisies and *horse-gowans*, he fell fast asleep, and dreamed that his father and he were defending the castle from a great company of pirates, with the old captain at the head of them.

CHAPTER XXXVI
THE THICK DARKNESS

The next day he was still better, and could not think why the doctor would not let him get up. As the day went on, he wondered yet more why Joan did not come to see him. Not once did the thought cross him that it was the doctor's doing. If it had, he would but have taken it for a precaution—as indeed it was, for the doctor's sake, not his. Jermyn would have as little intercourse between them as might be, till he should have sprung his spiritual mine. But he did all he could to prevent him from missing her, and the same night opened all his heart to Cosmo—that is, all the show-part of it.

In terms extravagant, which he seemed to use because he could not repress them, he told his frozen listener that his whole nature, heart and soul, had been for years bound up in Lady Joan; that he had again and again been tempted to deliver himself by death from despair; that if he had to live without her, he would be of no use in the world, but would cease to care for anything. He begged therefore his friend Cosmo Warlock, seeing he stood so well with the lady, to speak what he honestly could in his behalf; for if she would not favour him, he could no longer endure life. His had never been over full, for he had had a hard youth, in which he had often been driven to doubt whether there was indeed a God that cared how his creatures went on. He must not say all he felt, but life, he repeated, would be no longer worth leading without at least some show of favour from Lady Joan.

At any former time, such words would have been sufficient to displace Jermyn from the pedestal on which Cosmo had set him. What! If all the ladies in the world should forsake him, was not God yet the all in all? But now as he lay shivering, the words entering his ears seemed to issue from his soul. He listened like one whom the first sting has paralysed, but who feels the more every succeeding invasion of death. It was a silent, yet a mortal struggle. He held down his heart like a wild beast, which, if he let it up for one moment, would fly at his throat and strangle him. Nor could the practiced eye of the doctor fail to perceive what was going on in him. He only said to himself—"Better him than me!" He is young and will get over it better than I should." He read nobility and self-abnegation in every shadow that crossed the youth's countenance, telling of the hail mingled with fire that swept through his universe; and said to himself that all was on his side, that he had not miscalculated a hair's-breadth. He saw at the same time Cosmo's heroic efforts to hide his sufferings, and left him to imagine himself successful. But how Cosmo longed for his departure, that he might in peace despair!—for such seemed to himself his desire for solitude.

What is it in suffering that makes man and beast long for loneliness? I think it is an unknown something, more than self, calling out of the solitude—"Come to me!—Come!" How little of the tenderness our human souls need, and after which consciously or unconsciously they hunger, do we give or receive! The cry of the hurt heart for solitude, seems to me the call of the heart to God—changed by the echo of the tiny hollows of the heart of his creature—"Come out from among them: come to me, and I will give you rest!" He alone can give us the repose of love, the peace after which our nature yearns.

Hurt by the selfishness and greed of men, to escape from which we must needs go out of the world, worse hurt by our own indignation at their wrong, and our lack of patience under it, we are his creatures and his care still. The *right* he claims as his affair, and he will see it done; but the wrong is by us a thousand times well suffered, if it but drive us to him, that we may learn he is indeed our very lover.

That was a terrible night for Cosmo—a night billowy with black fire. It reminded him afterwards of nothing so much as that word of the Lord—*the power of darkness*. It was not merely darkness with no light in it, but darkness alive and operative. He hardly dared suspect the nature, and only now knew the force, and was about to prove the strength of the love with which he loved Joan. Great things may be foreseen, but they cannot be known until they arrive. His illness had been ripening him to this possibility of loss and suffering. His heart was now in blossom: for that some hearts must break;—I may not say in *full* blossom, for what the full blossom of the human heart is, the noblest saint with the mightiest imagination cannot know—he can but see it shine from afar.

It was a severe duty that was now required of him—I do not mean the performance of the final request the doctor had made—that Cosmo had forgotten, neither could have attempted with honesty; for the emotion he could not but betray, would have pleaded for himself, and not for his friend; it was enough that he must yield the lady of his dreams, become the lady as well of his waking and hoping soul. Perhaps she did not love Jermyn—he could not tell; but Jermyn was his friend and had trusted in him, confessing that his soul was bound up in the lady; one of them must go to the torture chamber, and when the *question* lay between him and another, Cosmo knew for which it must be. He alone was in Cosmo's hands; his own self was all he held and had power over, all he could offer, could yield. Mr. Simon had taught him that, as a mother gives her children money to give, so God gives his children *selves,* with their wishes and choices, that they may have the true offering to lay upon the true altar; for on that altar nothing else will burn than *selves.*

"Very hard! A tyrannical theory!" says my reader? So will it forever appear to the man who has neither the courage nor the sense of law to enable him to obey. But that man shall be the eternal slave who says to Duty *I will not.* Nor do I care to tell such a man of the *"thousand fold"*—of the truth concerning that altar, that it is indeed the nest of God's heart, in which the poor, unsightly, unfledged offering shall lie, until they come to shape and loveliness, and wings grow upon them to bear them back to us divinely precious. Cosmo thought none of all this now—it had vanished from his consciousness, but was present in his life—that is, in his action: he did not feel, he *did* it all—did it even when nothing seemed worth doing.

How much greater a man than he was Jermyn! How much more worthy of the love of a woman like Joan! How good he had been to him! What a horrible thing it would be if Jermyn had saved his life that he might destroy Jermyn's! Perhaps Joan might have come one day to love him; but in the meantime how miserable she was with her brother, and when could he have delivered her! while here was one, and a far better than he, who could, the moment she consented, take her to a house of her own where she would be a free woman! For him to come in the way, would be to put his hand also to the rack on which the life of Joan lay stretched!

Again I say I do not mean that all this passed consciously through the mind of Cosmo during that fearful night. His suffering was too intense, and any doubt concerning duty too far from him, to allow of anything that could be called thought; but such were the fundamental facts that lay below his unselfquestioned resolve—such was the soil in which grew the fruits, that is, the deeds, the outcome of his nature. For himself, the darkness billowed and rolled about him, and life was a frightful thing.

For where was God this awful time? Nowhere within the ken of the banished youth. In his own feeling Cosmo was outside the city of life—not even among the dogs—outside with bare nothingness—cold negation. Alas for him who had so lately offered to help another to pray, thinking the hour would never come to him when he could not pray! It had *come!* He did not try to pray. The thought of prayer did not wake in him! Let no one say he was punished for his overconfidence—for his presumption! There was no presumption in the matter; there was only ignorance. He had not learned—nor has any one learned more than in part—what awful possibilities lie in the existence we call *we.* He had but spoken from what he knew—that hitherto life for him had seemed inseparable from prayer to his Father. And was it separable?

Surely not. He could not pray, true—but neither was he alive. To live, one must choose to live. He was dead with a death that was heavy upon him. There is a far worse death—the death that is content and suffers nothing; but annihilation is not death—is nothing like it. Cosmo's condition had no evil in it—only a ghastly imperfection—an abyssmal lack—an exhaustion at the very roots of being. God seemed away, as he could never be and be God. But every commonest day of his life, he who would be a live child of the living has to fight with the God-denying look of things, and believe that in spite of that look, seeming ever to assert that God has nothing to do with them, God has his own way—the best, the only, the live way, of being in everything, and taking his own pure, saving will in them; and now for a season Cosmo had fallen in the fight, and God seemed gone, and *things* rushed in upon him and overwhelmed him. It was death. He did not yet know it—but it was not the loss of Joan, but the seeming loss of his God, that hollowed the last depth of his misery. But that is of all things the surest to pass; for God changing not, his life must destroy every false show of him. Cosmo was now one of those holy children who are bound hand and foot in the furnace, until the fire shall have consumed their bonds that they may pace their prison. Stifled with the smoke and the glow, he must yet for a time lie helpless; not yet could he lift up his voice and call upon the ice and the cold, the frost and the snow to bless the Lord, to praise and exalt him forever. But God was not far from him. Feelings are not scientific instruments for that which surrounds them; but they speak of themselves when they say, "I am cold; I am dark." Perhaps the final perfection will be when our faith is utterly and absolutely independent of our feelings. I dare to imagine this the final victory of our Lord, when he followed the cry of *Why hast thou forsaken me?* with the words, *Father, into thy hands I commend my spirit.*

Shall we then bemoan any darkness? Shall we not rather gird up our strength to encounter it, that we too from our side may break the passage for the light beyond? He who fights with the dark shall know the gentleness that makes man great—the dawning countenance of the God of hope. But that was not for Cosmo just yet. The night must fulfil its hours. Men are meant and sent to be troubled—that they may rise above the whole region of storm, above all possibility of being troubled.

CHAPTER XXXVII
THE DAWN

Strange to say, there was no return of his fever. He seemed, through the utter carelessness of mental agony, so to have abandoned his body, that he no longer affected it. A man must have some hope, to be aware of his body at all. As the darkness began to yield he fell asleep.

Then came a curious dream. For ages Joan had been persuading him to go with her, and the old captain to go with him—the latter angry and pulling him, the former weeping and imploring. He would go with neither, and at last they vanished both. He sat solitary on the side of a bare hill, and below him was all that remained of Castle Warlock. He had been dead so many years, that it was now but a half-shapeless ruin of roofless walls, haggard and hollow and gray and desolate. It stood on its ridge like a solitary tooth in the jaw of some skeleton beast. But where was his father? How was it he had not yet found him, if he had been so long dead? He must rise and seek him! He must be somewhere in the universe! Therewith came softly stealing up, at first hardly audible, a strain of music from the valley bellow. He listened. It grew as it rose, and held him bound. Like an upward river, it rose, and grew with a strong rushing, until it flooded all his heart and brain, working in him a marvellous good, which yet he did not understand. And all the time, his eyes were upon the dead home of his fathers. Wonder of wonders, it began to change—to grow before his eyes! It was growing out of the earth like a plant! It grew and grew until it was as high as in the old days, and then it grew yet higher! A roof came upon it, and turrets and battlements—all to the sound of that creative music; and like fresh shoots from its stem, out from it went wings and walls. Like a great flower it was rushing visibly on to some mighty blossom of grandeur, when the dream suddenly left him, and he woke.

But instead of the enemy coming in upon him like a flood as his consciousness returned, to his astonishment he found his soul as calm as it was sad. God had given him while he slept, and he knew him near as his own heart! The first *thought* that came was, that his God was Joan's God too, and therefore all was well; so long as God took care of her, and was with him, and his will was done in them both, all was on the way to be well so as nothing could be better. And with that he knew what he had to do—knew it without thinking—and proceeded at once to do it. He rose, and dressed himself.

It was still the gray sunless morning. The dream, with its dream-ages of duration, had not crossed the shallows of the dawn. Quickly he gathered his few things into his knapsack—fortunately their number had nowise increased—took his great-uncle's bamboo, saw that his money was safe, stole quietly down the stair, and softly and safely out of the house, and, ere any of its inhabitants were astir, had left the village by the southward road.

When he had walked about a mile, he turned into a road leading eastward, with the design of going a few miles in that direction, and then turning to the north. When he had travelled what to his weakness was a long distance, all at once, with the dismay of a perverse dream, rose above the trees the towers of Cairncarque. Was he never to escape them, in the body any more than in the spirit? He turned back, and again southwards.

But now he had often to sit down; as often, however, he was able to get up and walk. Coming to a village he learned that a coach for the north would pass within an hour, and going to the inn had some breakfast, and waited for it. Finding it would pass through the village he had left, he took an inside place; and when it stopped for a moment in the one street of it, saw Charles Jermyn cross it, evidently without a suspicion that his guest was not where he had left him.

When he had travelled some fifty miles, partly to save his money, partly because he felt the need of exercise, not to stifle thought, but to clear it, he left the coach, and betook himself to his feet. Alternately walking and riding, he found his strength increase as he went on; and his sorrow continued to be that of a cloudy summer day, nor was ever, so long as the journey lasted, again that of the fierce wintry tempest.

At length he drew nigh the city where he had spent his student years. On foot, weary, and dusty, and worn, he entered it like a returning prodigal. Few Scotchmen would think he had made good use of his learning! But he had made the use of it God required, and some Scotchmen, with and without other learning, have learned to think that a good use, and in itself a sufficient success—for that man came into the world not to make money, but to seek the kingdom and righteousness of God.

He walked straight into Mr. Burns's shop.

The jeweller did not know him at first; but the moment he spoke, recognized him. Cosmo had been dubious what his reception might be—after the way in which their intimacy had closed; but Mr. Burns held out his hand as if they had parted only the day before, and said,

"I thought of the two you would be here before Death! Man, you ought to give a body time."

"Mr. Burns," replied Cosmo, "I am very sorry I behaved to you as I did. I am not sorry I said what I did, for I am no less sure about that than I was then; but I am sorry I never came again to see you. Perhaps we did not quite understand on either side."

"We shall understand each other better now, I fancy," said Mr. Burns. "I am glad you have not changed your opinion, for I have changed mine. If it weren't for you, I should be retired by this time, and you would have found another name over the door. But we'll have a talk about all that. Allow me to ask you whither you are bound."

"I am on my way home," answered Cosmo. "I have not seen my father for several—for more than two years."

"You'll do me the honour to put up at my house to-night, will you not? I am a bachelor, as you know, but will do my best to make you comfortable."

Cosmo gladly assented; and as it was now evening, Mr. Burns hastened the shutting of his shop; and in a few minutes they were seated at supper.

As soon as the servant left them, they turned to talk of divine righteousness in business; and thence to speak of the jeweller's; after which Cosmo introduced that of the ring. Giving a short narrative of the finding of it, and explaining the position of Lady Joan with regard to it, so that his host might have no fear of compromising himself, he ended with telling him he had brought it to him, and with what object.

"I am extremely obliged to you, Mr. Warlock," responded the jeweller, "for placing such confidence in me, and that notwithstanding the mistaken principles I used to advocate. I have seen a little farther since then, I am happy to say; and this is how it was: the words you then spoke, and I took so ill, would keep coming into my mind, and that at the most inconvenient moments, until at last I resolved to look the thing in the face, and think it fairly out. The result is, that, although I daresay nobody has recognized any difference in my way of doing business, there is one who must know a great difference: I now think of my neighbour's side of the bargain as well as of my own, and abstain from doing what it would vex me to find I had not been sharp enough to prevent him from doing with me. In consequence, I am not so rich this day as I might otherwise have been, but I enjoy life more, and hope the days of my ignorance God has winked at."

Cosmo could not reply for pleasure. Mr. Burns saw his emotion, and understood it. From that hour they were friends who loved each other.

"And now for the ring!" said the jeweller.

Cosmo produced it.

Mr. Burns looked at it as if his keen eyes would pierce to the very heart of its mystery, turned it every way, examined it in every position relative to the light, removed it from its setting, went through the diamond catechism with it afresh, then weighed it, thought over it, and said,

"What do you take the stone to be worth, Mr. Warlock?"

"I can only guess, of course," replied Cosmo; "but the impression on my mind is, that it is worth more nearly two hundred than a hundred and fifty pounds."

"You are right," answered Mr. Burns, "and you ought to have followed my trade; I could make a good jeweller of you. This ring is worth two hundred guineas, fair market-value. But as I can ask from no one more than it is absolutely worth, I must take my profit off you: do you think that is fair?"

"Perfectly," answered Cosmo.

"Then I must give you only two hundred pounds for it, and take the shillings myself. You see it may be some time before I get my money again, so I think five per cent on the amount is not more than the fair thing."

"It seems to me perfectly fair, and very moderate," replied Cosmo.

As soon as dinner was over, he sat down to write to Joan. While there was nothing that must be said, he had feared writing. This was what he wrote:

"My dearest Joan,

"As you have trusted me hitherto, so trust me still, and wait for an explanation of my peculiar behaviour in going away without bidding you good-by, till the proper time comes—which must come one day, for our master said, more than once, that there was nothing covered which should not be revealed, neither hid that should not be known. I feel sure therefore, of being allowed to tell you everything sometime.

"I herewith send you a cheque as good as bank-notes, much safer to send, and hardly more difficult for Dr. Jermyn to turn into sovereigns.

"I borrowed of him fifteen pounds—a good deal more than I wanted. I have therefore got Mr. Burns, my friend, the jeweller, in this city, to add five pounds to the two hundred which he gives for the ring, and beg you, Joan, for the sake of old times, and new also, to pay for me the fifteen pounds to Dr. Jermyn, which I would much rather owe to you than to him. The rest of it, the other ten pounds, I will pay you when I can—it may not be in this world. And in the next—what then, Joan? Why then—but for that we will wait—who more earnestly than I?

"To all the coming eternity, dear Joan, I shall never cease to love you—first for yourself, then for your great lovely goodness to me. May the only perfection, whose only being is love, take you to his heart—as he is always trying to do with all of us! I mean to let him have me out and out.

"Dearest Joan, Your far-off cousin, but near friend,

"Cosmo Warlock."

CHAPTER XXXVIII
HOME AGAIN

Early the next day, while the sun was yet casting huge diagonal shadows across the wide street, Cosmo climbed to the roof of the Defiance coach, his heart swelling at the thought of being so soon in his father's arms. It was a lovely summer morning, cool and dewy, fit for any Sunday—whence the eyes and mind of Cosmo turned to the remnants of night that banded the street, and from them he sank into metaphysics, chequered with the champing clank of the bits, the voices of the ostlers, passengers, and guard, and the perpendicular silence of the coachman, who sat like a statue in front of him.

How dark were the shadows the sun was casting!

Absurd! the sun casts no shadows—only light.

How so? Were the sun not shining, would there be one single shadow?

Yes; there would be just one single shadow; all would be shadow.

There would be none of those things we call shadows.

True; all would be shade; there would be no shadows.

By such a little stair was Cosmo landed at a door of deep question. For now *evil* took the place of shadow in his *solo* disputation, and the law and the light and the shadow and the sin went thinking about with each other in his mind; and he saw how the Jews came to attribute evil to the hand of God as well as good, and how St. Paul said that the law gave life to sin—as by the sun is the shadow. He saw too that in the spiritual world we need a live sun strong enough to burn up all the shadows by shining through the things that cast them, and compelling their transparency—and that sun is the God who is light, and in whom is no darkness at all—which truth is the gospel according to St. John. And where there is no longer anything covered or hid, could sin live at all? These and such like thoughts held him long—till the noisy streets of the granite city lay far behind.

Swiftly the road flew from under the sixteen flashing shoes of the thorough-breds that bore him along. The light and hope and strength of the new-born day were stirring, mounting, swelling—even in the heart of the sad lover; in every *honest* heart more or less, whether young or old, feeble or strong, the new summer day stirs, and will stir while the sun has heat enough for men to live on the earth. Surely the live God is not absent from the symbol of his glory! The light and the hope are not there without him! When strength wakes in my heart, shall I be the slave to imagine it comes only as the sap rises in the stem of the reviving plant, or the mercury in the tube of the thermometer? that there is no essential life within my conscious life, no spirit within my spirit? If my origin be not life, I am the poorest of slaves!

Cosmo had changed since first he sat behind such horses, on his way to the university; it was the change of growth, but he felt it like that of decay—as if he had been young then and was old now. Little could he yet imagine what age means! Devout youth as he was, he little understood how much more than he his father felt his dependence on, that is his strength in God. Many years had yet to pass ere he should feel the splendour of an existence rooted in changeless Life ripening through the growing weakness of the body! It is the strength of God that informs every muscle and arture[9] of the youth, but it is so much his own—looks so natural to him—as it well may, being God's idea for him—that, in the glory of its possession, he does not feel it *as* the presence of the making God. But when weakness begins to show itself,—a shadow-back-

9 ARTURE: MacDonald believed this word to be Shakespearean invention. In his own 1885 annotated edition of Hamlet, he observes "I do not know if a list has ever been gathered of the words made by Shakspere: here is one of them—arture, from the same root as artus, a joint—arcere, to hold together, adjective arctus, tight. Arture, then, stands for juncture."

ground, against which the strength is known and outlined—when every movement begins to demand a distinct effort of the will, and the earthly house presses, a conscious weight, not upon its own parts only, but upon the spirit within, then indeed must a man *have* God, believe in him with an entireness independent of feeling, and going beyond all theory, or be devoured by despair. In the growing feebleness of old age, a man may well come to accept life only because it is the will of God; but the weakness of such a man is the matrix of a divine strength, whence a gladness unspeakable shall ere long be born—the life which it is God's intent to share with his children.

Cosmo was on the way to know all this, but now his trouble sat sometimes heavy upon him. Indeed the young straight back, if it feels the weight less, feels the irksomeness of the burden more than the old bowed one. With strength goes the wild love of movement, and the cross that prevents the free play of a single muscle is felt grievous as the fetter that chains a man to the oar. But this day—and what man has to do with yesterday and to-morrow?—the sun shone as if he knew nothing, or as if he knew all, and knew it to be well; and Cosmo was going home, and the love of his father was a deep gladness, even in the presence of love's lack. Seldom is it so, but between the true father, and true son it always will be so.

When he came within a mile of Muir of Warlock, he left the coach, and would walk the rest of the way. He desired to enjoy, in gentle, unruffled flow, the thoughts that like swallows kept coming and going between him and his nest as he approached it. Everything, the commonest, that met him as he went, had a strange beauty, as if, although he had known it so long, now first was its innermost revealed by some polarized light from source unseen. How small and poor the cottages looked—but how home-like! and how sweet the smoke of their chimneys! How cold they must be in winter—but how warm were the hearts inside them! There was Jean Elder's Sunday linen spread like snow on her gooseberry bushes; there was the shoemaker's cow eating her hardest, as if she would devour the very turf that made a border to the road—held from the corn on the other side of the low fence by a strong chain in the hand of a child of seven; and there was the first dahlia of the season in Jonathan Japp's garden! As he entered the village, the road, which was at once its street and the queen's highway, was empty of life save for one half-grown pig—"prospecting," a hen or two picking about, and several cats that lay in the sun. "There must be some redemption for the feline races," thought Cosmo, "when the cats have learned so much to love the sun!—But, alas! It is only his heat, not his light they love!" He looked neither on this side nor that as he walked, for he was in no mood for the delay of converse, but he wondered nevertheless that he saw nobody. It was the general dinner hour, true, but that would scarcely account for the deserted look of the street! Any passing stranger was usually enough to bring people to their doors—their windows not being of much use for looking out of! Sheltered behind rose-trees or geraniums or hydrangeas, however, not a few of whom he saw nothing were peering at him out of those windows as he passed.

The villagers had learned from some one on the coach that the young laird was coming. But, strange to say, a feeling had got abroad amongst them to his prejudice. They had looked to hear great things of their favourite, but he had not made the success they expected, and from their disappointment they imagined his blame. It troubled them to think of the old man, whom they all honoured, sending his son to college on the golden horse, whose history had ever since been the cherished romance of the place, and after all getting no good of him! so when they saw him coming along, dusty and shabby—not so well dressed indeed as would have contented one of themselves on a Sunday, they drew back from their peep-holes with a sigh, let him pass, and then looked again.

Nothing of all this however did Cosmo suspect, but held on his way unconscious of the regards that pursued him as a prodigal returning the less satisfactorily that he had not been guilty enough to repent.

CHAPTER XXXIX
THE SHADOW OF DEATH

Every step Cosmo took after leaving the village, was like a revelation and a memory in one. When he turned out of the main road, the hills came rushing to meet and welcome him, yet it was only that they stood there changeless, eternally the same, just as they had been: that was the welcome with which they met the heart that had always loved them.

When first he opened his eyes, they were as the nursing arms the world spread out to take him; and now, returning from the far countries where they were unknown, they spread them out afresh to receive him home. The next turn was home itself, for that turn was at the base of the ridge on which the castle stood.

The moment he took it, a strange feeling of stillness came over him, and as he drew nearer, it deepened. When he entered the gate of the close, it was a sense, and had grown almost appalling. With sudden inroad his dream returned! Was the place empty utterly? Was there no life in it? Not yet had he heard a sound; there was no sign from cow-house or stable. A cart with one wheel stood in the cart-shed; a harrow lay, spikes upward, where he had hollowed the mound of snow. The fields themselves had an unwonted, a haggard sort of look. A crop of oats was ripening in that nearest the close, but they covered only the half of it: the rest was in potatoes, and amongst them, sole show of labour or life, he saw Aggie: she was pulling the *plums* off their stems. The doors were shut all round the close—all but the kitchen-door; that stood as usual wide open. A sickening fear came upon Cosmo; it was more than a week since he had heard from home! In that time his father might be dead, and therefore the place be so desolate! He dared not enter the house. He would go first into the garden, and there pray, and gather courage.

He went round the kitchen-tower, as the nearest block was called, and made for his old seat, the big, smooth stone. Some one was sitting there, with his head bent forward on his knees! By the red night-cap it must be his father, but how changed the whole aspect of the good man! His look was that of a worn-out labourer—one who has borne the burden and heat of the day, and is already half asleep, waiting for the night. Motionless as a statue of weariness he sat; on the ground lay a spade which looked as if it had dropped from his hand as he sat upon the stone; and beside him on that lay his Marion's Bible. Cosmo's heart sank within him, and for a moment he stood motionless.

But the first movement he made forward, the old man lifted his head with an expectant look, then rose in haste, and, unable to straighten himself, hurried, stooping, with short steps, to meet him. Placing his hands on his son's shoulders, he raised himself up, and laid his face to his; then for a few moments they were silent, each in the other's arms.

The laird drew back his head and looked his son in the face. A heavenly smile crossed the sadness of his countenance, and his wrinkled old hand closed tremulous on Cosmo's shoulder.

<table>
<tr><td>"They canna tak frae me my son!" he murmured—and from that time rarely spoke to him save in the mother-tongue.</td><td>"They can't take from me my son!" he murmured—and from that time rarely spoke to him save in the mother-tongue</td></tr>
</table>

Then he led him to the stone, where there was just room enough for two that loved each other, and they sat down together.

The laird put his hand on his son's knee, as, when a boy, Cosmo used to put his on his father's.

<table>
<tr><td>"Are ye the same, Cosmo?" he asked. "Are ye my ain bairn?"</td><td>"Are you the same, Cosmo?" he asked. "Are you my own child?"</td></tr>
</table>

"Father," returned Cosmo, "gien it be possible, I loe ye mair nor ever. I'm come hame to ye, no to lea' ye again sae lang as ye live. Gien ye be in ony want, I s' better 't gien I can, an' share 't ony gait. Ay, I may weel say I'm the same, only mair o' 't."

"Father," returned Cosmo, "if it be possible, I love you more than ever. I'm come home to you, not to leave you again so long as you live. If you be in any want, I'll better it if I can, and share it anyway. Ay, I may well say I'm the same, only more of it."

"The Lord's name be praist!" murmured the laird. "—But do ye loe *him* the same as ever, Cosmo?" again he asked.

"The Lord's name be praised!" murmured the laird. "—But do you love *him* the same as ever, Cosmo?" again he asked.

"Father, I dinna loe him the same—I loe him a heap better. He kens noo 'at he may tak his wull o' me. Naething 'at I ken o' comes 'atween him an' me."

"Father, I don't love him the same—I love him much more. He knows now that he may have his will with me. Nothing that I know of comes between him and me."

The old man raised his arm, and put it round his boy's shoulders: he was not one of the many Scotch fathers who make their children fear more than love them.

"Then, Lord, let me die in peace," he said, "for mine eyes hae seen thy salvation!—But ye dinna luik freely the same, Cosmo!—Hoo is 't?"

"Then, Lord, let me die in peace," he said, "for mine eyes have seen thy salvation!—But you don't look quite the same, Cosmo!—How is it?"

"I hae come throuw a heap, lately, father," answered Cosmo. "I hae been ailin' in body, an' sair harassed in hert. I'll tell ye a' aboot it, whan we hae time—and o' that we'll hae plenty, I s' warran, for I tell ye I winna lea' ye again; an' gien ye had only latten me ken ye was failin', I wad hae come hame lang syne. It was sair agen the grain 'at I bade awa'."

"I have come through a lot, lately, father," answered Cosmo. "I have been ailing in body, and sorely harassed in heart. I'll tell you all about it, when we have time—and of that we'll have plenty, I'm sure, for I tell you I won't leave you again; and if you had only let me know you were failing, I would have come home long since. It was far from easy, staying away."

"The auld sudna lie upo' the tap o' the yoong, Cosmo, my son."

"The old shouldn't lie upon the top of the young, Cosmo, my son."

"Father, I wad willin'ly be a bed to ye to lie upo', gien that wad ease ye; but I'm thinkin' we baith may lie saft upo' the wull o' the great Father, e'en whan that's hardest."

"Father, I would willingly be a bed for you to lie on, if that would ease you; but I'm thinking we both may lie soft upon the the will of the great Father, even when that's hardest."

"True as trowth!" returned the laird. "—But ye're luikin' some tired-like, Cosmo!"

"True as truth!" returned the laird. "—But you're looking very tired, Cosmo!"

"I *am* some tired, an' unco dry. I wad fain hae a drink o' milk."

"I *am* very tired, and very thirsty. I would be glad of a drink of milk."

The old man's head dropped again on his bosom, and so for the space of about a minute he sat. Then he lifted it up, and said, looking with calm clear eyes in those of his son,

"I winna greit, Cosmo; I'll say yet, the will o' the Lord be dune, though it be sair upo' me the noo, whan I haena a drap o' milk aboot the place to set afore my only-begotten son whan he comes hame to me frae a far country!—Eh, Lord! whan yer ain son cam hame frae his sair warstle an' lang sojourn amo' them 'at kenned na him nor thee, it wasna til an auld shabby man he cam hame, but til the Lord o'

"I won't cry, Cosmo; I'll say yet, the will of the Lord be done, though it be hard upon me now, when I don't have a drop of milk about the place to set before my only—begotten son when he comes home to me from a far country!—Eh, Lord! when your own son came home from his great struggle and long sojourn among them that knew neither him nor thee, it wasn't to an old shabby man he came home,

glory an' o' micht! An' whan we a' win hame til the Father o' a', it'll be to the leevin' stren'th o' the universe.—Cosmo, the han' o' man's been that heavy upo' me 'at coo efter coo's gane frae me, an' the last o' them, bonny Yally, left only thestreen. Ye'll hae to drink cauld watter, my bairn!"

but to the Lord of glory and of might! And when we all win home to the Father of all, it'll be to the living strength of the universe.—Cosmo, the hand of man's been that heavy upon me that cow after cow's gone from me, and the last of them, bonny Yally, left only yesterday. You'll have to drink cold water, my child!"

Again the old man's heart overcame him; his head sank, and he murmured,—"Lord, I haena a drap o' milk to gie my bairn—me 'at wad gie 'im my hert's bluid! But, Lord, wha am I to speyk like that to thee, wha didst lat thine ain poor oot his verra sowl's bluid for him an' me!"

Again the old man's heart overcame him; his head sank, and he murmured,—"Lord, I haven't a drop of milk to give my child—me that would give him my heart's blood! But, Lord, who am I to speak like that to thee, who didst let thine own pour out his very soul's blood for him and me!"

"Father," said Cosmo, "I can du wi' watter as weel's onybody. Du ye think I'm nae mair o' a man nor to care what I pit intil me? Gien ye be puirer nor ever, I'm prooder nor ever to share wi' ye. Bide ye here, an' I'll jist rin an' get a drink, an' come back to ye."

"Father," said Cosmo, "I can do with water as well as anyone. Do you think I'm no more of a man than to care what I put into me? If you be poorer than ever, I'm prouder than ever to share with you. Wait here, and I'll just run and get a drink, and come back to you."

"Na; I maun gang wi' ye, man," answered the laird, rising. "Grizzie's a heap taen up wi' yer gran'mither. She's been weirin' awa', this fortnicht back. She's no in pain, the Lord be praised! an' she'll never ken the straits her hoose is come till! Cosmo, I hae been a terrible cooard—dreidin' day an' nicht yer hame-comin', no submittin' 'at ye sud see sic a broken man to the father o' ye! But noo it's ower, an' here ye are, an' my hert's lichter nor it's been this mony a lang!"

"No; I must go with you, man," answered the laird, rising. "Grizzie's much taken up with your grandmother. She's been wearing away, this fortnight back. She's not in pain, the Lord be praised! and she'll never know the straits her house is come to! Cosmo, I have been a terrible coward—dreading day and night your home-coming, not submitting to the thought of you seeing your father such a broken man! But now it's over, and here you are, and my heart's lighter than it's been for many a day!"

Cosmo's own sorrow drew back into the distance from before the face of his father's, and he felt that the business, not the accident of his life, must henceforth be to support and comfort him. And with that it was as if a new well of life sprung up suddenly in his being.

"Father," he said, "we'll haud on thegither i' the stret ro'd. There's room for twa abreist in 't—ance ye're in!"

"Father," he said, "we'll hold on together in the straight road. There's room for two abreast in it—once you're in!"

"Ay! ay!" returned the laird with a smile; "that's the bonniest word ye cud hae come hame wi' til me! We maun jist perk up a bit, and be patient, that patience may hae her perfe't wark. I s' hae anither try—an' weel I may, for the licht o' my auld e'en is this day restored til me!"

"Ay! ay!" returned the laird with a smile; "that's the bonniest word you could have come home with to me! We'll just have to perk up a bit, and be patient, that patience may have her perfect work. I'll have another try—and well I may, for the light of my old eyes is this day restored to me!"

"An' sae gran'mother's weirin awa', father!"

"And so grandmother's wearing away, father!"

"To the lan' o' the leal, laddie."

"To the land of the true, laddie."

"Wull she ken me?"

"Na, she winna ken ye; she'll never ken onybody mair i' this warl'; but she'll ken plenty whaur she's gaein'!"

He rose, and they walked together towards the kitchen. There was nobody there, but they heard steps going to and fro in the room above. The laird made haste, but before he could lay his hand on a vessel, to get for Cosmo the water he so much desired, Grizzie appeared on the stair, descending. She hurried down, and across the floor to Cosmo, and seizing him by the hand, looked him in the face with the anxiety of an angel-hen. Her look said what his father's voice had said just before—"Are ye a' there—a' 'at there used to be?"

"Hoo's gran'mamma?" asked Cosmo.

"Ow, duin' weel eneuch, sir—weirin' awa' bonny. She has neither pang nor knowledge o' sorrow to tribble her. The Lord grant the sowls o' 's a' sic anither lowsin'!"

"Hae ye naething better nor cauld watter to gie 'im a drink o', Grizzie, wuman?" asked the laird, but in mere despair.

"Nae 'cep he wad condescen' til a grainie meal intil 't," returned Grizzie mournfully, and she looked at him again, with an anxious deprecating look now, as if before the heir she was ashamed of the poverty of the house, and dreaded blame. "—But laird," she resumed, turning to her master, "ye hae surely a drap o' something i' yer cellar! Weel I wat ye hae made awa' wi' nane o' 't yersel'!"

"Weel, there ye wat wrang, Grizzie, my bonny wuman!" replied the laird, with the flicker of a humorous smile on his wrinkled face, "for I sellt the last bottle oot o' 't a month ago to Stronach o' the distillery. I thought it cudna du muckle ill there, for it wadna make his nose sae reid as his ain whusky. Whaur, think ye, wad the sma' things ye wantit for my mother hae come frae, gien I hadna happent to hae that property left? We're weel taen care o', ye see, Grizzie! That wad hae tried my faith, to hae my mother gang wi'oot things! But he never suffers us to be tried ayont what we're

"Will she know me?"

"Na, she won't know you; she'll never know anybody more in this world; but she'll know plenty where she's going!"

He rose, and they walked together towards the kitchen. There was nobody there, but they heard steps going to and fro in the room above. The laird made haste, but before he could lay his hand on a vessel, to get for Cosmo the water he so much desired, Grizzie appeared on the stair, descending. She hurried down, and across the floor to Cosmo, and seizing him by the hand, looked him in the face with the anxiety of an angel-hen. Her look said what his father's voice had said just before— "Are you all there—all that there used to be?"

"How's grandmamma?" asked Cosmo.

"Oh, doing well enough, sir—wearing away bonnily. She has neither pang nor knowledge of sorrow to trouble her. The Lord grant the souls of us all such a release!"

"Have you nothing better than cold water to give him a drink of, Grizzie, woman?" asked the laird, but in mere despair.

"Not unless he would condescend to a wee grain of meal in it," returned Grizzie mournfully, and she looked at him again, with an anxious deprecating look now, as if before the heir she was ashamed of the poverty of the house, and dreaded blame. "—But, laird," she resumed, turning to her master, "surely you have a drop of something in your cellar! I know you won't have made away with any yourself!"

"Well, there your knowledge fails you Grizzie, my bonny woman!" replied the laird, with the flicker of a humorous smile on his wrinkled face, "for I sold the last bottle out of it a month ago to Stronach of the distillery. I thought it couldn't do much ill there, for it wouldn't make his nose so red as his own whisky. Where, do you think, would the small things you wanted for my mother have come from, if I hadn't happened to have that property left? We're well taken care of, you see, Grizzie! That would have tried my faith, to have my mother go without things! But

able to beir; an' sae lang as my faith hauds the grup, I carena for back nor belly! Cosmo, I can bide better 'at ye sud want. Ye're mair like my ain nor even my mother, an' sae we bide it thegither. It maun be 'cause ye're pairt o' my Marion as weel's o' mysel'. Eh, man! but this o' families is a wonerfu' Godlike contrivance! Gien he had taen ony ither w'y o' makin' fowk, whaur wad I hae been this day wantin' you, Cosmo?"

he never suffers us to be tried beyond what we're able to bear; and so long as my faith stays strong, I don't care for back nor belly! Cosmo, I can better stand that you should want. You're more like my own than even my mother, and so we stand it together. It must be because you're part of my Marion as well as of myself. Eh, man! but this family way of things is a wonderful Godlike contrivance! If he had taken any other way of making folk, where would I have been this day without you, Cosmo?"

While he spoke, Cosmo was drinking the water Grizzie had brought him—with a little meal on the top of it—the same drink he used to give his old mare, now long departed to the place prepared for her, when they were out spending the day together.

"There's this to be said for the water, father," he remarked, as he set down the wooden bowl in which Grizzie had thought proper to supply it, "that it comes mair direc' frae the han' o' God himsel'—maybe nor even the milk. But I dinna ken; for I doobt organic chemistry maun efter a' be nearer his han' nor inorganic! Ony gait, I never drank better drink; an' gien ae day he but saitisfee my sowl's hunger efter his richteousness as he has this minute saitisfeed my body's drowth efter watter, I s' be a happier man nor ever sat still ohn danced an' sung."

"There's this to be said for the water, father," he remarked, as he set down the wooden bowl in which Grizzie had thought proper to supply it, "that it comes more direct from the hand of God himself—maybe than even the milk. But I don't know; for I suspect organic chemistry must after all be nearer his hand than inorganic! Anyway, I never drank better drink; and if one day he but satisfy my soul's hunger after his righteousness as he has this minute satisfied my body's thirst for water, I'll be a happier man than ever sat still without dancing and singing."

"It's an innocent cratur' at gies thanks for cauld watter—I hae aye remarkit that!" said Grizzie. "But I maun awa' to my bairn up the stair; an' may it please the Lord to lift her or lang, for they maun be luikin for her yont the burn by this time. Whan she wauks i' the mornin', the' 'ill be nae mair scornin'!"

"It's an innocent creature that gives thanks for cold water—I have always remarked that!" said Grizzie. "But I must go to my child upstairs; and may it please the Lord to lift her ere long, for they must be looking for her beyond the river by this time. When she wakes in the morning, there'll be no more scorning!"

This was Grizzie's last against her mistress. The laird took no notice of it: he knew Grizzie's devotion, and, well as he loved his mother, could not but know also that there was some ground for her undevised couplet.

Scarcely a minute had passed when the voice of the old woman came from the top of the stair, calling aloud and in perturbation,

"Laird! laird! come up direc'ly. Come up, lairds baith! She's comin' til hersel'!"

"Laird! laird! come up directly. Come up, lairds both! She's coming to herself!"

They hastened up, Cosmo helping his father, and approached the bed together.

With smooth, colourless face, unearthly to look upon, the old lady lay motionless, her eyes wide open, looking up as if they saw something beyond the tester of the bed, her lips moving, but uttering no sound. At last came a murmur, in which Cosmo's ears alone were keen enough to discern the articulation.

"Mar'on, Mar'on," she said, "ye're i' the lan' o' forgiveness! I hae dune the lad no ill. He'll come hame to ye nane the waur for ony words o' mine. We're no' a' made sae guid to begin wi' as yersel', Mar'on!"

"Marion, Marion," she said, "you're in the land of forgiveness! I have done the lad no ill. He'll come home to you none the worse for any words of mine. We're not all made so good to begin with as yourself, Marion!"

Here her voice became a mere murmur, so far as human ears could distinguish, and presently ceased. A minute or so more and her breathing grew intermittent. After a few long respirations, at long intervals, it stopped.

"She'll be haein' 't oot wi' my ain mistress or lang!" remarked Grizzie to herself as she closed her eyes.

"She'll be having it out with my own mistress before long!" remarked Grizzie to herself as she closed her eyes.

"Mother! mother!" cried the laird, and kneeled by the bedside. Cosmo kneeled also, but no word of the prayers that ascended was audible. The laird was giving thanks that another was gone home, and Cosmo was praying for help to be to his father a true son, such as the Son of Man was to the Father of Man. They rose from their knees, and went quietly down the stair; and as they went from the room, they heard Grizzie say to herself,

"She's gane whaur there's mair—eneuch an' to spare!"

"She's gone where there's more—a fathomless store!"

The remains of Lady Joan's ten pounds was enough to bury her.

They invited none, but all the village came to her funeral.

CHAPTER XL
THE LABOURER

Such power had been accumulated and brought to bear against Glenwarlock, that at length he was reduced almost to the last extremity. He had had to part with his horses before even his crops were all sown, and had therefore dismissed his men, and tried to sell what there was as it stood, and get some neighbouring farmer to undertake the rest of the land for the one harvest left him; but those who might otherwise have bought and cultivated were afraid of offending Lord Lick-my-loof, whose hand was pretty generally seen in the turn of affairs, and also of involving themselves in an unsecure agreement. So things had come to a bad pass with the laird and his household. A small crop of oats and one of potatoes were coming on, for which the laird did what little he could, assisted by Grizzie and Aggie at such times when they could leave their respective charges, but in the meantime the stock of meal was getting low, and the laird did not see where more was to come from. He and Grizzie had only porridge, with a little salt butter, for two, and not unfrequently the third also of their daily meals. Grizzie for a while managed to keep alive a few fowls that picked about everywhere, finally making of them broth for her invalid, and persuading the laird to eat the little that was not boiled away, till at length there was neither cackle nor crow about the place, so that to Cosmo it seemed dying out into absolute silence—after which would come the decay and the crumbling, until the castle stood like the great hollow mammoth-tooth he had looked down upon in his dream.

At once he proceeded to do what little could yet be done for the on-coming crops, resolving to hire himself out for the harvest to some place later than Glenwarlock, so that he might be able to mow the oats before leaving, when his father and Grizzie with the help of Aggie would secure them.

Nothing could now prevent the closing of the net of the last mortgage about them; and the uttermost Cosmo could hope for thereafter was simply to keep his father and Grizzie alive to the end of their natural days. Shelter was secure, for the castle was free. The winter was drawing on, but there would be the oats and the potatoes, with what kail the garden would yield them, and they had, he thought, plenty of peats. Yet not unfrequently, as he wandered aimless through the dreary silence, he would be speculating how long, by a judiciously ordered consumption of the place, he could keep his father warm. The stables and cow-houses would afford a large quantity of fuel; the barn too had a great deal of heavy wood-work about it; and there was the third tower or block of the castle, for many years used for nothing but stowage, whose whole thick floors he would thankfully honour, burning them to ashes in such a cause. In the spring there would be no land left them, but so long as he could save the house and garden, and find means of keeping his two alive in them, he would not grieve over that.

Agnes was a little shy of Cosmo—he had been away so long! but at intervals her shyness would yield and she would talk to him with much the same freedom as of old when they went to school together. In his rambles Cosmo would not pass her grandfather's cottage without going in to inquire after him and his wife, and having a little chat with Aggie. Her true-hearted ways made her, next to his father and Mr. Simon, the best comforter he had.

She was now a strong, well-grown, sunburnt woman, with rough hands and tender eyes. Occasionally she would yet give a sharp merry answer, but life and its needs and struggles had made her grave, and in general she would, like a soft cloud, brood a little before she gave a reply. She had by nature such a well balanced mind, and had set herself so strenuously to do the right thing, that her cross seemed already her natural choice, as indeed it always is—of the deeper nature. In her Cosmo always found what strengthened him for the life he had now to lead, though, so long as at any hour he could have his father's company, and saw the old man plainly reviving in his presence, he could not for a moment call or think it hard, save in so far as he could not make his father's as easy as he would.

When the laird heard that his son, the heir of Glenwarlock, had hired himself for the harvest on a neighbouring farm, he was dumb for a season. It was heavy both on the love and the pride of the father, which in this case were one, to think of his son as a hired servant—and that of a rough, swearing man, who had made money as a butcher. The farm too was at such distance that he could not well come home to sleep! But the season of this dumbness, measured by the clock, at least, was but of a few minutes' duration; for presently the laird was on his knees thanking God that he had given him a son who would be an honour to any family out of heaven: in there, he knew, every one was an honour to every other!

Before the harvest on the farm of Stanewhuns arrived, Cosmo, to his desire, had cut their own corn, with Grizzie to gather, Aggie to bind, and his father to stook, and so got himself into some measure of training. He found it harder, it is true, at Stanewhuns, where he must keep up with more experienced scythe-men, but, just equal to it at first, in two days he was little more than equal, and able to set his father's heart at ease concerning his toil.

With all his troubles, it had been a blessed time so long as he spent most of the day and every evening in his father's company. Not unfrequently would Mr. Simon make one, seated with them in the old drawing-room or on some hillside, taking wisest share in every subject of talk that came up. In the little council Cosmo represented the rising generation with its new thought, its new consciousness of need, and its new difficulties; and was delighted to find how readily his notions were received, how far from strange they were to his old-fashioned friends, especially his preceptor, and how greatly true wisdom suffices for the hearing and understanding of new cries after the truth. For what all men need is the same—only the look of it changes as its nature expands before the growing soul or the growing generation, whose hunger and thirst at the same time grow with it. And, coming from the higher to the lower, it must be ever in the shape of difficulty that the most precious revelations first appear. Even Mary, to whom first the highest revelation came, and came closer than to any other, had to sit and ponder over the great matter, yea and have the sword pass through her soul, ere the thoughts of her heart could be revealed to her. But Cosmo of the new time, found himself at home with the men of the next older time, because both he and they were true; for in the truth there is neither old nor new; the well instructed scribe of the kingdom is familiar with the new as well as old shapes of it, and can bring either kind from his treasury. There was not a question Cosmo could start, but Mr. Simon had something at hand to the point, and plenty more within digging-scope of his thought-spade.

But now that he had to work all day, and at night see no one with whom to take sweet counsel, Cosmo did feel lonely—yet was it an unfailing comfort to remember that his father was within his reach, and he would see him the next Sunday. And the one thing he had dreaded was spared him—namely, to share a room with several other men, who might prove worse than undesirable company. For the ex-butcher, the man who was a byword in the country-side for his rough speech, in this showed himself capable of becoming a gentleman: he would neither allow Cosmo to eat with the labourers—to which Cosmo himself had no objection, nor would hear of his sleeping anywhere but in the best bedroom they had in the house. Also, from respect to the heir of a decayed family and valueless inheritance, he modified even his own habits so far as almost to cease swearing in his presence. Appreciating this genuine kindness, Cosmo in his turn tried to be agreeable to those around him, and in their short evenings, for, being weary, they retired early, would in his talk make such good use of his superior knowledge as to interest the whole family, so that afterwards most of them declared it the pleasantest harvest-time they had ever had. Perhaps it was a consequence that the youngest daughter, who had been to a boarding-school, and had never before appeared in any harvest-field, betook herself to that in which they were at work towards the end of the first week, and *gathered* behind Cosmo's scythe. But Cosmo was far too much occupied—thinking to the rhythmic swing of his scythe, to be aware of the honour done him. Still farther was he from suspecting that it had anything to do with the appearing of Agnes one afternoon, bringing him a letter from his father, with which she had armed herself by telling him she was going thitherward, and could take a message to the young laird.

The harvest began upon a Monday, and the week passed without his once seeing his father. On the Sunday he rose early, and set out for Castle Warlock. He would have gone the night before, but at the request of his master remained to witness the signing of his will. As he walked he found the week had given him such a consciousness of power as he had never had before: with the labour of his own hands he knew himself capable of earning bread for more than himself; while his limbs themselves seemed to know themselves stronger than hitherto. On the other hand he was conscious in his gait of the intrusion of the workman's plodding swing upon the easy walk of the student.

His way was mostly by footpaths, often up and down hill, now over a moor, now through a valley by a small stream. The freshness of the morning he found no less reviving than in the old boyish days, and sang as he walked, taking huge breaths of the life that lay on the heathery hill-top. And as he sang the words came—nearly like the following. He had never wondered at the powers of the *improvvisatore*. It was easy to him to extemporize.

Win' that blaws the simmer plaid,
Ower the hie hill's shouthers laid,
Green wi' gerse, an' reid wi' heather,
Welcome wi' yer soul-like weather!
Mony a win' there has been sent
Oot aneth the firmament;
Ilka ane its story has;
Ilka ane began an' was;
Ilka ane fell quaiet an' mute
Whan its angel wark was oot.
First gaed ane oot ower the mirk,
Whan the maker gan to work;
Ower it gaed and ower the sea,
An' the warl' begud to be.
Mony ane has come an' gane
Sin' the time there was but ane:
Ane was great an' strong, an' rent
Rocks an' mountains as it went
Afore the Lord, his trumpeter,
Waukin' up the prophet's ear;
Ane was like a steppin' soun'
I' the mulberry taps abune;
Them the Lord's ain steps did swing,
Walkin' on afore his king;
Ane lay doon like scoldit pup
At his feet an' gatna up.
Whan the word the maister spak
Drave the wull-cat billows back;
Ane gaed frae his lips, an' dang

Wind that blows the summer plaid,
Over the high hill's shoulders laid,
Green with grass, and red with heather,
Welcome with your soul-like weather!
Many a wind there has been sent
Out beneath the firmament;
Every one its story has;
Every one began and was;
Every one fell quiet and mute
When its angel work was out.
First went one across the dark
When the maker 'gan to work;
Over it went and over the sea,
And the world began to be.
Many more have come and gone
Since the time there was but one:
One was great and strong, and rent
Rocks and mountains as it went
Before the Lord, his trumpeter,
Waking up the prophet's ear;
One was like a stepping sound
High in the mulberry tops around;
Them the Lord's own steps did swing,
Walking on before his king;
One lay down like scolded pup
At his feet, nor thence got up,
When at the word the master spoke
The wild-cat billows were revoked;
One went from his lips and threw

To the earth the sodger thrang;
Ane comes frae his hert to mine,
Ilka day, to mak it fine.
Breath o' God, eh! come an' blaw
Frae my hert ilk fog awa';
Wauk me up, an' mak me strang,
Fill my hert wi' mony a sang,
Frae my lips again to stert,
Fillin' sails o' mony a hert,
Blawin' them ower seas dividin'
To the only place to bide in.

"Eh, Mr. Warlock! is that you singin' o' the Sawbath day?" said the voice of a young woman behind him, in a tone of gentle raillery rather than expostulation.

Cosmo turned and saw Elspeth, his master's daughter already mentioned.

"Whaur's the wrang o' that, Miss Elsie?" he answered. "Arena we tellt to sing an' mak melody to the Lord?"

"Ay, but i' yer hert, no lood oot—'cep' it be i' the kirk. That's the place to sing upo' Sundays. Yon wasna a psalm-tune ye was at!"

"Maybe no. Maybe I was a bit ower happy for ony tune i' the tune-buiks, an' bude to hae ane 'at cam o' itsel'!"

"An' what wad mak ye sae happy—gien a body micht speir?" asked Elspeth, peeping from under long lashes, with a shy, half frightened, sidelong glance at the youth.

To the earth the soldier crew;
One comes from his heart to mine,
Every day, to make it fine.
Breath of God, ah! Blow apart
Each fog that settles o'er my heart;
Wake me up, and make me strong,
Fill my heart with many a song,
From my lips again to start,
Filling sails of many a heart,
Blowing them over seas dividing
To the only place to hide in.

"Eh, Mr. Warlock! is that you singing on the Sabbath day?" said the voice of a young woman behind him, in a tone of gentle raillery rather than expostulation.

Cosmo turned and saw Elspeth, his master's daughter already mentioned.

"Where's the wrong in that, Miss Elsie?" he answered. "Aren't we told to sing and make melody to the Lord?"

"Ay, but in your heart, not out loud—except it be in church. That's the place to sing on Sundays. That wasn't a psalm-tune you were singing!"

"Maybe not. Maybe I was a bit too happy for any tune in the tune-books, and had to have one that came of itself!"

"And what would make you so happy—if a person might ask?" asked Elspeth, peeping from under long lashes, with a shy, half frightened, sidelong glance at the youth.

She was a handsome girl of the milkmaid type, who wore a bonnet with pretty ribbons, thought of herself as a young lady, and had many admirers, whence she had grown a little bold, without knowing it.

"Ye haena ower muckle at hame to make ye blithe, gien a' be true," she added sympathetically.

"I hae a'thing at hame to make me blithe—'cep' it be a wheen mair siller," answered Cosmo; "but maybe that'll come neist—wha kens?"

"Ay! wha kens?" returned the girl with a sigh. "There's mony ane doubtless wad be ready eneuch wi' the siller anent what ye hae wantin 't!"

"I hae naething but an auld hoose—no sae auld as lat the win' blaw through 't, though,"

"You haven't much at home to make you blithe, if all be true," she added sympathetically.

"I have everything at home to make me blithe—except it be a bit more money," answered Cosmo; "but maybe that'll come next—who knows?"

"Ay! who knows?" returned the girl with a sigh. "There's many that would doubtless be ready enough with the money for what you have without it!"

"I have nothing but an old house—not so old as to let the wind blow through it though," said Cosmo, amused. "But whaur are ye for sae ear, Miss Elsie?"

said Cosmo, amused. "But where are you headed so early, Miss Elsie?"

"I'm for the Muir o' Warlock, to see my sister, the schuilmaister's wife. Puir man! he's been ailin' ever sin' the spring. I little thoucht I was to hae sic guid company upo' the ro'd! Ye hae made an unco differ upo' my father, Mr. Warlock. I never saw man sae altert. In ae single ook!"

"I'm going to the Muir o' Warlock, to see my sister, the schoolmaster's wife. Poor man! he's been ailing ever since the spring. I little thought I was to have such good company upon the road! You've made a great difference to my father, Mr. Warlock. I never saw man so altered. In one single week!"

She had heard Cosmo say he much preferred good Scotch to would-be English, and therefore spoke with what breadth she could compass. In her head, notwithstanding, she despised everything homely, for she had been to school, in the city, where, if she had learned nothing else, she had learned the ambition to *appear;* of *being* anything she had no notion. She had a loving heart, though—small for her size, but lively. Of what really goes to make a *lady*—the end of her aspiration—she had no more idea than the swearing father of whom, while she loved him, as did all his family, she was not a little ashamed. She was an honest girl too in a manner, and had by nature a fair share of modesty; but now her heart was sadly fluttered, for the week that had wrought such a change on her father, had not been without its effect upon her—witness her talking *vulgar, broad Scotch!*

"Your father is very kind to me. So are you all," said Cosmo. "My father will be grateful to you for being so friendly to me."

"Your father is very kind to me. So are you all," said Cosmo. "My father will be grateful to you for being so friendly to me."

"Some wad be gien they daured!" faltered Elspeth. "Was ye content wi' my getherin' to ye—to your scythe, I mean, laird?"

"Some would be if they dared!" faltered Elspeth. "Were you content with my gathering to you—to your scythe, I mean, laird?"

"Wha could hae been ither, Miss Elsie? Try 'at I wad, I couldna lea' ye ahin' me."

"Who could have been other, Miss Elsie? Try as I would, I couldn't leave you behind me."

"Did ye want to lea' me ahin' ye?" rejoined Elsie, with a sidelong look and a blush, which Cosmo never saw. "I wadna seek a better to gether til.—But maybe ye dinna like my han's!"

"Did you want to leave me behind you?" rejoined Elsie, with a sidelong look and a blush, which Cosmo never saw. "I wouldn't seek a better to gather to.—But maybe you don't like my hands!"

So far as I can see, the suggestion was entirely irrelevant to the gathering, for what could it matter to the mower what sort of hands the woman had who gathered his swath. But then Miss Elspeth had, if not very pretty, at least very small hands, and smallness was the only merit she knew of in a hand.

What Cosmo might have answered, or in what perplexity between truth and unwillingness to hurt she might have landed him before long, I need not speculate, seeing all danger was suddenly swept away by a second voice, addressing Cosmo as unexpectedly as the first.

They had just passed a great stone on the roadside, at the foot of which Aggie had been for some time seated, waiting for Cosmo, whom she expected with the greater confidence that, having come to meet him the night before, and sat where she now was till it was dark, she had had to walk back without him. Recognizing the voices that neared her, she waited until the pair had passed her shelter, and then addressed Cosmo with a familiarity she had not used since his return—for which Aggie had her reasons.

"Cosmo!" she called, rising as she spoke, "winna ye bide for me? Ye hae a word for twa

"Cosmo!" she called, rising as she spoke, "won't you wait for me? You have a

as weel 's for ane. The same sairs whaur baith hae lugs."

The moment Cosmo heard her voice, he turned to meet her, glad enough.

"Eh, Aggie!" he said, "I'm pleased to see ye. It was richt guid o' ye to come to meet me! Hoo's your father, an' hoo's mine?"

"They're baith brawly," she answered, "an' blithe eneuch, baith, at the thoucht o' seein' ye. Gien ye couldna luik in upo' mine the day, he wad stap doon to the castle. Sin' yesterday mornin' the laird, Grizzie tells me, hasna ristit a minute in ae place, 'cep' in his bed. What for camna ye thestreen?"

word for two as well as for one. The same serves where both have ears."

The moment Cosmo heard her voice, he turned to meet her, glad enough.

"Eh, Aggie!" he said, "I'm pleased to see you. It was very good of you to come to meet me! How's your father, and how's mine?"

"They're both grand," she answered, "and blithe enough, both, at the thought of seeing you. If you can't look in upon mine today, he'll step down to the castle. Since yesterday morning the laird, Grizzie tells me, hasn't rested a minute in one place, except in his bed. Why didn't you come last night?"

As he was answering her question, Aggie cast a keen searching look at his companion: Elsie's face was as red as fire could have reddened it, and tears of vexation were gathering in her eyes. She turned her head away and bit her lip.

The two girls were hardly acquainted, nor would Elsie have dreamed of familiarity with the daughter of a poor cotter. Aggie seemed much farther below her, than she below the young laird of Glenwarlock. Yet here was the rude girl addressing him as Cosmo—with the boldness of a sister, in fact! and he taking it as a matter of course, and answering in similar style! It was unnatural! Indignation grew fierce within her. What might she not have waked in him before they parted but for this shameless hussy!

"Ye'll be gaein' to see yer sister, Miss Elsie?" said Agnes, after a moment's pause.

"You'll be going to see your sister, Miss Elsie?" said Agnes, after a moment's pause.

Elspeth kept her head turned away, and made her no answer. Aggie smiled to herself, and reverting to Cosmo, presently set before him a difficulty she had met with in her algebra, a study which, at such few times as she could spare, she still prosecuted with the help of Mr. Simon. So Elsie, who understood nothing of the subject, was thrown out. She dropped a little behind, and took the role of the abandoned one. When Cosmo saw this, he stopped, and they waited for her. When she came up,

"Are we gaein' ower fest for ye, Miss Elsie?" he said.

"Not at all;" she answered, English again; "I can walk as fast as any one."

Cosmo turned to Aggie and said,

"Aggie, we're i' the wrang. We had no richt to speik aboot things 'at only twa kent, whan there was three walkin' thegither.—Ye see, Miss Elsie, her an' me was at the schuil thegither, an' we happent to tak' up wi' the same kin' o' thing, partic'larly algebra an' geometry, an' can ill haud oor tongues frae them whan we forgather. The day, it's been to the prejudice o' oor mainners, an' I beg ye to owerluik it."

"I didn't think it was profitable conversation for the Sabbath day," said Elsie,

"Are we going too fast for you, Miss Elsie?" he said.

"Not at all;" she answered, English again; "I can walk as fast as any one."

Cosmo turned to Aggie and said,

"Aggie, we're in the wrong. We had no right to speak about things that only two knew, when there were three walking together.—You see, Miss Elsie, she and I were at the school together, and we happened to take up with the same kind of thing, particularly algebra and geometry, and can hardly resist talking of them when we meet. Today, it's been to the prejudice of our manners, and I beg you to overlook it."

"I didn't think it was profitable conversation for the Sabbath day," said Elsie, with a smile meant to be chastened, but which Aggie took for bitter, and laughed in her sleeve. A few minutes more and the two were again absorbed, this time with a point in conic sections, on which Aggie professed to require enlightenment, and again Elsie was left out. Nor did this occur either through returning forgetfulness on the part of Aggie; or the naturally strong undertow of the tide of science in her brain. Once more Elsie adopted the *neglected* role, but being allowed to play it in reality, dropped farther and farther behind, until its earnest grew heavy on her soul, and she sat down by the roadside and wept—then rising in anger, turned back, and took another way to the village.

with a smile meant to be chastened, but which Aggie took for bitter, and laughed in her sleeve. A few minutes more and the two were again absorbed, this time with a point in conic sections, on which Aggie professed to require enlightenment, and again Elsie was left out. Nor did this occur either through returning forgetfulness on the part of Aggie; or the naturally strong undertow of the tide of science in her brain. Once more Elsie adopted the *neglected* role, but being allowed to play it in reality, dropped farther and farther behind, until its earnest grew heavy on her soul, and she sat down by the roadside and wept—then rising in anger, turned back, and took another way to the village.

Poor girl-heart! How many tears do not fancies doomed to pass cost those who give them but as it were a night's lodging! And the tears are bitter enough, although neither the love, and therefore the sorrow, may have had time to develop much individuality. One fairest soap-bubble, one sweetly devised universe vanishes with those tears; and it may be never another is blown with so many colours, and such enchanting changes! What is the bubble but air parted from the air, individualized by thinnest skin of slightly glutinous water! Does not swift comfort and ready substitution show first love rather the passion between man and woman than between a man and a woman? How speedily is even a Romeo consoled to oblivion for the loss of a Rosaline by the gain of a Juliet! And yet I mourn over even such evanishment; mourn although I know that the bubble of paradise, swift revolving to annihilation, is never a wasted thing: its influence, its educating power on the human soul, which must at all risks be freed of its shell and taught to live, remains in that soul, to be, I trust, in riper worlds, an eternal joy. At the same time therefore I would not be too sad over such as Elsie, now seated by a little stream, in a solitary hollow, alone with her mortification—bathing her red eyes with her soaked handkerchief, that she might appear without danger of inquisition before the sister whom marriage had not made more tender, or happiness more sympathetic.

But how is it that girls ready to cry more than their eyes out for what they call love when the case is their own, are so often hard-hearted when the case is that of another? There is something here to be looked into—if not by an old surmiser, yet by the young women themselves! Why are such relentless towards every slightest relaxation of self restraint, who would themselves dare not a little upon occasion? Here was Agnes, not otherwise an ill-natured girl, positively exultant over Elsie's discomfiture and disappearance! The girl had done her no wrong, and she had had her desire upon her: she had defeated her, and was triumphant; yet this was how she talked of her to her own inner ear:

"The impudent limmer!—makin' up til a gentleman like oor laird 'at is to be! Cudna he be doon a meenute but she maun be upon 'im to devoor 'im!—an' her father naething but the cursin' flesher o' Stanedyhes!—forby 'at a'body kens she was promised to Jock Rantle, the mason lad, an wad hae hed him, gien the father o' her hadna sworn at them that awfu' 'at neither o' them daured gang a fit further! Gien

"The impudent jade!—making up to a gentleman like our laird that's to be! Couldn't he be down a minute but she must be upon him to devour him!—and her father nothing but the cursing butcher of Stanedyhes!—besides the fact that everyone knows she was promised to Jock Rantle, the mason lad, and would have had him, if her father hadn't sworn at them so badly that neither of them dared go a foot

I had loed a lad like Jock, wad I hae latten him gang for a screed o' ill words! They micht hae sworn 'at likit for me! I wad hae latten them sweir! Na, na! Cosmo's for Elsie's betters!"

further! If I had loved a lad like Jock, would I have let him go for a whole list of ill words! Any who liked might have sworn for me! I would have let them swear! Na, na! Cosmo's for Elsie's betters!"

Elsie appeared no more in any field that season—staid at Muir o' Warlock, indeed, till the harvest was over.

But what a day was that Sunday to Cosmo! Labour is the pursuivant of joy to prepare the way before him. His father received him like a king come home with victory. And was he not a king? Did not the Lord say he was a king, because he came into the world to bear witness to the truth?

They walked together to church—and home again as happy as two boys let out of school—home to their poor dinner of new potatoes and a little milk, the latter brought by Aggie with her father's compliments "to his lairdship," as Grizzie gave the message. What! Was I traitor bad enough to call it a poor dinner? Truth and Scotland forgive me, for I know none so good! And after their dinner immediately, for there was no toddy now for the laird, they went to the drawing-room—an altogether pleasant place now in the summer, and full of the scent of the homely flowers Grizzie arranged in the old vases on the chimney-piece—and the laird laid himself down on the brocade-covered sofa, and Cosmo sat close beside him on a low chair, and talked, and told him this and that, and read to him, till at last the old man fell asleep, and then Cosmo, having softly spread a covering upon him, sat brooding over things sad and pleasant, until he too fell asleep, to be with Joan in his dreams.

At length the harvest was over, and Cosmo went home again, and in poverty-stricken Castle Warlock dwelt the most peaceful, contented household imaginable. But in it reigned a stillness most awful. So great indeed was the silence that Grizzie averred she had to make much more noise than needful about her affairs that she might not hear the ghosts. She did not mind them, she said, at night; they were natural then; but it was *ugsome* (horrible) to hear them in the day-time! The poorer their fare, the more pains Grizzie took to make it palatable. The gruel the laird now had always for his supper, was cooked with love rather than fuel. With what a tender hand she washed his feet! What miracles of the laundress-art were the old shirts he wore! Now that he had no other woman to look after him, she was to him like a mother to a delicate child, in all but the mother's familiarity. But the cloud was cold to her also; she seldom rimed now; and except when unusually excited, never returned a sharp answer.

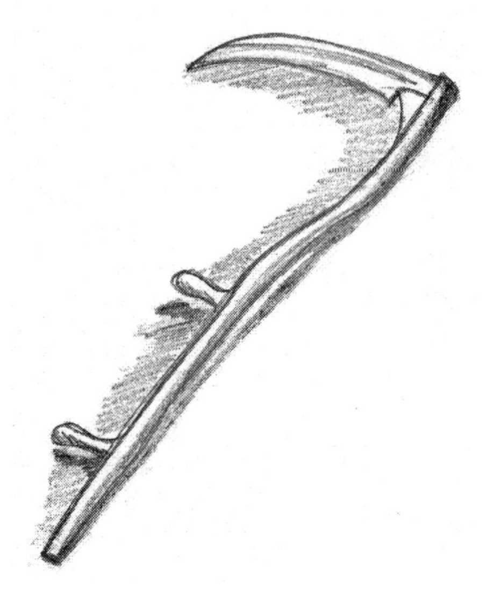

CHAPTER XLI
THE SCHOOLMASTER

It is time I told my readers something about Joan. But it is not much I have to tell. Cosmo received from her an answer to his letter concerning the ring within a week; and this is what she wrote:

"MY DEAR COSMO,

of course I cannot understand why you went away as you did. It makes me very unhappy, lest I should be somehow to blame. But I trust you entirely. I too hope for the day when it will be impossible to hide anything. I always find myself when I wake in the morning, trying to understand why you went away so, and one reason after another comes, but I have not got the real one yet—at least I think not. I will pay Dr. Jermyn the money with all my heart. I cannot pay him just yet, because the same day you left he was called to London upon medical business, and has not yet returned. Give my love to your father. I hope you are safe and happy with him by this time. I wish I were with you! Will that day ever come again? I cannot tell you how I miss you. It is not wonderful, if you will only think of it. I hope, dear Cosmo, it was not my fault that you went away. I know my behaviour was such as to most people would have seemed very strange, but you are not most people, and I did and do think you understood it, and made all the allowance for me that could be made. I had almost forgot to thank you for the money. I do thank you, Cosmo, but I should have been much more grateful had you kept it. It is all so stupid—and next to no use without you or your father! And to know I have such a large sum in the house that my brother knows nothing about, quite frightens me sometimes. I wish you had left me the horse to hide it in. I feel very much like a thief, and I am sure my brother would think of me as one if he knew. I feel sometimes as if there were an evil imp in the drawer where it lies. Mind you do not make the slightest allusion to it in any of your letters, and ask your father not to do so either. It has just one comfort in it—that I could now, if driven to it, run away. My love to your father. Your loving cousin,

JOAN."

Long before this letter arrived, Cosmo had told his father everything; and he, although he could not believe there was anything between Joan and the doctor, quite approved of his conduct.

"Wait upon the Lord," he said, after listening with the excitement of a young heart, the ache of an old one, and the hope of a strong one, to his son's narrative; "wait patiently on him, and he will give thee thy heart's desire."

They waited, and patiently.

What was there now that Cosmo could do to make a little money? With Mr. Simon he held many an anxious conference on the matter, but nothing could either think of except the heart—wearing endeavour after favour with one or other of the magazines—involving an outlay of much time, a sick deferment of hope, and great discouragement; for how small were the chances of his work proving acceptable to this or that man who, with the best intentions for the *success* of the magazine in his charge, and a keen enough perception of the unworthy in literature, had most likely no special love for the truth, or care to teach it, and was besides under the incapacitating influence, the deadening, debilitating, stupefying effect of having continually to judge—not to mention the enervating hopelessness that at length falls, I presume, upon every editor of a popular magazine, of finding one pearl among the cartloads of oysters sent him by unknown divers in the gulf of literature—filling him with amazement that there should be so many to write so well, and so few to write better. Mr. Simon nevertheless encouraged Cosmo to make the attempt, seeing that to one who had nothing else to do, it involved no loss, and would be certain gain to both head and heart, with just the possibility as well of a little return in money. So he set to work, and wrote, and wrote, and sent, and sent, but heard nothing and nothing.

The weeks came and went, and the frosts came and went, and then came and staid: and the snow fell and melted, and then fell and lay; and winter settled down with moveless rigour upon Castle Warlock. Nor had it lasted long, before it became evident that the natural powers of the laird had begun to fail more rapidly. But sufficient unto the day is the evil thereof, and that in the matter of death as well as of life; if we are not to forestall the difficulties of living, surely we are not to forestall the difficulties of dying. There was one thing, however, that did trouble him: the good old man's appetite had begun to fail, and how was he to get for him what might tempt him to eat? He was always contented, nor ever expressed a desire for anything not in the house; but this was what sent Cosmo on his knees oftenest of all—oftener even than his own spiritual necessities.

Never surely did household, even in Scotland, live upon less! Cosmo had to watch Grizzie to know that she ate at all, and once came nearly to the conclusion that she ate only dry meal. He would have had his father take his grandmother's room now she was gone, but he would not leave the one he had last occupied with his wife. From that he would go, he said, as she had gone. So Cosmo took his grandmother's, and there wrote and read—and when his father could not, in the very cold weather, leave his bed, was within the call of the slightest knock upon his floor. But every now and then, when the cold would abate a little, the laird would revive, and hope grow strong in the mind of his son: his father was by no means an old man yet, he would persuade himself, and might be intended to live many years; and thereupon he would set to work with fresh vigour. But it is hard to labour without encouragement, or apparent prospect of result.

Many a time did the Gracies go without milk that they might send for the laird the little their cow gave; but, though Cosmo never refused their kindness, as indeed he had no right, it went to his heart that the two old people should go without what was as needful for them as for his father. Mr. Simon too would every now and then send something from his house or from the village—oftener than Cosmo knew, for he had taken Grizzie into his confidence, and she was discreet. But now at length fell a heavenly crumb to keep the human sparrows picking.

The schoolmaster at the Muir, he who had behaved so insolently to the Warlocks, father and son, had returned to his duties at the end of the *harvest-holiday,* but had been getting worse for some time, and was at length unable to go on. He must therefore provide a substitute, and Cosmo heard that he was on the outlook for one.

Now Cosmo knew that, if he had desired to be made parish-schoolmaster, the influence of Lord Lick-my-loof would have been too strong against him, but it seemed possible that his old master might have so far forgotten by-gones as to be willing to employ him. He went to him therefore the same hour, and being shown into the room where he sat wrapt in blankets, laid before him his petition.

Now the schoolmaster, although both worldly in his judgement, and hasty in his temper, was not a heartless man. Keen feelings are not always dissociated from brutality even. One thing will reach the heart that another will not; and much that looks like heartlessness, may be mainly stupidity. He had never ceased, after the first rush of passion, to regret he had used the word that incensed the boy; and although he had never to his own heart confessed himself wrong in knocking down the violator of the sacredness of the master's person, yet, unconsciously to himself, he had for that been sorry also. Had he been sorrier, his pride would yet have come between him and confession. When the boy, then, on whom for years he had not set his eyes, stood unexpectedly before him, a fine youth, down in the world, and come, as he anticipated the moment he saw him, to beg a favour—behold an opportunity, not only of reparation without confession, but of induing the dignity of forgiveness! He received Cosmo, therefore, with the stiffness of a condescending inferior, it is true, but with kindness notwithstanding, and, having heard his request, accorded immediately a gracious assent, which so filled Cosmo with gratitude that he could not help showing some emotion, whereupon the heart of the schoolmaster in its turn asserted itself; and from that moment friendly relations were established between them.

Things were soon arranged. Cosmo was to be paid by the week, and should commence his work the next morning. He returned therefore in great consolation, carrying with him for his father one or two simple luxuries the village afforded. That night he could hardly sleep for joy.

He set about his new duties with zeal. Teaching itself is far from easy work to anyone anxious to make it genuine; and Cosmo had besides to leave home early in all kinds of wintry weather, and walk to it through the bitterness of *black frost,* the shifting toil of deep snow, or the assault of fierce storm. But he thought nothing of the labour or its accessories of discomfort; the only thing he felt hard was having to leave his father all the winter-day alone, for it was generally five o'clock before he got back to him.

And now in the heart of the laird arose a fresh gratitude for the son God had given him. His hours passed mainly in devotion and anticipation. Every time he received his son from the arms of the winter to his own, it was like the welcoming of one lost and found again.

Into the stern weather of their need had stolen a summer-day to keep hope alive. Cosmo gave up his writing, and spent all the time he had at home in waiting with mind and body upon his father. He read to him—sometimes his own poetry,—and that his father liked best of all, because therein he came nearer to his boy; now and then, when he was too weary for thought, he would play backgammon with him; and sometimes, when he was himself more tired than usual, would get Grizzie to come and tell yet again the stories she used to tell him when he was a child—some of which his father enjoyed the more that he remembered having heard them when he was himself a child. Upon one of these occasions, Grizzie brought from her treasury a tale which the laird remembered his grandmother's saying she too had heard when she was a child, and therewith it came into Cosmo's head to write it out, as nearly as he could, in Grizzie's words, and try a magazine with it. For the first time he received an answer—the most agreeable part of which was a small cheque, and the next most agreebale the request that he would send another paper of like character. Grizzie's face, when she learned in what way, and how largely, as it seemed to her, she had commenced contributing to the income of the family, was a sight worth a good deal more than a good dinner to both father and son. At first she imagined Cosmo was making game of her, and stood upon the dignity of her legends; but convinced at length of the fact of the case, she stared into nowhere for a minute, and then said,

"Eh, sirs! Oot o' the moo' o' babes an' sucklin's! The Lord be praist, whan herts is raist!"

"Eh, sirs! Out of the mouths of babes and sucklings! The Lord be praised, when hearts are raised!"

"Amen, Grizzie!" responded the laird. "Eh, wuman? gien ever ane wan a place in a faimily, her ain by foreordeenment o' the fatherly providence 'at luiks efter the faimilies o' men, Grizzie, ye're that wuman!"

"Amen, Grizzie!" responded the laird. "Eh, woman? if ever any won a place in a family, her own by foreordainment of the fatherly providence that looks after the families of men, Grizzie, you're that woman!"

Word to please Grizzie better the laird could not have found. It sunk in and in, for her pleasure could make no show, there being no room for any growth in the devotion of her ministrations.

And now Cosmo would take no more of the Gracies' milk, but got Aggie to go every day to a farm near, and buy what was required for his father, and Aggie was regular as the clock, sunshine or storm.

But there was another thing in which she was not quite so regular, but which yet she never missed when she could help it; so that, as often as three and occasionally four times in the week, Cosmo would find her waiting for him somewhere on his way home, now just outside the village, now nearer Glenwarlock, according to the hour when she had got through her work. The village talked, and Aggie knew it, but did not heed it; for she had now in her own feeling recovered her former position towards him; and it was one of the comforts of Cosmo's labour, when the dullness or contrariety of the human animal began to be too much for him, to think of the talk with Agnes he might hope was waiting him. Under Mr. Simon she had made much progress, and was now a companion fit for any thinking man. The road home was not half the length to Cosmo when Agnes walked it too. Thinking inside, and labouring outside, she was, in virtue of the necessities of her life, such a woman as not the most vaunted means of education, without the weight and seeming hindrances of struggle, can produce. One of the immortal women she was—for she had set out to grow forevermore—for whom none can predict an adequate future, save him who knows what he is making of her.

Her behaviour to Cosmo was that of a half sister, who, born in a humbler position, from which she could not rise, was none the less his sister, and none the less loved him. Whether she had anything to struggle with in order to keep this position, I am not prepared to say; but I have a suspicion that the behaviour of Elspeth, which so roused her scorn, had something to do with the restoring of the old relation between them. The most jealous of *reasonable* mothers could hardly have complained of her behaviour in Comso's company, however much she might have disapproved of her seeking it as she did. But it is well that God, and not even reasonable mothers, has the ordering of those things in which they consider themselves most interested, and are not unfrequently intrusive. Next to his father and Mr. Simon, Agnes Gracie was the most valued of Cosmo's friends. Mr. Burns came next. For Lady Joan, he never thought of her by the side of anybody else. If he had not learned to love her, I think he might now very well have loved Agnes. And if Cosmo had asked her now, when marriage was impossible, to marry him when he could marry, I do not know what Agnes might have answered. But he did not, and they remained the best of trusting friends.

CHAPTER XLII
GRANNIE AND THE STICK

This winter, the wind that drops the ripened fruit not plucked before, blew hard upon old Grannie, who had now passed her hundredth year. For some time Agnes had not been able to do much for her, but another great-grandchild, herself a widow and a mother, was spending the winter with her. On his way to or from school, Cosmo every day looked in to see or enquire after her; and when he heard she had had a bad night, he would always think how with her would fail the earthly knowledge of not a little of the past of his family, and upon one of these occasions resolved that he would at least find out whether she remembered the bamboo he had brought from Cairncarque.

Calling when school was over, he heard she was a little better, and the next morning brought with him the cane. In the afternoon he learned that she had had a better night, and going in found her in her chair by the fireside, and took his place by her so that the light from the window at her back should fall upon the stick.

He had not sat more than a minute, when he saw her eyes fixed upon the horse.

"What's that ye hae there, Cosmo?" she said.

"What's that you have there, Cosmo?" she said.

"This?" returned Cosmo. "It's a cane I pickit up upo' my traivels. What think ye o' 't?"

"This?" returned Cosmo. "It's a cane I picked up in my travels. What do you think of it?"

He held it out to her, but she did not move her hand towards it.

"Whaur got ye 't?" she asked, her eyes growing larger as she looked.

"Where did you get it?" she asked, her eyes growing larger as she looked.

"What gars ye speir, grannie?" he returned, with assumed indifference.

"What makes you ask, grannie?" he returned, with assumed indifference.

"I dinna believe there was anither like the ane that's like," she replied.

"I don't believe there was another like the one that's like," she replied.

"In which case," rejoined Cosmo, "it maun be the same. Ken ye onything aboot it?"

"In which case," rejoined Cosmo, "it must be the same. Do you know anything about it?"

"Ay; an' sae du ye, or ye hae less sense nor I wad hae mintit o' a Warlock. That stick's no a stick like ither sticks, an' I wuss I was nearer hame."

"Ay; and so do you, or you have less sense than I would have expected of a Warlock. That stick's not like other sticks, and I wish I was nearer home."

"Ye dinna mean, grannie, there's onything no canny aboot the stick?" said Cosmo.

"You don't mean, grannie, there's anything uncanny about the stick?" said Cosmo.

"I wadna like to think him near me 'at aucht it," she replied.

"I wouldn't like to think him near me that owned it," she replied.

"Wha aucht it, grannie?"

"Who owned it, grannie?"

"Rive 't a' to bits, laddie; there's something by ordnar aboot it. The auld captain made o' 't as gien it had been his graven image. That was his stick ye hae i' yer han', whaurever ye got it; an' it was seldom oot o' his frae mornin' till nicht. Some wad hae't he tuik it til 's bed wi' him. I kenna aboot that; but gien by ony accident he set it oot frae 'atween his knees, it

"Rive it all to bits, laddie; there's something not natural about it. The old captain treated it like his graven image. That was his stick you have in your hand, wherever you got it; and it was seldom out of his from morning to night. Some would have it he took it to his bed with him. I don't know about that; but if by any accident he set it out

was never oot o' the sicht o' his e'en. I hae seen him mysel', missin 't like, luik up o' a suddent as gien his sowl hed been requiret o' 'im, an' grip at it as gien it had been his proadigal son come hame oonexpeckit.

from between his knees, it was never out of the sight of his eyes. I've seen him myself, missing it, look up all of a sudden as if his soul had been required of him, and grip it as if it had been his prodigal son come home unlooked-for."

Cosmo told her where he had found it.

"I tellt ye sae!" she cried. "The murderin' villain cairriet it wi' him, weel kenning what was intil 't!"

Cosmo told her where he had found it.

"I told you so!" she cried. "The murdering villain carried it with him, well knowing what was in it!"

Cosmo showed her the joints and their boxes, telling her he had searched them all, but had found nothing. She shook her head.

"Ower late! ower late!" she murmured. "The rievin' English lord was aforehan' wi' the heir!"

"Too late! too late!" she murmured. "The thieving English lord stole a march on the heir!"

She seemed then to fall into a kind of lethargic musing, and as Cosmo had not yet made up his mind to show her the paper he had found in the top of the cane, and ask her opinion concerning it, for the present he bade her good-night—little thinking he was not to see her again in this world. For that same night she died.

And now when his opportunity was over, and he could learn no more from her, the mind of Cosmo was exercised afresh concerning the bamboo. According to Grannie, its owner habitually showed anxiety for its safety, and had it continually under his eye. It did not seem likely that the rings had been in it long when it was taken from him, neither that at any time he would have chosen to carry like valuables about with him in such a receptacle. It could hardly therefore be because of those or of similar precious things concealed in it, that he was always so watchful over it. It was possible, indeed, that from often using it for temporary concealment, he had come to regard it with constant anxiety; but the conjecture did not satisfy Cosmo. And as often as he turned the thing over in his mind, his speculation invariably settled on the unintelligible paper. It was true the said paper had seemed not so much there for its own safety, as by chance employment for the protection of the jewels round which it was, after all, rather squeezed than folded; but a man may crumple up his notes and thrust them in his pocket, yet care more for them than for anything else in the same place.

Thinking of the thing one night after he was in bed, it occurred to him suddenly to ask himself what he had done with the paper, for he could not remember when he had last seen it. He got up, took the stick, which being Joan's gift he always carried to his room, and opening the horse, which he could now do without his eyes, found it empty. This made him uneasy, and he lay down again to think what he could have done with it. It was dark night, and his anxiety was not so great but that sleep presented its claim upon him. He resisted it however, unwilling to yield until he had at least thought of some probability with regard to the paper. But, like a soundless tide, sleep kept creeping upon him, and he kept starting from it with successive spur-pricks of the will which had not yet consented to the nightly annihilation. Bethinking himself in one of these revivals that he might have put it in his pocket-book, he stretched his hand to the chair beside the bed on which lay his clothes. Then came a gap in his consciousness, and the next thing he knew was the pocket-book in his hand, with the memory or the dream, he could not afterwards tell which, of having searched it in vain.

He now felt so anxious that he could rest no longer, but must get up and look for the paper until he found it. He rose and lighted his candle, went down the stair to the kitchen, and out of the house—then began to doubt whether he was awake, but, like one compelled, went on to the great door, and up to the drawing-room, when first he became aware that the moon was shining, and all at once remembered a former dream, and knew it was coming to him again: there it was!—the old captain, seated in his chair, with the moon on his face, and a ghastly look! He felt his hair about to stand on end with terror, but resisted with all his might. The rugged, scarred countenance gazed fixedly at him, and he did his best to return the gaze. The appearance rose, and walked from the room, and Cosmo knew he had to follow it to the room above, which he had not once entered since his return. There, as before, it went to the other side of the bed, and disappeared. But this time the dream went a little farther. Despite his fear, Cosmo followed, and in the wall, by the head of the bed, saw an open door. He hurried up to it, but seemed to strike against the wall, and woke. He was in bed, but his heart was beating a terribly quick march. His pocket-book was in his hand: he struck a light, and searching in it, found the missing paper.

The next night, he told his dream to his father and Mr. Simon, and they had a talk about dreams and apparitions; then all three pored over the paper, but far from arriving at any conclusion, seemed hardly to get a glimpse of anything that could be called light upon its meaning.

CHAPTER XLIII
OBSTRUCTION

All this time Cosmo had never written again to Joan; both his father and he thought it better the former only should for the present keep up the correspondence. But months had passed without their hearing from her. The laird had written the third time, and received no answer.

The day was now close upon them when the last of their land would be taken, leaving them nothing but the kitchen-garden—a piece of ground of about half an acre, the little terraced flower-garden to the south of the castle, and the croft tenanted by James Gracie. They applied to Lord Lick-my-loof to grant them a lease of the one field next the castle, which the laird with the help of the two women had cultivated the spring before, but he would not—his resentment being as strong as ever, and his design deeper than they saw.

The formal proceedings took their legal course; and upon and after a certain day Lord Lick-my-loof might have been seen from not a few of the windows of the castle, walking the fields to the north and east, and giving orders to his bailiff concerning them. Within a fortnight those to the north were no more to be entered from the precincts of the castle except by climbing over a *dry-stane-dyke* (dry-stone-wall); and before many additional days were gone by, they found him more determined than they could have imagined, to give them annoyance.

He had procured a copy of an old plan of the property, and therein discovered, as he had expected and hoped, that that part of the road from the glen of the Warlock which passed the gate of the castle, had been made by the present laird only about thirty years before; whereupon—whether he was within his legal rights or not, I do not know, but everybody knew the laird could not go to law—he gave orders that it should be broken up from the old point of departure, and a dry dyke built across the gate. But the persons to whom the job was committed, either ashamed or afaid, took advantage of an evening on which Cosmo had a class for farm-labourers, to do the work after dark; whence it came that, plodding homewards without a suspicion, he found himself as he approached the gate all at once floundering among stones and broken ground, and presently brought up standing, a man built out from his own house by a mushroom wall—the entrance gone which seemed to him as old as the hills around it, for it was older than his earthly life. With a great shove he hurled half the height of it over, and walking in, appeared before his father in such a rage as bewildered and troubled him far more than any insolence of Lord Lick-my-loof could have done.

"The scoundrel!" cried Cosmo; "I should like to give him a good drubbing—only he's an old man! But I'll make him repent it—and heartily, too!"

"Cosmo, my boy," said the old man, "you are meddling with what does not belong to you."

"I know it's your business, father, not mine; but—"

"It's no more my business than yours, my son! *'Vengeance is mine, saith the Lord.'*—An' the best o' 't is," he went on, willing, by a touch of humour in the truth he had to speak, to help turn the tide of Cosmo's wrath, "he'll tak' no more than's guid for the sinner; whereas yersel', Cosmo, i' the tune ye're in noo, wad damn puir auld Lick-my-loof for ever and ever! Man, he canna hurt me to the worth o' sic a heap o' firin'!" Then changing his tone to absolute seriousness, "Min' ye tu, Cosmo," he went on, "'at the maister never threatent but

"It's no more my business than yours, my son! *'Vengeance is mine, saith the Lord.'*—And the best of it is," he went on, willing, by a touch of humour in the truth he had to speak, to help turn the tide of Cosmo's wrath, "he'll take no more than is good for the sinner, whereas you, Cosmo, in the tune you're in now, would damn poor old Lick-my-loof for ever and ever! Man, he can't hurt me to the worth of such a heap of firing!" Then changing his tone to absolute seriousness, "Remember too, Cosmo," he went on, "that the master never threatened but aye left the thing, whatever it was, to him 'at judges richteously. Ye want nothing but fair play, my son, an' whether ye get it frae Lick-my-loof or no, there's ane winna haud it frae ye. Ye 's get it, my son; ye 's get it! The maister 'll hae a'thing set richt at the lang last; an' gien he binna in a hurry, we may weel bide. For mysel', the man has smitten me upo' the tae cheek, an' may hae the tither to lat drive at whan he likes. It's no worth liftin' my auld airm to haud aff the smack."

always left the thing, whatever it was, to him that judges righteously. You want nothing but fair play, my son, and whether you get it from Lick-my-loof or not, there's one who won't keep it from you. You'll get it, my son; you'll get it! The master will have all things set right at the long last; and if he isn't in a hurry, we may well wait. For myself, the man has smitten me upon the one cheek, and may have the other to strike at when he likes. It's not worth lifting my old arm to hold off the smack."

He laughed, and Cosmo laughed too—but grimly and out of tune. Then the laird told him that just that piece of the road was an improvement of his own, and had cost him a good bit of blasting: it used to cross the stream twice before it got to the yard-gate. He hardly thought, he said, that his lordship would like to have to restore it; for, besides the expense, it would cost him so much out of one of his best fields. In the meantime they must contrive how to connect themselves with that part of the road which he dared not touch. The worst of it was that there was no longer any direct communication across the fields with James Gracie's cottage. To follow the road was to make a tremendous round.

Grizzie being already in bed when Cosmo came home, learned nothing that night of the evil news.

At break of day Cosmo was up to see what could be done, and found that a few steps cut in the rocky terraces of the garden would bring one with ease to the road. He set about it immediately, and before breakfast-time had finished the job.

The rage and indignation of Grizzie when she learned what had been done, far surpassed Cosmo's, and served to secure him from any return of the attack. The flood of poetic abuse that she poured out seemed inexhaustible, sweeping along with it tale after tale to the prejudice of "that leein' Lick-my-loof." ("that lying Lick-my-loof.") But, poetic as was her speech, not a single rime did she utter for the space of an hour during which she thus unloaded her heart.

"Ay!" she concluded, and thereafter sank into smouldering silence, "there was a footpath there afore ye was born, laird, blast or no blast; an' to that I can fess them 'at can beir testimony, ane o' them bein' nane ither nor Jeames Gracie himsel', wha's ten lang years aheid o' yer lairdship! An' lat me see man or dog 'at 'll haud me ohn taen my wull o' my richts intil 't! They canna hang me, and for less I carena."

"Ay!" she concluded, and thereafter sank into smouldering silence, "there was a footpath there before you were born, laird, blast or no blast; and to that I can bring them that can bear testimony, one of them being none other than Jeames Gracie himself, who's ten long years ahead of your lairdship! And let me see man or dog that will keep me from taking my rights in the matter! They can't hang me, and for less I don't care."

The schoolmaster was at length fit to resume his labours, and about a week after the event just recorded, Cosmo ceased to attend the school in his stead.

CHAPTER XLIV
GRIZZIE'S RIGHTS

In those days Mistress Gracie fell sick, and though for a while neither husband nor granddaughter thought seriously of her ailment, it proved more than her age, worn with labour, could endure, and she began to sink. Then Grizzie must go and help nurse her, for, Cosmo being at home all day long, the laird could well enough spare her.

Father and son were now seldom out of each other's sight. When Cosmo was writing, the laird would be reading in the same room; and when, after their dinner, the laird slept, Cosmo would generally read his New-Testament beside him, and as often as he woke fresh from his nap, the two would talk about what the one had been reading, and Cosmo would impart what fresh light the Greek had given him. The capacity of the old man for taking in what was new, was wonderful, and yet not to be wondered at, seeing it was the natural result of the constant practice of what he learned—for all truth understood becomes duty. To him that obeys well, the tuth comes easy; to him who does not obey, it comes not, or comes in forms of fear and dismay. The true, that is the obedient man, cannot help seeing the truth, for it is the very business of his being—the natural concern, the correlate of his soul. The religion of these two was obedience and prayer; their theories only the print of their spiritual feet as they walked homeward.

The road which Lord Lick-my-loof had broken up, went nearly in a straight line from Castle Warlock to the cottage of the Gracies, where it joined the road that passed his lodge. And now came Grizzie's call to action! The moment she found her services required for Mistress Gracie, she climbed the gate of the close, from the top of it stepped upon the new wall, thence let herself down on the disfeatured road, and set out to follow its track, turn for turn, through the ploughed land. In the evening she came back the same way, scrambled over the wall and the gate, and said never a word, nor was asked a question. To visit his tenants the laird himself went a mile about, but most likely he was not prepared to strain his authority with Grizzie, and therefore was as one who knew nothing.

Before the week was out, her steps, and hers alone, had worn a visible and very practicable footpath across the enemy's field; and whether Lord Lick-my-loof was from home, or that he willed the trespass to assume its most defined form and yield personal detection ere he moved in the matter, the week went by without notice taken.

On the Sunday morning however, as Grizzie was on her way to the cottage, she suddenly spied, over the edge of a hollow through which her path ran, the head of Lord Lick-my-loof: he was following the track she had made, and would presently meet her. Wide spread her nostrils, like those of the war-horse, for she too smelt the battle from afar.

"Here's auld Belzebub at last! gaein' to an' fro i' the earth, an' walkin' up an' doon intil 't!" she said to herself. "Noo's for me to priv the trowth o' Scriptur! Whether he'll flee or no, we'll see: I s' resist him. It's no me 'at'll rin, ony gait!"

"Here's old Beelzebub at last! going to and fro in the earth, and walking up and down in it!" she said to herself. "Now's for me to prove the truth of Scripture! Whether he'll flee or not, we'll see: I'll resist him. It's not me that'll run, anyway!"

His lordship had been standing by his lodge on the outlook, and when he saw Grizzie approaching, had started to encounter her. As she drew near he stopped, and stood in the path motionless. On she came till within a single space of him. He did not move. She stopped.

"I doobt, my lord," she said, "I'll hae to mak the ro'd a bit wider. There's hardly room for yer lordship an' anither. But I'm getting' on fine!"

"I think, my lord," she said, "I'll have to make the road a bit wider. There's hardly room for your lordship and another. But I'm getting on fine!"

"Is the woman an idiot!" exclaimed his lordship.

"Muckle siclike 's yersel', my lord!" answered Grizzie;—"no that muckle wit but I might hae mair, to guide my steps throuw the wilderness ye wad mak o' no an ill warl'."

"Are you aware, woman, that you have made yourself liable to a heavy fine for trespass? This field is mine!"

"An' this fitpath's mine, my lord—made wi' my ain feet, an' I coonsel ye to stan' aside, an' lat me by."

"Woman, you are insolent."

"Troth, I needna yer lordship to tell me that! Nane the less ae auld wife may say 'at she likes til anither."

"I tell you there is no thoroughfare here."

"An' I tell you there *is* a thoroughfare, an' ye hae but to wull the trowth to ken 'at there is. There was a ro'd here lang or yer lordship's father was merried upo' yer lorship's mither, an' the law—what o' 't yer lordship hasna the makin' o'—is deid agen ye: that I can priv. Hae me up: I can tak my aith as weel's onybody whan I'm sure."

"I will do so; but in the meantime you must get off my property."

"Weel, stan' by, an' I s' be aff o' 't in less time nor yer lordship."

"You must go back."

"Hooly an' fairly! Bide till the gloamin' an' I s' gang back—never fear. I' the mids o' the meantime I'm gaein' aff o' yer property the nearest gait—an' that's straucht efter my nose."

"Is the woman an idiot!" exclaimed his lordship.

"Much the same as yourself, my lord!" answered Grizzie;—"not that much wit but I might have more, to guide my steps through the wilderness you would make of not such a bad world."

"Are you aware, woman, that you have made yourself liable to a heavy fine for trespass? This field is mine!"

"And this footpath's mine, my lord—made with my own feet, and I advise you to stand aside, and let me by."

"Woman, you are insolent."

"Indeed, I don't need your lordship to tell me that! Still, one old wife can say what she likes to another."

"I tell you there is no thoroughfare here."

"And I tell you there *is* a thoroughfare, and you have but to will the truth to know that there is. There was a road here long before your lordship's father was married to your lordship's mother, and the law—what of it your lordship hasn't the making of—is dead against you: that I can prove. Have me up: I can take my oath as well as anybody when I'm sure.

"I will do so; but in the meantime you must get off my property."

"Well, stand by, and I'll be off it in less time than your lordship."

"You must go back."

"Steady and fairly! Wait till it's dark and I'll go back—never fear. In the meantime I'm going off your property the nearest way—and that's straight after my nose."

She tried, for the tenth time or so, to pass, but turn as she might, he confronted her. She persevered. He raised the stick he carried, perhaps involuntarily, perhaps thinking to intimidate her. Then was the air rent with such an outcry of assault as grievously shook the nerves of his lordship.

"Hold your tongue, you howling jade!" he cried—and the epithet sufficed to destroy every possible remnant of forebearance in the mind of Grizzie.

"There's them 'at tells me, my lord," she said with sudden calm, "'at that's hoo ye misca'd Annie Fyfe, puir lass, whan she cam

"Hold your tongue, you howling jade!" he cried—and the epithet sufficed to destroy every possible remnant of forebearance in the mind of Grizzie.

"There's those that tell me, my lord," she said with sudden calm, "that's the name you called Annie Fyfe, poor lass, when she came efter ye, fifty year ago, to yer father's hoose, an' gat na a plack to haud her an' her bairn frae the roadside! Ye needna girn like that, my lord! Spare yer auld teeth for the gnashin' they'll *hae* to du. Though ye fear na God nor regaird man, yer hoor 'll come, an' yer no like to bid it welcome."

after you, fifty years ago, to your father's house and got never a penny to keep her and her child from the roadside! You needn't pull that face, my lord! Spare your old teeth for the gnashing they'll *have* to do. Though you don't fear God nor regard man, your hour will come, and you're not likely to bid it welcome."

Beside himself with rage, Lord Lick-my-loof would have laid hold of her, but she uttered a louder cry than before—so loud that James Gracie's deaf colley heard her, and, having a great sense of justice, more courage than teeth, and as little regard to the law of trespass as Grizzie herself, came, not bounding, but tearing over the land to her rescue, as if a fox were at one of his sheep. He made straight for his lordship.

Now this dog was one of the chief offences of the cottage, for he had the moral instinct to know and hate a bad man, and could not abide Lord Lick-my-loof. He had never attacked him, for the colley cultivated self-restraint, but he had made his lordship aware that there was no friendship in his heart towards him.

Silent almost as swift, he was nearly on the enemy before either he or Grizzie saw him. His lordship staggered from the path, and raised his stick with trembling hand.

"Doon wi' ye! doon, Covenant! doon, ye tyke!" cried Grizzie. "Haud yer teeth gien ye wad keep the feow ye hae! Deil a bite but banes is there i' the breeks o' 'im!"

"Down with you! Down, Covenant! down, dog!" cried Grizzie. "Hold your teeth if you would keep the few you have! Devil a bite but bones is there in his trousers!"

The dog had obeyed, and now stood worshipping her with his tail, while with his eyes he watched the enemy and his stick.

"Hark ye, Covenant," she went on, "whan his sowl he selled him, the deevil telled him, 'at never mair sud he turn a hair at cry or moanin' in highway or loanin', for greitin' or sweirin' or grane o' despair. Haud frae him, Covenant, my fine fallow, haud frae him."

"Listen, Covenant," she went on, "when his soul he sold, the devil him told, that from that day hence, he would lose his sense to hear cry or moaning in highway or loaning (cattle-track), crying or swearing or groan of despair. Keep away from him, Covenant, my fine fellow, keep away from him."

Grizzie talked to the dog nor lifted her eyes. When she looked up, Lord Lick-my-loof was beyond the hollow, hurrying as if to fetch help. In a few minutes she was safe in the cottage, out of breath, but in high spirits; and even the dying woman laughed at her tale of how she had served his lordship.

"But ye ken, Grizzie," suggested Jeames, "we're no to return evil for evil, nor flytin' for flytin'!"

"But you know, Grizzie," suggested Jeames, "we're not to return evil for evil, nor scolding with scolding!"

"Ca' ye that flytin'?" cried Grizzie. "Ye sud hear what I didna say! That was flytin'! We'll be tried by what we *can* do, no by what we canna! An' for returnin' evil, did I no haud the dog frae the deith-shanks o' him?"

"Do you call that scolding?" cried Grizzie. "You should hear what I didn't say! That was scolding! We'll be tried by what we *can* do, not by what we can't! And for returning evil, didn't I keep the dog off those bony legs of his?"

The laird and Cosmo had spent as usual a quiet and happy Sunday. It was now halfway down the gloamin' towards night, and they sat together in the drawing-room, the laird on the sofa, and Cosmo at one of the windows. The sky was a cold clear calm of thin blue and translucent green, with a certain stillness which in my mind will more or less forever be associated with a Scotch Sunday. A long low cloud of dark purple hung like a baldachin over the yet glimmering coals on the altar of sunset, and the sky above it was like a pale molten mass of jewels that had run together with heat, and was still too bright for the stars to show. They were both looking out at the sky, and a peace as of the unbeginnings of eternity was sinking into their hearts. The laird's thoughts were with his Marion in the region beyond the dream; Cosmo's with Joan in the dream that had vanished into itself. If love be religion, what matter whether its object be in heaven or on the earth! Love itself is the only true nearness. He who thinks of his Saviour as far away can have made little progress in the need of him; and he who does not need much cannot know much, any more than he who is not forgiven much can love much. They sat silent, their souls belonging rather to the heaven over their heads than the earth under their feet, when suddenly the world of stillness was invaded with hideous discord, above which almost immediately rose the well known voice of Grizzie in fierce opposition. They rushed out. Over the gate and obstructing wall they descried, indistinct in the dull light, several heads, and hurrying thither, found Grizzie in the grasp of Lord Lick-my-loof's bailiff, and his lordship looking on with his hands in his pockets and the smile that was his own. But it was not for her own sake Grizzie cried out: there were two more in the group—two of the dog-kind, worrying each other with all the fierceness of the devotion which renders a master's quarrel more than the dog's own. They were, however, far from equally matched, and that was the cause of Grizzie's cry; for the one was the somewhat ancient colley named Covenant, whose teeth were not what they had been, and the other a mastiff belonging to Lord Lick-my-loof, young and malevolent, loosed from the chain the first time that night for a month. It looked ill for Covenant, but he was a brave dog, incapable of turning his back on death itself when duty called him, and what more is required of dog or man! Both the dogs were well bred each in its kind; Covenant was the more human, Dander the more devilish; and the battle was fierce.

The moment Cosmo descried who the combatants were, he knew that Covenant had no fair chance, and was over the wall, and had thrown himself upon them to part them; whereupon the bailiff, knowing his master desired the death of Covenant, let Grizzie go, and would have rushed upon Cosmo. But it was Grizzie's turn now, and she clung to the bailiff like an anaconda. He cursed and swore; nor were there lacking on Grizzie's body the next day certain bruises of which she said nothing except to Aggie; but she had got hold of his cravat, and did her best to throttle him. Cosmo did the same for the mastiff with less effect, and had to stun him with a blow on the head from a great stone, when he caught up Covenant in his arms, and handed him over the wall and the gate to his father. The same moment the bailiff got away from Grizzie, and made at him, calling to the mastiff. But the dog, only half recovered from the effects of Cosmo's blow, either mistaking through bewilderment, or moved by some influence ill explicable, instead of attacking Cosmo, rushed at his master. Rage recalls dislike, and it may be he remembered bygone irritations and teasings. His lordship, however, suddenly became aware of his treacherous intent, and in a moment his legs had *saved themselves* over wall and gate, and he stood panting and shaking beside the laird, in his turn the trespasser. The dog would have been over after him, had not Cosmo, turning his back on the bailiff, who had not observed his master's danger, knocked the dog, in the act of leaping, once more to the earth, when a rush of stones that came with him, and partly fell upon him, had its share in cowing him.

"Haud him! haud him! haud the deevil, ye brute! Haud the brute, ye deevil!" cried his lordship.

"It's yer ain dog, my lord," said the bailiff, whatever consolation there might be in the assurance, as he took him by the collar.

"Hold him! hold him! hold the devil, you brute! Hold the brute, you devil!" cried his lordship.

"It's your own dog, my lord," said the bailiff, whatever consolation there might be in the assurance, as he took him by the collar.

"Am I to be worriet 'cause the dog's my ain? Haud him the sickerer. He s' be ayont mischeef the morn!"

"Am I to be attacked because the dog's my own? Hold him tighter. He'll be beyond mischief tomorrow!"

"He's the true dog 'at sides wi' the richt; he'll be in bliss afore his maister," said Grizzie, as she descended from the gate, and stood on her own side of the fence.

"He's the true dog that sides with the right; he'll be in bliss before his master," said Grizzie, as she descended from the gate, and stood on her own side of the fence.

But the laird was welcoming his lordship with the heartiness of one receiving an unexpected favour in the visit.

"Weel loupen, my lord!" he said. "Come in an' rist yersel' a bit, an' I s' tak ye back on to yer ain property an easier gait nor ower a dry-stane-dyke."

"Well leaped, my lord!" he said. "Come in and rest yourself a bit, and I'll take you back on to your own property an easier way than over a dry-stone-wall."

"Gien it *be* my property," returned his lordship, "I wad be obleeged to ye, laird, to haud yer fowk aff o' 't!"

"If it *be* my property," returned his lordship, "I would be obliged to you, laird, to keep your folk off it!"

"Grizzie, wuman," said the laird, turning to her, "ye dinna surely want to bring me to disgrace! The lan' 's his lordship's—bought and paid for, an' I hae no more richt ower 't nor Jeames Gracie's colley here, puir beast!"

"Grizzie, woman," said the laird, turning to her, "ye surely don't want to bring me to disgrace! The land's his lordship's—bought and paid for, and I have no more right over it than Jeames Gracie's colley here, poor beast!"

"Ye may be richt aboot the lan', laird, the mair's the pity!" answered Grizzie; "but the futpath, beggin' the pardon o' baith lairdship and lordship, belangs to me as muckle as to aither o' ye. Here I stan', alane for mysel'! That ro'd 's my neebor, an' I'm bun' to see til 't, for it wad be a sair vex to mony a puir body like mysel' to louse the richt til 't."

"You may be right about the land, laird, the more's the pity!" answered Grizzie; "but the footpath, begging the pardon of both lairdship and lordship, belongs to me as much as to either of you. Here I stand, alone for myself! That road's my neighbour, and I'm bound to give it my attention, for it would sorely vex many a poor body like myself to lose the right to it."

"You'll have to prove what you say, woman," said his lordship.

"You'll have to prove what you say, woman," said his lordship.

"Surely, Grizzie," expostulated the laird, "his lordship maun un'erstan' affairs o' this natur', as well 's you or me!"

"Surely, Grizzie," expostulated the laird, "his lordship must understand affairs of this nature, as well as you or me!"

"As to the un'erstan'in' o' them, laird, I mak nae doobt," returned Grizzie; "an' as little 'at he's o' the wrang side o' the wa' this time."

"As to the understanding of them, laird, I make no doubt," returned Grizzie; "and as little that he's on the wrong side of the wall this time."

"Na, Grizzie—for he's upo' my side o' 't, an' walcome."

"Na, Grizzie—for he's on my side of it, and welcome."

"He's jist as walcome, naither mair nor less, to the path I made wi' my ain feet throuw the rouchest pleughed lan' I ever crossed."

"He's just as welcome, neither more nor less, to the path I made with my own feet through the roughest ploughed land I ever crossed."

Therewith Grizzie, who hated compromise, turned away, and went into the kitchen.

"Come this way, my lord," said the laird.

"Come this way, my lord," said the laird.

"Take the dog home," said his lordship to the bailiff. "Have him shot the first thing to—

"Take the dog home," said his lordship to the bailiff. "Have him shot the first thing to—

morrow morning. If it weren't the Sabbath, I'd have it done to-night."

"He's good watch, my lord," interceded the man.

"He may be a good watch, but he's a bad dog," replied his lordship. "I'll have neither man nor dog about me that doesn't know his master. You may poison him if you prefer it."

"Come awa, come awa', my lord!" said the laird. "This, as ye hae said, 's the Sabbath-nicht, an' the thoucht o' 't sud mak us mercifu'. I hae naething to offer ye but a cheir to rest ye in, an syne we'll tak the ro'd like neebors thegither an' I'll shaw ye the w'y hame."

morrow morning. If it weren't the Sabbath, I'd have it done to-night."

"He's good watch, my lord," interceded the man.

"He may be a good watch, but he's a bad dog," replied his lordship. "I'll have neither dog nor man about me that doesn't know his master. You may poison him if you prefer it."

"Come now, my lord!" said the laird. "This, as you have said, is the Sabbath-night, and the thought of it should make us merciful. I have nothing to offer you but a chair to rest you in, and then we'll take the road like neighbours together and I'll show you the way home."

His lordship yielded, for his poor thin legs were yet trembling with the successful effort they had made under the inspiration of fear, and now that spur was gone, the dyke seemed a rampart insurmountable, and he dared not attempt it.

"What are you keeping that cursed dog there for?" he said, catching sight, as he turned, of Cosmo, who held Covenant by the back of the neck.

"I am only waiting till your lordship's mastiff is out of the way," answered Cosmo.

"That you may set him at me again, as that old hag of yours did this morning!" As he spoke they had neared the kitchen-door, open as usual, and Grizzie heard what he said.

"That's as big a lee as ever your lordship h'ard tell i' the coort," she cried. "It's the natur o' dougs to tak scunners. They see far ben. Fess the beast in here, Cosmo; I s' be answerable for 'im. The puir animal canna bide my lord."

"Hoot, hoot, Grizzie," began the laird anew, with displeasure in his tone, but already the dog was in, and the kitchen door closed.

"Leave her alone, Mr. Warlock, if you don't want to have the worst of it," said his lordship, trying to laugh. "But seriously, laird," he went on, "it is not neighbourly to treat me like this. Oblige me by giving orders to your people not to trespass on my property. I have paid my money for it, and must be allowed to do with it as I please."

"My lord," returned the laird, "I have not given, and will not give you the smallest annoyance in my own person.—I hope yet to possess the earth," he interjected, half unconsciously, to himself, but aloud. "But—"

"What are you keeping that cursed dog there for?" he said, catching sight, as he turned, of Cosmo, who held Covenant by the back of the neck.

"I am only waiting till your lordship's mastiff is out of the way," answered Cosmo.

"That you may set him at me again, as that old hag of yours did this morning!" As he spoke they had neared the kitchen-door, open as usual, and Grizzie heard what he said.

"That's as big a lie as ever your lordship heard tell in the court," she cried. "It's the nature of dogs to form dislikes. They have great insight. Bring him in here, Cosmo; I'll be answerable for him. The poor animal can't stand my lord."

"Come, come, Grizzie," began the laird anew, with displeasure in his tone, but already the dog was in, and the kitchen door closed.

"Leave her alone, Mr. Warlock, if you don't want to have the worst of it," said his lordship, trying to laugh. "But seriously, laird," he went on, "it is not neighbourly to treat me like this. Oblige me by giving orders to your people not to trespass on my property. I have paid my money for it, and must be allowed to do with it as I please."

"My lord," returned the laird, "I have not given, and will not give you the smallest annoyance in my own person.—I hope yet to possess the earth," he interjected, half unconsciously, to himself, but aloud. "But—"

"Hey! hey!" said his lordship, thinking the man was sending his reason after his property.

"But," continued the laird, "I cannot interfere with the rights of my neighbours. If Grizzie says she has a right of way—and I think very probably she knows what she is about—I have no business to interfere."

"Hey! hey!" said his lordship, thinking the man was sending his reason after his property.

"But," continued the laird, "I cannot interfere with the rights of my neighbours. If Grizzie says she has a right of way—and I think very probably she knows what she is about—I have no business to interfere."

"Confound your cant!" cried his lordship. "You care no more for your neighbours than I do. You only want to make yourself unpleasant to me. Show me the way out, and be damned."

"My lord," said Cosmo, "if you weren't an old man, I would show you the quickest way out! How dare you speak so to a man like my father!"

"Hold your tongue, you young fool! *You* stand up for your father!—idling about at home and eating him up! Why don't you list? With your education you could work your way up. I warn you, if you fall into my hands, I will not spare you. The country will be better to live in when such as you are scarcer."

"Cosmo," said his father, "do not answer him. Show his lordship the way out, and let him go."

As they went through the garden, Lord Lick-my-loof sought to renew the conversation, but Cosmo maintained a stern silence, and his lordship went home incensed more than ever with the contumacious paupers.

But the path in which Grizzie gloried as the work of her own feet, hardened and broadened, and that although she herself had very little *foot* in it any more. For the following week Mistress Gracie died; and the day after she was buried, the old cotter came to the laird, and begged him to yield, if he pleased, the contested point, and part with the bit of land he occupied. For all the neighbours knew his lordship greatly coveted it, though none of them were aware what a price he had offered for it.

"Ye see, sir," he said, "noo 'at *she's* gane, it matters naething to Aggie or me whaur we are or what comes o' 's."

"But wadna she hae said the same, gien it had been you 'at was gane, Jeames?" asked the laird.

"'Deed wad she! She was aye a'thing for ither folk, an' naething for hersel'! The mair cause she sud be considered the noo!"

"An' ca' ye that considerin' her—to du the minute she's gane the thing wad hae grieved her by ordinar' whan she was wi' ye?"

"Whan we war thegither," returned Jeames with solemnity, "there was a heap o' things worth a hantle; noo 'at we're pairted there's jist nearhan' as mony 'at's no worth a strae."

"Weel du I un'erstan' ye, Jeames!" returned the laird with a sigh. "But what wad come o' yersel' an' Aggie wi'oot a place to lay yer heid? We're no to mak oorsel's a' sae ill aff as was the Maister; we maun lea' that to his wull.

"You see, sir," he said, "now that *she's* gone, it matters nothing to Aggie or me where we are or what comes of us."

"But wouldn't she have said the same, if it had been you that was gone, Jeames?" asked the laird

"Indeed she would! She was always all for others, and nothing for herself! The more cause she should be considered now!"

"And call you that considering her—to do the minute she's gone the thing that would have grieved her so much when she was with you?"

"When we were together," returned Jeames with solemnity, "there was a heap of things worth quite a bit; now that we're parted there's almost as many that aren't worth a straw."

"Well do I understand you, Jeames!" returned the laird with a sigh. "But what would come of yourself and Aggie without a place to lay your head? We're not to make ourselves all so badly off as was the Master; we

Ye wadna hae *her* luik doon an' see ye in less comfort nor whan she was wi' ye!"

"Thereanent, sir, I had a word o' proposal to mak," rejoined Jeames. "Ye hae nae men aboot the place: what for sudna Aggie an' me come and bide i' the men's quarters, and be at han' to len' a han' whan it was wantit? Aggie an' me wad help to get mair oot o' the gairden; I wad hae mair time for weyvin'; an' ye wad get a heap for the bit grun' fra Lick-my-loof. It wadna be an ill muv, I do believe, laird, for aither pairt. Consider o' 't, sir."

must leave that to his will. You wouldn't have *her* look down and see you in less comfort than when she was with you!

"About that, sir, I had a word of proposal to make," rejoined Jeames. "You have no men about the place: why shouldn't Aggie and I come and live in the men's quarters, and be at hand to lend a hand when it was wanted? Aggie and I would help to get more out of the garden; I would have more time for weaving; and you would get a lot for the ground from Lick-my-loof. It wouldn't be a bad move, for either of us. Consider of it, sir."

The laird saw that they might at least be better accommodated at the castle than the cottage. He would consult his son, he said. Cosmo in his turn consulted Aggie, and was satisfied. In the winter the wind blew through the cottage bitterly, she said.

As soon as it was settled, Cosmo went to call on his lordship, and was shown into his library.

His lordship guessed his errand, for his keen eye had that same morning perceived signs of change about the cottage. He received him with politeness, and begged to know wherein he could serve him. From his changed behaviour Cosmo thought he must be sorry for the way he had spoken to the laird.

"My father sent me," he said, "to inform your lordship that he is now at length in a position to treat with your lordship concerning the proposal to purchase Jeames Gracie's croft."

"I am greatly obliged to your father," replied Lord Lick-my-loof, softly wiping one hand with the other, "for his attention, but I have no longer any desire to secure the land. It has been so long denied me, that at length I have grown indifferent to the possession of it. That is a merciful provision of the Creator, that the human mind should have the faculty of accommodating itself to circumstances, even of positive nuisance."

Cosmo rose.

"As soon as you have made up your mind," added his lordship, rising also, "to part with what remains of the property, *including the castle,* I should be glad to have the refusal of that. It would make a picturesque ruin from certain points of view on the estate."

Cosmo bowed, and left his lordship grinning with pleasure.

CHAPTER XLV
ANOTHER HARVEST

The harvest brought again the opportunity of earning a pound or two, and Cosmo was not the man to let it slip. But he would not go so far from home again, for, though his father never pined or complained, Cosmo could see that his days shrunk more rapidly when he was not with him: left alone, he began at once to go home the faster—as if another dragging anchor were cast loose, and he was drawn the more swiftly whither sets the tide of life. To the old and weary man the life to come showed as rest; to the young and active Cosmo it promised more work. It is all one; what we need for rest as well as for labour is life; more life we want, and that is everything. That which is would be more. The eternal root causes us to long for more existence, more being, more of God's making, less of our own unmaking. Our very desire after rest comes of life, life so strong that it recoils from weariness. The imperfect needs to be more—must grow. The sense of growth, of ever enlarging existence, is essential to the created children of an infinite Father; for in the children the paternal infinite goes on working—by them recognizable, not as infinitude, but as growth.

The best thing in sight for both father and son seemed to Cosmo a place in Lord Lick-my-loof's harvest—an engagement to reap, amongst the rest, the fields that had so lately been his own. He would then be almost within sight of his father when not with him. He applied, therefore, to the *grieve,*[10] the same man with whom he had all but fought that memorable Sunday of Trespass. Though of a coarse, the man was not of a spiteful nature, and that he had quarrelled with another was not to him sufficient reason for hating him ever after; yet, as he carried the application to his lordship, for he dared not without his master's leave engage to his service the man he counted his enemy, it gave him pleasure to see what he called poor pride brought to the shame of what he called beggary—as if the labour of a gentleman's hands were not a good deal further from beggary than the living upon money gained anyhow by his ancestors!

Lord Lick-my-loof smouldered awhile before giving an answer. The question was, which would most gratify the feelings he cherished towards the man of old blood, high station, and evil fortunes—to accept or refuse the offered toil. His deliberation ended in his giving orders to the bailiff to *fee* the young laird, but to mind he did not pay workmen's wages for gentleman's work—which injunction the bailiff allowed to reach Cosmo's ears.

The young laird, as they all called him, was a favourite with his enemy's men—partly, that they did not love their master, and were the more ready to side with the man he oppressed; partly, because they admired the gentleman who so cheerfully descended to their level, and, showing neither condescension nor chagrin, was in all simplicity friendly with them; and partly, because some of them had been to his evening-school the last winter, and had become attached to him. No honest heart indeed could be near Cosmo long and not love him—for the one reason that humanity was in him so largely developed. To him a man was a man whatever his position or calling; he beheld neither in the great man a divinity, nor in the small man a slave; but honoured in his heart every image of the living God it pleased that God to make—honoured every man as, if not already such in the highest sense, yet destined to be one day a brother of Jesus Christ.

In the arrangement of the mowers, the grieve placed Cosmo last, as presumably the least capable, that he might not lower the rate of the field. But presently Cosmo contrived to make his neighbour in front a little uneasy about his legs, and when the man humorously objected to

10 GRIEVE: a farm manager or foreman.

having them cut off, asked him, for the joke of the thing, to change places with him. The man at once consented; the rest behaved with equal courtesy, showing no desire to contest with him the precedence of labour; before the end of the long bout, Cosmo swung the leading scythe; and many were the compliments he received from his companions, as they stood sharpening for the next, in which they were of one mind he must take the lead, some begging him however to be considerate, as they were not all so young as he, while others warned him that, if he went on as he had begun, he could not keep it up, but the first would be last before the day was over. Cosmo listened, and thereafter restrained himself, having no right to overwork his companions; yet notwithstanding he had cause, many a time in after life, to remember the too great exertion of that day. Even in the matter of work a man has to learn that he is not his own, but has a master, whom he must not serve as if he were a hard one. When our will goes hand in hand with God's, then are we fellow-workers with him in the affairs of the universe—not mere discoverers of his ways, watching at the outskirts of things, but labourers with him at the heart of them.

The next day Lord Lick-my-loof's shadow was upon the field, and there he spent some time watching how things went.

Now Grizzie and Aggie, irrespective of Cosmo's engagement, of which at the time they were unaware, had laid their heads together, and concluded that, although they could not both be at once away from the castle, they might between them, with the connivance of the bailiff, do a day's work and earn a day's wages; and although the grieve would certainly have listened to no such request from Grizzie in person, he was incapable of refusing it to Aggie. Hence it followed that Grizzie, in her turn that morning, was gathering to Cosmo's scythe, hanging her labour on that of the young laird with as devoted a heart as if he had been a priest at the high altar, and she his loving acolyte. I doubt if his lordship would have just then approached Cosmo, had he noted who the woman was that went stooping along behind the late heir of the land, now a labourer upon it for the bread of his household.

"Weel, Glenwarlock!" said the old man, giving a lick to the palm of his right hand as he stopped in front of the nearing mower, "ye're a famous han' at the scythe! The corn boos doon afore ye like the stooks to Joseph."	"Well, Glenwarlock!" said the old man, giving a lick to the palm of his right hand as he stopped in front of the nearing mower, "you're a famous hand at the scythe! The corn bows down before you like the sheaves to Joseph."
"I hae a guid arm an' a sharp scythe, my lord," answered Cosmo cheerily.	"I have a good arm and a sharp scythe, my lord," answered Cosmo cheerily.
"Whisht, whisht, my lord!" said Grizzie. "Gien the corn hear ye, it'll stan' up an' cry out. Hearken til 't."	"Quiet, quiet, my lord!" said Grizzie. "If the corn hears you, it'll stand up and cry out. Hearken to it."

The morning had been very still, but that moment a gust of wind came and set all the corn rustling.

"What! *you* here!—Crawford, you rascal!" cried his lordship, looking round, "turn this old cat out of the field."	"What! *you* here!—Crawford, you rascal!" cried his lordship, looking round, "turn this old cat out of the field."
But he looked in vain; the grieve was nowhere in sight.	But he looked in vain; the grieve was nowhere in sight.
"The deil sew up yer lordship's moo' wi' an awn o' beer!" cried Grizzie. "Haith, gien I be a cat, ye s' hear me curse!"	"The devil sew up your lordship's mouth with a beard of barley!" cried Grizzie. "Faith, if I be a cat, you shall hear me curse!"

His lordship bethought himself that she would certainly disgrace him in the hearing of his labourers if he provoked her further, for a former encounter had revealed that she knew things not to his credit. They were all working away as if they had not an ear amongst them, but almost all of them heard every word.

"Hoots, wuman!" he said, in an altered tone, "canna ye tak a jeist?"

"Na; there's ower mony o' yer lordship's jeists hae turnt fearsome earnest to them at tuik them!"

"What do you mean, woman?"

"Wuman! quo' he? My name's Grisel Grant. Wha kens na auld Grizzie, 'at never turnt her back on freen' or foe? But I'm no gaein til affront yer lordship wi' the sicht o' yersel' afore fowk—sae long, that is, as ye haud a quaiet souch. But gie the young laird there ony o' the dirt ye're aye lickin' oot o' yer loof, an' the auld cat 'll be cryin' upo' the hoose-tap!"

"Grizzie! Grizzie!" cried Cosmo, ceasing his work and coming back to where they stood, "ye'll ruin' a'!"

"What is there to ruin 'at he can ruin mair?" returned Grizzie. "Whan yer back's to the wa', ye canna fa'. An angry chiel' 'ill ca' up the deil; but an angry wife 'll gar him rin for 's life. When I'm angert, I fear no aiven his lordship there!"

"Heavens, woman!" he said, in an altered tone, "can't you take a jest?"

"Na; there's too many of your lordship's jests have turned deadly earnest to those on the receiving end!"

"What do you mean, woman?"

"Woman! said he? My name's Grisel Grant. Who doesn't know old Grizzie, that never turned her back on friend or foe? But I'm not going to affront your lordship with the sight of yourself before folk—so long, that is, as you hold your own tongue. But give the young laird there any of the dirt you're always licking out of your palm, and the old cat'll be crying from the roof-top!"

"Grizzie! Grizzie!" cried Cosmo, ceasing his work and coming back to where they stood, "you'll ruin all!"

"What is there to ruin that he can ruin more?" returned Grizzie. "When your back's to the wall, then you can't fall. When a man's in a rage, the devil's engaged; but an angry wife will make him run for his life. When I'm angered, I fear not even his lordship there!"

Lord Lick-my-loof turned and went, and Grizzie set to work like a fury, probably stung by the sense that she had gone too far. Old woman as she was, she had soon overtaken Cosmo, but he was sorely vexed, and did not speak to her. When after a while the heat of her wrath was abated, Grizzie could not endure the silence, for in every motion of Cosmo's body before her she read that she had hurt him grievously.

"Laird!" she cried at last, "my stren'th's gane frae me. Gien ye dinna speyk to me, I'll drap."

Cosmo stopped his scythe in mid swing, and turned to her. How could he resist such an appeal!

"Grizzie," he said, "I winna deny 'at ye hae vexed me,—"

"Ye needna; I wadna believe ye. But ye dinna ken yon man as I du, or ye wadna be sae sair angert at onything wuman cud say til 'im. Gien I was to tell ye what I ken o' 'im, ye wad be affrontit afore me, auld wife as I am. Haith, ye wadna du anither strok for 'im!"

"It's for the siller, no for *him,* Grizzie. But gien he war as ill as ye ca' 'im, a' the same, as ye weel ken, the Lord maks his sun to rise on the evil an' on the good, an' sen's rain on the just an' on the unjust!"

"Laird!" she cried at last, "my strength's gone from me. If you don't speak to me, I'll drop."

Cosmo stopped his scythe in mid swing, and turned to her. How could he resist such an appeal!

"Grizzie," he said, "I won't deny that you have vexed me,—"

"You needn't; I wouldn't believe you. But you don't know that man as I do, or you wouldn't be angered so much at anything woman could say to him. If I was to tell you what I know of him, you would be affronted before me, old wife as I am. Faith, you wouldn't do another stroke for him!"

"It's for the money, not for *him,* Grizzie. But if he were as bad as you say, all the same, as you well know, the Lord makes his sun to rise on the evil and on the good, and sends rain on the just and on the unjust!"

"Ow ay! the Lord can afoord it!" remarked Grizzie.

"Oh ay! the Lord can afford it!" remarked Grizzie.

"An' them 'at wad be his, maun affoord it tu, Grizzie!" returned Cosmo. "Whaur's the guid o' ca'in ill names, 'uman?"

"And those that would be his, must afford it too, Grizzie!" returned Cosmo. "Where's the good of calling ill names, woman?"

"I'll's the trowth o' them 'at 's ill. What for no set ill names to ill duers?"

"Ill's the truth of those with ill natures. Why not give evil names to evil doers?"

"'Cause a Christian 's bun' to destroy the warks o' the evil ane; an' ca'in' names raises mair o' them. The only thing 'at maks awa' wi' ill, is the man himsel' turnin' again 't, an' that he'll never du for ill names. Ye wad never gar me repent that gait, Grizzie. Hae mercy upo' the auld sinner, 'uman."

"Because a Christian must destroy the works of the evil one; and calling names raises more of them. The only thing that does away with ill, is the man himself turning against it, and that he'll never do for ill names. You would never make me repent that way, Grizzie. Have mercy on the old sinner, woman."

The pace at which they were making up for lost time was telling upon Grizzie, and she was silent. When she spoke again it was upon another subject.

"I cud jest throttle that grieve there!" she said. "To see 'im the nicht afore last come hame to the verra yet wi' Aggie, was enouch to anger the sanct 'at I'm no."

"I could just throttle that grieve there!" she said. "To see him the night before last come home to the very gate with Aggie, was enough to anger the saint that I'm not."

Jealousy sent a pang through the heart of Cosmo. Was not Aggie one of the family—more like a sister to him than any other could ever be? The thought of her and a man like Crawford was unendurable.

"She cudna weel help hersel'," he rejoined; "an' whaur's the matter, sae lang as she has naething to say til 'im?"

"She could hardly help herself," he rejoined; "and where's the harm, so long as she has nothing to say to him?"

"An' wha kens hoo lang that may be?" returned Grizzie. "The hert o' a wuman 's no deceitfu' as the Buik says o' a man's, an sae 's a heap the easier deceivt. The chield's no ill-luikin'! an' I s' warran' he's no sae rouch wi' a yoong lass as wi' an auld wife."

"And who knows how long that may be?" returned Grizzie. "The heart of a woman isn't deceitful as the Book says of a man's, and so is all the more easily deceived. The fellow's not bad-looking! and I'll wager he's not so rough with a young lass as with an old woman."

"Grizzie, ye wadna mint 'at oor Aggie's ane to be ta'en wi' the luiks o' a man!"

"Grizzie, you wouldn't suggest that our Aggie's one to be taken with the looks of a man!"

"What for no—whan it's a' the man has! A wuman's hert's that saft, whiles, 'at she'll jist tak 'im, no to be sair upon 'im. I wadna warran' ony lass! Gien the fallow cairry a fair face, she'll sweir her conscience doon he maun hae a guid hert."

"Why not—when it's all the man has! A woman's heart's that soft, sometimes, that she'll just take him, so as not to be hard on him. I wouldn't count any lass safe on that score! If the fellow carries a fair face, she'll swear her conscience down he must have a good heart."

Thus Grizzie turned the tables upon Cosmo, and sheltered herself behind them. Scarcely a word did he speak the rest of the morning.

At noon, when toil gladly made way for dinner, they all sat down among the stooks to eat and drink—all except Grizzie, who, appropriating an oatcake the food she and Aggie had a right to between them, carried it home, and laid the greater part aside. Cosmo ate and drank with the rest of the labourers, and enjoyed the homely repast as much as any of them. By the time the meal was over, Aggie had arrived to take Grizzie's place.

It was a sultry afternoon; and what with the heat and the annoyance of the morning from Grizzie's tongue and her talk concerning Agnes, the scythe hung heavy in Cosmo's hands, nor had Aggie to work her hardest to keep up with him. But she was careful to maintain her proper distance from him, for she knew that the least suspicion of relaxing effort would set him off like a thrashing machine. He led the field, nevertheless, at fair speed; his fellow labourers were content; and the bailiff made no remark. But he was so silent, and prolonged silence was so unusual between them, that Aggie was disquieted.

"Are ye no weel, Cosmo?" she asked.

"Aren't you well, Cosmo?" she asked

"Weel eneuch, Aggie," he answered. "What gars ye speir?"

"Well enough, Aggie," he answered. "What makes you ask?"

"Ye're haudin' yer tongue sae sair.—And," she added, for she caught sight of the bailiff approaching, "ye hae lost the last inch or twa o' yer stroke."

"You're being so quiet.—And," she added, for she caught sight of the bailiff approaching, "you've lost the last inch or two of your stroke."

"I'll tell ye a' aboot it as we gang hame," he answered, swinging his scythe in the arc of a larger circle.

"I'll tell you all about it as we go home," he answered, swinging his scythe in the arc of a larger circle.

The bailiff came up.

The bailiff came up.

"Dinna warstle yersel' to death, Aggie," he said.

"Don't work yourself to death, Aggie," he said.

"I maun haud up wi' my man," she replied.

"I must keep up with my man," she replied.

"He's a het man at the scythe—ower het! He'll be fit for naething or the week be oot. He canna haud on at this rate!"

"He's a hot man at the scythe—too hot! He'll be fit for nothing before the week's out. He can't keep on at this rate!"

"Ay can he—fine that! Ye dinna ken oor yoong laird. He's worth twa ordinar' men. An' gien ye dinna think me fit to gather til 'im, I s' lat ye see ye're mistaen, Mr Crawford."

"Ay he can—very well! You don't know our young laird. He's worth two ordinary men. And if you don't think me fit to gather to him, I shall let you see you're mistaken, Mr. Crawford."

And Aggie went on gathering faster and faster.

And Aggie went on gathering faster and faster.

"Hoots!" said the bailiff, going up to her, and laying his hand on her shoulder, "I ken weel ye hae the spunk to work till ye drap. But there's nae occasion the noo. Sit ye doon an' tak yer breath a meenute—here i' the shaidow o' this stook. Whan Glenwarlock's at the tither en', we'll set tu thegither an' be up wi' him afore he's had time to put a fresh edge on 's scythe. Come, Aggie! I hae lang been thinkin' lang to hae a word wi' ye. Ye left me or I kent whaur I was the ither nicht."

"Heavens!" said the bailiff, going up to her, and laying his hand on her shoulder, "I know well enough you have the spunk to work till you drop. But there's no occasion just now. Sit yourself down and take your breath a minute—here in the shadow of this stook. When Glenwarlock's at the other end, we'll set to together and be up with him before he's had time to put a fresh edge on his scythe. Come, Aggie! I've been longing to have a word with you for some time. You left me before I knew where I was the other night."

"My time's no my ain," answered Aggie.

"My time's not my own," answered Aggie.

"Whause is 't than?"

"Whose is it then?"

"Whiles it's the laird's, an' whiles it's my father's, an' noo it's his lordship's."

"Sometimes it's the laird's, and sometimes it's my father's, and now it's his lordship's."

"It's yer ain sae lang's I'm at the heid o' 's lordship's affairs."

"It's your own so long as I'm at the head of his lordship's affairs."

"Na; that canna be. He's boucht my time, an' he'll pey me for 't, an' he s' hae his ain."

"Na; that can't be. He's bought my time, and he'll pay me for it, and he shall have what's his."

"Ye needna consider 'im mair nor rizzon: he's been nae freen' to you or yours."

"You needn't consider him beyond reason: he's been no friend to you or yours."

"What's that to the p'int?"

"What has that to do with it?"

"A'thing to the p'int—wi' me here to haud it richt atween ye."

"Everything—with me here to keep it right between you."

"Ca' ye that haudin' o' 't richt, to temp' me to wrang 'im?" said Aggie, going steadily on at her gathering, while the grieve kept following her step by step.

"Do you call that keeping it right, to tempt me to wrong him?" said Aggie, going steadily on at her gathering, while the grieve kept following her step by step.

"Ye're unco short wi' a body, Aggie!"

"You're very short with a man, Aggie!"

"I weel may be, whan a body wad hae me neglec' my paid wark."

"I well may be, when a man would have me neglect my paid work."

"Weel, I reckon ye're i' the richt o' 't efter a', sae I'll jist fa' tu, an' len' ye a han'."

"Well, I reckon you're in the right of it after all, so I'll just fall to, and lend you a hand."

He had so far hindered her that Cosmo had gained a little; and now in pretending to help, he contrived to hinder her yet more. Still she kept near enough to Cosmo to prevent the grieve from saying much, and by and by he left her.

When they dropped work for the night, he would have accompanied her home, but she never left Cosmo's side, and they went away together.

"Aggie," said Cosmo, as soon as there was no one within hearing. "I dinna like that chield hingin' aboot ye—glowerin' at ye as gien he wad ate ye."

"Aggie," said Cosmo, as soon as there was no one within hearing. "I don't like that fellow hanging about you—looking at you as if he would eat you."

"He winna du that, Cosmo; he's ceevil eneuch."

"He won't do that, Cosmo; he's civil enough."

"Ye sud hae seen sae rouch as he was to Grizzie!"

"You should have seen how rough he was to Grizzie!"

"Grizzie's some rouch hersel' whiles," remarked Aggie quietly.

"Grizzie's pretty rough herself sometimes," remarked Aggie quietly.

"That's ower true," assented Cosmo; "but a man sud never behave like that til a wuman."

"That's only too true," assented Cosmo; "but a man should never behave like that to a woman."

"Say that to the man," rejoined Aggie. "The wuman can haud aff o' hersel'."

"Say that to the man," rejoined Aggie. "The woman can hold off by herself."

"Grizzie, I grant ye, 's mair nor a match for ony man; but ye're no sae lang i' the tongue, Aggie."

"Grizzie, I grant you, is more than a match for any man; but you're not so long in the tongue, Aggie."

"Think ye a lang tongue 's a lass's safety, Cosmo? I wad awe nane til 't! But what's ta'en ye the nicht, at ye speyk to me sae? I ken no occasion."

"Do you think a long tongue is a lass's safety, Cosmo? I would owe none to it! But what's possessed you tonight, that you speak to me so? I know no occasion."

"Aggie, I wadna willin'ly say a word to vex ye," answered Cosmo,; "but I hae notit an

"Aggie, I wouldn't willingly say a word to vex you," answered Cosmo,; "but I have noted

h'ard 'at the best o' wumen whiles tak oonaccoontable fancies to men no fit to haud a can'le to them."

and heard that the best of women sometimes take unaccountable fancies to men not fit to hold a candle to them."

Aggie turned her head aside.

Aggie turned her head aside.

"I wad ill like you, for instance, to be drawn to yon Crawford," he went on. "It's eneuch to me 'at he's been lang the factotum o' an ill man."

"I wouldn't like you, for instance, to be drawn to that Crawford," he went on. "It's enough to me that he's long been the factotum of a bad man."

A slight convulsive movement passed across Aggie's face, leaving behind it a shadow of hurtless resentment, yielding presently to a curious smile.

"I micht mak a better man o' 'im," she said, and again looked away.

"I might make a better man of him," she said, and again looked away.

"They a' think that, I'm thinkin'!" returned Cosmo with a sad bitterness. "An' sae they wull, to the warl's en'.—But, Aggie," he added, after a pause, "ye ken ye're no to be oonaiqually yokit."

"They all think that, I'm thinking!" returned Cosmo with a sad bitterness. "And so they will, to the world's end.—But, Aggie," he added, after a pause, "you know you're not to be unequally yoked."

"That's what I hae to heed, I ken," murmured Aggie. "But what do ye un'erstan' by 't, Cosmo? There's nae worshippers o' idols the noo, as i' the days whan the apostle said that."

"That's what I have to heed, I know," murmured Aggie. "But what do you understand by it, Cosmo? There's no idol-worshippers now, as in the days when the apostle said that."

"There's idols visible, an' idols invisible," answered Cosmo. "There's heaps o' idols amo' them 'at ca's themsel's an' 's coontit Christians. Gien a man set himsel' to lay by siller, he's the worshipper o' as oogly an idol as gien he said his prayers to the fish-tailt god o' the Philistines."

"There's idols visible, and idols invisible," answered Cosmo. "There are many idols among those who call themselves and are counted Christians. If a man sets himself to horde up money, he's the worshipper of as ugly an idol as if he said his prayers to the fish-tailed god of the Philistines."

"Weel I wat that!" returned Agnes, and a silence followed.

"I'm well aware of that!" returned Agnes, and a silence followed.

"You an' me's aye been true til ane anither, Aggie," resumed Cosmo at length, "an' I wad fain hae a promise frae ye—jist to content me."

"You and I have always been true to one another, Aggie," resumed Cosmo at length, "and I would fain have a promise from you—just to content me."

"What aboot, Cosmo?"

"What about, Cosmo?"

"Promise, an' I'll tell ye, as the bairnies say."

"Promise, and I'll tell you, as the children say."

"But we're no bairnies, Cosmo, an' I daurna—even to you 'at I wad trust like the Bible. Tell me what it is, an' gien I may, I wull."

"But we're not children, Cosmo, and I daren't—even to you that I would trust like the Bible. Tell me what it is, and if I may, I will."

"It's no muckle atween you an' me, Aggie. It's only this—'at gien ever ye fa' in love wi' onybody, ye'll let me ken."

"It's not much between you and me, Aggie. It's only this—that if ever you fall in love with anybody, you'll let me know."

Agnes was silent for a moment; then, with a tremble in her voice, which in vain she sought to smooth out, and again turning her head away, answered:

"Cosmo, I daurna."

"Cosmo, I daren't."

"I want naething mair," said Cosmo, thinking she must have misapprehended, "nor the promise 'at what ye ken I sall ken. I wad fain be wi' ye at sic a time."

"I want nothing more," said Cosmo, thinking she must have misapprehended, "than the promise that what you know I shall know. I would fain be with you at such a time."

"Cosmo," said Aggie with much solemnity, "there's ane 'at's aye at han', ane that sticketh closer nor a brither. The thing ye require o' me, micht be what a lass could tell to nane but the father o' her—him 'at's in haiven."

"Cosmo," said Aggie with much solemnity, "there's one who's always at hand, one who sticketh closer than a brother. The thing you require of me, might be what a lass could tell to none but her father—he who's in heaven."

Cosmo was silenced, as indeed it was time and reason he should be; for had she been his daughter, he would have had no right to make such a request of her. He did it all in innocence, and might well have asked her to tell him, but not to promise to tell him. He did not yet understand however that he was wrong, and was the more troubled about her, feeling as if, for the first time in their lives, Aggie and he had begun to be divided.

They entered the kitchen. Aggie hastened to help Grizzie lay the cloth for supper. Her grandfather looked up with a smile from the newspaper he was reading in the window. The laird, who had an old book in his hand, called out,

"Here, Cosmo! Jist hearken to this bit o' wisdom, my man—frae a hert doobtless praisin' God this mony a day in higher warl's:—'He that would always know before he trusts, who would have from his God a promise before he will expect, is the slayer of his own eternity.'"

"Here, Cosmo! Just hearken to this bit of wisdom, my man—from a heart doubtless praising God this many a day in higher worlds:—'He that would always know before he trusts, who would have from his God a promise before he will expect, is the slayer of his own eternity.'"

The words mingled strangely with what had just passed between him and Agnes. Both they and that gave him food for thought, but could not keep him awake.

The bailiff continued to haunt the goings and comings of Agnes, but few supposed his attentions acceptable to her. Cosmo continued more or less uneasy.

The harvest was over at length, and the little money earned mostly laid aside for the sad winter, once more on its way. But no good hope dies without leaving a child, a younger and fresher hope, behind it. The year's fruit must fall that the next year's may come, and the winter is the only way to the spring.

CHAPTER XLVI
THE FINAL CONFLICT

As there was no more weekly pay for teaching, and no extra hands were longer wanted for farm-labour, Cosmo, hearing there was a press of work and a scarcity of workmen in the building-line, offered his services, at what wages he should upon trial judge them worth, to Sandy Shand, the mason, then erecting a house in the village for a certain Mr. Pennycuik—a native of the same, who, having left it long ago, and returned from India laden with riches, now desired, if not to end, yet to spend his days amid the associations of his youth. Upon this house, his offer accepted, Cosmo laboured, now doing the work of a mason, now of a carpenter, and receiving fair wages, until such time when the weather put a stop to all but indoor work of the kind. But the strange thing was, that, instead of reaping golden opinions for his readiness to turn his hand to anything honest by which he could earn a shilling, Cosmo became in consequence the object of endless blame—that a young man of his abilities, with a college-education, should spend his time—*waste* it, people said—at home, pottering about at work that was a disgrace to a gentleman, instead of going away and devoting himself to some *honourable calling.* "Look at Mr. Pennycuik!" they said. "See how he has raised himself in the social scale, and that without one of the young laird's advantages! There he stands, a rich man and employer of labour, while the poor-spirited gentleman is one of his hired labourers!" Such is the mean idea most men have of the self-raising that is the duty of a man! They speak after their kind, putting ambition in the place of aspiration. Not knowing the spirit they were of, these would have had Cosmo say to his father, *Korban*. They knew nothing of, and were incapable of taking into the account certain moral refinements and delicate difficulties entailed upon him by that father, such as might indeed bring him to beggary, but could never allow him to gather riches like those of Mr. Pennycuik. Like his father he had a holy weakness for the purity that gives arms of the things within us. If there is one thing a Christian soul recoils from, it is meanness—of action, of thought, of judgement. What a heaven some must think to be saved into! At the same time Cosmo would not have left his father to make a fortune the most honourable.

Through stress of weather, Cosmo was therefore thrown back once more upon his writing. But still, whether it was that there was too little of Grizzie or too much of himself in these later stories, his work seemed to have lost either the power or the peculiarity that had recommended it. Things therefore did not look promising. But they had a fair stock of oatmeal laid in, and that was the staff of life, also a tolerable supply of fuel, which neighbours had lent them horses to bring from the peat-moss.

With the cold weather the laird began again to fail, and Cosmo to fear that this would be the last of the good man's winters. As the best protection from the cold he betook himself to bed, and Cosmo spent his life almost in the room, reading aloud when the old man was able to listen, and reading to himself or writing when he was not. The other three of the household were mostly in the kitchen, saving fuel, and keeping each other company. And thus the little garrison awaited the closer siege of the slow-beleaguering winter, most of them in their hearts making themselves strong to resist the more terrible enemies which all winter-armies bring flying on their flanks—the haggard fiends of doubt and dismay—which creep through the strongest walls. To trust in spite of the look of being forgotten; to keep crying out into the vast whence comes no voice, and where seems no hearing; to struggle after light, where is no glimmer to guide; at every turn to find a doorless wall, yet ever seek a door; to see the machinery of the world pauseless grinding on as if self-moved, caring for no life, nor shifting a hair's-breadth for all entreaty, and yet believe that God is awake and utterly loving; to desire nothing but what comes meant for us from his hand; to wait patiently, willing to die of hunger, fearing only lest faith should fail—such is the victory that overcometh the world, such is faith indeed. After such victory Cosmo had to strive and pray hard, sometimes deep sunk in the wave while his father floated calm on its crest: the old man's discipline had been longer; a continuous communion had for many years been growing closer between him and the heart whence he came.

"As I lie here, warm and free of pain," he said once to his son, "expecting the redemption of my body, I cannot tell you how happy I am. I cannot think how ever in my life I feared anything. God knows it was my obligation to others that oppressed me, but now, in my utter incapacity, I am able to trust him with my honour, and my duty, as well as my sin."

"Look here, Cosmo," he said another time; "I had temptations such as you would hardly think, to better my worldly condition, and redeem the land of my ancestors, and the world would have commended, not blamed me, had I yielded. But my God was with me all the time, and I am dying a poorer man than my father left me, leaving you a poorer man still, but, praised be God, an honest one. Be very sure, my son, God is the only adviser to be trusted, and you must do what he tells you, even if it lead you to a stake, to be burned by the slow fire of poverty.—O my Father!" cried the old man, breaking out suddenly in prayer, "my soul is a flickering flame of which thou art the eternal, inextinguishable fire. I am blessed because thou art. Because thou art life, I live. Nothing can hurt me, because nothing can hurt thee. To thy care I leave my son, for thou lovest him as thou hast loved me. Deal with him as thou hast dealt with me. I ask for nothing, care for nothing but thy will. Strength is gone from me, but my life is hid in thee. I am a feeble old man, but I am dying into the eternal day of thy strength."

Cosmo stood and listened with holy awe and growing faith. For what can help our faith like the faith of the one we must love, when, sorely tried, it is yet sound and strong!

But there was still one earthly clod clinging to the heart of Cosmo. There was no essential evil in it, yet not the less it held him back from the freedom of the man who, having parted with everything, possesses all things. The place, the things, the immediate world in which he was born and had grown up, crowded with the memories and associations of childhood and youth, amongst them the shadowy loveliness of Lady Joan, had a hold of his heart that savoured of idolatry. The love was born in him, had come down into him through generation after generation of ancestors, had a power over him for whose existence he was not accountable, but for whose continuance, as soon as he became aware of its existence, he would know himself accountable. For Cosmo was not one of those weaklings who, finding in themselves certain tendencies with whose existence they had nothing to do, and therefore in whose presence they have no blame, say to themselves, "I cannot help it," and at once create evil, and make it their own, by obeying the inborn impulse. Inheritors of a lovely estate, with a dragon in a den, which they have to kill that the brood may perish, they make friends with the dragon, and so think to save themselves trouble.

But I would not be misunderstood; I do not think Cosmo loved his home too much; I only think he did not love it enough in God. To love a thing divinely, is to be ready to yield it without a pang when God wills it; but to Cosmo, the thought of parting with the house of his fathers and the rag of land that yet remained to it, was torture. This hero of mine, instead of sleeping the perfect sleep of faith, would lie open-eyed through half the night, hatching scheme after scheme—not for the redemption of the property—even to him that seemed hopeless, but for the retention of the house. Might it not at least go to ruin under eyes that loved it, and with the ministration of tender hands that yet could not fast enough close the slow-yawning chasms of decay? His dream haunted him, and he felt that, if it came true, he would rather live in the dungeon wine-cellar of the mouldering mammoth-tooth, than forsake the old stones to live elsewhere in a palace. The love of his soul for Castle Warlock was like the love of the Psalmist for Jerusalem: when he looked on a stone of its walls, it was dear to him. But the love of Jerusalem became an idolatry, for the Jews no longer loved it because the living God dwelt therein, but because it was *theirs,* and then it was doomed, for it was an idol. The thing was somewhat different with Cosmo: the house was almost a part of himself—an extension of his own body, as much his as the shell of a snail is his. But because into this shell were not continued those nerves of life which give the consciousness of the body, and there was therefore no reaction from it of those feelings of weakness and need which, to such a man as Cosmo, soon reveal the fact that he is not lord of his body, that he cannot add to it one cubit, or make one hair white or black, and must therefore leave the care of it to him who made it, he had to learn in other ways that his castle of stone was God's also. His truth and humility and love had not yet reached to the quickening of the idea of the old house with the feeling that God was in it with him, giving it to him. Not yet possessing therefore the soul of the house, its greatest bliss, which nothing could take from him, he naturally could not be content to part with it. It seemed an impossibility that it should be taken from him—a wrong to things, to men, to nature, that a man like Lick-my-loof should obtain the lordship over it. As he lay in the night, in the heart of the old pile, and heard the wind roaring about its stone-mailed roofs, the thought of losing it would sting him almost to madness,—hurling him from his bed to the floor, to pace up and down the room, burning, in the coldest midnight of winter, like one of the children in the fiery furnace, only the furnace was of worse fire, being the wrath which worketh not the righteousness of God.

Suddenly one such night he became aware that he could not pray—that in this mood he never prayed. In every other trouble he prayed—felt it the one natural thing to pray! Why not in this? Something must be wrong—terribly wrong!

It was a stormy night; the snow-burdened wind was raving; and Cosmo would have been striding about the room but that now he was in his father's, and dreaded disturbing him. He lay still, with a stone on his heart, for he was now awake to the fact that he could not say, "Thy will be done." He tried sore to lift up his heart, but could not. Something rose ever between him and his God, and beat back his prayer. A thick fog was about him—no air wherewith to make a cry! In his heart not one prayer would come to life; it was like an old nest without bird or egg in it.

It was too terrible! Here was a schism at the very root of his being. The love of things was closer to him than the love of God. Between him and God rose the rude bulk of a castle of stone! He crept out of bed, laid himself on his face on the floor, and prayed in an agony. The wind roared and howled, but the desolation in his heart made of the storm a mere play of the elements. How few of my readers will understand even the possibility of such a state! How many of them will scorn the idea of it, as that of a man on the high road to insanity!

"God," he cried, "I thought I knew thee, and sought thy will; and I have sought thy will in greater things than this wherein I now lie ashamed before thee. I cannot even pray to thee. But hear thou the deepest will in me, which, thou knowest, must bow before thine, when once thou hast uttered it. Hear the prayer I cannot offer. Be my perfect Father to fulfil the imperfection of thy child. Be God after thy own nature, beyond my feeling, beyond my prayer—according to that will in me which now, for all my trying, refuses to awake and arise from the dead. O Christ, who knowest me better a thousand times than I know myself, whose I am, divinely beyond my notions of thee and me, hear and save me eternally, out of thy eternal might whereby thou didst make me and give thyself to me. Make me strong to yield all to thee. I have no way of confessing thee before men, but in the depth of my thought I would confess thee, yielding everything but the truth, which is thyself; and therefore, even while my heart hangs back, I force my mouth to say the words—*Take from me what thou wilt, only make me clean, pure, divine.* To thee I yield the house and all that is in it. It is thine, not mine. Give it to whom thou wilt. I would have nothing but what thou choosest shall be mine. I have thee, and all things are mine."

Thus he prayed, thus he strove with a reluctant heart, forcing its will by the might of a deeper will, that *would* be for God and freedom, in spite of the cleaving of his soul to the dust.

Then for a time thought ceased in exhaustion. When it returned, lo! he was in peace, in the heart of a calm unspeakable. How it came he could not tell, for he had not been aware of its approach; but the contest was over, and in a few minutes he was fast asleep—ten times his own because a thousand times another's—one with him whom all men in one could not comprehend, whom yet the heart of every true child lays hold upon and understands.

I would not have it supposed that, although the crisis was past, there was no more stormy weather. Often it blew a gale—often a blast would come creeping in—almost always in the skirts of the hope that God would never require such a sacrifice of him. But he never again found he could not pray. Recalling the strife and the great peace, he made haste to his master, compelling the refractory slave in his heart to be free, and cry, "Do thy will, not mine." Then would the enemy withdraw, and again he breathed the air of the eternal.

When a man comes to the point that he will no longer receive anything save from the hands of him who has the right to withhold, and in whose giving alone lies the value of possession, then is he approaching the inheritance of the saints in light, of those whose strength is made perfect in weakness. But there are those who for the present it is needless to trouble any more than the chickens about the yard. Their hour will come, and in the meantime they are counted the fortunate ones of the earth.

CHAPTER XLVII
A REST

But now James Gracie fell sick. They removed him therefore from the men's quarters, and gave him Cosmo's room, that he might be better attended to, and warmer than in his own. Cosmo put up a bed for himself in his father's room, and Grizzie and Aggie slept together; so that the household was gathered literally under one roof—that of the kitchen-tower, as it had been called for centuries.

James's attack was serious, requiring much attention, and involving an increase of expenditure which it needed faith to face. But of course Cosmo did not shrink from it: so long as his money lasted, his money should go. James himself objected bitterly to such waste, as he called it, saying what remained of his life was not worth it. But the laird, learning the mood the old man was in, rose, and climbed the stair, and stood before his bed, and said to him solemnly,

"Jeames, wha are ye to tell the Lord it's time he sud tak ye? what *kin'* o' faith is 't, to refuse a sup, 'cause ye see na anither spunefu' upo' the ro'd ahin' 't?"	"Jeames, who are you to tell the Lord it's time he should take you? what *kind* of faith is it, to refuse a sup, because you can't see another spoonful upon the road behind it?"

James hid his old face in his old hands. The laird went back to his bed, and nothing more ever passed on the subject.

The days went on, the money ran fast away, no prospect appeared of more, but still they had enough to eat.

One morning in the month of January, still and cold, and dark overhead, a cheerless day in whose bosom a storm was coming to life, Cosmo, sitting at his usual breakfast of brose, the simplest of all preparations of oatmeal, bethought himself whether some of the curiosities in the cabinets in the drawing-room might not, with the help of his friend the jeweller, be turned to account. Not waiting to finish his breakfast, for which that day he had but little relish, he rose and went at once to examine the family treasures in the light of necessity.

The drawing-room felt freezing—dank like a tomb, and looked weary of its memories. It was so still that it seemed as if sound would die in it. Not a mouse stirred. The few pictures on the walls looked perishing with cold and changelessness. The very shine of the old damask was wintry. But Cosmo did not long stand gazing. He crossed to one of the shrines of his childhood's reverence, opened it, and began to examine the things with the eye of a seller. Once they had seemed treasures inestimable, now he feared they might bring him nothing in his sore need. Scarce a sorrow at the thought of parting with them woke in him, as one after another he set those aside, and took these from their places and put them on a table. He was like a miner searching for golden ore, not a miser whom hunger had dominated. The sole question with him was, would this or that bring money. When he had gone through the cabinet, he turned from it to regard what he had found. There was a dagger in a sheath of silver of raised work, with a hilt cunningly wrought of the same; a goblet of iron with a rich pattern in gold beaten into it; a snuff-box with a few diamonds set round a monogram in gold in the lid: these, with several other smaller things that had an air of promise about them, he thought it might be worth while to make the trial with, and packed them carefully, thinking to take them at once to Muir of Warlock, and commit them to the care of the carrier. But when he returned to his father, he found he had been missing him, and put off going till the next day.

As the sun went down, the wind rose, and the storm in the bosom of the stillness came to life—the worst of that winter. It reminded both father and son of the terrible night when Lord Mergwain went out into the deep. The morning came, fierce with gray cold age, a tumult of wind and snow. There seemed little chance the carrier would go for days to come. But the storm might have been more severe upon their hills than in the opener country, and Cosmo would go and see. Certain things too had to be got for the invalids.

It was with no small difficulty he made his way through the snow to the village, and there also he found it so deep, that the question would have been how to get the cart out of the shed, not whether the horses were likely to get it through the Glens o' Fowdlan. He left the parcel therefore with the carrier's wife, and proceeded, somewhat sad at heart, to spend the last of his money, amounting to half-a-crown. Having done so, he set out for home, the wind blowing fierce, and the snow falling thick.

Just outside the village he met a miserable-looking woman, with a child in her arms. How she came to be there he could not think. She moved him with the sense of community in suffering: hers was the greater share, and he gave her the twopence he had left. Prudence is but one of the minor divinities, if indeed she be anything better than the shadow of a virtue, and he took no counsel with her, knowing that the real divinity, Love, would not cast him out for the deed. The widow who gave the two mites was by no means a prudent person. Upon a certain ancient cabinet of carved oak is represented *Charity,* gazing at the child she holds on her arm, and beside her *Prudence,* regarding herself in a mirror.

Cosmo had not gone far, battling with wind and snow above and beneath, before he began to feel his strength failing him. It had indeed been failing for some time. Grizzie knew, although he himself did not, that he had not of late been eating so well; and he had never quite recovered his exertions in Lord Lick-my-loof's harvest-fields. Now, for the first time in his life, he began to find his strength unequal to elemental war. But he laughed at the idea, and held on. The wind was right in his face, and the cold was bitter. Nor was there within him, though plenty of courage, good spirits enough to supply any lack of physical energy. His breath grew short, and his head began to ache. He longed for home that he might lie down and breathe, but a long way and a great snowy wind were betwixt him and rest. He fell into a reverie, and seemed to get on better for not thinking about the exertion he had to make. The monotony of it at the same time favoured the gradual absorption of his thoughts in a dreamy meditation. Alternately sunk in himself for minutes, and waking for a moment to the consciousness of what was around him, he had walked, as it seemed, for hours, and at length, all notion of time and distance gone, began to wonder whether he must not be near the place where the parish-road turned off. He stood, and sent sight into his eyes, but nothing was to be seen through the drift save more drift behind it. Was he upon the road at all? He sought this way and that, but could find neither ditch nor dyke. He was lost! He knew well the danger of sitting down, knew on the other hand that the more exhausted he was when he succumbed, the sooner would the cold get the better of him, and that even now he might be wandering from the abodes of men, diminishing with every step the likelihood of being found. He turned his back to the wind and stood—how long he did not know, but while he stood thus 'twixt waking and sleeping, he received a heavy blow on the head—or so it seemed—from something soft. It dazed him, and the rest was like a dream, in which he walked on and on for ages, falling and rising again, following something, he never knew what. There all memory of consciousness ceased. He came to himself in bed.

Aggie was the first to get anxious about him. They had expected him home to dinner, and when it began to grow dark and he had not come, she could bear it no longer, and set out to meet him. But she had not far to go, for she had scarcely left the kitchen-door when she saw someone leaning over the gate. Through the gathering twilight and the storm she could distinguish nothing more, but she never doubted it was the young laird, though whether in the body or out of it she did doubt not a little. She hurried to the gate, and found him standing between it and the wall. She thought at first he was dead, for there came no answer when she spoke; but presently she heard him murmur something about conic sections. She opened the gate gently. He would have fallen as it yielded, but she held him. Her touch seemed to bring him a little to himself. She supported and encouraged him; he obeyed her, and she succeeded in getting him into the house. It was long ere Grizzie and she could make him warm before the kitchen-fire, but at last he came to himself sufficiently to walk up the stairs to bed, though afterwards he remembered nothing of it.

He was recovering before they let the laird understand in what a dangerous plight Aggie had found him, but the moment he learned that his son was ailing, the old man seemed to regain a portion of his strength. He rose from his bed, and for the two days and three nights during which Cosmo was feverish and wandering, slept only in snatches. On the third day Cosmo himself persuaded him to return to his bed.

The women had now their hands full—all the men in the house laid up, and they two only to do everything! The first night, when they had got Cosmo comfortable in bed, and had together gone down again to the kitchen, in the middle of the floor they stopped, and looked at each other: their turn had come! They understood each other, and words were needless. Each had saved a little money—and now no questions would be asked! Aggie left the room and came back with her store, which she put into Grizzie's hand. Grizzie laid it on the table, went in her turn to her box, brought thence her store, laid it on the other, took both up, closed her hands over them, shook them together, murmered over them, like an incantation, the words, "It's nae mair mine, an' it's nae mair thine, but belongs to a', whatever befa'," ("It's no more mine, and it's no more thine, but belongs to all, whatever befall.") and put all in her pocket under her winsey petticoat. Thence, for a time, the invalids wanted nothing—after the moderate ideas of need, that is, ruling in the house.

When Cosmo came to himself on the third day, he found that self possessed by a wondrous peace. It was as if he were dead, and had to rest till his strength, exhausted with dying, came back to him. Bodiless he seemed, and without responsibility of action, with that only of thought. Those verses in *The Ancient Marniner* came to him as if he spoke them for himself:

> "I thought that I had died in sleep,
> And was a blessed ghost."

His soul was calm and trusting like that of a bird on her eggs, who knows her one grand duty in the economy of the creation is repose. How it was he never could quite satisfy himself, but, remembering he had spent their last penny, he yet felt no anxiety; neither, when Grizzie brought him food, felt inclination to ask her how she had procured it. The atmosphere was that of the fairy-palace of his childish-visions, only his feelings were more solemn, and the fairy, instead of being beautiful, was—well, was dear old Grizzie. His sole concern was his father, and the cheerful voice that invariably answered his every inquiry was sufficient reassurance.

For three days more he lay in a kind of blessed lethargy, with little or no suffering. He fancied he could not recover, nor did he desire to recover, but to go with his father to the old world, and learn its ways from his mother. In his half slumbers he seemed ever to be gently floating down a great gray river, on which thousands more were likewise floating, each by himself, some in canoes, some in boats, some in the water without even an oar; every now and then one would be lifted and disappear, none saw how, but each knew that his turn would come, when he too would be laid hold of; in the meantime all floated helpless onward, some full of alarm at the unknown before them, others indifferent, and some filled with solemn expectation; he himself floated on gently waiting: the unseen hand would come with the hour, and give him to his mother.

On the seventh day he began to regard the things around him with some interest, began to be aware of returning strength, and the approach of duty: presently he must rise, and do his part to keep things going! Still he felt no anxiety, for the alarum of duty had not yet called him.

And now, as he lay passive to the influences of restoring strength, his father from his bed would tell him old tales he had heard from his grandmother; and sometimes they made Grizzie sit between the two beds, and tell them stories she had heard in her childhood. Her stock seemed never exhausted. Now one, now the other would say,

"There, Grizzie! I never heard that before!" and Grizzie would answer, "I daursay no, sir. Hoo sud ye than? I had forgotten 't mysel'!"

"There, Grizzie! I never heard that before!" and Grizzie would answer, "I daresay not, sir. How should you then? I had forgotten it myself!"

Here is one of the stories Grizzie told them.

Here is one of the stories Grizzie told them.

"In a cauld how, far amo' the hills, whaur the winter was a sair thing, there leevit an honest couple, a man 'at had a gey lot o' sheep, an' his wife—fowk weel aff in respec' o' this warld's gear, an' luikit up til amo' the neebours, but no to be envied, seein' they had lost a hail bonny family, ane efter the ither, till there was na ane left i' the hoose but jist ae laddie, the bonniest an' the best o' a', an' as a matter o' coorse, the verra aipple o' their e'e.—Amo the three o' 's, laird," here Grizzie paused in her tale to remark, "Ye'll be the only ane 'at can fully un'erstan' hoo the hert o' a parent maun cleave to the last o' his flock.—Weel, whether it was 'at their herts was ower muckle wrappit up i' this ae human cratur for the growth o' their sowls, I dinna ken—there bude to be some rizzon for 't—this last ane o' a' begud in his turn to dwine an' dwin'le like the lave; an' whauriver thae twa puir fowk turnt themsel's i' their pangs, there stude deith, glowerin' at them oot o' his toom e'en. Pray they did, ye may be sure, an' greit whan a' was mirk, but prayers nor tears made nae differ; the bairn was sent for, an' awa' the bairn maun gang. An' whan at len'th he lay streekit in his last clean claes till the robe o' richteousness 'at wants na washin' was put upon 'im, what cud they but think the warl' was dune for them!

"In a cold hollow, far among the hills, where the winter was severe, there lived an honest couple, a man that had a great flock of sheep, and his wife—folk well off in respect of this world's wealth, and looked up to amongst the neighbours, but not to be envied, seeing they had lost a whole bonny family, one after the other, till there was none left in the house but just one laddie, the bonniest and the best of all, and as a matter of course, the very apple of their eye.—Among the three of us, laird," here Grizzie paused in her tale to remark, "You'll be the only one that can fully understand how the heart of a parent must cleave to the last of his flock.—Well, whether it was that their hearts were too much wrapped up in this one human creature for the growth of their souls, I don't know—there must be some reason for it—this last one of all began in his turn to waste and dwindle like the rest; and wherever those two poor folk turned themselves in their pangs, there stood death, glowering at them out of his empty eyes. Pray they did, you may be sure, and cry when all was dark, but prayers nor tears made any difference; the child was sent for, and away the child must go. And when at length he lay stretched out in his last clean clothes till the robe of righteousness that wants no washing was put upon him, what could they think but that their lives were over!

"But the warl' maun wag, though the hert may sag; an' whan the deid lies streekit, there's a hoose to be theekit. An' the freens an' the neebours gaithert frae near an' frae far, till there was a heap o' fowk i' the hoose, come to the beeryin' o' the bonny bairn. An' fowk maun ait an' live nane the less 'at the matter they come upo' be deith; an' sae the nicht afore the yerdin', their denner the neist day whan

"But on the world goes, despite heart's woes; and when we lay out the dead, we must earn our bread. And the friends and the neighbours gathered from near and from far, till there was a throng of folk in the house, come to the burying of the bonny boy. And folk must eat and live none the less that the matter they come upon be death; and so the night before the burial, their dinner the next day when they cam back frae the grave, had to be foreordeent.

"It was i' the spring-time o' the year, unco late i' thae pairts. The maist o' the lambs hed come, but the storms war laith to lea' the laps o' the hills, an' lang efter it begud to be something like weather laicher doon, the sheep cudna be lippent oot to pick their bit mait for themsel's, but had to be keepit i' the cot. Sae to the cot the gudeman wad gang, to fess hame a lamb for the freens an' the neebours' denners. An' as it fell oot, it was a fearsome nicht o' win' an' drivin' snaw—waur, I wad reckon, nor onything we hae hereawa'. But he turnt na aside for win' or snaw, for little cared he what cam til 'im or o' 'im, wi' sic a how in his hert. O' the contrar' the storm was like a freenly cloak til's grief, for upo' the r'od he fell a greitin' an' compleenin' an' lamentin' lood, jeedgin' nae doubt, gien he thoucht at a', he micht du as he likit wi' naebody nigh. To the sheep cot, I say, he gaed wailin' an cryin' alood efter bonny bairn, the last o' his flock, oontimeous wis taen.

"Half blin' wi' the nicht an' the snaw an' his ain tears, he cam at last to the door o' the sheep-cot. An' what sud he see there but a man stan'in' afore the door—straucht up, an' still i' the mirk! It was 'maist fearsome to see onybody there—sae far frae ony place—no to say upo' sic a nicht! The stranger was robed in some kin' o' a plaid, like the gudeman himsel', but whether a lowlan' or a hielan' plaid, he cudna tell. But the face o' the man—that was ane no to be forgotten—an' that for the verra freenliness o' 't! An' whan he spak, it was as gien a' the v'ices o' them 'at had gane afore, war made up intil ane, for the sweetness an' the pooer o' the same.

" 'What mak ye here in sic a storm, man?' he said. An the soon' o' his v'ice was aye safter nor the words o' his mooth.

" 'I cam for a lamb,' answered he.

" 'What kin' o' a lamb?' askit the stranger.

" 'The verra best I can lay my han's upo' i' the cot,' answered he , 'for it's to lay afore my freens and neebours. I houp, sir, ye'll come

they came back from the grave, had to be prepared.

"It was in the spring-time of the year, very late in those parts. Most of the lambs had come, but the storms were loath to leave the laps of the hills, and long after it began to be something like weather lower down, the sheep couldn't be allowed out to graze for themselves, but had to be kept in the cot. So to the cot the goodman would go, to bring home a lamb for the friends and the neighbours' dinners. And as it fell out, it was a fearsome night of wind and driving snow—worse, I would reckon, than anything we have hereabouts. But he turned not aside for wind or snow, for little cared he what came to him or of him, with such a void in his heart. On the contrary, the storm was like a friendly cloak to his grief, for upon the road he fell a crying and complaining and lamenting loudly, judging no doubt, if he thought at all, he might do as he liked with nobody nigh. To the sheep cot, I say, he went wailing and crying aloud after bonny boy, the last of his flock, was taken so young.

"Half blind with the night and the snow and his own tears, he came at last to the door of the sheep-cot. And what should he see there but a man standing before the door—straight up, and still in the dark! It was almost fearsome to see anybody there—so far from any place—not to say upon such a night! The stranger was robed in some kind of a plaid, like the goodman himself, but whether a lowland or a highland plaid, he couldn't tell. But the face of the man—that was one not to be forgotten—and that for the very friendliness of it! And when he spoke, it was as if all the voices of those who had gone before, were made up into one, for the sweetness and power of the same.

" 'What make you here in such a storm, man?' he said. And the sound of his voice was still softer than the words of his mouth.

" 'I came for a lamb,' answered he.

" 'What kind of lamb?' asked the stranger.

" 'The very best I can lay my hands upon in the cot,' answered he, 'for it's to lay before my friends and neighbours. I hope, sir, you'll hame wi' me an' share o' 't. Ye s' be welcome.'

" 'Du yer sheep mak ony resistance whan ye tak the lamb? Or whan it's gane, du they mak an outcry?'

" 'No, sir—never.'

"The stranger gae a kin' o' a sigh, an' says he,

" 'That's no hoo they trait me! Whan I gang to my sheep-fold, an tak the best an' the fittest, my ears are deavt an' my hert torn wi' the clamours—the bleatin', an' ba'in o' my sheep—my ain sheep! compleenin' sair agen me;—an' me feedin' them, an' cleedin' them, an' haudin' the tod frae them, a' their lives, frae the first to the last! It's some oongratefu', an some sair to bide.'

"By this time the man's heid was hingin' doon; but whan the v'ice ceased, he luikit up in amaze. The stranger was na there. Like ane in a dream wharin he kenned na joy frae sorrow, or pleesur' frae pain, the man gaed into the cot, an' grat ower the heids o' the 'oo'y craters 'at cam croodin' aboot 'im; but he soucht the best lamb nane the less, an' cairriet it wi' 'im. An' the next day he came hame frae the funeral wi' a smile upo' the face whaur had been nane for mony a lang; an the neist Sunday they h'ard him singin' i' the kirk as naebody had ever h'ard him sing afore. An' never frae that time was there a moan or complaint to be h'ard frae the lips o' aither o' the twa. They hadna a bairn to close their e'en whan their turn sud come, but whaur there's nane ahin' there's mair to fin'."

come home with me and share of it. You shall be welcome.'

" 'Do your sheep make any resistance when you take the lamb? or when it's gone, do they make an outcry?'

" 'No, sir—never.'

"The stranger gave a kind of sigh, and said,

" 'That's not how they treat me! When I go to my sheep-fold, and take the best and the fittest, my ears are plagued and my heart torn with the clamours—the bleating, and baaing of my sheep—my own sheep! complaining sore against me;—and me feeding them, and clothing them, and keeping the fox from them, all their lives, from the first to the last! It's very ungrateful, and hard to bear.'

"By this time the man's head was hanging down; but when the voice ceased, he looked up in amaze. The stranger wasn't there. Like one in a dream wherein he knew not joy from sorrow, or pleasure from pain, the man went into the cot, and cried over the heads of the wooly creatures that came crowding about him; but he sought the best lamb none the less, and carried it with him. And the next day he came home from the funeral with a smile upon the face where had been none for many a day; and the next Sunday they heard him singing in the church as nobody had ever heard him sing before. And never from that time was there a moan or complaint to be heard from the lips of either of the two. They hadn't a child to close their eyes when their turn should come, but where there's none behind, there's the more to find."

Grizzie ceased, and the others were silent, for the old legend had touched the deepest in them.

Many years after, Cosmo discovered that she had not told it quite right, for having been brought up in the Lowlands, she did not thoroughly know the ancient customs of the Highlands. But she had told it well after her own fashion, and she could not have had a fitter audience.

"It's whiles i' the storm, whiles i' the desert, whiles i' the agony, an' whiles i' the calm, whauriver he gets them richt themlanes, 'at the Lord visits his people—in person, as a body micht say," remarked the laird, after a long pause.

"It's now in the storm, now in the desert, now in the agony, and now in the calm, wherever he gets them all alone, that the Lord visits his people—in person, as one might say," remarked the laird, after a long pause.

Cosmo did not get well so fast as he had begun to expect. Nothing very definite seemed the matter with him; it was rather as if life itself had been checked at the spring, therefore his senses dulled, and his blood made thick and slow. A sleepy weariness possessed him, in which he would lie for hours, supine and motionless, desiring nothing, fearing nothing, suffering nothing, only loving. The time would come when he must be up and doing, but now he would not think of work; he would fancy himself a bird in God's nest—the nest into which the great brother would have gathered all the children of Jerusalem. Poems would come to him—little songs and little prayers—spiritual butterflies, with wings whose spots matched; sometimes humorous little parables concerning life and its affairs would come; but the pity was that none of them would stay; never, do what he might, could he remember so as to recall one of them, and had to comfort himself with the thought that nothing true can ever be lost; if one form of it go, it is that a better may come in its place. He doubted if the best could be forgotten. A thing may be invaluable, he thought, and the form in which it presents itself worth but little, however at the moment it may share the look of the invaluable within it. But happy is the half-sleeper whose brain is a thoroughfare for lovely things—all to be caught in the nets of Life, for Life is the one miser that never loses, never can lose.

When he was able to get up for a while every day, Grizzie yielded a portion of her right of nursing to Aggie, and now that he was able to talk a little, the change was a pleasant one. And now first the laird began to discover how much there was in Aggie, and expressing his admiration of her knowledge and good sense, her intellect and insight, was a little surprised that Cosmo did not seem so much struck with them as himself. Cosmo, however, explained that her gifts were no discovery to him, as he had been aware of them from childhood.

"There are few like her, father," he said. "Mony's the time she's hauden me up whan I was ready to sink."

"The Lord reward her!" responded the laird.

"There are few like her, father," he said. "Many's the time she's held me up when I was ready to sink."

"The Lord reward her!" responded the laird.

All sicknesses are like aquatic plants of evil growth: their hour comes, and they wither and die, and leave the channels free. Life returns—in slow, soft ripples at first, but not the less in irresistible tide, and at last in pulses of mighty throb through every pipe. Death is the final failure of all sickness, the clearing away of the very soil in which the seed of the ill plant takes root and prevails.

By degrees Cosmo recovered strength, nor left behind him the peace that had pervaded his weakness. The time for action was at hand. For weeks he had been fed like the young ravens in the nest, and, knowing he could do nothing, had not troubled himself with the useless *how;* but it was time once more to understand, that he might be ready to act. Mechanically almost, he opened his bureau: there was not a penny there. He knew there could not be—except some angel had visited it while he lay, and that he had not looked for. He closed it, and sat down to think. There was no work to be had he knew of; there was little strength to do it with, had there been any. As the spring came on, there would be labour in the fields, and that he would keep in view, but the question was of present or all but present need. One thing only he would not do. There were many in the country around on friendly terms with his father and himself, but his very soul revolted from any endeavour to borrow money while he saw no prospect of repaying it. He would carry the traditions of his family no further in that direction. Literally, he would rather die. But rather than his father should want, he would beg. "Where borrowing is dishonest," he said to himself, "begging may be honourable. The man who scorns to accept a gift of money, and does not scruple to borrow, knowing no chance of repaying, is simply a thief; the man who has no way of earning the day's bread, *has a divine right to beg.*" In Cosmo's case, however, there was this difficulty: he could easily make a living of some sort, would he but leave his father, and that he was determined not to do. Before absolute want could arrive, they must have parted with everything, and then he would take him to some city or town, where they two would live like birds in a cage. No; he was not ready yet to take his pack and make the rounds of the farm-houses to receive from each his dole of a handful of meal! But then again, what?

Once more he fell a thinking; but it was only to find himself again helplessly afloat where no shore of ways or means was visible. Nothing but beggary in fact, and that for the immediate future, showed in sight. Could it be that God verily intended for him this last humiliation of all? But again, would such humiliation be equal to that under which they had bowed for so many long years—the humiliation of owing and not being able to pay? What a man gives, he gives, but what a man lends, he lends expecting to be repaid! A beggar may be under endless obligation, but a debtor who cannot pay is a slave! He may be God's free man all the while—that depends on causes and conditions, but not the less is he his fellow's slave! His slavery may be to him a light burden, or a sickening misery, according to the character of his creditor—but, except indeed there be absolute brotherhood between them, he is all the same a slave!

Again the immediately practical had vanished, lost in reasoning, and once more he tried to return to it. But it was like trying to see through a brick wall. No man can invent needs for others that he may supply them. To write again to Mr. Burns would be too near the begging on which he had not yet resolved. He never suspected that the parcel he had left at the carrier's house was lying there still—safe in his wife's press, under a summer-shawl! He could not go to Mr. Simon, for he too was poor, and had now for some time been far from well, fears being by the doctor acknowledged as to the state of his lungs. He would go without necessaries even to help them, and that was an insurmountable reason against acquainting him with their condition!

All at once a thought came to him: why should he not, for present need, pledge the labour of his body in the coming harvest? That would be but to act on a reasonable probability, nor need he be ashamed to make the offer to any man who knew him enough to be friendly. He would ask but a part of the fee in advance, and a charitable or kindly disposed man would surely venture the amount of risk involved! True, when the time came he might be as much in want of money as he was now, and there would be little or none to receive, but on the other hand, if he did not have help now, he could never reach that want, and when he did, there might be other help! Better beg then than now! He would make the attempt, and that the first day he was strong enough to walk the necessary distance! In the meantime, he would have a peep into the meal-chest!

It stood in a dark corner of the kitchen, and he had to put his hand in to learn its condition. He found a not very shallow layer of meal in the bottom. How there could be so much after his long illness, he scarcely dared imagine. He must ask Grizzie, he said to himself, but he shrank in his heart from questioning her.

There came now a spell of warm weather, and all the invalids improved. Cosmo was able to go out, and every day had a little walk by himself. Naturally he thought of the only other time in his life when he first walked out after an illness. Joan had been so near him then it scarce seemed anything could part them, and now she seemed an eternity away! For months he had heard nothing of her. She must be married, and, knowing well his feelings, must think it kinder not to write! Then the justice of his soul turned to the devotion of the two women who had in this trouble tended him, though the half of it he did not yet know; and from that he turned to the source of all devotion, and made himself strong in the thought of the eternal love.

From that time, the weather continuing moderate, he made rapid progress, and the week following judged himself equal to a long walk.

CHAPTER XLVIII
HELP

He had come to the resolve to carry his petition first to the farmer in whose fields he had laboured the harvest before the last. The distance was rather great, but he flattered himself he would be able to walk home every night. In the present state of his strength, however, he found it a long trudge indeed; and before the house came in sight, was very weary. But he bore up and held on.

"I was almost as ill-off," he said to himself, "when I came here for work the first time, yet here I am—alive, and likely to work again! It's just like going on and on in a dream, wondering what we are coming to next."

He was shown into the parlour, and had not waited long when the farmer came. He scarcely welcomed him, but by degrees his manner grew more cordial. Still the coldness with which he had been received caused Cosmo to hesitate, and a pause ensued. The farmer broke it.

"Ye didna gie's the fawvour o' yer company last hairst!" he said. "I wad hae thought ye micht hae f'un' yersel' fully mair at hame wi' the like o' us nor wi' that ill-tongued vratch, Lord Lick-my-loof! Nane o' 's tuik it ower weel 'at ye gied na's the chance o' yer guid company."

"You didn't give us the favour of your company last harvest!" he said. "I would have thought you might have found yourself much more at home with the likes of us than with that ill-tongued wretch, Lord Lick-my-loof! None of us took it over well that you denied us the chance of your good company."

This explained his reception, and Cosmo made haste in his turn to explain his conduct.

This explained his reception, and Cosmo made haste in his turn to explain his conduct.

"Ye may be sure," he answered, "it gaed some agen the grain to seek wark frae him, an' I had no rizzon upon earth for no comin' to you first but that I didna want to be sae far, at nicht especially, frae my father. He's no the man he was."

"You may be sure," he answered, "it went quite against the grain to seek work from him, and I had no reason upon earth for not coming to you first but that I didn't want to be so far, at night especially, from my father. He's not the man he was."

"Verra nait'ral!" responded the farmer heartily, and wondered in himself whether any of his sons would have considered him so much. "Weel," he went on, "I'm jist relieved to un'erstan' the thing; for the lasses wad hae perswaudit me I hed gien ye some offence wi' my free-spoken w'y, whan I'm sure naething cud hae been far'er frae the thoucht o' my hert."

"Very natural!" responded the farmer heartily, and wondered in himself whether any of his sons would have considered him so much. "Well," he went on, "I'm just relieved to understand the thing; for the lasses would have persuaded me I had given you some offence with my free-spoken way, when I'm sure nothing could have been further from the thought of my heart."

"Indeed," said Cosmo, half rising in his eagerness, "I assure you, Mr. Henderson, there is not a man from whom I should be less ready to imagine offence than yourself. I do not know how to express my feeling of the kindness with which you always treated me. Nor could I have given you a better proof that I mean what I say than by coming to you first, the moment I was able for the walk, with the request I have now to make. Will you engage me for the coming harvest, and pay me a part of the fee in advance? I know it is a strange request, and if you refuse it, I doubt if there is another to whom I shall venture to make it. I confess also that I have been very ill, but I am now fairly on the mend, and there is a long time to recover my strength in before the harvest. To tell you the truth, we are much in want of a little money at the castle. We are not greatly in debt now, but we have lost all our land; and a house, however good, won't grow corn. Something in my mind tells me that my father, unlikely as it may seem, will yet pay everything; and anyhow we want to hold on as long as we can. I am sure, if you were in our place, you would not be willing to part with the house a moment before you were absolutely compelled."

"But, laird," said the farmer, who had listened with the utmost attention, "hoo can the thing be, 'at amo' a' the great fowk ye hae kent, there sud be nane to say, 'Help yersel' '? I canna un'erstan' hoo the last o' sic an auld faimily sud na hae a han' held oot to help them!"

"It is not so very hard to explain," replied Cosmo. "Almost all my father's old friends are dead or gone, and a man like him, especially in straitened circumstances, does not readily make new friends. Almost the only person he has been intimate with of late years is Mr. Simon, whom I daresay you know. Then he has what many people count peculiar notions—so peculiar, indeed, that I have heard of some calling him a fool behind his back because he paid themselves certain moneys his father owed them. I believe if he had rich friends they would say it was no use trying to help such a man."

"Weel!" exclaimed the farmer, "it jist blecks me to ken hoo there can be ony trowth i' the Bible, whan a man like that comes sae near to beggin' his breid!"

"He is very near it, certainly," assented Cosmo, "but why not he as well as another?"

"'Cause they tell me the Bible says the richteous man sall never come to beg his breid."

"Well, *near* is not *there*. But I fancy there must be a mistake. The writer of one of the psalms—I do not know whether David or another, says he never saw the righteous forsaken or his seed begging bread; but though he may not have seen it, another may."

"Weel, I fancy gien he hed, he wadna hae been lang in puttin' a stop til 't! Laird, gien a sma' maitter o' fifty poun' or sae wad tide ye ower the trible—weel, ye cud pay me whan ye likit."

"But, laird," said the farmer, who had listened with the utmost attention, "how can the thing be, that among all the great folk you have known, there should be none to say, 'Help yourself'? I can't understand how the last of such an old family shouldn't have a hand held out to help them!"

"It is not so very hard to explain," replied Cosmo. "Almost all my father's old friends are dead or gone, and a man like him, especially in straitened circumstances, does not readily make new friends. Almost the only person he has been intimate with of late years is Mr. Simon, whom I daresay you know. Then he has what many people count peculiar notions—so peculiar, indeed, that I have heard of some calling him a fool behind his back because he paid themselves certain moneys his father owed them. I believe if he had rich friends they would say it was no use trying to help such a man."

"Well!" exclaimed the farmer, "it just baffles me to know how there can be any truth in the Bible, when a man like that comes so near to begging his bread!"

"He is very near it, certainly," assented Cosmo, "but why not he as well as another?"

"'Cause they tell me the Bible says the righteous man shall never come to beg his bread."

"Well, *near* is not *there*. But I fancy there must be a mistake. The writer of one of the psalms—I do not know whether David or another, says he never saw the righteous forsaken or his seed begging bread; but though he may not have seen it, another may."

"Well, I fancy if he had, he wouldn't have been long in putting a stop to it! Laird, if a small matter of fifty pounds or so would tide you over the trouble—well, you could pay me when you liked."

It was a moment or two before Cosmo could speak. A long conversation followed, rising almost to fierceness, certainly to oaths, on the part of the farmer, because of Cosmo's refusal to accept the offered loan.

"I do see my way," persisted Cosmo, "to paying for my wages with my work, but I see it to nothing more. Lend me two pounds, Mr. Henderson, on the understanding that I am to work it out in the harvest, and I shall be debtor to your kindness to all eternity; but more I cannot and will not accept."

Grumbling heavily, the farmer at length handed him the two pounds, but obstinately refused any written acknowledgement or agreement.

Neither of them knew that, all the time the friendly altercation proceeded, there was Elsie listening at the door, her colour coming and going like the shadows in a day of sun and wind. Entering at its close she asked Cosmo to stop and take tea with them, and the farmer following it up, he accepted the invitation, and indeed was glad to make a good meal. Elsie was sorely disappointed that her father had not succeeded in making him his debtor to a larger extent, but the meal passed with pleasure to all, for the relief of having two pounds in his pocket, and those granted with such genuine kindness, put Cosmo in great spirits, and made him more than usually agreeable. The old farmer wondered admiringly at the spirit of the youth who in such hardship could yet afford to be merry. But I cannot help thinking that a perfect faith would work at last thorough good spirits, as well as everything else that is good.

Cosmo sat with his kind neighbours till the gloaming began to fall. When he rose to go, they all rose with him, and accompanied him fully half-way home. When they took their leave of him, and he was again alone, his heart grew so glad that, weak as he yet was, and the mists rising along his path, he never felt the slightest chill, but trudged cheerily on, praying and singing and *making*[11] all the way, until at length he was surprised to find how short it had been.

For a great part of it, after his friends left him, he had glimpses now and then of some one before him that looked like Aggie, but the distance between them gradually lengthened, and before he reached home he had lost sight of her. When he entered the kitchen, Aggie was there.

"Was yon you upo' the ro'd afore me, Aggie?"

"Ay, was't."

"What for didna ye bide?"

"Ye had yer company the first half o' the ro'd, an' yer sangs the last, an' I didna think ye wantit me."

"Was that you upon the road before me, Aggie?" he said.

"Ay, it was."

"Why didn't you wait?"

"You had your company the first half of the way, and your songs the last, and I didn't think you wanted me."

So saying she went up the stair.

As Cosmo followed, he turned and put his hand into the meal-chest. It was empty! There was not enough to make their supper. He smiled in his heart, and said to himself,

"The links of the story hold yet! When one breaks, the world will drift."

Going up to his father, he had to pass the door of his own room, now occupied by James Gracie. As he drew near it, he heard the voice of Aggie speaking to her grandfather. What she said he did not know, but he heard the answer.

"Lassie," said the old man, "ye can never see by the Lord to ken whaur he's takin' ye. Ye may jist as weel close yer e'en. His garment spreads ower a' the ro'd, an' what we hae to du is to haud a grip o' 't—no to try an' see ayont it."

Cosmo hastened up, and told his father what he had overheard.

"Lassie," said the old man, "you can never see past the Lord to know where he's taking you. You may just as well close your eyes. His garment spreads over all the road, and what we have to do is to keep a grip of it—not to try and see beyond it."

Cosmo hastened up, and told his father what he had overheard.

11 MAKING: from the Scots word 'makar'/'maker', meaning a poet. Here Cosmo is *making* his own poetry as he walks.

"There's naething like faith for makin' o' poets, Cosmo!" said the laird. "Jeames never appeart to me to hae mair o' what's ca'd intellec' nor an ord'nar' share; but ye see the man 'at has faith he's aye growin', an' sae may come to something even i' this warl'. An' whan ye think o' the ages to come, truly it wad seem to maitter little what intellec' a man may start wi'. I kenned mysel' ane 'at in ord'nar' affairs was coontit little better nor an idiot, 'maist turn a prophet whan he gaed doon upo' his knees. Ay! fowk may lauch at what they haena a glimp o', but it'll be lang or their political economy du sae muckle for sic a man! The economist wad wuss his neck had been thrawn whan he was born."

"There's nothing like faith for making poets, Cosmo!" said the laird. "Jeames never appeared to me to have more of what's called intellect than an ordinary share; but you see the man that has faith he's always growing, and so may come to something even in this world. And when you think of the ages to come, truly it would seem to matter little what intellect a man may start with. I myself knew one that in ordinary affairs was counted little better than an idiot, almost turn a prophet when he went down upon his knees. Ay! folk may laugh at what they haven't a glimpse of, but it'll be long before their political economy does so much for such a man! The economist would wish his neck had been wrung when he was born."

Here Cosmo heard Grizzie come in, and went down to her. She was sitting in his father's chair by the fire, and did not turn her face when he spoke. She was either tired or vexed, he thought. Aggie was also now in the kitchen again.

"Here, Grizzie!" said Cosmo, "here's twa poun'; an' ye'll need to gar't gang far'er nor it can, I'm thinkin', for I dinna ken whaur we're to get the neist."

"Here, Grizzie!" said Cosmo, "here's two pounds; and you'll need to make it go further than it can, I'm thinking, for I don't know where we're to get the next."

"Ken ye whaur ye got the last?" muttered Grizzie, and made haste to cover the words:

"Do you know where you got the last?" muttered Grizzie, and made haste to cover the words:

"Whaur got ye that, Cosmo?" she said.

"Where did you get that, Cosmo?" she said.

"What gien I dinna tell ye, Grizzie?" he returned, willing to rouse her with a little teasing.

"What if I don't tell you, Grizzie?" he returned, willing to rouse her with a little teasing.

"That's as ye see proper, sir," she answered. "Naebody has a richt to say til anither 'Whaur got ye that?' 'cep' they doobt ye hae been stealin'."

"That's as you see proper, sir," she answered. "Nobody has a right to say to another 'Where did you get that?' except they suspect you've been stealing."

It was a somewhat strange answer, but there was no end to the strange things Grizzie would say: it was one of her charms! Cosmo told her at once where and how he had got the money; for with such true comrades, although not yet did he know how true, he felt almost that a secret would be a sin.

But the moment Grizzie heard where Cosmo had engaged himself, and from whom on the pledge of that engagement he had borrowed money, she started from her chair, and cried, with clenched and outstretched hand,

"Glenwarlock, yoong sir, ken ye what ye're duin'?—The Lord preserve 's! he's an innocent!" she added, turning with an expression of despair to Aggie, who regarded the two with a strange look.

"Glenwarlock, young sir, do you know what you're doing?—The Lord preserve us! he's an innocent!" she added, turning with an expression of despair to Aggie, who regarded the two with a strange look.

"Grizzie!" cried Cosmo, in no little astonishment, "what on earth gars ye luik like that at the mention o' ane wha has this moment helpit us oot o' the warst strait ever we war in!"

"Gien there had been naebody nearer hame to help ye oot o' waur straits, it's waur straits ye wad be in. An' it's waur straits ye'll be in yet, gien that man gets his wull o' ye!"

"He's a fine, honest chiel'! An' for waur straits, Grizzie,—are na ye at the verra last wi' yer meal?"

"Grizzie!" cried Cosmo, in no little astonishment, "what on earth makes you look like that at the mention of one who has this moment helped us out of the worst strait ever we were in!"

"If there had been nobody nearer home to help you out of worse straits, it's worse straits you would be in. And it's worse straits you'll be in yet, if that man gets his way with you!"

"He's a fine, honest man! And for worse straits, Grizzie—aren't you at the very last with your meal?"

As he spoke he turned, and, in bodily reference to fact, went to the chest into which he had looked but a few minutes before. To his astonishment, there was enough in it for a good many meals! He turned again, and stared at Grizzie. But she had once more seated herself in his father's chair, with her back to him, and before he could speak she went on thus:

"Shame fa' him, say I, 'at made his siller as a flesher i' the wast wyn' o' Howglen, to ettle at a gentleman o' a thoosan' year for ane o' his queans! But, please the Lord, we s' haud clear o' 'im yet!"

"Hoot toot, Grizzie! ye canna surely think ony sic man wad regaird the like o' me as worth luikin' efter for a son-in-law! He wadna be sic a gowk!"

"Gowk here, gowk there! he kens what ye are an' what ye're worth—weel that! Hasna he seen ye at the scythe? Disna he ken there's ten times mair to be made o' ae gentleman like you, wi' siller at his back, nor ten common men sic as he's like to get for his dothers? Weel kens he it's nae faut o' you or yours 'at ye're no freely sae weel aff as some 'at oucht an' wull be waur, gien it be the Lord's wull, or a' be dune! Disna he ken 'at Castle Warlock itsel' wad be a warl's honour to ony leddy—no to say a lass broucht up ower a slauchter-hoose? Shame upo' him an' his!"

"Weel, Grizzie," rejoined Cosmo, "ye may say 'at ye like, but I dinna believe he wad hae dune what he has dune—"

"Cha!" interrupted Grizzie; "what has he dune? Disna he ken the word o' a Warlock's as guid as gowd? Disna he ken your wark, what wi' yer pride an' what wi' yer ill-placed gratitude, 'ill be worth til 'im that o' twa men? The man's nae coof! He kens what he's aboot!

"Shame on him, say I, who made his money as a butcher in the west end of Howglen, for trying to catch a gentleman of a thousand years for one of his daughters!" But, please the Lord, we shall keep clear of him yet!"

"Pooh pooh, Grizzie! you can't surely think any such man would regard the likes of me as worth looking after for a son-in-law! He wouldn't be such a fool!"

"Fool here, fool there! he knows what you are and what you're worth—very well! Hasn't he seen you at the scythe? Doesn't he know there's ten times more to be made of one gentleman like you, with money at his back, than ten common men such as he's like to get for his daughters? Well he knows it's no fault of you or yours that you're not just as well off as some who ought and will be worse, if it be the Lord's will, before all's done! Doesn't he know that Castle Warlock itself would be a world's honour to any lady—not to say a lass brought up over a slaughter-house? Shame upon him and his!"

"Well, Grizzie," rejoined Cosmo, "you may say what you like, but I don't believe he would have done what he has done—"

"Humph!" interrupted Grizzie; "what has he done? Doesn't he know the word of a Warlock's as good as gold? Doesn't he know your work, what with your pride and what with your ill-placed gratitude, will be worth to him that of two men? The man's no dunce! He knows what he's about! Faith, you

Haith, ye needna waur muckle graititude upo' sic benefactions!"

"To show you, Grizzie, that you are unfair to him, I feel bound to tell you that he pressed on me the loan of fifty pounds."

"I tell ye sae!" screamed Grizzie, starting again to her feet. "God forbid ye took 'im at his offer!"

"I did not," answered Cosmo; "but all the same—"

"The Lord be praised for his abundant an' great mercy!" cried Grizzie, more heartily than devoutly. "We may contrive to win ower the twa poun', even sud ye no work it oot; but *fifty!*—the Lord be aboot us frae ill! so sure 's deith, ye wad hae had to tak the lass!—Cosmo, ye canna but ken the auld tale o' muckle-moo'd Meg?"

"Weel that," replied Cosmo. "But ye'll alloo, Grizzie, times are altert sin' the day whan the laird cud gie a ch'ice atween a wife an' the wuddie! Mr. Hen'erson canna weel hang me gien I sud say *no*."

"Say ye *no*, come o' the hangin' what like," rejoined Grizzie.

"But, Grizzie," said Cosmo, "I wad fain ken whaur that meal i' the kist cam frae. There was nane intil 't an hoor ago."

needn't spend much gratitude upon those benefactions!"

"To show you, Grizzie, that you are unfair to him, I feel bound to tell you that he pressed on me the loan of fifty pounds."

"I tell you so!" screamed Grizzie, starting again to her feet. "God forbid you took him at his offer!"

"I did not," answered Cosmo; "but all the same—"

"The Lord be praised for his abundant and great mercy!" cried Grizzie, more heartily than devoutly. "We may contrive to pay back the two pounds, even should you not work it out; but *fifty!*—the Lord protect us from ill! as sure as death, you would have had to take the lass!—Cosmo, you can't but know the old tale of big-mouthed Meg?"

"I know it well," replied Cosmo. "But you'll allow, Grizzie, times are altered since the day when the laird could give a choice between a wife and the gallows! Mr. Henderson can't very well hang me if I should say *no*."

"Say *no*, come of the hanging what may," rejoined Grizzie.

"But, Grizzie," said Cosmo, "I would fain know where that meal in the chest came from. There was none inside it an hour ago."

With all her faults of temper and tongue, there was one evil word Grizzie could not speak. In the course of a not very brief life she had tried a good many times to tell a lie, but had never been able; and now, determined not to tell where the meal had come from, she naturally paused unprepared. It was but for a moment. Out came the following utterance.

"Some fowk says, sir, 'at the age o' miracles is ower. For mysel' I dinna preten' to ony opingon; but sae lang as the needcessity was the same, I wad be laith to think Providence wadna be consistent wi' itsel'. Ye maun min' the tale, better nor I can tell't ye, concernin' yon meal-girnel—muckle sic like, I daursay, as oor ain, though it be ca'd a barrel i' the Buik—hit 'at never wastit, ye ken, an' the uily-pig an' a'—ye'll min' weel—though what ony wuman in her senses cud want wi' sic a sicht o' ile's mair nor I ever cud faddom! Eh, but a happy wuman was she 'at had but to tak her bowl an' gang to the girnel, as I micht tak my pail an' gang to the wall! An' what for michtna the Almichty mak a meal-wall as weel's a watter-wall, I wad like to ken! What for no a wall 'at

"Some folk say, sir, that the age of miracles is over. For myself I don't pretend to any opinion; but so long as the necessity was the same, I would be loath to think Providence wouldn't be consistent with itself. You must remember the tale, better than I can tell you it, concerning that meal-chest—much the same, I daresay, as our own, though it be called a barrel in the Book—the one that never wasted, you know, and the oil-pig and all—you'll remember well—though what any woman in her senses could want with such a lot of oil's more than I ever could fathom! Eh, but a happy woman was she who had but to take her bowl and go to the chest, as I might take my pail and go to the well! And why might the Almighty not make a meal-well as soon as a sud rin ile—or say milk, which wad be mair to the purpose? Ae thing maun be jist as easy to him as anither—jist as ae thing's as hard to us as anither! Eh, but we're helpless creturs!"

water-well, I would like to know! Why not a well that should run oil—or say milk, which would be more to the purpose? One thing must be just as easy to him as another—just as one thing's as hard to us as another! Eh, but we're helpless creatures!"

"I' your w'y, Grizzie, ye wad keep us as helpless as ever, for ye wad hae a' thing hauden oot to oor han', like to the bairnie in his mither's lap! It's o' the mercy o' the Lord 'at he wad mak men an' women o' 's—no haud 's bairns for ever!"

"In your way, Grizzie, you would keep us as helpless as ever, for you would have everything held out to our hand, like to the baby in his mother's lap! It's of the mercy of the Lord that he would make men and women of us—not keep us children for ever!"

"It may be as ye say, Cosmo; but whiles I cud maist wuss I was a bairn again, an' had to luik to my mither for a' thing."

"It may be as you say, Cosmo; but sometimes I could almost wish I were a child again, and had to look to my mother for everything."

"An' isna that siclike as the Lord wad hae o' 's, Grizzie? We canna aye be bairns to oor mithers—an' for me I wasna ane lang—but we can an' maun aye be bairns to the great Father o' 's."

"And isn't that such as the Lord would have of us, Grizzie? We can't always be children to our mothers—and for me I wasn't one long—but we can and must always be children to the great Father of us."

"I hae an ill hert, I doobt, Cosmo, for I'm unco hard to content. An' I'm ower auld noo, I fear, to mak muckle better o'. But maybe some kinly body like yersel' 'ill tak me in han' whan I'm deid, an' put some sense intil me!"

"I have a bad heart, I suspect, Cosmo, for I'm very hard to content. And I'm too old now, I fear, to be made much better. But maybe some kindly person like yourself will take me in hand when I'm dead, and put some sense into me!"

"Ye hae sense eneuch, Grizzie, an' to spare, gien only ye wad—"

"You have sense enough, Grizzie, and to spare, if only you would—"

"Guide my tongue a wee better, ye wad say! But little ye ken the temptation o' ane 'at has but ae solitary wapon, to mak use o' that same! An' the gift ye hae ye're no to despise; ye maun turn a' til accoont."

"Guide my tongue a bit better, you would say! But little do you know the temptation of one who has but a single weapon, to make use of that same! And the gift you have you're not to despise; you must turn all to account."

Cosmo did not care to reason with her further, and went back to his father.

Grizzie had gained her point; which was to turn him aside from questions about the meal.

For a little while they had now wherewith to live; and if it seem to my reader that the horizon of hope was narrowing around them, it does not follow that it must have seemed so to them. For what is the extent of our merely rational horizon at any time? But for faith and imagination it would be a narrow one indeed! Even what we call experience is but a stupid kind of faith. It is a trusting in impetus instead of in love. And those days were fashioning an eternal joy to father and son, for they were loving each other a little more ere each day's close, and were thus putting time, despite of fortune, to its highest use.

CHAPTER XLIX
A COMMON MIRACLE

Until he was laid up, Cosmo had all the winter, and especially after his old master was taken ill, gone often to see Mr. Simon. The good man was now beginning, chiefly from the effects of his complaint, to feel the approach of age; but he was cheerful and hopeful as ever, and more expectant. As soon as he was able Cosmo renewed his visits, but seldom stayed long with him, both because Mr. Simon could not bear much talking, and because he knew his father would be watching for his return.

One day it had rained before sunrise, and a soft spring wind had been blowing ever since, a soothing and persuading wind, that seemed to draw out the buds from the secret places of the dry twigs, and whisper to the roots of the rose-trees that their flowers would be wanted by and by. And now the sun was near the foot of the western slope, and there was a mellow, tearful look about earth and sky, when Grizzie, entering the room where Cosmo was reading to his father, as he sat in his easy chair by the fireside, told them she had just heard that Mr. Simon had had a bad night and was worse. The laird begged Cosmo to go at once and inquire after him.

The wind kept him company as he walked, flitting softly about him, like an attendant that needed more motion than his pace would afford, and seemed so full of thought and love, that, for the thousandth time, he wondered whether there could be anything but spirit, and what we call matter might not be merely the consequence of our human way of looking at the wrong side of the golden tissue. Then came the thought of the infinitude of our moods, of the hues and shades and endless kinds and varieties of feeling, especially in our dreams; and he said to himself how rich God must be, since from him we come capable of such inconceivable differences of conscious life!

"How poor and helpless," he said to himself, "how mere a pilgrim and a stranger in a world over which he has no rule, must he be who has not God all one with him! Not otherwise can his life be free save as moving in loveliest harmony with the will and life of the only Freedom—that which wills and we are!"

"How would it be," he thought again, "if things were to come and go as they pleased in my mind and brain? Would that not be madness? For is it not the essence of madness, that things thrust themselves upon one, and by very persistence of seeming, compel and absorb the attention, drowning faith and will in a false conviction? The soul that is empty, swept, and garnished, is the soul which adorns itself, where God is not, and where therefore other souls come and go as they please, drawn by the very selfhood, and make the man the slave of their suggestions. Oneness with the mighty All is at the one end of life; distraction, things going at a thousand foolish wills, at the other. God or chaos is the alternative; all thou hast, or no Christ!"

And as he walked thinking thus, the stream was by his side, tumbling out its music as it ran to find its eternity. And the wind blew on from the moist west, where the gold and purple had fallen together in a ruined heap over the tomb of the sun. And the stars came thinking out of the heavens, and the things of earth withdrew into the great nest of the dark. And so he found himself at the door of the cottage, where lay one of the heirs of all things, waiting to receive his inheritance.

But the news he heard was that the master was better; and the old woman showed him at once to his room, saying she knew he would be glad to see him. When he entered the study, in which, because of his long illness and need of air, Mr. Simon lay, the room seemed to grow radiant, filled with the smile that greeted him from the pillow. The sufferer held out his hand almost eagerly.

"Come, come!" he said; "I want to tell you something—a little experience I have just had—an event of my illness. Outwardly it is nothing, but to you it will not be nothing.—It was blowing a great wind last night."

"So my father tells me," answered Cosmo, "but for my part I slept too sound to hear it."

"It grew calm with the morning. As the light came the wind fell. Indeed I think it lasted only about three hours altogether."

"I have of late been suffering a good deal with my breathing, and it has always been worst when the wind was high. Last night I lay awake in the middle of the night, very weary, and longing for the sleep which seemed as if it would never come. I thought of Sir Philip Sidney, how, as he lay dying, he was troubled, because, for all his praying, God would not let him sleep; it was not the want of sleep that troubled him, but that God would not give it him; and I was trying hard to make myself strong to trust in God whatever came to me, sleep or waking weariness or slow death, when all at once up got the wind with a great roar, as if the prince of the power of the air were mocking my prayers. And I thought with myself, 'It is then the will of God that I shall neither sleep nor lie at peace this night!' and I said 'Thy will be done!' and laid myself out to be quiet, expecting, as on former occasions, my breathing would begin to grow thick and hard, and by and by I should have to struggle for every lungful. So I lay waiting. But still as I waited, I kept breathing softly. No iron band ringed itself about my chest; no sand filled up the passages of my lungs!

"The cottage is not very tight, and I felt the wind blowing all about me as I lay. But instead of beginning to cough and wheeze, I began to breathe better than before. Soon I fell fast asleep, and when I woke I seemed a new man almost, so much better did I feel. It was a wind of God, and had been blowing all about me as I slept, renewing me! It was so strange, and so delightful! Where I dreaded evil, there had come good! So, perchance, it will be when the time which the flesh dreads is drawing nigh: we shall see the pale damps of the grave approaching, but they will never reach us; we shall hear ghastly winds issuing from the mouth of the tomb, but when they blow upon us they shall be sweet—the waving of the wings of the angels that sit in the antechamber of the hall of life, once the sepulchre of our Lord. And when we die, instead of finding we are dead, we shall have waked better!"

It was an experience that would have been nothing to most men beyond its relief, but to Peter Simon it was a word from the eternal heart, which, in every true and quiet mood, speaks into the hearts of men. When we cease listening to the cries of self-seeking and self-care, then the voice that was there all the time enters into our ears. It is the voice of the Father speaking to his child, never known for what it is until the child begins to obey it. To him who has not ears to hear God will not reveal himself: it would be to slay him with terror.

Cosmo sat a long time talking with his friend, for now there seemed no danger of hurting him, so much better was he. It was late therefore when he rose to return.

CHAPTER L
DEFIANCE

Aggie was in the kitchen when he entered. She was making the porridge.

"What's come o' Grizzie?" asked Cosmo.

"What's become of Grizzie?" asked Cosmo.

"Ye dinna like my parritch sae weel as hers!" returned Agnes.

"You don't like my porridge so well as hers!" returned Agnes.

"Jist as weel, Aggie," answered Cosmo.

"Just as well, Aggie," answered Cosmo.

"Dinna ye tell Grizzie that."

"Don't you tell Grizzie that."

"What for no?"

"Why not?"

"She wad be angert first, an' syne her hert wad be like to brak."

"She would be angry first, and then her heart would be like to break."

"There's nae occasion to say't," conceded Cosmo.

"There's no occasion to say it," conceded Cosmo.

"But what's come o' her the nicht?" he went on. "It's some dark, an I doobt she'll—"

"But where is she tonight?" he went on. "It's pretty dark, and I expect she'll—"

"The ro'd atween this an' the Muir's no easy to lowse," said Aggie.

"The road between here and the Muir's not easy to lose," said Aggie.

But the same instant her face flushed hotter than ever fire or cooking made it; what she had said was in itself true, but what she had not said, yet meant him to understand, was not true, for Grizzie had gone nowhere near Muir o' Warlock. Aggie had never told a lie in her life, and almost before the words were out of her mouth, she felt as if the solid earth were sinking from under her feet. She left the spurtle sticking in the porridge, and dropped into the laird's chair.

"What's the maitter wi' ye, Aggie?" said Cosmo, hastening to her in alarm, for her face was now white, and her head was hanging down.

"What's the matter with you, Aggie?" said Cosmo, hastening to her in alarm, for her face was now white, and her head was hanging down.

"This is no to be borne!" she cried, and started to her feet. "—Cosmo, I tellt ye a lee."

"This is not to be borne!" she cried, and started to her feet. "—Cosmo, I told you a lie."

"Aggie!" cried Cosmo, dismayed, "ye never tellt me a lee i' yer life."

"Aggie!" cried Cosmo, dismayed, "you never told me a lie in your life."

"Never afore," she answered; "but I hae tellt ye ane noo—no to live through! Grizzie's no gane to Muir o' Warlock."

"Never before," she answered; "but I have told you one now—not to live through! Grizzie's not gone to Muir of Warlock."

"What care I whaur Grizzie's gane!" rejoined Cosmo. "tell me or no tell me as ye like."

"What care I where Grizzie's gone!" rejoined Cosmo. "tell me or don't tell me as you like."

Aggie burst into tears.

Aggie burst into tears.

"Haud yer tongue, Aggie," said Cosmo, trying to soothe her, himself troubled with her trouble, for he too was sorry she should *almost* have told him a lie, and his heart was sore for her misery. Well he knew how she must suffer, having done a thing so foreign to her nature! "It *could* be little mair at the warst," he went on, "than a slip o'the wull, seein ye made sic haste to set it richt again. For mysel', I s' bainish the thoucht o' the thing."

"Hold your tongue, Aggie," said Cosmo, trying to soothe her, himself troubled with her trouble, for he too was sorry she should *almost* have told him a lie, and his heart was sore for her misery. Well he knew how she must suffer, having done a thing so foreign to her nature! "It *could* be little more at the worst," he went on, "than a slip of the will, seeing you made such haste to set it right again. For myself, I shall banish the thought of the thing."

"I thank ye, Cosmo. Ye wad aye du like the Lord himsel'. But there's mair intil 't. I dinna ken what to du or say. It's a sair thing to stan' atween twa, an' no ken what to du ohn dune mischeef—maybe wrang!—There's something it 'maist seems to me ye hae a richt to ken, but I canna be sure; an yet—"

"I thank you, Cosmo. You would always do like the Lord himself. But there's more to it. I don't know what to do or say. It's hard to stand between two, and not know what to do without doing mischief—maybe wrong!—There's something it almost seems to me you have a right to know, but I can't be sure; and yet—"

She was interrupted by the hurried opening of the door. Grizzie came staggering in, with a face of terror.

"Tu wi' the door!" she cried, almost speechless, and sank in her turn upon a chair, gasping for breath, and dropping at her feet a canvas bag, about the size of a pillow-case.

She was interrupted by the hurried opening of the door. Grizzie came staggering in, with a face of terror.

"Shut the door!" she cried, almost speechless, and sank in her turn upon a chair, gasping for breath, and dropping at her feet a canvas bag, about the size of a pillow-case.

Cosmo closed the door as she requested, and Aggie made haste to get her some water, which she drank eagerly. After a time of panting and sighing, she seemed to come to herself, and rose, saying, as if nothing had happened,

"I maun see to the supper."

"I must see to the supper."

Cosmo stooped and would have taken up the bag, but she pounced upon it, and carried it with her to the corner of the fire, where she placed it beyond her. In the meantime the porridge had begun to burn.

"Eh, sirs!" she cried, "the parritch 'll be a' sung—no to mention the waste o' guid meal! Aggie, hoo cud ye be sae careless!"

"It was eneuch to gar onybody forget the pot to see you come in like that, Grizzie!" said Cosmo.

"An' what'll ye say to the tale I bring ye!" rejoined Grizzie, as she turned the porridge into a dish, careful not to scrape too hard on the bottom of the pot.

"Tell's a' aboot it, Grizzie, an' bena lang aither, for I maun gang to my father."

"Gang til 'im. Here's naebody wad keep ye frae 'im!"

"Eh, sirs!" she cried, "the porridge will be all burned—not to mention the waste of good meal! Aggie, how could you be so careless!"

"It was enough to make anybody forget the pot to see you come in like that, Grizzie!" said Cosmo.

"And what'll you say to the tale I bring you!" rejoined Grizzie, as she turned the porridge into a dish, careful not to scrape too hard on the bottom of the pot.

"Tell us all about it Grizzie, and don't take long either, for I must go to my father."

"Go to him. No one here would keep you from him!

Cosmo was surprised at her tone, for although she took abundant liberty with the young laird, he had not since boyhood known her rude to him.

"No till I hear yer tale, Grizzie," he answered.

"An' I wad fain ken what ye'll say til 't, for ye never wad alloo o' kelpies; an' there's me been followed by a sure ane, this last half-hoor—or it may be less!"

"Hoo kenned ye it was a kelpie—it's maist as dark 's pick?"

"Kenned! quo' he? Didna I hear the deevil ahin' me—the tramp o' a' the fower feet o' 'im, as gien they had been fower an' twinty!"

"Not till I hear your tale, Grizzie," he answered.

"And I fain would know what you'll say to it, for you never believed in kelpies; and I've just been followed by a sure one, this last half-hour—or it may be less!"

"How did you know it was a kelpie—it's about as dark as pitch?"

"Knew! said he? Didn't I hear the devil behind me—the tramp of all his four feet, as if they had been four-and-twenty!"

"I won'er he didna win up wi ye than, Grizzie!" suggested Cosmo.

"Guid kens hoo he didna; I won'er mysel'. But I trow I ran; an' I tak ye to witness I garred ye steik the door."

"But they say," objected Cosmo, who could not fail to perceive from what Aggie said that there was something going on which it behooved him to know, "that the kelpie wons aye by some watterside."

"Weel, cam I no by the tarn o' the tap o' Stieve Know?"

"What on earth was ye duin' there after dark, Grizzie?"

"What was I duin'? I saidna I was there efter dark, but the cratur micht hae seen me pass weel eneuch. Wasna I ower the hill to my ain fowk i' the How o' Hap? An' didna I come hame by Luck's Lift? Mair by token, wadna the guidman o' that same hae me du what I haena dune this twae year, or maybe twenty—tak a dram? An' didna I tak it? An' was I no in need o' 't? An' didna I come hame a' the better for 't?"

An' get a sicht o' the kelpy intil the bargain—eh, Grizzie?" suggested Cosmo.

"Hoots! gang awa up to the laird, an' lea' me to get my breath an' your supper thegither," said Grizzie, who saw to what she had exposed herself. "An' I wuss ye may see the neist kelpy yersel'! Only whatever ye du, Cosmo, dinna m'unt upo' the back o' 'im, for he'll cairry ye straucht hame til 's maister; an' we a' ken wha *he* is."

"I'm no gaein'," said Cosmo, as soon as the torrent of her speech allowed him room to answer, "till I ken what ye hae i' that pock o' yours."

"Hoot!" cried Grizzie, and snatching up the bag, held it behind her back, "ye wad never mint at luikin' intil an auld wife's pock! What ken ye what she michtna hae there?"

"It luiks to me naither mair nor less nor a meal-pock," said Cosmo.

"Meal-pock!" returned Grizzie with contempt: "what neist!"

"I wonder he didn't catch up with you then, Grizzie!" suggested Cosmo.

"Lord knows how he didn't; I wonder myself. But I believe I ran; and I take you to witness I made you shut the door."

"But they say," objected Cosmo, who could not fail to perceive from what Aggie said that there was something going on which it behooved him to know, "that the kelpie always lives by some waterside."

"Well, didn't I come by the tarn on the top of Stieve Hill?"

"What on earth were you doing there after dark, Grizzie?"

"What was I doing? I didn't say I was there after dark, but the creature might have seen me pass well enough. Wasn't I over the hill to my own folk in the Hap Valley? And didn't I come home by Luck's Lift? Moreover, wouldn't the goodman there have me do what I haven't done these two years, or maybe twenty—take a dram? And didn't I take it? And wasn't I in need of it? And didn't I come home all the better for it?"

"And get a sight of the kelpy into the bargain—eh, Grizzie?" suggested Cosmo.

"Heavens! go away up to the laird, and leave me to get my breath and your supper together," said Grizzie, who saw to what she had exposed herself. "And I wish you may see the next kelpy yourself! Only whatever you do, Cosmo, don't mount upon his back, for he'll carry you straight home to his master; and we all know who *he* is."

"I'm not going," said Cosmo, as soon as the torrent of her speech allowed him room to answer, "till I know what you have in that bag of yours."

"Heavens!" cried Grizzie, and snatching up the bag, held it behind her back, "you would never try to look into an old wife's bag! You never know what she might not have there!"

"It looks to me neither more nor less than a meal-bag," said Cosmo.

"Meal-bag!" returned Grizzie with contempt: "what next!"

He made another movement to seize the bag, but she caught the spurtle from the empty porridge-pot and showed fight with it, genuine earnest beyond a doubt for the defence of her bag. Whatever the secret was, it looked as if the bag were somehow connected with it. Cosmo began to grow very uncomfortable. So strange were his nascent suspicions that he dared not for a time allow them to take shape in his brain lest they should thereby start at once into the life of fact. His mind had, for the last few days, been much occupied with the question of miracles. Why, he thought with himself, should one believing there is in very truth a live, thinking, perfect Power at the heart and head of affairs, count it impossible that, in their great and manifest need, their meal-chest should be supplied like that of the widow of Zarephath? If he could believe the thing was done then, there could be nothing absurd in hoping the thing might be done now. If it was possible once, it was possible in the same circumstances always. It was impossible, however, for him or any human being to determine concerning any circumstances whether they were or were not the same. Wherever the thing was not done, did it not follow that the circumstances could not be the same? One thing he was able to see—that, in the altered relations of man's mind to the facts of Nature, a larger faith is necessary to believe in the constantly present and ordering will of the Father of men, than in the unusual phenomenon of a miracle. In the meantime it was a fact that they had all hitherto had their daily bread.

But now this strange behaviour of Grizzie set him thinking of something very different. And why did not the jeweller make some reply to his request concerning the things he had sent him? He said to himself for the hundredth time that he must have found it impossible to do anything with them, and have delayed writing from unwillingness to cause him disappointment, but he could not help a growing soreness that his friend should take no notice of the straits he had confessed himself in. The conclusion of the whole matter was, that it must be the design of Providence to make him part with the last clog that fettered him; he was to have no ease in life until he had yielded the castle! If it were so, then the longer he delayed the greater would be the loss. To sell everything in it first would but put off the evil day, preparing for them so much the more poverty when it should come; whereas if he were to part with the house, and take his father where he could find work, they would be able to have some of the old things about them still, to tincture strangeness with home. The more he thought the more it seemed his duty to put a stop to the hopeless struggle by consenting in full and without reserve to the social degradation and heart-sorrow to which it seemed the will of God to bring them. Then with new courage he might commence a new endeavour, no more on the slippery slope of descent, but with the firm ground of the Valley of Humiliation under their feet. Long they could not go on as now, and he was ready to do whatever was required of him, only he wished God would make it plain. The part of discipline he liked least—a part of which doubtless we do not yet at all understand the good or necessity—was uncertainty of duty, the uncertainty of what it was God's will he should do. But on the other hand, perhaps the cause of that uncertainty was the lack of perfect readiness; perhaps all that was wanted to make duty plain was absolute will to do it.

These and other such thoughts went flowing and ebbing for hours in his mind that night, until at last he bethought himself that his immediate duty was plain enough—namely, to go to sleep. He yielded his consciousness therefore to him from whom it came, and fell asleep.

CHAPTER LI
DISCOVERY AND CONFESSION

In the morning he woke wondering whether God would that day let him know what he had to do. He was certain he would not have him leave his father; anything else in the way of trouble he could believe possible.

The season was now approaching the nominal commencement of summer, but the morning was very cold. He went to the window. Air and earth had the look of a black frost—the most ungenial, the most killing of weathers. Alas! that was his father's breathing: his bronchitis was worse! He made haste to fetch fuel and light the fire, then leaving him still asleep, went down stairs. He was earlier than usual, and Grizzie was later; only Aggie was in the kitchen. Her grandfather was worse also. Everything pointed to severer straitening and stronger necessity: this must be how God was letting him know what he had to do!

He sat down and suddenly, for a moment, felt as if he were sitting on the opposite bank of the Warlock river, looking up at the house where he was born and had spent his days—now the property of another, and closed to him forever! Within those walls he could not order the removal of a straw! could not chop a stick to warm his father! "The will of God be done!" he said, and the vision was gone.

Aggie was busy getting his porridge ready—which Cosmo had by this time learned to eat without any accompaniment—and he bethought himself that here was a chance of questioning her before Grizzie should appear.

"Come, Aggie," he said abruptly, "I want to ken what for Grizzie was in sic a terror aboot her pock last nicht. I'm thinkin' I hae a richt to ken."

"I wish ye wadna speir," returned Aggie, after but a moment's pause.

"Aggie," said Cosmo, "gien ye tell me it's nane o' my business, I winna speir again."

"Ye *are* guid, Cosmo, efter the w'y I behaved to ye last nicht," she answered, with a tremble in her voice.

"Dinna think o' 't nae mair, Aggie. To me it is as gien it had never been. My hert's the same to ye as afore—an' justly. I believe I un'erstan' ye whiles 'maist as well as ye du yersel'."

"I houp whiles ye un'erstan' me better," answered Aggie. "Sair do I m'urn 'at the shaidow o' that lee ever crossed my min'."

"It was but a shaidow," said Cosmo.

"But what wad ye think o' yersel, gien it had been you 'at sae near—na, I winna nibble at the trowth ony mair—gien it had been you, I wull say't, 'at lee'd that lee—sic an ane as it was?"

"I wad say to mysel' 'at wi God's help I was the less lik'ly ever to tell a lee again; for that

"Come, Aggie," he said abruptly, "I want to know why Grizzie was in such terror about her bag last night. I think I have a right to know."

"I wish you wouldn't ask," returned Aggie, after but a moment's pause.

"Aggie," said Cosmo, "if you tell me it's none of my business, I won't ask again."

"You *are* good, Cosmo, after the way I behaved to you last night," she answered, with a tremble in her voice.

"Don't think of it any more, Aggie. To me it's as if it had never been. My heart's the same to you as before—and justly. I believe I understand you sometimes almost as well as you do yourself."

"I hope sometimes you understand me better," answered Aggie. "I wish from my soul that the shadow of that lie never crossed my mind."

"It was but a shadow," said Cosmo.

"But what would you think of yourself, if it had been you that so nearly—na, I won't nibble at the truth any more—if it had been you, I will say it, that lied that lie—such a one as it was?"

"I would say to myself that with God's help I was the less likely ever to tell a lie again;

noo I un'erstude better hoo a temptation micht come upon a body a' at ance, ohn gien 'im time to reflec'—an' sae my responsibility was the greater."

"Thank ye, Cosmo," said Aggie humbly, and was silent.

"But," resumed Cosmo, "ye haena tellt me yet 'at it's nane o' my business what Grizzie had in her pock last nicht."

"Na, I cudna tell ye that, 'cause it wadna be true. It is yer business."

"What was i' the pock than?"

"Weel, Cosmo, ye put me in a great diffeeculty; for though I never said to Grizzie I wadna tell, I made nae objection—though at the time I didna like it—whan she tellt me what she was gaein' to du; an' sae I canna help fearin' it may be fause to her to tell ye. Besides, I hae latten 't gang sae lang ohn said a word, 'at the guid auld body cud never jaloose I wad turn upon her noo an' tell!"

"You are dreadfully mysterious, Aggie," said Cosmo, "and in truth you make me more than a little uncomfortable. What can it be that has been going on so long, and had better not be told me! Have I a right to know or have I not?"

"Ye hae a richt to ken, I do believe, else I wadna tell ye," answered Aggie. "I was terrified, frae the first, to think what ye wad say til 't! But ye see, what was there left? You, an' the laird, an' my father was a' laid up thegither, heaps o' things wantit, the meal dune, an' life depen'in' upo' fowk haein' what they cud ait an' drink!"

because now I understood better how a temptation might come upon someone all at once, without giving him time to reflect—and so my responsibility was the greater."

"Thank you, Cosmo," said Aggie humbly, and was silent.

"But," resumed Cosmo, "you haven't told me yet that it's none of my business what Grizzie had in her bag last night."

"Na, I couldn't tell you that, because it wouldn't be true. It is your business."

"What was in the bag then?"

"Well, Cosmo, you put me in a great difficulty; for though I never said to Grizzie I wouldn't tell, I made no objection—though at the time I didn't like it—when she told me what she was going to do; and so I can't help fearing it may be false to her to tell you. Besides, I have let it go so long without saying a word, that the good old woman could never suspect I would turn upon her now and tell!"

"You are dreadfully mysterious, Aggie," said Cosmo, "and in truth you make me more than a little uncomfortable. What can it be that has been going on so long, and had better not be told me! Have I a right to know or have I not?"

"You have a right to know, I do believe, else I wouldn't tell you," answered Aggie. "I was terrified, from the first, to think what you would say about it! But you see, what was there left? You, and the laird, and my father were all laid up together, heaps of things wanted, the meal finished, and life depending upon folk having what they could eat and drink!"

As she spoke, shadowy horror was deepening to monster presence; the incredible was gradually assuming shape and fact; the hair of Cosmo's head seemed rising up. He asked no more questions, but sat waiting the worst.

"Dinna be ower hard upo' Grizzie an' me, Cosmo," Aggie went on, "It wansa for oorsel's we wad hae dune sic a thing; an' maybe there was nane but them we did it for 'at we wad hae been able to du't for. But I hae no richt to say *we*. Blame, gien there be ony, I hae my share o'; but praise, gien there be ony, she has't a'; for, that the warst michtna come to the warst, at the last she took the meal-pock," said Aggie, and burst into tears as she said it, "An' gaed oot wi' 't."

"Don't be too hard upon Grizzie and me, Cosmo," Aggie went on. "It wasn't for ourselves we would have done such a thing; and maybe there were none but those we did it for that we would have been able to do it for. But I have no right to say *we*. Blame, if there be any, I have my share of; but praise, if there be any, she has it all; for, that the worst mightn't come to the worst, at the last she took the meal-bag," said Aggie, and burst into tears as she said it, "And went out with it."

"Good God!" cried Cosmo, and for some moments was dumb. "Lassie!" he said at length, in a voice that was not like his own, "didna ye ken i' yer ain sowl we wad raither hae dee'd?"

"There 'tis! That's jist what for Grizzie wadna hae ye tellt! But dinna think she gaed to ony place whaur she was kent," sobbed Agnes, "or appeart to ony to be ither than a puir auld body 'at gaed aboot for hersel'. Dinna think aither 'at ever she tellt a lee, or said a word to gar fowk pity her. She had aye afore her the possibility o' bein' ca'd til accoont some day. But I'm thinkin' gien ye had applyt to her an' no to me, ye wad hae h'ard anither mak o' a defence frae mine! Ae thing ye may be sure o'—there's no a body a hair the wiser."

"What difference does that make?" cried Cosmo. "The fact remains."

"Hoot, Cosmo!" said Agnes, with a revival of old authority, "ye're takin' the thing in a fashion no worthy o' a philosopher—no to say a Christian. Ye tak it as gien there was shame intil 't! An' gien there wasna shame, I daur ye to priv there can be ony disgrace! Gien ye come to that wi' 't, hoo was the Lord o' a' himsel' supportit whan he gaed aboot cleanin' oot the warl'? Wasna it the women 'at gaed wi' 'im 'at providit a' thing?"

"Good God!" cried Cosmo, and for some moments was dumb. "Lassie!" he said at length, in a voice that was not like his own, "didn't you know in your own soul we would rather have died?"

"There it is! That's just why Grizzie wouldn't have you told! But don't think she went to any place where she was known," sobbed Agnes, "or appeared to any to be other than a poor old woman who went about for herself. Don't think either that she ever told a lie, or said a word to make folk pity her. She had always before her the possibility of being called to account some day. But I'm thinking if you had applied to her and not to me, you would have heard another style of a defence from mine! One thing you may be sure of—there's nobody one hair the wiser."

"What difference does that make?" cried Cosmo. "The fact remains."

"Heavens, Cosmo!" said Agnes, with a revival of old authority, "you're taking the thing in a fashion not worthy of a philosopher—not to say a Christian. You take it as if there was shame in it! And if there wasn't shame, I dare you to prove there can be any disgrace! If you come to that, how was the Lord of all himself supported when he went about cleaning out the world? Wasn't it the women who went with him who provided everything?"

"True; but that was very different! They knew him, all of them, and loved him—knew that he was doing what no money could pay for; that he was working himself to death for them and for their people—that he was earning the whole world. Or at least they had a far off notion that he was doing as never man did, for they knew he spake as never man spake. Besides there was no begging there. He never asked them for anything."—Here Aggie shook her head in unbelief, but Cosmo went on—"And those women, some of them anyhow, were rich, and proud to do what they did for the best and grandest of men. But what have we done for the world that we should dare to look up to it to help us?"

"For that maitter, Cosmo, are na we a' brithers an' sisters? A' body's brithers an' sisters wi' a' body. It's but a kin' o' a some mean pride 'at wadna be obleeged to yer ain fowk, efter ye hae dune yer best. Cosmo! ilka han'fu' o' meal gi'en i' this or ony hoose by them 'at wadna in like need accep' the same, is an affront frae brither to brither. Them 'at wadna tak, I say, has no richt to gie."

"But nobody knew the truth of where their handful of meal was going. They thought

"For that matter, Cosmo, aren't we all brothers and sisters? Each is brother and sister to each. It's but a kind of meanest pride that wouldn't be obliged to your own folk, after you have done your best. Cosmo! every handful of meal given in this or any house by those who wouldn't in like need accept the same, is an affront from brother to brother. Those who wouldn't take, I say, have no right to give."

"But nobody knew the truth of where their handful of meal was going. They thought they were giving it to a poor old woman, when they were in fact giving it to men with a great house over their heads. It's a disgrace, an' hard to beir, Aggie!"

"'Deed, the thing's hard upon 's a! but whaur the disgrace is, I will not condescen' to see. Men in a muckle hoose! Twa o' them auld, an' a' three i' their beds, no fit to muv! Div ye think there's ane o' them 'at gied to Grizzie, 'at wad hae gi'en less—though what less nor the han'fu' o' meal, which was a' she ever got, it wad be hard to imaigine—had they kent it was for the life o' auld Glenwarlock—a name respeckit, an' mair nor respeckit, whaurever it's h'ard?—or for the life o' the yoong laird, vroucht to deith wi' labourers' wark, an syne 'maist smoored i' storm?—or for auld Jeames Gracie, 'at's led a God-fearin' life till he's 'maist ower auld to live ony langer? I say naething aboot Grizzie an' me, wha cud aye tak care o' oorsel's gien we hadna three dowie men to luik efter. We did oor best, but whan a' oor ain siller was awa' efter the lave, we cudna win awa' oorsel's to win mair. Gien you three cud hae dune for yersel's, we wad hae been sen'in' ye hame something."

"You tell me," said Cosmo, as if in a painful dream, through which flashed lovely lights, "that you and Grizzie spent all your own money upon us, and then Grizzie went out and begged for us?"

"'Deed, there's no anither word for't—nor was there ae thing ither to be dune!" Aggie drew herself up, and went on with solemnity. "Div ye think, Cosmo, whaur heid or hert or fit or han' cud du onything to waur off want or tribble frae you or the laird, 'at Grizzie or mysel' wad be wantin' that day? I beg o' yer grace ye winna lay to oor chairge what we war driven til. As Grizzie says, we war jist at ane mair wi' desperation."

they were giving it to a poor old woman, when they were in fact giving it to men with a great house over their heads. It's a disgrace, and hard to bear, Aggie!"

"Indeed, the thing's hard upon us all! but where the disgrace is, I will not condescend to see. Men in a great house! Two of them old, and all three in their beds, not fit to move! Do you think there's one of those who gave to Grizzie, who would have given less—though what less than the handful of meal, which was all she ever got, it would be hard to imagine—had they known it was for the life of old Glenwarlock—a name respected, and more than respected, wherever it's heard?—or for the life of the young laird, wrought to death with labourers' work, and then all but smothered in storm?—or for old Jeames Gracie, who's led a God-fearing life till he's almost too old to live any longer? I say nothing about Grizzie and me, who could always take care of ourselves if we hadn't three sick men to look after. We did our best, but when all our own money was away after the rest, we couldn't get away ourselves to earn more. If you three could have managed alone, we would have been sending you home something."

"You tell me," said Cosmo, as if in a painful dream, through which flashed lovely lights, "that you and Grizzie spent all your own money upon us, and then Grizzie went out and begged for us?"

"Indeed, there's no other word for it—nor was there one thing other to be done!" Aggie drew herself up, and went on with solemnity. "Do you think, Cosmo, where head or heart or foot or hand could do anything to ward off want or trouble from you or the laird, that Grizzie or I would be wanting that day? I beg of your grace not to lay to our charge what we were driven to. As Grizzie says, we were just beside ourselves with desperation."

Cosmo's heart was full. He dared not speak. He came to Aggie, and taking her hand, looked her in the face with eyes full of tears. She had been pale as sun-browned could be, but now she grew red as a misty dawn. Her eyes fell, and she began to pull at the hem of her apron. Grizzie's step was on the stair, and Cosmo, not quite prepared to meet her, walked out.

The morning was neither so black nor so cold as he had imagined it. He went into the garden, to the nook between the two blocks, there sat down, and tried to think. The sun was not far above the horizon, and he was in the cold shade of the kitchen-tower, but he felt nothing, and sat there motionless. The sun came southward, looked round the corner, and found him there. He brought with him a lovely fresh day. The leaves were struggling out, and the birds had begun to sing. Ah! what a day was here, had the hope of the boy been still swelling in his bosom! But the decree had gone forth! no doubt remained! no refuge of uncertainty was left! The house must follow the land! Castle Warlock and the last foothold of soil must go, that wrong should not follow ruin! Were those divine women to spend money, time, and labour, that he and his father should hold what they had no longer any right to hold? Or in beggary, were they to hide themselves in the yet lower depth of begging by proxy, in their grim stronghold, living upon unacknowledged charity, as their ancestors on plunder! He dared not tell his father what he had discovered until he had taken at least the first step towards putting an end to the whole falsehood. To delay due action was of all things what Cosmo dreaded; and as the loss mainly affected himself, the yielding of the castle must primarily be his deed and not his father's. He rose at once to do it.

The same moment the incubus of Grizzie's meal-bag was lifted from his bosom. The shame was, if shame was any, that they should have been living in such a house while the thing was done. When the house was sold, let people say what they would! In proportion as a man cares to do what he ought, he ceases to care how it may be judged. Of all things why should a true man heed the unjust judgement?

"If there be any stain upon us," he said to himself, "God will see that we have the chance of wiping it out!"

With that he got over gate and wall, and took his way along Grizzie's path, once more, for the time at least, an undisputed possession of the people.

But while he was thinking in the garden, Grizzie, who knew from Aggie that her secret was such no more, was in dire distress in the kitchen, fearing she had offended the young laird beyond remedy. In great anxiety she kept going every minute to the door, to see if he were not coming in to have his breakfast. But the first she saw of him was his back, as he leaped from the top of the wall. She ran after him to the gate.

"Sir! sir!" she cried, "come back; come back, an' I'll gang doon upo' my auld knees to beg yer pardon."	"Sir! sir!" she cried, "come back; come back, and I'll go down upon my old knees to beg your pardon."

Cosmo turned the moment he heard her, and went back.

When he reached the wall, over the top of the gate he saw Grizzie on her knees upon the round paving stones of the yard, stretching up her old hands to him, as if he were some heavenly messenger just descended, whose wrath she deprecated. He jumped over wall and gate, ran to her, and lifted her to her feet, saying,

"Grizzie, wuman, what are ye aboot! Bless ye, Grizzie, I wad 'maist as sune strive wi' my ain mither whaur she shines i' glory, as wi' you!"	"Grizzie, woman, what are you about! Bless you, Grizzie, I would almost as soon strive with my own mother where she shines in glory, as with you!"

Grizzie's face began to work like that of a child in an agony between pride and tears, just ere he breaks into a howl. She gripped his arm hard with both hands, and at length faltered out, gathering composure as she proceeded,

"Cosmo, ye're like an angel o' God to a' 'at hae to du wi' ye! Eh, sic an accoont o' ye as I'll hae to gie to the mither o' ye whan I win to see her! For surely they'll lat me see her, though they may weel no think me guid eneuch to bide wi' her up there, for as lang as we was	"Cosmo, you're like an angel of the Lord to all that have to do with you! Eh, such an account of you as I'll have to give to your mother when I reach her! For surely they'll let me see her, though they may well not think me good enough to stay with her up there, for as

thegither doon here! Tell me, sir, what wad ye hae me du. But jist ae thing I maun say:—gien I hadna dune as I did du, I do not see hoo we cud hae won throu' the winter."

"Grizzie," said Cosmo, "I ken ye did a' for the best, an' maybe it was the best. The day may come, Grizzie, whan we'll gang thegither to ca' upo' them 'at pat the meal i' yer pock, an' return them thanks for their kin'ness."

"Eh, na, sir! That wad never du! What for sud they ken onything aboot it! They war jist kin'-like at lairge, an' no to naebody in partic'lar, like the man wi' his sweirin'. They gae to me jist as they wad to ony unco beggar wife. It was to me they gae't, no to you. Lat it a' lie upo' me."

"That canna be, Grizzie," said Cosmo. "Ye see ye're ane o' the faimily, an' whatever ye du, I maun haud my face til."

"God bless ye, sir!" exclaimed Grizzie, and turned towards the house, entirely relieved and satisfied.

"But eh, sir!" she cried, turning again, "ye haena broken yer fast the day!"

"I'll be back in a feow minutes, an' mak a brakfast o' 't by or'nar'," answered Cosmo, and hastened away up the hill.

long as we were together down here! Tell me, sir, what would you have me do. But just one thing I must say:—if I hadn't done as I did, I do not see how we could have made it through the winter."

"Grizzie," said Cosmo, "I know you did all for the best, and maybe it was the best. The day may come, Grizzie, when we'll go together to call upon those who put the meal in your bag, and return them thanks for their kindness."

"Eh, na, sir! That would never do! Why should they know anything about it! They were just generally kind, and not to anybody in particular, like the man with his swearing. They gave to me just as they would to any strange beggar-wife. It was to me they gave it, not to you. Let it all lie upon me."

"That can't be, Grizzie," said Cosmo. "You see you're one of the family, and whatever you do, I must hold my face to."

"God bless you, sir!" exclaimed Grizzie, and turned towards the house, entirely relieved and satisfied.

"But eh, sir!" she cried, turning again, "you haven't broken your fast today!"

"I'll be back in a few minutes, and have a breakfast to remember," answered Cosmo, and hastened away up the hill.

CHAPTER LII
IT IS NAUGHT, SAITH THE BUYER.

When Cosmo reached the gate of his lordship's *policy*, he found it closed, and although he both rang the bell, and called lustily to the gate-keeper, no one appeared. He put a hand on the top of the gate, and lightly vaulted clean over it. But just as he lighted, who should come round a bend in the drive a few yards off, but lord Lick-my-loof himself, out for his morning-walk! His irritable cantankerous nature would have been annoyed at sight of anyone treating his gate with such disrespect, but when he saw who it was that thus made nothing of it—clearing it with as much contempt as a lawyer would a quibble not his own—his displeasure grew to indignation and anger.

"I beg your pardon, my lord," said Cosmo, taking the first word that apology might be immediate, "I could make no one hear me, and therefore took the liberty of describing a parabola over your gate."

"A verra ill fashiont parabola in my judgement, Mr. Warlock! I fear you have been learning of late to think too little of the rights of property."

"A very ill fashioned parabola in my judgement, Mr. Warlock! I fear you have been learning of late to think too little of the rights of property."

"If I had put my foot on your new paint, my lord, I should have been to blame; but I vaulted clean over, and touched nothing more than if the gate had been opened to me."

"I'll have an iron gate!"

"Not on my account, my lord, I hope; for I have come to ask you to put it out of my power to offend any more, by enabling me to leave Glenwarlock."

"Well?" returned his lordship, and waited.

"I find myself compelled at last," said Cosmo, not without some tremor in his voice, which he did his best to quench, "to give you the refusal, according to your request, of the remainder of my father's property."

"House and all?"

"Everything except the furniture."

"Which I do not want."

A silence followed.

"May I ask if your lordship is prepared to make me an offer?—or will you call on my father when you have made up your mind?"

"I will give you two hundred pounds for the lot."

"Two hundred pounds!" repeated Cosmo, who had not expected a large offer, but was unprepared for one so small; "why, my lord, the bare building material would be worth more than that!"

"Not to take it down. I might as well blast it fresh from the quarry. I know the sort of thing those walls of yours are! Vitrified with age, by George! But I don't want to build, and standing the place is of no use to me. I should but let it crumble away at its leisure!"

Cosmo's dream rose again before his mind's eye; but it was no more with pain; for if the dear old place was to pass from their hands, what other end could be desired for it!

"But the sum you mention, my lord, would not, after paying the little we owe, leave us enough to take us from the place!"

"That I should be sorry for; but as to paying, many a better man has never done that. You have my offer: take it or leave it. You'll not get half as much if it come to the hammer. To whom else would it be worth anything, bedded in my property? If I say I don't want it, see if anybody will!"

Cosmo's heart sank afresh. He dared not part with the place off hand on such terms, but must consult his father: his power of action was for the time exhausted; he could do no more alone—not even to spare his father.

"I must speak to the laird," he said. "I doubt if he will accept your offer."

"As he pleases. But I do not promise to let the offer stand. I make it now—not to-morrow, or an hour hence."

"I must run the risk," answered Cosmo. "Will you allow me to jump the gate?"

But his lordship had a key, and preferred opening it.

When Cosmo reached his father's room, he found him not yet thinking of getting up, and sat down and told him all—to what straits they were reduced; what Grizzie had felt herself compelled to do in his illness; how his mind and heart and conscience had been exercised concerning the castle; how all his life, for so it seemed now, the love of it had held him to the dust; where and on what errand he had been that morning, with the result of his interview with Lord Lick-my-loof. He had fought hard, he said, and through the grace of God had overcome his weakness—so far at least that it should no more influence his action; but now he could go no further without his father. He was equal to no more.

"I would not willingly be left out of your troubles, my son," said the old man, cheerfully. "Leave me alone a little. There is one, you know, who is nearer to each of us than we are to each other: I must talk to him—your father and my father, in whom you and I are brothers."

Cosmo bowed in reverence, and withdrew.

After the space of nearly half an hour, he heard the signal with which his father was in the habit of calling him, and hastened to him.

The laird held out his old hand to him.

"Come, my son," he said, "and let us talk together as two of the heirs of all things. It's unco easy for me to regaird wi' equanimity the loss o' a place I am on the point o' leavin' for the hame o' a' hames—the dwellin' o' a' the loves, withoot the dim memory or foresicht o' which—I'm thinkin' they maun be aboot the same thing—we could never hae lo'ed this auld place as we du, an' whaur, ance I'm in, a'thing doon here maun dwindle ootworthied by reason o' the glory that excelleth—I dinna mean the glory o' pearls an' gowd, or even o' licht, but the glory o' love an' trowth. But gien I've ever had onything to ca' an ambition, Cosmo, it has been that my son should be ane o' the wise, wi' faith to believe what his father had learned afore him, an' sae start farther on upo' the narrow way than his father had startit. My ambition has been that my endeavours and my experience should in such measure avail for my boy, as that he should begin to make his own endeavours and gather his own experience a little nearer that perfection o' life efter which oor divine nature groans an' cries, even while unable to know what it wants. Blessed be the voice that tells us we maun

"Come, my son," he said, "and let us talk together as two of the heirs of all things. It's very easy for me to regard with equanimity the loss of a place I am on the point of leaving for the home of all homes—the dwelling of all the loves, without the dim memory or foresight of which—I think they must be about the same thing—we could never have loved this old place as we do, and where, once I'm in, everything down here must dwindle outworthied by reason of the glory that excelleth—I don't mean the glory of pearls and gold, or even of light, but the glory of love and truth. But if ever I had anything to call an ambition, Cosmo, it has been that my son should be one of the wise, with faith to believe what his father had learned before him, and so start farther on upon the narrow way than his father had started. My ambition has been that my endeavours and my experience should in such measure avail for my boy, as that he should begin to make his own endeavours and gather his own experience a little nearer that perfection of life after which our divine nature groans and cries, even while unable to know what it wants. Blessed

forsake all, and take up our cross, and follow him, losing our life that we may find it! For whaur wad he hae us follow him but til his ain hame, to the verra bosom o' his God an' oor God, there to be ane wi' the Love essential!"

be the voice that tells us we must forsake all, and take up our cross, and follow him, losing our life that we may find it! For where would he have us follow him but to his own home, to the very bosom of his God and our God, there to be one with the Love essential!"

Such a son as Cosmo could not listen to such a father saying such things, and not drop the world as if it were no better than the burnt out cinder of the moon.

"When men desire great things, then is God ready to hear them," he said; "and so it is, I think, father, that he has granted your desires for me: I desire nothing but to fulfil my calling."

"Then ye can pairt wi' the auld hoose ohn grutten?"

"As easy, father, as wi' a piece whan I wasna hungry. I do not say that another mood may not come, for you know the flesh lusteth against the spirit as well as the spirit against the flesh; but in my present mood of light and peace, I rejoice to part with the house as a victory of the spirit. Shall I go to his lordship at once and accept his offer? I am ready."

"Do, my son. I think I have not long to live, and the money, though a little, is large in this, that it will enable me to pay the last of my debts, and die in the knowledge that I leave you a free man. You will easily provide for yourself when I am gone, and I know you will not forget Grizzie. For Jeames Gracie, he maun hae his share o' the siller because o' the croft: we maun calculate it fairly. He'll no want muckle mair i' this warl'. Aggie 'ill be as safe's an angel ony gait. An', Cosmo, whatever God may mean to du wi' you i' this warl', ye'll hae an abundant entrance ministered to ye intil the kingdom o' oor Lord an' Saviour. Wha daur luik for a better fate nor that o' the Lord himsel'! But there was them 'at by faith obtained kingdoms, as weel as them wha by faith were sawn asunder: they war baith martryrdoms; an' whatever God sen's, we s' tak."

"Then you accept the two hundred for croft and all, father?"

"Dinna ettle at a penny more; he micht gang back upo 't. Regaird it as his final offer."

"When men desire great things, then is God ready to hear them," he said; "and so it is, I think, father, that he has granted your desires for me: I desire nothing but to fulfil my calling."

"Then you can part with the old house without a tear?"

"As easily, father, as with a snack when I wasn't hungry. I do not say that another mood may not come, for you know the flesh lusteth against the spirit as well as the spirit against the flesh; but in my present mood of light and peace, I rejoice to part with the house as a victory of the spirit. Shall I go to his lordship at once and accept his offer? I am ready."

"Do, my son. I think I have not long to live, and the money, though a little, is large in this, that it will enable me to pay the last of my debts, and die in the knowledge that I leave you a free man. You will easily provide for yourself when I am gone, and I know you will not forget Grizzie. For Jeames Gracie, he must have his share of the money because of the croft: we must calculate it fairly. He won't want much more in this world. Aggie'll be as safe as an angel anyway. And, Cosmo, whatever God may mean to do with you in this world, you'll have an abundant entrance ministered to you in the kingdom of our Lord and Saviour. Who would dare look for a better fate than that of the Lord himself! But there were those who by faith obtained kingdoms, as well as those who by faith were sawn asunder: they were both martyrdoms; and whatever God sends, we'll take."

"Then you accept the two hundred for croft and all, father?"

"Don't aim for a penny more; he might go back upon it. Regard it as his final offer."

Cosmo rose and went, strong-hearted, and without a single thought that pulled back from the sacrifice. There was even a certain pleasure in doing the thing just because in another and lower mood it would have torn his heart: the spirit was rejoicing against the flesh. To be rid of the castle would be to feel, far off, as the young man would have felt had he given all to the poor and followed the master. With the strength of a young giant he strode along.

When he reached the gate, there was my lord leaning over it.

"I thought you would be back soon! I knew the old cock would have more sense than the young one; and I didn't want my gate scrambled over again," he said, but without moving to open it.

"My father will take your lordship's offer," said Cosmo.

"I was on the point of making a fool of myself, and adding another fifty to be certain of getting rid of you; but I came to the conclusion it was a piece of cowardice, and that, as I had so long stood the dirty hovel at my gate because I couldn't help it, I might just as well let you find your way out of the parish."

"I am sure from your lordship's point of view you were right," said Cosmo. "We shall content ourselves, anyhow, with the two hundred."

"Indeed you will not! Did I not tell you I would not be bound by the offer? I have changed my mind, and mean to wait for the sale."

"I beg your pardon. I did not quite understand your lordship."

"You do now, I trust!"

"Perfectly, my lord," replied Cosmo, and turning away left his lordship grinning over the gate. But he had a curious look, almost as if he were a little ashamed of himself—as if he had only been teasing the young fellow, and thought perhaps he had gone too far. For Cosmo, in such peace was his heart, that he was not even angry with the man.

On his way home, the hope awoke, and began once more to whisper itself, that they might not be able to sell the place at all; that some other way would be provided for their leaving it; and that, when he was an old man, he would be allowed to return to die in it. But up started his conscience, jealously watchful lest hope should undermine submission, or weaken resolve. God *might* indeed intend they should not be driven from the old house! but he kept Abraham going from place to place, and never let him own a foot of land, except so much as was needful to bury his dead. And there was our Lord: he had not a place to lay his head, and had to go out of doors to pray to his father in secret! The only things to be anxious about were, that God's will should be done, and that it should not be modified by any want of faith or obedience or submission on his part. Then it would be God's very own will that was done, and not something composite, in part rendered necessary by his opposition. If God's pure will was done, he must equally rejoice whether that will took or gave the castle!

And so he returned to his father.

When he told him the result of his visit, the laird expressed no surprise.

"He maketh the wrath o' man to praise him," he said. "This will be for our good."

The whole day after, there was not between them another allusion to the matter. Cosmo read to his father a ballad he had just written. The old man was pleased with it; for what most would have counted a great defect in Cosmo's imagination was none to him—this namely, that he never could get room for it in this world; to his way of feeling, the end of things never came here; what end, or seeming end came, was not worth setting before his art as a goal for which to make; in its very nature it was no *finis* at all, only the merest close of a chapter.

This was the ballad, in great part the result of a certain talk with Mr. Simon.

The miser he lay on his lonely bed,
Life's candle was burning dim,

His heart in his iron chest was hid,
Under heaps of gold and a well locked lid,
And whether it were alive or dead,
It never troubled him.

Slowly out of his body he crept,
Said he, "I am all the same!
Only I want my heart in my breast;
I will go and fetch it out of the chest."
Swift to the place of his gold he stept—
He was dead but had no shame!

He opened the lid—oh, hell and night!
For a ghost can see no gold;
Empty and swept—not a coin was there!
His heart lay alone in the chest so bare!
He felt with his hands, but they had no might
To finger or clasp or hold!

At his heart in the bottom he made a clutch—
A heart or a puff-ball of sin?
Eaten with moths, and fretted with rust,
He grasped but a handful of dry-rotted dust:
It was a horrible thing to touch,
But he hid it his breast within.

And now there are some that see him sit
In the charnel house alone,
Counting what seems to him shining gold,
Heap upon heap, a sum ne'er told:
Alas, the dead, how they lack of wit!
They are not even bits of bone!

Another miser has got his chest,
And his painfully hoarded store;
Like ferrets his hands go in and out,
Burrowing, tossing the gold about;
And his heart too is out of his breast,
Hid in the yellow ore.

Which is the better—the ghost that sits
Counting shadowy coin all day,
Or the man that puts his hope and trust
In a thing whose value is only his lust?
Nothing he has when out he flits
But a heart all eaten away.

That night, as he lay thinking, Cosmo resolved to set out on the morrow for the city, on foot, and begging his way if necessary. There he would acquaint Mr. Burns with the straits they were in, and require of him his best advice how to make a living for himself and his father and Grizzie. As for James and Agnes, they might stay at the castle, where he would do his best to help them. As soon as his father had had his breakfast, he would let him know his resolve, and with his assent, would depart at once. His spirits rose as he brooded. What a happy thing it was that Lord Lick-my-loof had not accepted their offer! all the time they saw themselves in a poor lodging in a noisy street, they would know they had their own strong silent castle waiting to receive them, as soon as they should be able to return to it! Then the words came to him: "Here we have no continuing city, but we seek one to come."

The special discipline for some people would seem to be that they shall never settle down, or feel as if they were at home, until they are at home in very fact.

"Anyhow," said Cosmo to himself, "such a castle we have!"

To be lord of space, a man must be free of all bonds of place. To be heir of all things, his heart must have no *things* in it. He must be like him who makes things, not like one who would put everything in his pocket. He must stand on the upper, not the lower side of them. He must be as the man who makes poems, not the man who gathers books of verse. God, having made a sunset, lets it pass, and makes such a sunset no more. He has no picture-gallery, no library. What if in heaven men shall be so busy growing, that they have not time to write or to read!

How blessed Cosmo would live, with his father and Grizzie and his books, in the great city—in some such place as he had occupied when at the university! The one sad thing was that he could not be with his father all day; but so much the happier would be the home-coming at night! Thus imagining, he fell fast asleep.

He dreamed that he had a barrow of oranges, with which he had been going about the streets all day, trying in vain to sell them. He was now returning home, the barrow piled, as when he set out in the morning, with the golden fruit. He consoled himself however with the thought, that his father was fond of oranges, and now might have as many as he pleased. But as he wheeled the barrow along, it seemed to grow heavier and heavier, and he feared his strength was failing him, and he would never get back to his father. Heavier and heavier it grew, until at last, although he had it on the pavement—for it was now the dead of the night—he could but just push it along. At last he reached the door, and having laboriously wheeled it into a shed, proceeded to pick from it a few of the best oranges to take up to his father. But when he came to lift one from the heap, lo, it was a lump of gold! He tried another and another: every one of them was a lump of solid gold. It was a dream-version of the golden horse. Then all at once he said to himself, nor knew why, "My father is dead!" and woke in misery. It was many moments before he quite persuaded himself that he had but dreamed. He rose, went to his father's bedside, found him sleeping peacefully, and lay down comforted, nor that night dreamed any more.

"What," he said to himself, "would money be to me without my father!"

Some of us shrink from making plans because experience has shown us how seldom they are realised. Not the less are the plans we do make just as subject to overthrow as the plans of the most prolific and minute of projectors. It was long since Cosmo had made any, and the resolve with which he now fell asleep was as modest as wise man could well cherish; the morning nevertheless went differently from his intent and expectation.

CHAPTER LIII
AN OLD STORY

He was roused before sunrise by his father's cough. After a bad fit, he was very weary and restless. Now, in such a condition, Cosmo could almost always put him to sleep by reading to him, and he therefore got a short story, and began to read. At first it had the desired effect, but in a little while he woke, and asked him to go on. The story was of a king's ship so disguising herself that a pirate took her for a merchant-man; and Cosmo, to whom it naturally recalled the Old Captain, made some remark about him.

"You mustn't believe," said his father, "all they told you when a boy about that uncle of ours. No doubt he was a rough sailor fellow, but I do not believe there was any ground for calling him a pirate. I don't suppose he was anything worse than a privateer, which, God knows, is bad enough. I fancy, however, for the most of his sea-life he was captain of an East Indiaman, probably trading on his own account at the same time. That he made money I do not doubt, but very likely he lost it all before he came home, and was too cunning, in view of his probable reception, to confess it."

"I remember your once telling me an amusing story of an adventure—let me see—yes, that was in an East Indiaman: was he the captain of that one?"

"No—a very different man—a cousin of your mother's that was. I was thinking of it a minute ago; it has certain points, if not of resemblance, then of contrast with the story you have just been reading."

"I should like much to hear it again, when you are able to tell it."

"I have got it all in writing. It was amongst my Marion's papers. You will find, in the bureau in the book-closet, in the pigeon-hole farthest to the left, a packet tied with red tape: bring that, and I will find it for you."

Cosmo brought the bundle of papers, and his father handed him one of them, saying, "This narrative was written by a brother of your mother's. The captain Macintosh who is the hero of the story, was a cousin of her mother, and at the time of the event related must have been somewhat advanced in years, for he had now returned to his former profession after having lost largely in an attempt to establish a brewery on the island of St. Helena!"

Cosmo unfolded the manuscript, and read as follows:

" 'An incident occurring on the voyage to India when my brother went out, exhibits captain Macintosh's character very practically, and not a little to his professional credit.

" 'On a fine evening some days after rounding the cape of Good Hope, sailing with a light breeze and smooth water, a strange sail of large size hove in sight, and apparently bearing down direct upon the "Union," Captain Macintosh's ship; evidently a ship of war, but showing *no colours*—a very suspicious fact. All English ships at that time trading to and from India, by admiralty rules, were obliged to carry armaments proportioned to their tonnage, and crew sufficient to man and work the guns carried. The strange sail was *nearing* them, or "the big stranger," as the seamen immediately named her. My brother, many years afterwards, more than once told me, that the change, or rather the *transformation,* which Captain Macintosh *under*went, was one of the most remarkable facts he had ever witnessed; more bordering on the *marvellous,* than anything else. When he had carefully and deliberately viewed the "big stranger," and deliberately laying down his glass, his eyes seemed to have catched *fire!* and his whole countenance lighted up; a new spirit seemed to possess him, while he preserved the utmost coolness: advancing deliberately to what is called the poop railing, and steadily looking forward—"Boatswain! Pipe to quarters." Muster roll called.—"Now, my men, we shall *fight!* I know you will do it well!—Clear ship for action!" I have certainly but my brother's word and judgement upon the fact, who had never been *under fire;* but his opinion was, that no British ship of war could have been more speedily, or more completely cleared for action, both in rigging, decks, and guns,—guns *double shotted* and run out into position. "The big stranger" was now *nearing,*—no ports opened, and no colours shewn—*all,* increased cause of suspicion that there was some ill intent in the wind—and it was very evident, from the *size* of the "big stranger"—nearly *thrice* the size of the little "Union,"—that, one broad side from the former, might send the latter at once to the bottom:—the whole crew, my brother related, were in the highest spirits, more as if preparing for a *dance,* than for work of life and death. Suddenly, the captain gives the command—"Boarders,—prepare to board!—Lower away, boarding Boats"—and no sooner said than done. The stranger was now at musket-shot. It was worthy the courage of a *Nelson* or a *Cochrane,* to think of boarding at such odds;—a mere handful of men, to a full complement of a heavy Frigate's crew! The idea was altogether in keeping with the best naval tactics and skill. Foreseeing that one broadside from such an enemy would sink him, he must *anticipate* such a crisis. Boarding would at least divert the enemy from their *guns;* and he knew what British seamen could do, in clearing an enemy's decks! *There* was British spirit in those days. Let us hope it shall again appear, should the occasion arise. The captain himself was the first in the foremost Boarding Boat—and the first in the enemy's main chains, and to set his foot on the enemy's main deck! when a most magic-like scene saluted the Boarders; but did not *yet* allay suspicion:—not a single enemy on deck!—Here, a characteristic act of a British *tar*—the Union's Boatswain,—must not be omitted—an old man of war's man:—no sooner had his foot touched the *enemy's* deck, than *rushing aft*—(or towards the ship's *stern*)—to the *wheel,*—the *only man on deck* being he at the wheel,—a big, lubbery looking man,—the Union's boatswain in less than a *moment* had his hands to the steersman's throat,—and with one *fell shove*, sent him spinning, heels over head—all the full length of the ship's quarter-deck, to land on the main-deck;—one may suppose rather *astonished!* The manly boatswain himself was the only man *hurt* in the affair—his boarding pistol, by some untoward accident, went off,—its double shot running up his fore-arm, and lodging in the bones of his elbow. Amputation became necessary; and the dear old fellow soon afterwards died.

" 'But what did all this *hullybaloo* come to? Breathe—and we shall hear! "The Big Stranger" turned out to be a large, heavy armed Portuguese Frigate!—Actually the *war-ship solitary* of the Portuguese navy then afloat!—a fine specimen of Portuguese naval discipline, no doubt!—not a watch even on deck!—They had seen immediately on seeing her, that the "Union" was *English,* and a merchant ship—which a practised seaman's eye can do at once; and they had quietly gone to take their *siesta,* after their country's fashion—Portugal, at that time, being one of Britain's allies, and not an enemy;—a grievous *disappointment* to the crew of the "Union." '

"My uncle seems to have got excited as he went on," said Cosmo, "to judge by the number of words he has underlined!"

"He enters into the spirit of the thing pretty well for a clergyman!" said the laird.

CHAPTER LIV
A SMALL DISCOVERY

When they had had a little talk over the narrative, the laird desired Cosmo to replace the papers, and rising he went to obey. As he approached the closet, the first beams of the rising sun were shining upon the door of it. The window through which they entered was a small one, and the mornings of the year in which they so fell were not many. When he opened the door, they shot straight to the back of the closet, lighting with rare illumination the little place, commonly so dusky that in it one book could hardly be distinguished from another. It was as if a sudden angel had entered a dungeon. When the door fell to behind him, as was its custom, the place felt so dark that he seemed to have lost memory as well as sight, and not to know where he was. He set it open again, and having checked it so, proceeded to replace the papers. But the strangeness of the presence there of such a light took so great a hold on his imagination, and it was such a rare thing to see what the musty dingy little closet, which to Cosmo had always been the treasure-chamber of the house, was like, that he stood for a moment with his hand on the cover of the bureau, gazing into the light-invaded corners as if he had suddenly found himself in a department of Aladdin's cave. Old to him beyond all memory, it yet looked new and wonderful, much that had hitherto been scarcely known but to his hands now suddenly revealed in radiance to his eyes also. Amongst other facts he discovered that the bureau stood, not against a rough wall as he had imagined, but against a plain surface of wood. In mild surprise he tapped it with his knuckles, and almost started at the hollow sound it returned.

"What can there be ahin' the bureau, father?" he asked, re-entering the room.

"What can there be behind the bureau, father?" he asked, re-entering the room.

"I dinna ken o' onything," answered the laird. "The desk stan's close again' the wa', does na't?"

"I don't know of anything," answered the laird. "The desk stands close against the wall, doesn't it?"

"Ay, but the wa' 's timmer, an' soon's how."

"Ay, but the wall's wooden, and sounds hollow."

"It may be but a wainscotin'; an' gien there was but an inch atween hit an' the stane, it wad soon' like that."

"It may be but a wainscoting; and if there was but an inch between it and the stone, it would sound like that."

"I wad like to draw the desk oot a bit, an' hae a nearer luik. It fills up a' the space, 'at I canna weel win at it."

"I would like to draw the desk out a bit, and have a nearer look. It fills up all the space, so that I can hardly get to it."

"Du as ye like, laddie. The hoose is mair yours nor mine. But noo ye hae putten't i' my heid, I min' my mother sayin' 'at there was ance a passage atween the twa blocks o' the hoose: could it be there? I aye thoucht it had been atween the kitchen an' the dinin' room. My father, she said, had it closed up."

"Do as you like, laddie. The house is more yours than mine. But now you've put it in my head, I recall my mother saying that there was once a passage between the two blocks of the house: could it be there? I always thought it had been between the kitchen and the dining room. My father, she said, had it closed up."

Said Cosmo, who had been gazing toward the closet from where he stood by the bedside,

"It seems to gang farther back nor the thickness o' the wa'!" He went and looked out of the western window, then turned again towards the closet. "I canna think," he resumed, with something like annoyance in

Said Cosmo, who had been gazing toward the closet from where he stood by the bedside,

"It seems to go farther back than the thickness of the wall!" He went and looked out of the western window, then turned again towards the closet. "I can't think," he resumed, with something like annoyance in his tone, his tone, "hoo it cud be 'at I never noticed that afore! A body wad think I had nae heid for what I prided mysel' upo'—an un'erstan'in' o' hoo things are putten thegither, specially i' the w'y o' stane an' lime! The closet rins richt intil the great blin' wa' atween the twa hooses! I thoucht that wa' had been naething but a kin' o' a curtain o' defence, but there may weel be a passage i' the thickness o' 't!"

"how it could be that I never noticed that before! You would think I had no head for what I prided myself upon—an understanding of how things are put together, especially with regard to stone and lime! The closet runs right into the great blind wall between the two houses! I thought that wall had been nothing but a kind of curtain of defence, but there may well be a passage in the thickness of it!"

So saying he re-entered the closet, and proceeded to move the bureau. The task was not an easy one. The bureau was large, and so nearly filled the breadth of the closet, that he could attack it nowhere but in front, and had to drag it forward, laying hold of it where he could, over a much-worn oak floor. The sun had long deserted him before he got behind it.

"I wad sair like to brak throu the buirds, father?" he said, going again to the laird.

"I'm very tempted to break through the boards, father?" he said, going again to the laird.

"Onything ye like, I tell ye, laddie! I'm growin' curious mysel'," he answered.

"Anything you like, I tell you, laddie! I'm growing curious myself," he answered.

"I'm feart for makin' ower muckle din, father."

"I'm afraid I'll make too much noise, father."

"Nae fear, nae fear! I haena a sair heid. The Lord be praist, that's a thing I'm seldom triblet wi'. Gang an' get ye what tools ye want, an' gang at it, an' dinna spare. Gien the hole sud lat in the win', ye'll mar nae mair, I'm thinkin', nor ye'll be able to mak again. What timmer is 't o'?"

"No fear, no fear! I haven't a sore head. The Lord be praised, that's a thing I'm seldom troubled with. Go and get whatever tools you want, and go at it, and don't spare. If the hole should let in the wind, you'll mar no more, I think, than you'll be able to make again. What wood is it made of?"

"Only deal, sae far as I can judge."

"Only deal, so far as I can judge."

Cosmo went and fetched his tool-basket, and set to work. The partition was strong, of good sound pine, neither rotten nor worm-eaten—inch-boards matched with groove and tongue, not quite easy to break through. But having, with a centre-bit and brace, bored several holes near each other, he knocked out the pieces between, and introducing a saw, soon made an opening large enough to creep through. A cold air met him, as if from a cellar, and on the other side he seemed in another climate.

Feeling with his hands, for there was scarcely any light, he discovered that the space he had entered was not a closet, inasmuch as there was no shelf, or anything in it, whatever. It was certainly most like the end of a deserted passage. His feet told him the floor was of wood, and his hands that the walls were of rough stone without plaster, cold and damp. With outstretched arms he could easily touch both at once. Advancing thus a few paces, he struck his head against wood, felt panels, and concluded a door. There was a lock, but the handle was gone. He went back a little, and threw himself against it. Lock and hinges too gave way, and it fell right out before him. He went staggering on, and was brought up by a bed, half-falling across it. He was in the spare room, the gruesome centre of legend, the dwelling of ghostly awe. Not yet apparently had its numen forsaken it, for through him passed a thrill at the discovery. From his father's familiar room to this, was like some marvellous transition in a fairy-tale; the one was home, a place of use and daily custom; the other a hollow in the far-away past, an ancient cave of Time, full of withering history. Its windows being all to the north and long unopened, it was lustreless, dark, and musty with decay.

Cosmo stood motionless a while, gazing about him as if, from being wide awake, he suddenly found himself in a dream. Then he turned as if to see how he had got into it. There lay the door, and there was the open passage! He lifted the door: the other side of it was covered with the same paper as the wall, from which it had brought with it several ragged pieces. He went back, crept through, and rejoined his father.

In eager excitement, he told him the discovery he had made.

"I heard the noise of the falling door," said his father quietly. "I should not wonder now," he added, "if we discovered a way through to the third block."

"Oh, father," said Cosmo with a sigh, "what a comfort this door would have so often been! and now, just as we are like to leave the house forever, we first discover it!"

"How well we have got on without it!" returned his father.

"But what could have made grandfather close it up?"

"There was, I believe, some foolish ghost-story connected with it—perhaps the same old Grannie told you."

"I wonder grandmamma never spoke of it!"

"My impression is she never cared to refer to it."

"I daresay she believed it."

"Weel, I daursay! I wadna won'er!"

"Well, I daresay! I wouldn't wonder!"

"What for did ye ca' 't foolish, father?"

"Why did you call it foolish, father?"

"Jist for thouchtlessness, I doobt. But wha could hae imagined to kep a ghaist by paperin' ower a door, whan, gien there be ony trowth i' sic tales, the ghaist gangs throu a stane wa' jist as easy 's open air! But surely o' a' fules a ghaist maun be the warst 'at hings on aboot a place!"

"Just by thoughtlessness, I think. But who could have imagined restraining a ghost by papering over a door, when, if there be any truth in such tales, the ghost goes through a stone wall just as easily as open air! But surely of all fools a ghost that never leaves a place must be the worst!"

"Maybe it's to haud away frae a waur. The queer thing, father, to me wad be 'at the ghaist, frae bein' a fule a' his life, sud grow a wise man the minute he was deid! Michtna it be a pairt o' his punishment to be garred see hoo things gang on efter he's deid! What could be sairer, for instance, upon a miser, nor to see his heir gang to the deevil by scatterin' what he gaed to the deevil by gatherin'?"

"Maybe it's to keep away from a worse. The queer thing, father, to me would be that the ghost, from being a fool all his life, should grow a wise man the minute he was dead! Mightn't it be a part of his punishment to be made to see how things go on after he's dead! What could be harder, for instance, upon a miser, than to see his heir go to the devil by scattering what he went to the devil by gathering?"

"'Deed, ye're richt eneuch there, my son!" answered the old man. Then after a pause he resumed. "It's aye siller or banes 'at fesses them back. I can weel un'erstan' a great reluctance to tak their last leave o' the siller, but for the banes—eh, but I'll be unco pleased to be rid o' mine!"

"Indeed, you're right enough there, my son!" answered the old man. Then after a pause he resumed. "It's always money or bones that brings them back. I can well understand a great reluctance to take their last leave of the money, but for the bones—eh, but I'll be well pleased to be rid of mine!"

"But whaur banes are concernt, hasna there aye been fause play?" suggested Cosmo.

"But where bones are concerned, hasn't there always been false play?" suggested Cosmo.

"Wad it be revenge, than, think ye?"

"Would it be revenge then, think you?"

"It micht be: maist o' the stories o' that kin' en' wi' bringin' the murderer an' justice acquant. But the human bein' seems in a' ages

"It might be: most of the stories of that kind end with bringing the murderer to justice. But the human being seems in all

to hae a grit dislike to the thoucht o' his banes bein' left lyin' aboot. I hae h'ard gran'mamma say the dirtiest servan' was aye clean twa days o' her time—the day she cam an' the day she gaed."

ages to have a great dislike to the thought of his bones being left lying about. I have heard grandmamma say the dirtiest servant was always clean two days of her time—the day she came and the day she went."

"Ye hae thoucht mair aboot it nor me, laddie! But what ye say wadna haud wi' the Parsees, 'at lay oot their deid to be devoored by the birds o' the air."

"You have thought more about it than me, laddie! But what you say wouldn't hold with the Parsees, who lay out their dead to be devoured by the birds of the air."

"They swipe up their banes at the last. An' though the livin' expose the deid, the deid mayna like it."

"They swipe up their bones at the last. And though the living expose the dead, the dead may not like it."

"I daursay. Ony gait it maun be a fine thing to lea' as little dirt as possible ahin' ye, an' tak nane wi' ye. I wad fain gang clean an' lea' clean!"

"I daresay. Anyway it must be a fine thing to leave as little dirt as possible behind you, and take none with you. I would fain live clean and leave clean!"

"Gien onybody gang clean an' lea' clean, father, ye wull."

"If anybody live clean and leave clean, father, you will."

"I luik to the Lord, my son.—But noo, whan a body thinks o' 't," he went on after a pause, "there wad seem something curious i' thae tales concernin' the auld captain! Sometime we'll tak Grizzie intil oor coonsel, an' see hoo mony we can gaither, an' what we can mak o' them whan we lay them a' thegither. Gien the Lord hae't in his min' to keep 's i' this place, yon passage may turn oot a great convanience."

"I look to the Lord, my son.—But now, when a man thinks of it," he went on after a pause, "there would seem something curious in those tales concerning the old captain! Sometime we'll take Grizzie into our counsel, and see how many we can gather, and what we can make of them when we lay them all together. If the Lord has it in his mind to keep us in this place, that passage may turn out a great convenience."

"Ye dinna think it wad be worth while openin' 't up direc'ly?"

"You don't think it would be worth while opening it up at once?"

"I wad bide for warmer weather. I think the room's jist some caller now by rizzon o' 't."

"I would wait for warmer weather. I think the room's grown quite cool now because of it."

"I'll close 't up at ance," said Cosmo.

"I'll close it up at once," said Cosmo.

In a few minutes he had screwed a box-lid over the hole in the partition, and shut the door of the closet.

"Noo," he said, "I'll gang an' set up the door on the ither side."

"Now," he said, "I'll go and set up the door on the other side."

Before he went however, he told his father what he had been thinking of, saying, if he approved and was well enough, he should like to go the next day.

"It's no an ill idea," said the laird; "but we'll see what the morn may be like."

"It's not a bad idea," said the laird; "but we'll see what tomorrow may be like."

When Cosmo entered the great bedroom of the house from the other side, he stood for a moment staring at the open passage and prostrate door as if he saw them for the first time, then proceeded to examine the hinges. They were broken; the half of each remained fast to the door-post, the other half to the door. New hinges were necessary; in the meantime he must prop it up. This he did; and before he left the room, as it was much in want of fresh air, he opened all the windows.

His father continuing better through that day, he went to bed early that he might start at sunrise.

CHAPTER LV
A GREATER DISCOVERY

In the middle of the night he was awakened by a loud noise. Its nature he had been too sound asleep to recognise; he only knew it had waked him. He sprang out of bed, was glad to find his father undisturbed, and stood for a few moments wondering. All at once he remembered that he had left the windows of the best bedroom open; the wind had risen, and was now blowing what sailors would call a gale: probably something had been blown down! He would go and see. Taking a scrap of candle, all he had, he crept down the stair and out to the great door.

As he approached that of the room he sought, the faint horror he felt of it when a boy suddenly returned upon him as fresh as ever, and for a moment he hesitated, almost doubting whether he were not dreaming: was he actually there in the middle of the night? But with an effort he dismissed the folly, was himself again, entering the room, if not with indifference yet with composure. There was just light enough to see the curtains of the terrible bed waving wide in the stream of wind that followed the opening of the door. He shut the windows, lighted his candle, and then saw the door he had set up so carefully flat on the floor: the chair he had put against it for a buttress, he thought, had not proved high enough, and it had fallen down over the top of it. He placed his candle beside it, and proceeded once more to raise it. But, casting his eyes up to mark the direction, he caught a sight which made him lay it down again and rise without it. The candle on the floor shone half-way into the passage, lighting up a part of one wall of it, and showing plainly the rough gray stones of which it was built. Something in the shapes and arrangement of the stones drew and fixed Cosmo's attention. He took the candle, examined the wall, came from the passage with his eyes shining, and his lips firmly closed, left the room, and went up a story higher to that over it, still called his. There he took from his old secretary the unintelligible drawing hid in the handle of the bamboo, and with beating heart unfolded it. Certainly its lines did, more or less, correspond with the shapes of those stones! He must bring them face to face!

Down the stair he went again. It was the dead of the night, but every remnant of childhood's awe was gone in the excitement of the hoped discovery. He stood once more in the passage, the candle in one hand, the paper in the other, and his eyes going and coming steadily between it and the wall, as if reading the rough stones by some heiroglyphic key. The lines on the paper and the joints of the stones corresponded with almost absolute accuracy.

But another thing had caught his eye—a thing yet more promising, though he delayed examining it until fully satisfied of the correspondence he sought to establish: on one of the stones, one remarkable neither by position nor shape, he spied what seemed the rude drawing of a horse, but as it was higher than his head, and the candle cast up shadows from the rough surfaces, he could not see it well. Now he got a chair, and, standing on it, saw that it was plainly enough a horse, like one a child might have made who, with a gift for drawing, had had no instruction. It was scratched on the stone. Beneath it, legible enough to one who knew them so well, were the lines—

catch your Nag, & pull his Tail	catch your Horse, & pull his Tail
in his hind Heel caw a Nail	in his hind Heel drive a Nail
rug his Lugs frae ane anither	pull his Ears from one another
stand up, & ca' the King yer Brither	stand up, & call the King your Brother

How these directions were to be followed with such a horse as the one on the flat before him would be scanned! Probably the wall must be broken into at that spot. In the meantime he would set up the door again, and go to bed.

For he was alarmed at the turmoil the sight of these signs caused him. He dreaded *possession* by any spirit but the one. Whatever he did now he must do calmly. Therefore to bed he went. But before he gave himself up to sleep, he prayed God to watch him, lest the commotion in his heart and the giddiness of hope should make something rise that would come between him and the light eternal. The man in whom any earthly hope dims the heavenly presence and weakens the mastery of himself, is on the by-way through the meadow to the castle of Giant Despair.

In the morning he rose early, and went to see what might be attempted for the removing of the stone. He found it, as he had feared, so close-jointed with its neighbours that none of his tools would serve. He went to Grizzie and got from her a thin old knife; but the mortar had got so hard since those noises the servants used to hear in the old captain's room, that he could not make much impression upon it, and the job was likely to be a long one. He said to himself it might be the breaking through of the wall of his father's prison and his own, and wrought eagerly.

As soon as his father had had his breakfast, he told him what he had discovered during the dark hours. The laird listened with the light of a smile, not the smile itself, upon his face, and made no answer; but Cosmo could see by the all but imperceptible motion of his lips that he was praying.

"I wish I were able to join you," he said at length.

"There is na room for mair nor ane at a time, father," answered Cosmo; "an' I houp to get the stane oot afore I'm tired. You can be Moses praying, while I am Joshua fighting."

"An' prayin' again waur enemies nor ever Joshua warstled wi'," returned his father; "for whan I think o' the rebound o' the spirit, even in this my auld age, that cudna but follow the mere liftin' o' the weicht o' debt, I feel as gien my sowl wad be tum'led aboot like a bledder, an' its auld wings tak to lang slow flaggin' strokes i' the ower thin aether o' joy. The great God protec' 's frae his ain gifts! Wi'oot him they're ten times waur nor ony wiles o' the deevil's ain. But I'll pray, Cosmo; I'll pray."

"There isn't room for more than one at a time, father," answered Cosmo; "and I hope to get the stone out before I'm tired. You can be Moses praying, while I am Joshua fighting."

"And praying against worse enemies than ever Joshua fought with," returned his father; "for when I think of the rebound of the spirit, even in this my old age, that couldn't but follow the mere lifting of the weight of debt, I feel as if my soul would be tumbled about like a bladder, and its old wings take to long slow flagging strokes in the over-thin aether of joy. The great God protect us from his own gifts! Without him they're ten times worse than any wiles of the devil's own. But I'll pray, Cosmo; I'll pray."

The real might of temptation is in the lower and seemingly nearer loveliness as against the higher and seemingly farther.

Cosmo went back to his work. But he got tired of the old knife-it was not tool enough, and had to fashion on the grindstone a screw-driver to a special implement. With that he got on better.

The stone,—whether by the old captain's own hands, his ghost best knew—was both well fitted and fixed, but after Cosmo had worked at it for about three hours his tool suddenly went through. It was then easy to knock away from the edge gained, and on the first attempt to prize it out, it yielded so far that he got a hold with his fingers, and the rest was soon done. It disclosed a cavity in the wall, but the light was not enough to let him see into it, and he went to get a candle.

Now Grizzie had a curious dislike to any admission of the povery of the house even to those most interested, and having but one small candle-end left, was unwilling both to yield it, and to confess it her last.

"Them 'at burns daylicht, sune they'll hae nae licht!" she said. "What wad ye want wi' a can'le? I'll haud a fir-can'le to ye, gien ye like."

"Those who burn the light of day, soon will walk in night alway!" she said. "What would you want with a candle? I'll hold a fir-candle to you, if you like."

"Grizzie," repeated Cosmo, "I want a can'le."

"Grizzie," repeated Cosmo, "I want a candle."

She went grumbling, and brought him the miserable end.

She went grumbling, and brought him the miserable end.

"Hoot, Grizzie!" he expostulated, "dinna be sae near. Ye wadna, gien ye kenned what I was aboot."

"Heavens, Grizzie!" he expostulated, "don't be so miserly. You wouldn't, if you knew what I was about."

"Eh! what are ye aboot, sir?"

"Eh! what are you about, sir?"

"I'm no gaein' to tell ye yet. Ye maun hae patience, an' I maun hae a can'le."

"I'm not going to tell you yet. You must have patience, and I must have a candle."

"Ye maun tak what's offert ye."

"You must take what you're offered."

"Grizzie, I'm in earnest."

"Grizzie, I'm in earnest."

"'Deed an' sae am I! Ye s' hae nae mair nor that—no gien it was to scrape the girnel—an' that's dune lang syne, an' twise ower!"

"Indeed, so am I! You shall have no more than that—not if it was to scrape the meal-chest—and that's done long ago, and twice over!"

"Grizzie, I'm feart ye'll anger me."

"Grizzie, I'm afraid you'll anger me."

"Ye s' get nae mair!"

"You shall get no more!"

Cosmo burst out laughing.

Cosmo burst out laughing.

"Grizzie," he said, "I dinna believe ye hae an inch mair can'le i' the hoose!"

"Grizzie," he said, "I don't believe you have an inch more candle in the house!"

"It needs na a Warlock to tell that! Gien I had it, what for sud na ye hae 't 'at has the best richt?"

"It doesn't take a Warlock to tell that! If I had it, why shouldn't you have it who have the best right?"

Cosmo took his candle, and was as sparing of it as Grizzie herself could have wished.

CHAPTER LVI
A GREAT DISCOVERY

The instant the rays of the candle-end were thrown into the cavity, he saw what, expectant as he was, made him utter a cry. He seemed to be looking through a small window into a toy-stable—a large one for a toy. Immediately before him was a stall, in which stood a horse, with his tail towards the window. He put in his hand and felt it over. For a toy it would have been of the largest size below a rocking horse. It was covered with a hairy skin. So far all was satisfactory, but alas! more stones must be removed ere it could be taken from its prison stall, where, like the horses of Charlemagne, it had been buried so many years. He extinguished the precious candle-end, and set to work once more with a will and what light the day afforded. Nor was the task much easier than before. Every one of the stones was partly imbedded in the solid of the wall, projecting but a portion of its bulk over the hollow of the stable. The old captain must indeed have worked hard: for assuredly he was not the man to call for help where he desired secrecy—though doubtless it was his sudden death, and the nature of it, which prevented him from making disclosure concerning the matter before he left the world: the rime, the drawing, the scratches on the stone, all indicated the intention. Cosmo took pleasure in thinking that, if indeed his ghost did "walk," as Grannie and others had affirmed, it must be more from desire to reveal where his money was hid, than from any gloating over the imagined possession of it.

But it was now dinner-time, and he must rest, for he was tired as well as hungry—and no wonder, the work having been so awkward as well as continuous! He locked the door of the room, went first to tell his father what he had further found, and then made haste over his meal, for the night was coming, and there were no candles. Persistently he laboured; "the toil-drops fell from his brow like rain;" and at last he laid hold of the patient animal by the hind legs, with purpose to draw it gently from the stall. A little way it came, then no farther, and he had to light the candle. Peeping into the stall he perceived a chain stretching from its head to where the manger might be. This he dared not try to break, lest he might injure the mechanism he hoped to find in it. But clearly the horse could not have been so fastened as the stall then stood. The stall must have been completed after the horse was thus secured. More than ever he now needed a candle—and indeed one held for him; but he was not prepared either to take Grizzie into his confidence, or to hurt her by preferring Agnes. He therefore examined the two stones forming the sides of the stall, and led by the appearance of one of them, proceeded to attempt its removal almost in the dark, compelled indeed now and then to feel for the proper spot where to set his tool before he struck it. For some time he seemed to make little or no progress; but who would be discouraged with the end in sight!

The stone at length moved, and in a minute he had it out. For the last time he lighted his candle, and there was just enough of it left to show him how the chain was fastened. With a pair of pincers he detached it from the wall—and I may mention that his life after he wore it at his watch.

And now he had the horse in his arms and would have borne it straight to his father, in whose presence it must be searched, but that, unwilling to carry it through the kitchen, he must first go to the other end of the passage and open that way.

The laird was seated by the fire when Cosmo went through, and returning with the horse, placed it on a chair beside him. They looked it all over, wondering whether the old captain could have made it himself, and Cosmo thought his father prolonged the inquiry from a wish to still his son's impatience. But at length he said,

"Noo, Cosmo, i' the name o' God, the giver o' ilka guid an' perfect gift, see gien ye	"Now, Cosmo, in the name of God, the giver of every good and perfect gift, see if you

can win at the entrails o' the animal. It canna be fu' o' men like the Trojan horse, or they maun be enchantit sma', like the deevils whan they war ower mony for the cooncil ha'; but what's intil 't may carry a heap waur danger to you an' me nor ony nummer o' airmit men!"

can find the entrails of the animal. It can't be full of men like the Trojan horse, or they must be enchanted small, like the devils when they were too many for the council hall; but what's inside it may carry a much worse danger to you and me than any number of armed men!"

"Ye min' the rime, father?" asked Cosmo.

"You remember the rime, father?" asked Cosmo.

"No sae weel as the twenty-third psalm," replied the laird with a smile.

"Not so well as the twenty-third psalm," replied the laird with a smile.

"Weel, the first line o' 't is, 'Catch yer naig, an' pu' his tail.' Wi' muckle diffeeclety we hae catcht him, an' noo for the tail o' 'im!—There! that's dune!—though there's no muckle to shaw for 't. The neist direction is—'In his hin' heel caw a nail:' we s' turn up a' his fower feet thegither, 'cause they're co-operant; an' noo lat's see the proper spot whaur to caw the said nail!"

"Well, the first line of it is, 'Catch your horse, and pull his tail.' With much difficulty we have caught him, and now for his tail!—There! that's done!—though there's not much to show for it. The next direction is—'In his hind heel drive a nail:' we'll turn up all his four feet together, as they're co-operant; and now let's see the proper spot where to drive the said nail!"

The horse's shoes were large, and the hole where a nail was missing had not to be sought. Cosmo took a fine bradawl, and pushed it gently into the hoof. A loud, whirring noise followed, but with no visible result.

"The next direction," said Cosmo, "is—'Rug his lugs frae ane anither.' Noo, father, God be wi' 's! an' gien it please him we be dis-ap'intit, may he gie 's grace to beir 't as he wad hae 's beir 't."

"The next direction," said Cosmo, "is—'Pull his ears from one another.' Now, father, God be with us! and if it please him we be disappointed, may he give us grace to bear it as he would have us bear it."

"I pray the same," said the laird.

"I pray the same," said the laird.

Cosmo pulled the two ears of the animal in opposite directions. The back began to open, slowly, as if through the long years the cleft had begun to grow together. He sprang from his seat. The laird looked after him with a gentle surprise. But it was not to rush from the room, nor yet to perform a frantic dance with the horse for a partner.

One of the windows looked westward into the court, and at this season of the year, the setting sun looked in at the window. He was looking in now; his rays made a glowing pool of light in the middle of the ancient carpet. Beside this pool Cosmo dropped on the floor like a child with his toy, and pulled lustily at its ears. All at once into the pool of light began to tumble a cataract as of shattered rainbows, only brighter, flashing all the colours visible to human eye. It ceased. Cosmo turned the horse upside down, and a few stray drops followed. He shook it, and tapped it, like Grizzie when she emptied the basin of meal into the porridge-pot, then flung it from him. But the cataract had not vanished. There it lay heaped and spread, a storm of conflicting yet harmonious hues, with a foamy spray of spiky flashes, and spots that ate into the eyes with their fierce colour. In every direction shot the rays from it, blinding; for it was a mound of stones of all the shapes into which diamonds are fashioned. It makes my heart beat but to imagine the glorious show of deep-hued burning, flashing, stinging light! The heaviest of its hues was borne light as those of a foam-bubble on the strength of its triumphing radiance. There pulsed the mystic glowing red, heart and lord of colour; there the jubilant yellow, light—glorified to ethereal gold; there the loveliest blue, the truth unfathomable, profounder yet than the human red; there the green, that haunts the brain with Nature's soundless secrets! all together striving, yet atoning, fighting and fleeing and following, parting and blending, with illimitable play of infinite force and endlessly delicate gradation. Scattered here and there were a few of all the coloured gems—sapphires, emeralds, and rubies; but they were scarce of note in the mass of ever new-born, ever dying colour that gushed from the fountains of the light-dividing diamonds.

Cosmo rose, left the glory where it lay, and returning to his father, sat down beside him. For a few moments they regarded in silence the shining mound, where, like an altar of sacrifice, it smoked with light and colour. The eyes of the old man as he looked seemed at once to sparkle with pleasure, and quail with some kind of fear. He turned to Cosmo and said,

"Cosmo, are they what they luik?"

"Cosmo, are they what they look?"

"What they luik, father?" asked Cosmo.

"What they look, father?" asked Cosmo.

"Bonny bits o' glaiss they luik," answered the old man. "But," he went on, "I canna but believe them something better, they come til's in sic a time o' sair need. But, be they this or be they that, the Lord's wull be done—noo an' for ever, be it, I say, what it like!"

"Bonny bits of glass they look," answered the old man. "But," he went on, "I can't but believe them something better, they come to us in such a time of sore need. But, be they this or be they that, the Lord's will be done—now and for ever, be it, I say, what it like!"

"I wuss it, father!" rejoined Cosmo. "But I ken something aboot sic-like things, frae bein' sae muckle in Mr. Burns's shop, an' hauding a heap o' conference wi' 'im about them; an' I tell ye, sir, they're maistly a' di'mon's; an' the nummer o' thoosan' poun' they maun be worth gien they be worth a saxpence, I daurna guess!"

"I wish it, father!" rejoined Cosmo. "But I know something about such things, from being so much in Mr. Burns's shop, and speaking so much with him about them; and I tell you, sir, they're mostly all diamonds; and the number of thousand pounds they must be worth if they be worth a sixpence, I daren't guess!"

"They'll be eneuch to pey oor debts ony gait, ye think, Cosmo?"

"They'll be enough to pay our debts anyway, you think, Cosmo?"

"Ay, that wull they—an' mony a hun'er times ower. They're maistly a guid size, an' no a feow o' them lairge."

"Ay, that they will—and many a hundred times over. They're mostly a good size, and not a few of them large."

"Cosmo, we're ower lang ohn thankit. Come here, my son; gang down upo' yer knees, an' lat's say to the Lord what we're thinkin'."

"Cosmo, we've delayed thanks too long. Come here, my son; go down on your knees, and let's say to the Lord what we're thinking."

Cosmo obeyed, and knelt at his father's knee, and his father laid his hand upon his head that so they might pray more in one.

"Lord," he said, "though naething a man can tak in his han's can ever be his ain, no bein' o' his nature, that is, made i' thy image, yet, O Lord, the thing 'at's thine, made by thee efter thy holy wull an' pleesur, man may touch an' no be defiled. Yea, he may tak pleesur baith in itsel' an' in its use, sae lang as he han'les 't i' the how o' thy han', no grippin' at it an' ca'in' 't his ain, an' lik a rouch bairn seekin' to snap it awa' 'at he may hae his fule wull o' 't. O God, they're bonny stanes an' fu' o' licht: forbid 'at their licht sud breed darkness i' the hert o' Cosmo an' me. O God, raither nor we sud du or feel ae thing i' consequence o' this thy gift, that thoo wadna hae us do or feel, we wud hae

"Lord," he said, "though nothing a man can take in his hands can ever be his own, not being of his nature, that is, made in thy image, yet, O Lord, the thing that's thine, made by thee after thy holy will and pleasure, man may touch and not be defiled. Yea, he may take pleasure both in itself and in its use, so long as he handles it in the hollow of thy hand, not gripping at it and calling it his own, and like a rough child seeking to snap it away that he may have his foolish will of it. O God, they're bonny stones and full of light: forbid that their light should breed darkness in the heart of Cosmo and me. O God, rather than we should do or feel one thing in consequence of this thy

thee tak again the gift; an' gien i' thy mercy, for it's a' mercy wi' thee, it sud turn oot, efter a', 'at they're no stanes o' thy makin', but coonterfeit o' glaiss, the produc' o' airt an' man's device, we'll lay them a' thegither, an' keep them safe, an' luik upon them as a token o' what thoo wad hae dune for 's gien it hadna been 'at we warna yet to be trustit wi' sae muckle , an' that for the safety an' clean-throuness o' oor sowls. O God, latna the sunshiny Mammon creep intil my Cosmo's hert an' mak a' mirk; latna the licht that is in him turn to darkness. God hae mercy on his wee bairns, an' no lat the playocks he gies them tak their e'en aff o' the giein' han'! May the licht noo streamin' frae the hert o' the bonny stanes be the bodily presence o' thy speerit, as ance was the doo' 'at descendit upo' the maister, an' the buss 'at burned wi' fire an' wasna consumed. Thou art the father o' lichts, an' a' licht is thine. Gar oor herts burn like them—a' licht an' nae reek! An' gien ony o' them cam in at a wrang door, may they a' gang oot at a richt ane. Thy wull be dune, which is the purifyin' fire o' a' thing, an' a' sowl! Amen."

gift, that thou would not have us do or feel, we would have thee take again the gift; and if in thy mercy, for it's all mercy with thee, it should turn out, after all, that they're not stones of thy making, but glass counterfeits, the product of art and man's device, we'll lay them all together, and keep them safe, and look upon them as a token of what thou would have done for us had it not been that we were not yet to be trusted with so much, and that for the safety and sanctity of our souls. O God, let not the sunshiny Mammon creep into my Cosmo's heart and make all dark; let not the light that is in him turn to darkness. God have mercy on his little ones, and not let the toys he gives them take their eyes off the giving hand! May the light now streaming from the heart of the bonny stones be the bodily presence of thy spirit, as once was the dove that descended upon the master, and the bush that burned with fire and was not consumed. Thou art the father of lights, and all light is thine. Make our hearts burn like them—all light and no smoke! And if any of them came in at a wrong door, may they all go out at a right one. Thy will be done, which is the purifying fire of every thing, and every soul! Amen."

He ceased, and was silent, praying still. Nor did Cosmo yet rise from his knees: the joy, and yet more the relief at his heart filled him afresh with fear, lest, no longer spurred by the same sense of need, he should the less run after him from whom help had come so plentifully. Alas! how is it with our hearts that in trouble they cry, and in joy forget! that we think it hard of God not to hear, and when he has answered abundantly, turn away as if we wanted him no more!

When Cosmo rose from his knees, he looked his father in the face with wet eyes.

"Oh, father!" he said, "how the fear and oppression of ages are gone like a cloud swallowed up of space. Oh, father! are not all human ills doomed thus to vanish at last in the eternal fire of the love-burning God?—An' noo, father, what 'll we du neist?" resumed Cosmo after a pause, turning his eyes again on the heap of jewels. The sunrays had now left them, and they lay cold and almost colourless, though bright still: even in the dark some of them would shine! "It pleases me, father," he went on, "to see nane o' them set. It pruvs naething, but maks 't jist a wheen mair likly he got them first han' like. Eh, the queer things! sae hard, an' yet 'maist bodiless! naething but skinfu's o' licht!"

"Oh, father!" he said, "how the fear and oppression of ages are gone like a cloud swallowed up of space. Oh, father! are not all human ills doomed thus to vanish at last in the eternal fire of the love-burning God?—And now, father, what will we do next?" resumed Cosmo after a pause, turning his eyes again on the heap of jewels. The sunrays had now left them, and they lay cold and almost colourless, though bright still: even in the dark some of them would shine! "It pleases me, father," he went on, "to see none of them set. It proves nothing, but makes it just a bit more likely he got them first hand. Eh, the queer things! so hard, and yet almost bodiless! nothing but skinfuls of light!"

"Hooever they war gotten," rejoined the laird, "there can be no question but the only w'y o' cleansin' them is to put them to the best use we possibly can."

"However obtained," rejoined the laird, "there can be no question but the only way of cleansing them is to put them to the best use we possibly can."

"An' what wad ye ca' the best use, father?"

"And what would you call the best use, father?"

"Whatever maks o' a man a neebour. A true life efter God's notion is the sairest bash to Sawtan. To gie yer siller to ither fowk to spread is to jink the wark laid oot for ye. I' the meantime hadna ye better beery yer deid again? They maun lie i' the dark, like human sowls, till they're broucht to du the deeds o' licht."

"Whatever makes of a man a neighbour. A true life after God's notion is the hardest blow to Satan. To give your money to other folk to spread is to dodge the work laid out for you. In the meantime hadn't you better bury your dead again? They must lie in the dark, like human souls, till they're brought to do the deeds of light."

"Dinna ye think," said Cosmo, "I micht set oot the morn efter a', though on a different eeran', an' gang straucht to Mr. Burns? He'll sune put 's i' the w'y to turn them til accoont. They're o' sma' avail as they lie there."

"Don't you think," said Cosmo, "I might set out tomorrow after all, though on a different errand, and go straight to Mr. Burns? He'll soon show us how to turn them to account. They're of small use as they lie there."

"Ye canna du better, my son," answered the old man.

"You can't do better, my son," answered the old man.

So Cosmo gathered the gems together into the horse, lifting them in handfuls. But, peering first into the hollow of the animal, to make sure he had found all that was in it, he caught sight of a bit of paper that had got stuck, and found it a Bank of England note for five hundred pounds. This in itself would have been riches an hour ago—now it was only a convenience.

"It's queer to think," said Cosmo, "'at though we hae a' this siller, I maun tramp it the morn like ony caird. Wha is there in Muir o' Warlock could change 't, an' wha wad I gang til wi' 't gien he could?"

"It's queer to think," said Cosmo, "that though we have all this money, I must tramp it tomorrow like any tinker. Who is there in Muir of Warlock could change it, and who would I go to if he could?"

His father replied with a smile,

His father replied with a smile,

"It brings to my min' the words o' the apostle—'Noo I say, that the heir, sae lang as he's but a bairn, differeth naething frae a servan', though he be lord o' a'. Eh, Cosmo, but the word admits o' curious illustration!"

"It brings to my mind the words of the apostle—'Now I say, that the heir, so long as he's but a child, differeth nothing from a servant, though he be lord of all.' Eh, Cosmo, but the word admits of curious illustration!"

Cosmo set the horse, as soon as he had done giving him his supper of diamonds, again in his old stall, and replaced the stones that had shut him in as well as he could. Then he wedged up the door, and having nothing to make paste, glued the paper again to the wall which it had carried with it. He next sought the kitchen and Grizzie.

CHAPTER LVII
MR. BURNS

"Grizzie," he said, "I'm gaein' a lang tramp the morn, an' I'll need a great poochfu' o' cakes."

"Eh, sirs! An' what's takin' ye frae hame this time, sir?"

"I'm no gaein' to tell ye the nicht, Grizzie. It's my turn to hae a secret noo! But ye ken weel it's lang sin' there's been onything to be gotten by bidin' at hame."

"Eh, but, sir! ye're never gaein' to lea' the laird! Bide an' dee wi' him, sir."

"God bless ye, Grizzie! Hae ye ony baubees?"

"Ay; what for no! I hae sax shillin's, fower pennies, an' a baubee fardin'!" answered Grizzie, in the tone of a millionaire.

"Weel, ye maun jist len' me half a croon o' 't."

"Half a croon!" echoed Grizzie, staggered at the largeness of the demand. "Haith, sir, ye're no blate!"

"I dinna think it's ower muckle," said Cosmo, "seein I hae to tramp five an' thirty mile the morn. But bake ye plenty o' breid, an' that'll haud doon the expence. Only, gien he can help it, a body sudna be wantin' a baubee in 's pooch. Gien ye had nane to gie me, I wad set oot bare. But jist as ye like, Grizzie! I cud beg to be sure—noo ye hae shawn the gait," he added, taking the old woman by the arm with a laugh, that she might not be hurt, "but whan ye ken ye sudna speir, an' whan ye hae, ye hae no richt to beg."

"Weel, I'll gie ye auchteen pence, an' considerin' a' 'at 's to be dune wi' what's left, ye'll hae to grant it 's no an oonfair portion."

"Weel, weel, Grizzie! I'm thinkin' I'll hae to be content."

"'Deed, an' ye wull, sir! Ye s' hae nae mair."

"Grizzie," he said, "I'm going on a long tramp tomorrow, and I'll need a great pocketful of cakes."

"Eh, sirs! And what's taking you from home this time, sir?"

"I'm not going to tell you tonight, Grizzie. It's my turn to have a secret now! But you know well it's long since there's been anything to be had by staying at home."

"Eh, but, sir! you're never going to leave the laird! Stay and die with him, sir."

"God bless you, Grizzie! Have you any halfpence?"

"Ay; why not! I have six shillings, four pennies, and a halfpenny farthing!" answered Grizzie, in the tone of a millionaire.

"Well, you must lend me half a crown of it."

"Half a crown!" echoed Grizzie, staggered at the largeness of the demand. "Faith, sir, you aren't bashful!"

"I don't think it's too much," said Cosmo, "seeing I have to tramp five and thirty miles tomorrow. But bake plenty of bread, and that'll keep the expense down. Only, if he can help it, a man shouldn't be wanting a ha'penny in his pocket. If you had none to give me, I would set out bare. But just as you like, Grizzie! I could beg to be sure—now you have shown the way," he added, taking the old woman by the arm with a laugh, that she might not be hurt, "but when you know you shouldn't ask, and when you have, you have no right to beg."

"Well, I'll give you eighteen pence, and considering all that's to be done with what's left, you'll have to admit it's not an unfair portion."

"Well, well, Grizzie! I'm thinking I'll have to be content."

"That you will, sir! You shall have no more."

That night the old laird slept soundly, but Cosmo, ever on the brink of unconsciousness, was blown back by a fresh gust of gladness. The morning came golden and brave, and his father was well enough to admit of his leaving him. So he set out, and in the strength of his relief walked all the way without spending a penny of Grizzie's eighteen pence: two days before, he would consult his friend how to avoid the bitterest dregs of poverty; now he must find from him how to make his riches best available!

He did not tell Mr. Burns, however, what his final object was—only begged him, for the sake of friendship and old times, to go with him for a day or two to his father's.

"But, Mr. Warlock," objected the jeweller, "that would be taking the play, and we've got to be diligent in business."

"The thing I want you for is business," replied Cosmo.

"But what's to be done with the shop? I have no assistant I can trust."

"Then shut it up, and give your men a holiday. You can put up a notice informing the great public when you will be back."

"Such a thing was never heard of!"

"It is quite time it should be heard of then. Why, sir, your business is not like a doctor's, or even a baker's. People can live without diamonds!"

"Don't speak disrespectfully of diamonds, Mr. Warlock. If you knew them as I do, you would know they had a thing or two to say."

"Speak of them disrespectfully you never heard me, Mr. Burns."

"Never, I confess. I was only talking from the diamond side. Like all things else, they give us according to what we have. To him that hath shall be given. The fine lady may see in her fine diamonds only victory over a rival; the philosopher may read embodied in them law inexorably beautiful; and the Christian poet—oh, I have read my Spenser, Mr. Warlock!—will choose the diamond for its many qualities, as the best and only substance wherein to represent the shield of the faith that overcometh the world. Like the gospel itself, diamonds are a savour of life unto life, or a savour of death unto death, according to the character of them that look on them."

"That is true enough. Every gift of God is good that is received with faith and thanksgiving, and whatsoever is not of faith is sin. But will you come?"

Mr. Burns did at length actually consent to close his shop for three days, and go with Cosmo.

"It will not be a bad beginning," he said, as if in justification of himself to himself, "towards retiring from business altogether—which I might have done long ago," he added, "but for you, sir!"

"It is very well for me you did not," rejoined Cosmo, but declined to explain. This piqued Mr. Burns's curiosity, and he set about his preparations at once.

In the mean time things went well at Castle Warlock, with—shall I say?—one exception: Grizzie had a severe fit of repentance, mourning bitterly that she had sent away the youth she worshipped with only eighteen pence in his pocket.

"He's sure to come to grief for the want o' jist that ae shillin' mair!" she said over and over to herself; "an' it'll be a' an' only my wite! What gien we never see 'im again! Eh, sirs! it's a terrible thing to be made sae contrairy! What'll come o' me in the neist warl', it wad be hard for onybody to say!"

"He's sure to come to grief for the want of just that one shilling more!" she said over and over to herself; "and it'll be all and only my fault! What if we never see him again! Eh, sirs! it's a terrible thing to be made so contrairy! What'll become of me in the next world, it would be hard for anybody to say!"

On the evening of the second day, however, while she was "washing up" in the gloomiest frame of mind, in walked Cosmo, and a gentleman after him.

"Hoo's my father, Grizzie?" asked Cosmo.

"How's my father, Grizzie?" asked Cosmo.

"Won'erfu' weel, sir," answered Grizzie, with a little more show of respect than usual.

"Wonderfully well, sir," answered Grizzie, with a little more show of respect than usual.

"This is Grizzie, Mr. Burns," said Cosmo. "I have told you about Grizzie that takes care of us all!"

"How do you do, Grizzie?" said Mr. Burns, and shook hands with her. "I am glad to make your acquaintance."

"Here, Grizzie!" said Cosmo; "here's the auchteen pence ye gae me for expences: say ye're pleased I haena waured it.—Jist a word wi' ye, Grizzie!—Luik here—only dinna tell!"

"This is Grizzie, Mr. Burns," said Cosmo. "I have told you about Grizzie that takes care of us all!"

"How do you do, Grizzie?" said Mr. Burns, and shook hands with her. "I am glad to make your acquaintance."

"Here, Grizzie!" said Cosmo; "here's the eighteen pence you gave me for expenses: say you're pleased I haven't wasted it.—Just a word with you, Grizzie!—Look here—only don't tell!"

He had drawn her aside to the corner where stood the meal-chest, and now showed her a bunch of bank-notes. So many she had never seen—not to say in a bunch, but scattered over all her life! He took from the bunch ten pounds and gave her.

"Mr. Burns," he said aloud, "will be staying over to-morrow, I hope."

Grizzie *glowered* at the money as if such a sum could not be canny, but the next moment, like one suddenly raised to dignity and power, she began to order Aggie about as if she were her mistress, and an imperious one. Within ten minutes she had her bonnet on, and was setting out for Muir o' Warlock to make purchases.

But oh the pride and victory that rose and towered and sank weary, only to rise and tower again in Grizzie's mind, as she walked to the village with all that money in her pocket! The dignity of the house of Warlock had rushed aloft like a sudden tidal wave, and on its very crest Grizzie was borne triumphing heavenwards. From one who begged at strange doors for the daily bread of a decayed family, all at once she was the housekeeper of the most ancient and honourable castle in all Scotland, steering the great ship of its fortunes! With a reserve and a dignity as impressive as provoking to the gossips of the village, from one shop to another she went, buying carefully but freely, rousing endless curiosity by her look of mystery, and her evident consciousness of infinite resource. But when at last she went to the Warlock Arms, and bought a half dozen of port at the incredible price of six shillings a bottle, there was not a doubt left in the Muir that "the old laird" had at last and somehow come in for a great fortune. Grizzie returned laden herself, and driving before her two boys carrying a large basket between them. Now she was equal to the proper entertainment of the visitor, for whom, while she was away, Aggie, obedient to her orders, was preparing the state bedroom,—thinking all the time of that night long ago when she and Cosmo got it ready for Lord Mergwain.

Cosmo and Mr. Burns found the laird seated by the fire in his room; and there Cosmo recounted the whole story of the finding of the gems, beginning far back with the tales concerning the old captain, as they had come to his knowledge, just touching on the acquisition of the bamboo, and the discovery of its contents, and so descending to the revelations of the previous two days. But all the time he never gave the jeweller a hint of what was coming. In relating the nearer events, he led him from place to place, acting his part in them ,and forestalling nothing, never once mentioning stone or gem, then suddenly poured out the diamonds on the rug in the firelight.

Leaving the result to the imagination of my reader, I will now tell him a thing that took place while Cosmo was away.

CHAPTER LVIII
TOO SURE COMES TOO LATE

The same day Cosmo left, Lord Lick-my-loof sent to the castle the message that he wanted to see young Mr. Warlock. The laird returned the answer that Cosmo was from home, and would not be back till the days following.

In the afternoon came his lordship, desiring an interview with the laird; which, not a little against his liking, the laird granted.

"Sit ye doon, my lord," said Grizzie, "an' rist yer shins. The ro'd atween this an' the ludge, maun be slithery."

"Have a seat, my lord," said Grizzie, "and rest your shins. The road between here and the lodge, must be slithery."

His lordship yielded and took the chair she offered, for he would rather propitiate than annoy her, seeing he was more afraid of Grizzie than aught in creation except dogs. And Grizzie, appreciating his behaviour, had compassion upon him and spared him.

"His lairdship," she said, "maunna be hurried puttin' on his dressin'-goon. He's no used to see onybody sae ear'. I s' gang an' see gien I can help him; he never wad hae a man aboot 'im 'cep' the yoong laird himsel'."

"His lairdship," she said, "mustn't be hurried putting on his dressing-gown. He's not used to seeing anybody so early. I'll go and see if I can help him; he never would have a man about him except the young laird himself."

Relieved by her departure, his lordship began to look about the kitchen, and seeing Aggie, asked after her father. She replied that he was but poorly.

"Getting old!"

"Surely, my lord. He's makin' ready to gang."

"Poor old man!"

"What wad yer lordship hae? Ye wadna gang on i' this warl' for ever?"

"'Deed and I would have no objection—so long as there were pretty girls like you in it."

"Suppose the lasses had a ch'ice tu, my lord?"

"What would they do?"

"Gang, I'm thinkin'."

"What makes you so spiteful, Aggie? I never did you any harm that I know of."

"Ye ken the story o' the guid Samaritan, my lord?" said Aggie.

"I read my Bible, I hope."

"Weel, I'll tell ye a bit mair o' 't nor ye'll get there. The Levite an' the Pharisee—naebody ever said yer lordship was like aither o' them—"

"No, thank God! nobody could."

"—they gaed by o' the ither side, an' loot him lie. But there was ane cam up, an' tuik 'im by the legs, 'cause he lay upo' his lan', an' wad hae pu'd him aff. But jist i' the nick o' time by

"Getting old!"

"Surely, my lord. He's making ready to go."

"Poor old man!"

"What would your lordship have? You wouldn't go on in this world forever?"

"Indeed, I would have no objection—so long as there were pretty girls like you in it."

"Suppose the lasses had a choice too, my lord?"

"What would they do?"

"Go, I think."

"What makes you so spiteful, Aggie? I never did you any harm that I know of."

"You know the story of the good Samaritan, my lord?" said Aggie.

"I read my Bible, I hope."

"Well, I'll tell you a bit more of it than you'll get there. The Levite and the Pharisee—nobody ever said your lordship was like either of them—"

"No, thank God! nobody could."

"—they went by on the other side, and let him lie. But there was one came up, and took him by the legs, because he lay upon his land, and would have pulled him off. But just in the

cam the guid Samaritan, an' set him rinnin'. Sae it was sune a sma' maitter to onybody but the ill neebour, wha couldna weel gang straucht to Paradise. Abraham wad hae a fine time o' 't wi' sic a bairn in 's bosom!"

nick of time, by came the good Samaritan, and set him running. So it was soon a small matter to anybody but the bad neighbour, who couldn't well go straight to Paradise. Abraham would have a fine time of it with such a child in his bosom!"

"Damn the women! Young and old they're too many for me!" said his lordship to himself,—and just then Grizzie returning invited him to walk up to the laird's room, where he made haste to set forth the object of his visit.

"I said to your son, Glenwarlock, when he came to me the other morning, that I would not buy."

"Yes, my lord."

"I have however, lawyer though I be, changed my mind, and am come to renew my offer."

"In the meantime, however, we have changed our minds, my lord, and will not sell."

"That's very foolish of you."

"It may seem so, my lord; but you must allow us to do the best with what modicum of judgement we possess."

"What can have induced you to come to such a fatal resolution! I am thoroughly acquainted with the value of the land all about here, and am convinced you will not get such a price from another, be he who he may."

"You may be right, my lord, but we do not want to sell."

"Nobody, I repeat, will make you a better—I mean an equal offer."

"I could well believe it might not be worth more to anyone else—so long, that is, as your lordship's property shuts it in on every side; but to your lordship—"

"That is my affair; what it is worth to you is the question."

"It is worth more to us than you can calculate."

"I daresay, where sentiment sends prices up! But that is not in the market. Take my advice and a good offer. You can't go on like this, you know. You will lose your position entirely. Why, what are you thinking of!"

"I am thinking, my lord, that you have scarcely been such a neighbour to induce us to confide our plans to you. I have said we will not sell—and as I am something of an invalid—"

Lord Lick-my-loof rose, feeling fooled—and annoyed with himself and everybody in "the cursed place."

"Good morning, Glenwarlock," he said. "You will live to repent this morning."

"I hope not, my lord. I have lived nearly long enough. Good morning!"

His lordship went softly down the stair, hurried through the kitchen, and walked slowly home, thinking whether it might not be worth his while to buy up Glenwarlock's few remaining debts.

CHAPTER LIX
A LITTLE LIFE WELL ROUNDED

"Pirate or not, the old gentleman was a good judge of diamonds!" said Mr. Burns, laying down one of the largest. "Not an inferior one in all I have gone over! Your uncle was a knowing man, sir: diamonds are worth much more now than when he brought them home. These rough ones will, I trust, turn out well: we cannot be so sure of them."

"How much suffering the earlier possession of them would have prevented!" said the laird. "And now they are ten times more welcome that we have the good of that first."

"Sapphires and all of the finest quality!" continued Mr. Burns, in no mood for reflection. "I'll tell you what you must do, Mr. Cosmo: you must get a few sheets of tissue paper, and wrap every stone up separately—a long job, but the better worth doing! There must be a thousand of them!"

"How can they hurt, being the hardest things in the world?" said Cosmo.

"Put them in any other company you please—wheel them to the equator in a barrowful of gravel, or line their box with sand-paper, and you may leave them naked as they were born! But, bless thy five wits! did you never hear the proverb, 'Diamond cut diamond?' They're all of a sort, you see! I'd as soon shut up a thousand game-cocks in the same cellar. If they don't scratch each other, they may, or they might, or they could, or they would, or at any rate they should scratch each other. It was all very well so long as they lay in the wall of this your old diamond-mine. But now you'll be forever playing with them! No, no! wrap each one up by itself, I say."

"We're so far from likely to keep fingering them, Mr. Burns," said Cosmo, "that our chief reason for wishing you to see them was that you might, if you would oblige us, take them away, and dispose of them for us!"

"A-ah!" rejoined Mr. Burns, "I fear I am getting too old for a transaction of such extent! I should have to go to London—to Paris—to Amsterdam—who knows where?—that is, to make the best of them—perhaps to America! And here was I thinking of retiring!"

"Then let this be your last business transaction. It will not be a bad one to finish up with. You can make it a good thing for yourself as well as for us."

"If I undertake it, it shall be at a fixed percentage."

"Ten?" suggested Cosmo.

"No; there is no risk, only labour in this. When I took ten for that other diamond, I paid you the money for it, you will remember: that makes a difference. I wish you would come with me; I could help you to see a little of the world."

"I should like it greatly, but I could not leave my father."

Mr. Burns was a little nervous about the safety of the portmanteau that held such a number of tiny parcels in silver paper, and would not go inside the coach although it rained, but took a place in sight of his luggage. I will not say what the diamonds brought. I would not have my book bristle with pounds like a French novel with francs. They more than answered even Mr. Burns's expectations.

When he was gone, and all hope for this world vanished in the fruition of assured solvency, the laird began to fail. While Cosmo was yet on the way with Mr. Burns and the portmanteau to meet the coach, he said to his faithful old friend,

"I'm tired, Grizzie; I'll gang to my bed, I think. Gien ye'll gie me a han', I winna bide for Cosmo."

"Eh, sir, what for sud ye be in sic a hurry to sleep awa' the bonny daylicht?" remonstrated

"I'm tired, Grizzie; I'll go to my bed, I think. If you'll give me a hand, I won't wait for Cosmo."

"Eh, sir, why should you be in such a hurry to sleep away the bonny daylight?"

Grizzie, shot through with sudden fear, nor daring allow to herself she was afraid. "Bide till the yoong laird comes back wi' the news: he winna be lang."

"Gien ye haena time, Grizzie, I can manage for mysel'. Gang yer wa's, lass. Ye hae been a richt guid freen' to yer auld mistress! Ye hae dune yer best for him 'at she left!"

"Eh, sir! dinna speyk like that. It's terrible to hearken til!—I' the verra face o' the providence 'at's been takin' sic pains to mak up to ye for a' ye hae gane throu'—noo whan a' 's weel, an' like to be weel, to turn roon' like this, an' speyk o' gaein' to yer bed! It's no worthy o' ye, laird!"

remonstrated Grizzie, shot through with sudden fear, nor daring allow to herself she was afraid. "Wait till the young laird comes back with the news: he won't be long."

"If you don't have time, Grizzie, I can manage for myself. Go, lass. You have been a true, staunch friend to your old mistress! You have done your best for him that she left!"

"Eh, sir! don't speak like that. It's terrible to listen to!—In the very face of the providence that's been taking such pains to make up to you for all you have gone through—now when all's well, and like to be well, to turn round like this, and speak of going to your bed! It's not worthy of you, laird!"

He was so amused with her expostulation that he laughed heartily, brightened up, and did not go to bed before Cosmo came—kept up, indeed, a good part of the day, and retired with the sun shining in at his western window.

The next day, however, he did not rise. But he had no suffering to speak of, and his face was serene as the gathering of the sunrays to go down together; a perfect yet deepening peace was upon it. Cosmo scarcely left him, but watched and waited, with a cold spot at his heart, which kept growing bigger and bigger, as he saw his father slowly drifting out on the ebb-tide of this earthly life. Cosmo had now to go through that most painful experience of all—when the loved seem gradually withdrawing from human contact and human desires, their cares parting slowly farther and farther from the cares of those they leave—a gulf ever widening between, already impassable as lapsing ages can make it. But when final departure had left the mind free to work for the heart, Cosmo said to himself—"What if the dying who seem thus divided from us, are but looking over the tops of insignificant earthly things? What if the heart within them is lying content in a closer contact with ours than our dull fears and too level outlook will allow us to share? One thing their apparent withdrawal means—that we must go over to them; they cannot retrace, for that would be to retrograde. They have already begun to learn the language and ways of the old world, begun to be children there afresh, while we remain still the slaves of new, low-bred habits of unbelief and self-preservation, which already to them look as unwise as unlovely. But our turn will come, and we shall go after, and be taught of them. In the meantime let us so live that it may be the easier for us in dying to let the loved ones know that we are loving them all the time."

The laird ceased to eat, and spoke seldom, but would often smile—only there was in his smile too that far-off something which troubled his son. One word he often murmured—*peace.* Two or three times there came as it were a check in the drift seaward, and he spoke plainly. This is very near what he said on one of these occasions:

"Peace! peace! Cosmo, my son, ye dinna ken hoo strong it can be! Naebody can ken what it's like till it comes. I hae been troubled a' my life, an' noo the verra peace is 'maist ower muckle for me! It's like as gien the sun wad put oot the fire. I jist seem whiles to be lyin' here waitin' for ye to come intil my peace, an' be ane wi' me! But ye hae a lang this warl's life afore ye yet. Eh! winna it be gran' whan it's

"Peace! peace! Cosmo, my son, you don't know how strong it can be! Nobody can know what it's like till it comes. I have been troubled all my life, and now the very peace is almost too much for me! It's as if the sun would put out the fire. I just seem sometimes to be lying here waiting for you to come into my peace, and be one with me! But you have a long life in this world before you yet. Eh! won't it be grand

weel ower, an' ye come! You an' me an' yer mother an' God an' a'! But somehoo I dinna seem to be lea'in you aither—no half sae muckle as whan ye gaed awa' to the college, an' that although ye're ten times mair to me noo than ye war than. Deith canna weel be muckle like onything we think aboot it; but there maun surely be a heap o' fowk unco dreary an' fusionless i' the warl' deith taks us til; an' the mair I think aboot it, the mair likly it seems we'll hae a heap to du wi' them—a sair wark tryin' to lat them ken what they are, an' whaur they cam frae, an' hoo they maun gang to win hame—for deith can no more be yer hame nor a sair fa' upo' the ro'd be yer bed. There may be mony ane there we ca'd auld here, 'at we'll hae to tak like a bairn upo' oor knees an' bring up. I see na anither w'y o''t. The Lord may ken a better, but I think he's shawn me this. For them 'at are Christ's maun hae wark like his to du, an' what for no the personal ministration o' redemption to them 'at are deid, that they may come alive by kennin' him? Auld bairns as weel as yoong hae to be fed wi' the spune."

when it's well over, and you come! You and me and your mother and God and all! But somehow I don't seem to be leaving you either—not half so much as when you went away to the college, and that although you're ten times more to me now than you were then. Death can't well be much like anything we think about it; but there must surely be masses of dreary and spiritless folk in the world death takes us to; and the more I think about it, the more likely it seems we'll have a power of work to do with them—trying to let them know what they are, and where they came from, and how they must set about returning home—for death can no more be your home than a nasty fall upon the road be your bed. There may be many there we called old here, that we'll have to take like a child on our knees and bring up. I see no other way. The Lord may know a better, but I think he's shown me this. For those that are Christ's must have work like his to do, and why not the personal ministration of redemption to those that are dead, that they may come alive by knowing him? Old children as well as young have to be fed with the spoon."

The day before that on which he went, he seemed to wake up suddenly, and said,—

"Cosmo, I'm no inclined to mak a promise wi' regaird to ony possible communication wi' ye frae the ither warl', nor do I the least expec' to appear or speyk to ye. But ye needna for that conclude me awa' frae ye a'thegither. Fowk may hae a hantle o' communication ohn aither o' them kent it at the time, I'm thinkin'. Min' this ony gait: God's oor hame, an' gien ye be at hame an' I be at hame, we canna be far sun'ert!"

The day before that on which he went, he seemed to wake up suddenly, and said,—

"Cosmo, I'm not inclined to make a promise with regard to any possible communication with you from the other world, nor do I the least expect to appear or speak to you. But you needn't on that account conclude me away from you altogether. Folk may have a deal of communication without either of them knowing it at the time, I'm thinking. Remember this anyway: God's our home, and if you be at home, and I be at home, we can't be far sundered!"

As the sun was going down, closing a lovely day of promise, the boat of sleep, with a gentle wind of life and birth filling its sail, bore, softly gliding, the old pilgrim across the faint border between this and that. It may be that then, for a time, like a babe new-born, he needed careful hands and gentle nursing; and if so, there was his wife, who must surely by now have had time to grow strong. Cosmo wept and was lonely, but not broken-hearted; for he was a live man with a mighty hope and great duties, each of them ready to become a great joy. Such a man I do not think even diamonds could hurt, although, where breathes no wind of life, those very crystals of light are amongst the worst in Beelzebub's army to flyblow a soul into a thing of hate and horror.

CHAPTER LX
A BREAKING UP

Things in the castle went on in the same quiet way as before for some time. Cosmo settled himself in his father's room, and read and wrote, and pondered and aspired. The household led the same homely simple life, only fared better. The housekeeping was in Grizzie's hands, and she was a liberal soul—a true *bread-giver.*

James Gracie did not linger long behind his friend. His last words were, "I won'er gien I hae a chance o' winnin' up wi' the laird!"

James Gracie did not linger long behind his friend. His last words were, "I wonder if I have a chance of winning up with the laird!"

On the morning that followed his funeral, as soon as breakfast was over, Aggie sought Cosmo, where he sat in the garden with a book in his hand.

"Whaur are ye gaein' Aggie?" he said, as she approached prepared for walking.

"Where are you going, Aggie?" he said, as she approached prepared for walking.

"*My* hoor's come," she answered. "It's time I was awa'."

"*My* hour's come," she answered. "It's time I was away."

"I dinna un'erstan' ye, Aggie," he returned.

"I don't understand you, Aggie," he returned.

"Hoo sud ye, sir? Ilka body kens, or sud ken, what lies to their ain han'. It lies to mine to gang. I'm no wantit langer. Ye wadna hae me ait the breid o' idleness?"

"How should you, sir? Everybody knows, or should know, what lies to their own hand. It lies to mine to go. I'm not wanted longer. You wouldn't have me eat the bread of idleness?"

"But, Aggie," remonstrated Cosmo, "ye're ane o' the faimily! I wad as sune think o' seein' my ain sister, gien I had ane, gang fra hame for sic a nae rizzon at a'!"

"But, Aggie," remonstrated Cosmo, "you're one of the family! I would as soon think of seeing my own sister, if I had one, leave home for such a no reason at all!"

The tears rose in her eyes, and her voice trembled:

The tears rose in her eyes, and her voice trembled:

"It canna be helpit; I maun gang," she said.

"It can't be helped; I must go," she said.

Cosmo was dumb for many moments; he had never thought of such a possibility; and Aggie stood silent before him.

"What hae ye i' yer heid, Aggie? What thoucht ye o' duin' wi' yersel'?" he asked at length, his heart swelling so that he could scarcely bring out the words.

"What are your plans, Aggie? What do you think of doing with yourself?" he asked at length, his heart swelling so that he could scarcely bring out the words.

"I'm gaein' to luik for a place."

"I'm going to look for a place."

"But, Aggie, gien it canna be helpit; and gang ye maun, *ye* ken I'm rich, an' *I* ken there's naebody i' the warl' wi' a better richt to share in what I hae: wadna ye like to gang til a ladies' school, an' learn a heap o' things?"

"But, Aggie, if it can't be helped, and go you must, *you* know I'm rich, and *I* know there's nobody in the world with a better right to share in what I have: wouldn't you like to go to a ladies' school, and learn a heap of things?"

"Na, I wadna. It's hard wark I need to haud me i' the richt ro'd. I can aye learn what I hunger for, an' what ye dinna desire ye'll never learn. Thanks to yersel' an' Maister Simon, ye hae putten me i' the w'y o' that! It's no kennin'

"No, I wouldn't. It's hard work I need to keep me on the right road. I can always learn what I hunger for, and what you don't desire you'll never learn. Thanks to you and Master Simon, you've set me up for that! It's not things—it's kennin' things upo' the ro'd ye gang, 'at's o' consequence to ye. The lave I mak naething o'."

knowing things—it's knowing things upon your own road, that matters to you. The rest I make nothing of."

"But a time micht come whan ye wad want mony a thing ye micht hae learnt afore."

"But a time might come when you would want many a thing you might have learned before."

"Whan that time comes, I'll learn them than, wi' half the trouble, an' in half the time,—no to mention the pleesur o' learnin' them. Noo, they wad but tak me frae the things I can an' maun mak use o'. Na, Cosmo, I'm b'un to du something wi' what I hae, an' no bide till I get mair. I'll be aye gettin'."

"When that time comes, I'll learn them then, with half the trouble, and in half the time,—not to mention the pleasure of learning them. Now, they would but take me from the things I can and must make use of. No, Cosmo, I'm bound to do something with what I have, and not wait till I get more—and more I'll always be getting."

"Weel, Aggie, I daurna temp' ye to bide gien ye oucht to gang; an' ye wad but despise me gien I was fule eneuch to try 't. But ye canna refuse to share wi' me. That wadna be like ane 'at had the same father an' the same maister. Tak a thoosan' poun' to begin wi', an' gang an'—an' du onything ye like, only dinna work yersel' to deith wi' rouch wark. I canna bide to think o' 't."

"Well, Aggie, I daren't tempt you to stay if you ought to go; and you would but despise me if I was fool enough to try it. But you can't refuse to share with me. That wouldn't be like one that had the same father and the same master. Take a thousand pounds to begin with, and go and—and do anything you like, only don't work yourself to death with rough work. I can't stand the thought of it."

"A thousan' poun'! No ae baubee! Cosmo, I wad hae thoucht ye had mair sense! What wad baudrins there du wi' a silk goon? Ye can gie me the twa poun' ten I gae to Grizzie to help haud the life in 's a'. A body maun hae something i' their pooch gien they can, an' gien they canna, they maun du wi' naething. It's won'erfu' hoo little 's railly wantit!"

"A thousand pounds! Not one ha'penny! Cosmo, I would have thought you had more sense! What would the cat there do with a silk gown? You can give me the two pounds ten I gave to Grizzie to help keep us all alive. I must have something in my pocket if I can, and if I can't, I must do with nothing. It's wonderful how little is really wanted!"

Cosmo felt miserable.

Cosmo felt miserable.

"Ye winna surely gang ohn seein' Maister Simon!"

"You surely won't go without seeing Master Simon!"

"I tried to see him last nicht, but auld Dorty wadna lat me near him. I *wad* fain say fareweel til him."

"I tried to see him last night, but old Dorty wouldn't let me near him. I *would* fain say farewell to him."

"Weel, put aff gaein' awa' till the morn, an' we'll gang thegither the nicht an' see him. Dorty winna haud *me* oot."

"Well, put off going away till tomorrow, and we'll go together tonight and see him. Dorty won't keep *me* out."

Aggie hesitated, thought, and consented. Leaving Cosmo more distressed than she knew, she went to the kitchen, took off her bonnet, and telling Grizzie she was not going till the morrow, sat down, and proceeded to pare the potatoes.

"Ance mair," said Grizzie, resuming an unclosed difference, "what for ye sud gang's clean ayont me. It's true the auld men are awa', but here's the auld wife left, an' she'll be a mither to ye, as weel's she kens hoo, an' a lass o' your sense is easy to mither. I' the name o'

"Once more," said Grizzie, resuming an unclosed difference, "why you should go is clean beyond me. It's true the old men are away, but here's the old wife left, and she'll be a mother to you, as well as she knows how, and a lass of your sense is easy to mother. In

God I say ’t, the warl’ micht as weel objec’ to twa angels bidin’ i’ h’aven thegither as you an’ the yoong laird in ae hoose! Say ’at they like, ye’re but a servan’ lass, an’ here am I ower ye! Aggie, I’m growin’ auld, an’ railly no fit to mak a bed my lane—no to mention scoorin’ the flure! It’s no considerate o’ ye, Aggie!—jist ’cause yer father—hoots, he was but yer gran’father!—’s deid o’ a guid auld age, an’ gaithert til *his* fathers, to gang an’ lea’ me my lane! Whaur am I to get a body I cud bide to hae i’ my sicht, an’ you awa’—you ’at’s been like bane o’ my bane to me! It’s no guid o’ ye, Aggie! There maun be temper intil ’t! I’m sure I ken no cause ever I gae ye.”

the name of God I say it, the world might as well object to two angels living in heaven together as you and the young laird in one house! Say what they like, you’re but a servant lass, and here am I over you! Aggie, I’m growing old, and really not fit to make a bed myself—not to mention scouring the floor! It’s not considerate of you, Aggie!—just because your father—heavens, he was but your grandfather!—is dead of a good old age, and gathered to *his* fathers, to go and leave me by myself! Where am I to get someone I could stand to have in my sight, with you gone—you who have been like bone of my bone to me! It’s not good of you, Aggie! There must be temper in it! I’m sure I know no cause I ever gave you.”

Aggie said not a word; she had said all she could say, over and over; so now she pared her potatoes, and was silent. Her heart was sore, but her mind was clear, and her will strong.

Up and down the little garden Cosmo walked, revolving many things. “What is this world and its ways,” he said, “but a dream that dreams itself out and is gone!”

The majority of men, whether they think or not, worship solidity and fact: to such Cosmo’s conclusion must seem both foolish and dangerous—though a dream may be filled with truth, and a fact be a mere shred for the winds of the limbo of vanities. Everything that *can* pass belongs to the same category with the dream. The question is whether the passing body leaves a live soul; whether the dream has been dreamed, the life lived aright. For there is a reality beyond all facts of suns and systems; solidity itself is but the shadow of a divine necessity; and there may be more truth in a fable than in a whole biography. Where life and truth are one, there is no passing, no dreaming more. To that waking all dreams truly dreamed are guiding the dreamer. But the last thing—and this was the conclusion of Cosmo’s meditation—any dreamer needs regard, is the judgement of other dreamers upon his dreams. The all-pervading, ill-odoured phantom called Society is but the ghost of a false God. The fear of man, the trust in man, the deference to the opinion of man, is the merest worship of a rag-stuffed idol. The man who *seeks* the judgement of God can well smile at the unsolicited approval or condemnation of self-styled Society. There *is* a true society—quite another thing. Doubtless the judgement of the world is of even moral value to those capable of regarding it. To deprive a thief of the restraining influence of the code of thieves’ honour, would be to do him irreparable wrong; so with the tradesman whose law is the custom of trade; but God demands an honesty, a dignity, a beauty of being, altogether different from that demanded by man of his fellow; and he who is taught of God is set out of sight above such law as that of thieves’ honour, trade-custom, or social recognition—all of the same quality—subjected instead to a law which obeyed is liberty, disobeyed is a hell deeper than Society’s attendant slums.

“Here is a woman,” said Cosmo to himself, “who, with her earnings and her labour both, ministered to the very bodily life of my father and myself! She has been in the house the angel of God—the noblest, truest of women! She has ten times as much genuine education as most men who have been to college! Her brain is second only to her heart!—If it had but pleased God to make her my sister! But there is a way of pulling out the tongue of Slander!”

The evening was Mr. Simon’s best time, and they therefore let the sun go down before they left the castle to visit him. On their way they had a right pleasant talk about old things, now the one now the other bringing some half faded event from the store-closet of memory.

"I doobt ye winna min' me takin' ye oot o' the Warlock ae day there was a gey bit o' a spait on?" said Agnes at length, looking up in Cosmo's face.

"Eh, I never h'ard o' that, Aggie!" replied Cosmo.

"I canna think to this day hoo it was ye fell in," she went on: "I hadna the chairge o' ye at the time. Ye maun hae run oot o' the hoose, an' me efter ye. I was verra near taen awa wi' ye. Hoo we wan oot o' the watter I canna un'erstan'. A' 'at I ken is 'at whan I cam to mysel', we war lyin' grippit til ane anither upon a laich bit o' the bank."

"But hoo was't 'at naebody ever said a word aboot it efterhin'?" asked Cosmo.

"I never tellt onybody, an' ye wasna auld eneuch no to forget a' aboot it."

"What for didna ye tell?"

"I was feart they wad think it my wite, an' no lat me tak chairge o' ye ony mair, whauras I kent ye was safer wi' me nor wi' ony ither aboot the place. Gien it had been my wite, I cudna hae hauden my tongue; but as it was, I didna see I was b'un to tell."

"Hoo did ye hide it?"

"I ran wi' ye hame to oor ain hoose. There was naebody there. I tuik aff yer weet claes, an' pat ye intil my bed till I got them dry."

"An' hoo did ye wi' yer ain?"

"By the time yours was dry, mine was dry tu."

"I don't expect you'll remember me taking you out of the Warlock one day it was fairly in spate?" said Agnes at length, looking up in Cosmo's face.

"Eh, I never heard of that, Aggie!" replied Cosmo.

"I can't think to this day how it was you fell in," she went on: "I didn't have charge of you at the time. You must have run out of the house, and me after you. I was very nearly swept away with you. How we escaped the water I can't understand. All that I know is that when I came to myself, we were lying gripping each other upon a low bit of the bank."

"But how was it that nobody ever said a word about it afterwards?" asked Cosmo.

"I never told anybody, and you weren't old enough not to forget all about it."

"Why didn't you tell?"

"I was afraid they would think it my fault, and not let me take charge of you any more, whereas I knew you were safer with me than with any other about the place. If it had been my fault, I couldn't have held my tongue; but as it was, I didn't think I had to tell."

"How did you hide it?"

"I ran with you home to our own house. There was nobody there. I took off your wet clothes, and put you into my bed till I got them dry."

"And what about your own?"

"By the time yours were dry, mine were dry too."

When they arrived at the cottage, Dorty demurred, but her master heard Cosmo's voice and rang his bell.

"I little thought your father would have gone before me," said Mr. Simon. "I think I was aware of his death. I saw nothing, heard nothing, neither was I thinking about him at the moment; but he seemed to come to me, and I said to myself, 'He is on his way home.' I shall have a talk with him by and by."

Agnes told him she had come to bid him good-bye; she was going after a place.

"Well," he answered, after a thoughtful pause, "so long as we obey the light in us, and that light is not darkness, we can't go wrong. If we should mistake, he will turn things round for us; and if we be to blame, he will let us see it."

He was weak, and they did not stay long.

"Don't judge my heart by my words, my dear scholars," he said. "My heart is right toward you, but I am too weary to show it. God bless you both. I may not see you again, Agnes, but I shall think of you there, and if I can do anything for you, be sure I will."

When they left the cottage, the twilight was half-way toward the night, and a vague softness in the east prophesied the moon. Cosmo led Agnes through the fields to the little hollow where she had so often gone to seek him. There they sat down in the grass, and waited for the moon. Cosmo pointed out the exact spot where she rose that night she looked at him through the legs of the cow.

"Ye min' Grizzie's rime," he said:	"You remember Grizzie's rime," he said:
" 'Whan the coo loups ower the mune, The reid gowd rains intil men's shune'?	" 'When the cow leaps over the moon, The red gold rains into men's shoes'?
I believe Grizzie took the queer sicht for a guid omen. It's unco strange hoo fowk'll mix up God an' chance, seein' there could hardly be twa mair contradictory ideas! I min' ance hearin' a man say, 'It's almost a providence!'"	I believe Grizzie took the queer sight for a good omen. It's very strange how folk will mix up God and chance, seeing there could hardly be two more contradictory ideas! I remember once hearing a man say, 'It's almost a providence!'"
"I doobt wi' maist fowk," said Aggie, "it's only 'There's almost a God.' For my pairt I see nae room atween no believin' in him at a', an' believin' in him a'thegither an' lattin' him du what he likes wi' 's."	"I expect with most folk," said Aggie, "it's only 'There's almost a God.' For my part I see no room between not believing in him at all, and believing in him altogether and letting him do what he likes with us."
"I'm o' your min' there, Aggie, oot an' oot," responded Cosmo.	"I'm of your mind there, Aggie, out and out." responded Cosmo.

As he spoke the moon came peering up, and, turning to Agnes to share the sight with her, he saw the yellow light reflected from tears.

"Aggie! Aggie!" he said, in much concern, "what are ye grietin' for?"	"Aggie! Aggie!" he said, in much concern, "what are you crying for?"

She made no answer, but wiped away her tears, and tried to smile. After a little pause,

"Ony body wad think, Cosmo," she said, "'at gien I believed in a God, he maun be a sma' ane! What for sud onybody griet 'at has but a far awa' notion o' sic a God as you an' the laird an' Maister Simon believes in!"	"Anybody would think, Cosmo," she said, "that if I believed in a God, he must be a small one! Why should anybody cry who has but a far off notion of such a God as you and the laird and Master Simon believe in!"
"Ye may weel say that, Aggie!" rejoined Cosmo—yet sighed as he said it, for he thought of Lady Joan. A long pause followed, and then he spoke again.	"You may well say that, Aggie!" rejoined Cosmo—yet sighed as he said it, for he thought of Lady Joan. A long pause followed, and then he spoke again.
"Aggie," he said, "there canna weel be twa i' this warl' 'at ken ane anither better nor you an' me. We hae been bairns thegither; we hae been to the schuil thegither; we hae had the same maister; we hae come throu dour times thegither—I doobt we hae been hungry thegither, though ye saidna a word; we hae warstlet wi' poverty, an' maybe wi' unbelief; we loe the same fowk best; an' abune a' we set the wull o' God. It wad be sair upo' baith o' 's to pairt—an' to me a vex forby 'at the first thing w'alth did for me sud be to tak you awa'. It wad 'maist brak my hert to think 'at her 'at cam throu the lan' o drowth wi' me—ay, tuik me throu 't for, wantin' her, I wad hae fa'en to	"Aggie," he said, "there can't well be two in this world who know one another better than you and I. We have been children together; we have been to school together; we have had the same master; we have come through hard times together—I suspect we have been hungry together, though you didn't speak of it; we have fought with poverty, and maybe with unbelief; we love the same folk best; and above all we set the will of God. It would be hard upon both of us to part—and to me a vex besides that the first thing wealth did for me should be to take you away. It would almost break my heart to think that she who came through the land of drought with me—ay,

rise nae mair, sud gang on climmin' the dry hill-ro'd, an' me lyin' i' the bonny meadow-gerse at the fut o' 't. It canna be rizzon, Aggie! What for sud ye gang? Merry me, Aggie, an' bide—bide an' ca' the castel yer ain."

took me through it for, without her, I would have fallen to rise no more, should go on climbing the dry hill-road, while I lay in the bonny meadow-grass at the foot of it. It can't be sense, Aggie! Why should you go? Marry me, Aggie, and stay—stay and call the castle your own."

"Hoots! wad ye merry yer mither!" cried Agnes, and to Cosmo's fresh dismay burst into laughter and tears together. I believe it was the sole time in her life she ever gave way to discordant emotion.

"Heavens! would you marry your mother!" cried Agnes, and to Cosmo's fresh dismay burst into laughter and tears together. I believe it was the sole time in her life she ever gave way to discordant emotion.

Cosmo stared speechless. It was as if an angel had made a poor human joke! He was much too bewildered to feel hurt, especially as he was aware of no committed absurdity.

But Aggie was not pleased with herself. She choked her tears, crushed down her laughter, and conquered. She took his hand in hers.

"I beg yer pardon, Cosmo," she said; "I shouldna hae lauchen. Lauchin', I'm sure, 's far eneuch frae my hert! I kenna hoo I cam to du 't. But ye're sic a bairn, Cosmo! Ye dinna ken what ye wad hae! An' bein' a kin' o' a mither to ye a' yer life, I maun lat ye see what ye're aboot—I wadna insist ower sair upo' the years atween 's, though that's no a sma' maitter, but surely ye haena to be tellt at this time o' day, 'at for fowk to merry 'at dinna loe ane anither, is little gien it be onything short o' a sin."

"I beg your pardon, Cosmo," she said; "I shouldn't have laughed. Laughing, I'm sure, is far enough from my heart! I don't know why I did it. But you're such a child, Cosmo! You don't know what you would have! And being a sort of mother to you all your life, I must let you see what you're about—I wouldn't insist over much upon the years between us, though that's not a small matter, but surely you don't need telling at this time of day, that for folk to marry who don't love one another, is little if it be anything short of a sin."

"I hae loed *you,* Aggie," said Cosmo, with some reproach in his tone.

"I have loved *you,* Aggie," said Cosmo, with some reproach in his tone.

"Weel du I ken that. An ill hert wad be mine gien it didna tell me that! But, Cosmo, whan ye said the word, didna *your* hert tell ye ye meant by 't something no jist the verra same as ye inten'it me to un'erstan' by 't?"

"Well do I know that. Mine would be a bad heart if it didn't tell me that! But, Cosmo, when you said the word, didn't *your* heart tell you you meant by it something not precisely the same as you intended me to understand by it?"

"Aggie, Aggie!" sighed Cosmo, "I wad aye loe ye better an' better."

"Aggie! Aggie!" sighed Cosmo, "I would always love you more and more."

"Ay, ye wad, gien ye cud, Cosmo. But ye're ower honest to see throu' yersel'; an' I'm no sae honest but I can see throu' you. Ye wad merry me 'cause ye're no wullin' to pairt wi' me, likin' me better nor ony but ane, an' her ye canna get! Gien I was a leddy, Cosmo, maybe I michtna be ower prood to tak ye upo' thae terms, but no bein' what I am. It wad need love as roon 's a sphere for that. Eh, but there micht come a time o' sair repentace! Ance merried upo' you, gien I war to tak it intil my heid 'at I

"Ay, you would, if you could, Cosmo. But you're too honest to see through yourself; and I'm not so honest but I can see through you. You would marry me because you're not willing to part with me, liking me better than any but one, and her you can't get! If I was a lady, Cosmo, perhaps I mightn't be too proud to take you upon those terms, but not being what I am. It would need love as round as a sphere for that. Eh, but there might come a time of sore repentance! Once married to you,

was ae hair i' yer gait, or 'at ye was ae hair freer like wi me oot o' yer sicht, I wad be like to rin to the verra back-wa' o' creation! Na; it was weel eneuch as we hae been, but *merried!* Ye wad be guid to me aye, I ken that, but I wad be aye wantin' to be deid, 'at ye micht loe me a wee better. I say naething o' what the warl' wad say to the laird o' Glenwarlock merryin' his servan' lass; for ye care as little for the warl' as I du, an' we're baith some wiser nor it. But efter a', Cosmo, I wad be some oot o' my place—wadna I noo? The hen-birds nae doobt are aye the soberer to luik at, an' haena the gran' colours nor the gran' w'ys wi' them 'at the cocks hae; but still there's a measure in a'thing: it wad ill set a common hen to hae a peacock for her man. My sowl, I ken, wad gang han' in han', in a heumble w'y, wi' yours, for I un'erstan' ye, Cosmo; an' the day may come whan I'll luik fitter for yer company nor I can the noo; but wha like me could help a sense o' unfitness, gien it war but gaein' to the kirk side by side wi' you? Luik at the twa o' 's noo i' the munelicht thegither! Dinna ye see 'at we dinna match?"

if I were to take it into my head that I was one hair in your way, or that you were one hair freer with me out of your sight, I would be like to run to the very back-wall of creation! Na; it was well enough as we've been, but *married!* You would be good to me always, I know that, but I would ever be wanting to die, that you might love me a bit better. I say nothing of what the world would say to the laird of Glenwarlock marrying his servant lass; for you care as little for the world as I do, and we're both much wiser than it. But after all, Cosmo, I would be out of my element—wouldn't I now? The hen-birds no doubt are always the soberer to look at, and haven't the grand colours or the grand ways with them that the cocks have; but still there's a measure in everything: it would ill fit a common hen to have a peacock for her mate. My soul, I know, would go hand in hand, in a humble way, with yours, for I understand you, Cosmo; and the day may come when I'll look fitter for your company than I can now; but who like me could help a sense of unfitness, if it were but going to church side by side with you? Look at the two of us now in the moonlight together! Don't you see that we don't match?"

"A' that wad be naething gien ye loed me, Aggie."

"Gien *ye* loed *me,* say, Cosmo—loed me eneuch to be prood o' me! But that ye dinna. Exem' yer ain hert, an' ye'll see 'at ye dinna.—An' what for sud ye!"

"All that would be nothing if you loved me, Aggie."

"If *you* loved *me,* say, Cosmo—loved me enough to be proud of me! But that you don't. Search your own heart, and you'll see that you don't.—And why should you!"

Here Aggie broke down. A burst of silent weeping, like that of one desiring no comfort, followed. Suddenly she ceased and rose, and they walked home without a word.

When Cosmo came down in the morning, Aggie was gone.

CHAPTER LXI
REPOSE

Cosmo had no need of a very searching examination of his heart to know that it was mainly the wish to make her some poor return for her devotion, conjoined with the sincere desire to retain her company, that had influenced him in the offer she had been too wise and too genuinely loving to accept. He did not fall into any depths of self-blame, for, whatever its kind, his love was of quality pure and good. The only bitterness his offer bore was its justification of Agnes's departure.

But Grizzie saw no justification of it anywhere.

"What I'm to du wantin' her, I div not ken. *No becomin'*, quo' he, *for a lass like her to bide wi' a bachelor like himsel'!*"

"H'ard ever onybody sic styte! As gien she had been a lady forsooth! I micht wi' jist as muckle sense objec' to bidin' wi' him mysel'! But I s' du what I like, an' lat fowk say 'at they like, sae lang as I'm na fule i' my ain e'en!

I'm ower white, Mr. Gled, for you.
Ow na! ye're no that, bonny doo."

"What I'm to do without her, I do not know. *Not becoming*, said he, *for a lass like her to live with a bachelor like himself!*"

"Who ever heard such nonsense! As if she had been a lady forsooth! I might with just as much sense object to living with him myself! But I shall do what I like, and let folk say what they like, so long as I see no stain in myself!

I'm too white, Mr. Hawk, for your nest above.
Oh no! that you're not, bonny dove."

But by degrees Cosmo grew gently ashamed of himself that he had so addressed Agnes. He saw in the thing a failure in respect, a wrong to her dignity. That she had taken it so sweetly did not alter its character. Seeming at the time to himself to be going against the judgement of the world, and treating it with the contempt it always more or less deserves, he had in reality been acting in no small measure according to it! For had there not been in him a vague condescension operant all the time? Had he not been all but conscious of the feeling that his position made up for any want in his love? Had she been conventionally a lady, instead of an angel in peasant form, would he have been so ready to return her kindness with an offer of marriage? There was little conceit in supposing that some, even of higher position than his own, would have accepted the offer on lower terms; but knowing Aggie as he did, he ought not to have made it to her: she was too large and too fine for such an experiment. This he now fully understood; and had he not been brought up with her from childhood as with an elder sister, she might even now have begun to be a formidable rival to the sweet memories of Joan's ladyhood. For he saw in her that which is at the root, not only of all virtue, but of all beauty, of all grandeur, of all growth, of all attraction. Every charm—in its essence, in its development, in its embodiment, is a flower of the tree of life, whose root is the truth. I see the smile of the shallow philosopher, thinking of a certain lady to him full of charm, who has no more love for the truth than a mole for the light. But that lady's charm does not spring out of her; it has been put upon her, and she will soon destroy it. It comes of truth otherwhere, and will one day leave her naked and not lovely. The truth was in Agnes merely supreme. To have asked such a one to marry him for reasons lower than the highest was good ground for shame. Not therefore even then was he *painfully* ashamed, for he felt safe with Agnes, as with the elder sister that pardons everything.

It was some little time before they had any news of her; but they heard at last that she had rented Grannie's cottage from her grand-daughter, her own aunt, and was going to have a school there for young children. Cosmo was greatly pleased, for the work would give scope to some of her highest gifts and best qualities, while it would keep her within reach of possible service. Nothing however can part those who are of the true mind towards the things that *are*.

Cosmo betook himself heartily to study, and not only read but wrote regularly every day—no more with the design of printing, but in the hope of shaping more thoroughly and so testing more truly his contemplations and conclusions. I scorn the idea that a man cannot think without words, but Cosmo thus improved his thinking, and learned to utter accurately, that is, to say the thing he meant, and keep from saying the thing he did not mean.

The room over the kitchen, which had first in his memory been his grandmother's, then became his own, and returned to his disposal when James Gracie died, he made his study; and from it to the drawing-room, with the assistance of a village mason, excavated a passage—for it was little less than excavation—in the wall connecting the two blocks, under the passage in which had lain the treasure.

The main issue Grizzie's new command of money found was in a torrent of cleaning. If she could have had her way, I think she would have put up scaffold all over the outside of the house, and scrubbed it down from chimneys to foundations.

On the opposite side of the Warlock river, the laird rented a meadow, and there Grizzie had the long disused satisfaction of seeing two cows she could call hers, the finest cows in the country, feeding with a vague satisfaction in the general order of things. The stable housed a horse after Cosmo's own heart, on which he made excursions into the country round, partly in the hope of coming upon some place not too far off where there was land to be bought.

All that was known of the change in in his circumstances was that he had come into a large fortune by the death—date not mentioned—of a relative with whom his father had not for years had communication, and Cosmo never any. Lord Lick-my-loof, after repeated endeavours to get some information about this relative, was perplexed, and vaguely suspicious.

How the spending of the money thus committed to him was to change the earthly issues of his life, Cosmo had not yet learned, and was waiting for light on the matter. For a man is not bound to walk in the dark, neither must, for the sake of doing something, run the risk of doing wrong. He that believeth shall not make haste; and he that believeth not shall come no speed. He had nothing of the common mammonistic feeling of the enormous importance of money, neither felt that it laid upon him a heavier weight of duty than any other of the gifts of God. And if a poet is not bound to rush into the world with his poem, surely a rich man is not bound to rush into the world with his money. Rather set a herd of wild horses loose in a city! A man must know first how to *use* his money, before he begin to spend it. And the way to use money is not so easily discovered as some would think, for it is not one of God's ready means of doing good. The rich man as such has no reason to look upon himself as specially favoured. He has reason to think himself specially tried. Jesus, loving a certain youth, did him the greatest kindness he had in his power, telling him to give his wealth to the poor, and follow him in poverty. The first question is not how to do good with money, but how to keep from doing harm with it. Whether rich or poor, a man must first of all do justice, love mercy, and walk humbly with his God; then, if he be rich, God will let him know how to spend. There must be ways in which, even now, a man may give the half, or even the whole of his goods to the poor, without helping the devil. Cosmo, I repeat, was in no haste: it is not because of God's poverty that the world is so slowly redeemed. Not the most righteous expenditure of money will save it, but that of life and soul and spirit—it may be, to that, of nerve and muscle, blood and brain. All these our Lord spent—but no money. Therefore I say, that of all means for saving the world, or doing good, as it is called, money comes last in order, and far behind.

Out of the loneliness in which his father left him, grew a great peace and new strength. More real than ever was the other world to him now. His father could not have vanished like a sea-bubble on the sand! To have known a great man—perhaps I do not mean such a man as my reader may be thinking of—is to have some assurance of immortality. One of the best of men said to me once that he did not feel any longing after immortality, but, when he thought of certain persons, he could not for a moment believe they had ceased. He had beheld the lovely, believed therefore in the endless.

Castle Warlock was scarcely altered in appearance. In its worst poverty it had always looked dignified. There was more life about it and freedom, but not so much happiness. The diamonds had come, but his father was gone, Aggie was gone, Mr. Simon was going, and Joan would not come! Cosmo had scarce a hope for this world; yet not the less did he await the will of the Will. What that was, time would show, for God works in time.

CHAPTER LXII
THE THIRD HARVEST

As the days went by, Cosmo saw his engagement to Mr. Henderson drawing near, nor had the smallest inclination to back out of it. The farmer would have let him off at once, no doubt, but he felt, without thinking, that it would be undignified, morally speaking, to avoid, because he was now in plenty, the engagement granted by friendship to his need. Nor was this all, for, so doing, he would seem to allow that, driven by necessity, he had undertaken a thing unworthy, or degrading; for Cosmo would never have allowed that any degree of hunger could justify a poor man in doing a thing disgraceful to a rich man. No true man will ever ask of fellow creature, man or woman, on terms however extravagant, the doing of a thing he could not do himself without a sense of degradation. There is no leveller like Christianity—but it levels by lifting to a lofty table-land, accessible only to humility. He only who is humble can rise, and rising lift.

In thus holding to what he had undertaken, a man of lower nature might have had respect to the example he would so give: Cosmo thought only of honourable and grateful fulfilment of his contract. Not only would it have been a poor return for Mr. Henderson's kindness to treat his service as something beneath him now, but, worst of all, it would have been to accept ennoblement at the hands of Mammon, as of a power able to alter his station in God's world. To change the spirit of one's ways because of money, is to confess onesself a born slave, a thing of outsides, a knight of Riches, with a maggot for his crest.

When the time came, therefore, Cosmo presnted himself. With a look of astonishment shodowed by disappointment, the worthy farmer held out his hand.

"Laird," he said, "I didna expec' *you!*"

"Laird," he said, "I didn't expect *you!*"

"What for no?" returned Cosmo. "Haena I been yer fee'd man for months!"

"Why not?" returned Cosmo. "Haven't I been your fee'd man for months!"

"Ye put me in a kin' o' a painfu' doobt, laird. Fowk tellt me ye had fa'en heir til a sicht o' siller!"

"You put me in a kind of painful doubt, laird. Folk told me you had fallen heir to a great fortune!"

"But alloin', hoo sud that affec' my bargain wi' you Mr. Henderson? Siller i' the pooch canna tak obligation frae the back."

"But if so, how should that affect my bargain with you, Mr. Henderson? Money in the pocket can't take obligation from the back."

"Drivin' things to the wa', nae doobt!" returned the farmer. "I micht certainly hae ta'en the law o' ye, failin' yer appearance. But amo' freen's, that cudna be; an' 'deed, Mr. Warlock, gien a body wad be captious, michtna he say it wad hae been mair freen'ly to beg aff?"

"Driving things to the wall, no doubt!" returned the farmer. "I might certainly have taken you to court if you failed to appear. But among friends, that couldn't be; and indeed, Mr. Warlock, a captious man might say it would have been more friendly not to come."

"A bargain's a bargain," answered Cosmo; "an' to beg aff o' ane 'cause I was nae langer i' the same necessity as whan I made it, wad hae been a mere shame. Gien my father hed been wi' me, an' no weel eneuch to like me oot o' 's sicht, I wad hae beggit aff fest eneuch, but wi' no rizzon it wad hae been ill-mainnert, not to say dishonest an' oongratefu'. Gien ye hae

"A bargain's a bargain," answered Cosmo; "and not to come because I was no longer in the same necessity as when I made it, would have been a mere shame. If my father had been with me, and not well enough for me to leave him, I would soon have asked leave to stay away, but with no reason it would have been ill-mannered, not to say dishonest and

spoken to ony ither i' my place, he s' hae the fee, an' I s' hae the wark. Lat things stan', Mr. Henderson."

ungrateful. If you've engaged anyone in my place, he shall have the fee, and I shall have the work. Let things stand, Mr. Henderson."

"Laird!" answered the farmer, not a little moved, "there's no a man I wad raither see at my wark nor yersel'. A' o' them, men an' women, work the better whan ye're amo' them. They wad be affrontit no to haud up wi' a gentleman! Sae come awa' an' walcome!—ye'll tak something afore we fa' tu?"

"Laird!" answered the farmer, not a little moved, "there's not a man I would rather see at my work than yourself. All of them, men and women, work the better when you're among them. They would be affronted not to keep up with a gentleman! So join us, and welcome!—you'll take refreshment before we start?"

Cosmo accepted a jug of milk, half cream, from the hand of Elsie.

The girl was much improved, having partially unlearned a good deal of the nonsense gathered at school, and come to take a fair share with her sisters in the work of the house and farm—enlightened thereto doubtless by her admiration for Cosmo. It is not from those they marry people always learn most.

When Cosmo reached the end of the first bout, and stood to sharpen his scythe, he was startled to see, a little way off, gathering after one of the scythes, a form he could not mistake. She had known he would keep his troth! She did not look up, but he knew her figure and every motion of it too well to take her for another than Aggie.

That she thus exposed herself to misrepresentation, Aggie was well enough aware, but with the knowledge of how things stood between her and Cosmo, she was far above heeding the danger. Those who do the truth are raised even above defying the world. Defiance betrays a latent respect, but Aggie gave herself no more trouble about the opinion of the world than that of a lower animal. Those who are of the world may defy, but they cannot ignore it.

She had declined being a party to Cosmo's marrying his mother, but was not therefore prepared to expose him undefended to any one whatever who might wish to take him, even should she be of age unobjectionable; and she knew one who would at least be hampered by no scruples arising from conscious unfitness. Agnes might well have thought it better he should marry the cottar's than the farmer's daughter! Anyhow she was resolved to keep an eye on the young woman so long as Cosmo was within her swoop. He was chivalrous and credulous, and who could tell what Elsie might not dare! Her refusal to be his wife did not deprive her of antecedent rights. And there she was, gathering behind Cosmo, as two years ago!

The instant she was free, Aggie set out for home, not having exchanged a word with Cosmo, but intending to linger on the way in the hope of his overtaking her. The Hendersons would have had him stay the night, but he had given his man orders to wait him with his horse at a certain point on the road; and Aggie had not gone far before he got up with her.

Whatever was or had been the state of her feelings towards Cosmo, she had never mistaken his towards her; neither had she failed to see that his heart was nowise wounded by her refusal of his offer: it would have been a little comfort to her, having to be severe with herself, to see some sign of suffering in him, but she had got over much, and now was nowise annoyed at the cheery unembarrassed tone in which he called out when he saw her, and turning greeted him with the same absence of constraint.

"An' sae ye're gaein' to tak the bairnies un'er yer wing, Aggie!" said Cosmo, as they walked along. "They're lucky little things 'at'll gang to your schuil! What pat it i' yer heid?"

"And so you're going to take the children under your wing, Aggie!" said Cosmo, as they walked along. "They're lucky little things that'll go to your school! What made you think of it?"

"Mr. Simon advised it," answered Aggie; "but I believe I pat it in his heid first, sayin'

"Mr. Simon advised it," answered Aggie; "but I believe I gave him the notion hoo little was dune for the bairnies jist at the time they war easiest to guide. Rouch wark maks the han's rouch, and rouch words maks the hert rouch."

"The haill country-side 'ill be gratefu' to ye, Aggie.—Ye'll lat me come an' see ye whiles?"

"Nane sae welcome," answered Aggie. "But wull ye be bidin' on, noo 'at ye haena him 'at's gane? Winna ye be gaein' awa', to write buiks, an' gar fowk fin' oot what's the maitter wi' them?"

"I dinna ken what I'm gaein' to du," answered Cosmo. "But for writin' buiks, I could do that better at hame nor ony ither gate, wi' a'thing min'in' me o' my father, an' you nearhan' to gie me coonsel."

"I hae aye been yours to comman', Cosmo," replied Aggie, looking down for one moment, then immediately up again in his face.

"An' ye're no angert wi' me, Aggie?"

"Angert!" repeated Aggie, and looked at him with a glow angelic in her honest, handsome face, and her eyes as true as the heavens. "It was only 'at ye didna ken what ye were aboot, an' bein' sae muckle yoonger nor mysel', I was b'un to tak care o' ye; for a wuman as weel's a man maun be her brither's keeper. Ye see yersel' I was richt!"

"Ay, was ye, Aggie," answered Cosmo, ashamed and almost vexed at having to make the confession.

first, saying how little was done for the children just at the time they were easiest to guide. Rough work makes the hands rough, and rough words make the heart rough."

"The whole country-side will be grateful to you, Aggie.—You'll let me come and see you sometimes?"

"None so welcome," answered Aggie. "But will you be staying on, now that you've lost him that's gone? Won't you be going away, to write books, and teach folk the way to self-knowledge?"

"I don't know what I'm going to do," answered Cosmo. "But for writing books, I could do that better at home than anywhere else, with everything reminding me of my father, and you close by to give me counsel."

"I have always been yours to command, Cosmo," replied Aggie, looking down for one moment, then immediately up again in his face.

"And you're not angry with me, Aggie?"

"Angry!" repeated Aggie, and looked at him with a glow angelic in her honest, handsome face, and her eyes as true as the heavens. "It was only that you didn't know what you were about, and being so much younger than me, I was bound to take care of you; for a woman as well as a man must be her brother's keeper. You see I was right!"

"Ay, you were, Aggie," answered Cosmo, ashamed and almost vexed at having to make the confession.

He did not see the heave of Aggie's bosom, nor how she held back and broke into nothing the sigh that would have followed.

"But," she resumed, after a moment's pause, "a' lasses michtna ken sae weel what was fittin' them, nor care sae muckle what was guid for you; naebody livin' can ken ye as I du! an' gien ye war to lat a lass think ye cared aboot her—it micht be but as a freen', but she micht be sae ta'en wi' ye—'at—'at maybe she micht gar ye think 'at hoo she cudna live wantin' ye—an' syne what wad ye du than, Cosmo?"

"But," she resumed, after a moment's pause, "all lasses might not know so well what befitted them, nor care so much what was good for you; nobody living can know you as I do! and if you were to let a lass think you cared about her—it might be but as a friend, but she might be so taken with you—that—that maybe she would convince you she couldn't live without you—and what would you do then, Cosmo?"

It was a situation in which Cosmo had never imagined himself, and he looked at Aggie a little surprised.

"I dinna freely un'erstan' ye," he said.

"I don't quite understand you," he said.

"Na, I reckon no! Hoo sud ye! Ye're jist ower semple for this warl', Cosmo! But I'll put it plainer:—what wad ye du gien a lass was to fa' a greitin', an' a wailin', an fling hersel' i' yer airms, an' mak as gien she wad dee?—what wad ye du wi' her, Cosmo?"

"Na, I reckon not! How should you! You're just too innocent for this world, Cosmo! But I'll put it plainer:—what would you do if a lass were to fall a weeping, and a wailing, and fling herself in your arms, and make as if she would die?—what would you do with her, Cosmo?"

"'Deed I dinna ken," replied Cosmo with some embarrassment. "What wad ye hae me du, Aggie?"

"Indeed, I don't know," replied Cosmo with some embarrassment. "What would you have me do, Aggie?"

"I wad hae ye set her doon whaur ye stude, gien upo' the ro'd, than upo' the dyke, gien i' the hoose, than upo' the nearest chair, and tak to yer legs an' rin. Bide na to tak yer bonnet, but rin an' rin till ye're better nor sure she can never win up wi' ye. An' specially gien the name o' the lass sud begin wi' an *E* an' gang on till an *l*, I wad hae ye rin as gien the auld captain was efter ye."

"I would have you set her down where you stood, if upon the road, then upon the wall, if in the house, then upon the nearest chair, and take to your legs and run. Leave your bonnet, and run and run till you're more than sure she can never catch you. And specially if the lass's name begins with an *E* and goes on to an *l*, I would have you run as if the old captain were after you."

"I hae had sma' occasion," said Cosmo, "to rin fra *him*."

"I have had small occasion," said Cosmo, "to run from *him*."

And therewith, partly to change the subject, for he now understood Aggie, and did not feel it right to talk about any girl as if she could behave in the manner supposed, partly because he had long desired an opportunity of telling her, he began, and gave her the whole history of the diamonds, omitting nothing, even where the tale concerned Lady Joan. Before he got to the end of it, they were at the place where the man was waiting with his horse, and as that was the place where Aggie had to turn off to go to Muir o' Warlock, there they parted.

CHAPTER LXIII
A DUET, TRIO, AND QUARTET'

The next day things went much the same, only that Elsie was not in the field. Cosmo, who had been thinking much over what Aggie had said, and was not flattered that she should take him for the goose he did not know himself to be, could hardly wait for the evening to have another talk with her.

"Aggie," he said, as he overtook her in a hollow not many yards from the verge of the farm, "I dinna like ye to think me sic a gowk! What gars ye suppose a lass could hae her wull o' me in sic a w'y 's yon? No 'at I believe ony lass wad behave like that! It's no like yersel' to fancy sae ill o' yer ain kin'! I'm sure ye didna discover thae things i' yer ain hert! There's nae sic a lass."

"Aggie," he said, as he overtook her in a hollow not many yards from the verge of the farm, "I don't like you to think me such a fool! What makes you suppose a lass could manipulate me that way? Not that I believe any lass would behave like that! It's not like you to have such ill fancies about your own kind! I'm sure you didn't discover those things in your own heart! There's no such lass."

"What maitter whether there be sic a lass or no, sae lang as gien there was ane, she wad be ower muckle for ye?"

"What matter if there be such a lass or not, so long as if there were one, she would be too much for you?"

"That's ower again—what I'm compleenin' o'! an' gien it war onybody but yersel' 'at has a richt, I wad be angry, Aggie."

"That's it again—what I'm complaining of! and if it were anybody but you, who have a right, I would be angry, Aggie."

"Cosmo," said Agnes solemnly, "ye're ower saft-hertit to the women-fowk. I do believe—an' I tell ye't again in as mony words—ye wad merry ony lass raither nor see her in trible on your accoont."

"Cosmo," said Agnes solemnly, "you're too soft-hearted with the women-folk. I do believe—and I tell you it again in as many words—you would marry any lass rather than see her in trouble on your account."

"Ance mair, Aggie, what gies ye a richt to think sae ill o' me?" demanded Cosmo.

"Once more, Aggie, what gives you a right to think so ill of me?" demanded Cosmo.

"Jist the w'y ye behaved to mysel'."

"Just the way you behaved to me."

"*Ye* never tellt me ye couldna du wantin' me!"

"*You* never told me you couldn't live without me!"

"I houp no, for it wadna hae been true. I can du wantin' ye weel eneuch. But ye allooed ye wasna richt!"

"I hope not, for it wouldn't have been true. I can live without you well enough. But you admitted you were wrong!"

"Ay—it was a presumption."

"Ay—it was a presumption."

"Ay! but what made it a presumption?"

"Ay! but what made it a presumption?"

Cosmo could not bear to say plainly to the girl he loved so much, that he had not loved her so as to have a right to ask her to marry him. He hesitated.

"Ye didna loe me eneuch," said Aggie, looking up in his face.

"You didn't love me enough," said Aggie, looking up in his face.

"Aggie," returned Cosmo, "I'm ready to merry ye the morn gien ye'll hae me!"

"Aggie," returned Cosmo, "I'm ready to marry you tomorrow if you'll have me!"

"There noo!" exclaimed Aggie, in a sort of provoked triumph, "didna I tell ye! There ye are, duin 't a' ower again! Wasna I richt? Ye're fit to tak care o' onybody but yersel'—an' the

"There now!" exclaimed Aggie, in a sort of provoked triumph, "didn't I tell you! There you are, doing it all over again! Wasn't I right? You're fit to take care of anybody but yourself—

lass 'at wad fain hae ye! Eh, but sair ye need a sensible mitherly body like mysel' to luik efter ye!"

"Tak me, than, an' luik efter me at yer wull, Aggie; I mean what I say!" persisted Cosmo, bewildered with embarrassment and a momentary stupidity.

"Ance mair, Cosmo, dinna be a gowk," said Agnes with severity. "Ye loe me ower little, an' I loe *you* ower muckle for that."

"Ye're no angry at me, Aggie?" said Cosmo, almost timidly.

"Angry at ye, my bonny lad!" cried Aggie, and looking up with a world of tenderness in her eyes, and a divine glow of affection, for hers was the love so sure of itself that it maketh not ashamed, she threw her two strong, shapely honest arms round his neck; he bent his head, she kissed him heartily on the mouth, and burst into tears. Surely but for that other love that lay patient and hopeless in the depth of Cosmo's heart, he would now have loved Aggie in a way to satisfy her, and to justify him in saying he loved her! And to that it might have come in time, but where is the use of saying what might have been, when all things are ever moving towards the highest and best for the individual as well as for the universe!—not the less that hell may be the only path to it for some—the hell of an absolute self-loathing.

and the lass that would fain have you! Eh, but you've sore need of a sensible motherly type like myself to look after you!"

"Take me, then, and look after me at your will, Aggie; I mean what I say!" persisted Cosmo, bewildered with embarrassment and a momentary stupidity.

"Once more Cosmo, don't be foolish," said Agnes with severity. "You love me too little, and I love *you* too much for that."

"You're not angry with me, Aggie?" said Cosmo, almost timidly.

"Angry with you, my bonny lad!" cried Aggie, and looking up with a world of tenderness in her eyes, and a divine glow of affection, for hers was the love so sure of itself that it maketh not ashamed, she threw her two strong, shapely honest arms round his neck; he bent his head, she kissed him heartily on the mouth, and burst into tears. Surely but for that other love that lay patient and hopeless in the depth of Cosmo's heart, he would now have loved Aggie in a way to satisfy her, and to justify him in saying he loved her! And to that it might have come in time, but where is the use of saying what might have been, when all things are ever moving towards the highest and best for the individual as well as for the universe!—not the less that hell may be the only path to it for some—the hell of an absolute self-loathing.

Just at that moment, who should appear on the top of a broken mound of the moorland, where she stood in the light of the setting sun, but Elsie, neatly dressed, glowing and handsome! A moment she stood, then descended, a dark scorn shadowing in her eyes, and a smile on her mouth showing the whitest of teeth.

"Mr. Warlock," she said, and took no notice of his humble companion, "my father sent me after you in a hurry as you may see," —and she heaved a deep breath—"to say he doesn't think the bear o' the Gowan Brae, 'ill be fit for cutting this two days, an' they'll gang to the corn upo' the heuch instead. He was going to tell you himself, but ye was in such a hurry!"

"I'm muckle obleeged to ye, Miss Elsie," replied Cosmo. "It'll save me a half-mile i' the mornin'."

"Mr. Warlock," she said, and took no notice of his humble companion, "my father sent me after you in a hurry as you may see,"—and she heaved a deep breath—"to say he doesn't think the Gowan Hill barley will be fit for cutting these two days, and they'll go to the corn on the cliffside instead. He was going to tell you himself, but you were in such a hurry!"

"I'm much obliged to you, Miss Elsie," replied Cosmo. "It'll save me a half-mile in the morning."

"An' my father says," resumed Elsie, addressing Agnes, "yer wark's no worth yer wages."

"And my father says," resumed Elsie, addressing Agnes, "your work's not worth your wages."

Aggie turned upon her with flashing eyes and glowing face.

Aggie turned upon her with flashing eyes and glowing face.

"I dinna believe ye, Miss Elsie," she said. "I dinna believe yer father said ever sic a word. He kens my wark's worth my wages whatever he likes to set me til. Mair by token he wad hae tellt me himsel'! I s' jist gang straucht back an' speir."

"I don't believe you. Miss Elsie," she said. "I don't believe your father ever said such a word. He knows my work's worth my wages whatever he likes to set me to. What's more he would have told me himself! I'll just go straight back and ask."

She turned, evidently in thorough earnest, and set off at a rapid pace back towards the house. Cosmo glanced at Elsie. She had turned white—with the whiteness of fear, not of wrath. She had not expected such action on the part of Aggie. She would be at once found out! Her father was a man terrible in his anger, and her conscience told her he would be angry indeed, angrier than she had ever seen him! She stood like a statue, her eyes fixed on the retreating form of the indignant Agnes, who reached the top of the rising ground, and was beginning to disappear, before the spell of her terror gave way. She turned with clasped hands to Cosmo, and murmured, her white lips hardly able to fashion the words,

"Mr. Warlock, for God's sake, cry her back. Dinna lat her gang to my father."

"Mr. Warlock, for God's sake, call her back. Don't let her go to my father."

"Was the thing ye said no true?" asked Cosmo.

"Was the thing you said not true?" asked Cosmo.

"Weel," faltered Elsie, searching inside for some escape from admission, "maybe he didna jist say the verra words,—"

"Well," faltered Elsie, searching inside for some escape from admission, "maybe he didn't just say the very words,—"

"Aggie maun gang," interrupted Cosmo. "She maunna lat it pass."

"Aggie must go," interrupted Cosmo. "She mustn't let it pass."

"It was a lee! It was a lee!"

"It was a lie! It was a lie!"

Cosmo ran, and from the top of the rise called aloud,

Cosmo ran, and from the top of the rise called aloud,

"Aggie! Aggie! come back."

"Aggie! Aggie! come back."

Beyond her he saw another country girl approaching, but took little heed of her. Aggie turned at his call, and came to him quickly.

"She confesses it's a lee, Aggie," he said.

"She confesses it's a lie, Aggie," he said.

"She wadna, gien she hadna seen I was gaein' straucht til her father!" returned Agnes.

"She wouldn't, if she hadn't seen I was going straight to her father!" returned Agnes.

"I daursay; but God only kens hoo to mak the true differ 'atween what we du o' oorsel's, an' what we're gart. We maun hae mercy, an' i' the meantime she's ashamed eneuch. At least she has the luik o' 't."

"I daresay; but God only knows how to truly judge what we do of ourselves and what we're made to do. We must have mercy, and in the meantime she's ashamed enough. At least she looks it."

"It's ae thing to be ashamed 'cause ye hae dune wrang, an' anither to be ashamed 'cause ye're f'un' oot!"

"It's one thing to be ashamed because you've done wrong, and another to be ashamed because you're found out!"

"Cosmo, ye ken maist aboot the guid in fowk, an' I ken maist aboot the ill," said Aggie.

"Cosmo, you know most about the good in folk, and I know most about the bad," said Aggie.

Here the young woman who had been nearing them scarce observed while they talked, came up, and they turning to go back to Elsie, where she still stood motionless, followed them at her own pace behind.

"I beg yer pardon, Aggie," said Elsie, holding out her hand. "I was ill-natert, an' said the thing wasna true. My father says there isna a better gatherer i' the countryside nor yersel'." Aggie took her offered hand and said,

"I beg your pardon, Aggie," said Elsie, holding out her hand. "I was ill-natured, and said the thing that wasn't true. My father says there isn't a better gatherer in the countryside than you are." Aggie took her offered hand and said,

"Lat by-ganes be by-ganes. Be true to me an' I'll be true to you. An' I winna lee whether or no."

"Let by-gones be by-gones. Be true to me and I'll be true to you. And I won't lie either way."

Here the stranger joined them. She was a young woman in the garb of a peasant, but with something about her not belonging to the peasant. To the first glance she was more like a superior servant out for a holiday, but a second glance was bewildering. She stopped with a half timid but quiet look, then dropped her eyes with a flush.

"Will you please tell me if I am on the way to Castle Warlock?" she said, with a quiver about her mouth which made her like a child trying not to smile.

Cosmo had been gazing at her: she reminded him very strangely of Joan; but the moment he heard her voice, which was as different from that of a Scotch peasant as Tennyson's verse is from that of Burns, he gave a cry, and was on his knees before her.

"Joan!" he gasped, and seizing her hand, drew it to his lips, and held it there.

She made no sound or movement. Her colour went and came. Her head drooped. She would have fallen, but Cosmo received her, and rising with her, as one might with a child in his arms, turned, and began to walk swiftly homeward.

Aggie had a short fierce struggle with her rising heart, then turned to Elsie, and said quietly,

"Ye see we're no wantit!"

"You see we're not wanted!"

"I see," returned Elsie. "But eh! she's a puir cratur."

"I see," returned Elsie. "But eh! she's a poor creature."

"No sae puir!" answered Aggie. "Wad *ye* dress up like a gran' leddy to gang efter yer yoong man?"

"Not so poor!" answered Aggie. "Would *you* dress up like a grand lady to go after your young man?"

"Ay wad I—fest eneuch!" answered Elsie with scorn.

"Ay, I would—fast enough!" answered Elsie with scorn.

Aggie saw her mistake.

Aggie saw her mistake.

"Did ye tak notice o' her han's?" she said.

"Did you notice her hands?" she said.

"No, I didna."

"No, I didn't."

"Ye never saw sic han's! Did ye tak notice o' her feet?"

"You never saw such hands! Did you notice her feet?"

"No, I didna."

"No, I didn't."

"Ye never saw sic feet! Yon 's ane 'at canna gather, nor stook, nor bin', but she's bonny a' throu', an' her v'ice is a sang, an' she'll gang throu' fire an' watter ohn blinkit for her love's sake. Yon's the lass for oor laird! The like o' you an' me sud trible heid nor hert aboot the likes o' *him*."

"You never saw such feet! There's one who can't gather, stook, nor bind, but she's bonny all through, and her voice is a song, and she'll go through fire and water without blinking for her love's sake. She's the lass for our laird! The likes of you and me shouldn't trouble head or heart about the likes of *him*."

"Speyk for yersel', lass," said Elsie.

"Speak for yourself, lass," said Elsie.

"I tellt ye," returned Aggie, quietly but with something like scorn, "'at gien ye wad be true to me, I wad be true to you; but gie yersel' airs, an' I say guid nicht, an' gang efter my fowk."

"I told you," returned Aggie, quietly but with something like scorn, "that if you would be true to me, I would be true to you; but give yourself airs, and I say good night, and go after my folk."

She turned and departed, leaving Elsie more annoyed than repentant: it may take a whole life to render a person capable of shame, not to say sorrow, for the meanest thing of many he has done.

And now, Aggie's heart lying stone-like within her as she followed Cosmo with his treasure, her brain was alive and active for his sake. Joan was herself again, Cosmo had set her down, and they were walking side by side. "What are they going to do?" thought Aggie. "Are they going straight home together? Why does she come now the old laird is gone?" Such and many other questions she kept asking herself in her carefulness over Cosmo.

They passed the turning Aggie would have taken to go home; she passed it too, following them steadily.—That old Grizzie was no good! She must go home with them herself! If the reason for which she left the castle was a wise one, she must now, for the same reason, go back to it! Those two must not be there with nobody to make them feel comfortable and taken care of! They must not be left to feel awkward together! She must be a human atmosphere about them, to shield them, and make home for them! Love itself may be too lonely. It needs some reflection of its too lavish radiation.—This was practically though not altogether in form what Agnes thought.

In the meantime, the first whelming joy-wave having retired, and life and thought resumed their operations, they had begun to talk.

"Where have you come from?" asked Cosmo.

"From Cairntod, the place I came from that wild winter night," answered Joan.

"But you are...when were you...how long...have you been married?"

"Married!" echoed Joan. "Cosmo, how could you!"

She looked up in his face wild and frightened.

"Well, you never wrote! and—"

"It was you never wrote!"

"I did not, but my father did, and got no answer."

"I wrote again and again, and begged for an answer, but none came. If it hadn't been for the way I dreamed about you, I don't know what would have become of me!"

"The devil has been at old tricks, Joan!"

"Doubtless—and I fear I have hardly to discover his agent."

"And Mr. Jermyn?" said Cosmo, with a look half shy, half fearful, as if after all some bolt must be about to fall.

"I can tell you very little about him. I have scarcely seen him since he brought me the money."

"Then he didn't…?"

"Well, what didn't he?"

"I have no right to ask."

"Ask me *anything.*"

"Didn't he ask you to marry him?"

Joan laughed.

"I had begun to be afraid he had something of the kind in his head, when all at once I saw no more of him."

"How was that?"

"I can only guess: he may have spoken to my brother, and that was enough."

"Didn't you miss him?"
"Life *was* a little duller."
"If he *had* asked you to marry him, Joan?"
"Well?"
"Would you?"
"Cosmo!"
"You told me I might ask you anything!"
She stood, turned to the roadside, and sat down on the low earth-dyke. Her face was white.
"Joan! Joan!" cried Cosmo, darting to her side; "what is it, Joan?"
"Nothing; only a little faintness. I have walked a long way and am getting tired."
"What a brute I am!" said Cosmo, "to let you walk! I will carry you again."
"Indeed you will not!" she answered, moving a little from him.
"Do you think you could ride on a man's saddle?"
"I think so. I could well enough if I were not tired. But let me be quiet a little."
They were very near the place where Cosmo's horse must be waiting him. He ran to take him and send the groom home with a message.

To Joan it was a terrible moment. Had she, most frightful of thoughts! been acting on a holy faith that yet had no foundation? She had come to a man who asked her whether she would not have married his friend! She had taken so much for understood that had not been understood!

When Joan sat down Agnes stopped—a good way off: till the moment of service arrived she would be nothing. Several times she started to run to her, for she feared something had gone wrong, but checked herself lest she should cause more mischief by interfering. When she saw her sink sideways on the dyke, she did run, but seeing Cosmo hurrying back to her, stopped again.

Before Cosmo reached her Joan had sat up. The same faith, or perhaps rather hope, which had taken shape in her dreams, now woke to meet the necessity of the hour. She rose as Cosmo came near, saying she felt better now, and let him put her on the horse.

But now Joan was determined to face the worst, to learn her position and know what she must do.

"Has the day not come yet, Cosmo?" she said. "Cannot you now tell me why you left me so suddenly?"
"It may come with your answer to the question I put to you," replied Cosmo.
"You are cruel, Cosmo!"
"Am I? How? I do not understand."
This was worse and worse, and Joan grew rather more than almost angry. It is so horrid when the man you love will be stupid! She turned her face away, and was silent. A man must sometimes take his life in his hand, and at the risk of even unpardonable presumption, suppose a thing yielded, that he may know whether it be or not. But Cosmo was something of the innocent Aggie took him for.

"Joan, I don't see how I am wrong, after the permission you gave me," persisted he, too modest. "Agnes would have answered me straight out."
He forgot.
"How do you know that? What have you ever asked her?"
Joan, for one who refused an answer, was tolerably exacting in her questions. And as she spoke she moved involuntarily a step farther from him.
"I asked her to marry me," replied Cosmo.
"You asked her to marry you?"
"Yes, but she wouldn't."

"Why wouldn't she?"

Joan's face was now red as fire, and she was biting her lip hard.

"She had more reasons against it than one. Oh, Joan, she is so good!"

"And are you going to marry her?"

Instead of answering her question, Cosmo turned and called to Agnes, some thirty yards behind them:

"Come here, Aggie."

Agnes came quickly.

"Tell Lady Joan," he said, "what for ye wadna merry me."

"'Deed, my lady," said Agnes, her face also like a setting sun, "ye may believe onything he tells ye, jist as gien it war gospel. He disna ken hoo to mak a lee."

"I know that as well as you," replied Lady Joan.

"Na, ye canna du that, 'cause ye haena kent him sae lang."

"Will you tell me why you would not marry him?"

"For ae thing, 'cause he likit you better nor me, only he thoucht ye was merried, an' he didna like lattin' me gang from the hoose."

"Thank you, Agnes," said Joan, with a smile nothing less than heavenly. "He was so obstinate!"

"Tell Lady Joan," he said, "why you wouldn't marry me."

"Indeed, my lady," said Agnes, her face also like a setting sun, "you may believe anything he tells you, just as if it were gospel. He doesn't know how to form a lie."

"I know that as well as you," replied Lady Joan.

"Na, you can't possibly, because you haven't known him so long."

"Will you tell me why you would not marry him?"

"For one thing, because he liked you better than me, only he thought you were married, and he didn't like letting me leave the house."

"Thank you, Agnes," said Joan, with a smile nothing less than heavenly. "He was so obstinate!"

And with that she slipped from the saddle, threw her arms round Aggie's neck, and kissed her.

Aggie returned her embrace, with simple truth, then drawing gently away, said, putting her hand before her eyes as if she found the sun too strong,

"It's verra weel for you, my lady; but it's some sair upo' me; for I tellt him he sudna merry his mither, an' ye're full as auld as I am."

Joan gave a sigh.

"I am a year older, I believe," she answered, "but I cannot help it. Nor would I if I could, for three years ago I was still less worthy of him than I am now; and after all it is but a trifle."

"Na, my leddy, it's no a trifle, only some fowk carry their years better nor ithers."

Here Cosmo set Joan up again, and a full explanation followed between them, neither thinking of suppression because of Aggie's presence. She would indeed have fallen behind again, but Joan would not let her, so she walked side by side with them, and amongst the rest of the story heard Cosmo tell how he had yielded

"It's very well for you, my lady; but it's hard enough upon me; for I told him he shouldn't marry his mother, and you're fully as old as I am."

Joan gave a sigh.

"I am a year older, I believe," she answered, "but I cannot help it. Nor would I if I could, for three years ago I was still less worthy of him than I am now; and after all it is but a trifle."

"No, my lady, it's not a trifle, only some folk carry their years better than others."

Here Cosmo set Joan up again, and a full explanation followed between them, neither thinking of suppression because of Aggie's presence. She would indeed have fallen behind again, but Joan would not let her, so she walked side by side with them, and amongst the rest of the story heard Cosmo tell how he had yielded

Joan because poor Jermyn loved her. Agnes both laughed and cried as she listened, and when Cosmo ceased, threw her arms once more around him, saying, "Cosmo, ye're worth it a'!" then releasing him, turned to Joan and said,

"My lady, I dinna grudge him to ye a bit. Noo 'at he's yours, an a' 's come roon' as it sud, I'll be mysel' again—an' that ye'll see! But ye'll mak allooance, my lady; for ye hae a true hert, an' maun ken 'at whan a wuman sees a man beirin' a'thing as gien it was naething, 'maist like a God, no kennin' he's duin' onything by or'nar', she can no more help loein' him nor the mither 'at bore her, or the God 'at made her. An' mair, my lady, I mean to loe him yet; but, as them 'at God has j'ined man nor wuman maunna sun'er, I winna pairt ye even in my min'; whan I think o' the tane, it'll be to think o' the tither, an' the love 'at gangs to him 'ill aye rin ower upo' you—forby what I beir ye on yer ain accoont. Noo ye'll gang on thegither again, an' I'll come ahin'."

Joan because poor Jermyn loved her. Agnes both laughed and cried as she listened, and when Cosmo ceased, threw her arms once more around him, saying, "Cosmo, you're worth it all!" then releasing him, turned to Joan and said,

"My lady, I don't grudge him to you a bit. Now that he's yours, and all's come round as it should, I'll be myself again—and that you'll see! But you'll make allowance, my lady; for you have a true heart, and must know that when a woman sees a man bearing everything as if it were nothing, almost like a God, not knowing that he's doing anything special, she can no more help loving him than the mother that bore her, or the God that made her. And more, my lady, I mean to love him yet; but, as those God has joined none must sunder, I won't part you even in my mind; when I think of the one, it'll be to think of the other, and the love due to him will always run over upon you—besides what I bear you on your own account. Now you'll go on together again, and I'll come behind."

It was now to Aggie as if they were all dead and in the blessed world together, only she had brought with her an ache which it would need time to tune. All pain is discord.

"Ye see, my lady," she said, as she turned aside and sat down on the bordering turf, "I hae been a mither til 'im!"

"You see, my lady," she said, as she turned aside and sat down on the bordering turf, "I have been a mother to him!"

Who will care to hear further explanation!—how Joan went to visit distant relatives who had all at once begun to take notice of her; how she had come with them, more gladly than they knew, on a visit to Cairntod; and how such a longing seized her there that, careless of consequences, she donned a peasant's dress and set out for Castle Warlock; how she had lost her way, and was growing very uneasy when suddenly she saw Cosmo before her!

"But what am I to do now, Cosmo?" she said. "What account of myself can I give my people?"

"You can tell them you met an old lover, and finding him now a rich man, like a prudent woman, consented at once to marry him."

"I must not tell a story."

"Pray who asks you to tell a story?"

"You do, telling me to say I have a rich lover."

"I do not. I am rich."

"Not in money?"

"Yes, in money."

"Why didn't you tell me before?"

"I forgot. How could I think of riches with you filling up all the thinking-place!"

"But what am I to do to-night?"

"To-night?—oh!—I hadn't thought of that!—We'll ask Aggie."

So Aggie was once more called, and consulted. She thought for a minute, then said,—

"Cosmo, as sune's ye're hame, ye'll sen' yer man strauch awa' upo' the horse to lat my lady's fowk ken. She better write them a bit letter, an' tell them she's fa'en in wi' an auld acquaintance, a lass ca'd Agnes Gracie, a dacent young wuman, an' haein' lost her ro'd an' bein' unco' tired, she's gaein' hame wi' her to sleep; an' the laird o' Glenwarlock was sae kin' 's to sen' his man upo' his horse to cairry the letter. That w'y there'll be nae lees tellt, an' no ower muckle o' the trowth."

"Cosmo, as soon as you're home, you'll send your man straight away upon the horse to let my lady's folk know. She'd better write them a letter, and tell them she's fallen in with an old acquaintance, a lass called Agnes Gracie, a decent young woman, and having lost her road and being very tired, she's going home with her to sleep; and the laird of Glenwarlock was so kind as to send his man upon his horse to carry the letter. That way there'll be no lies told, and not too much of the truth."

Cosmo began to criticise, but Joan insisted it should be as Aggie said.

When they arrived at the castle, Grizzie was not a little scandalised to see her young master with a country lass on his horse, and making so much of her. But when she came to understand who she was, and that she had dressed up to get the easier to Castle Warlock she was filled with approbation even to delight.

"Eh, but ye're a lass to mak a man prood! I cudna hae dune better mysel' gien I had been a gran' lady wi' a' the wits o' a puir wife! Sit ye doon, my lady, an' be richt walcome! Eh, but ye're bonny, as ever was ony! an eh, but ye're steady as never was leddy! May the Lord bless ye, an' the laird kiss ye!"

"Eh, but you're a lass to make a man proud! I couldn't have done better myself if I had been a grand lady with all the wits of a poor woman! Take a seat, my lady, and be truly welcome! Eh, but you're bonny, as ever was any! and eh, but you've grace, as befitting your place! May the Lord bless you, and the laird kiss you!"

This outbreak of benediction rather confused Cosmo, but Joan laughed merrily, being happy as a child. Aggie turned her face to Grizzie in dread of more; but the true improviser seldom, I fancy, utters more than six lines. They had supper, and then a cart came rumbling to the door, half full of straw, into which Joan got with Aggie. A few things the latter had borrowed of Grizzie to help make the former comfortable, were handed in and they set out for Muir o' Warlock. In the morning Lady Joan declared she had never slept better than in old Grannie's box-bed.

They were married almost immediately, and nobody's leave asked. Cosmo wrote to acquaint Lord Mergwain with the event, and had in return, from his lordship's secretary, an acknowledgement of the receipt of his letter.

Of what they had to tell each other, of the way they lived, of how blessed they were even when not altogether happy—of these matters I say nothing, leaving them to the imagination of him who has any, while for him who has none I grudge the labour, thinking too he would very likely rather hear how much Cosmo got for his diamonds, and whether, if Lord Mergwain should not marry, Cairncarque will come to Lady Joan. But such things even he is capable of employing his fancy upon, and it would be a pity to prevent him from doing what he can.

I will close my book with a little poem that Cosmo wrote—not that night, but soon after. The poet may, in the height of joy, give out an extempore flash or two, but he writes no poem then. The joy must have begun to be garnered, before the soul can sing about it. How we shall sing when we absolutely believe that *Our life is hid with Christ in God!*

Here is my spiritual colophon.

All things are shadows of thee, Lord;
The sun himself is but a shade;
My soul is but the shadow of thy word,
A candle sun-bedayed!

Diamonds are shadows of the sun;
They drink his rays and show a spark:
My soul some gleams of thy great shine hath won,
And round me slays the dark.

All knowledge is but broken shades—
In gulfs of dark a wandering horde:
Together rush the parted glory-grades—
And lo, thy garment, Lord!

My soul, the shadow, still is light,
Because the shadow falls from thee;
I turn, dull candle, to the centre bright,
And home flit shadowy.

Shine, shine; make me thy shadow still—
The brighter still the more thy shade;
My motion be thy lovely moveless will:
My darkness, light delayed!

(THE END.)

Other titles available in the
WORKS OF MACDONALD
TRANSLATION SERIES:

COMING SOON:
'SIR GIBBIE'
(CHRISTMAS 2018)

To order, go to
The Works of MacDonald
website:
www.worksofmacdonald.com/products/robert-falconer

or order on Amazon:
https://goo.gl/VzoEGh (U.S.)
https://goo.gl/M9Shz1 (U.K)

Made in the USA
Lexington, KY
16 May 2019